WHISPER OF THE RAVENS
ANSUZ

MALENE SØLVSTEN

WHISPER OF THE RAVENS
ANSUZ

Translated from the Danish
by Adrienne Alair

Arctis

TRANSLATOR'S NOTE: The passages from "Völuspá" and the Ballad of
Vafthruthnir are based on the translation of the *Poetic Edda* by
Henry Adams Bellows, which is in the public domain. They have been changed
in some places to align more closely with the Danish version of the text.

W1-Media, Inc.
Arctis Books USA
Stamford, CT, USA

Visit our website at www.arctis-books.com

1 3 5 7 9 8 6 4 2

The Library of Congress Control Number: 2022951141

ISBN 978-1-64690-026-8
eBook ISBN 978-1-64690-623-9

English translation copyright © Adrienne Alair, 2023

Printed in China

MIX
Paper | Supporting
responsible forestry
FSC® C020056

To my mother,
who loves fantastical stories.

PART I

HEAVEN'S RIM

The sun, the sibling
of the moon, from the south
Its right hand cast
Over heaven's rim;
No knowledge it had
where its home should be,
The moon knew not
What might it had,
The stars knew not
Where their stations were

Völuspá
10th century

PROLOGUE

*I have always been able to see the past. And right then, I was having
a vision. Normally, I don't get scared when I see past events. I can't
change them anyway, and they can't hurt me. But this vision made my
heart pound, and I could barely breathe for fear.*

*I was barefoot and felt the winter chill creeping up my legs, but still, I
knew I was not really there.*

*A girl walked right past me. Her face was hidden by her loose, matted
hair, which appeared pale gray in the sparse light of the moon.*

*I found myself at the edge of a forest. A sharp scent of spruce tickled
my nostrils, and through the trees, I glimpsed snow-covered fields, glowing coldly in the moonlight.*

A man walked through me.

What the hell?

*The man followed the girl with the matted hair, and his boots crushed
the dry branches with each step.*

*The girl did not react to the sound but continued onward like a sleep-
walker. Her white-and-dark-gray dress, which clung to her body, was
made of a thin, almost transparent material.*

*The man's clothing was timeless. Dark pants and a light-colored
jacket with a hood that was pulled up, so I could not see his face, either.*

I spotted the leather cord in his hand.

*He shouted something I couldn't hear, but it made the girl stop next to
a spindly birch tree. The only one among the robust spruces. The birch
tree was only a little taller than she was, and it had a delicate trunk that
reached up toward the dark sky.*

The girl's slim neck was exposed above the low neckline of her dress, and it glowed nearly white in the light of the moon.

A stream of icy fear ran through my chest as the man grabbed an end of the cord in each hand and pulled it taut before him.

"Watch out," I shouted uselessly. She could not hear me, after all. I was not there, and this had already happened, maybe a few months ago, maybe hundreds of years.

The man came close to the girl's back and laid his cheek against her hair.

She did not react.

He whispered something in her ear and placed the leather cord around her throat. Gently, almost like a caress.

The man pulled, but the girl neither resisted nor moved.

I shouted again and again that she needed to run, kick, hit. Do something. Anything.

After several very long seconds, the girl sank to her knees and landed facedown on the layer of dry spruce needles covering the forest floor.

The man went down with her, and she flailed her arms weakly but managed only to sweep away some of the spruce needles surrounding her.

Finally, the girl was still.

The man sat hunched over with one knee on either side of the thin body, and he let out a desperate cry as he used both hands to rip her dress apart. His arms moved in strange jerking motions over her body before he stood and reached out to the little birch tree for balance. It snapped in half, and the top dangled from a thin strip of bark. On shaky legs, he disappeared into the adjacent field and out of sight.

The girl lay on her stomach, an arm sticking out at an unnatural angle. Her hair covered her face, which was turned away from me.

A terrified sound forced its way up my throat and out past my lips before I could stop it.

Her back had a symbol carved into it. It resembled a distorted "F," but the two horizontal strokes sloped downward. Around the symbol were dark, glistening smears of blood.

I wanted to run, but I did not move. The girl's mutilated back was the only thing I could see.

"Help," I yelled. "Help me."

I was pushed hard from the side and tumbled to the forest floor.

A gigantic, hairy head gave me another shove.

CHAPTER 1

Monster pushed me with his snout. He didn't put his whole weight into it, but still, each shove nearly rolled me over onto my stomach. Standing on all fours by the side of my bed, he looked down at me, which should say something about his size.

When people ask what breed my dog is, I usually say he's an Irish Wolfhound mix. What I don't say is that he's definitively not mine—he's very much his own—and I suspect he's only 0.001% Irish Wolfhound, the rest of him a combination of grizzly bear and mammoth. I tend to keep that part to myself.

"Was I screaming in my sleep, Monster?" I stroked his large head with a limp hand.

He nodded.

No, I corrected myself. Obviously, dogs do not nod.

The August morning sun was bursting through the window, and the clock read 7:30 a.m. *Oh no!* It was half an hour before I had to show up to my first day of high school.

Here in Denmark, high school lasts for three years, starting at the age of sixteen or seventeen. If my elementary and middle school years were any indication, this was not going to be easy.

I straightened my back, let out a deep breath, and dug around in my closet for a pair of black jeans and a black hoodie.

Monster placed his paw on the chair where I had laid out a yellow T-shirt, so that, for once, I would not greet the world dressed entirely in black. He tilted his head.

"I can't do it after all," I told him.

He sighed. This dog seemed to have a very un-dog-like interest in my clothes. And perhaps I assigned him some qualities he could not possibly possess.

"Another day," I promised as I got dressed. Then I lay down on the floor and started doing push-ups. I did only fifty because I was in a hurry.

We shuffled the few steps to the kitchen. Everything but the toilet and shower were in the same room. I opened a package of chocolate cookies and held one out to Monster. He gave it a resigned look but, with a crunch, began to chew.

I also took a bite, but then put the cookie down. My stomach was already in knots. Instead, I went into the bathroom.

As always, my reflection seemed just a bit foreign. The girl looking back at me had raven-black hair; milk-white skin; large, slightly protruding blue-green eyes; a long, pointed nose; and strong, dark eyebrows—a scar running through one of them.

I have not been lucky with my looks. Or much else.

Out of habit, I let my finger glide along the long, twisted scar that runs from the middle of my chest down between my breasts, ending just above my navel. I have no idea where it came from. The one in my eyebrow, however, I have no doubts about.

Using black eyeliner and mascara, I camouflaged my ugly features. Then I stomped out of the bathroom. With my bag in hand, I shouted to Monster: "Are you coming?"

Monster ran alongside my bike the whole way to the high school, but I did not know what he would do while I endured the day inside. When I parked, he kept running toward Kraghede Forest, the edge of which stretches along the high school's soccer fields. I watched him and wondered, as always, if it would be the last time I saw him. At the start of the forest, he turned around and gave a loud bark before running off between the trees.

Ravensted High School resembles a handful of gigantic reddish-brown LEGO blocks assembled haphazardly by a giant child. On one side of the high school sits one of the city's two elementary schools. I attended both briefly. On the other side sits Kraghede Forest. I once saw a map of the city and thought that, from above, the forest resembles an arm hugging Ravensted in a semicircle. The forest's broad forearm encircles the city to the east, thins out over the northern part, and ends in a finger pointing accusingly toward the west. After this, there is nothing but the boglands of Store Vildmose, ghost towns, and vacation homes, until you hit the west coast and the town of Jagd.

Inside the school, I studied the letter containing practical information and enthusiastic words of welcome that the school had sent.

People gave me a wide berth—aside from the one person whose shoulder bumped painfully into mine. I wasn't sure if it was intentional or if she simply didn't notice me. The few who looked in my direction turned up their noses at my black outfit and dark makeup. Or maybe they were simply turning up their noses at me in general.

I retreated against the wall and tried to ignore the other students. The first thing I needed to do was find Orange Hall, room 20.

After walking a short distance, glancing at the map I'd been given, I found out why it was called Orange Hall. *Good God.* Never in the history of orange had the color been misused to such an extent. The walls, doors, and ceiling were painted in varying shades of the color. Even the acrylic carpeting was tangerine. The pictures that hung on the walls had clearly been selected from the same color spectrum. Someone had taped a piece of paper to the door of room 2O that said, in a variety of colors, "Welcome 1B." The last thing this aesthetically challenged hallway needed was more bright hues.

I entered the room, which, to my surprise, was half-empty. Even though I had overslept, I managed to arrive with ten minutes to spare. The few people in the room put their heads together, whispering, without saying hello.

Welcome to high school.

The tables were arranged in a horseshoe shape, and I chose a seat at the one with the greatest number of empty chairs. Feeling my chest tightening, I sat on the edge of the chair and kept my eyes on my hands, which were curled into fists on the table.

As the room gradually filled, I could feel the past pressing in. Or rather, the *pasts*.

I can feel a little from almost everyone. Some more than others. There are very few whose pasts I cannot see at all. For instance, my only friend, Arthur. I can often sense a person's feelings with only a one-second delay, and I can feel most people's basic mood. Meaning, the dominant feelings in their life. You could call them auras, although I don't see rainbows around people. From some, I also get images that resemble little movies. I can bring up flashes from a person's past if I touch them, so I avoid that, or if they touch me, which *they* pretty much always do.

Little Mads sat down across from me and didn't talk to anyone, either. We'd both had a hard time in class the year I lived in Vringelby, but we never joined forces. From a distance, I had witnessed his painful transition from tall child to tall teenager. His growth had clearly not stopped after I left Vringelby Village School a little over three years ago, and with a height well over six-foot-five, he was the bearer of the region's most ironic nickname. Nicknames are like a sport up here. There's not much else to do. I've been given my fair share, too. *Psycho* is the one that stuck.

Peter walked in, and at once my entire body was ready to fight. The boy who had taught me to fight—let's just say as a sparring partner—had become a young man, but his eyes were the same.

15

Malicious and combative. Or maybe that was just when he was looking at me.

I remembered the time he and two other boys chased me through Kraghede Forest.

Being unable to run away from him and his mob had cost me a split eyebrow, four sprained ribs, and a whole lot of pride.

I looked at his somewhat flattened nose, which ruined an otherwise attractive face. He hadn't been so tough when I first took the bat from him that day, around three years after the attack in the forest. It was stupid of him to go after me alone. Now I caught his eye and rubbed the straight bridge of my own nose. Imagine, he beats me up and bullies me for years, and I smash his nose with a bat *one time*, and I'm the one who ends up in juvenile detention.

Peter held my gaze and tapped a finger over his eye in the place where the scar shone through my brow.

I vaguely knew others in the room. Mina Ostergaard came gliding in aristocratically. I also saw Niller, Suzuki, Johnny-Bum from Rakkeby, and Alice with the long red hair. I remembered Alice as a quiet girl from the half year I had class with her in North Lyngby. She had never spoken to me or bothered me. I appreciated both facts.

The seats filled up, but the ones on my side of the table were the least popular. In the end, only two empty spots were left.

Exactly.

A chubby boy stuck his head in the doorway and looked around for a free seat. He took a couple of hesitant steps in the direction of the empty chairs on either side of me.

"Thomas, you can sit here," a blond girl offered.

The relief in his face was palpable as he trudged over to his savior and sat at the corner of the horseshoe, uncomfortably straddling a table leg.

My eyes downcast, I resisted the urge to bang my head on the table.

"Can I sit here?" asked a melodic voice.

I looked up and into a pair of shining blue eyes surrounded by long lashes in the most perfect face I had ever seen. The nose was straight, and the eyes were deep-set above high cheekbones. The lips were shapely and full, the teeth pearly white, and the face surrounded by golden hair. This was, without compare, the most beautiful boy I'd ever seen in my life.

He smiled, but he could have just as well planted a fist in my solar plexus. I thought I heard a synchronized sigh from every girl in the room.

I realized he was still looking at me expectantly, so I gave a brief nod toward the chair.

"I'm Mathias. I just moved here. What's your name?" He sat down.

What was my name again?

I looked at him with furrowed brows. He was probably wondering if I was all right in the head. The answer would be *no*, but I'm not mute, either.

"Anna Sakarias," I stammered.

Mathias held out his hand, which seemed a bit old-fashioned, but when a guy like that offers you his hand, you take it.

I got the strangest pictures from him when our hands met. His past was like a series of photos where the images were out of order. I saw the usual little movie, but then suddenly, there were blind spots and missing links in the chain of events. The action stopped abruptly, and I was shut out.

"I've been looking forward to meeting the girl who beat up the city's biggest bully, burned her foster family's house down, and lives with a killer dog." He rolled his eyes dramatically.

I didn't know how to respond to his stream of words, which were incidentally delivered in a flat Copenhagen accent. The story with Peter and the bat had become a local legend, and in the retelling, a silly broken nose had been transformed into a lengthy

17

torture session. My foster family's house had burned down, that was correct, but I was not the one who set it on fire. In fact, I had gotten the entire family out in time, including their elderly hamster. And Monster had not killed anyone. Not while he had been living with me, in any case. Or at least, I didn't think so.

"Voilà," was the only thing I could think to say. I pointed at myself with my right thumb, which could actually be interpreted as me confirming my reputation.

Mathias raised his well-shaped eyebrows, impressed. Something in the doorway caused his face to stiffen in a surprised grimace, which did not make him any less pleasing to look at.

I followed his eyes and saw a girl walking into the room. No. *Sashaying* was more like it, with hazelnut skin and a cloud of dark corkscrew curls around her head. Her eyes were large and round and the color of maple syrup. Her lips were soft, and her body was narrow and wide in all the right places. A tight neon-yellow-and-royal-blue dress appeared to be painted onto her, and a chain with large purple stones hung around her neck, almost reaching her waist. A violently orange bag was slung across her torso, so its strap accentuated the cleft between her well-formed breasts. I had never seen such a horrifying color combination with such a successful result.

Mathias's mouth hung open slightly.

She headed directly for us, and what she did when she arrived at our table took me completely by surprise.

She hugged me.

CHAPTER 2

I sat stiff as a statue as the strange girl wrapped her slim brown arms around me. No one, and I mean absolutely no one, hugs me. Ever. I am not used to physical contact, and her—let's just say *aura*—hit me like a freight train. It was crackling, electric, creative, and bubbly.

She took my hands as she sat. "You're Anna."

It wasn't a question, so I didn't nod.

"I'm Luna." She might as well have added a *ta-daaa*.

I looked at her blankly.

"I'm *that* Luna."

"Should I know who you are?" I tried not to reveal my bewilderment as I discreetly eased my hands out of her grasp.

The girl only tightened her grip on me. "My parents are your parents' best friends."

My face froze in disbelief.

Luna was about to say something more, but at that moment, our homeroom teacher arrived. He introduced himself as Mr. Nielsen, immediately launching into a long explanation of schedules, where we should pick up our books in the basement, and how we could always come to him with our problems. If I had a dollar for every time an adult had assured me of this, I would be pretty well-off. I could double my fortune with every time that turned out not to be the case. When his eyes fell on me, he hurried to look away. It was barely noticeable. That's how it usually goes when people look at me.

My parents. My only relationship to them was that once, a little less than eighteen years ago, they dumped me into the world and left me.

I wasn't the only one who wasn't listening. To my right, Luna was openly staring at me. To my left, Mathias was doing whatever he could to catch a glimpse of Luna.

Mr. Nielsen started to call out our names. "Mathias Jarl Hedskov."

Mathias raised a muscular arm without taking his eyes off Luna.

When Mr. Nielsen came to Luna, he had to stop and read the name to himself first. "Luna Asfrid Villum Sekibo."

Mr. Nielsen announced that there would be a short break before we would all introduce ourselves to the class.

Luna was about to say something to me, but I stood up. It is rare for me to be around a lot of people, and even rarer for people to talk to me. So far, the day had been an unfortunate combination of both situations, and it was only 9:00 a. m. I stormed toward the door.

I turned and saw that behind me, Mathias had seized the opportunity, stolen my seat, and started talking to Luna.

When I swung out into Orange Hall, I ran right into a dark-haired boy. It felt like I had torpedoed into a concrete wall, and I nearly toppled over.

With a firm grip on my shoulders, he held me upright. I was hit with a strong scent of forest and fresh air and something I couldn't identify. He looked down at me with intense, dark eyes. No pictures came from him, but I could sense that he had an important task. A man on a mission.

"Sorry," I mumbled and tried to slip away. He looked gruffly at me but did not release my shoulders from his iron grasp. He stared at my face and squinted in recognition. I truly was infamous in Ravensted now. Had my reputation really gotten so far ahead of me?

"Varnar!" Janitor Preben stood a short way down the hall. I knew who Preben was. Everyone knows everyone in this small town. But I had never seen this boy before.

He let me go and walked off with fluid, feline steps. It was only then that I saw the green work pants.

"They hire a criminal as an assistant janitor every year." Peter leaned against the doorway. "When I saw you here, I actually thought you had gotten the job."

"Maybe I could make your nose look normal again if I smashed it one more time?" I wondered aloud.

"Maybe you would be less repulsive if I gave you a matching scar in your other eyebrow?" he bit back, but then shook his head. "No, you're so hideous, even your own parents couldn't bear to look at you."

He was going to say something else, but his voice broke with a cough.

Behind him stood Luna, her arms at her sides.

Peter looked over his shoulder and smiled. His face changed and suddenly became almost pleasant.

"You're new here in town, so let me give you a word of advice," he said to Luna. "Stay away from this one and hang out with us normal people."

She looked at him with her beautiful cognac-colored eyes. If looks could kill, Peter would have been lying dead on the orange acrylic carpet.

"I would rather drink piss in a pigsty with a bunch of perverted farmers," she said.

His smile stiffened and he coughed as if he were finding it hard to breathe.

"That can certainly be arranged," Niller said with a grin as he passed us.

Peter was still coughing when Mr. Nielsen called us back into the classroom.

"Instead of introducing yourselves to the entire classroom, please do so in groups of three. You will then introduce one another to the class," he said.

Mathias and Luna leaned in to me, and easy as that, our group was formed. It felt strange after a whole lifetime of various teachers having to convince reluctant groups to take me in.

"Who was that idiot?" asked Luna.

"An old friend." I looked down at the table.

"If that's one of your friends, I'd hate to meet your enemies."

Mathias squinted his eyes at Luna. "I'm confused. You know Anna, but she doesn't know you?"

"I don't get it. Why haven't you ever heard of me?" asked Luna. "Haven't Mia and Jens talked about me?"

I jerked my head up to look at her. How did she know my first foster family?

"It's been thirteen years since they threw me out. I haven't seen them since."

"Why did they throw you out?" asked Luna. I could tell Mathias was ready to kick her under the table, but she continued. "The agreement was that you would live with Mia and Jens until either my parents or your mother could come get you."

She pursed her full lips and tapped them with a pink finger-nail.

I looked down again and inhaled sharply.

Mathias mercifully changed the topic. "What's your story, Luna?"

Luna leaned back in her chair. "I'm seventeen years old. My parents lived here in town until about six months before I was born. My mom is from Ravensted. My dad is from West Africa, but he spent most of his life in France. They're aid workers, so we've traveled all around the world. Now that I'm starting high school, my mom wanted to come back home."

Wow. I was clearly not the only one who had lived in a billion

22

different places. But at least Luna had had her parents along for the ride.

When it seemed like Luna had nothing more to say, we both looked at Mathias.

"I'm from Copenhagen," he started.

"It's pretty clear that you're not from here." Luna laughed.

He stared in fascination at her smiling mouth for a moment before he could continue. "My mom has always worked in hair salons, but she'd never had the means to buy one herself. About three months ago, she was contacted by a man from up here. He had bought an old salon and wanted her to run it. It sounded a little sketchy, but we decided to take the chance. And the guy has stayed away so far, so I think it's okay."

"Where's your dad?" asked Luna.

I was beginning to suspect that she didn't have the world's best situational awareness.

Mathias's face grew dark, and he crossed his arms. "I don't know who he is."

"Haven't you asked your mom? Do you even know his name?" Luna pressed.

I was about to put my hand over her mouth, as the expression on Mathias's face was almost unbearable. My own had probably looked about the same five minutes earlier. I came to his rescue.

"Who's going to say what about whom?" I asked.

Mathias and I exchanged a glance. Neither of us wanted Luna to introduce us to the class. Lord only knew what she would come up with.

"Should I just introduce all three of us?" asked Mathias.

I was more than willing to stay seated, and Luna shrugged her shoulders and nodded.

People began their introductions, red-cheeked and giggling. A sour-looking girl named Maja introduced Little Mads, which appeared to cause her physical pain. When it was Mathias's turn to do the talking, he described me as local and supersweet, and Luna he characterized as a globe-trotter.

I don't think anyone had ever called me supersweet before.

I tried to keep to myself for the rest of the day, but Mathias and Luna were always around me. They didn't give up, and they didn't appear to tire of my one-word answers.

When I finally walked out of the school, Monster was waiting for me in the parking lot. Mathias and Luna, who were trailing at my heels and talking, stopped when they saw the enormous dog.

"Shut *up*," Mathias exclaimed.

I pet Monster on the head and walked over to my bike.

"Don't you want to come down to Frank's Diner?" Luna shouted after me.

She unlocked a battered Long John–style cargo bike, with a box in front large enough to hold a small human.

I had heard the two of them talking about wanting to go to a café, but by no means had I thought their plans included me.

"And if you don't want to come, you could at least say goodbye," Luna continued.

Oh right. Normal people probably say a friendly goodbye to one another.

Too bad I'm not normal.

Without a word, I rode away with Monster galloping at my side.

The next morning, we stood in Brown Hall, waiting to be let in for our first history lesson.

For what it's worth: If you ever need to decorate a high school and get the idea to design it around an already-dubious color theme, for God's sake, skip the color brown.

I was having a hard time concentrating in my brown surroundings, and I rubbed my eyes to wake myself up a bit.

The night before, I had once again had the vision of the girl being strangled and mutilated, and again I woke up crying and shaking from fear. This was the first time I had had the same vision twice in a row.

On the color front, Luna gave Brown Hall a run for its money in her orange top, green pants, and purple shoes.

"You're coming home with me today." This was a command, not an invitation.

Mathias paced around us.

"I have to do something," I mumbled.

Luna rolled her eyes.

Mathias began to chatter about something I didn't quite register, trying with a strained smile to get our attention.

Luna did not back down. "My parents want to meet you."

I looked down at the toes of my black shoes and counted silently to ten.

"They're making dinner."

I made a face. "Isn't that what parents do every night?"

"They want to get to know you. They want to help you. They want to take care of you."

With each of Luna's statements, it felt like a balloon inside me was inflating more and more. Her final sentence caused it to pop.

"You can tell *your* parents," I hissed, "that I don't want any more biological, step-, adoptive, foster, or surrogate parents. More parents are actually the very thing I would most like to be free of. Tell them they're too late. Seventeen years too late." And before I could applaud myself for the longest cohesive string of words I had directed toward another person in months, I stormed down Brown Hall. Out of the corner of my eye, I saw that Luna tried to come after me, but Mathias held her back. I ran toward the exit, which was shaped like a little tunnel, and pushed open the first door, but before I made it to freedom, the other door opened, and the young assistant janitor entered. For the second time, I barged right into him.

The small passageway filled with his scent.

"Where are you going?" He had a slight Scandinavian-sounding accent.

"It doesn't concern you." I tried to go around him. He stepped to the side and obstructed my path. I went to the other side, but again he blocked me.

"Move," I growled.

"It's safest if you stay inside." He spoke quietly, but there was determination behind his words.

I pushed him with both hands, but he didn't move an inch. I pushed him again and felt, like the first time I'd run into him, an iron wall of a body. He was slim and only a head taller than me, but I could not move him from where he stood. I saw now that his black T-shirt was taut across his muscular torso.

He caught my eye with his intense gaze. His dark, longish hair framed his face.

While I'm quite sure I could take—or at least be a worthy opponent against—Peter and most other men, I was one hundred percent sure that I would not stand a chance against Varnar, as I'd just remembered Janitor Preben calling him. It wasn't just his strong body, although that in and of itself would be pretty difficult to get past. It was his gaze. I could see a willpower much like my own in Varnar's eyes, but his was stronger. But that did not mean I was thinking of giving up. If I couldn't hit him, I could insult him.

"Since when are you a police officer? Aren't you just an assistant janitor?"

A smile flew across Varnar's lips, and for a split second, his face changed markedly. It was as if I were struck by a fleeting sunbeam. "Yes, right now I am an assistant janitor." He said the word as if it were foreign in his mouth. His eyes grew even darker than before.

"Go back."

He took a step in my direction and towered over me.

I had to fight hard not to step back or cast my eyes down.

At that moment, Mathias joined us. He looked at Varnar, who was blocking my way out.

Although I would put my money on Varnar every time if they really came to blows, he cast his eyes down as a sign of capitulation. At the same time, Mathias decided that Varnar had stopped my flight, and that the two of them were therefore allies. Against me, of course. He held out his hand.

"Mathias."

Varnar took it and introduced himself.

"Anna, won't you come back? Class just started. You can make it without getting marked absent," Mathias whispered, which was completely pointless in the little tunnel. "Luna didn't mean to upset you. She just really wants to be your friend."

"Yes, Anna. Mathias is right. Go back," Varnar said before he turned and disappeared the same way he had come, with a you-take-it-from-here look to Mathias.

"I'm not used to having friends." I pressed my lips together. Why wouldn't they just leave me alone?

"No one can go through life without friends," Mathias said gently.

"I've gotten along just fine." I let my eyes come to rest on a point far beyond the glass door.

"Just because you're not used to having friends, that doesn't mean we can't be good for you, and you for us."

I looked at him when he said *us*.

He nudged my shoulder. "Come on, Anna. What's the worst that could happen?"

"As soon as I start to care about you guys, you'll decide you don't want to be my friends anymore." The words were out before I could stop them, and my voice cracked a little.

The teasing tone was completely gone when Mathias spoke: "Oh, Anna . . . That won't happen."

I straightened my back and looked straight into his blue eyes. "I just don't understand why you want to be friends with me."

Mathias smiled his most charming smile, and my knees grew weak. This asshole knew exactly what he was doing.

"Luna, because she's Luna, and because in her mind, you were already friends before you were born. She's fantastic, Anna. You should really give her a chance."

Okay. Someone had apparently grown fond of someone.

Mathias laughed. "And me, because you're different, and you make me curious. You're wild, and you don't take shit from anyone. And you have that totally crazy dog. You don't say a whole lot, but when you do, you're sharp and funny and sarcastic. And you don't talk like the others, all *hou a hou a hou.*" He mimicked the thick North Jutland accent.

I started laughing, and it broke my determination.

Mathias opened the door into the hallway, and I trudged after him back to Brown Hall and the history class that had already started.

During the long ten o'clock break, we sat in the school's café, which was called The Island. We had claimed a plush red three-person sofa that had seen better days.

Luna broke the ice. "It's fine. You don't have to come home with me today, but can't I still tell you what I know about your parents?"

Mathias, who sat between us like a mediator, leaned back in the sofa and busied himself reading a magazine.

"I don't want to know anything about them." I tried to sound decisive, without any hysterical undertone. "There's no reason to. They're gone."

"Okay." Luna looked like she had swallowed a lemon. "Okay. But it's not my fault that our parents screwed everything up. I don't know why we didn't come here sooner. My whole childhood I was

28

told, *Maybe we can go home and get Anna next year. Maybe it'll work out in the summer.* But for some reason or another, it never worked out. Until now."

She reached across Mathias and took my hand. I let her hold it, even though it felt strange. Once again, I felt her electric creativity and an immense strength.

"But we can still be good friends, anyway. I've never done anything to you. I can feel it, we have to be friends—we just *have* to."

To be fair, she *hadn't* done anything to me. What was so wrong with having a friend? Or two? Normal people have friends. Normal people actually like having friends and seek out the company of other people.

But I'm not normal.

Luna squeezed my hand, and my determination wavered. Suddenly, it was impossible to say no. *No thanks.* The words stayed on my tongue. *No thanks. Just say it, Anna.*

Luna smiled innocently. "Do you want to go down to Frank's after class?"

I wanted to say *no. No, no, no, and no.*

"Okay," I said. I was surprised to hear the word come out of my mouth.

Mathias smirked down into his magazine.

It was the first time I had been to Frank's Bar & Diner, which had in record time become a town institution. Frank's opened about three years ago. At that time, I was living in group home number two. Shortly before that, I had moved out of foster home number seven, after it had burned down. The reason for my exit. They thought I had set the fire. That was back when I was still trying to convince people of my innocence. Now I had reached the point where I couldn't even be bothered to try.

The whole interior of Frank's was stainless steel, chrome, and leather. The walls were lined with booths with red leather seats surrounding metal tables. The bar gave off a metallic shine, and next to it stood a jukebox that blasted 1950s music into the room.

I had no doubt that it was Frank who stood behind the bar. His dark-gray pomaded hair was combed back, the sleeves of his black T-shirt were rolled up, and sailor tattoos covered both arms. There was something youthful about him, though he looked like he was in his mid-fifties. The thing that endeared him to me the most was the warmth that twinkled in his eyes.

Luna ran up to the bar and gave him a hug. He returned it with one arm, while he used the other to hand a pint of beer across the counter to a woman, whom he winked at before turning his attention to Luna.

The woman hadn't seen me, but out of habit, I managed to jump to the side when she turned, before either of us could be doused with beer.

"I thought yesterday was your first time here?" I whispered to Mathias.

"It was. She could make friends with a wooden shoe. I've never seen anything like it."

We walked up to the counter, where Mathias shook Frank's hand.

Frank scratched at his wide sideburns before extending his hand to me. I took it and got a flash of intelligence and friendliness. I also saw a little boy, about five years old, and I felt a violent wave of love, longing, and sadness. Too bad for Frank. But he was far from the first father in history to be separated from his child. Or—I looked him up and down—maybe grandchild.

"And who are you, my dear?"

I let go of his hand immediately. "Anna. And I'm not your anything."

With a sour look on my face, I waited for Frank to wrinkle his nose or take a step back. But he just smiled at me.

Why are so many people suddenly noticing me?

"My my, she's a scrappy one." Frank wrenched me out of my musings and wiggled his eyebrows at Luna, who nodded with false resignation—like a mother who is confronted with her child's misconduct.

"We don't know what to do." She put her arm around Mathias's shoulder.

He quickly put his arm around her waist and beamed like the sun.

Luna continued: "We've tried everything. Homeopathic medicine, music therapy, exercise, fresh air . . ."

Frank placed his index finger on his chin and furrowed his brows, doctor-like. "It's her diet that's the problem. I'm prescribing a milkshake and a chiliburger with fries, stat."

I rolled my eyes. How nice that they could amuse themselves at my expense.

Before heading into the kitchen, he swung his head toward Luna. "Remember, you start tomorrow."

We turned to Luna, who gave us a goofy grin. "We agreed on it yesterday. I needed a job, and I thought this could be a fun place to work."

We sat in a booth. Luna and Mathias ordered only milkshakes because they would be eating dinner at home later. They had *families*, after all.

Mathias clucked. "Luna, you are impressive. Yesterday you managed to acquire a new class, two new friends, and a new boss. Who knows what you can achieve in a year."

She laid her hand on his, and he stiffened. "I got a new boss and a new friend. I don't know yet what you will be to me."

His cheeks burned, and a happy grin spread across his handsome face.

It suddenly felt quite warm in our little booth.

Fortunately, Frank came with the food and drinks just then, and the mood shifted. Luna dove into her milkshake and chattered

31

away. Mathias looked happy and smitten, and I felt a pinch of guilt because I was sitting there, eating food that had been prepared for me. I decided to splurge and buy some extra food to bring home to Monster.

I let Mathias and Luna leave the diner alone, and I walked up to Frank.

"I'd like another burger to go."

He turned and studied me.

"Still hungry?" He looked me up and down before smoothing his coiffed gray hair.

I shook my head. "Not for me."

"Who's the lucky person, if I may ask?" Frank leaned over the stainless bar with a hand beneath his chin.

"My dog," I said. "He won't eat dog food, I can't cook, and I only have chocolate cookies at home."

Frank let out a resounding laugh, and deep wrinkles surrounded his eyes.

He whistled toward the kitchen, and out trotted a rottweiler that, to my eyes, looked small and harmless, but on the other hand, I'm used to Monster. I'm sure to other people, Frank's rottweiler was a large and potentially very dangerous dog.

"This one won't touch dog food, either. No, you won't, will you? Oh no you won't." This last bit sounded like Frank was speaking to a baby.

"You know what?" Frank said. "We always have a ton of leftovers, and my dog can't eat them all, though he does try. If you give me five dollars a week, I'll have my cook put some aside for you every day. You can just pick them up whenever works for you. What kind of dog do you have?"

I looked out the glass door and saw Monster sitting patiently just across the street from Frank's. How did he find me? He sat near a dog-leash hitch on the wall, so it looked like he was tied up.

"See for yourself." I pointed.

Frank looked out and his face froze in surprise. "Let's make that ten dollars."

I left Frank's with a bag of food. When I got home and opened it up, between the mixed-up leftover fries, bread, and burger patties, I found a nicely wrapped chicken sandwich and a piece of pie. It's rare to come across kindness without ulterior motives, and as I ate the sandwich later that evening, I considered what Frank might want in return. Not that he would get it.

Monster was happy. Never in all the time he'd lived with me had he eaten so well. I gave him a plate on the table because he was horribly offended whenever I put his food on the floor. He is tall enough to sit on the floor and eat at my tiny dining table. He ate the entire bag's contents, and then we watched TV.

Monster laid his enormous head on my lap. An old movie was on, but I think Monster was paying more attention to it than I was.

Friends. I knew the word but didn't know quite what it meant. Mathias and Luna seemed to have decided that I would be their friend. But did I even know how to be one? There had been very few consistent people in my life. Arthur and Greta were actually the only stable people in my world. Greta was my caseworker, so she could hardly be classified as a friend. So Arthur was the only one I would ever put in that category. Even though he was almost too weird to be.

I laid my head on Monster's shoulder and closed my eyes. When I opened them again, I was standing in the forest.

The man placed the cord around the girl's neck, and I prepared myself for what I was about to see. What I would be forced to bear witness to. I cursed the fact that I was involuntarily admitted to this horrific performance. And to have to see it again and again.

Why did I keep seeing it?

33

I watched the scene with as much calm as I could muster, focusing to see if I could recognize anything. But spruce forests all look the same. Through the trees, I saw a field. It followed an upward curve and ended on a hilltop. At the top sat a small white house.

The man tightened the cord around the girl's neck, and she made a gurgling noise.

Instinctively, I shouted for her to watch out. *Anna, you idiot.* Even though my brain coolly informed me that I might as well be shouting at characters in a film, I couldn't stop myself.

The girl sank to her knees. Her arms slumped down at her sides, and she hit the ground with a thump.

I started to scream. Either in my head or out loud, I begged: *Wake me up, Monster. Please? Before he gets the knife.*

A cold snout prodded me.

I woke with a start in the same position I had fallen asleep in. I wiped my cheeks with the back of my hand.

This didn't feel like my other visions. Something about it was totally off. To clear my mind, I grabbed the remote and switched over to the news channel.

The yellow graphic on the screen announced breaking news. I wanted to switch back to the movie, but when I heard the presenter mention the town of Hjallerup, my finger paused over the button. I had lived there, the year I stayed in group home number one. Nothing much ever happened out there, and the town's name sounded foreign in the news anchor's mouth.

"The girl was found this evening on the side of the road near Hjallerup in North Jutland." Photos of a redheaded girl flashed across the screen. She was sixteen, or maybe a little older. The news ran in a loop, and the presenter started from the beginning.

"We have news that a teenage girl was found dead this evening in North Jutland." The young journalist wearing pastel colors and horn-rimmed glasses held a dramatic pause. "A jogger found the body of seventeen-year-old Tenna Smith Jensen in a ditch just outside Hjallerup in North Jutland. Tenna Smith Jensen had been reported missing two days ago, but this evening, authorities announced that she was found dead. The police believe that foul play was involved in her death."

The news cut to pictures of a residential building at dusk. I recognized it immediately.

"Tenna Smith Jensen lived in Kobbelgården Group Home and had not been seen since the day before yesterday." The pictures I had already seen of the girl and the policeman talking about the cause of death flashed across the screen again.

My old superintendent appeared on the screen. He said what was expected. They were shaken up. They didn't think Tenna had any enemies. His thoughts went out to her loved ones.

Monster looked intensely at the TV, and once again the cavalcade of images streamed across the screen. No, I didn't know her. But it was strange, nevertheless.

I turned off the TV while the anchor was mid-sentence.

However many months, years, or centuries apart we were, there was something about Tenna Smith Jensen's fate that reminded me of the girl from my vision.

CHAPTER 3

Arthur was standing outside my door when Monster and I came back from our morning run.

"Did you hear?" Arthur didn't bother with introductory pleasantries.

He didn't need to, either, because I knew what he was talking about.

"Saw it on the news yesterday." I unlocked the door and ushered him in.

Monster looked around as if to locate something before throwing himself on the floor.

I kicked off my running shoes in the hall.

Arthur is older than me. I don't know exactly how old he is, but I met him in the orphanage I was brought to as a four-year-old when I was taken from Jens and Mia's home. Back then, he must have been an older teenager—I don't remember much from that time—but from the start, he took on a kind of older-brother role. He visited me in the various foster homes, and many nights he sat by my bed if I couldn't sleep and told me stories and sang me songs.

His skin was always fair—even more so than mine—but today he was extra pallid.

"She was the same age as you."

"It's sad, but it's not like I knew her or anything," I said as I reached for an apple on the kitchen table.

Monster lifted his large head.

"It's okay," I told the dog. "Did you know her?" I asked Arthur and bit into the apple.

Arthur shook his head. "Nah. Still horrible though."

He mussed his red hair and shivered as if he were freezing. He always goes around in the same worn-out winter coat—even in summer. I've teased him about it many times, but he always brushes me off with a smile. I envy his ability to be completely unconcerned with what others think of him.

"I see you've got a new roommate," said Arthur. "Where did he come from?"

"He just showed up about six months ago."

Arthur eyed the giant dog, who furrowed his bushy eyebrows. "And so you just let him move in?"

"It was more like he followed me in one day and never left."

"I thought you liked to live alone."

"It's just that I like animals better than people," I said with a grimace.

Arthur gave me a broad smile. "I'm glad he's here. He can take care of you."

"Are you thinking about the murdered girl?" How overprotective was Arthur allowed to be? "It must have been someone she knew. And it was all the way over in Hjallerup."

Monster looked up, sensing my irritation.

"It's okay, Monster," I said again. *Relax, dog.*

"You call him Monster?" Arthur burst out laughing.

"Well, it's not like he can tell me his name." I took two pieces of rye bread and slapped a slice of cheese between them.

Monster looked miserably at the sandwich but took it in his teeth.

Arthur raised an eyebrow but didn't comment on it. He turned back to the other subject.

"Hjallerup is only fifteen miles away. We don't know who or what is on the loose. I would be happy if you were extra careful for a little while. When you aren't at school, have your dog with you." He said *dog* as though he didn't think it was a wholly accurate descriptor. "Will you promise me that? Then I'll be able to rest a little easier." He smiled to himself.

"I'm pretty much always with Monster. So okay."

"Good. Thank you, Anna. I have to go now, but I'll stop by again soon."

I smiled at him.

"It's so nice to see you smile. You don't do it all that often." Arthur looked at me warmly.

I opened the door for him, and he ran down the stairs with a wave. Monster looked out the door after him.

Tenna was the big topic of conversation when I got to school. Those who had not yet heard what happened received vivid accounts of the few details that had been released. No one knew Tenna except our classmate, Tine, who turned out to be her second cousin.

Tine enjoyed her place in the spotlight, and she gladly shared what she knew about Tenna's alcoholic father. The three younger siblings. The forced removal. Tine insinuated incest, her eyes gleaming with sensationalism.

Mr. Nielsen entered the classroom. "I'm sure you have already heard what happened in Hjallerup. I understand, Tine, that you were related to the girl."

Tine hung her head and looked suitably shaken.

Mr. Nielsen's face shone with sympathy. "You take it easy today. I hope the rest of you will show Tine some extra care in the coming days and weeks."

I concentrated on Tine and reached out with my power. It was not often that I searched for something specific in a person's past, but it was actually easy to sort through the memories and find what I was looking for. It might have helped that, right now, Tine was thinking about her second cousin.

Tine had met Tenna only twice in her life. She felt nothing more than indifference and a touch of embarrassment for her.

"And uh . . ." For once, Mr. Nielsen focused on me.

"What was your name? Anna . . . you lived at Kobbelgården, didn't you?" The question tore me away from spying on Tine's past. "You must also be shocked by what happened."

Stop trying to disguise curiosity as compassion, Mr. Nielsen. He certainly was not the first adult to have tried that trick on me.

Without answering, I vaguely shrugged my shoulders.

Mr. Nielsen's eyes quickly flickered away from me, as if he had forgotten that he had just spoken to me. He looked back out over the class. "I think you should talk to each other about this." He gave us an admonishing look. "And you should look out for one another. None of this walking home alone at night from Frank's or other places. We don't know who did this or what was behind it."

Mr. Nielsen echoed Arthur's concern. An adult concern. I don't think anyone in the room, even for a second, saw themselves suffering the same fate as Tenna.

The mood was strange that day. The teachers didn't feel like teaching, but they also didn't want to release us from the protective walls of the school. Most of the day, we hung out on the sofas in The Island under the pretense of doing group work.

Luna stretched.

Mathias's eyes lingered on her, but he managed to tear them away. "I know you don't necessarily know everyone who ever lived in that institution, Anna, but did you know her?"

I ran my fingers through my hair. "I didn't know her. But everyone's acting like I did."

He didn't say anything more. Something made me look up, and I saw Varnar leaning against the wall just down the hall and staring angrily at me. What had I ever done to him? I held his gaze with a hard look.

Luna looked in his direction and leaned toward me. "That guy's really hot. He's, like, real bad-boy hot."

Mathias looked, horrified, from Luna to Varnar.

She whacked him on the arm. "Not for me. For Anna. Are you interested in him?" This last bit was directed at me.

Where the hell did that come from? Here I was, trying to send him a death glare, and Luna interpreted it as my being interested? Maybe this experiment with having friends had turned me soft.

"No, absolutely not," I said. "I'm just wondering why he's looking at me like that. As far as I know, I've never done anything to him. Maybe I beat up a brother of his?"

Luna gaped. "Beat up?"

Oops.

Mathias didn't look surprised.

"Anna, have you been going around beating people up?" asked Luna. "It's one thing to defend yourself. Gods know, you've probably needed to." She looked out the corner of her eyes at Peter, who sat nearby. "But have you actually sought out . . . violence?"

I smiled darkly. "I didn't have much of a choice."

"But violence is powerlessness and destruction."

"No, Luna. Violence is a tool. If I want to be left in peace, I sometimes have to strike first. If I don't go after them, sooner or later, they come after me."

"You reap what you sow. And if you want to reap peace, it's not a good idea to sow violence and hatred," said Luna. "Can't you see that? Think of that girl."

"Save it for the Peace March, Luna. It's wasted on me." We sat for a while without saying anything.

Mathias started to study for class, but he was flipping through the history book so quickly that he couldn't possibly have been taking it all in. Maybe he was hoping to skim so much that he could come up with some kind of answer if he was called on in the next class.

It was blazing hot out, and Luna had on royal-blue hot pants that very few girls could have gotten away with wearing. Luna got away with it. Her top was red with yellow polka dots, and she wore a narrow orange belt. To complete the look, she had tucked her dark curls into a green turban.

"Anna, why do you always dress in black?" she asked suddenly.

Mathias's eyes stopped on the page, and he struggled to suppress a laugh.

I looked at Luna's color bomb of an outfit and considered how to answer diplomatically. "I just like that color the best."

Luna looked thoughtful. "Did you know that black isn't really a color? It's actually the absence of light. Black strangles the light and symbolizes destruction. That's why I don't like to wear black."

Sometimes Luna sounded like a middle-aged alternative healer.

"Maybe I like destruction." I turned up my lips in a sadistic smile.

Luna opened her mouth to say something, but Mathias slammed his book on the table.

"And did you know that in the Viking Age, there was a group of warriors called berserkers?" He was clearly trying to get us to talk about something else.

Luna took the book and looked through it, while Mathias continued. "*Berserker* was the name of a type of Viking warrior that fought in an almost trancelike state with such a violent fervor that most of their enemies ended up in pieces. They felt neither pain nor fear, and they threw themselves into battle without any form of protection. Oftentimes, they dressed themselves in wolf skins, thus inspiring the first legends of werewolves. They thought violence and destruction were a means to . . ." He stopped, as if only then realizing the parallel to the conversation Luna and I had been having just a few minutes before.

"Are you saying I'm a berserker?" I had read about the berserkers the previous evening. As far as I remembered, they fought wearing nothing but animal hides, in a state of euphoric intoxication caused by a fungus.

Luna looked up from the book. "You quoted the text word-for-word. How did you memorize all that?"

"I have a photographic memory. It's totally normal."

"But how could you have read it so quickly?" I asked. I had seen him flipping through the book, and it seemed as though he had barely let his eyes rest on each page.

"I read fast. That's also totally normal."

"I don't think it's normal to be able to read so quickly," I said.

Mathias pressed his lips together. I recognized that facial expression as one of my own, from when I didn't want to talk about a given topic anymore. So I turned back to the colors.

"Luna, I've noticed that you wear some very colorful clothes. I don't know what it's like in the places you've lived, but in this country . . ." I gestured at some of the other students, who, despite the season, were dressed in black, dark blue, and one daring girl in white.

Luna played with her beaded necklace. "The different colors have an effect on me. Every morning, I assess how I feel and put on the colors I need. Today, for example, we have history. There's a lot of stuff I have to memorize, and blue makes me focused." She pointed to the tight blue hot pants. "So I put these on to help me concentrate."

"They have the exact opposite effect on me." Mathias eyed the article of clothing in question.

Luna moved on the sofa so she could drape her legs over Mathias's lap, and he carefully placed his hand on her smooth brown shin.

Her hands glided across her top and belt. "The colors of fire give thanks to the sun because it shines and gives us life. I knew we had French class, and so I was a little amped-up. The green color," she touched the turban, "calms me."

Mathias seemed to lose his ability to speak after this tour of Luna's well-sculpted body, so I spoke up. "So you self-medicate with colors?"

"You could say that. I don't know if you've noticed, but I struggle a bit with controlling my feelings."

No, we certainly hadn't noticed that.

"You can't imagine the things I say and do if I don't take these precautions."

No, we absolutely could not imagine.

"Maybe you use black in the same way, Anna," she said. "Maybe you use black as a shield, because you're preparing yourself for the next attack, and you have no idea where it'll come from."

CHAPTER 4

It was Friday. I was in gym class, and I was trying to devise a plan to get out of the morning assembly during the upcoming free period. If I put myself in a room with over five hundred people and their pasts, it would end in catastrophe.

I rubbed my eyes. The previous night I had had the vision twice, and Monster had to wake me because I was crying in my sleep. I was now on my fifth day without a full night's uninterrupted sleep, and I was ready to scream with frustration.

Our gym teacher, Mrs. Hansen, was in her mid-fifties. She walked around the gym with upbeat and decisive strides. Luna was standing next to me wearing a tight yellow jumpsuit. People stared, and some of the girls laughed. She laughed back, unaware that they were laughing at her, not with her. She grabbed my upper arm.

"Nice muscles. Do you work out a lot?"

"Yes."

"What do you do?"

"Every morning, I go for a bike ride or run six to nine miles. Then I box with my punching bag." I saw no reason to admit that I was blacklisted from every martial arts club in the region. "I also do a hundred push-ups and sit-ups."

"Every day?"

I nodded.

Mathias joined us. "What does Anna do every day? Aside from provoking at least three people."

"She runs, boxes, and does a hundred push-ups." Luna did some feminine boxing punches in the air.

Mathias whistled. "Damn. What are you training for?"

My gaze flickered in Peter's direction. Mathias followed it.

"Let's hope it doesn't come to that." He took me by the shoulders and turned me around, so I had my back to Peter.

At that moment, the teacher called us to attention. The mere sight of her accommodating smile made me tired.

"We're going to do trust exercises. Divide yourselves into groups of four."

Uh-oh. I turned to head for the exit.

Mathias grabbed me by the arm and dragged Luna up from the lotus pose she had placed herself in on the floor.

"I get the feeling you have some issues in this area," he whispered.

"Thanks," I mumbled.

"We're missing one." Luna ran over to Little Mads, who stood by himself. I don't know if he was happy or terrified to be part of our mysterious group. His face, way up there above me, was impossible to read.

Mrs. Hansen instructed us to put our backs to the group and—in an insane show of trust—let ourselves fall into their arms. The group would lower the person to the floor and lift them back up to their feet.

Luna dropped at once, before we were ready, and Mathias barely managed to grab her before she hit the floor. He deftly got her back on her feet. Little Mads and I hadn't even registered her throwing herself backward.

Mathias looked over his shoulder and leaned back. We grabbed him, lowered him, and got him back up again with no problems.

Mads cleared his throat. "Maybe it's best if we skip me," he said with his deep voice. He wasn't fat by any means, but he resembled a trick photo of a regular guy who'd been blown up and photoshopped in with the rest of us.

45

Mathias and I exchanged a look. We were inclined to agree, but Luna assured him that we could surely lift him.

I tensed all my muscles and prepared myself.

Mads cautiously leaned back into our arms, and we moaned under the weight. He was still holding back some.

"Come on, Mads," encouraged Luna. "Just let yourself fall. We can definitely hold you."

Shut up, Luna.

Mads relaxed, and we felt his full weight. I feared that all four of us would end up in one big pile. We lowered him carefully. He hung, swinging slightly above the ground, and I was ready to give up and just lay him down on the floor. I didn't have any more strength to give. But Mathias emitted a very manly *huugghh* and took the last of the weight, and somehow, we got Mads upright again.

My turn. I tried to refuse, but Luna was impossible to deny, so I positioned myself with my back to the others.

Come on, Anna, you can do it.

"Come on, Anna." Luna echoed my thoughts.

I took a deep breath and let myself fall. At least, I thought I did.

I tried again, but I just stood there stiff as a board. "Come on, Anna." I could hardly hear Luna's voice anymore. Peter walked by at that moment.

"You need help with everything," he said and pushed me hard in the chest, and I toppled backward.

I stepped on Mathias's toes and banged my head into Luna's chin before landing on the floor. I shot up lightning fast, my hands clenched into fists, and had almost reached Peter when Mads grabbed me around the waist and held my arms at my sides.

"Let me go," I hissed, but he held tight. The close contact between us sent waves of images from him to me. I saw him alone on the playground, and I felt his sadness. I heard the children's vicious shouts, and I saw myself as a child fighting bitterly against

46

some bullies. I sensed him debating whether he should help me, and his guilt over not getting involved.

"We just started here. Stop trying to ruin it already," he whispered.

Mathias went right up to Peter. "What the hell are you doing?"

"What do you mean?"

"You pushed her." Mathias pointed at me.

"Psycho?" Peter looked at Mathias, uncomprehending. "She fell. Honestly, I don't think she's entirely sober."

Luna was also there now. "You leave her alone."

"I'll do what I want to do." Peter took a step toward me, and suddenly I was highly aware that I was standing with my arms pinned to my sides. But before Peter reached me, it appeared as though he had hit a glass wall.

"You leave her alone," came Luna's voice again.

And to my surprise, he actually turned around and swept across the room.

"What did you do to make him hate you so much?" Luna asked.

She watched him go and squinted her eyes. At that moment, Peter stumbled and nearly fell.

Mads let me go and looked down. Mathias coughed quietly.

Luna looked at them. "What?"

"I hit him in the head with a bat and broke his nose and one cheekbone. He was out of school with a bad concussion for two months and got so far behind, he had to repeat the year." Expecting a lecture on peace and love, I looked calmly at Luna.

"I'm sure you had your reasons," she said.

Morning assembly. Students streamed toward the large auditorium. Only a few times in my life had I been somewhere with over two hundred people. I tried to scurry in the opposite direction. No one would notice if one person was missing, right? But Luna grabbed my arm.

47

"Where are you going?"

I writhed. "Uh, I just thought . . ."

"Come on." Luna pulled me toward the auditorium.

The physical contact made it hard for me to refuse her. Actually, when I tried, I was completely unable to turn around. I wondered at this as she hauled me into the enormous room, where I was immediately attacked from all sides.

I saw funerals; a raised, defensive hand right before a blow; and a summer meadow with storm clouds overhead. I felt anger and joy, heard children crying, saw a smiling grandmother. It became more incoherent and all-encompassing as people trickled in, and I was bombarded with pasts from every direction.

Mathias sat on the other side of Luna. She said something to him, but I only saw her lips moving. With eyes closed, I leaned forward. The voices in my head grew louder, the images clearer, and the feelings overpowered my own.

Then it all disappeared. For a moment, there was blessed quiet inside my head. Then I heard music.

I cautiously opened my eyes.

The room had changed. I was still in Ravensted High School's auditorium, but it looked nothing like it had just a few seconds before. Whereas I had previously been sitting among rows of hundreds of students and teachers, the room was now cleared of chairs and decorated for a dance. Around me, young people danced to a song that was already an oldie when I was a kid.

What time am I in?

I noticed a little group of three standing with their backs to me. Two girls and a boy. One girl had long, ash-blond hair, the other had black shoulder-length curls. Something about the boy was familiar, even though I could see only his slim silhouette in the dim light.

Someone started to shout hysterically. "They're hanging outside in the tree. They're dead."

48

The three raised their heads and looked around.

Everything went black again.

"Is she still unconscious?" Mathias's voice verged on hysteria. My hands found something cold. Tiles. I looked up cautiously and discovered that I was lying on the floor of the girls' bathroom, and that Luna and Mathias stood over me.

"Are you awake? I was about to slap you or pour a bucket of water over your head," Luna laughed nervously.

I wanted to say something, but the nausea came on so quickly that I barely made it to one of the toilets before I threw up.

Luna was immediately at my side, holding my hair back.

I'm not used to people taking care of me, but I was grateful to her for making sure I didn't get vomit in my hair. When I was done, I laid my forehead against the cool toilet seat, until I remembered what body part is usually in contact with it. I leaned back.

"Should we call a doctor?" I heard Mathias ask in the background.

"I'm okay." Now that the nausea was letting up, the shame came on with a vengeance. "What happened?"

"I could ask you the same thing." Luna laid a hand on my cheek, and it felt so good that I didn't protest. "We were sitting in the auditorium, and your eyes were closed. Then you opened them, but it was as if you weren't even there. Mathias practically had to carry you out." Luna giggled. "Just so you know, people might think you guys are an item now."

Mathias jumped in. "I didn't have a choice. From what I know of you, having an attack in front of five hundred people is not like you."

"I have social phobia," I lied. "I always feel sick when I'm around a lot of people."

Luna crawled backward out of the little stall.

49

"My dad can cure phobias with hypnosis." She stopped when she remembered my resistance toward her parents. "Is there anything I can get you?"

"A soda." I needed sugar.

Luna flitted away and I was alone with Mathias. I sat across the stall, pulled my legs up, and leaned my head back against the thin wall.

"Who is dead?" asked Mathias.

I looked up at him.

He looked me up and down, his arms crossed. "When I carried you out, you were whispering, *They're dead, they're dead. They're hanging outside in the tree.*"

I didn't reply.

"Social phobia, my ass," he said.

"Photographic memory, *my* ass," I replied.

We held each other's gaze, neither of us saying anything. Mathias's blue eyes sparkled.

Then Luna came in with a soda in her hand and saw us staring at one another.

"Damn, you would think you two really were an item." She handed me the soda. "Or that you're about to rip each other's heads off."

I always recover quickly after a vision, so I did not go home. My theory is that my brain simply overheats. The more people, the worse it is. But for the rest of the day, I kept going back to the three young people I had seen in the vision.

When I finally left school, there were two peculiar-looking people standing in the parking lot. My first impression was that they were . . . colorful, and that they looked like no one else I had ever met. There were two things I was sure of: these were Luna's parents, and they were waiting for me. This was a take-the-bull-by-the-horns-or-flee situation, so I walked directly over to them.

On my way, I kept my eyes on the people who, according to Luna, had been my absent parents' best friends.

The woman was so pale that her skin had an almost bluish tint. Her hair was long and silvery white. Her features were delicate, and her large eyes were cornflower blue. Bare feet stuck out from under a floor-length purple dress, and she smiled a cautious but warm smile. The man's coloring was the opposite of hers. Chocolate and mahogany. His dreadlocks went down to his waist, and a silver ring shone against the dark skin of his nose. His red shirt was unbuttoned at the top, exposing a tattooed chest. He opened his mouth slightly, which revealed several gold teeth.

The couple leaned toward one another without touching, as if they were two magnets affected by each other's force field. They were the least parent-like parents I had ever seen.

I reached them and tried to look gruff, but the woman's smile made it difficult.

She spoke. "Dearest Anna Stella, I have longed for this day."

My eyes watered when she said my seldom-used middle name. I furiously blinked the feeling away.

"Well, until a few days ago, I had no idea you existed. So why don't you do us all a favor and scurry back to your hippie commune."

The man's full lips pulled back in a broad and slightly menacing smile. I saw something in his face. Recognition?

His voice was deep and had a strong accent. "I'm Benedict—Ben—and Rebecca here is Luna's mother."

I felt the same kind of persuasion from him as I did from Luna. The feeling of not being able to refuse him. I threw all my mental power behind blocking that feeling.

"Anna. I gave my word to your mother and father nearly eighteen years ago. I cannot break my word."

"I consider it broken."

He looked at me with his eyes squeezed halfway shut. "It's not your decision."

I wanted to know exactly what this man had promised my mother and father when I was a baby, so I reached out with my extrasensory ability. Like I was sniffing, listening, or feeling around for something. Or trying to tune in to a specific frequency on a radio. But I hit a wall. There was nothing. Not even a baseline mood. I tried again, with a little more concentration. Nothing.

With all my strength, I flung my clairvoyance at him.

He swayed slightly, as though I had poked him in the chest with a finger. Smiling, he bent his head.

"You are your mother's daughter," he said. "No doubt about that."

Rebecca grasped my hands, as Luna had done that first day. The same electric and creative current flowed from her to me. I got a bit more from her than from Ben, a friendly yet sad baseline, but there was also the same barricade.

What I was doing was something close to assault, but I did not expect her to notice. Through Rebecca's hand, I hammered my power into her. It forced its way up through her arm and into her chest to wrest something of the past out of her.

She made a sound as if she'd been thrown into ice-cold water.

I got a flash. Just one. Of a woman with curly black hair and furious brown eyes. She held a tiny, bloody baby in her arms. "Take her," she hissed.

Ben pried our hands apart and stepped between me and Rebecca. The image of the woman disappeared, and an invisible wall formed between us. It threatened to bring me to my knees.

"Who the hell are you people?"

They weren't able to answer because, at that moment, Luna arrived. "Mom. Dad. What's going on?"

I, too, wanted to know. This was the first time anyone had noticed that I was digging around in their past.

But Ben and Rebecca were not about to reveal anything. Luna's mother smiled at her daughter and smoothed her unruly curls.

"Luna, honey. We were just trying to convince Anna to come visit us."

Ben turned to me. "Luna tells us you're mad at us. We understand."

"You don't understand shit," I said quietly and turned to leave.

Luna grabbed my arm. "You can't go, Anna."

Again, as from Ben, I felt a wave of persuasion emanating from her. But whereas—if I used all my strength—I could shut her father out, I was unable to resist Luna.

I stayed.

"Anna," Luna continued, "just listen to them."

I turned back toward Ben and Rebecca.

"Thank you, *chérie*." Ben looked at his daughter, surprised. I thought I saw pride in his gaze. "We heard what happened with the girl, and we aren't comfortable with you living all alone."

Ah, this again. An adult's concern.

At that moment, Monster came galloping from the forest and sat at my side. Rebecca closed her eyes, and Ben's mouth hung open. Monster looked directly at them.

Ha!

"I don't live alone," I said.

"You surprise me," said Ben. I didn't know if he was talking to Monster or to me.

Mathias joined us, and once again, both Ben and Rebecca looked clearly taken aback. There was nothing strange about that. I was yet to witness anyone who wasn't bowled over by Mathias's beauty the first time they saw him. Except for Luna, of course.

Mathias reached his hand out to Ben, who took it.

"I have been looking forward to meeting Luna's parents," he said formally.

Kiss-ass.

He also extended a hand to Rebecca. She and Ben exchanged a glance.

"Likewise," she said. "Luna's friends are our friends, too."

Varnar walked out of the school's red front door and stared at our little flock.

Ben, Rebecca, Luna, and Mathias didn't notice him, but Monster immediately stood alert. He followed Varnar with his large eyes, and the hairs on the back of his neck rose slightly.

"Well, nice meeting you," I said and started walking away from the group. This time, not even Luna's powers of persuasion could stop me.

"Come, Monster," I called over my shoulder.

He remained sitting majestically in front of Ben and Rebecca. This stupid dog totally ruined my exit.

"Come on, Monster."

He didn't move.

All right, he could suit himself. I continued toward the bike racks with determined strides.

Finally, Monster ran and joined me. I realized that I had been holding my breath.

Ben shouted after me. "Isn't there anything we can give you to convince you to give us a chance?"

I turned and sent him the iciest glare I could find in my arsenal.

He seemed to sincerely want to be in my life. Maybe, for the first time, I had the chance to be part of a family that actually wanted me around. I looked at them as they all stood there watching me.

"No," I shouted back, wanting to get away from them. This time I didn't plan to stop.

Ben closed his eyes and sniffed. Though the air was still, a light breeze reached me from across the parking lot.

He opened his eyes and shouted: "What about your very own house?"

CHAPTER 5

A house. I don't think anything else Ben could have said would have gotten me to listen to him, but I stood there as if cemented to the gray pavement.

Ben made his way over to me in just a few long strides. What he had to say was obviously not suitable to shout across the parking lot.

"Your mother left us their house. It is rightfully yours. We would have waited until you came of age, but if that's what it takes, you can have it now."

"What do you want in return for giving it to me four months early?"

Ben flashed a wild, gold-flecked smile. "Come to dinner at our house tonight."

"Just dinner?"

He nodded. "Just dinner. Bring the dog."

"I don't want to hear anything about my parents. Nothing."

"We won't mention them."

"And Mathias has to come, too," I negotiated.

Ben nodded and held out his hand so we could shake on it. I took his hand and felt it sealed either my, his, or perhaps both of our fates.

Without another word, he left me and Monster. He made a waving motion with his large arm, signaling his family to follow him. When Rebecca turned, I shuddered at the sight of the long white hair that flowed down her back. I was almost certain she was one of the three people I had seen in my vision at the morning assembly. The atypical family clambered into an orange Volkswagen bus, which Ben deftly navigated out of the parking lot.

"Did you hear that, Anna? We're going to their house tonight. We're going to Luna's house. Should I pick you up so we can go together? They live a little outside of town. I have the address." Mathias was speaking quickly and practically jumping up and down.

I sighed. "Okay, Romeo. Pick me up at six."

It wasn't until I was riding my bike home with Monster running at my side that I realized Ben had said my *mother* had given them the house.

In one of the very few pieces of information I had about my progenitors, my father's absence was glaring.

I was dressed—in black—had brushed my thick hair, and, as always, had gone all in with the dark makeup, when there was a knock on my door just before dinnertime.

Mathias had put on a collared shirt and arranged his golden hair in a side part. With his Grecian nose, sapphire-blue eyes, and prominent jawline, he looked like something from a fashion magazine. In his hand, he held a bouquet of flowers.

What would it be like if someone went so far out of their way for my sake? I looked at the flowers.

"You really shouldn't have, Mathias," I said.

His facial expression was priceless, and my irony sailed right over his head without so much as mussing his well-coiffed hair.

"They're for Luna's mom. I promise you, you will get a bouquet of flowers another day." He laughed when he saw I was joking. "May I see where you live?"

I stepped to the side so he could enter my minimal apartment. Monster alone took up the entire kitchen area. My punching bag hung in the middle of the living space, and my sofa bed and table filled what was left. Mathias and I stood crammed in the entryway.

"Well, this place is . . . tidy."

I'm not so dumb that I can't recognize criticism camouflaged as a compliment.

"You don't like my home?"

Mathias looked around. "Maybe a picture or a couple plants," he tried. "It's a little impersonal. I can only see things that have a function. Something you can sit on, lie on, or eat at. And something you can," he eyed the punching bag, "practice on."

"Why should I have something that doesn't serve a function?" In the kitchen I thought I saw Monster roll his eyes.

"I don't know. Maybe because most people like to have nice things in their home. You should hang up something pretty."

I gave him a grim smile.

"I can pin you up on the wall." I spread out my arms and assumed a Jesus-on-the-cross position.

Mathias paled. "It makes me very uneasy to hear you say that."

I shook my head. "I don't like to have a bunch of knickknacks. It's way too much trouble when . . ." I stopped.

Mathias finished my sentence for me. "When you have to move again."

"Yeah." With a cough, I tried to keep my voice steady.

"How many places have you lived?"

"Fourteen." I tried to make it sound totally normal. Mathias had enough tact to not ask any more questions.

About one mile outside of Ravensted sat Luna's house. It was one of those former farms the area is full of. The old structures remain and have been, depending on the owners' financial means and ambition, more or less restored. People live in the old farmhouses and have filled the former barns and stables with junk. All the land is usually sold off. Maybe the owners keep a single field or two.

Luna's parents' house belonged to the category of "not-so-restored." The roof was covered in moss, and the white lime plaster was flaking off the walls, which in several places were painted with strange symbols and figures. In the trees along the dirt road that ran from Kraghede Road to the house hung dream catchers, a couple of bird skeletons, animal skulls, and a single round loaf of wheat bread tied with blue ribbon.

Mathias and I looked up in wonder as we rode past, with Monster trotting alongside us. When we parked our bikes against the peeling wall, Luna came bounding out, and Ben appeared in the doorframe. He welcomed us solemnly with his deep bass voice.

It was less run-down inside—cozy and clean—but filled with too many things for my taste. A sweet-and-spicy scent hung over the home. The kitchen was made of solid, weathered wood with curtains in front of the shelves under the countertop. Jars of herbs and dried flowers piled up in the windowsills and on the counter, and more hung from the ceiling to dry. In the living room, the walls were covered in masks, antlers, painted fabric, and maps. On shelves and on the floor sat urns, statues, and taxidermic animals. In one corner stood a large loom with a half-finished weaving project.

Mathias and I had a hard time finding the right words.

"What a lovely home," Mathias stammered and ceremoniously handed the bouquet to Rebecca, who accepted it with a nod.

She found an orange string, wrapped it around the bouquet, and hung it upside down from the ceiling among the other dried flowers and herbs, while we tried to act like it was normal for a mother to accept a bouquet of flowers from her daughter's suitor in such a way.

Luna showed us up a narrow wooden staircase. "Come, you have to see my room."

Monster stayed downstairs.

Luna pulled us into a room that was an explosion of colors and objects. A sewing machine stood amid the chaos, and it was clear that she was in the middle of a project. Maybe even several projects. On a dress form hung a half-finished wine-red dress with tulle and lace. On hangers all around were more pieces of clothing in different colors. Leaning against the wall stood a painting that depicted the view from her window. There were fields, and behind them on a hilltop was a little white house. The bright blue sky filled the top three-quarters of the image, and the house resembled a tiny white pearl amid the blue.

Luna flung out her arms. "What do you think?"

Mathias looked around. "Wow."

It was a *wow* that could be interpreted in several different ways, but Luna gave a wide smile. "Thanks."

"Did you make all this yourself?" I pointed at the clothes.

"Of course! I sew all my clothes myself."

I stroked the red dress.

"Do you like it?" asked Luna, suddenly seeming a little self-conscious.

"Yes." Oddly enough, I had never seen a dress like it before. "Why didn't you tell us you were so creative?"

"I don't know. I just have to do it. There's this energy inside me that comes out when I paint and sew. And when I sing and write music."

"Is there anything you can't do?" Mathias gaped.

She grabbed the guitar with a smile, sat cross-legged on the floor, and began to play. She sang something in French that I didn't understand, but her voice was lovely.

Mathias and I stood spellbound.

"Beautiful, *chérie*," someone said from behind us when Luna's voice faded away. Mathias and I jumped, startled.

Ben stood in the doorway. "Are you coming down?"

We trundled single file down the narrow staircase.

Monster sat in the kitchen. He looked pretty relaxed there, and Rebecca did not appear to have anything against the giant dog's presence.

She turned to us. "Luna and Mathias, would you help me make a salad?"

I could smell that this was a diversion tactic from a mile away.

Luna leapt into the kitchen and started pulling out various food items. Mathias gladly took the food and set it on the table as I wondered what dark chocolate and chorizo would be doing in a salad.

To pass the time while the others prepared the food, I looked around the living room. I picked up a statuette that stood on a shelf flanked by a small skull with sharp teeth and a figure of Ganesh. The statuette was the same size as my hand and clearly of African origin. It depicted a man who had an unsettling resemblance to Ben in miniature.

Rebecca turned around. "Please put him back, Anna, dear. That's Augustin Odion, and he's a little . . . grouchy."

I looked at her, mystified, but returned the figure to its place. Ben put his hand on my shoulder. A wave of his wild energy shot down into my arm.

"Would you like to see the house?"

"What? Now?"

Ben laughed his deep laugh. "Yes, it's just on the other side of that field."

I looked out the kitchen window. The two pale fields bordering Ben and Rebecca's lot stretched, as I had seen in Luna's painting, up toward a hilltop, on which stood a small white house. Behind the hill spread Kraghede Forest.

"Shall we?" He waved a broad hand toward the door.

This man—I looked at Ben—had promised my parents that he would take care of me in their absence. A promise he was just now fulfilling, nearly eighteen years after he had made it. I honestly did not think too highly of any of them, but I wasn't going to say no to a house. As far as I was concerned, the devil himself could have lived there. So, wordlessly and with an icy look, I walked past him. Monster jumped up and ambled at my side.

After wading through tall wheat, the three of us turned onto a small path that ran along the windbreak between the fields that lay parallel between the two houses.

Along the way, Ben provided brief snippets of information. He pointed to the left. "Our field." He pointed to the right. "Your field."

"Who planted them?"

Ben did not turn to reply, instead speaking straight out into the air. I had no difficulty hearing his powerful bass voice.

"When we left, we transferred the land to Paul Ostergaard." He pointed down the hill, to where the Ostergaard property was. "You go to school with his daughter, Mina. We know Paul from the old days."

I was well aware of Paul Ostergaard. He was known locally as the Earl because he owned so much land and was so wealthy.

The path turned sharply and went up a steep incline, and I thanked my physical fitness that I was able to follow Ben's long strides without gasping for breath. Then we reached a little house.

The property consisted of a farmhouse with an extension at one end, which I assumed was a former stable or barn. The paint on the exterior walls was peeling slightly, and although the roof had spots of moss here and there, it appeared to be watertight. *Odinmont* was written on the side of the house in letters made of iron.

I said the name aloud.

"This place has been called that since long before the house was built," said Ben.

Many places in Denmark are named after Norse gods, and as far as I was concerned, the hill could be called Donald Duck as long as I was allowed to live there in peace.

Ben stopped a few steps from the royal-blue front door. *Did I hear him whisper something very quietly?* He inserted a key into the lock, which clicked before we entered the house.

From the foyer, we walked into the kitchen, which, like Ben and Rebecca's house, was an integrated part of the living room. This, however, was where all similarities ended. Where Ben and Rebecca's house was stuffed to the gills with trinkets and decorative items, there was a total lack of anything that wasn't functional in this house. I don't know if it irritated me or pleased me. An antique and rather battered spear hung on one of the walls and appeared to be the only thing without a clear function. At one end of the little low-ceilinged living room stood a large, heavy dining table with simple but massive wooden chairs. A deep crack ran along the length of the tabletop. At the other end of the living room stood an old wooden bench. I was surprised that there was no sofa but decided that the bench took the place of one. My parents were obviously not the leisurely type. On a bookshelf stood a colossus of a system with a record player, cassette player, and CD player. Two of the shelves were filled with a ton of LPs and just a few CDs.

"Did you get the house ready for me, or has someone lived here in the meantime?" I had expected the house to be in poor condition after all these years. Smashed windows, a thick layer of dust, and the tracks of uninvited guests. But it was clean and smelled as if it had recently been aired out.

"The house has been unoccupied, but it's ready for you now," said Ben cryptically.

From the foyer, a door led into the bathroom, which looked nice but a little old-fashioned with dark green tiles and louvered cabinet doors.

Upstairs there were just two rooms connected by a short hallway. One room was a classic bedroom, its furnishings blessedly simple with a double bed, a small vanity with a chair and mirror, and an old wardrobe. In the other, I stopped in the doorway, unable to step inside.

There was a large crib and a wide changing table. On the table lay two identical onesies. It was almost as if they had been laid out, and the house's inhabitants had just gone out for a moment. A moment that had lasted eighteen years.

I pushed the raw lump in my throat as far down as I could and tore my eyes away from the baby clothes.

Someone had painted a pretty valley under a blue sky directly on the wall. Animals—horses, I think—were spread across the green carpet of grass. In the middle of the valley was a lake, exactly the same color as the sky. At the end of the valley was a dark forest, which shone almost like cold metal. The scene looked like something from a fairy tale.

I turned abruptly toward Ben. "When can I move in?"

"I have to speak with your legal guardian, Greta, first. But maybe in a couple of weeks."

"And the house is in your custody until then?"

Ben nodded.

"Will you do something for me before I move in?"

Ben nodded again, and I noted that he hadn't asked what I wanted before agreeing.

"Will you clear out this room?" I pointed over my shoulder with my thumb.

"Of course." His expression didn't change.

I didn't look into the room again. But when I reached the stairs, I looked down the little hall.

Monster was still standing in the doorway, staring into the nursery. If a dog can be lost in thought, then that's what he was.

On the way back, I asked the question I had been pondering the past few hours. "Why are you giving me this house?"

"Odinmont has been yours since you were born."

"Right, but why are you transferring it to me now? I could have gotten it when I come of age. You could have just let Greta take care of it."

Ben sniffed the air, as if breathing something in. Then he replied. "I think you're safer here. I would have preferred to have you move in with us, but I know I can't get you to do that. This is the next best thing."

"What do you mean, *safer*?"

"Something evil has come to this area, and I believe that the young girls' deaths have something to do with it."

A little guiltily, I realized I hadn't really given much thought to Tenna Smith Jensen. My own problems—which in comparison were quite small, considering I was still breathing—had overshadowed everything else.

Hey, wait a second.

"*Girls*? There was only Tenna."

Ben turned and towered over me with a crazed look on his face. I took a step back.

"No," he rumbled. "There was another. Six months ago. Naja Holm."

Though I was generally not aware of the people around me, I still would have noticed a murdered teenage girl. I shook my head in denial.

"She was found not far from where you were living at the time. Outside of Jerslev."

Oh, her.

"She wasn't murdered. They said on the news it was a hit-and-run."

Ben's eyes turned a shade darker.

"That's not what I'm hearing. They think she was murdered." He turned suddenly and kept walking.

As I stumbled trying to keep pace with Ben's long legs, I wondered who *they* were. Who had told him that Naja was murdered?

The rest of the visit passed relatively painlessly.

When Ben and I got back, I saw the table was set for six. The sixth plate turned out to be for Monster. Mathias looked appalled when the large dog sat at the end of the table, but no one else seemed to notice it.

We ate a somewhat unusual but surprisingly delicious dinner. Luna's salad was the pièce de résistance. I'm no culinary expert, but I got a clear sense that this household had an unconventional approach to preparing food. And it worked out pretty well for them.

Before the meal, Rebecca said grace. I gritted my teeth. Foster family number six were members of an evangelical church, and their entire world was organized around religious rituals. I did not last very long with foster family number six.

Rebecca placed her hands together with her fingertips toward the ceiling. Her smooth white hair surrounded her face. She gave thanks to the chicken and the pig who gave their lives so that we could eat, and thanks to the vegetables for having grown in the life-giving earth. Mathias and I exchanged a glance, and I had to bite my lip to keep from laughing.

Mathias turned up the charm as much as he could, and it had a dazzling effect on both Rebecca and Ben. I was grateful that he took the spotlight and that no one pressured me to participate in the conversation.

The only moment the mood turned a bit tense was when Luna, Mathias, and I retreated upstairs. When I went to use the bathroom, I discovered a small green-walled room next to Ben and Rebecca's bedroom. A large mattress lay on the floor. It was covered in colorful blankets and pillows, and on the walls hung framed paintings of landscapes from all over the world.

"Whose room is that next door?" I asked when I plopped back down on the floor with Luna and Mathias.

A strange expression flitted across Luna's face. "I thought you were going to live here."

Without saying a word, I looked down at the floor and wished it would swallow me whole.

Luna continued hastily. "My mom and dad said I should tread carefully with you. That you might not want to live here. Something about how your mom is really tough, and if you're anything like her, you have your own ideas about things. But, on the other hand, if you resemble your dad . . ." Luna bit her lip. "Oh, right. You don't want to know anything about them."

Too late. I exhaled hard.

"But I didn't really believe them. So the first thing I did when we moved in was decorate your room." She laughs a bit nervously. "Do you like it?"

My body prepared to jump up and storm out.

Mathias rolled his eyes. "Jeez, you two." He leaned slightly toward me and put on a girly voice: "Ohhh, thanks, Luna. I really appreciate it, even though I was planning to live by myself." Then he leaned toward Luna and said with a slightly deeper, yet still girly, voice, "No, thank *you*, Anna. I might have jumped the gun a little, but it's only because I so badly want to be friends with you. But I'm happy for you that you've found a good place to live."

He grabbed my hand and forced it into Luna's. He was shockingly strong.

A wave of Luna's creative and wild energy shot into my hand, and I got some of the little picture show from Mathias's grasp on my wrist. I shuddered and pulled back my hand, but I managed to laugh with them, even if it was a bit forced.

As Mathias and I biked away, I pointed in the direction of my future home.

Mathias whistled. "Your own house. Sweet."

The evening had not been quite as terrible as I had feared, but I was looking forward to being alone with Monster after a very long and peopley week.

But when we climbed up the stairs—Mathias had revealed yet another very old-fashioned trait by insisting on escorting me home—Arthur stood leaning against my door. He looked at Mathias, who returned his gaze.

"Hey, Arthur," I said. I may have sounded a little tired.

"Hey," Mathias said to Arthur and held out his hand.

In all the years I'd known him, I had never seen that expression on Arthur's face. He looked astonished but tentatively took Mathias's hand.

"This is Mathias. We go to school together," I said by way of introduction.

"Arthur," Arthur said shakily. It was obviously completely unfathomable to him that I had made a new friend.

"How do you know Anna?" asked Mathias.

"Oh, you know, around," Arthur evaded.

Mathias clearly didn't know what to say.

The three of us—four if you count Monster—stood and looked at one another.

Monster looked around as if to locate something or other.

"Well, anywaaaay . . ." I hinted to both Arthur and Mathias.

"Do you guys want to go to Frank's and have a beer?" Mathias gave us one of his most charming smiles.

"I don't drink, but I'd like to come," Arthur replied quickly, which left me in a bit of a bind. One one hand, a crowded bar was overwhelming, but the idea of Arthur and Mathias going alone and potentially gossiping about me behind my back was not appealing, either.

I sighed. "Okay, as long as we sit outside."

Monster stayed home.

I lagged a bit behind and looked up at the sky. It had a mint-green tinge, even though it was almost ten o'clock. It was one of those summer evenings in August when the air is mild and people panic that the warm weather could be the last of the year, so they swarm out onto the streets in droves. The majority of Frank's customers that evening were therefore sitting outside in the little space in front of the bar, where there were tables and chairs set up.

After Arthur had recovered from his obvious shock that I had made a new friend, he seemed very chatty. Unbelievably chatty, actually. He and Mathias fortunately did not talk about me, but about old music from the nineties.

Mathias went to get beers. After a look from me, he was quick to volunteer to join the long line in front of the bar, where people were pushing each other to reach the front.

"He seems nice." There was care in Arthur's voice.

I nodded. "He's in love with a girl named Luna."

"Are you sad about that?" Arthur asked cautiously.

"No, not at all. She's really sweet."

Arthur eyed me without saying anything more.

I recognized several people at the other tables. Some of them snuck glances at us. Others stared blatantly. Every time I said something to Arthur, eyes flicked in our direction. Peter, who was sitting with Niller, looked me straight in the eyes, put his finger to his temple, and made a swirling motion. Varnar was there, too. He looked at me out of the corner of his eye, but quickly turned his head when I looked at him. A girl his age joined him and placed two beers on the table. Her short dark-brown hair was slicked back, and her coloring was dark like Varnar's. She looked at me with a curious expression.

I swallowed and wrested my eyes away.

"Earth to Anna." Arthur waved a hand in front of my face. "Don't you want to tell me about your friend Luna?" he asked, evidently for the second time.

"I go to school with her. We were at her house tonight."

"Were her parents there?"

"Yeah, and they made some really bizarre food."

Arthur chuckled. "Really?"

I nodded. "Yeah. Who mixes together chicken, cinnamon, chocolate, and raisins?"

Arthur laughed again.

Maybe I was paranoid, but I felt like people were still staring at me. Most people usually treated me like I was invisible. If they didn't get aggressive at the mere sight of me. I looked around again, agitated. People should mind their own business.

"Did they seem happy?" asked Arthur.

"Who?"

"Luna's parents."

This was a strange question. But I knew Arthur. It was easier to answer him than argue.

"Sure. But also worried. Especially Luna's dad. He brought up the dead girls."

"I've been thinking about them, too," said Arthur.

It was sad, but I couldn't see how it affected me in any way.

"Wait, how did you know there's more than one dead girl?"

Arthur was about to answer, but at that moment Mathias came back.

"Are you sure you don't want anything? I can get you a soda."

Arthur shook his head but looked longingly at the beers. Mathias sat down.

"Are you in school, or do you have a job, Arthur?"

"No." Arthur did not elaborate.

"So what do you do?"

"I make the time pass in other ways."

Mathias left it alone. "How old are you?" he asked instead.

Even I didn't know the answer to that. He had always been an adult in my eyes.

Arthur cleared his throat. "I'm twenty-seven."

Hmm. I actually thought he was older. I had perceived him as an adult when I'd first met him, but maybe he'd seemed that way only because I'd been a child myself.

"How old are you?" Arthur asked Mathias.

"I just turned eighteen," said Mathias. "I started high school last year, but then I dropped out and worked in a café. I'm a couple of years older than the other people in my class."

"I'm turning eighteen soon, too," I said. "But I also spent a year doing something else." I thought of Nordreslev Youth Center, the juvenile detention center where I was placed after I hit Peter with the bat.

Arthur, who knew that story, did me the favor of changing the subject. "Before you got here, Anna was saying that you had visited your friend Luna this evening."

If he was counting on getting more out of Mathias about the evening's events than from me, he was right. Just hearing Luna's name apparently set off fireworks in his heart. Fireworks that overshadowed any ability to think rationally.

"Did you know Luna's parents gave Anna a house?"

Arthur's smile disappeared. "They did what?"

Mathias continued, and I had a strong suspicion that Luna had infected him with verbal diarrhea.

"They know Anna's parents, so they gave her their old house. Anna's going to be Luna's neighbor." Mathias looked at me enviously.

"Anna's parents. Did they say anything about them?"

"No, because I asked them not to," I cut in, and sent Mathias a furious look.

He slapped his hand across his shapely mouth. "Maybe you wanted to tell Arthur yourself."

More like *not tell him at all.* Arthur was at times a bit overprotective, and he definitely was not going to like the idea of me living alone in the country. Not that it had anything to do with him. I hadn't planned to say anything. Once I had moved, it would be too late for him to say anything. But now I could expect hundreds of questions from him.

He asked only one. "Why didn't you want to know anything about your parents?"

"Why would I want to hear about two people who got rid of me?"

Mathias looked down in his beer. "Maybe there was a reason why they did what they did. Maybe Ben and Rebecca could tell you something that might make you like them."

"I don't want to like them," I nearly shouted.

Again, Arthur responded with a question. "Why not?"

This time I wasn't dumb enough to answer. I just looked breathlessly down into my beer, my cheeks burning.

Arthur was about to say something more, but suddenly he shivered, as if a cold wind had struck him on this warm summer evening.

And then the screaming began.

CHAPTER 6

The screams were coming from the back alley behind Frank's.

Arthur, Mathias, and I were the first ones to reach the girl, who stood paralyzed, screaming. On the ground in front of us lay another girl. I realized it was Alice from my class at the same time I noticed blood flowing from a gaping wound in her neck. Her aura had been extinguished like a broken light bulb.

The pool of blood was getting bigger and bigger, and it darkened Alice's carrot-colored hair. I started to inch backward when it came near my feet.

I lost feeling in my face, fingers, and legs, and my breathing became rapid.

All at once, a large group of people arrived; moments before, they had been enjoying themselves inside and in front of the bar. I tried to take another step back, but I was pushed forward, and the weight of all those people bombarded my head. I could see the very recent past playing out.

Just above Alice's body, I saw a translucent, dying version of Alice writhing. She grabbed her neck as if to close the gruesome wound. I heard an awful gurgling sound when she tried to breathe.

Mathias had his arms around the still-screaming girl, who I just now realized was Kamilla—another classmate. Her screams turned to fragmented sentences.

"He . . . he came . . . out of nowhere. All of a sudden. He didn't even look at me," sobbed Kamilla. "He dragged her back here.

And cut her. Then . . . he was gone." Her eyes were wide, and she inhaled in great gulps.

I saw the images simultaneously, and Kamilla's words served as disjointed subtitles.

The man was tall and had long hair, a beard, and wild eyes. I could smell him. Sweat and alcohol. He grabbed Alice by the throat with an enormous hand, pushed her backward into the alley, and shoved her up against the wall. Without hesitation, he lifted a gigantic knife and nearly decapitated her with it. While still holding her up with one hand on her jaw, he tucked the knife into his belt with the other hand and wiped his fingers on her white shirt. Then he dropped her on the ground and was gone. It took twenty seconds, max. At first, Alice's expression was one of surprise, but it quickly slid into panic as she fought to breathe.

Dark spots began to dance in front of my eyes. I looked for Arthur, but he was gone.

The throng pressed me forward, and I could sense their fear— and lust for the sensational. Faintly, I heard people screaming when they caught sight of Alice.

Mathias was holding the shocked Kamilla upright. No help to be found there.

My own legs were starting to give out, and my ears were ringing, but I could not get away.

Frank stuck his head out the back entrance, and his smile lines dissolved into shock when he saw the dead girl on the ground. His horror washed over me.

I tried to focus on Alice's blood-smeared white T-shirt, just to hold on to something. Suddenly, the marks left by the man's fingers did not look random. They consisted of one long stroke and two smaller ones tilting downward. It looked unmistakably similar to the symbol, the crooked F, that the killer carved into the girl's back in my recurring vision.

73

My last attempt to keep my head up and my legs down was unsuccessful. My consciousness flickered one last time before I lurched forward toward the ground, the pool of blood, and Alice.

I landed in a pair of strong arms.

My eyes were already closed, so I recognized Varnar only from his scent. Before I blacked out, I managed to wonder how he was able to take in the bloody scene, assess more than a hundred people, and react when he saw me about to pass out.

I heard the characteristic thrumming of a large group of people without being able to pick out individual words. When I faint, my sense of hearing is the first to return, and for a moment I am blind, mute, paralyzed, and confused as hell. Then my body tingles, and my senses come back but I'm still confused. I'm used to fainting. It's one of the fringe benefits of my power. Is it any wonder I stay far away from other people?

This time I was lying down, and my head was resting on something soft. A cushion. As fainting episodes go, this was one of the better ones. But that was only until I remembered what I had just seen. I opened my eyes and looked up at a man dressed in white and orange, who was in the middle of taking my blood pressure. Mathias and Arthur were watching over his shoulder. Arthur's red hair was sticking out in every direction, and Varnar was nowhere to be seen.

"That really isn't necessary." I tried weakly to push him away. If I was really unlucky, I would throw up soon.

"I'm just checking to make sure you're okay." He avoided my gaze.

"Shouldn't you be taking care of the girl out there?"

"There's not too much I can do for her." He looked briefly up at the ceiling.

"The other girl. Kamilla."

"Other people are taking care of your friend."

74

"She's not my friend. None of them are. Were." I closed my eyes again. "I'm okay. I just got scared."

"We have a crisis counselor, if either of you wants to talk to someone."

I shook my head.

"Can you sit up?" he asked.

I propped myself up, while the EMT turned to Mathias. "You should call her parents."

Mathias's eyes flicked toward me, perplexed. "We can take care of her."

"We?" The EMT shook his head and continued. "If you're the next of kin, then you need to get her home. Stay with her tonight and call for help if she starts to feel cold or faint. And be sure to take care of yourself, too." He looked sternly at Mathias, who nodded obediently.

The white-and-orange-clad man spoke to me—again without looking me in the eye. "You should go to the doctor on Monday. You might need crisis counseling later."

I nodded, well aware that I would not go to the doctor unless I was at death's door, and probably not even then.

He gave several more instructions to Mathias, but Arthur did not seem to notice being overlooked.

Mathias pulled me up to my feet. "That was the second time today."

"The second time what?" Arthur asked sharply.

"The second time she's fainted," said Mathias.

Shut up, Mathias!

"Is there something wrong with you? Did you take something?" Arthur's voice was piercing.

"You know I never do drugs. Earlier today I went to an assembly."

"Well, why did you do that?" he wondered. "You know what happens."

"I don't know. Maybe I've started following the rules."

Arthur started to laugh, but it faded quickly. This was not an evening that invited laughter. "Come on, let's get you home to bed."

Mathias protested. "He said I should do it."

"I'm taking her." Arthur's voice did not leave room for discussion.

Arthur sat next to the bed, while Monster lay on the floor and looked at me, worried. Arthur took my hand.

My body continued vibrating, even though I ordered it to lie still.

"Did you see the murderer?"

Arthur was the only person who knew I was clairvoyant.

"Yes," I whispered.

"Describe him to me."

I closed my eyes and recalled the grim vision. "He was huge and had long hair. Matted. And a long beard. He stank, and his eyes were wild. Like he was on drugs or something." I opened my eyes again.

Even though the room was as dark as it could get on a Scandinavian summer night, I saw the terror in Arthur's face. He was even more pale than usual, if that was possible, and his freckles stood in sharp contrast to his light skin.

"Do you know him?" I asked.

"I know his type." He closed his eyes. "Listen up, Anna. This is very important." He opened his green eyes. "Keep Monster with you at all times. And go to Ben and Rebecca's as often as possible. You should not be alone. And if he or anyone else comes after you, call for me. I will always hear you."

"How can you hear me if we're not together?"

"Just promise me you'll call if you have problems." Arthur's facial expression showed that this was not up for debate, and I knew him well enough to know that he did not intend to elaborate.

"I promise," I sighed.

76

"Thank you. Go to sleep now. You need to rest." He kissed me on the forehead.

Before I fell asleep, I sniffed my shirt. It smelled like Varnar.

Immediately, I was standing in the spruce forest. *Damn!* I would obviously not be getting a break today.

The girl was about six feet from the little birch tree. Which meant I had about ten seconds before the man would show up and do what I knew he was going to do. I took a step to the side to avoid having him walk through me. I knew the scene so well by now that I had time to look around more, even though I knew what was coming.

The forest looked like any other spruce forest. Trees aren't too different from one to the next. I looked past them, out to the open fields. The moon was not quite full, and I glimpsed the little house that sat slightly above where I was standing. It looked familiar now. Where had I seen it before? I searched my brain but it was blurry. As if I were not myself.

Then I heard the man's crunching footsteps. I turned to see his face, but he was looking down and his hood was pulled up. He had the cord, and for the second time in mere hours, I saw a young girl lose her life.

Someone shook me, and Arthur's voice broke through. "Anna, wake up. You're crying."

I gasped as if about to drown. Arthur's green eyes bored into mine, and I clutched his cool arm.

"What did you see?"

My answer was instinctive. "He's strangling a girl. And then he cuts her. I see it every night." I knocked my knuckles against my temple.

Arthur held my hands so that I couldn't hit myself.

"You don't usually see the same vision multiple times," he said. "When did you start seeing the girl getting strangled?"

I looked down at the comforter. When I was younger, I didn't know that I was the only one who could see the past, but I quickly found out that I made people uncomfortable when I opened my mouth. I just didn't know which of the things I said they were reacting to. Eventually, I didn't dare say anything at all.

"Tell me about the vision with the girl," Arthur pressed again.

I told him as calmly as I could.

"Do you know the girl?" Arthur looked at me without blinking.

"I can't see her face. Just her back. She has long hair, maybe a little longer than mine." I twirled a black tendril between my fingers. "But it's a light color, I think. It's hard to see because it's at night."

"Could it be red?" Arthur asked quietly and let go of my hands.

"Yeah, it very well could be."

"More." He made a continuing motion with his hand. "Fat, thin, tall, short?"

"She's slim, about my height."

"What about the man?"

"I can't see him."

Arthur looked like he was holding his breath. "Have you ever seen the future?"

"No, never. I only see useless glimpses of the past." I punched a fist into the comforter. "What the hell can I do with that?"

"So, she's already dead."

"Of course she's dead. She's dead as a stone."

Arthur's face shut down. "You need to sleep, Anna."

He moved to the window and looked out, lost in thought. His hair shone slightly in the light of the streetlamps.

I closed my eyes, and I don't think it took more than a couple of seconds before I fell asleep.

When I woke up at eleven o'clock the next morning, Arthur was gone. He had probably figured the period for potential shock was over.

Monster and I walked to the bakery, where people pushed in front of me in line without so much as looking in my direction. Alice's face smiled at me from every front page. I picked up a newspaper. Under Alice's photo there were two other pictures of young, smiling girls. The headline read SAME MURDERER? One of the girls was Tenna Smith Jensen. The other one I didn't recognize, but Ben had mentioned her name the day before. Naja Holm. When I saw the girls side by side, the similarity was unmistakable. All three of them were redheads. Beneath the photos, the text said the police were now reopening the Naja Holm case, especially due to the similarity between the girls, but there were other details they did not want to release in light of the investigation. They suspected that a serial killer with a fetish for red-haired teenage girls was on the loose. The idea was plausible, and I remembered Arthur's question, whether the girl in my vision could have red hair. Were there four girls instead of three?

While I waited my turn, I thought about how I should spend the day. I decided to go for a bike ride, and I knew exactly where to go.

The sun was shining from a cloudless, brilliant blue sky, and the heat radiated off the asphalt as I flew down Kraghede Road with Monster behind me. I passed Luna's house but did not slow down. My destination was someplace else entirely.

The little dirt road that started at the foot of the hill led up to my soon-to-be home. The hill was so steep that I had to stand up on the pedals. At the top, I leaned my bike against the wall and admired the view.

The entire northwestern section of Denmark is flat as a pancake, this hill being one of the few exceptions. From here, the left side of the hill sloped down toward Ben and Rebecca's house. Behind me, the dirt driveway led down to Kraghede Road. In front of me, the fields stretched down to the Earl's large property, Ostergaard, and to my right, the hill tilted sharply, ending at the outer edge of Kraghede Forest. The forest lay like a dark, sleeping giant at the end of the golden wheat field.

Monster did his best sheepdog impression and had to jump to move through the tall grain. I laughed, and he stopped. It looked as if his large mouth had broken into a grin. I ran out into the field.

"You silly dog." I caught up to him, knelt, and put my arms around him. He laid his enormous head on my shoulder.

"I'm so glad you're here," I whispered. In response, he breathed into my ear.

I patted his head, stood, and turned to walk back up the hill toward the house but stiffened when I looked up there. It all clicked into place in my head, and I turned back toward the forest. Without thinking, I started to run. Monster ran after me with a confused bark.

It was like going from day to night, because I was coming from the sharp sunlight. At first, I could barely see anything in the dim forest as my eyes adjusted to the greenish light. It was cooler, and the hairs stood up on my bare arms and legs. Or maybe that was because my surroundings were starting to look more and more familiar.

Forests are almost all alike, but if you've tried to memorize landmarks in one, you can quickly recognize where you are. I had had plenty of time to memorize each stone and spruce tree, so I did not doubt for a second that I had been in this forest, in this spot, before. Many times before.

My heart pounded as I walked toward the place where I had seen the girl fall. The chill of anxiety swept over my arms, but I kept going.

I prepared myself to see the vision again, now that I was physically in the place where it had happened. But I saw nothing.

I placed a hand on the ground and concentrated, but I got nothing more than still images of the changing seasons and people passing by. A deep calm flowed from the earth and up into my hand. Nature is in no hurry.

I saw no strangled girls or murderers. No backs with F-shaped scars. I placed myself where the vision normally began, and I trembled involuntarily. My entire body was screaming at me to run away, but I forced myself to keep standing there.

When a bird fluttered past me, I jumped and had to convince my pounding heart to remain inside my rib cage, even though it seemed determined to break out of my body and flee without me. After a few deep breaths, I stared ahead.

Aside from the fact that it was summer and daytime, the scene was identical to my vision—but I did not feel anything with my powers.

Monster ran in wide circles around me, as if scanning the perimeter.

Why was the vision hidden from me? It was like staring at a spot-the-difference picture. I could see that there were differences, but I couldn't figure out what they were. With eyes closed, I recalled the vision. I looked forward again and saw the same scene before me in daylight.

I kicked off my shoes so that the soles of my bare feet touched the mossy forest floor. Frustrated, I closed my eyes again and fully opened all my other senses in the hopes of getting just a tiny hint.

The forest told me nothing, but I captured something else. The footsteps were silent, but I clearly sensed the aura of someone moving quickly in my direction.

Someone with a very focused and aggressive energy placed themselves right behind me.

CHAPTER 7

I whipped around and went on the offensive without thinking. One of my fists flew toward the man's face, and the other toward his stomach.

He avoided my blows with an elegant ease and caught both of my hands in his. My sudden attack threw both of us off balance, however, and we tumbled to the forest floor. I landed on top of him, but he quickly rolled us over, so he sat straddling me and held my hands over my head. It was only then that I recognized him.

Varnar's face was so close to mine that the tips of his dark hair brushed my cheekbones.

"What are you doing here?" His voice was strained from the effort of holding me down, and again I could hear his slight accent.

I tried to twist myself free: "What's it to you? What are *you* doing here?"

He said nothing, but his eyes glimmered threateningly, and I was suddenly highly aware of the fact that I'd never seen the face of the man in my vision. Varnar was still holding my hands above my head, and he was too strong for me to break free. At the same time, he was pinning me to the ground with his strong gaze.

I had only one chance, so I gathered all the courage I had and slung my face toward Varnar's to headbutt him. He quickly turned his head, so I missed. At the same time, he grabbed my hair and held both my head and my hands down, while his legs tightened their grip around my torso.

I gasped for air in frustration, but I was unable to move.

The close physical contact between us allowed me to sense his feelings more intensely than I had ever felt anyone's before, and although I did not see concrete images from his past, I sensed his extreme determination. I was paralyzed by his strong emotions, and for a moment I lay completely still.

He opened his mouth to say something, but just then he was tackled from the side. Suddenly he was the one lying on his back. Monster's jaws were locked around his neck. Varnar struggled to breathe but had the good sense to lie completely still.

Monster's eyes met mine. If I said the word, he would crush Varnar's throat.

With my head tilted, I rubbed my wrists, trying to hide how freaked out I was at having been so close to Varnar.

"What should I do now?" I said aloud.

Varnar did not respond, but Monster growled, and I sensed clearly what *he* wanted to do.

Then I heard a voice behind me, speaking a Scandinavian language. The strange words sounded stern, like an order. I turned around and saw the girl who had been sitting with Varnar at Frank's the previous evening. His girlfriend, I assumed. Monster moved his eyes from me to her and reluctantly loosened his grip on Varnar, who quickly rolled away and jumped to his feet with a feline grace.

The four of us looked at one another. The silence hung between us for several very long seconds. I felt someone should say something, but I personally had no idea what to say after what had just happened. Monster couldn't talk, and Varnar appeared to be too furious to say anything. Mercifully, the girl began to speak.

"I'm Aella. It's nice to meet you." She smiled, which was not quite what I was expecting after my dog had nearly mauled her boyfriend. She spoke with the same accent as Varnar. "I'm sure Varnar is sorry to have frightened you."

He didn't look the least bit sorry.

"Why did you sneak up on me?" I asked.

"You were the one who attacked me," he spat. "I had to hold you down so you wouldn't hurt me or yourself."

Now that I thought about it, he actually hadn't done anything to me aside from walking silently and standing behind me.

"You startled me," I said sharply.

"Do you always attack people who startle you?"

I shrugged. I guess I did, as a general rule.

Aella raised her hands and stood between us.

"But nothing happened, did it, Varnar? Anna doesn't seem to have hurt anything but your pride." She gave him a teasing smile and turned to me. "It's totally understandable that you would be on edge after what happened yesterday."

I didn't ask how she knew my name, nor did I tell her that my reaction had nothing to do with Alice's fate, as brutal as it was. But I did ask, "What are you even doing here?"

Aella leaned her head to one side and looked at me in a way that made me feel shy. "We live nearby."

Aside from Ostergaard, Odinmont, and Luna's parents' house, I was not aware of any habitable properties within a half-mile radius.

"Define *nearby*."

"We're currently staying at Kraghede Manor," she said innocently.

"The dilapidated estate in the forest? Isn't it on the brink of collapse?"

"Only the east wing. The rest is fine. There's a roof over our heads, and the oven still works." She looked at Varnar. "We don't need anything else."

They were clearly in love. They even looked alike, in that non-sibling way that couples come to resemble one another.

"You should come visit us someday." Aella's gaze lingered on my face just a little too long. "We're going to be neighbors, after all."

84

"Where did you hear that?"

"I listened to your conversation with your friend yesterday," she replied shamelessly.

I squeezed my eyes shut. Compared to people's normal reaction to me, she was far too nice, and she was also staring at me much more than everyone else—combined—did.

"Well, don't expect me to come borrow a cup of sugar from you anytime soon." I grimaced and stole a quick peek at Varnar, who by all accounts seemed to share my feelings toward Aella's invitation. I picked up my shoes and marched out of the forest with as much dignity as I could manage with leaves in my hair and dirt smeared up my arms and legs. Once again, Varnar's scent lingered in my clothes. I cursed it.

Monster trotted at my side and nudged me with his snout. "Traitor," I mumbled. "Can't you do what *I* ask? Or would you rather obey some random girl?"

For obvious reasons, Monster did not reply, but he snorted loudly.

We passed my former and future home. A closer inspection would have to wait. I climbed onto my bike and steered it homeward, not caring whether Monster followed.

If he no longer wanted to live with me, there was certainly plenty of space at Kraghede Manor.

For the rest of the weekend, I could not get Varnar's dark eyes out of my head—and his fleeting smile the day he tried to keep me from leaving the high school. Every time he appeared in my mind's eye, I reminded myself of Aella. And of the fact that I had crashed into him twice now, fainted in his arms, and attacked him, after which my dog nearly bit off his head. He surely thought I was an idiot, and I was inclined to agree with him.

On Monday morning, the school was, as expected, all abuzz about Alice.

A camera crew had taken up residence in the parking lot and was interviewing the students most eager to be filmed. None of Alice's closest friends volunteered.

We were called into the auditorium so the principal could update us. I hid behind the gym during the assembly, but I got the summary from Luna and Mathias afterward.

The few times I saw Varnar, he scowled at me. I tried to ignore him, even though the butterflies in my stomach were fluttering like crazy.

Later that day, it was time for my monthly visit to my caseworker, Greta. My sneakers made little squeaking noises against the linoleum floor as I walked down the halls of Ravensted Social Center. The meeting had been the only recurring event in my life for as long as I could remember. Over the years, I had come here with various foster parents, but in recent years, I had handled the visits alone.

When I reached Greta's door, I saw it was closed, which meant she was speaking with a client. I heard a deep voice behind the door and prepared myself for some poor guy to come lurching out. I admired Greta's courage to be alone with some of the types that came to the center. Of course, to many people, I myself was one of those types.

To my surprise, Ben came out. Next to Greta, he resembled a large, colorful bird with his long dreadlocks, red corduroy pants, and unbuttoned sky-blue shirt, which showed off all the tattoos on his chest. I noticed now that they were small symbols arranged in strange patterns.

He smiled broadly at me, and his gold teeth sparkled in the fluorescent lighting.

"Anna, I just talked to Greta about how the house will be transferred to you. We agreed that you should move out there as soon as possible."

Standing next to him, Greta looked to be anything but in agreement, but she said nothing.

"I have temporarily transferred the deed to Greta, because she is still your guardian." He seemed a bit irritated by this. Then he turned to Greta. "I know that I can trust you on this," he said gravely. "You will let Anna move as soon as possible, and you will transfer the deed to her the day she turns eighteen."

His eyes bored into hers and she nodded like a marionette, even though the look on her face said the exact opposite. Ben released Greta from his spell and flashed me another big gold-flecked smile.

"See you, Anna." He patted me on the shoulder before he left, humming down the hall.

The people he passed turned around to look at him.

Greta shivered, showed me into her office, and sat behind her computer. I pulled up the chair to the corner of her desk.

"He's always made me uncomfortable." She began to type.

"You've met Ben before?"

"He was here when you were little and were put into the foster system," she said absently as she typed away.

This information was completely new to me, but I knew nothing about how I had ended up a ward of the state.

"That was when you had to be removed from Mia and Jens's care. Ben knew your parents, after all."

I held up a hand.

Greta shook her head. She seemed a little out of it. I hoped Ben hadn't caused her lasting harm with his hypnosis, or whatever it was he did to her.

"Sorry. I shouldn't have mentioned your parents."

She smoothed her straight hair, which hung on either side of her narrow face in a pageboy style. Her brown turtleneck sweater was loose on her, though it couldn't have been bigger than a size small. She pushed her glasses up the bridge of her nose and sniffed.

87

"Well then, congratulations on the house. Ben is very intent on you moving as soon as possible, although I don't think a young girl has any business living alone in a house that far out in the country. Especially not as things stand right now. The only reason I'm allowing it is that you have your large dog."

This was the first time she had spoken positively about Monster. Who would have thought this would go so smoothly?

Greta looked at me sternly. "Of course, there are some conditions."

Okay, here it comes.

"I expect to be able to visit you out there and check that you're keeping it neat and clean. These will be unannounced visits," she lifted a finger, "and I will not allow for other people to live or stay in your house for long periods."

"No problem."

"And you need to have a job."

I was horrified. "But . . . I get money from the government."

"Anna, it's expensive to own a house. Even if you get it for free. It's a much bigger responsibility than renting. You will not be allowed to move out there until you have a job."

I could tell that she meant it.

"Where the hell am I supposed to find a job? There aren't even enough jobs for normal people right now."

Greta looked back to her computer. "I can find a placement for you. You could be a cashier at the supermarket. We provide a subsidy to companies that hire at-risk youth."

It was hard enough to be surrounded by people at school all day. The thought of spending my afternoons in the supermarket with even more people was unbearable.

"Wouldn't it be easier if you just gave me the extra money? Don't you think they'll be afraid that I'll steal from the cash register? People know about my past, after all."

"As far as I know, you've never stolen anything. But yes, they might think you have." Greta looked intently at the screen through her thick glasses. "We'll eliminate places with cash held on the premises, but it's important that you join the workforce." She rubbed her upper lip with her thumb and index finger. "You could also work at DTF."

"The knife factory? Me and a bunch of knives?"

"No, that won't work, either." Greta continued clicking. "The preschool? Or the nursing home?"

"Would you entrust your children to someone like me? Or your aging husband?"

"Well, I have neither children nor a husband," Greta said pointedly. "But you're probably right. We'll avoid cash, knives, children, and the elderly."

We both sat and thought about it. I couldn't think of any place that didn't involve other people—who I wanted to avoid coming in contact with—or cash, potential weapons, children, or the elderly—who other people wanted to keep me from coming in contact with.

"We can talk about it next month."

I shook my head imperceptibly. I just needed to survive the next few months, and then I could drop out of school, and Monster and I would happily live out the rest of our lives in Odinmont.

It's funny how we always think "the rest of our lives" extends so far into the future.

I walked to Frank's to pick up the day's ration of dog food. On the way, I recounted my conversation with Greta to Monster. It's stupid to talk to a dog, but even I need someone to talk to.

Frank was in the middle of putting bottles away but turned when he saw me come in.

"Food for the dog?" He stuck his head into the kitchen and shouted something. "Have a seat while Milas packs it up." He smoothed his gray pompadour. "There hasn't been a soul in here all day. I think it's because of what happened Friday." His forehead creased slightly.

I nodded and climbed up on a barstool.

Frank looked at me. "You look even more dour than usual. What's wrong?"

"You don't need to worry about my problems."

Frank's eyes were directed at me, and he leaned his head back slightly. "Maybe I can help."

"It's because . . ." I started. "No, it doesn't matter."

He scratched his tattooed arm and leaned over the counter. "Come on. Tell me. I'm curious, and I'm bored. Make an old man happy?" This last bit was said with smiling eyes, furrowed with deep wrinkles.

I sighed. "I've been given a house."

"Not a bad problem to have." The corners of his mouth turned up in suppressed amusement.

"That's not it. It's not a hundred percent mine until I turn eighteen." I made a face. "My caseworker says I have to get a job before I can move in."

Frank narrowed his eyes. "Caseworker?"

I waved my hand to indicate that I did not wish to comment.

He dropped it. "How hard can it be to get a job?"

"No one dares to allow me in the vicinity of valuables or anything I can use as a weapon. Caring for children and the infirm is also a no-go. That leaves very few possibilities."

"Can you cook?"

I laughed. Frank stared at me, and I realized that I laugh so infrequently that people are shocked when it finally happens.

I composed myself. "No, I can't cook. I'm a disaster in the kitchen."

"It's nice to see you cheerful for once." My cheeks grew warm. I wanted to get up and stomp out, but Frank laid a hand on my arm. I was struck by a flash of caring with an undercurrent of sorrow.

"I take it back. Go ahead and sulk." He let go of me. "Can you chop vegetables?"

"You mean can I destroy something with a knife? Yeah, I think I can figure that out."

Frank tilted his head. "I can see why people are sometimes a little scared of you." He scratched his cheek. "But if you want to wash dishes and chop vegetables, I have a job for you a couple of times a week."

I thought about it for a moment, though just a very brief moment, before I nodded. "If you dare to let me handle a knife, then you're a rare breed."

"I'll take the risk. And I'm actually pretty handy with a knife myself," he teased.

"Can you call her?" I reached for a pen behind the bar and wrote Greta's number on a scrap of paper. You know you have serious problems when you've memorized your social worker's phone number. "You need to tell her you hired me. She'll probably think it's a prank call."

Again, Frank gave me a strange look. "Write down your own number, too."

"I don't have a phone, but I can give you my school email."

"No phone? I thought kids from your generation were born with cell phones in their hands." He walked into the kitchen and came back with a bag full of food.

The orange afternoon sunlight washed over Ben and Rebecca's house like flames licking up the walls. I parked my bike and walked up to their door with Monster at my side. I studied some strange drawings that surrounded the doorframe. They depicted a slew of red snakes writhing on top of one another. I hadn't seen them the last time I was out here.

"It's a serpent knot," came Rebecca's gentle voice from behind me. I hadn't even noticed her.

In her light ankle-length dress and bare feet, and with her silver hair draped around her like a cloak, she looked like a storybook angel, minus the wings.

"What's a serpent knot?"

"The serpent knot symbolizes evil. Whoever walks through the serpent knot leaves evil behind them. I painted it here so that we and our guests will always enter our home with only goodness in our hearts." She took me by the arm, which amazed me, considering how I had behaved the first time we had physical contact. She led me around the house and showed me the different drawings on the walls.

"This is a gripping beast." She stopped in front of a whimsical little creature painted in green and blue.

The creature looked like a monkey with four arms. It had a goofy grin and, with all four hands, had a firm grip on itself—around its neck, arms, and wrists.

Rebecca stroked her slim fingers across the drawing. "The gripping beast symbolizes a complex person who represses themselves without realizing they're doing it." She looked at me with her large cornflower-blue eyes. "Everyone has this side, but in some people it's stronger. Do you understand, Anna?"

I nodded. "Leave evil behind me. Don't get in my own way. Yes. Check."

Monster snorted irritably, but Rebecca smiled to herself.

I turned toward the trees along the dirt road, where animal bones and various food items were still dangling. "Why is all that stuff hanging in your trees?"

Rebecca turned her gaze down the road. "We held a blót ceremony. At the blót, we make offerings to the gods."

"The gods?" I leaned away from her slightly, but she was still holding on to my arm.

"Odin, above all. Can't forget him," she smiled, as if I obviously knew what she was talking about, "but most often we turn to Freyr and Freyja. The gods of fertility and love. And Heimdall—the mystical god."

"Uh-huh."

"Ben also honors Tyr and Thor for their strength and bravery. Ben is much more combative than I am. You should have seen him and your mother sometimes." Rebecca giggled.

I twisted myself out of her grasp. The lady was totally nuts. I nudged Monster, who looked back at me. I think he was excited to see what I would do. I myself wasn't sure if I should run away, ask Rebecca to elaborate, or call a doctor.

Fortunately, Ben came up to us at that moment.

Rebecca turned to him. "I was just telling Anna about our last blót."

Ben looked at me, slightly alarmed. In contrast to Rebecca, he seemed to understand that normal people found it strange to believe in Odin and Thor and hang food and skeletons from the trees.

Time to change the subject. "Ben, it's okay with Greta for me to move in next weekend."

Ben lit up with a large, white smile flecked with gold—which, if not for the warmth in his eyes, would have been pretty terrifying.

"Should I come over Saturday morning and help?"

I nodded. "And I actually need to speak with Luna, if she's here."

"I knew you two would become friends," said Rebecca.

"I just need to ask her for a favor."

"She's in her room. Just go on up," said Ben.

Glad to be able to turn my back on the two crazies, I walked through the serpent knot—and thereby, apparently, the world's evil—and took the stairs two at a time.

Luna came bouncing out of her room. "Anna." She smiled. "What are you doing here?"

I bit my lip, not entirely sure how to ask. "If I ask you a favor,

93

what percent chance is there that you'll just do it without asking questions, and keep it a secret afterward?"

"A hundred. I trust you," she said without hesitation.

I don't always trust *myself*, so I had no idea what she was basing this on, but that was her problem.

"I need you to draw a picture of a man. I'll tell you what he looks like, and you'll draw him. Can you do that?"

Luna kept her promise to not ask questions. She just nodded, went into her room, and dug through the piles for paper and a pencil.

"I'm ready."

I sat down next to her, closed my eyes, and tried to remember "the Savage," as I had dubbed him in my mind.

"He has long hair. It goes down past his shoulders," I began. "Very thick eyebrows. Broad jaw and small, narrow eyes. They're close together. And uh . . . full beard."

I described the man as well as I could, and Luna's pencil scratched across the paper. When I finished, I opened my eyes and saw five drawings spread out across the table. I don't have a creative bone in my body, and I studied the faces, impressed. I picked one up.

"Maybe a little broader here." I pointed to the cheekbones. "And the hairline is farther down."

Luna began again, then stopped. "This is probably going to sound a little weird."

After what your mom just spouted, nothing can shock me.

"I think that if I touch you, I'll be able to draw him better."

The ends justify the means, so I nodded, and Luna snaked a bare foot toward my toes. The familiar tingling creativity flowed from her. She began to draw again, and in no time, she showed me a perfect portrait of the man who had killed Alice. Even his wild look was captured in the drawing.

She handed it to me.

"Thanks," I mumbled, and stood to leave.

"Won't you stay longer?"

I fidgeted with the paper without answering.

"I want to show you something." Luna rooted around in her closet and pulled out something fluffy. "I finished the dress."

I recognized the red dress that had been in progress the last time I was there.

"What do you think?" She seemed a little anxious.

I took the dress and studied it. It was made of wine-red silk, lace, and tulle, and had a wealth of small black beads. It sparkled when I turned it in the late-afternoon sun, which was streaming in through the window. The bodice was pure lace apart from a piece of silk across the chest. The back was open down to the waist, where it turned into a foam of soft tulle. Around the arms and down the sides, the black beading was shaped into two snakes. They curved softly around the breasts, and their heads ended at each hip. Their eyes were icy-blue beads. Though it was miles away from my standard worn-out black outfit, I loved it.

"It's for you," said Luna. "I started sewing it before we met, but it only really came together in the past week."

"Why?"

She fingered a bead. "I get the impression you don't have a lot of things that were made especially for you."

I wanted to throw the dress down and run screaming out of the room.

"Don't you want to try it on?" Luna caught my eye.

No, no, no. I held the dress out to her and tried to appear dismissive and determined, but it was too late. Her persuasive power streamed into me.

Shit. Why wasn't I immune to this like with her dad? I pulled off my clothes, and Luna's eyes flickered over the long scar on my chest, but she didn't say anything. She just silently helped me into the dress.

95

It fit perfectly.

She took a step back. "Oh."

I looked in the large mirror that hung on one wall, and I barely recognized myself. The dress was spectacular. If I made the slightest movement, it looked like the snakes were writhing around my body, and the wine-red color made my pale skin look like ivory. The black beads were the exact same color as my hair. In spite of myself, I loved how I looked in this dress.

Voices sounded from the bottom of the stairs. Rebecca called up: "Luna, you have one more guest."

"Hey, Anna and Luna. I hope I'm not interrupting . . ." Mathias stopped when he saw me and was unable to close his mouth. "You look beautiful, Anna," he breathed.

"She is soooo hot in this dress. I knew it." Luna jumped up and down and flung an arm around Mathias, who hastened to put his own arm around her.

"Stop." I waved a hand. "Can you not?"

Mathias looked at me as if studying a rare animal. "That color suits you."

"Thank you, thank you, show's over now. Both of you out so I can change."

Giggling and closely intertwined, they walked out the door.

I allowed myself one last look in the mirror. One. Then I pulled off the dress and put my normal clothes back on. I carefully laid the dress on the bed and stroked it with one hand.

Outside, they were all sitting at a battered patio table, talking and laughing. Even Monster, who sat at the end of the table, seemed to be having fun. I walked past them with my hood pulled up around my face.

Monster jumped up and ran after me.

I'm not completely devoid of manners, so I waved to them over my shoulder as I shoved off down the dirt road on my bike.

Luna and I sat at a table in one of the high school's common areas with books spread around us. Her ancient relic of a laptop whined, exhausted.

I read aloud from a book. "The Vikings were the people who lived in Scandinavia from the eighth century to the end of the eleventh century. They were characterized by a combination of honor and raw brutality. They believed that a person's fate was predestined from birth."

We were writing an assignment about the Viking Age. It was due the next day, we were nowhere near finished, and I could barely keep myself awake. It was as if the vision had become more insistent and frequent, and I woke up screaming several times each night.

"Then what, Anna?"

I focused on Luna, who looked at me through a pair of enormous nonprescription glasses with purple plastic frames.

"What?"

Her hands hovered over the keyboard. "What should I write next?"

"Uh." I looked down. The letters resembled a smear of ants. "The Vikings developed a wide variety of gods in a religion known as Norse paganism or Asatru. The most important gods are the main god, Odin; his sons, Thor and Baldr; and his wife, Frigg. Plus the Æsir Tyr, Heimdall, Loki, Njord, and his twins, Freyr and Freyja."

Luna snorted as she hit the keys.

"Is there something wrong?" I asked wearily.

"Loki's not a god, he's a Jotun."

"It says here that he is." I tapped my fingertip on the page. "It's probably best if we write what it says."

"And Njord, Freyr, and Freyja aren't Æsir, they're Vanir."

"Von what?" I rubbed my eyes.

"Vanir. It's a different type of god than the Æsir." She rolled her eyes as if she had just explained to me that two plus two equals four.

"Should I continue?" I tried to conceal a yawn with my hand.

Luna nodded, pained. "If we absolutely must."

"In Norse mythology, there are also Jotun. Jotun are giants . . ."

"Not all of them," Luna muttered through clenched teeth.

I ignored her and continued. "Among the Jotun, the proto-Jotun Ymir is the most famous, along with Loki's children: the monstrous Midgard Serpent, Fenrir, and the goddess of the under-world, Hel." I read a bit further to myself. "It also says something about slaves—thralls. They're called Þjálfi and Röskva."

Luna stood up abruptly, her chair clattering behind her. She tore the book out of my hands and threw it in the nearest trash can.

I pulled it back out. "I'll get a fine, Luna."

Peter walked past us just then.

"Are you looking for food in there?" He laughed. "You don't get enough from welfare?"

I raised the book to throw it at him, but Luna grabbed my arm. I pulled it back before she could do any persuasive hocus-pocus. "Thanks for nothing, Luna," I hissed. "Can't we just get this done?"

Tears gathered in Luna's large golden eyes. "It's just not true, what it says."

"So?"

"Only Þjálfi is a thrall. Röskva is free."

"Again—so what?" I rubbed my forehead.

Luna put her arms straight down at her sides and made her hands into fists like a small child. "I don't want to write that they're both thralls."

"Okay," I said, defeated. "So we'll write that one is a thrall, and the other is free."

"Thank you." Her lower lip was about to start trembling.

"Why are you all wound up today? Did you forget to wear something green?"

For a moment she stared at me, but then she broke into uncontrollable laughter. She lifted her glasses and wiped her eyes. The crisis appeared to be over. She dug around in her bag, fished out a green scarf, and wrapped it around her head.

"That helped."

I refrained from telling her that I had meant it as a joke. "Why is this stuff so important to you?"

Luna straightened her spine. "Well, it is our religion."

I remembered the bits of food hanging in the trees outside her house.

"Are you really pagan?"

Luna held her head high. "Yes. We follow the ancient Norse beliefs."

Surprised, I searched for the right words to say. "So . . . your whole family?"

Luna looked at her thoughtfully. "I think my dad had to be convinced. He has a totally different background, of course. But that was before I was born."

"How was he convinced?"

"I don't know, but if I did, I probably wouldn't be able to tell you, anyway."

"Why not?"

"Because I think it has something to do with your parents."

Hmm, all right then. My curiosity and principles fought it out in my inner boxing ring. My principles won by a landslide.

"You're right, I don't want to know anything." I rubbed my eyes. "If you know so much about this, then we don't even need the books. Can you just explain it and I'll write it down?"

"Good idea. We'll start with Odin, the All-Father. I've always been a little scared of him. He's so strict and serious. He has two ravens named Huginn and Muninn. Huginn can see the future, and Muninn can see the past. They sit on Odin's shoulders and whisper to him everything that has happened and will happen in all the worlds." She didn't get any further before Mathias came stomping up to us.

He held out his phone, his arm outstretched. "I was just reading the news."

We looked at the screen. Luna's drawing of Alice's murderer looked back at us, manic. We both busied ourselves with looking at the books and the computer. Mathias pointed at Luna.

"Did you draw this?" He waved his phone.

I cursed silently. I had given it to the police in secret. I had not taken Mathias's hyperawareness of Luna into account. Of course he would recognize her drawing style.

Luna looked calmly at Mathias. "I don't want to lie to you. So don't ask me."

Mathias opened his mouth to say something.

She held up a hand. "Don't ask me."

It looked like the words got caught in Mathias's throat. Actually, it looked like they were painfully stuck down there. So he turned to me. "Do you have something to do with this?"

Unlike Luna, I had no problem lying to Mathias. I looked him straight in the eyes.

"I have no idea what you're talking about. And how would Luna know what the murderer looks like? She was at home, sleeping, when Alice was killed."

Next to me, Luna sniffed and wrinkled her nose.

Mathias did not want to drop it. "Anna, did you see him that night?"

Now Luna got involved. "Mathias, do you know what characterizes best friends?"

He shook his head.

"Best friends are the ones who don't ask a million questions."

"Exactly," I continued. "They just help move the body and never mention it again."

Both Luna and Mathias looked at me, shocked.

"What?" I shrugged. "It's just an expression."

"Not one I've ever heard," said Luna.

Was I the only one with a sense of humor?

Mathias sat down.

"I will probably figure this out," he said but dropped the subject nonetheless. "How far have you gotten with the assignment? Mads and I are almost done."

While Mathias and Luna chatted, I discreetly pulled Mathias's phone in front of me.

Who Knows the Pippi Killer? was the headline of the article. It stated that the drawing had come into the hands of police, and that Kamilla had confirmed the likeness. The police were very eager to get in contact with the person who had made the drawing.

Mathias wiggled his phone out of my hands.

"Does it say anything you didn't already know?" He thought he was about to figure out what was going on. He had no idea.

"I didn't know they're calling him the Pippi Killer."

Mathias raised his eyebrows. His expression said: *But you knew all the rest?*

"Why are they calling him the Pippi Killer?" Our wordless conversation had gone over Luna's head.

"After Pippi Longstocking because the victims have red hair like her." We sat for a while, thinking.

Mathias changed the subject. "What are you doing today, Anna?"

"I have my first shift at Frank's after school. And tonight I have to pack."

Luna jumped in her chair. "Oh right, I forgot to ask what time my dad should be there on Saturday."

"The sooner the better. Eight, if that's not too early."

"Not at all. He always gets up at sunrise to welcome the day."

At Frank's, I was put to work by the cook, Milas. It was nothing I hadn't done before in various foster families and group homes. After having demonstrated my knife skills to him and Frank, I was praised for my speed, precision, and versatility. They took a step back when, with a flick of my wrist, I flung the knife into the cutting board so that the tip went down close to an inch into the wood.

Okay, maybe that was a bit too much, but I got carried away.

"I can see why there aren't many people willing to put a knife in your hand," Frank said. "I thought you were joking."

I laughed. It was meant as a friendly chuckle, but I could see from the men's faces that they perceived it as frightening.

Milas glanced at Frank, who gave him a reassuring pat on the shoulder. Milas's vibe told me he was more than skeptical about the thought of working with me.

"You can start by taking out the trash." His accent was thick. When I walked past him, I caught a glimpse of the horrors he had experienced in the Balkan war. I stopped instinctively and looked at him, terrified, impressed that he was still in one piece. Sort of. His aura had some seriously frayed edges. I shook it off, lifted the two large black garbage bags, and walked out into the courtyard behind Frank's.

A scream left my lips as Alice's murderer, the Savage, came running directly toward me with his giant knife held aloft.

CHAPTER 8

The Savage pushed Alice into the alley and slit her throat. Then he drew the strange F on her T-shirt with blood and dropped her in front of me, and then he was gone.

A version of Alice became transparent and disappeared at my feet. I remained standing there, hyperventilating. The trash had spilled and lay scattered around me.

Milas and Frank came running. They had heard my screams.

"What's going on?" Frank grabbed me by the shoulders. Protective instinct and images of a little boy poured from him into me.

I shook myself free.

"A rat," I stammered. "A big black rat."

"You don't seem like the type of person who'd be scared of rats."

I tried to look terrified, which was not difficult. The vision had happened so quickly, I hadn't even realized it was a vision.

"Oh, yeah. Super scared." I knelt to gather up the food scraps. "I'm okay now."

"Call the municipality and tell them we have rats, Milas," said Frank before going back inside.

Milas remained, with his hand resting on the doorknob.

"I've heard people scream like that before." He hesitated before continuing. "When it was the last sound they made."

I ignored him. After a while, I heard the door close. I placed my fingertips on the pavement, bent my head down, and exhaled.

Now there were two more names on the list of people who were deeply freaked out by me.

I was at the top of that list.

At eight o'clock on Saturday morning, Ben arrived in the orange Volkswagen bus.

Mathias was there five minutes later. I hadn't asked him to help, but he probably came just to kiss up to Luna's dad.

My entire life could fit in the back of Ben's car. And there was still room for Mathias's bike and Monster. Squeezed together in the front seat, we drove toward Odinmont, where Luna and her mother were waiting in the yard. Rebecca looked festive, with a big basket in her arms.

Luna hugged us all. She held Mathias's hand in hers, and he didn't look like he intended to let go of it—ever. We carried my things into the house in no time. Ben had kept his promise. The nursery had been cleared out, although the mural still adorned the one wall. We carried my futon inside, and I hung up my punching bag. It would be a combination guest room and workout room— not that I was counting on having all that many guests.

When we were done, Rebecca clapped her hands. "Outside, everyone. We must gain the favor of the gods for your move to Odinmont. We will hold a færa-blót."

I cringed so hard, it probably looked like I was having a muscle spasm. I looked pleadingly at Mathias, but he just looked back at me with a defiant grin.

"What does a færa-blót entail?" he asked on the way out.

"Blót is a ritual in which we offer the gods and other beings a sacrifice in exchange for their goodwill." We had reached the yard. "Færa is the Old Norse word for 'to move.'"

Rebecca's eyes flickered.

"What does it mean besides 'to move'?" I asked, suspicious.

"'To prevent,'" Ben's deep voice rumbled behind me.

"Prevent what?"

He did not reply, and Rebecca busied herself with digging around in her basket. She handed us each a chicken egg that had been painted with runes.

"Stand in a circle." She waved her hand.

We obediently formed a circle.

"Hear me, oh beings, hear me, oh gods, hear me, oh spirits, hear me, oh All-Father. We have formed a circle to blót for Anna's life in this house, the glory of the gods, the protection of the spirits, and her good fortune. I declare this circle sacred." Rebecca's voice was steady and clear. "Give Anna a peaceful and happy life here at Odinmont. May she reap what she sows."

Luna looked at me with concern. Rebecca flung her egg on the ground so it splatted across the gravel. Mathias let out a little yip of alarm.

"Hear me, oh beings, hear me, oh gods, hear me, oh spirits, hear me, oh All-Father. Accept our offering," she shouted loud enough that it must have been audible all the way in Ravensted.

Ben and Luna also threw their eggs on the ground and looked expectantly at Mathias and me. We followed suit, and I began to back out of the circle.

"Hear me, oh beings, hear me, oh gods, hear me, oh spirits, hear me, oh All-Father," roared Rebecca with arms raised, and I scurried back into the circle.

The yellow yolks were slowly sucked down as if through an underground straw. The earth vibrated beneath my feet, and the hairs on the back of my neck began to stand up.

Rebecca lowered her arms.

"This blót is complete, and the circle can now be broken." She smiled. "It wouldn't be a feast without food and drink," she said cheerfully, and led us into the house.

As we followed her, I saw that Mathias's eyes were wide and shining blue.

Monster and I were alone in the house, and I lay down on the bench and felt like I was finally able to exhale.

The house emanated a calm I had not felt in many other places. I didn't feel so much as a hint of what had happened back when my parents lived here. Just a sense of peace and happiness.

Monster snored from the floor, exceedingly content with this upgrade in habitat.

Because I knew what awaited me, I did not want to go to bed, but my eyelids felt like lead after the many nights of interrupted sleep.

Forest. Night. Winter. The girl's hand brushed against mine.

Shit. I must have fallen asleep.

"Stop it. I don't want to see this anymore," I screamed at the sky and sank to the ice-cold forest floor.

The man passed just then, but I almost didn't notice him.

"I'm so tired," I whispered. "Whatever message I'm supposed to be getting, I don't understand it." I didn't know who I was speaking to. "Let me dream something nice."

I stubbornly squeezed my eyes shut, lay down, and placed my hands on the frozen ground. But the ground was no longer cold. It was smooth and soft, and warmth radiated toward me.

I cautiously opened one eye and found that I was lying in a large bed, on the softest sheets I had ever touched. The walls of the room were draped with tapestries, and the floor was made of stone. Flames roared in an open fireplace. A man stood in front of it with his back toward me.

Dear lord. I had wandered into a knight-in-shining-armor fantasy. True, I had asked for a nice dream, but this was just cheesy.

The man turned.

It was Varnar.

I held my breath. His hair was longer, and his face was not sullen, but otherwise he looked like himself. Then he smiled, and the smile warmed me more than the fire in the hearth. In two long strides, he was next to the bed.

Okay. I was in a knight-in-shining-armor fantasy, where Varnar played the leading role. I considered pinching myself on the arm, but the look on his face made that unnecessary. This was definitely, one hundred percent, a dream. Varnar would never look at me like that in real life.

He leaned toward me, but I didn't dare move for fear of waking myself up.

"I've been waiting for this. For so long." He spoke slowly, but there was an intensity in his voice.

The bed rocked when he lay down next to me, but I was too surprised to move.

I was enveloped in his characteristic scent, and he leaned in closer to me. When his lips nearly touched mine, I made a strangled sound.

I was pulled out of the dream.

No, no, no. I want to go back. Monster nudged me with his snout, and no matter how hard I tried to hold on to the dream, it disappeared like sand between my fingers.

"Why did you wake me up?" I yelled.

Monster took a step back and turned his giant head almost 180 degrees.

"Was I making strange noises in my sleep again?"

His eyes confirmed it.

"It wasn't in the same way, Monster. It was . . ." How was he supposed to understand? "It doesn't matter. Sorry."

No one can make you feel guilty like a dog giving you that wounded look. I reached out and stroked his head. He leaned toward my hand and breathed into it.

"Come on, let's go to bed."

I crawled into the large double bed, and Monster turned himself around several times before plopping down with a thud.

Then I closed my eyes and slept the whole night without dreaming anything at all.

The following days, my head was in a fog, and at school I could not stop looking for Varnar.

The only time my head was somewhat clear was when I was pounding away at my punching bag, doing push-ups, or running. I therefore did little else when I wasn't at school or work. My appetite was nonexistent, so I ate nothing. Monster paced nervously around me with large, worried eyes.

I was glad when we had gym class on Friday. Finally, a few hours where time would not drag on while I fought to stay focused.

Our gym teacher herded us outside in high spirits, which I tried to ignore.

The low early-September sun lay across the large grass fields. A cool breeze had just begun to creep in, but now it seemed late summer was refusing to admit it would soon be over.

The teacher announced a running test. She held a stopwatch and an air horn in her hands, which she waved enthusiastically.

First, we had a minute to run across the soccer field. In the next round, we had fifty-five seconds. She would take five seconds off every time we crossed the field. Those who did not reach the goal by the time she sounded the air horn were out.

We got started, and everyone reached the goal. In the second round, there was only one person who didn't make it. Thomas lumbered off the field, breathless and red-faced. When we were down to thirty-five seconds, half of the group had been eliminated. Some didn't reach the goal in time, others simply gave up along the way and left the field, panting.

Mathias, Peter, and I led the pack every time.

Luna ran off the field just before the goal when we were supposed to cross the field in thirty seconds. She threw herself onto the grass and moaned. Mathias watched her but kept running. Only he, Peter, and I remained at twenty seconds.

The taste of blood permeated my mouth, my legs burned, and sharp jabs pierced my side. Under normal circumstances, I would have given up, but with Peter at my heels and in my eagerness to cast Varnar out of my mind, I kept going.

Mathias and I made it to the goal before the air horn sounded.

Peter did not. As he left the field, cursing, I wondered how he would exact his revenge.

Mathias and I took off again.

I was running with everything I had, but alongside me, Mathias wasn't even winded. I was starting to see white spots in the corners of my vision when Mathias overtook me. We both made it in fifteen seconds. Me just barely, Mathias with no problem.

I took a few large gulps of air to prepare myself for the next round.

Ten seconds. It was impossible. But I wanted to at least try to overtake Mathias.

He was ahead of me immediately.

The teacher and our class looked like they were watching a rocket being launched into space. Open mouths and wondering eyes.

Mathias noticed, too.

I know this because a feeling of uncertainty or embarrassment swept off him and hit me in his wake. He slowed down deliberately. I passed him and was a few feet ahead of him when the horn blasted.

Moaning, I sank down to the grass. I panted and could feel my pulse in my temples. Behind me, I heard Mathias's heavy breathing, and through the spots that were dancing before my eyes, I saw the others running toward us.

"Cut the bullshit, Mathias."

"Why are you mad? You won."

I couldn't get up, so I scowled sideways back at him.

"Only because you let me win." I struggled to breathe. It's difficult to scold someone and gasp for air at the same time. "And stop acting like you're out of breath."

He said nothing, but his breathing grew silent.

The rest of our class arrived.

The teacher was ecstatic. "I've never seen anything like it. No one has ever made fifteen seconds before. I've taught gym for twenty-three years. And you almost did it in ten, which is barely even humanly possible."

I glanced at Mathias, who looked down at the grass.

Luna's fire-engine-red sneakers jumped up and down right next to my ear.

"You're so cool, both of you." She threw herself down between us and hugged us so Mathias toppled backward.

"Mathias, you are in incredibly good shape." The teacher looked him up and down.

He flashed her a smile, complete with sparkling white teeth. This seemed to send her into a different galaxy. It was so unfair that he could do that.

"Not as good as Anna, apparently. Anna, was it ten miles you said you run every day?"

And in that way, Mathias changed the subject from his own noteworthy physique so that the focus was on me.

He would pay for that.

I refused to speak to Mathias for the rest of the day. After school I had a shift at Frank's, and Mathias and Luna sat with Little Mads in the café while I chopped vegetables and cleaned like crazy in the kitchen. A couple of times, I had to go into the crowd to clear tables because Frank and the other bartender were busy. I would have a word with Frank about that later. I didn't remember bussing tables being part of my job description.

Peter sat with two other guys. One of them seemed slightly familiar.

Oh. It was Markus, one-third of the gang of twerps that had followed me into Kraghede Forest many years ago. He didn't appear to have accomplished much more than riding a souped-up moped and extorting people.

The other guy I didn't know. And after one look, I knew I had no desire to know him. Almost all his visible skin was tattooed, even his shaved head and one cheek. His eyes were a watery pale blue, and I caught a whiff of pure psychopath when I passed him.

At another table sat Varnar and Aella. Aella smiled at me as I passed them, while Varnar looked stiffly down at the table.

"Hey, neighbor, you should smile more. You look like you're pining for someone," she said.

I stopped and looked at her suspiciously before I shifted my gaze onto Varnar. Obviously, it was clear to him that I thought of him constantly, but to tell that to his girlfriend, who then openly made fun of me? That was malicious of both of them.

Aella leaned back.

"Our invitation still stands," she said with a defiant look.

Varnar looked up at me. His dark hair framed his face. His expression was neutral, but I could sense that he was hesitant. I looked straight into his eyes. The dream returned in a flash.

"You can both go to hell," I hissed, and saw two sets of eyebrows shoot up before I stomped off.

I entered the kitchen with the overloaded tray that was so heavy my arms were trembling. Mathias came running after me.

"Anna, I don't understand why you're mad at me." He gave me his most effective smile, but I was too angry to let it affect me. *Okay.* I was so angry that I refused to let him see how it affected me.

He took the tray from me and held it in one hand. I started chopping a cucumber as if the poor vegetable were my mortal enemy. Mathias set down the tray and laid a hand on my arm. I waved him away and ended up swinging the sharp knife in his direction. He jumped back but did not seem particularly upset that I waved an eight-inch kitchen knife toward his gorgeous face.

"What's wrong?"

"There's something mysterious about you. Something you haven't told me."

Mathias coughed out a scornful laugh. "Right, because you've told me *everything*."

I sniffed. "I don't have to tell you anything."

"Why do my secrets have anything to do with you?"

"You're dating Luna. That's why."

"With all due respect, I don't think this is about Luna."

I turned back to the cucumber, which was now nearly pulverized. Mathias leaned toward me.

"I think you're curious, and I feel exactly the same way about you," he said. "There's something different about you, and I want to know what it is."

The knife stopped over the cucumber. I hadn't even considered talking to Mathias about my defect. I had no clue how to respond. "Uhh, well . . ." I delayed, the knife landing on the cutting board with a clatter. Then I pulled the black garbage bag out of its stand even though it was only half-full, flung open the back door, and ran out into the back alley, where I threw it into the dumpster.

In the quiet late-summer evening, I took a few deep breaths and looked up. The stars were just about to appear in the turquoise sky.

When I looked straight ahead again, the Savage was coming right toward me.

I simply did not have the patience for a vision right now. I waved my hand in the air in front of me.

"Go away."

He continued toward me.

I walked forward and flapped both hands. "Shoooo, get out of here."

The Savage tilted his head and opened his mouth as if he were straining to understand what I said.

CHAPTER 9

We looked at one another.

The Savage, whom I was absolutely looking at in the present, had the same crazed eyes I remembered from the night he killed Alice. The sharp odor of unwashed body struck me. He was dressed in strange leather clothing, and the giant knife in his belt made my chef's knife look like a paring knife.

He slowly came closer, like an animal investigating something unfamiliar. Curious and reserved at the same time.

I took a tentative step toward the door, but he suddenly moved and blocked my escape route, almost elegantly. The adrenaline rushed through my veins and commanded me to run, but I forced myself to stay. I considered shouting for help, but only for a split second. I would be dead before help could get here.

He reached out, took a lock of my black hair, and twisted it between his fingers.

To my great irritation, I made a noise. A mix between a whimper and a gasp. If I was going to die, I had no intention of sniveling while it happened, so I pressed my lips together and stared him straight in the eyes. He was easy to read. His aura was animalistic and aggressive, and the images that poured out of him were clear.

I saw him bash the back of Naja Holm's head on the asphalt, and I felt his glee at causing her harm. With blood-smeared fingers, he drew the F on her black jacket. I saw him cut Alice's throat again. But then I realized what I *wasn't* seeing. I did not see Tenna or the girl in the woods.

Mathias's aura appeared behind me. Just on the other side of the door.

"Get out of here," I whispered, counting on him hearing me even though there was a door between us.

It creaked, and Mathias stepped out.

For God's sake, Mathias.

He threw himself between me and the Savage and shoved him in the chest. This was a very brave and unbelievably stupid thing to do. The Savage hurtled backward and snarled, spraying saliva. He gripped his knife and raised it toward Mathias, who could now probably kiss his shapely rear end goodbye.

But all at once, there was an empty space in front of me—aura-wise, that is. Mathias's aura disappeared. And not only that. He doubled in size, and small, pale-green, ethereal threads radiated from him.

What on earth?

Then he roared, though it didn't sound like anything a living creature would produce. More mechanical. Like the deep tones of a braking train. The sound made the ground sway, and the air that streamed out of Mathias's mouth struck the Savage in the head and blew him over. A nauseating scent of cooked flesh spread through the air, and when the Savage leapt to his feet, I saw that his face was horribly burned. Had Mathias's breath . . . *scalded* him?

The Savage did not scream. Anyone else would have squealed like a stuck pig, but he just traced a finger over his burnt skin with wide-open eyes. Then he ran.

Mathias collapsed in front of me.

I faintly heard people spilling out onto the street on the other side of Frank's. Some screamed. One person shouted, "Earthquake!"

Mathias lay with his eyes closed. He was back to his normal size, and his aura had returned. I sat down next to him—mostly because my legs could no longer support me.

"What was that?" I tried to keep the shock out of my voice and laid a hand on his shoulder, but his panic welled up in me, so I took my hand away.

Mathias looked up at me with burning blue eyes. "There's something inside me that's fighting to get out. I try to keep it down, but sometimes I just can't."

I exhaled and squeezed my trembling hands together. "Whatever it is, it just saved our lives."

"I'm afraid I'll hurt someone I care about."

"Has that ever happened?"

People were still shouting, but I couldn't deal with that right now. Mathias shook his head. He slowly propped himself up and leaned against the wall.

"It's always been there, but it's getting stronger and stronger."

"Have you talked to anyone about it?"

A bitter laugh escaped Mathias's lips. "I didn't really work in a café last year."

I had figured as much. "So what were you doing?"

"First I was in custody, but then they put me in the psych ward."

"What did you do?" I hastened to rephrase. "What did they *think* you did?"

Mathias gave me a smile I could almost recognize as his usual one, and we shared a brief moment of mutual understanding. "They thought I'd shot a . . . I don't know what I should call him." He rubbed his forehead. "A thug."

I gaped. "Jesus Christ."

He nodded. "Yep. Jesus effing Christ."

"How could they think you would do that?"

"Because they saw the hole. It went straight through his chest."

"Did you really shoot someone?"

"I was just keeping him away from me when he tried to start a fight. I didn't mean for my hand to go through his chest."

Okay. All right, then.

"Why did they commit you?" I asked as calmly as I could as I dragged myself over to him and leaned against the wall.

"Because I told the truth. They dropped the charges real quick when they couldn't find any proof that I'd shot him. But by then I had already tried to explain."

You should never try to explain.

"They thought you were sick in the head," I said.

"Paranoid with schizophrenic tendencies and a distorted perception of reality," he corrected.

I shrugged. "Sick in the head."

On the street, I could still hear a tumult. People were very busy panicking, so no one bothered us in the back alley. Mathias didn't seem to register the here and now at all.

He continued: "I took my pills and sat through my electro-shocks, but I couldn't tell a difference. I learned to pretend I was doped up or unconscious. They released me when I acted like a good patient and stopped talking about superpowers and inner demons."

I looked at Mathias's profile in the sharp overhead light of the bare bulb above the diner's back entrance. In that moment, he was impossibly beautiful. Almost otherworldly.

"So, you moved to get a change of scenery after all that went down?" I asked.

"No," Mathias replied absently. "We moved when his friends came after me."

"But you didn't have anything to do with them, did you?"

"No. It was a coincidence that I even got near them in the first place. The guy didn't die, but he was pretty pissed when he came to. He probably couldn't remember much, but when he woke up, his rib cage was shattered, and he had a punctured lung. He thought I was responsible for both. And he evidently has some very loyal friends. I'm sorry I lied to you."

"It's okay. I lie to you all the time."

He looked at me angrily but then softened. "I thought you might be like me. The whole story with Peter. The drawing of Alice's killer. And you can run really fast. I thought you had some answers. But all I did was make you scared of me." It seemed as if he had finally registered the panicked shouts from the street and turned his head in the direction of the sound.

"Sorry to disappoint you, but I'm not scared of you. And I don't know what you are." I flexed my biceps. "And there're no super-powers here."

"But you are . . . *something*." He proceeded cautiously.

I hesitated but then nodded in response. My power was nothing compared to his boiling breath and bone-crushing fingers. But if I could help even a little . . .

"I sometimes see things that have already happened. I also see people's baseline mood or aura. It sounds stupid, but I don't know what else to call it."

"You saw Alice from our class," said Mathias. "And that's why you get sick when there's a lot of people around. You can sense them."

I gave him an ironic thumbs-up.

"What about me? Can you see what I am?" He leaned forward slightly.

I weighed my words before I spoke.

"Yes, I can see your past," I said eventually.

"But I seem normal?"

"Everyone's different," I said, sidestepping the question.

"Can't you just tell me the truth? I have to find out what I am."

"Okay, Mathias. You are different. Your past is full of holes, like a colander, and just now, when you went into superhero mode, you dropped off my radar entirely. I know your aura, and it was gone. Now it's back again."

Mathias was silent.

The sharp smells of old food and beer began to force their way through to me. I wished I had kept my mouth shut, and I was about to say something—I didn't know what, just something re-assuring—when Varnar arrived. He came running into the back alley and looked around with a wild look in his eyes.

"Where is he?"

I played dumb. "Where is who?"

"I know he was here."

"He ran off," said Mathias.

Now keep your mouth shut, Mathias, if you want your little secret to stay between us.

Varnar squinted at Mathias.

"He ran off?" he repeated skeptically. Then he turned his attention back to me, which made my heart flop in my chest. "Did he do anything to you? Did he touch you? Are you hurt?" The words were caring, but he delivered them like an accusation.

I stood up and felt like I was a hundred and eighty years old.

"It was lucky Mathias came. Otherwise, I would probably be dead now." I dragged my index finger across my throat. "He's gone, and we're alive. End of story."

Aella tumbled into the alley.

Over his shoulder, Varnar said, "He saw Anna. I was too late."

No kidding!

"If you want to be my secret protector, I have to say, you're horrible at it," I grumbled. "It's a good thing you have your jani-torial job to fall back on, because you're the worst bodyguard I've ever met."

Varnar looked at me, his mouth open. I turned around and walked back into the kitchen.

Before the door slammed behind me, I heard Aella laughing loudly.

CHAPTER 10

I stretched out in bed. On the floor, Monster smacked his lips. It was Saturday morning, I hadn't dreamed about the girl in the woods in a week, and although I had been plagued by thoughts of Varnar during pretty much all my waking hours, I was no longer in a sleep deficit.

We trudged downstairs, and I came as close to culinary brilliance as is possible for me: I boiled water in a pot and mixed it with instant coffee in a cup. I opened the double doors that led from the living room out into the little garden, which I had thus far neglected to make use of.

Outside the doors was a small stone-paved patio, where there stood a beat-up table with four equally beat-up chairs around it. The rest of the garden was a wilderness of flowers and plants. To my astonishment, the lawn looked freshly mowed and well-maintained, though it had a few yellow spots. Had Ben hired someone to take care of it while the house was empty? Surrounding it all was a hedge that someone—probably Ben—had given a half-hearted trim, and at the end of the hedge was a small opening to the drive leading from Kraghede Road up to my house.

I sat in the sun wearing nothing but a camisole and shorts and looked out at the scenery. I sat a little higher up than the hedge, so I could easily see over it.

With the house's placement on the only hill in a several-mile radius, I had a fantastic view over the flat landscape. As far west as my eyes could see, there were fields and whitewashed houses and farms. In several places, the horizon was interrupted by tall wind-mills, their blades spinning calmly. To the east was Ravensted, and in a half-moon around the town lay Kraghede Forest, but the town and the better part of the forest were hidden behind the other side of my house. I could see only the little, narrow strip of forest, one end of the half-moon, which ran to the end of my field. The sun was still strong, even though it was September, and today it shone unabashedly from a cloudless sky.

I sipped the coffee and allowed myself to enjoy a moment of contentment. The feeling sat strangely in my body. Monster came lumbering over, sat down, and majestically surveyed the scene.

"What should we do today?" I pet him on his large head, and he leaned into my hand.

"Let's start with some breakfast," came a voice from the other side of the hedge.

I jumped up, the coffee splashing all over.

Aella came into view in the hedge opening and took in every inch of my disheveled appearance. Her eyes lingered a moment on the scar on my chest.

"What the hell are you doing here?" I sputtered.

"Good morning to you, too," she said cheerfully, swinging a bag that appeared to contain bread. She walked past me into the house.

I walked after her and stood with my hands on my hips. "You can't just barge in here. It is *my* home, you know."

"And congratulations on that, by the way," she said without an ounce of shame over rooting around in my cabinets and drawers. "Good, you have butter and cheese."

"What are you doing here?" I asked again. Monster accepted the croissant that Aella handed him.

"Monster, seriously," I said.

He paused with the croissant in the corner of his mouth. Then the thrill of food overpowered him, and as he chewed, dry flakes of croissant hitting my floor, I shot him a death glare.

Aella had found the things she was looking for and carried them outside. I walked after her, dumbfounded.

"Sorry for showing up unannounced. But we are neighbors, after all. And I need to talk to you about something." She patted a chair.

"Wouldn't you rather eat breakfast with your lover?"

Her face froze.

"How did you know . . ." Then her face transformed into a grin. "Wait, do you mean Varnar?"

I looked at her, confused, as she giggled.

"Did you think Varnar and I . . . that Varnar has a girlfriend?"

"Why is that funny?" I sat down with no idea of what to do about my uninvited guest.

She waved her hands dismissively.

"We feel bad that we didn't get there in time yesterday."

"That sucks for you."

"There's a murderer on the loose, and now he's seen you. Who knows if he'll get the idea to come after you again?" She tore open the paper bag and placed a roll on my plate. She continued more casually. "Varnar and I agreed: Now that we live so close by, we might as well keep an extra eye on you. Don't get weirded out if you see us on your land or at the edge of the forest."

She looked at me innocently and took a big bite of her roll.

Hmmm. She wasn't asking for permission. She was informing me that they were going to do that.

"And what makes you qualified to keep an eye on me? Considering there's a cold-blooded murderer at large," I asked.

"Let's just say we have experience."

I tried to reach out with my power. There was not much to be found. Like with Varnar, I detected no images.

Aella had finished eating and stood up.

"So, it's settled." She studied me. Something resembling pain flitted across her face. Then she reached out her hand to brush away a strand of my hair that had strayed down over one of my eyes. I instinctively jerked my head back, and her hand stopped mid-movement. Then she lowered it.

"You should smile more, Anna. You're so pretty when you smile." She turned and vanished through the hole in the hedge.

I sat back in my chair, stunned. This was the second time she had urged me to smile. I was pretty sure I had never smiled in Aella's presence, so I had no clue how she would have the slightest idea of what I looked like when I smiled.

Arthur came to visit in the afternoon.

I had had a wonderful day in the quiet of my house after a twelve-mile run, an extra-long session with the punching bag, a hundred crunches, and a hundred push-ups on my knuckles. Afterward, I cleaned and did laundry in the ancient washing machine in the bathroom, which, oddly enough, still worked perfectly. I hung the clothes to dry on the line back by the barn, which I hadn't had time to investigate yet. Then I washed all the windows in the house.

Okay, finding out that Aella and Varnar were not a couple had made a certain impression.

As always, Arthur made his entrance in silence, and I started slightly when he spoke. I was in the middle of taking dry, fresh-smelling clothes off the line when he suddenly appeared at my side.

"Congratulations on the house."

I didn't want to show how startled I was, so I replied as if I had been expecting him.

"Thanks. Do you like it?" I continued with my task.

Arthur looked around, taking in Odinmont.

"The window frames need painting, and the roof should be cleared of moss," he said. "And it needs better insulation. It'll be cold in winter."

I felt an enormous urge to defend my little house. "The roof is completely watertight. It rained the other day, and not a drop got in."

I tossed a black T-shirt into the woven basket I had found in the bedroom. Arthur turned to me and smiled his wide smile. His red hair shone in the sunlight.

"It's a nice house. It just needs a loving hand, but who doesn't?" He patted me on the shoulder. "Do *you* like it?"

"I love it." I had no other word for it.

"Can I come in?"

I replied by walking toward the house with the large basket of laundry in my arms.

Inside, I gave him a quick tour before we sat down at the large wooden table. Arthur's fingers found the deep crack in the table-top, and he ran his finger along it in the same way I did every time I sat there.

"Have you had the dream again?"

I shook my head. "It's stopped. I've slept really well for the past week."

Arthur exhaled cautiously before changing the subject. "Has anything else happened?"

"No, mostly just school and work," I lied.

Arthur nodded. "It's good that you have a job, but school is number one."

I made a *pff* sound. It was funny that Arthur was focused on my schooling. Considering his status as a self-sufficient loner, he was hardly a paragon of virtue.

I followed him to the door, where we stood for a moment at the threshold.

Arthur hesitated. "There's someone it's about time you meet. Ideally soon. I think he can give you some answers."

"And what do I need answers to?"

"You know, your dreams. The things you see." He looked out

over the field and down toward Kraghede Forest. "There's no guarantee that I'll always be here. I would really like for you to meet him now so you can go to him if you need anything. He knows pretty much everything."

I think my voice got a little shrill. "What do you mean, you won't always be here?" I had never considered a life for myself that Arthur wasn't a part of.

Arthur spread his arms and smiled. "It's just an extra precaution."

I relaxed a little. "When should I meet this mysterious person?"

"What about tomorrow?"

"And where are we going to meet him?"

"You mean where are *you* going? I'm not coming."

"I'm not going anywhere alone."

Arthur took my hand. "Do you trust me?"

I thought about it briefly. "Yes. You're actually the only person I trust. You and Monster."

He gave my hand a squeeze. "So will you do this for me?"

"Okay, fine. Where am I going?"

"You need to go to Jagd."

I had absolutely no desire to go to a little podunk town on the far west coast. And especially not to meet a man I didn't know. Did I really want to know more about my power? I saw the past once in a while. I couldn't change it or do anything about anything. *No*, I decided. I had no need to continue picking at this inflamed wound. But then I thought about Mathias. How he shook with fear at the part of himself he could not control. Maybe this man, whoever he was, could shed light on that mystery. Arthur had said he had answers for most things.

Okay, I'll do it, Arthur. But for your and Mathias's sake. Not for my own.

I took a shower, changed the sheets, and pulled on a freshly washed T-shirt. Having dried on the line earlier that day, my clothes and the linens had a scent of sun and fresh air that reminded me of Varnar. I had to admit I looked forward to diving under the duvet and reveling in that fragrance.

Before I got into bed, I sat at the vanity to untangle my wet hair. I grabbed the brush and looked in the mirror, but my hand stopped mid-movement.

I saw my face in the mirror, but the hair that fell around it in soft, completely dry waves was fiery red. A sudden chill hit me, like tiny ice crystals spreading through my veins. The face in the mirror was mine, but it was not me. The face, whose features mirrored my own exactly, smiled at me kindly; a smile that I'd never form with my own lips.

I stood so abruptly that the chair toppled noisily behind me.

Monster was up the stairs in three big leaps.

"In the mirror," I stammered. "I saw a face. My face. But with red hair."

Monster walked over to the mirror and looked into it. He emitted a low growl. I could see his reflection, but the angle prevented me from seeing my own.

Before I went to bed, I covered the mirror with a sheet. It was silly and childish, but I knew I would not get a wink of sleep otherwise.

I rode my bike to Jagd the following evening. It had been nearly impossible to do my makeup without looking, but I simply refused to use the mirror.

Monster ran alongside me the entire way.

The trip from Ravensted to Jagd was more than twenty miles, and I used it as a welcome opportunity to burn off some energy. I wasn't sure Monster felt the same way. His thick fur was disheveled, and he was panting heavily when we reached the destination, which is so far from everything that not even the crows venture there. This is seagull territory. There's not much else other than heather, sheep, and beach houses. The trees have been sheared flat on one side by the merciless and constant westerly wind.

Arthur had told me to show up at a bar called The Boatsman to meet the mysterious stranger. The bar has been there for generations and embraces both sides of the town's opposing personalities. Both tourists and locals love the place.

This area in the northwesternmost corner of Denmark has always been poor, but when I hopped off my bike and walked across the crunching gravel of the parking lot toward The Boatman, it wasn't centuries of despair that emanated from the ground and into me. It felt more like the sandy soil itself was made of a tough and stubborn substance that gave people who live on it an unshakable will to live—and live well—regardless of what nature dealt them. Even now, as year after year the sea claimed large chunks of the coastline, they stayed where they were until their houses fell over the edge.

The parking lot was full of cars, mopeds, and also a couple of tractors. I gave The Boatman a good look before I went in.

The bar sat near a cliff that dropped more than 150 feet down to the sea below. I felt like it could fall to the sea with the next sandslide. Built from heavy, dark logs and topped with a black roof made of wide planks, The Boatman resembled an ancient Viking castle.

Monster stayed outside when I went in. He sat nicely in front of the dog-leash hitch, but he sighed deeply.

With all my strength, I pushed on the heavy wooden door. I had to take a firm grip on the iron handle, which was cast in the shape of a boar's head.

The bar was packed with people. Although I had traveled a significant distance without seeing so much as one car on the road, I stepped into a jumble of people drinking beer and singing along with the live band. Being off season, the tourists had thinned out, and this evening it was clearly the local population who was letting loose.

The band was good, but I was able to appreciate the music for only a moment before images and emotions from the crowd bombarded my brain. The headache set in in a matter of seconds. I did not have long to locate this mysterious friend of Arthur's.

I walked around the large, round bar that formed the center of The Boatman. Behind it stood two bartenders. One, a small woman with long black hair, emanated aggression. Her arms were sinewy and tattooed from shoulder to wrist, and she had a thick ring through her nose like a bull and large wooden earrings in each ear that stretched her earlobes almost to their breaking point.

The other bartender was a tall man with long nearly white hair down to his waist. His skin was so pale it was almost transparent; his eyebrows and lashes were so white they could barely be seen. A calm energy flowed from him. The two bartenders were complete opposites in every way. Gender, coloring, height, and aura. Nevertheless, they somehow resembled each other.

I spent a couple of valuable seconds studying them before returning to my mission. I made a few fruitless laps around the room, not knowing who I was looking for.

Just as I decided to leave with an unfulfilled mission and a splitting headache, a young man stepped in front of me. He appeared to be in his early twenties, but after a quick scan, I knew his past stretched further back than that.

Maybe it was the effect of the crowd playing a trick on me. Out of curiosity, I reached out to touch him, and it felt as if I were sinking down into a bottomless swamp of mental quicksand. His baseline mood was permeated by an enormous appetite for everything life had to offer, with a strange undercurrent of sadness and loss. I got a few very clear images from him, and what I saw made my cheeks burn.

Dark blond curls formed an unruly cloud around his face, and his gray-blue eyes could be described only as bedroom eyes. The most alluring smile I had ever seen played across his soft lips, and he looked at me as if I were a delicious piece of chocolate he was about to sink his teeth into. No man had ever looked at me that way before. Aside from Varnar in the dream, and that didn't count.

He walked a circle around me before placing himself in front of me, his legs slightly spread. He bobbed his head in time with the music.

"Arthur should have told me to look for the prettiest girl in the bar. You would have been easier to find."

Was this the mysterious stranger I was supposed to meet? He didn't look like the oracle Arthur had advertised. He struck me as more of an annoying charlatan.

"Don't make fun of me," I said.

"I have never been more serious in my life." His eyes glimmered.

I rubbed my throbbing temple. "Okay, Papa Smurf, drop the lover boy act. If we're gonna talk, we're going outside."

"Papa Smurf?"

"Either you've been extremely busy for the past twenty years, or you're significantly older than you look."

His soft lips curled into a smile that was more calculating than alluring.

"It's true. You are a seeress." He stared intensely at me, and his face grew serious. "It's hard for you to be in here with all these people?"

I nodded. The pain pounded behind my eyes, and I felt like I was standing on a bouncing trampoline. A blackout was not far off.

He touched my cheek with one hand. I jerked my head back, but he quickly placed his thumb on my bottom lip and stroked it. His finger left a sticky fluid behind.

Without thinking, I licked my lips. He made a half-strangled noise, somewhere between a moan and a sigh.

"It's been years since I saw such an appetizing mouth," he whispered.

I was about to slug him, but then a miracle happened. All at once, I relaxed completely. The headache disappeared, and the images and emotions that had just been hammering against my mind were gone. I could not see the aura or the past of a single person in the room, neither the place itself. It was a liberation. Even when I'm all alone, I can always feel *something*. From the ground I walk on, from the chair I sit on, or from the building I'm inside of. There is always at least a trace of an event or emotion. It was like flipping the switch on a years-long case of tinnitus that I had gotten used to but still bothered me.

The man returned his hand to my cheek. He stepped close to me, but I didn't get anything from him. No images. No feelings. I could have screamed with relief, but I just looked drowsily up at him.

"What did you give me?" *Whatever it was, give me the whole bottle*.

"A present," he whispered in my ear. "But it would be polite of you to share." He gave me a questioning look.

Feeling pleasantly foggy, I nodded. He leaned over me and brushed my lips with his own.

Carefully, he licked some of the fluid off my lips. The substance, whatever it was, also worked on him. He relaxed noticeably against my body. He let his mouth rest against mine for a moment. Then he kissed me. He KISSED me!

No one had ever kissed me before, and I didn't even know his name. But I was so relaxed and comfortable that I just leaned into it. The room swirled around me, and my knees buckled.

I had no desire to stop, until I realized I saw Varnar in my mind's eye while I kissed this stranger. I pulled back and blinked a couple times.

"Delicious," he said. Whether he was talking about the kiss or the drug, I had no idea.

I shook my head to clear my mind and pushed him away with a flat hand.

"I don't know what you're doing, but I'm leaving now." I tried to walk past him, but he grabbed my hand.

"I'm sorry, I couldn't stand seeing you in pain. It's better now, isn't it?"

I nodded.

"But Arthur will be furious if he finds out about this." I pointed back and forth between our lips, referring to both the kiss and the drug.

The man laughed.

"I've known Arthur a long time, and it's a fact that he won't succumb to rage. Or to anything else." He traced his index finger thoughtfully over his lips. "But I also know that he won't like it, so let's not mention it to him."

"What kind of shitty friend are you? Why did he send me up here to meet you?"

"I'm not Arthur's friend," said the man. "You aren't here to meet me."

I glared at him. "You aren't the one I'm supposed to meet? Then who are you?"

"I'm just the welcome committee."

"And who are you welcoming me on behalf of?"

"Someone who's been looking for you a long time. And we shouldn't make him wait any longer."

"Who is he?"

The man squeezed my hand, which I had forgotten he was holding.

I quickly pulled it back.

"You'll find out soon," he said.

"And who are you?"

"I'm Elias Eriksen," he said and bowed politely. "Welcoming committee, lover boy, and apparently also Papa Smurf."

"And pusher of strange narcotics."

"That's just the tip of the iceberg. I'm all that and more."

He came even closer. "I can be whatever you want."

"Oh, stop it." Elias was getting on my nerves, and I regretted letting him kiss me. I had the feeling it would come to haunt me. "Just take me to him."

Elias bowed his head with a smile and pointed to the exit.

Outside, Monster jumped up and ran toward us. Elias flinched and pushed me behind him with one arm. Monster growled as they stared at each other.

"It's okay. Both of you," I said. I hopped out from behind Elias's back and walked over to Monster.

Elias's face was unreadable. He turned and waved for us to follow him.

We walked behind The Boatman and toward the cliff that created a steep drop to the beach far below. The spiky lyme grass came up to my thighs, and I let my hands glide over the top of it. The blades cut the palms of my hands like little razors.

The North Sea lay like a carpet ahead of us and stretched smoothly toward the sky, meeting it far out on the horizon. Here and there, small waves were topped with glimmers of orange. The sun, which was enormous and fiery red, lay low in the sky and prepared for a bombastic landing in the sea.

Right by the cliff, with the tips of his toes practically sticking out over the edge, stood a man with his back to us. He was bathed in the beams of the setting sun, and his silhouette stood out sharply. He was tall, and his contours indicated a strong and muscular body, like a dancer or a swimmer, with broad shoulders and a straight posture.

Monster stayed behind a bit, but Elias followed me all the way up to the man.

We stood behind him, and he turned his head slightly. Dark hair brushed his shoulders in shining waves that would be any hairdresser's wet dream. I caught only a glimpse of his profile, but what I saw made me gasp for air. He turned his face back toward the sea.

"Elias, I assume you have taken good care of my guest." His voice was deep and a little hoarse.

Elias and I exchanged a glance.

"He's taken good care of me," I said. "Enough about that. I want to know why I'm here."

The man laughed softly. "Leave us, Elias."

Elias did a strange half bow and took a few steps back.

I pointed at him with a grimace to signal I wanted to speak to him again. He nodded, turned around, and went to join Monster.

I stood next to the man in the orange evening light, which now caressed us both.

His hair partially covered his face, but what I could see of it was nothing less than beautiful. His nose looked like it was drawn with a ruler, his jawline and chin were sharply defined, and his lips formed a soft arc. I tried to use my power but got nothing from him. Elias's drug must still be working.

"This place was several miles inland not so long ago," he said. "The sea is voracious."

I looked out over the cliff, and my stomach flipped. Below, an old sewage pipe and some steel wires stuck out into the air. A flock of seagulls were down there. Far beneath us lay the beach.

"So we're standing on the brink of the abyss," I said.

"I prefer to call it Denmark's crowning glory."

I had biked more than twenty miles, had willingly entered a venue with over a hundred people, had been drugged, and had gotten my first kiss—for *this*.

"Thanks for that, *Visit North Jutland*." My voice was despondent. "Do you have more tourism slogans on your mind, or are you ready to talk about what I actually came here for?"

The man was quiet for a moment. "No one has spoken so disrespectfully to me in over seventeen years."

"You've done nothing to earn my respect, so you don't have it. I don't even know what your name is."

He turned directly toward me, and I was almost bowled over by his beauty. His features were exquisite, with blue-green, deep-set eyes and high cheekbones. Even though they looked nothing alike, he reminded me of Mathias.

I couldn't pull my gaze away, so I looked him straight in the eyes. I felt like I was being sucked down by the undercurrent in the sea. He gave a soft smile that made me feel like I was the most important person in the world. In that second, I would have followed him to the ends of the earth, committed murder, or died for him, if need be.

I broke eye contact and looked out at the sea while I tried to regain control of my pounding heart. This was a dangerous man.

Is now the time for me to run away?

But Arthur had wanted me to meet him; he had asked me to trust him. I could feel the man's gaze on me, although I was careful not to look directly at him again. Better to look straight into the setting sun.

"My name is Od." He looked back out at the horizon.

I exhaled. I had apparently been holding my breath.

"You've been well hidden, Anna. I have been searching for you for many years."

Od. I tasted the strange name in my mouth.

"It shouldn't have been that hard to find me," I said.

As a case number in the system, I had lived almost a semipublic life.

"It was harder than you'd think. People thought it was too dangerous for you to have contact with me."

"By *people*, do you mean Arthur?"

"Among others."

"And why do these *people* think it's not dangerous anymore?"

"The rules of the game are changing. I'm not saying it isn't still dangerous for you. I'm saying it's more dangerous for you to do nothing."

I didn't feel like I was gaining a better understanding of things from talking with Od. Quite the opposite.

"I didn't even know there was a game in progress," I said.

"It's been in progress since before you were born."

My patience snapped. He could be as terrifying and handsome as he wanted. I couldn't stand this cryptic conversation anymore.

"Listen. Arthur wanted me to talk to you. You've been looking for me. I'm here now. So spit it out already, whatever this big reveal is."

Od's hoarse laughter flowed over me. "I would love to tell you everything you need to know. But you need to be ready for it, and I needed to be sure that you were the right person."

"So am I the right person?"

He laughed again. "You are. No doubt about it. But you're not ready for the truth."

I threw my hands up in the air, frustrated. "Great. Well, thanks for this. I'm glad we were able to waste my time and yours."

I turned to leave.

"I don't think you want to know more right now."

I stopped. "And how do you know what I want? I am gradually becoming aware that there is more between heaven and earth than meets the eye. You shouldn't be afraid of shocking me with the harsh, supernatural realities."

Od turned around, and once again I was caught in his gaze. He had turned down the charm, however, which made it easier for me to look him in the eyes and maintain my anger.

He looked at me tenderly. "You aren't ready to hear the truth because it requires that I tell you about your parents."

Why the hell would this strange man know anything about my treacherous parents?

"You're right." I clenched my fists. "I don't want to know anything about them."

"That's a shame."

I sensed that there was more to this than I perceived. I considered my real reason for being there. Mathias. If I left now, I might not be able to help him. I took a breath.

"I need to ask you for a favor."

Od tilted his head. I didn't think he was capable of being surprised, but he was as close as he could get. He nodded for me to continue.

"My friend has some problems. Can you talk to him?"

"I'm not some random psychologist you can just book a consultation with."

"I think his problems lie within your, uh . . . area of expertise." *Unexplained paranormal phenomena.* "I don't know who else he can go to."

Od stroked his chin. "A compromise?"

This time, I was the one who nodded for *him* to continue.

"I'm having a party soon. I would like for you to be there."

A *party?* Of all things, I would be subjected to a party. Surely with a ton of guests, which I suppose is what parties are all about. I couldn't remember ever having been to one, but I understood the basic concept.

Od continued. "I want you to come to the party with me."

"You don't seem like someone who has a hard time getting a date."

Od flashed a smile that nearly knocked me over. "It's not a romantic rendezvous. It's politics. Do we have an agreement?"

"Deal." *You owe me big time, Mathias.* "What order are we doing this in?"

"First the party. You'll receive an invitation."

Od turned his back to me again. While we were talking, the sun had dived headfirst into the waves. Darkness was falling. The sea suddenly looked gloomy and dangerous. The conversation was clearly over.

Od remained standing at the edge of the cliff, where he looked out inscrutably toward the horizon. *Denmark's crowning glory, my ass.*

I walked back to Monster and Elias, who were sitting in the spiky grass.

"Well, what did you get out of him?" Elias stood up. "I could see from all the way down here how frustrated Od was. What did you say to him?"

"It is absolutely none of your business," I snapped. Od had by no means appeared frustrated to me. I had had irritatingly little control over the conversation. And I didn't really know what I had gotten out of it, other than an unwanted invitation to a party.

Elias sniffed. "Relax, I'm just asking."

Which reminded me of something. "I also want to ask you something."

"Ask away."

"What was it you gave me?"

"Oh, that. There are other ways to dampen your senses, you know. Because that's what clairvoyance is. An overdeveloped sense. Clairvoyance is not magic."

New information. Maybe useful, but not right now. "You didn't answer my question. I want to know what it is. I want more. I'm willing to pay for it."

"It's called klinte. I can't sell it to you. I can only dispense it where there is a special need so it doesn't get misused."

"You manage that well," I said with a raised eyebrow.

Elias put his hand on his heart.

"I am only human." He said *human* as if it were not a given. "Temptation is every man's burden."

"Listen." I clawed desperately at my hair and felt like a junkie. "I can handle the regular days at school and work just fine. But there are situations where this would help me a lot."

Elias looked patiently at me. He had clearly heard it all before.

"I fainted twice in one day a few weeks ago," I blurted.

A glimmer of empathy ran across Elias's face.

"You faint?" He seemed to wage a bit of an internal battle with himself before coming to a decision. "I can teach you to control it better. I'll give you some klinte to hold you over until you learn to shield your powers. But you can't take it every day. Only in emergencies."

Hand it over. Give it to me. I held out my hand.

Elias produced a miniature ampoule with a tiny screw top.

"No more?" I said.

"You don't need to take a lot. I only gave you a drop tonight." He winked. "And we did share it."

He placed the ampoule in my palm and closed my fingers around it. He turned my hand over, lifted it to his lips, then kissed it.

I jerked my hand back.

"May I have your phone number?"

"No, you most certainly may not. And besides, I don't have a phone."

Elias squinted. "I didn't think it was possible to live without one these days."

"I get along just fine, thank you."

"Anyway, it's not for me, though I would love to have long conversations with you late into the night."

I could guess what Elias imagined these conversations would be about.

"Od wants it so I can call about the party."

"You don't seem like the type of guy who would let a lack of modern technology stop you. I'm sure you'll figure out some other way to invite me."

I was ready to go. I knew I should thank Elias for the klinte. But the words could not get past my lips.

"Bye," I said instead. Then I hurried off on my bike.

Elias shouted after me: "Anna. It's not true that the first fix is the best. It just gets better and better each time. You're going to ask me for more."

I was well aware that he had done me a favor.

"I'll be careful not to take too much." I waved the ampoule.

Elias blew me a kiss. "I wasn't talking about the klinte."

It took me a couple of days to process my meeting with Elias and Od. Od's words and tone had shaken me, and I went over our conversation in my head again and again. Elias's kiss had given me more fuel for my daydreams about Varnar, so I was foggy—to put it mildly—most of the time. Whenever I saw Varnar at school, I quickly looked away.

He did the same.

In Tuesday's French class, I sat down next to Mathias, exhausted. Luna was standing at the front and bombarding our teacher with a rapid stream of French, and the poor woman looked lost.

Mathias laid a warm hand on my shoulder. "You're looking a little rough today. Are you okay?"

I nodded distractedly. "I'm fine. How are you?"

He shrugged. "The weekend was hard to get through. I always have to spend some time pushing *it* back down. It helped to be with Luna." A goofy smile flew across his lips.

I shook my head with a smile. "You two . . ."

I knew exactly what *it* he was talking about. Maybe the klinte would work on Mathias? The little ampoule sat in my pocket, but I hadn't taken any more of it. The effect had waned after a couple of hours, and by Monday morning, my power was back at full strength. I had decided to ration the klinte since I didn't know if Elias would give me more.

"Did you tell Luna about it?"

"No, I can't. What if she runs away screaming?"

"Something tells me she's not the type to run away screaming."

"And your secret is safe with me," he continued.

"Good," I said.

The French teacher called the class to order, and Luna came dancing back to us. She sat next to Mathias and planted a kiss on his cheek.

He took her hand under the table.

I had been so busy with my own life, I hadn't been following their first forays into a relationship, though I didn't doubt for a second that was where they were heading. I didn't need to be clairvoyant to see what would happen between them.

The teacher asked for our attention. "Today we will start learning the past tense."

Mathias leaned toward me. "You should feel right at home with that."

I had a shift at Frank's that evening. The activity level had not fully returned to normal after Alice's death and the inexplicable "earthquake" a few days prior, so there weren't many patrons at the bar.

Through the swinging kitchen doors, I saw Peter sitting at a table with the face-tatted psychopath and an ultrathin girl with red hair. The table was covered in empty beer glasses, and the girl was visibly intoxicated. I knew her from somewhere but couldn't place it.

Frank nodded appreciatively when I voluntarily walked into the bar with a tray in my hand and began collecting empty glasses and bottles from the tables—while I snuck glances at the little group. I could handle it because there were so few guests in the room.

The intoxicated girl was wearing a faded pink top and ripped acid-wash jeans. She had a poorly executed scribble of a tattoo on her lower back. The psychopath ran a hand up her thigh under the table while he talked to Peter. She was chattering away, but neither of them was listening to her.

Peter looked at me with his teeth bared and said something to the psychopath, who trained his eyes on me.

When his watery eyes met mine, a chill went down my spine. Fortunately, he seemed only vaguely interested and quickly looked away again.

I looked at the girl again. I finally got it—she had been at Nordreslev Youth Center at the same time as me. She hadn't had red hair back then, but a new hair color can be purchased at any supermarket.

What was her name? Belinda something?

"Aren't you gonna say hi, Ugly-Anna?" she asked loudly.

Peter lifted his head with a caustic grin. "Yeah, Ugly-Anna, aren't you gonna say hi?"

I turned to seek refuge in the kitchen. Mostly to get away from Peter and his psychopath friend.

"You could at least say hi," Belinda called and started to follow me.

People started to look at her and giggle. The psychopath didn't like that and pulled hard on her arm. She hit the edge of the chair and toppled to the floor. On the way down, she tried to grab the table for stability, but it tipped, so the glasses rained down on her. She howled, and the psychopath took a firmer grip on her thin arm and dragged her out of Frank's.

Peter skulked after them and sent me an evil glare that said it was my fault his night out had been interrupted.

I got a dustpan, walked to the table, and began to gather the shards of glass. Frank came over to help.

"Do you know her?" He tilted his head toward the door.

"A little," I said evasively, but when Frank kept looking inquisitively at me, I continued.

"We were at Nordreslev together."

"The prison?" He whistled and scratched one of his sideburns with his thumb. "Why was she in there?"

I turned down the corners of my mouth. "No idea. She's always been in and out of the system."

Frank started to pick up the glass. "Doesn't she have a family?"

"I don't think so."

He weighed the sharp pieces of glass in his hand as he stared blankly out into space.

I stacked the last shards in the dustpan. "Shall I take those?" I pointed to his hand.

He dropped the glass into the pan with a rapid motion.

"Hey, careful not to cut yourself."

He laughed. "Don't you worry about me. I never get hurt." He motioned toward the kitchen. "Now get back to work!" This was followed by a friendly wink.

I stood up and tried to shake off my meeting with Belinda, even though it felt like I'd been punched in the gut.

"You're right. I have to be careful; my boss is crazy strict."

Frank stood and crossed his tattooed arms.

"So I've heard. He's said to be completely unpredictable. Brutal, even."

"I'd better . . ." I pointed toward the kitchen.

That night, the dream with the girl in the woods came back. Being unprepared, I screamed through it until Monster woke me up.

The next morning, Belinda was found strangled in her bed, and I was the last person she had spoken to aside from Peter and the psychopath.

PART II

THE RUNES
OF THE GODS

Of the runes of the gods
And the giants' race
The truth indeed can I tell,
(For to every world have I won;)
To nine worlds came I,
to Niflhel beneath,
The home where dead men dwell

Ballad of Vafthruthnir
10th century

CHAPTER 11

On Wednesday morning, our homeroom teacher, Mr. Nielsen, looked ten years older.

Everyone noticed Peter's empty chair. No one talked about it. Kamilla, who had only recently returned after Alice's death, resembled a frightened bird, and I sat slumped, exhausted, in my seat.

"For those who haven't heard what happened, this morning a girl named Belinda Jaeger was found dead. Someone got into her apartment and killed her. The police think it was the same person who killed . . ." Mr. Nielsen's professional facade cracked, and he looked at the ceiling. "Alice."

He breathed heavily in and out.

"Belinda was from here in town, but she lived elsewhere during several periods of her life." His gaze landed on me. "That reminds me. Anna . . ."

I lifted my tired head with a jerk, and everyone looked at me.

"There's someone who wants to speak with you. They're waiting in the principal's office."

The curiosity in the room bubbled toward me as I stood and walked to the door. Mathias and Luna looked questioningly at me, and I shrugged my shoulders in response.

The secretary, Mrs. Larsen, met me in front of the principal's office. Her eyes were agitated beneath her blue eye shadow, and her mouth pulled back in an expression of unease when she spoke to me.

"Good, you're here. The police have been waiting for you for half an hour."

The police?

Mrs. Larsen looked me up and down, from the black joggers to the worn black T-shirt with the silver skull print. She ended at my tired face.

"I'm sure they don't think you have anything to do with it."

Her facial expression, however, told me she thought I had everything to do with it.

Principal Holten stuck his head out of his door. His broad face was a grimace of concern. When he caught sight of me, he opened the door fully as a sign that I should come inside. I stepped forward, but he grabbed me by the arm.

"I will stay with you during the conversation." There was a promise in his words. He didn't care about my past, my appearance, and the discomfort I made him feel. I was a student at his school, his territory, and was therefore under his protection.

I nodded and walked past him into the room. At a table sat two policemen. I had seen them at school, the day we were informed of Alice's death. They stood, and the older one took the floor. He was tall, with an understated physical strength. Formerly attractive, but now ragged, with thin yellowish-gray hair.

"I'm Lars Guldager, and this is Hakim Murr," he said, gesturing to the younger man. "I am the chief investigator at the police station in Aalborg. Hakim is an officer at the local station in Ravensted. He is helping with the investigation into the murders of the redheaded girls. This is not an interrogation. We just want to talk to you. But Mr. Holten will stay. As your observer."

"Okay," I mumbled.

When I shook the young policeman's hand, I felt an energetic and ambitious aura, and I sensed an uncompromising nature from him. His gaze kept darting away from my face, but he stubbornly redirected his dark green eyes toward me with something that

146

resembled effort. He sat down and folded his muscular arms across a buff chest.

When I took the older officer's hand, a series of images, scents, and sounds shot into my head, and I had to fight the urge to pull my hand back. The sour smell of sweat. Sunrise over a field. Something above my head made a *whooooosh* sound. Another noise sounded like rain. Even though the sky was cloudless, red drops fell from it.

I released his hand and blinked to focus on the here and now.

We sat down.

"*Um* . . ." He looked down at his papers to find my name. "Anna." He coughed lightly before continuing. "No one is accusing you of anything."

"I should think not. Because I haven't done anything." This came out sounding harsher than I had intended. What if the police had found out about the drawing? As long as they didn't bring Luna into it. This is what you get for trying to help.

It seemed as if the old policeman and Principal Holten had momentarily forgotten I was there.

"Do you even have any leads?" asked Principal Holten.

"Not a whole lot. You should advise the girls to be careful."

They continued talking.

Hmm.

I found myself looking at the young policeman—Hakim. With great concentration, he stared at me and exhaled frustratedly. I held his gaze with furrowed brows as Principal Holten and Lars Guldager prattled on without so much as looking in my direction.

Hakim rapped the table lightly with his knuckles. "Shall we continue our conversation with . . ." He stole a glance down at his neighbor's papers. "With Anna here?"

Lars focused on me again. "Right." He sat up a little straighter. "You spoke with Belinda yesterday. And you knew the other three murdered girls."

"No, I didn't. I didn't know any of them."

Hakim took over. Again, he forced himself to keep looking at me. "You lived with both Tenna and Belinda. Naja went to school with you in Jerslev, and Alice was in your class both at this high school and in Vringelby."

I shook my head. "I knew who Belinda and Alice were, but Tenna and I weren't at Kobbelgården at the same time. I never met her. And I can't remember ever having noticed Naja. I didn't live in Jerslev very long."

"Was it when you lived in Jerslev that you burned down your foster family's house?" Hakim said, without breaking his stare.

"Could I just show you something?" Principal Holten asked out of the blue.

The two older men rose and walked to the principal's desk, where he began to dig around in a drawer to pull something out.

For a second, Hakim began to follow them, but he forced himself back in his seat and composed himself.

Surprised that he would jump right into asking about the house, I replied in a way that could easily be misinterpreted: "No, that was a different foster family."

"What about Belinda?" pressed Hakim. "You were one of the last people to see her alive. Eyewitnesses say that you argued, and that you pushed her into a table."

I could pretty well guess who these eyewitnesses were. I clenched my fists under the table. "Do *all* the witnesses say I pushed her?"

Hakim turned around in his chair and snapped at his colleague: "Do you want to come back over here?"

The two older men came lumbering back.

"Anna Sakarias. There's something familiar about your last name. Where are your parents from?"

I shrugged as the heat rose in my cheeks and my heart pounded.

Fortunately, Lars let the whole name thing drop. "The thing is, we're looking for a connection between the four murders. We received a drawing of the murderer's likeness." He laid a copy of Luna's drawing in front of me. "Have you seen him before?"

I looked into the Savage's wild eyes, which Luna had captured so vividly.

"No," I lied.

"Does the letter F mean anything to you?" Hakim asked out of the blue.

"F?"

"An F, on its own. Does that mean anything to you? Do you know what it signifies?"

A strange feeling simmered in my stomach. "Why are you asking me that?"

The two policemen exchanged a look, and Lars shook his head imperceptibly.

At that moment, I wished I could touch one of them to get a clearer view, with my power, of what they knew. I contented myself with leaning toward Hakim just to catch something. And that was enough. I could barely hold back a terrified moan.

I saw Alice's T-shirt with the distorted F drawn in bloody finger paint. It was also carved into Tenna's stomach. Belinda's forehead bore it with fine little cuts that gaped a little, and it was painted onto Naja's jacket in blood. I got an image of Hakim, illuminating the black jacket with a special lamp so the F of dried blood glowed neon blue. His face was both horrified and triumphant. The symbols were identical to the one I saw again and again carved into the back of the girl from my vision. Why the hell had they kept that out of the media?

Hakim jumped ahead to the next topic, as if the F symbol were insignificant. I tried with all my might to keep my face neutral.

"What about these guys? Do you know them?" He laid two photographs in front of me. One of Peter and one of the psychopath. They were classic mug shots, and both had on the same clothes as the day before.

There was no reason to lie.

"Peter Nybo." I pointed at the first photo. When I discovered that my hand was shaking, I planted my finger firmly on the other picture to keep it steady. "I don't know this one's name, but he was with Peter at Frank's yesterday. They were sitting with Belinda."

"I suppose that's all," Lars said suddenly and stood halfway, but Hakim waved him back down.

"His name is Christian Mikkelsen," continued Hakim. He then pointed at the picture of Peter. "Is this the same Peter Nybo against whom you committed assault with a deadly weapon a few years ago?" He nudged the photo toward me.

Technically, Peter had been responsible for both the weapon and the assault, but they would never believe that.

"I was convicted of it, anyway," I said.

The two men spoke briefly with Principal Holten, and I took the opportunity to flee the office. No one noticed. Outside, I exhaled a few times before I walked back to the classroom. Mathias leaned toward me when I sat down.

"What happened? Who did you have to speak with?"

"The police." I slumped in my chair and rubbed my forehead.

"What did you say to them?" A faint nervousness vibrated from him.

"I just said I didn't know anything."

When I rode my bike up the dirt road to my house after school, a broad figure was standing in front of my blue front door. It was Hakim, the young police officer.

What the hell is he doing here?

His eyes widened when he saw Monster, who was galloping alongside me. Monster stopped when I got off the bike, and he stayed close by my side. A rumble sounded from his chest.

"It's okay." I laid my hand on his head.

Hakim shifted. Irritation and something else, uncertainty or frustration, emanated from him.

Stunned, I racked my brain to figure out what he wanted. I decided that an offensive was the best defense.

"Did Daddy Lars give you permission to come out here?" I asked calmly over my shoulder as I locked my bike.

"Lars doesn't know I'm here. I'm off duty. And don't call him that. We are colleagues and equals."

"Equals. I thought you were an intern. How old are you? Twenty?" I strained to keep my face neutral.

He clenched his fists. "I'm twenty-six. And you should know better than to speak that way to a policeman."

"You just said you were off duty." I walked past him and unlocked the door. I placed myself between the lock and Hakim to hide my trembling hands. A strange feeling made me look over my shoulder and down to the edge of the forest.

Varnar stood down there, looking up at my house.

"Come in," I said to Hakim as I stepped through the door. Varnar better not think he could decide who I did and didn't receive visits from.

I tossed my keys on the kitchen table and put on a pot of water to boil.

"Coffee?"

He nodded and looked around my sparsely furnished yet perfectly functional home. He paused at the large spear that hung on the wall. I was suddenly unsure whether it was even legal, but Hakim didn't mention it.

I set the cups, the pot of boiled water, and a glass of instant coffee granules on the large wooden table and waved him over.

"What didn't we cover earlier today?" I asked as I made a cup of coffee and held it out to him.

Hakim took the cup and wrapped his large hands around it. "The more I investigate the murdered girls, the more you show up."

Again, he pinned me down with his sharp, dark green gaze. It now seemed easier for him to focus on me.

"And you don't think I've just been around a lot? I've crossed paths to some extent with pretty much everyone in the region."

Hakim's green eyes glimmered. "That's what my colleagues said, too, after we read your case file."

He looked out my living room window. "I know there is a link between you and those girls."

"Then you see something I myself can't see."

"I believe that," Hakim said candidly. He took a sip of coffee. "I believe that you yourself don't know what the connection is. But I know it's there."

He took a brief pause, as if he was considering how much he should say.

"We have detained Peter Nybo and Christian Mikkelsen for the murder of Belinda Jaeger. But I don't think they were the ones who did it."

"Isn't it a little unprofessional for you to tell me that?"

"Unorthodox, maybe." He ran his finger along the cup's handle. "Do you share my view?"

I took a mouthful of coffee to give myself a little time to think. I had nothing to lose by telling the truth. "I don't think it was either of them."

"Why not?"

"Just a hunch."

"So how do you feel about them being suspects?"

"I don't care," I said without thinking, but then stopped. "No, I do care, if that means you don't catch the real murderer. But I don't feel bad for them."

"You have a history with Peter Nybo."

"You could certainly call it that."

"I don't think it was you who attacked him, back then," said Hakim.

My stomach churned a little in surprise. "Why not?"

"Just a hunch." He echoed my words from before.

Just then, there was a knock at the door. Monster jumped up and let out a single bark, causing the cups on the table to shake.

"Are you expecting guests?" Hakim turned in his chair.

"No." I stood to open the door.

Outside stood Varnar. "Is everything okay?"

Hakim came to my side, and the two men exchanged hostile glares. I looked from one to the other. What the hell did they think they were doing? Claiming their territory?

"Everything is okay, if you two would just leave me in peace."

Hakim cleared his throat and handed me his card. "We were finished anyway. But contact me if you think of anything that might help. I wasn't able to find your phone number anywhere. Can you write it down for me?"

"I don't have a phone," I said resignedly. My status as a non-phone-owner was starting to become a problem.

Hakim looked like he was about to say something, but then thought better of it. He probably thought my lack of phone was the least strange thing about me.

I was inclined to agree.

Hakim walked sideways out the door and gave Varnar a don't-try-any-bullshit look.

Varnar held Hakim's gaze with no hesitation. Hakim receded with heavy, crunching steps across my gravel driveway.

My heart was pounding heavily in my chest when I stood alone with Varnar. He ran a hand through his dark hair. It fell back and framed his face as usual.

"I thought he was bothering you."

"We were just talking. He's a cop; he's investigating the murders."

Varnar looked down. Then he raised his head and looked me directly in the eyes.

The butterflies in my stomach ran amok.

His intense, dark brown eyes bored into mine, and images from the dream I had had starring him flickered in my head. He seemed to want to say something, but then he turned abruptly and took off running toward Kraghede Forest without so much as a goodbye.

When I arrived at work on Thursday afternoon, Luna and Frank stood talking behind the bar, while Mathias sat on a barstool admiring Luna. In the kitchen, I nodded to Milas, tied an apron around my waist, and started chopping salad greens. Frank swung open the door and stuck his head in.

"There's someone who wants to talk to you."

Varnar? I walked into the café.

Elias.

He smiled just as flirtatiously as last time, while his eyes swept through Frank's—surely to take note of the female patrons. He ended on Luna, who he winked at.

Mathias straightened slightly on his stool.

"I think you've seen enough." I took Elias by the arm.

He turned to face me and spread his arms as if to give me a hug. I moved my hand to his chest and shook my head.

"Not a chance." Upon touching him, I heard a feminine moan from his very recent past. I quickly retracted my hand.

He sighed. "Must I really pine for you?"

"Something tells me you never pine for very long." I wiped my hand on my apron.

He smiled and scratched at his unruly curls. "All women are pearls, but you, Anna, are a sparkling diamond."

Yeah, yeah, that's a good one.

I nodded at a barstool, and he sat down. "What do you want?"

"I'm the invitation."

"To what?"

"To the annual equinox ball at The Boatman, of course."

I had completely forgotten that I had promised Od that I'd go to a party with him. "Why is it at The Boatman?"

"Od owns The Boatman? Did you not know that?"

"Until just over a week ago, I didn't even know Od existed."

Elias handed me an envelope that was closed with a wax seal. The signet depicted a boar's head.

I carefully broke the seal and pulled out a card. The same boar's head was embossed on the front of the thick, expensive paper. The invitation was written in red ink with beautiful penmanship. On Saturday, September 22, the day of the fall equinox, the annual ball would be held at The Boatman in Jagd. I would be picked up at seven o'clock. Guests were expected to come in formal attire.

Formal?

I waved the card in front of Elias's nose. "What does it mean by *formal?*"

"In my case, an outrageously expensive suit, in which I'll look so sexy it's not even fair. For you, the princess gown of your dreams."

"Do I look like someone who dreams of wearing a princess gown?"

"Do you *really* want to know what I think you dream about?" Elias asked with a smile.

I threw my hands up. It was one thing to have to go to a party and suffer through being around a ton of people, but wearing a dress was another. I clearly hadn't thought it all the way through when I said yes to Od.

Elias's face grew serious. "If you can't afford one, Od is happy to pay."

I remembered Luna's creation with the snakes and shook my head. It was the only piece of clothing in the "dress" category I would ever consider wearing. "I have one I got as a gift."

"Which reminds me . . ." He pulled out a rectangular package. "This is from Od."

I opened it and took out a brand-new cell phone, the most expensive model. I stroked a finger across the cool glass screen. "Why?"

"Od would like to be able to contact you without sending me every time. Although it is my exquisite pleasure, of course." Elias wiggled his eyebrows. "Actually, I'm amazed that you didn't have a phone already."

"No one ever wanted to call me." I looked Elias squarely in the eyes and made my voice firm. "What does Od want in return?" Might as well get it out in the open straight away.

"You are a very straightforward girl. I like that. You remind me of someone I used to know." He paused briefly. "Od wants your friendship."

"My friendship cannot be purchased with a cell phone, regardless of how expensive it is."

"He knows that. But the first step to a friendship with you is being able to get ahold of you. Just take it."

Of course I would take it. I just wanted to know the price. Not that Od should assume I would simply pay it. I put the phone back in the box.

"Then I guess we're done here." I turned to go back to the kitchen.

"There's just one more thing." Elias caught my arm, and I stopped with a jerk.

Out of the corner of my eye, I saw Frank looking sharply in our direction. He took a step toward us. I waved him away with one hand.

"What?" I asked.

"Do you have any klinte left?"

"I haven't taken any of what you gave me."

"Such willpower! Most people would have gone straight home and drank the whole bottle."

"By *most people* do you mean you?"

He didn't respond.

I continued: "As we agreed, I'm saving it for an emergency. Like this awful party, for example."

"There are people who have waited years to attend this ball."

"So give my invitation to them."

He chuckled and shook his head. "An agreement between you and Od isn't something I want to get in the middle of. No, I was wondering if I should teach you to shield your clairvoyance."

"Shhh." I looked around.

"It's nothing to be embarrassed about. You should be proud."

"Easy for you to say."

"I can help you."

I considered his offer for a moment. "What makes you an expert? Do you have the same power as me?"

Elias shook his head. "I can't do anything like that. I don't have a supernatural bone in my body, although a certain part of me is pretty magical."

He laughed cheekily, and I made a gagging noise.

"But I can coach people who," he lowered his voice, "can do things that are out of the ordinary. Shielding is the same, regardless of what one's powers are."

Ah, okay then.

"Can you come to my place on Sunday?" With Monster in the house, I would probably be safe from his advances.

Elias bowed. "It would be an honor. Can you write down your address? We've had a hard time locating you."

This surprised me. It was no secret where I lived.

When Elias saw what I had written, he looked blankly at the paper. "The circle closes."

I had no idea what he meant, and I also really didn't care.

"I have to get back." I pointed to the kitchen. "See you Sunday."

"Who were you talking to?" Luna asked when she came into the kitchen with a full tray an hour later.

"No one special. His name is Elias."

157

Luna took a couple of coffee cups and placed them in the dish-washer. "I thought you were into that hot janitor from school. But then this guy shows up."

I tried to play it cool, but silently cursed the fact that it was so obvious how I felt about Varnar. "Elias hits on everyone. It doesn't mean anything."

"Mhmm," she said. "Has anything happened with the other guy? He looks at you when you aren't watching."

My heart did a backward somersault.

"And I can tell how crazy you are about him." She laughed. "It's almost palpable."

"I'm not crazy about him," I whispered.

"I don't understand why you won't admit it. It's nice to be in love."

I couldn't disagree more. It was horrible to be in love. I couldn't eat, sleep, or think. And every time I saw him, I felt nauseous and my knees buckled.

And I've just admitted to myself that I'm in love with Varnar.

"How about you and Mathias? What's happening with you guys?" I tried desperately to change the subject.

She picked at her orange nail polish with a frown. "I really like him. He's so sweet."

"Then what's the matter?"

She blew away a dark ringlet that had strayed across one eye. "I'm scared that he might have a girlfriend in Copenhagen. He has some big secret that he doesn't want to share with me. I don't want to go any further with him until I know what it is."

I debated with myself over getting involved.

"I don't think he has another girl," I said cautiously. "He's really in love with you." I could certainly say that much. "Tell him you know he's hiding something, and that you can handle it, whatever it is. Because you can, right? Handle it, I mean. Regardless of what it is."

"Now you're making me think you know something."

I held my hands up.

"I know nothing," I lied.

Luna straightened. "You're right. This is Mathias we're talking about. How bad could it be?"

I thought back to the Savage's sizzling face, his skin hanging in tatters, and the nauseating smell of cooked flesh.

"I'm sure you're worrying about nothing," I said aloud.

That evening, Monster sat extra close to me on the bench while we watched TV. He laid his large head in my lap.

I enjoyed the warmth that flowed from his body. Even his loud snores, which almost drowned out the movie, had a calming effect on me. I felt a rare sense of peace and contentment. As if my life were finally beginning to take shape.

That night, the large dog crawled up into my bed and lay right up against me, his breath—which was shockingly fresh for a dog—blowing in my ear.

The next morning, he was gone.

I looked everywhere. I called his name but got no response.

It was like he had disappeared off the surface of the earth.

Friday went by at school while I hoped Monster would be waiting for me outside, as always, when classes were over.

Mathias asked me what was wrong. I didn't answer him, and he didn't ask again. I went to the morning assembly and took a little klinte beforehand. The klinte worked, but I felt no enjoyment at being free of my clairvoyance.

There was no giant dog at the bike shed when I left to go home.

On Saturday morning, I opened my eyes and was in a good mood for a split second, until I remembered that Monster was gone. I missed him all the way down to the marrow of my bones.

I did my homework in the morning because I had to work that evening. The shift at Frank's dragged by, and I nearly teared up when Milas held out a bag of leftovers to take home to Monster. I took the bag in case he showed up. But when I said goodbye to Frank, who sped off in his ancient pickup truck, and Milas, who was going home to his family, I stood alone unlocking my bike, knowing Monster would not come back. The feeling of being abandoned struck something deep inside me.

I pushed my bike through the alley from Algade to Grønnegade as I wiped my cheek with the back of my hand.

I heard footsteps behind me.

I stopped and looked over my shoulder.

"Oh, they let you out," I said when I spotted Peter.

He took a few steps toward me. "You blabbed to the police, psycho. It's your fault I sat rotting in a cell for three days."

"Everyone saw you with Belinda. I just confirmed what the police already knew."

Peter didn't hear a word I said. He continued toward me. "The big guy, the foreigner, wouldn't let us go, and he asked a whole lot of questions about you. You've always hated me. But to have me accused of murder?"

Getting blamed for everyone else's problems really was my specialty. I leaned my bike against the wall. No need for it to get scratched if he started to flail around.

"You need to be put in your place, psycho," he hissed.

"Peter, go home before I'm forced to hurt you," I said despondently.

"What about me?" said a voice behind me.

I turned toward the other end of the alley. Markus, Peter's sidekick, who had helped chase me into the forest when I was a kid, came sneaking up with a slouched posture.

I was starting to get a little worried—mostly for the fate of my bike. I could definitely handle Peter. With Markus, it was just a matter of gaining the mental advantage. Once I took care of Peter, Markus would split. That's how it was when we were kids, and that's how it was now.

Okay, Peter first. I ignored Markus and took a few steps toward Peter.

"And me," said someone in the courtyard behind Frank's. The psychopath, whose name was apparently Christian Mikkelsen, stepped out of the shadows.

With my back to the wall, I realized they had been waiting for me.

While I wasn't particularly worried about Peter and Markus, I wasn't so sure about Christian. His aura was rough like sandpaper, and I started to get several images from him. They weren't pretty. He was the type who kept punching until his opponent was on the ground, and then he put his boots to use. Mild fear simmered in my stomach.

The blow came quickly. Normally, I see my opponent gather their courage for the attack, but Christian hit me without warning.

I only just managed to duck, avoiding a second blow, and I sent a fist into Christian's chin. It didn't land with full force, so all I did was make him even more irate.

Markus howled like a hyena and came running up. Peter leaned closer.

"You're gonna get it now, psycho," he roared.

Christian struck me again, and this time he hit my cheekbone straight on.

Stars exploded in my field of vision, but I used the force from his blow to turn around and swing my leg in a roundhouse kick that hit him in the side. The kick landed perfectly, but I didn't pull my foot back quickly enough, and Christian got hold of my leg. He pulled, so I landed on my back and smacked my head on the asphalt.

Markus planted a kick in my side now that I was down.

A coward as always.

I grabbed Markus's leg and wrapped myself around it to throw him off balance. With my hand balled into a fist, I hit him in the knee, and his leg collapsed under him.

He landed on his ass, and I heard a sharp crack as his tailbone broke.

The other two circled closer.

I knew that I had lost. I knew that I was about to get the beating of my life. But I wouldn't go down without a fight. I pushed up Markus's pants leg and bit his shin as hard as I could, until I tasted blood.

He kicked his leg, trying to shake me off.

Peter threw himself on me. His hands hit and scratched at my face to get me away from Markus's leg. He finally succeeded, and for a brief moment, I lay in blessed peace while Peter and Markus retreated. My cheekbone and the back of my head were throbbing, and blood was cascading from my nose. The scratch marks stung across my face, and my side, stomach, and back were burning.

Black boots stopped next to my field of vision.

I looked up into Christian's crystal-clear eyes, and I knew what awaited me. Instinctively, I closed my eyes and curled up into a ball.

But the kicks didn't come. Instead, I heard something strange above me.

I looked up cautiously. Around me and almost directly above me, a man was performing what looked to be a cross between an assault and a dance.

I stared, fascinated. I had never seen anyone fight like that. Though "fight" is a strong word, as Peter, Markus, and Christian did not seem to present a challenge for my savior. In less than twenty seconds, all three of them lay spread on the ground as if they were sleeping. I had barely even registered what had happened.

The man stood for a moment with his back to me. Although he was motionless, the energy rolled off him. I recognized the aura.

Varnar turned and crossed the short distance to me. I was still lying on my side, blood streaming from my nose. I slowly pushed myself up.

He didn't help me, and I was grateful. I dragged myself to one of the alley's walls and propped myself against it, leaning my head back to stop the nosebleed.

Varnar gave me a piece of fabric, which I pressed to my nose.

"Thanks," I said. My voice sounded nasally through the fabric. I took it away, but the blood immediately began to pour down again. I tried to catch it with the cloth, but it ran down over my fingers.

Varnar squatted in front of me. He held my face in his hands and looked intensely at me. I think my heart stopped for a couple of seconds.

Then, with one hand, he took a firm hold of the bridge of my nose and squeezed.

I bit back a whimper, but tears formed in my eyes. The bleeding stopped immediately. Varnar let go of my nose and took the cloth from my hands. He carefully wiped the blood off my face. He pressed lightly on my cheekbone and turned my head from side to side. Then his fingers glided into my hair and pressed gently on my neck and the back of my head. Cautiously, he pulled his hands back, draping my long hair over one shoulder.

I sat quiet as a mouse.

"Lie down," he mumbled.

I did as he said. He carefully lifted my T-shirt and ran his hand across my stomach and sides. I sighed, but not from pain. It was almost unbearable, but I didn't want him to stop. He pulled my T-shirt back down and gestured for me to sit back up.

"We have to call an ambulance," I said.

"A what?" he asked as I slowly got to my feet.

"An ambulance. A doctor."

"You aren't seriously injured," he said.

"Not for me." I pointed at the three unconscious men. "For them."

Varnar's expression was uncomprehending. "They're your enemies."

"That may well be, but we can't just leave them there." I dug out my new phone, but my hands were shaking. Not so much from the blows I'd been dealt, but from Varnar's examination. "You'll need to do it."

I gave him the phone. He looked at it, mystified.

"Swipe your finger there to turn it on." I pointed at the glass screen. "And press 2-3-0-1. That's the code."

He brought the phone to life but looked at the keypad without doing anything.

"You need to press 9-1-1."

"Right." He pressed the correct numbers, and when a voice came through the phone, he held it up to my good cheek.

"Three men were assaulted in the alley behind Frank's Bar & Diner in Ravensted."

Varnar took the phone back and ended the call. I hoped that was enough information for the authorities to get the message.

We sat for a moment in silence.

"You can't keep fighting like this," Varnar said finally.

I looked at him, surprised. After the demonstration in the art of violence he had just performed, he was the last person I would have expected to say those words. It was like an echo of all the social workers, foster parents, and teachers I had ever come into contact with.

"I didn't have much of a choice. They came after me," I said.

Varnar furrowed his brows slightly. "That's not what I mean. You can't keep fighting *the way* you are fighting. I need to teach you to do it properly."

CHAPTER 12

We walked in silence along Kraghede Road. My cheekbone and the back of my head were still throbbing like hell.

We turned up the dirt driveway to Odinmont, and Varnar looked to the sky.

"Why are those guys your enemies?"

I shrugged.

"Two of them I've known most of my life. They've never liked me. The third, the one with the shaved head, I just met a few days ago." I made a face. "But it doesn't take much to make people hate me."

Varnar did not contradict me. "They thought you had turned them in."

"They think I told the police that they killed Belinda Jaeger." I stopped. We had made it halfway up the drive. "How do you know what they thought?"

Varnar stopped, too. "The guy who spoke to you first said so."

"Yes—*before* they attacked me."

Varnar looked blankly at me and nodded.

"That means . . . you were there the whole time?"

He nodded again.

I fumbled for the words. "You let them hit me and kick me before you stepped in."

"I needed to see how skilled you are at fighting. I wouldn't have let them seriously hurt you."

"You couldn't know that," I hissed and began to stomp toward my house. "You seem like you want oh so badly to be the big

165

protector, but the first time I had problems, you came too late. The second time, you let me get the crap half-beaten out of me before you did anything."

Varnar caught up to me and walked alongside me in long strides. "I still haven't forgiven myself for coming too late that time. But tonight, I made the right decision. I had to know how well you can protect yourself, so I can . . ." He closed his mouth tightly.

"So you can what?"

He threw up his hands. "It's nothing."

We had reached my front door. I turned to face him.

"Listen, I'm glad you helped me. But then next time you stumble upon a girl getting the shit kicked out of her by three men, I think you should help her from the start." I leaned my bike against the wall and got out my keys.

"I'm coming over tomorrow afternoon," said Varnar from behind me.

I turned, and we looked at one another in the moonlight.

"Why?" I asked.

"So we can start training. I never want to see you bite someone on the leg again. You're lucky he didn't kick you in the neck. You could have ended up paralyzed or dead."

I brought my hand to my throat. I hadn't thought of that. If Varnar hadn't come to my rescue—however slow he may have been to pull the trigger—I could be somewhere else and in an entirely different state than in front of my door with a few scratches. Plus, this was hardly the last time Peter and his ilk would mess with me. And now that I lived out here all alone—I sent a bleak thought to Monster—I needed to be able to defend myself.

"Great."

Varnar bowed his head before turning around and running. I watched him until he disappeared in the shadows of Kraghede Forest.

That night I dreamed I was looking at myself in a mirror.

My reflection looked sadly back at me, red tendrils falling around my face. My mirror image formed words I couldn't make out, and on my shoulder, Monster rested his head. He looked kindly at me from the mirror and exhaled into my mane.

The dream slipped into the night woods, and again I relived the girl's death. This time there was no one to wake me, and I saw the vision to the very end, crying and screaming. Dream and vision must have blended together, because when the murderer ran toward the edge of the forest, he turned and looked over his shoulder.

It was Varnar.

A loud noise thundered through the dream. I sat up in bed. It was morning. My cheeks were wet with tears, and I inhaled shakily.

Someone was pounding on my front door.

Bewildered, I tumbled out of bed, ran down the stairs, and flung the door open.

Outside in the morning sun stood Elias. His face bore its usual cheeky, flirtatious expression, but it changed to shock when he saw me.

"What in the gods' name happened?" he asked.

I touched my cheek, which in addition to being wet with tears was also sore as hell. I had bothered to only half-heartedly wash off the worst of the blood before falling into bed.

"I ran into some unpleasant characters yesterday evening," I said.

"Who was it?" Elias's voice demanded an answer.

"Just someone I go to school with—and his buddies."

He exhaled. "So you've known them for a long time?"

"It doesn't concern you." I tousled my hair. "What are you doing here?"

"We had an agreement."

"I totally forgot you were coming. Can we wait until another day?"

"You best believe we cannot. I'm not going anywhere until I've made sure you're okay." He walked past me, though I hadn't invited him in.

I threw my hands up in frustration.

"I'm okay," I shouted.

Elias stopped behind me and took me by the arm. He led me into the bathroom and planted me in front of the mirror.

I gathered myself before I looked. Fortunately, my hair was black, and my sullen facial expression was the same as usual, but all similarities with my normal appearance ended there. One cheekbone was purple and swollen, and my right eye was almost shut. I had dried blood in my nostrils, and there were clear tracks of Peter's nails on my forehead and lower lip and along my jawline. My uninjured eye was red and bloodshot, and my hair was one big, stiff, matted bird's nest.

"You are not okay. You look awful."

"You should see the other guys," I said with a smile, but the scratch on my lip didn't let it last long.

It wasn't a lie. Whatever Varnar had done to them single-handedly was far worse than what the three of them together had managed to do to me.

Elias lifted my camisole. Purple and blue blotches spread across my defined stomach muscles where Markus had kicked me.

"Your back doesn't look much better," he commented, stroking a warm hand across it. His aura, reminiscent of quicksand, billowed into me.

"They're just scratches." I removed his hand and took a step away.

"That may be, but I would like you to take a shower so I can see what's blood and dirt and what are real wounds."

I exhaled with a laugh. "I'm not taking my clothes off within a one-mile radius of you."

"Do you think I would take advantage of such a situation?"

"It's hard for me to assess what you would take advantage of."

"I promise I'm not a Peeping Tom." He looked a bit ashamed, nevertheless. "I'll make breakfast in the meantime," he said over his shoulder before closing the door behind him.

Only when I stood under the showerhead did I realize how sore I was. My back ached, my abdominal muscles and ribs burned sharply when I breathed, and I had a horrific headache. I had to wash my hair three times to get all the dried blood out.

When I was finally as clean as I was going to get—and smelling like my favorite coconut shampoo—I turned off the hot water and stepped out of the shower. I dried off and wrapped my hair in the towel. In front of the mirror, I wanted to inspect my injuries again, so I ran my hand across the glass to remove the steam.

A red mane blazed in the small strip of mirror, and I caught a glimpse of my own face, trying desperately to say something with soundless words.

I screamed, turned my back to the mirror, and hid my face in my hands.

Elias rushed through the door with my bread knife in his hand.

"What's going on?" He stared at me, and I stood there wearing nothing but the towel turban. Then he slapped a hand across his eyes and turned to leave, but he misjudged the distance and walked into the doorframe.

The knife clattered to the tile floor.

"OUT," I yelled.

"I thought there was someone in here with you." With his hands still covering his eyes, he snatched the knife off the floor and fumbled his way out.

I took a couple of breaths, wrapped the towel around myself, and limped to put some clothes on.

Downstairs, Elias sat at the dining table, which was set with coffee cups, plates, bread, and cheese. He lifted his hands in a defensive position.

"I'm sorry."

"It's fine. It was an accident." I sat at the table.

"What are the names of the people who did this? And are you gonna tell me why they did it?"

I looked down at the table. "Nope."

Elias dropped the subject.

"You look better," he said. "It's not as bad as I thought. But you will have the marks for a while if I don't do something."

"There's not so much you can do. I guess I'll just have to wait for them to go away."

"That's where you're wrong," he said, and produced a small ampoule that resembled the one he had given me with the klinte. The liquid in this ampoule, however, was a blinding shade of neon green. He handed me the ampoule. "Welcome to my world."

I turned the ampoule in my fingers. "And this is?"

"Laekna, it's called. It'll make you heal quicker. I could get a healer to cure you immediately, but that would be like using a sledgehammer to crack a nut."

"Healer?"

"Like I said: Welcome to my world. Which is also your world, now that I think about it. You just don't know it yet."

I turned the small ampoule over in my hand. "Do I just drink this?"

"Only a little. A bit more than the amount of klinte I gave you." He looked at me hopefully. "We can share it like last time."

"No, thanks," I said and shuddered. I was finding it hard enough to forget the first kiss, which I kept mixing up with my daydreams about Varnar.

Elias turned down the corners of his mouth in a scorned expression. "Give me your finger."

I stuck out my index finger, and he placed a drop of laekna on the tip. I put my finger in my mouth and sucked. The fluid had a strong flavor. Nothing like the sweet, floral klinte. More like horseradish or chili. Heat spread in a wave from my throat up into my head and out onto my face. It swept down my neck and into my arms, continuing downward to my stomach. When it reached me below the belt, I let out a little gasp.

Elias suppressed a smile by biting his lip.

The heat wave pulsated through my legs and down to my toes, and then it was gone.

I sat there, disoriented. Then I lifted my hand to my cheek. The tenderness had subsided significantly, and I could see out of my right eye again. I felt for the scratches on my face, but they were completely gone. I pulled up my T-shirt and saw that the violet bruises had disappeared. Only a faint greenish-yellow shadow remained.

Elias looked contentedly at me. "Much better. Tomorrow you won't see any of it."

"Do you have a magic potion for every scenario?" I asked as he closed the ampoule.

"It's not a magic potion. These are medicines. They're made from plant extracts and, in certain instances, more hard-hitting ingredients. But never with witchcraft."

I noticed he didn't answer my question. "Do you make them yourself?"

"I've spent many years refining the craft. It's my specialty."

"You said you've spent years refining what you do. How many years are we talking?"

Elias didn't reply; instead, he held out his hand. I looked down at the extended hand without moving. He gestured that I should take it.

"What now?"

"Try and see for yourself. I want to test your abilities."

"All right." I just had to gather myself before I took his hand in mine. It was warm and strong, and it actually felt nice to hold it. As soon as we touched, I was nearly sucked into Elias's deep, strange past.

"What do you see?"

I closed my eyes and concentrated. The images streamed toward me. I kept them at a slight distance and focused on the basic impulses I received from him.

"Your aura is like normal people's—but different."

"How is it different?"

"It has more . . . *volume*. It's all there. Sorrow, joy, love, longing, desire, hatred, sympathy. That's how it is with most people, though one feeling is usually dominant. But with you, there's more of everything. Like you've experienced everything double."

"Are you sure there isn't a dominant feeling? Go deeper." Elias's voice had a tense undertone.

I reached into him. As deep as I could. Deeper than I had gone into anyone's past. I sorted and grouped and compared the feelings. Sweat broke out on my forehead, and I was breathing heavily. The further back I got, the harder it was. It was like moving concrete blocks. Normally, I was overwhelmed by people's pasts, and I did what I could to hold them back. Now that I was intentionally digging around in someone's past, it was harder than I had thought it'd be. But finally, I bumped up against something. A kind of blockade. Was I in the epicenter of Elias's emotions?

"Which feeling?" Elias asked again.

"Insatiability." I investigated the blockade. "You desire everything and everyone. You want it all. All experiences and all people. You have enough desire for a hundred lifetimes."

Elias tightened his grip on my hand and started to say something. I shushed him.

"Wait, there's more. Why do you want to have and experience everything?" I prodded mentally at the feeling, which gave slightly. "There's something behind it."

I used all my strength and finally got it out of the way. I opened my eyes and looked straight into Elias's gray-blue ones. "It's loss. You lost something that's gone forever. Even if you live forever, experience everything and everyone, you will never get it back."

I saw tears glimmering in Elias's eyes for a split second before he turned his head. Then he let go of my hand and stood up. He stood by the glass door and stared out across the flat landscape from the lookout post that is my house.

Meanwhile, I wiped the sweat off my forehead and exhaled.

Finally, Elias turned back toward me, his eyes now completely dry. He gave me a straight-to-the-point look.

"Your retrocognition is strong. I've never seen it so strong in someone who hasn't received guidance. It may be more powerful than that of anyone I've ever met. Anything creative must be impossible for you."

"What do you mean?"

"People who can see the past aren't capable of creating anything." Elias shrugged his shoulders, as if he had just told me that C-A-T spells cat.

"Why not?"

"Time is both destructive and creative," Elias explained. "Going backward . . . it's the same as destruction in the most neutral sense of the word. For time to become past, the present must be destroyed. Therefore, people like you tend to be very much in touch with their destructive side and not so much with their creative side."

I let this fundamental aha moment concerning my personality settle as Elias continued.

"I would wager you're terrible at painting and drawing."

I nodded slowly. "And cooking is decidedly dangerous for both me and my surroundings."

Elias's mouth pulled into a crooked smile. "It's a good thing you have so many other assets."

I ignored his comment. "Have you known many people like me?"

"Clairvoyants? Yeah, a few. Both of the past and the future. A handful are a combination, but with them, the gift is usually weaker because it's split. Clairvoyance is not an uncommon ability." He sat at the table and slapped his palms against it. "Let's get started teaching you to shield. Take my hand again."

I did as he said.

"How do you usually turn off your power?" he asked.

"I envision a hermetically sealed bubble around me, where nothing can get in. Sometimes I picture a shield made of iron."

"Does it work?"

"Not really. The only thing that works is to stay away from people, but even then, I get something from my surroundings."

"I think I can help you." He squeezed my hand. "Try doing the opposite. Open up like you did before."

"Why?"

"Just try it."

I activated my clairvoyance again and immediately got feelings and pictures from Elias. I saw the women. Lots of women. And I saw him bent over cauldrons and vats that boiled and bubbled. Also a glimpse of him embracing Od. *Weird.*

"Close your eyes," said Elias.

I obeyed.

"Start by accepting your clairvoyance. It's there, and it's okay."

I tried, but it was hard. I hated my curse. Elias waited patiently. Eventually I found a balance, where I tolerated the clairvoyance. Elias sensed that I was ready and continued.

"Now open your other senses. First smell."

I sniffed. The smell of coffee tickled my nostrils. I could also smell Elias's spicy and slightly sweet fragrance.

"Listen."

I listened and heard our breathing. The wind outside rustled through the trees, and a single bird cawed.

"See."

I opened my eyes, and Elias was holding a chain in the sunlight cascading in through the window. At the end of the chain hung a crystal. It caught the light and threw it back in different colors. I found myself smiling in fascination.

Elias smiled back. "Now try to go back to your clairvoyance. Don't try to induce it or shut it off. Just observe it, while you have your other senses open."

I reached out again. The clairvoyance was still there. I could feel it, but it was no longer active. It was as if it had fallen asleep.

"It's working," I whispered, nearly on the verge of tears with gratitude.

"Feel," Elias said hoarsely. He stroked the fingertips of his free hand up my forearm. It tickled in a pleasant way.

"I said it's working," I said, somewhat short of breath.

"I know," he whispered. "This is for my own sake."

He leaned forward.

I abruptly let go of his hand and jerked back. My clairvoyance flared up again, and Elias's feeling of losing everything burst into me.

"Why did you do that?" I shouted.

"I couldn't help it. You're so pretty with no makeup. Your smile is fantastic."

"I'm about to kick you out. Can you not do that all the time?"

He thought about it.

"I actually don't think I can. I'm used to getting what I want." He looked at me with large puppy-dog eyes.

"So get out and go get everything you want, if it's so easy for you."

"Everything I want right now is sitting in front of me."

"I've seen enough inside your sick head to know you only want me for twenty minutes, until someone new and more exciting shows up."

"You're probably right," he admitted. "Except you're underestimating me with regard to the twenty minutes."

After I had kicked Elias out, which I did very emphatically after his last comment, I was left sitting alone. It was the first time in my life that an empty room had felt empty. Normally it just felt peaceful.

All my senses were still wide open after Elias's exercise, and it was like I felt everything double. I began restlessly taking cups and food off the table. It was only ten o'clock. My stomach fluttered when I remembered that Varnar was coming later in the day. I ignored the impulse to put makeup on. I didn't have enough faith in my trembling hands to do it without looking, and I didn't dare get anywhere near the mirror.

A few hours later, there was a soft knock at the door.

I opened it, and as I expected, Varnar stood outside. He was wearing a pair of loose black pants and a close-fitting black shirt. It stretched tight across his broad shoulders. His dark hair was gathered in a knot that made his facial features clearly visible.

He looked intensely at me, which made me self-conscious, but I held his gaze.

"Your injuries are almost gone," he observed.

Something made me hesitant to mention Elias, so I said nothing.

"And you look different without makeup."

My heart beat a little faster. Elias had said I was pretty without makeup. Did Varnar think so, too?

"It was better the other way," he said. "You should keep painting your eyes."

"Okay," I mumbled behind pursed lips.

Varnar led me out into my small yard. I stood, somewhat at a loss, in the middle of the lawn with my arms hanging at my sides. I had no idea how we were going to do this. But it seemed that Varnar knew exactly how he wanted to tackle it.

"I've seen a bit of what you can do. Some things you need to unlearn, and some things you need to refine." He walked around me and stopped right in front of me. "I'm your opponent now. Imagine that you know a fight between us is inevitable. What do you do?"

I had to think about that. "I strike first, if I can get away with it."

Varnar nodded. I had answered correctly.

"How many times do you hit?"

"Just once. And then I wait. Sometimes that's enough for the other person to give up."

This time he shook his head. "More. Five to six punches or kicks to different parts of the body. The opponent feels surrounded and will often retreat."

I nodded. That made sense.

"Then you deal the deciding blow, here." He reached out his arm and placed the edge of his hand on my throat.

I shivered at his touch.

"Or here." He placed the heel of his hand on my temple.

The fine hairs on the back of my neck stood up. "Or here." He made a fist and moved his hand to just under my breastbone.

I worried that he could feel my heart pounding.

"Yesterday, you also used your legs." I was mostly trying to divert the attention away from myself. "You did somersaults and windmills, and you kicked. Can you teach me that?"

"You're not ready for that. You have a lot to learn. Because you kicked, your opponent got you down. That's one of the most important things. Never kick, hit, or stand in a way that might allow your opponent to bring you to the ground. Then you'll almost certainly lose the fight."

The critique stung, but I asked him to continue. "What else did I do wrong?"

"A lot," said Varnar, without the least regard for my feelings. "Your hands," he said, taking my hands in his. I exhaled carefully, and he continued. "They should always be near your face. As soon as you know the fight is unavoidable. Your elbows should be in at your sides and your hands up here." He lifted my hands in the air. "Tuck your chin to protect your neck. And never again try to head-butt someone's skull with your forehead."

I found myself smiling, thinking about the day I attacked him in the woods. After seeing him in action the previous evening, I now knew how hopeless my endeavor had been. Varnar's lips also parted in a smile, and again it was as if the smile were trying to outshine the sun. He laid his hands on either side of my head, up near the crown.

"Use these two areas." He pressed gently. So close-up, his aroma was overwhelming.

I looked up, and our eyes met.

The smile vanished, and he wrinkled his brows almost imperceptibly. Then he let go of me.

"We'll start with blocking," he said. His face was expressionless now. "I'll try to hit you."

In a flash, his hand flew forward, and I ducked instinctively. At the same moment, Varnar's knee hit my shoulder, and I tumbled backward and landed on my butt in the grass.

"No," he said. "Stay on your feet, hands up. Block my punch. Your natural reaction is to duck, and that's wrong. If you duck, you risk being brought down. It's better to take the hit and stay on your feet."

I stood up.

"Again," he commanded.

Irritation bubbled up in me, and I could feel my fighter spirit activating.

Varnar's hand flew forward again. This time I raised my arm, and he hit it instead of my face.

"Better, but you should use the force from my punch to either knock my arm away or turn it around and lock it in your armpit. Then you can get in a punch or a kick." He showed me. He took another swing with his right arm, and this time I locked it under my arm. He struck again with the other arm while I still had his right one locked.

I quickly copied the movement from before and locked his

left arm. Instinctively, I lifted my knee and rammed it into his stomach. He made a muffled noise.

I let go immediately. "Sorry. I don't know why I did that."

Varnar's eyes glimmered with recognition.

"It was a natural reaction, and those are the best. As long as you've learned the right reactions." He clutched his stomach. "But you landed wrong. The stomach is, in most people, protected by a strong layer of muscles." He hit himself there, and the strike made a sound that indicated exactly how well the stomach muscles in question were. "You need to land higher or lower. Higher, you can hit the ribs; in the middle, you hit the diaphragm. Or lower, so you hit the pelvis or groin."

We continued. Varnar hit and instructed me, and I blocked his blows. Several times, he reminded me that I needed to hold my hands and arms up in front of my face.

The sun beat down, and I eventually had to take my shirt off, even though I was embarrassed to be wearing only a camisole in front of him. Then I remembered he had more or less said I looked ugly without makeup. So what I was wearing was completely irrelevant, even if I were wearing only lingerie. I threw my shirt onto the patio and enjoyed feeling the air on my bare arms.

Varnar's eyes flitted briefly across the top of the long scar that peeked out above the neckline of my top. His forehead glistened with sweat.

"You're in good shape," he said. "Most people would be begging to stop now."

We had been at it for over an hour, and my energy was nowhere near depleted. "Am I not the first person you've trained?"

"No," he said curtly.

I waited for him to elaborate, but he didn't say anything. Instead, he grabbed his shirt and—help me God—pulled it over his head.

I gasped for air at the sight of his bare torso. His olive skin glimmered in the sun, and when he turned to toss the shirt onto the patio, he revealed a back that was one big mosaic of small muscles that rippled at his slightest movement. On his right bicep, he had something that looked like burn marks. Fine, small white scars that shone on his skin. I tried not to stare at them. Or at the rest of him.

Varnar turned toward me again. Some of his dark hair had fallen from the knot in damp tendrils around his face.

"You know what, I'm actually pretty wiped out," I lied. "It's probably best if we stop for today." *And it's probably also best if you put your shirt back on.*

Varnar's gaze rested on me for a moment. Then he nodded and walked into the house. Inside, I filled two glasses with water and gave him one, which he emptied in one gulp.

I watched him as he drank. "Why are you helping me?" I asked.

He looked down into the empty glass. "I figured you would ask at some point."

This wasn't an answer, so I looked at him expectantly.

But then there was a knock at the door. I cursed silently and went to open it. Quite a parade of guests I was having today.

Outside stood Mathias. He stepped inside and immediately started talking.

"I need advice about Luna." He stopped when he saw Varnar standing there with his impressive bare torso glistening with sweat in the middle of the kitchen. Mathias looked back at me and studied my flushed appearance.

I wanted to explain, say it wasn't what it looked like—but that would make it even more awkward. Varnar took his shirt and walked past us. He stopped in the doorway and turned toward me.

"You did well today. Shall we do it again tomorrow?"

Mathias looked at me, eyes wide.

I bit my lip. The awkwardness of the situation had not even occurred to Varnar.

"Yeah, sounds good. Just come over after school."

"Remember to stretch so you don't get sore later," he said. "Some of the positions you were in today are probably not ones your body's used to."

Varnar nodded as he passed Mathias, who was about to die of amusement.

When Varnar was gone, I held my head.

Mathias broke out in loud laughter. "What's going on between you two? I thought you were into that guy who came by Frank's the other day."

With my head still buried in my hands, I mumbled, "I'm not into anyone." I looked up over my fingers, but Mathias laughed even harder when we made eye contact. I buried my face again.

"Then you better explain what's going on, because it looks pretty suspicious."

I was uncertain of how I should explain it to Mathias, but he beat me to it. His sharp X-ray vision focused on my face. The grin stiffened on his lips.

"You've been hurt." He removed my hands and pointed to my cheekbone. "Who hit you?"

"Okay, I'll tell you the story, but swear you'll keep it a secret."

Mathias nodded immediately, and I told him the broad strokes. When I was done, he was sputtering with rage.

"Three against one. And a girl, no less. I'll kill Peter tomorrow."

I hadn't given a thought to whether Peter would come to school on Monday.

"You should report them to the police."

"I'm not going anywhere near the police if I can help it. I prefer to handle this myself."

"What if they go after you again, and neither I nor Monster nor Varnar are nearby?"

"That's why Varnar was here today. He's teaching me to fight."

"Ahh, that makes sense. It sounded like you'd been doing

something else." He winked. "But I thought you were already a pro at fighting."

"Not like Varnar. Not even close."

Mathias caught something in my face.

"You're crazy about him," he said.

I closed my eyes, extremely embarrassed of how obvious it was.

"Come on," said Mathias. He put an arm around my shoulder and pulled me over to the large table. "I think we both need to talk."

A couple of cups of coffee and a chocolate bar later, we had covered most of it. Even the fact of Monster's disappearance. Mathias said he was sure he would show up again, but he didn't sound convinced. I also told him about Od and Elias, but left out the kiss. Mathias was elated that Od was willing to speak with him but annoyed with me for promising to go to a party for his sake.

"You should have asked me first," he said.

"You would have just told me to stay home."

"Yes, of course. I can't let you put yourself through that."

"You need answers. And I believe Od can provide them. And I'm learning how to be around a lot of people."

"By taking drugs?"

"Among other things." I ignored his critical undertone. "But I'm also trying other tactics. Elias is helping me shut down my power."

"Elias. And you're not interested in him?"

"No! He's way too much. All the time. It's unbearable."

"Most girls would love to be admired like that."

"I think it's exhausting."

"What if it was Varnar treating you like that?"

I looked down at the table. "He would never do that."

"Why not?"

I couldn't look at Mathias.

"He said today that I'm not pretty without makeup. I'm quite sure he's not interested in me in that way." I could feel the tears in the corners of my eyes. I felt pathetic, but it was a relief to say it aloud.

Mathias gently placed his index finger under my chin and lifted my face. He looked at me with his beautiful blue eyes.

"When I came in here today, and I saw your face with no make-up, you were simply gorgeous. You are really a beautiful girl."

"You don't need to say that. I know I haven't been blessed in the looks department. People have always said I'm ugly."

Mathias let go of my chin.

He lowered his voice to a hiss. "Who are these people? People like Peter?"

"Not just him. Everyone thinks it. Even if they don't say it out-right, I can *sense* it."

"I'm not lying to you. You are insanely pretty. Sure, it's been a little hard to see it behind all the makeup and your constant frown, but you are. With a crazy hot body. I don't understand why Varnar said what he did. In any case, he was wrong."

"That's enough. It's sweet of you, but stop it."

Mathias didn't say any more.

"What was it you wanted to talk to me about?" I asked.

"Luna." Mathias's eyes rested on something outside my kitchen window. Ben and Rebecca's house at the foot of Odinmont. "I just want to be with her, but she's pulling away from me. I don't know why. I'm so in love with her, it almost hurts. It's been that way since the first time I saw her."

Mathias seemed to share my discomfort around love. He wrung his hands.

"I talked with Luna about you the other day."

Mathias's head gave a jerk. "What did she say?"

"She's in love with you. She said so."

Mathias's eyes lit up with his smile. He gestured with his hand for me to continue.

"She knows you have a secret. She doesn't want to move forward until she knows what it is."

Mathias's face fell, and he sank back in his chair. "If I don't tell her, she won't want to be with me, and if I do, she'll run away from me. I'll lose her either way."

"I actually think she'll be relieved. Right now, her theory is that you have a girlfriend."

"There's no one else. I've told her that."

"I'm just the messenger. This is something the two of you have to talk about. But I think you should tell her. Since she knows there's something you're keeping from her."

Mathias looked thoughtful. "Unless we say it *together*."

"No, no, no."

Mathias continued quickly. "She already practically thinks you can walk on water with how much she looks up to you. If she finds out you're also different, then maybe she won't be so scared about me."

"And she doesn't think you can walk on water?"

"Apparently not unless I reveal my secret. Come on, we'll do it together."

"Not a chance. This is something you two need to work out. I don't want to be involved."

Mathias's shoulders slumped. "You're right. That was selfish of me."

"Yes, it was selfish of you."

He sat for a while, thinking. Then he looked at his phone.

"I should go. It's almost nine. And you look really tired."

"I slept like crap last night. I had the dream again."

"What dream?" asked Mathias.

Oh right, how would he know about that?

I told him about both the vision and the red hair in the mirror. After a life of isolation with my secret, the more I talked with Mathias, the more I wanted to tell him.

"That's freaking creepy," he said when I was done. "How do you stand it?"

"I don't have much choice. And look at me." I made a zigzag with my finger across my tired face. "I'm avoiding mirrors. The one in my bedroom is covered, and I would appreciate it if you would throw a towel over the one in the bathroom before you leave. I'll have to do my makeup without looking tomorrow."

I massaged my temples.

Mathias went into the bathroom and came back quickly. "It's covered now."

"Thanks." I stood to walk him out. I was so tired, I felt like I could fall asleep standing up. It had been a long day, with more human contact than I usually had in an entire month.

Mathias turned at the door. "Get up half an hour before you usually do tomorrow."

"Why?"

"Just do it."

"Okay. Off you go." I shooed him away, but he pulled me into a warm embrace. I had never been given a hug like this before. Instinctively, I jerked away.

"No," whispered Mathias in my ear.

I forced myself to relax as he held me. His strange aura flowed into me. The images and emotions jumped around as usual, but then it was like the tempo slowed down. There was more time between the images, and eventually they were all gone, along with his aura.

I stood still but lifted my head.

Mathias was just as handsome as usual, but he was significantly taller. His chest was broader, and his eyes shone more intensely blue than normal. A greenish mist billowed from him and into me. He smiled at me, and in that moment, I knew I would walk through fire and water for him. I got a feeling of déjà vu.

He took a step back when he realized what had happened.

I grabbed him by the wrist. "I am not afraid of you. You won't do anything to me."

"No." His voice had more power than usual. "I won't do anything to you."

Slowly he became smaller, and the blue flames in his eyes diminished. From my grip on his wrist, I saw the images return. His aura looked like itself again.

"You have to tell Luna."

Mathias bowed his head. The golden hair swished down over his forehead.

"Yes, I'll talk to Luna."

# CHAPTER 13

I went for a long run the next morning. Dark clouds hung heavily over the landscape, and through them the sun cast a soft gray light across the fields, which were mostly covered in short stubble and dotted with large round bales of hay. This early in the day, there weren't many cars on the roads. Only once did I see, in the distance, a combine harvester rolling out onto a field. Far out on the western horizon, the windmills' blades turned steadily. They resembled stoic giants.

At around half past six, there was a knock at the door. Outside stood Mathias with a large black bag in one hand.

"What is that?"

"It's a cosmetics bag."

"A what?"

"M-a-k-e-u-p," said Mathias, as if I were a bit slow.

"Yes, I know what a cosmetics bag is, but what are you doing with it?"

"I practically grew up in beauty salons. They had me combing hair and painting nails when I was eight, and by the time I was twelve, I could get a bride ready for her big day. Hair, makeup, everything."

"And you're sure you're into girls?"

"I didn't have you pegged as the prejudiced type." He walked past me. "You can't do your own makeup because of the mirror issue, so I'll do it for you," he said over his shoulder.

Good point. "What are you planning to do?"

Mathias studied my face critically. "To be totally honest, I was thinking of giving you the full makeover treatment."

"You said yesterday that I'm pretty the way I am."

"You are pretty. But what that idiot Varnar said yesterday really pissed me off. I want to show him just how beautiful you can be. Come on. It'll be fun."

And it actually was fun.

Mathias had me lie on my back on the bench with a mask on my face and cotton pads soaked with some kind of serum on my eyes. As I lay there, he did my nails.

Blind as I was, I said several times, "Not pink. For God's sake, anything but pink."

Mathias just chuckled. "Wait and see."

When he removed the dried flakes of mud from my face, I saw that my nails had been filed into soft arcs and painted a dark wine red. Then he colored my eyelashes and brows. "I can't come over every day to do your makeup, so I'm dyeing your lashes black. So on the days you want to wear makeup, all you need to do is put on a little dark eye shadow. You can do that without a mirror," he said. He sat behind me with my head in his lap and began to squeeze and pinch.

"Ow, damn."

Mathias laughed. "You can take a beating from three grown men without wincing, but you can't handle having a single black-head extracted? Pull yourself together."

I bit back the pain. Even when he slapped a stinging liquid on my face.

The close physical contact between us allowed me to sense his strange aura, but I had gotten so used to it, it didn't feel invasive. As Mathias tinkered away, I experimented with Elias's trick. I inhaled the smell of the products and listened to Mathias's voice, and it actually worked. Eventually, my power practically lay down and went to sleep.

He set to work on my eyebrows with tweezers, and once again, I had to hold back several squeaks.

"When are you going to talk to Luna?"

Mathias continued his painful task. "Tomorrow. I sent her a text yesterday, after I left here, saying I needed to tell her something. She has to work today, but tomorrow she can hang out." He ripped out an extra-stubborn eyebrow hair.

Ow, for the love of . . . !

"I'm super nervous," he said.

"I'm sure she'll understand," I said through clenched teeth.

When Mathias was finally satisfied, he ordered me to sit up, and then he studied my face.

"You are the most beautiful canvas an artist could wish for." He dug around in his bag and pulled out brushes and tools, along with a mountain of makeup products.

The only makeup I owned was an eyeliner and a mascara, so many of the items were unfamiliar to me. For someone like me, who can slap on a bunch of makeup in thirty seconds, it was a mystery what he was doing as he brushed, smeared, and painted for an eternity. Finally, he admired his work.

"You are perfect."

"Too bad I can't see it for myself."

The time had flown by, and we ended up in a hurry to get going. Mathias called Luna and asked if we could ride to school with her. She met us with her cargo bike on Kraghede Road in front of Ben and Rebecca's house.

"Wow. You look amazing. Did you do this?" This last part was addressed to Mathias.

He nodded proudly, while I suppressed an overwhelming urge to bike home and wash the artwork off my face to smear on my usual war paint.

"It's not too much?" I asked Luna. "I haven't seen it myself."

"Why didn't you look in the mirror?"

Mathias looked at the ground. I shrugged.

She didn't probe any further. "It's totally perfect. You're wearing less than usual."

"Why did it take so long?" I asked Mathias.

"The art of subtlety," was all he said.

At school, people stared at me, which I was unaccustomed to. I kept my eyes aimed at the floor.

"What did you do?" I hissed at Mathias.

"You're destroying my artwork with that sulky face." He laughed. "I just used a few little tricks. People can't tell exactly what's different. They can just tell that you're glowing in a different way. I made sure to stay close to your normal style. Believe me, I would have rather put a reddish brown around your eyes to accentuate their color, but something tells me you would have killed me, so I chose charcoal gray."

We walked into the classroom, and several people looked up. Their eyes lingered on my face, and I was ready to sink into the floor. Little Mads smiled and laid his hand on his heart, and I got a direct flash of something I had never seen in him before. Warmth and friendliness instead of sadness and loneliness.

Luna had zoned out with her gaze fixed on me.

I shivered involuntarily.

She fingered her red beaded necklace. She was dressed in red from head to toe. Red floor-length dress, red ankle boots, and a red baseball cap with red studs in the shape of a heart. The cap looked like it belonged in a ten-year-old's wardrobe.

"Mathias, do you want to do me?" she asked

Mathias, who had just taken a sip of water, choked as it went down the wrong pipe.

"What?" he coughed.

"Do me. Like you did Anna. Makeup and hair." She thumped him on the back.

"Ohhh." He gasped for air. "That's what you meant."

"What else could I have meant?"

"Nothing." He had regained control of his breathing. "Of course, just let me know when."

Peter came limping in just before class started. One of his eyes was bruised and swollen. Mina dashed over and asked what had happened.

"I fell down the stairs," he mumbled as he threw me a hateful glare.

Our history teacher, Margit, came in with her gray hair in a bun and a large amber necklace around her neck. She started handing back last week's assignment on the Viking Age. She made brief comments each time she passed a paper to a group.

"Mina, Thomas, and Peter—very good. Niels and Ibrahim—read the book a little more carefully next time instead of watching Hollywood movies. Marvel got it all wrong when they put Thor together with Captain America."

She stopped in front of Luna and me. "Interesting paper you wrote. I liked your reinterpretation of the gods' relationship to mankind, and the idea that the different Norse races have children with each other left and right. And I'm impressed that you caught the errors in the book. Great source critique." She nodded approvingly.

"Wow, we got an A. Are we the best or what?" Luna practically shouted across the class. She waved the first page of our paper around, where the grade was written in bold red pen.

People scowled at us.

Hello, Luna. You're in Denmark. Northern Denmark, at that. She was clearly unfamiliar with our strict egalitarian social code.

"You earned it, Luna. You were the one who knew the most," I said.

After class, Mathias and Luna went ahead while I packed up. When I stepped into the hallway, Peter was waiting for me. On closer inspection, I saw that his bad eye was almost swollen shut and was entirely dark purple.

Peter grabbed me by the arm and yanked me down to the end of Brown Hall, which was now empty. His hostile mood shot into me like a toxic injection.

I tried to wriggle out of his grasp, but he held tight.

"If you so much as try anything, I'll smash that eye the rest of the way into your skull," I hissed.

He let go. "I just want to know what's going on."

"You're a total prick. That's what's going on. I can't believe you're still such a coward that you need to bring your buddies along when you attack me."

"I've gone after you by myself before."

"And remind me, how did that go?"

Peter raised his hand halfway to his nose. Then he lowered it again.

"You're one to talk about ganging up on people. I want to know who they were."

"Who?"

"The people who helped you. How many were there? Five or six? It was totally overkill. It was all planned. We just wanted to scare you."

"You can't control your psychopath friend. He would have killed me," I said. Peter shook his head, but I continued. "And maybe I handled you all by myself."

"The last thing I remember is that you were lying on the ground after taking one punch in the face and one in the stomach. I woke up in the hospital, and they said there must have been at least five people," Peter snapped back. With suspicion, he studied my obviously transformed and now scratch-free face. "By the way, taking a few blows to the head looks good on you. Let me know if you want some more."

I made no comment, just stared expressionlessly at Peter.

"I'm going to the police. Maybe Christian and Markus will, too," he added.

I shivered at the thought of where they would put me the next time, now that I was too old for juvenile detention. I tried to keep my voice steady.

"What are you going to say? That I was bleeding on the ground, after you had assaulted me, and that I called up five friends you never saw?"

Peter looked me up and down. "You don't have a scratch on you. We didn't do anything to you. Maybe you and your friends were lying in wait for us."

I froze internally. Imagine if Mathias and Luna got dragged into this. Suddenly, I wasn't so happy about Elias's healing concoction.

"You attacked me, and I beat all three of you. That's the truth," I said coldly before I turned and walked away.

"This is gonna cost you!" Peter shouted after me.

Mathias turned the corner at the same moment.

Oh no!

His face turned dark at the sight of Peter. "At least you're coming after her alone today."

Shut up, Mathias, I begged silently.

Peter widened his eyes. "I knew it. It was you on Saturday."

Mathias walked right up to Peter. His aura flickered a couple times before it disappeared. He grew slightly and stared Peter dead in the eyes, with a sapphire-blue gaze I was happy not to be on the receiving end of.

Peter flinched noticeably.

Mathias spoke, and his voice was deeper than usual. "I wasn't there when you were three guys against one girl. A girl I care a lot about. If I had been there, you wouldn't be standing here now. You would be lying in a temperature-controlled stainless-steel drawer in the basement of the local hospital."

Peter was unable to evade Mathias's gaze, seemingly about to crumble beneath it.

Mathias clenched his fists, which were now the size of dinner plates. "You leave Anna alone from now on. You do not speak to her, you do not look at her, and most importantly, you do not touch her. Understood?" The last word sounded like metal against metal.

Peter's entire body was shaking. I sidled up next to Mathias and took him by the arm, which was burning up. I was afraid that Peter would melt under Mathias's gaze.

"That's enough now," I said softly.

He shifted his shining blue eyes to me. They were otherworldly. I wavered as they bored into mine, but I maintained eye contact.

"Go, Peter. Now!" I commanded.

He broke into a run, as fast as his injured legs could carry him. I managed to hear him whisper, "You guys are totally sick," before he left Brown Hall.

Mathias's aura seeped back just as quietly, and he returned to his normal size. The arm I was holding felt once again like flesh and blood. The cool flames in his eyes died down.

"It's getting stronger, whatever's inside me," he said. "I can't control it anymore."

"Yes you can. The thing inside you is good. It protects people."

"It's dangerous."

"Yeah, dangerous to assholes."

At the end of the hall, I registered a figure. Varnar stood frozen in place, staring at us. I saw the alarm in his eyes sweeping from Mathias to me.

I nodded at him to indicate that everything was okay, and he disappeared around the corner. Had he seen Mathias's transformation? I wasn't too worried about what Peter thought. I don't think he noticed anything other than that Mathias was damn scary. But Varnar tended to have a different view of things than the average person. He had almost certainly observed that Mathias was different.

Before me, Mathias quivered precariously. I dragged him into an empty classroom, where he sank into a chair.

"What's happening to me? Am I crazy?"

"You're not crazy. I can see it when it happens."

"What does it look like?"

"You get bigger, your eyes shine, and sometimes you have a faint green glow," I said honestly.

Mathias's laughter ended in a kind of sob. "I'm the Hulk."

I also had to laugh. "Maybe. I'm trying to find out what you are. I'm going to that party with that guy Od. You'll talk to him afterward, and then we'll know a lot more."

"I know how hard it is for you." He wrinkled his handsome forehead. "You are a really good friend, with a big heart."

A lump traveled up my throat at a dangerously high speed.

"Pull yourself together, Mathias. Just because you might be running around with an alien inside you, you don't have the right to get all sentimental," I snapped.

A smile crossed Mathias's lips, but he said nothing more.

Varnar was waiting next to my bike when school let out. When I reached him, he looked intensely at me, as if he only then registered the change.

I raised my chin as defiance bubbled up in me.

"Better?" I pointed at my face.

He studied me without changing his expression.

"Yes, it's better," he said curtly. His dark brows approached one another. Then he turned around and began to run. I hopped on my bike and took off after him. He jogged silently alongside me all the way to Odinmont.

The day was not as hot as the one before, and the North Jutland wind blew across the flat landscape, which meant that we both kept our shirts on. I also found it easier to concentrate that way.

We picked up our training where we left off the day before. I waited for Varnar to mention Mathias, but he didn't say a word about him. Instead, he instructed me to parry hits and kicks and to move in relation to my opponent.

"You should never stand still. It's about confusing your opponent. And there can't be a system to your footwork. A talented opponent can read that and predict your next move."

Varnar corrected me when my defenses failed, and he reminded me of the most important thing in a fight. "You aren't of much use to yourself if you're lying on the ground."

Gradually, more time passed between his corrections, and I was proud of myself. My body refused to get tired, but after a couple hours, Varnar stopped.

"I can keep going," I protested.

"Your body can, but your mind is worn out. You're making more mistakes, and I don't want them to be encoded in you." His dark hair hung loose, and the wind grabbed at it.

I had a strong urge to run my fingers through my hair and comb out the knots, but instead I crossed my arms.

"What mistakes?"

"For the past half hour, you have consistently taken two steps to the right and then one to the left, after which you go backward and then forward." He tapped a finger on his temple. "The brain wants to create systems, even if you're not aware of it. You must train your mind to make your movements random." He brushed back his tangled hair. "We're done for today. Can you train tomorrow?"

I nodded silently.

Without so much as a nod to confirm our agreement, he disappeared, running through the gap in the hedge.

Afterward, I tried to do homework, but I soon gave up. I turned on the TV and clicked aimlessly though the channels. The energy was simmering inside me, and I had a hard time sitting still. I turned off the TV and looked at my phone. There was a text from

Luna. She wrote that it was dead slow at Frank's, and she asked if I wanted to come by.

I sat for a while with my phone in my hand. I needed to ask her if the dress was ready, anyway, so I stuffed the phone in one pocket and my wallet in the other.

I rode faster than ever and even took a longer route to burn off some of my excess energy, but I still felt a little hyperactive when I walked into Frank's, which, as Luna had said, was nearly empty.

Frank and Luna were hanging out behind the bar. They smiled when they saw me. I guessed Frank's smile was mostly because his bar was no longer completely abandoned.

"Anna, you came." Luna sounded amazed.

Frank studied me. "You're glowing, Anna. What happened?"

I shrugged.

He changed the subject tactfully.

"We really haven't had customers in several days." He shook his head, and a stressed expression flitted across his face. "Can you guys call some of your friends? Tell them they can eat for half price. We have to fill up the tables. It scares people away to see it so empty."

"We could call Mathias," Luna said hesitantly. She lit up. "And Little Mads."

I giggled.

Frank looked at us, uncomprehending.

"I have no friends," I explained, "and Luna hasn't even lived in this town for a month. There's a pretty limited number of people we can call."

"You do have friends," protested Luna. "You have Mathias and me—and that guy Arthur I haven't met yet."

"You're actually right," I mumbled, as a strange warmth spread through my stomach.

Frank looked back and forth between us without saying anything, then focused on me. "Are you here for food for your dog?"

I looked down at the bar and shook my head.

He turned abruptly to Luna. "Can you log in to our profile and write that everything on the menu is half off tonight?"

"That's a great idea." She danced down to the other end of the bar and opened the laptop that sat there.

I raised an eyebrow. "Profile?"

Frank rubbed his chin and smoothed his graying hair. He shot me a crooked smile. "Something tells me you aren't very active on social media."

I gave him a look of distaste. "It's hard enough being social in the real world."

Frank smiled warmly, but his face quickly grew serious again.

"What happened to your dog?" When I didn't answer, he continued: "Come on. I know a worried dog owner when I see one."

"He's gone," I whispered. I didn't dare speak louder, as I was afraid my voice would crack.

"Gone?"

"He was gone on Friday when I woke up."

Frank set an elbow on the bar and rested his chin in his hand. "My dog disappeared like that a couple of times. Once for a whole week. It was a nightmare."

"Really?"

"Yeah. And there was nothing I wouldn't have done to get him back." His brow furrowed, and for a moment, he was deep in thought. Then he smiled at me again with twinkling eyes. "Don't worry. You'll see him again."

It felt as if a hundred pounds were lifted off my shoulders.

Frank patted my hand. From his touch, I felt a sharp stab of pain, and images of the little boy appeared. The boy cried and shouted. Abruptly, Frank turned and walked into the kitchen.

Luna came back, and I told her my real purpose for coming to see her. She jumped, and her curls danced around her head.

"You're going to wear the dress. Yaaay! I'm so excited to see you in it. Where are you going to wear it?"

"To a party. A ball, actually. It's a long story."

"Is it at The Boatman in Jagd?"

"How did you know?"

"I'm going, too. My mom and dad have been talking about the parties at The Boatman for as long as I can remember, but they couldn't go, because we weren't in Denmark. This year, it's finally possible."

"Do they know Od?"

"Who's Od?"

"The guy who owns The Boatman."

Luna bit her lip. "I haven't heard that name before. But it's gonna be amazing. We can get ready together. We'll have Mathias do our makeup. We'll have fun."

Fun wasn't exactly the word I would have used.

I sat at my large dining table on Tuesday afternoon, struggling with my French homework. The assignment was to write ten sentences about myself in French.

It wasn't so much the language that gave me trouble; it was writing ten sentences about myself that I was comfortable sharing with others.

I looked down at my paper, where I had begun to write. My name is Anna. I am seventeen years old. I have black hair. I work in a café. *I am clairvoyant. I can see auras. My best friend is a missing giant dog. I am in love with a guy who can take down three men in thirty seconds.*

Outside, darkness had just begun to fall, and the wind rustled in the trees. I was paging idly through my grammar book when I heard voices outside.

Through my kitchen window, I saw Mathias storming up with Luna in tow. Without knocking, he yanked open my front door and barged in. Luna was wearing a bright-red wrap dress, red sneakers, and a red turban. I was starting to think she was going through a red phase.

"Sit down, both of you," Mathias practically shouted.

Something in his voice made us listen, and we sat on either side of the table.

He spoke to me. "You have to tell Luna about your power."

I pressed my lips together and shook my head.

He turned toward Luna. "Show Anna what you showed me."

Luna widened her cognac-colored eyes. "What if she gets scared?"

He laughed, hard. "Believe me. It takes a lot to scare Anna."

"Do you think she'll like it?" whispered Luna, as if I weren't there.

"She'll love it." Mathias took her hand and gave it a squeeze.

Luna smiled at him and then shifted her gaze, almost bashfully, to me.

What is going on?

She inhaled deeply, released Mathias's hand, and began to move her fingers in the air. Her wild energy became more intense. Then, the air around her sparkled.

Something vibrated beneath my palms. I looked down and discovered that the table was shaking slightly. My empty coffee cup trembled, and the teaspoon inside it rattled against the edge.

Then she pointed at my grammar book and moved her index finger in the air with small twitching motions.

The pages moved.

"What . . ." I exhaled.

Although the book was a couple of feet away from her, she was flipping through it. Luna stopped and looked at us with a cautious smile.

"How the hell did you do that?" I asked.

She shrugged her shoulders. "I've never shown anyone before. It's nothing special."

"You can move something without touching it. That is special!"

"I showed Mathias when he showed me," she paused briefly, "what he can do, turning green and all that."

From the end of the table, Mathias cleared his throat.

"He said you had also seen it." She cocked her head. "He said you also have a secret."

First Arthur, then Mathias, Od, and Elias, and now Luna.

I sighed. "I'm clairvoyant."

"You're what?"

"I can see the past."

Luna leaned forward with an expression of wonderment. "Can you see *everyone's* past?"

She did not even question whether it could be true.

"More or less. With some people it's not so clear. Like you, for example." Instinctively, I reached into her with my power.

She squirmed in her seat.

"It tickles," she giggled.

"Can you feel me?"

"Yes. But go ahead," she encouraged me and took my hand.

I shifted my attention to Mathias and investigated his shaky past. "Mathias, can you feel me now?"

He shook his head.

Luna bounced impatiently in her chair and shook my hand. "What about me?"

I closed my eyes and tried to read her again. She squirmed again and laughed.

"Eeee!" she squealed, as if I had actually tickled her physically. I rooted around in her mind without seeing anything concrete, but suddenly it was like she opened up so I could see in.

"What can you see?" she asked.

"A ton. Your house in Nepal was blue and white. And it smelled like sandalwood."

She nodded and put her hand on her forehead, as if she were trying to make sense of things.

"So, what exactly can you do? Can you read thoughts?"

I grimaced. "No, not at all. I can see people and sense their baseline moods. With most people, I can also see a kind of aura."

She lit up. "What color is mine? I hope it's every color of the rainbow."

"I don't see auras as colors. I see a texture and an energy. Yours looks like electricity."

"Can you see the future?"

I shook my head vehemently. "If only. That would be useful. Then I could predict the lotto numbers or prevent accidents. I can't do anything to change the past."

"You could become a detective," said Mathias. "Then you could solve murders."

"A little hard with the whole burden-of-proof thing," said Luna. Sometimes she was sharper than I expected. I could practically hear the pieces falling into place in her head.

"Alice's killer!" she exclaimed. "That was how you knew what he looked like."

"I knew that was you," said Mathias.

She clapped her hand flat on the tabletop.

"So you're clairvoyant, Anna." She was astonishingly quick to accept the inexplicable. "What about you, Mathias? I just saw you turn big and green. What are you?"

Mathias's shoulders sagged a little. "I don't know. It just pops up once in a while."

"I don't know what I am, either. You're lucky, Anna," said Luna.

Lucky was the last descriptor I would apply to myself.

"You knew about each other." Luna sounded a little wounded. "Why didn't you tell me?"

I looked down at the table. "I discovered Mathias's, uh . . . *tendencies* by chance." I didn't mention that he had seared the skin off the Savage's face. It would be up to him to tell Luna about that. "And he figured me out. Against my will."

"I really wanted to tell you, Luna." Mathias's voice was pleading. "But I was afraid of how you would react. If we had known that you were dealing with something similar, we would have told you sooner."

Speak for yourself!

Luna smiled slightly.

We all sat and looked at one another. The three freaks.

"Tell Luna about the dream," said Mathias.

"What dream?" asked Luna.

I scratched my scalp. "I have this recurring vision where I see a girl get killed. She's strangled by a man, but I can't see her face or his, even though I try every time I have the dream. He finishes by carving a symbol into the girl's back. I see it almost every night." I didn't mention that one time Varnar had been part of the dream.

Luna swallowed but kept her composure. "Do you usually see the same vision over and over?"

At her side, Mathias looked slightly pale.

"No. I rarely see the same scene once I've seen it already."

"Then it must be important in some way," Luna concluded. She adjusted her turban. "Could it have something to do with Alice and the other girls?"

"I had the same thought," I said. "Maybe there's one more girl, and they just haven't found her yet."

"And now she's haunting you, so you can find her, and she can have peace," said Luna dramatically.

Mathias tilted his head back, as if he were thinking, *Oh, come on.* "You believe in ghosts, too?" he asked.

Luna wiggled her shoulders. "Yes. Don't you guys?"

We both shook our heads.

"Are we not all three in a position where we should at least consider that they might exist?" She returned to the previous subject. "Are there other things that are different about the vision? What kind of symbol does he carve into her?"

"It's like a weird F. I think it's the killer's signature."

"Why?" Mathias shuddered.

"Well, when I spoke to the police, they asked me if the letter F meant anything to me. They didn't want to say more. So I poked around in their heads a little. I saw that the same F had been found on all the other girls. Tenna had it cut into her stomach. Belinda had it on her forehead."

At the end of the table, Mathias rolled his eyes. "Ugh, for God's sake."

I went on. "Naja and Alice had it drawn on their clothes in blood. I don't know how the police have managed to keep it secret."

"What does it look like?" Luna took my notepad and the pencil I had been using when I was trying to write about myself in French and handed them to me. "Try to draw it."

"It's lopsided. But he also doesn't seem very bright," I said, before taking the paper and trying to recreate the F.

Luna looked down at the paper when I pushed it back to her. Mathias scooted close to her and looked down at my unhelpful strokes.

"That guy Elias wasn't kidding when he said people who can see the past are utterly lacking in creative ability."

I grumbled. "That's what it looks like, though."

"Why an F?" he murmured. "Maybe his name starts with an F. Or maybe he's getting revenge on someone whose name starts with an F?"

"It's not an F," Luna said quietly. "It's an A."

Mathias and I looked down at the paper.

"How on earth do you get an A from that?" asked Mathias. "I mean, Anna's no artist, but still."

Luna traced the strokes with her fingers. "It's from the Elder Futhark. The oldest runic alphabet. It's our forefathers' symbol for the letter A. The rune is called Ansuz. It means 'god'."

"Do people still use runes?" Mathias's voice was a little rough.

"Yes, but not as a written language. We use them symbolically. According to our faith, the runes are magical. A gift from the gods. My mom says they give power to whatever object they're carved into."

"Oh God." Mathias squirmed in his seat. "He's into some kind of occult shit. He *is* a psychopath, after all."

I shook my head slowly. "I don't think so. My impression of him was that he's pretty dumb. Being a psychopath requires a certain intelligence."

Luna's dark skin had also paled. "My dad once said that there are people who practice Asatru in a different way than we do. More brutal. Maybe this is bigger than just one man."

The hairs on my arms stood up. "Bigger?"

Luna exhaled. "There are these religious circles. They sacrifice animals. Like how we sacrifice food. We always just take a portion of something we were going to eat anyway. We never kill for the purpose of making a sacrifice, but some people maintain the old customs and sacrifice piglets, chickens, and goats. When you think about it, it's no worse than what farmers do every day to thousands of animals. I don't think the animals suffer."

"But it's only animals they're sacrificing?" I asked.

"As far as I know. But in the Norse faith, you never let the sacrifice lie on the ground. It has to be either put in water or hung from a tree or some other high place, so the gods can get it. The higher the better. And there should also ideally be nine equal offerings. At least if it's for Odin."

"Isn't there something about this that reminds you of the Windmill Murders?" Mathias interrupted.

"The what?" asked Luna. "What are the Windmill Murders?"

"You've never heard of them?"

Luna shook her head.

"You must be the only person in Denmark who hasn't," said Mathias.

"Well, I haven't been *in* Denmark," said Luna.

Mathias and I shared a grim look.

"About twenty years ago, there was someone going around in this area killing animals and hanging them from trees. Always nine at a time." I stopped and prepared myself before continuing. "Finally, he killed nine people. They were found hanging from three windmills just outside Ravensted. One from each blade."

Luna opened her mouth, but nothing came out.

"Aaghh, it's so creepy," said Mathias.

"Did they find out who did it?" asked Luna.

"The murderer turned out to be a local nutjob. They sent him to the psychiatric hospital, and he's never getting out. It can't be him killing the girls now."

"Who were the dead people hanging from the windmills?"

I exhaled with pursed lips. "No children—fortunately. There was an old married couple. A couple of addicts who were friends with the murderer. Paul Ostergaard, the Earl, his wife was also one of them."

Luna gasped. "Mina's mom?"

I nodded. "Janitor Preben's son was there, too. He was probably in his early twenties then. The last three men were never identified."

None of us said anything. A branch slapped against my window in the wind.

Mathias changed the subject. "Should we tell the police that it's not an F? Maybe they can use that for something."

"What would we say to them, Mathias?" I asked. "They don't know that I know what the symbol looks like. Should I tell them I read their pasts and that I saw the symbol in a vision? No, thanks."

"If there's a link to the Windmill Murders, the police should know."

"But the guy responsible for those is behind lock and key," I said.

"The police figured it all out back then. And nothing has happened since."

"What about the girl you keep seeing? Maybe there are others no one's heard about," said Mathias. "Why do you see her again and again?"

"I don't know. It's really strange," I said. "I found the spot where it happened, down in the woods, but I couldn't see anything when I was actually there."

"It's right down there? You didn't tell me you'd found the place." Mathias looked like he had just bitten down on an ice cube and now had aching teeth.

"I didn't think it was important."

"I don't know if it's important, but it's damn creepy," he said.

"Should we go down there?" Luna looked from me to Mathias.

Mathias paled even further and glanced out the window.

"What good would it do?" I was starting to get goose bumps.

"It's dark out. Maybe you can see more now. Plus, we're here. Maybe our abilities can help. Like the time I sketched the murderer. I drew on your strength."

"You did? How do you do that?"

"I just do. It's like pulling lint off a piece of fabric. Anyway, I think we should go down there. Now."

Mathias and I exchanged a doubtful look.

"Come on." Luna had practically shouted, so we both jumped in our seats. "This is important. I can just feel that it is. Maybe her spirit can't cross over until we've gotten a specific message."

She stood.

"We're going now." She marched off, and I was hit with a cloud of her strange persuasive power as she passed me.

It must have hit Mathias, too, because he shot up from his chair and followed her.

"Goddamn it," I said as I ran after them.

I found a flashlight in a box in the hallway. I was amazed that it still worked after sitting there for eighteen years.

As we walked across the field, I lit our way with it. The short straw stubble crunched beneath our feet. A few days ago, a combine harvester had made an appearance and scalped my field entirely.

Mathias and Luna held hands.

At that moment, I secretly wished I had someone to hold mine. I thought of Varnar. He would never take my hand unless it was to pull me down and then berate me for not staying on my feet.

We entered Kraghede Forest, and it didn't take me long to find the spot. I pointed the flashlight's beam at the green forest floor next to the little birch tree.

"This is where she died," I said.

Luna, who was standing right were the girl fell, instinctively took a step back. Mathias started to glow slightly green.

"Can you turn up your light a little, Mathias? Then I can save some battery power," I said.

The others laughed nervously.

"Can you see anything, Anna?" asked Luna.

I focused, but like the first time I was there, I saw nothing but the steady changing of the seasons. I placed myself where I normally saw the vision—about fifteen feet from the birch tree—and turned off the flashlight.

Bathed in moonlight, the scene was eerily familiar, aside from the lack of snow.

My pulse rose. Luna and Mathias stood behind me, and I prepared myself to see the girl come walking by.

Nothing happened.

Behind me, I could tell that the others didn't want to disturb me and were trying to be completely still, but Luna's impatient energy bumped up against my back.

"Stop it, Luna."

"Stop what?"

"Being so eager. I can feel it."

"Sorry," she mumbled. "Can't you use my strength?"

I tried to draw strength from her aura. She made a *whoooii* sound and squirmed.

"It's not working. To be honest, you're a little distracting," I snapped.

"Okay, okay," she said, and they walked a little farther away.

I tried again. Still, nothing happened. I turned around and threw up my arms. "I don't know what's wrong. I can't see anything."

"What if we act out the scene?" Luna suggested.

I looked incredulously at her. "What do you mean?"

"Mathias and I. Maybe it'll shake something loose. You can direct us."

"No, that's way too macabre," Mathias exclaimed.

"Come on." Luna cast her power of persuasion—which I now strongly suspected was linked to her ability to flip through books from a couple of feet away—over us.

Mathias faltered mentally. Now that I was aware of it, I could plainly see Luna's influence attack his aura. I stared, fascinated.

"Do you see something now? You look completely different." Luna looked at me excitedly.

"No. But I see that you're using some kind of trick to convince us."

"Can you do that?" asked Mathias.

Luna looked a bit ashamed.

"You're the first person to notice," she said.

Mathias brushed off his arms as if to remove Luna's influence.

"I don't think that's helping," I told him.

"We might as well get it over with. Let's do what Luna says," he sighed.

I nodded my head. It couldn't do any harm. With my back to them, I directed: "Luna, walk past me."

She began to walk. When she passed, I gave a start, but the sight of her turban-clad head reassured me. She was also quite a bit taller than the girl in the vision.

"Walk a little slower, Luna."

She reduced her speed.

"Mathias, go after her. You should end up by the birch tree."

They walked dutifully in single file.

"Stop," I shouted when they reached the birch tree. "Act like you're strangling her, Mathias."

He placed his hands around Luna's neck. I hadn't told him the detail of the cord, but I assessed his height in relation to the birch tree. It fit with the man in the vision.

"Down on your knees, Luna. And you follow, Mathias." I watched them in their fictitious struggle. Still, nothing set off my clairvoyance.

"Then what happened?" Mathias yelled from his crouched position.

Luna lay still on the ground in a dead-girl pose.

I gave up and walked over to them. "It's no use. I don't see anything."

"Is there anything else in the vision?" said Luna from the forest floor.

I searched my memory. "Nothing happens except that the man cuts her, then he stands up and runs away."

Still in his role, Mathias obeyed me. He waved his arms over Luna's back and then reached for the birch tree to pull himself to his feet.

I stiffened.

"Oohhh," I exclaimed.

They both turned to me as the world spun around, and my entire body felt a chill.

"What's going on?" Mathias went into full protector mode and glowed fiercely green.

I tried to find the words. "The vision ends with the man stand-ing and grabbing on to the birch tree. But it breaks under his weight."

We all looked at the straight little tree.

"But it's not broken," Luna began.

Mathias met my gaze. "That's because it hasn't happened yet."

 # CHAPTER 14

The three of us sat, dazed, around my dining table.

When the realization hit us, we had abandoned all sense of dignity and bolted from the woods back to my house.

Indoors, in the warmth and light, I was a little embarrassed to have gotten so scared. The other two appeared to feel the same way. I went into the kitchen and put some water on to boil.

"Coffee or tea?"

"Don't you have anything stronger?" asked Mathias.

I rooted around in the kitchen cabinet where I had seen some dusty bottles. I pulled one out. It had no label, but a rune resembling a strange P was etched into the glass.

"This stuff gets better with age, right?"

"Yeah," said Mathias. "Bring it over."

After a brief struggle, I got the dry cork out of the way and poured a golden liquid into a few glasses. I handed one to Mathias, and he swirled it in circles so the liquid crawled up the sides. It left oily rings on the glass.

"Whatever it is, it has a high alcohol percentage. Just as I hoped." He took a little sip before closing his eyes and taking a large gulp. "Mmm."

I tried mine, too. It was stronger than wine, and it tasted spicy and sweet.

Luna took a large sip, rounded her lips in an O and exhaled in the same way as one does when drinking whiskey.

"I thought you couldn't see the future."

"I can't. Or at least I've never been able to before."

"Never ever?" She narrowed her eyes.

Something scratched at my memory. "There was one time. But I'm not sure. Have you both heard the story of my foster family's house that burned down?"

They nodded. A little too quickly. I was so eternally tired of being a local legend.

"The night the house burned down, I dreamed that I saw my foster mom come running toward me. She was on fire. She was a living torch. And someone kept shouting at me to wake up."

Mathias and Luna looked at me, eyes wide.

I continued and tried to keep my voice steady. "Fires had been set in five different parts of the house, but they hadn't really taken hold yet. I was able to get the whole family out, but the house burned down."

"And you were blamed for having started the fire," said Mathias.

"I always thought I had smelled the smoke in my sleep and that's why I dreamed what I did. But now I'm not sure."

"If that was a vision, it means you can change the future. Your foster mom didn't die in the fire, even though she died in your vision. You actually averted her death." Luna adjusted her turban, which was sitting slightly askew after our frantic flight. "So we can also prevent the murder in the woods."

"Maybe," I said.

"But what does the vision itself mean?" Mathias held his glass up to the ceiling lamp and examined it. Filtered through the liquid, golden light bathed his handsome face.

"It means that there's a girl who has a date with death," I said sharply.

Mathias gave me an irritated look. "I figured as much. What I mean is, why are you seeing it?"

"I think Anna is the one who has to stop it," said Luna.

"But then why didn't I see the others? Naja, Tenna, Alice, and

213

Belinda? If I had foreseen their deaths, maybe I could have helped them." My throat burned suddenly, and I had to lower my voice. "Why am I seeing this specific girl?"

No one had an answer, so no one said anything. I pictured Alice's kind smile, but I pushed the image away and emptied my glass.

"We can't really do anything about it now. And it's getting late." *Hint, hint: You can go now.*

Mathias and Luna also finished their drinks. Mathias shook his head and made a *brrrrrr* sound.

"That's strong. What is it?"

"No idea. It was in the cabinet." I put the cork back in the bottle.

"Are you okay being alone?" asked Luna. "You can sleep over at my house."

I shook my head.

"I'm used to it." I felt a jab of longing. "We can just talk about it tomorrow."

They got up and left my home, arm in arm.

We did not say much to one another the next day at school. Mathias and Luna looked as tired as I felt. But they'd started showing how they felt about each other. They held hands, and one time I saw them kiss. Their infatuation emanated from them like a heat wave. Sometimes I warmed myself in it; other times it felt like it singed me. They received jealous scowls from both the boys and the girls, but Luna and Mathias were too absorbed in each other to notice.

During our long morning break, we hung out in silence on the red sofa.

"Did you notice the moon in your vision?" Luna's question came out of the blue.

"What?"

"The moon. Is it full or half or what? And where is it in the sky?"

"Does that mean something?"

"We might be able to calculate when it happens." Luna's hand stroked her red beaded necklace.

I looked impatiently at her. "But how would we be able to figure that out?"

Luna tried to sound casual, but she spoke with a hint of pride. "My dad taught me to navigate based on the celestial bodies."

"During your many years at sea?" Mathias disguised a laugh by kissing her hand.

She pulled her hand away and smiled at him before slapping him with it.

"We've actually sailed a lot. And it's important not to be totally reliant on technology in case it stops working or you're stranded on a deserted island."

"In that case, you wouldn't have much need to navigate," I said dryly.

"Ugh, you two." Luna shoved us. "I'm serious. Anna, if you can try to measure the moon's position with your hand and remember its size and phase the next time you have the vision, I might be able to figure it out. It would help if we could calculate—even if only approximately—when it would happen. Maybe it would give us a chance to prevent the murder."

"It's cool that you know all that about the moon," Mathias said, wrapping his arms around her.

She smiled. "I'm not called Luna for nothing."

That afternoon, after pacing restlessly around my living room for almost an hour, there was finally a knock at the door. Varnar stood outside in loose workout pants and a sleeveless black shirt that put his muscular arms on merciless display. The pale scars on his right arm stood in contrast to his dark coloring, like small ridges in his silky skin. I imagined running a finger across them.

Clouds were gathering above him, and there were rumblings in the distance.

"Run," he said, before he turned around and sped toward the forest.

I stood, confused, as he took off across the bare field. Then I ran after him. It didn't take me long to catch up to him.

When I reached his side, he increased his speed. I matched his pace with no problem.

Small drops of rain began to fall, and a sharp bolt of lightning flashed in the sky, followed by an enormous thunderclap.

We soared into the woods. Varnar now ran even faster, and I did the same, trying to match his pace. I took a few sharp turns around the trees, and I managed to register briefly that we were running across the spot where the girl would be strangled, and where Luna, Mathias, and I had nearly been frightened to death the night before.

Above us, the rain began to fall hard, but in the forest, we were protected by the trees. Only a few drops found their way to us, but the thunder roared overhead. The smell of wet moss and bark was overpowering.

We reached the narrow path simultaneously, with heavy footfalls against the muddy ground. I got out in front of Varnar. Whenever he came up alongside me, I increased my pace, and I felt like we were flying. I looked back and grinned. A rare smile flitted across Varnar's lips.

"Where are we going?" I shouted.

"The manor," he shouted back.

I gave everything I had, with Varnar racing after me. I was almost disappointed when Kraghede Manor appeared at the end of the path. I slowed down and stopped at what was once the yard. Now it was an overgrown mess.

Varnar stopped behind me, and I was pleased to hear that he was gasping for breath. I, too, was breathing in sharp bursts. Here in the clearing around the manor, where there were no trees to shield us, the rain hit us in large splats.

Kraghede Manor—once the seat of the region's power—was in a sorry state. The four wings still stood, but with smashed windows and graffitied, peeling walls. The roofs hung like canopies, and in several places, they had collapsed entirely. I could sense the grandeur of the past, and impulses of activity flowed into me.

"We're going into the old riding hall," Varnar said, yanking me back to the present. His dark hair stuck to his forehead in wet clumps, and the rain made his shirt cling even more closely to his body.

I took a couple of large mouthfuls of moist air to clear my brain. Then I looked down at myself and saw I was equally soaked.

Varnar jogged across the yard and up to a dilapidated building, where he pulled open a large sliding door and went in.

Inside, I saw that it was an open hall with a floor covered in old sawdust. A past echo of neighing and hoofbeats rang in my head, and a flock of birds fluttered away when we walked through. They disappeared out one end of the building, where the roof had completely collapsed. Where we stood, the ceiling was intact, and I could hear the rain hammering against the tin roof.

I looked up to the rafters high above us. "What's keeping this end from falling down?"

"It's secure," said Varnar. "I've been up there."

I estimated that it was probably about thirty feet to the ceiling, and I tried to picture Varnar climbing around up there.

His fingers ran through his wet hair and squeezed it so the drops ran down his arms. Then he tied his hair in a knot with a leather cord and shook the water off his hands.

The sight of the leather string made me shudder.

"Are you ready?" he asked.

"Just a sec," I said, then I took my own long hair and twisted the water out before gathering it in a tight ponytail. My hoodie was heavy with rainwater, so I took it off and tossed it in the sawdust. "Now I am."

Varnar looked at me for a moment too long. A muscle tightened in his neck. Then he stood in front of me.

"First, we'll practice what I taught you yesterday. Then we'll continue with different ways of hitting." He took an imperceptible step toward me, and without thinking, I brought my hands in front of my face and took a swipe at him. He avoided it with ease and threw me a punch in return.

I grabbed his arm and locked it. He let me do it. It was a trap, but I realized it too late. He twisted his arm around my body and turned me around, so he was now holding me from behind. His chin rested on my shoulder.

"Good reactions, but you locked my arm too low. You made it easy for me to catch you and hold on to you." His breath tickled my ear.

I kicked backward, but he wrapped his leg around mine. I was now completely restrained, and I felt his warm chest against my back through our wet clothes. His scent seeped into my nostrils, and his focused aura enveloped me.

Then he released me, and I tumbled forward.

Get yourself together, Anna!

Just because I got weak in the knees over a guy, it shouldn't extend to my fighting skills. I cast away all thoughts of fragrant, rain-soaked hair and muscular arms, whipped around, and went after him again. This time I lashed out as quickly as I could.

Varnar evaded me and hit back. I parried with one arm while sending a blow to his solar plexus with the other. It landed, but he managed to step back, so it lost its force. He swept my arm to the side, and he gained direct access to strike me with a fist in the shoulder.

It hurt like hell, but I refused to show it. Instead, I used the force of his punch to spin around so I was positioned next to him, and I karate chopped him in the back.

His hand flew to my face, and the back of it hit me across one cheek and the side of my nose. It grew warm, and I sniffed. Blood dripped from it. I felt the will to fight rumbling inside me. Without thinking about it, I copied something he had done to Peter. I planted a hand on the ground and used my whole body as a lever so I could kick him. I hit him square in the jaw, and he grunted in pain.

A feeling of triumph ignited within me, but he turned around and swung his leg, sweeping both of mine out from under me.

I landed on my back in the damp sawdust. It stuck to my still-wet arms. He laughed, and I saw that his teeth were covered in blood. I cursed and tried to get up, well aware that if I stayed down, it would mean I had lost. I rolled sideways and slammed my knuckles into his knee with everything I had.

He let out an anguished sound and sank down to his knees above me. Now it was my turn to laugh, but only for a split second, because his hand came flying.

"Varnar," came a sharp voice from behind us.

Varnar's hand swayed in the air in front of my rib cage.

We both looked toward the door, where Aella stood sopping wet.

"You're supposed to protect Anna, not beat her half to death."

I wiped my nose with the back of my hand. The blood left a wide, dark red track across my skin. Varnar stood up but didn't put weight on the leg I had hit. I had to struggle to get up.

Aella marched over to us, and I felt like we were children who had been caught doing something forbidden.

"I can't learn to defend myself if we don't fight for real," I said defensively.

Aella's gaze moved to Varnar. "What kind of ideas have you put in her head?"

"I haven't put anything in her head. She learns unusually quickly when she tries things with her own body. I've never seen anything like it."

His words sent a wave of warmth over me. Something told me that it was more self-defense than genuine praise. But it meant something, nevertheless.

"We weren't hitting that hard," I said, but my assertion was spoiled by the blood that ran from my nose and down over my lips. I sniffed intently to stop the traitorous stream, while trying to keep my face in a neutral expression. I swallowed a large mouthful of spit with a strong taste of iron and nearly threw up.

Aella fixed her chocolate-brown eyes on me.

"I didn't think a person as incorrigible as Varnar existed, but I was mistaken." Varnar was about to say something, but she held a finger in the air to stop him. "I have always disagreed with your training methods, but I haven't gotten involved. It's a different story with Anna."

"Do I not have a say?" I asked.

"No," they said simultaneously as they stared angrily at each other.

"All right, well . . ." I collected my bloody, sawdust-covered hoodie from the ground. Outside, the rain was pounding down, and I wasn't looking forward to the journey home—but the urge to get away was stronger. I started to walk tentatively toward the door.

"You're not going anywhere," Aella shouted over her shoulder. "Come on, let's get you some dry clothes. Varnar can't be responsible for you getting pneumonia, too."

I sat on a rug in front of an open fireplace in what had once been the manor's sitting room. Now it was a dilapidated room with peeling wallpaper, battered furniture, and windows where someone had crudely nailed boards over the shattered panes. But it was dry and warm.

Aella had loaned me some loose green pants and a light brown shirt of a soft material. I shivered in the unfamiliar clothes. In my hand I held a mug of a hot, strong drink. I think it was the same as what Mathias, Luna, and I had drunk the night before. My wet clothes hung in front of the fireplace, the water evaporating.

Varnar had disappeared, and Aella was now standing in the shabby kitchen and fiddling with a large pot on the old-fashioned woodstove.

I sat wondering how exactly I had ended up there, when Varnar sat down next to me in one of his catlike and elegant movements. He handed me a bowl of soup and a piece of bread.

I tasted the soup and coughed. It had an aggressively strong flavor.

Varnar smiled fleetingly. "Aella isn't the best chef. She's refused to learn to cook out of principle."

I took a hasty sip of my hot drink, which was almost as strong, and I coughed again.

"What is this?" I waved the mug.

"It's mead."

I looked down into the cup. "I thought mead was the same as beer? This tastes nothing like beer."

"No, it's not the same."

I waited for an elaboration that never came. I nibbled at the bread, my mind blank of conversation topics. Varnar had nothing to say, either, so we just sat in silence and stared into the flames.

Several times, I almost asked him why he was training me, and why he and Aella lived in the abandoned manor house, but the words didn't leave my tongue. Finally, I set the half-eaten slice of bread on the plate before getting up to feel my clothes, which were almost dry. I wanted to go into the other room to change, but Varnar stopped me.

"What are you doing Friday?"

I looked down at him. His hair was dry now, but there were still small pieces of sawdust glowing in his dark strands. I suppressed an urge to remove them. He turned his head and looked up at me with his dark brown eyes, which I only now noticed had flecks of green in them.

I forced my voice to stay calm. "I have work."

"What about Saturday?"

"I'm going to a party that evening. A ball, actually."

"A ball? Where?"

"The Boatman, in Jagd. Do you know it?"

Varnar nodded with an expression I could not interpret.

"I've heard of it." He took a moment before he spoke again. "Who are you going with? That cop?"

Where did that come from? Shyly, I shifted my gaze away from him and let it rest on the flames instead.

"I'm going with a man named Od."

"Od Dinesen?"

"I don't know his last name, but he owns The Boatman," I said. "But I actually have no desire to go." The words flew out of my mouth.

"Why not?" Varnar straightened slightly.

Again, I spoke without thinking.

"I have to wear a dress," I said pathetically.

Beneath me, Varnar gave a surprised laugh. As always, the effect of seeing him smile nearly knocked my legs out from under me. He looked completely different when his hard features were erased.

"You'll go up against three men in a fight, but you're afraid to wear a dress?"

"I just don't like parties," I mumbled. Then I fled from the room.

In the kitchen, I bumped into Aella.

"Are you leaving already?"

"Yeah. I'll just change so you can have your clothes back."

She felt the slightly damp shirt I had over my arm. Then she shook her head.

"Just borrow what you have on. I don't want you going home in wet clothes."

I was about to protest.

Varnar's aura flickered behind me. "She can just give me your clothes next time we train."

My back grew warm in a way that was both wonderful and unsettling, and I picked at the sleeve of my shirt to hide how strongly I was affected by being close to him.

Aella narrowed her eyes slightly as she looked from him to me. Then she nodded.

"Deal," she said and turned brusquely toward the kitchen table, where she was busy cleaning the large cast-iron pot. "Are you walking Anna home, Varnar?" she said over her shoulder.

It was almost dark outside. The rain had stopped, and it smelled like damp forest.

"You don't need to come," I said.

"Yes, I do," said Varnar. He started walking away from the manor and into the woods.

I followed suit. I couldn't think of anything to say. I already wasn't one for small talk, and with Varnar, my quietness was multiplied tenfold.

He seemed to feel the same way, so neither of us said a word on the walk. When we finally reached Odinmont, he walked me all the way up to my blue front door.

I turned to him to say goodbye. Thanks for today. Nice of you to beat me up—anything. But the words got stuck in my throat.

He looked at me seriously, also seeming like he had something to say. Then he turned abruptly and ran back to the forest without so much as a word.

I stood in the kitchen at Frank's on Friday evening. The number of customers had started to bounce back over the past few days. The kitchen was closed, and Milas had left over an hour ago. All that was left to do was to clean up and wash the dishes, and this was my chance.

Out in the bar, I could hear laughter and conversation. The evening had slipped into the phase where the music was turned up and the beers were slung across the bar in a steady stream, and Frank was in better spirits than I had seen him in a long time. He even danced his Elvis dance in front of the whole crowd, to great applause.

It had been over a week since Belinda died, and the media had quickly moved on to other and more current news, so the hype about the Pippi Killer of North Jutland had died down. The town's teenage girls still traveled in packs or were escorted by boyfriends, brothers, or fathers, even though these well-meaning men wouldn't stand a chance against the Savage if his gaze were to fall on some poor redhead. Not that there were many of them left in the area. Redheads, that is. Mathias said his mom was exceptionally busy in the salon, dyeing the hair of the region's women and girls any color but red. *One man's loss is another's gain.*

I heard Luna's voice. She wasn't working, so I wondered what she was doing at Frank's. Through the window in the swinging door, I saw her come charging behind the bar toward the kitchen door wearing an oversized orange jumpsuit with the hood pulled up around her face. Mathias was right behind her, and he had an uneasy expression on his face.

She flashed me a big smile when they entered the kitchen.

"I have something to show you." She pulled down the hood to reveal an impressive mane of bright red hair. The curls bounced around her face when she shook her head toward me. "Isn't it awesome?"

I stared at her, dumbfounded. "What the hell are you thinking?"

The smile stiffened on Luna's lips. "You don't like it?"

"No," I shouted. "Are you a total idiot?"

Tears sprung to her eyes, and her lower lip trembled slightly.

Mathias stood between us. "That's enough, Anna."

"Are you on her side? Don't you think it's crazy for her to dye her hair red when there's a murderer on the loose with a fetish for cutting the heads off red-haired girls? Weren't you the one who said anyone with so much as a hint of red is dyeing their hair a different color? Do you realize that Luna is now practically the only red-haired teenage girl in North Jutland?" It's rare for me to say so many sentences in a row, but this was an emergency.

Mathias's face fell more and more with each word I spoke. His cheeks flushed with shame, and I caught a short film from his head, in which Luna sat with her back to a sink while he rinsed red hair dye out of her hair.

I opened my mouth. He took a step back, as if he feared I would hit him.

"You did not," I said

"She did that persuasion hocus-pocus on me," he squeaked.

I turned back to face Luna. "Why did you do that?"

She looked down at the ground. "It just popped into my head a few days ago. My hair just needed to be red. The dark color was blocking all the energy, so I couldn't think clearly."

"Well, you're right about that at least. You weren't thinking clearly. If you were tired of the dark brown, why not blond, blue, green? It doesn't even matter. Just not red."

Luna, her voice thin, said, "You know how it is with me and colors. Only red can help me think properly. Otherwise, I'll never be able to figure out the thing with the moon. That was why I decided to dye it."

"You're putting your life in danger to help a hypothetical girl avoid her hypothetical death?"

"Yes, of course." She looked down at her green sneakers. "All week I've tried to wear all the red clothes I have, but it hasn't helped. It's like the universe intended for my hair to be red. It's color magic. You have no idea what a relief it is to have it colored now. I . . ."

Shit. Luna had so much faith that my vision was correct, she was willing to risk her life for it. I took my head in both hands.

"The universe's intention. Color magic. Can you stop it with the hippie talk? Girls have been killed. And you know that it's not over yet." I scowled at Mathias. "Say something to her. Join the fight."

He crumpled.

"What is it with you?" I shouted at him.

"You're really scary when you're mad."

"Oh, fry me."

Luna looked confused. "Why would he *fry* you?"

Mathias sent me a blazing blue look.

At that moment, Frank came into the kitchen. He stopped at the sight of Luna's hair.

"Oh, wow," he said. "Are you sure this is the time to dye your hair red?"

Luna gave him a stubborn pout.

I turned to Mathias. "You have to fix it."

He threw up his arms. "I can't. Only if Luna wants it."

She shook her head, and the curls flew in all directions. Frank backed away toward the door, clearly uncomfortable with our drama.

"Mathias, promise me you'll take the girls home?" He glanced at Luna's red curls. "Are you on your bikes?"

We nodded in unison, and Frank fled back into the noisy bar. I gave up on convincing Luna for now.

"I'm busy, actually," I said. "You don't need to wait for me. I can certainly ride home alone."

"You close in half an hour. We can wait," said Mathias.

"Luna, can you put your hood back up to at least hide your hair?"

They walked out into the bar as Luna pulled her jumpsuit's hood over her head and stuffed her curls inside it. She looked like a giant orange baby with a penchant for hip-hop.

When Frank had finally kicked out the last of the drunk patrons, Luna, Mathias, and I sat on barstools in the closed bar. Frank allowed us each a forbidden after-hours beer.

"You do know it's illegal to serve alcohol to people under eighteen?" Luna said with a smile and drew a circle in the air between herself and me when he handed us the beers.

"Eh, I've done worse," he said and winked at her. Then he turned and returned a stray vodka bottle to its place on the shelf. I caught a glimpse of his reflection in the mirrored wall behind the liquor bottles. Deep furrows stretched across his forehead, and his brows were lowered. He turned toward us again and ran a hand over his gray coif. In the dim lighting, it glinted like silver. "What do you guys think? Are people scared out there?"

Mathias set his beer on the bar.

"They're starting to calm down now. But the girls are nervous." He glanced at me and Luna. "Some of them, anyway. And people with teenage daughters are worried. People are talking about what they'll do to him if they catch him. And let me tell you, 'bring him to the police' is pretty far down on the list."

"I hope he stops soon." Frank shuddered and leaned tiredly against the bar. "If for no other reason than he's bad for business."

"And for health," I added and ran my index finger across my neck.

The other three looked at me.

"What? He is."

Frank sighed. "Anna, this is serious. It's not a joke."

I thought of my recurring vision. No, it was definitely not a joke.

We finished our drinks and left Frank's. Outside, we walked over to our bikes while Frank locked up. I stopped in front of my red racing bike with a little yelp.

The front wheel was folded in on itself, and the back tire was cut up. I touched it. It buzzed with aggressive energy. Then I tried something new. I tried to see what had happened. I almost asked it. Finally, I got a glimpse of Christian Mikkelsen kicking my bike.

"What happened?" asked Luna, though it was pretty obvious.

"It's a message," I said.

"About what?" Luna tried unsuccessfully to straighten the front wheel by tugging on it.

Mathias met my gaze. "Was it Peter?"

I shook my head. "It was Christian."

"Should I talk to him?" He grew slightly.

"No. They already think I brought friends to beat them up that night. No reason to draw their attention to you."

"I don't care," he nearly shouted.

"You don't, Mathias? Do you really want him to talk to the police and for them to start digging around in your past?"

Luna looked like a giant question mark. "What past? And why can't the police dig around? Is there something I still don't know?"

Loads, Luna.

Mathias bent his head. "Yes, there is more I haven't told you."

I didn't belong in this conversation, and I considered how I should make my exit. Without my bike, I felt like I was missing a limb.

Fortunately, Frank arrived at that moment. He whistled when he saw Christian's work.

"Is that yours?"

"Yep."

"Do you know who might've done something like that?" There was a threat in Frank's question.

"No," I lied. "Probably some drunk asshole who didn't score tonight and took it out on my bike."

To Mathias and Luna, who were having a wordless conversation next to us with wide eyes and flailing arms, I said, "You guys can ride your bikes. I'll run home."

"No, no, no," protested Frank. "I'm driving you."

"You really don't need to. I can take care of myself."

"Will you please just go with him, Anna?" said Mathias.

Luna cast a cloud of persuasion over me.

I nodded in resignation. "Okay, fine."

We said goodbye while Frank moved my poor bike into the back alley, where it could stay until I could get it to the repair shop.

"Don't forget we're coming over at noon tomorrow," Luna shouted after me.

"What are you doing tomorrow at noon?" asked Frank as we walked to his car.

I scratched my forehead. "We have to get ready for a party."

"When's the party?"

"Not until the evening."

"It must be quite some party if you need a whole day to doll your-selves up."

I shivered in my faded black denim jacket. "It's in Jagd."

Frank looked pointedly at me. "Are you going to the equinox ball at The Boatman?"

I nodded.

"How in the hell did you get an invitation to that?"

"Do you know about it?"

"Do I! I've been trying to attend it for years." He looked at me in awe. "Do you have someone to go with?"

"I would bring you if I could, but I'm supposed to go with the guy who owns The Boatman." I was a hundred times more comfortable in Frank's company than in Od's.

Frank gasped for air. "You're going with Od Dinesen? Are you friends?"

"He's more of a friend of a friend," I said evasively.

We crawled into Frank's old pickup, and when he took off down the street, I leaned back in the soft seat and enjoyed the unfamiliar sixties music he had put on. The truck felt safe and homey. Then I realized it was because it smelled like dog.

I looked at Frank in profile. His hair lay in a soft arc over his forehead, and he mouthed soundlessly along with the song. The smile lines around his eyes formed pronounced shadows every time we passed a streetlamp.

I turned my face and looked out the window.

"Anna?" Frank's voice was hesitant.

"What is it?"

"I know you girls hear this over and over these days, but will you please take a little better care of yourself?"

We drove past the sign for Ravensted, thereby leaving the last streetlamp behind us. Aside from the truck's headlights, it was pitch-black on the country road. Darkness fell in the car, too. I could only faintly see Frank's face in the dim light of the dashboard.

"I do take care of myself."

Frank let out a little laugh.

"You take out the trash even though I've said Milas should do it. You want to run home alone in the middle of the night. You live way out in the middle of nowhere, right up against a large forest." He paused briefly. "I'm just worried about what's out there."

He turned up Kraghede Road, and we passed Ben and Rebecca's house, its windows glowing faintly.

"But I don't have red hair," was the only thing I could spit out.

"No, but you're something special."

"What are you talking about?"

"Most people look right through you, and others hate you instinctively."

I tried to soften the mood. "Not you. You've always been sweet to me."

Again, Frank furrowed his brows. "I've always liked you."

Before Luna, Mathias, and Frank came into the picture, no one aside from Arthur had been nice to me.

"I've thought about who he could be," Frank continued. His voice was a bit hoarse. "I think he's new to the area. It's the way

230

he chooses his victims. It seems random. Like he's just taking samples."

"They all have red hair. That doesn't seem random."

"What I mean is that I'm convinced he's not local. And you've been around the area quite a bit in your life. So you can easily spot new faces. I think those are the ones you should be on the lookout for. The new faces, I mean." He swung up the dirt road that led to Odinmont. The truck bumped and creaked on the uneven road.

"But we know what he looks like. The drawing. So there's no reason to look out for new faces."

Frank looked out into the dark. "I think there's more evil out there than just him."

A figure stood waiting at my front door. My heart jumped when I saw that it was Varnar. What was he doing at my house at two o'clock in the morning? I opened the door to hop out, but Frank put his hand on my shoulder and stopped me.

"How well do you know that guy?" He nodded toward Varnar, and his grip tightened, as if he were afraid to let me leave the truck.

"I've really just met him," I answered honestly. "But he's okay."

Varnar approached the truck. I knew his mannerisms well enough to know that he was preparing for an attack. He didn't like that Frank had a hold of my arm.

I removed Frank's fingers. His grip was so tight it was uncomfortable.

"Frank, he's okay," I repeated.

Frank scowled at Varnar, who stared back.

"He'd better be."

I smiled and waved at Varnar to signal that there were no problems. I also flashed Frank a grin.

"I'll pass it along." I hopped out of the truck and walked over to Varnar. I waved Frank off with both hands. He put the truck in reverse and pulled backward down the drive.

I stood in front of Varnar. "What are you doing here?"

"I wanted to make sure you got home safe. Was he bothering you?"

"He's my boss, Varnar. As you can see, I made it home in one piece. And you, as usual, are late when it comes to taking care of me. What if Frank was the crazed murderer? I was completely alone with him, way out in the country, in the middle of the night." I rolled my eyes dramatically.

Varnar made a frustrated sound. "You have no idea how hard you are to keep tabs on."

I raised my eyebrows in surprise. "Are you keeping tabs on me?"

Varnar looked up at the moon. The silvery light caressed his face, and I caught myself feeling deeply envious of the moon.

"I have to tell you something."

My heart did backflips in my chest.

"What?" I tried to keep my voice steady.

Varnar still didn't look at me. His eyebrows drew together almost imperceptibly. By now I knew they did that when he was struggling with what he wanted to say. As usual, he said nothing.

"I'm going to bed now. You can tell me when you're ready." I sighed, turned my back to him, and fished my keys out of my pocket.

"Monday evening," he said behind me.

I turned halfway around. "Monday evening what?"

"I'll come over Monday evening around dinnertime. Then I'll tell you."

I was about to reply, but he had already run off down the moonlit field toward the forest.

I was jittery and couldn't sit still. All through the night, I had tossed and turned and speculated over what Varnar wanted to tell me. I fantasized about him declaring his undying love for me. *Ha.* I laughed to myself. *What are you thinking?* Then the thoughts started all over again.

At five o'clock in the morning, I admitted defeat and got up. A long run, a proper training session, and all my homework later, it was still only nine o'clock. My untouched and now-cold cup of coffee sat before me on the kitchen table.

I pushed my palms against the tabletop and stood up. Armed with my flashlight, I headed for the barn. The sliding door stuck, and I yanked on it with all my strength until, with a screech, it allowed me to pry it open a crack.

I shined the light around. The barn was full of junk. There was row upon row of gardening tools, and the large crib had been placed right inside the door. My throat scratched and I quickly looked away from the bed and the two small blankets lying inside it. A blue chest with a rounded lid caught my attention. I stepped over some paint cans and knelt next to it. A thick layer of dust and spiderwebs covered its sides and top. The hinges gave out when I opened the lid. There were a bunch of things inside. A coat, a cast-iron pot, a book, a box covered in green velour, and more of the bottles of mead that also sat in my kitchen cabinet. I opened an envelope but closed it quickly when I glimpsed a photo of Ben and Rebecca. Rebecca's face was youthfully smooth in the picture. I put the box and the book inside the pot and draped the coat over my arm. Then I picked my way back across the floor. In the doorway, I squinted against the light.

"Find anything exciting in there?"

I let out a little howl in fright.

"Sorry," said Arthur. "I didn't mean to scare you."

"Well, you did." I set the pot on the ground, turned off the flashlight, and tossed it in with the box and the book. With great difficulty, I pulled the sliding door closed. "Are you gonna help me or what?"

Arthur took the coat and walked toward my front door.

Wow, how chivalrous, Arthur, I thought as I struggled with the iron pot.

Inside, Arthur carefully laid the coat on the bench, as if it were a fragile baby.

"Maybe it fits you?" he wondered aloud.

I went to the bench, picked up the long coat, and turned it in the light from the glass door. It had dark embroidery that was almost invisible against the black background. The embroidery resembled the paintings on Ben and Rebecca's house. A gripping beast, serpents, and dragons.

"Try it on," said Arthur.

I swung it around and slipped into the sleeves. The lining was made of red suede so soft it caressed my arms.

Arthur watched me with a strange look in his eye.

"It looks great on you," he said finally. "Try looking in the mirror."

"Not right now," I said, taking the coat off and tossing it onto the bench.

Arthur smoothed it gently.

"How do you know Od?" I put my hands on my hips.

Arthur's face grew attentive. "Did he tell you something? What happened?"

"He said I was who he thought I was, but that I wasn't ready to hear the truth. So, to answer your question, he didn't tell me shit, and not much happened other than him inviting me to the equinox ball at The Boatman."

Arthur widened his eyes. "You can't go alone."

"I won't. He asked me to go with him."

"With Od? I wonder why?"

"Because of my sparkling personality, perhaps."

Arthur smiled. "There's nothing wrong with your personality."

More than a dozen social workers, ex-foster parents, and teachers I've left in my wake would strongly disagree with that statement.

Arthur continued: "But Od never does anything that doesn't have a deeper meaning."

234

I could tell Od where to shove his deeper meaning. I was going only for Mathias's sake.

"You didn't answer my question of how you know him."

Arthur winced. "I'll tell you some other time."

I sniffed. "And Elias said that you and he have known each other for a long time."

Arthur's eyes narrowed. "Was Elias there? What did he do?"

I hadn't planned on saying anything, but it was interesting that Arthur automatically assumed that Elias had done something wrong.

"He said that you two aren't friends."

"We certainly are not."

"I mean, I know he's a little annoying, but he seems all right. He's helped me learn to shield."

Arthur closed his eyes as if trying to control his temper.

"Anna, the only person Elias really does anything for is Elias. If he's helping you, it's because he wants something in return. You must never be alone with him."

I stuck my chin out defiantly. "I already have been, several times. He's been here, too."

Arthur clenched his fists. "He's been here, in this house?"

I nodded.

"I forbid it." His voice was shrill. "He cannot come here again."

I burst out laughing. "You can't forbid anything, Arthur. This is my home, and I decide for myself who comes to visit."

"Just promise me you won't let your guard down with him. He can't be trusted."

"Whatever." Then I thought of something. "Arthur, do you remember that dream I've been having?"

"Have you had it again?"

"Yes. But it's not that. You know how I said that the girl is already dead? That it happened a long time ago? I think I was wrong."

"What are you saying?"

"I don't think it's happened yet. I'm actually pretty sure of it."

Arthur stared at me. "She's not dead?"

"Yet," I said. "The vision doesn't change."

A look of pure joy flew across Arthur's face.

"But we might be able to change it." He took a few long strides toward the door. Then he turned around, came back to me, and laid a hand on each of my shoulders. "Have fun tonight. But take care of yourself, okay?"

I wanted to say that he should stay out of it, but his green eyes shone with such care that I didn't have the heart.

"Of course, Arthur."

He stroked my cheek. "When did you get so grown up? You're not a little girl anymore. I'm very proud of you."

A lump formed in my throat, and I had no idea what to say.

He kissed my forehead, then let go and left soundlessly through my front door.

I stood there with my arms hanging at my sides. Then I shook off my emotions, walked to the kitchen table, and looked down into the cast-iron pot. First, I pulled out the book. It was bound in red leather embossed with something resembling an African mask. When I opened the book, I saw it was full of handwritten notes that mostly looked like recipes. Dried flowers and leaves were stuck between pages, and several pages were decorated with drawings. I flipped to the first page. *Pour Rebecca de Benedict Omikha Sekibo*, it said in beautiful, curved handwriting.

Feeling like I was snooping in someone else's private life, I closed the book and set it on the table. I pulled out the box instead. It creaked a bit when I opened it. Inside lay a piece of jewelry. A necklace with a pendant. The chain was made of thick rings in a material resembling matte gold, and the pendant was a red crystalline stone in the shape of a heart. Encircling the heart vertically, between the two arcs at the top and down to the point, ran a narrow gold band. The piece was beautiful in a strange way. It was both rough and fine, fragile and strong at the same time. I lifted it carefully and held it in my hand.

Something, an energy or power, coursed from the jewel and into my hand. I received no images from it, but it was as if the necklace itself had a soul. *Strange.*

I laid it back in the box and closed it with a snap.

"Up."

"Down."

Luna and Mathias stood bent over me, each grasping a handful of my hair. Mathias had a makeup brush in his other hand. The back of his hand was covered with lines and splotches of different colors. I sat on a chair in the middle of my living room wearing the red dress with the snake embroidery, holding my fingers out so the wet nail polish—the exact same ice-blue color as the snakes' eyes—could dry.

"Down and curled." Luna pressed her lips together stubbornly.

"But if it's up, you can see the back neckline. And curls are too dramatic. The dress is plenty dramatic on its own."

"What is that supposed to mean? Is there something wrong with the dress?"

"Can't I decide for myself?" I tried. "I would prefer to wear it down. No curls."

They ignored me.

Mathias took Luna by the hand and pulled her away. "There is nothing wrong with the dress. It's beautiful. And you're beautiful."

He kissed her on the cheek. She giggled. Their infatuation flowed over me, but I tried to ignore it.

Luna was wearing a gold floor-length silk dress with a plunging neckline, which in my opinion, belonged in the back. On her head she wore a purple turban, which we had insisted on to hide her red hair.

Mathias continued: "Anna is also pretty dramatic in her own right."

"Hey, I'm sitting right here."

They ignored me again. Luna bit her lip, as if she were thinking about it.

"I chose her dress, so you can choose her hair."

"Can I choose something myself? Anything?"

Finally, they looked at me. Then they grinned at one another, as if I were a three-year-old who had said something cute but highly unrealistic.

After another two hours of work, in which Mathias also did Luna's makeup, they finally declared me done. I couldn't look at myself, with good reason, but I used my hand to feel my hair, which Mathias had worked on for an eternity. He had teased, braided, and sprayed, and now it sat high on top of my head in a coiffure I could only guess at the appearance of.

"Done," he said. "You are my masterpiece."

Luna stood before me and looked at me. Then she smiled at Mathias. "And you thought curls would be too dramatic."

He shrugged. "I got carried away. Anna has such nice hair."

What? I patted desperately at my hair to get an idea of how it looked.

"Aaaah, don't touch!" shouted Mathias.

"Don't worry. It's unbelievably beautiful," said Luna.

I shook my head. "Glad that's over with. I'm getting picked up soon."

"Why aren't you riding with us? There's plenty of room in the car."

"It says on my invitation that I'm getting picked up. I'd better keep my end of the agreement so that Od keeps his."

Mathias bowed his head. "I'm sorry you have to do this for me."

"Yeah, I sure as hell am, too. But I'm doing it now, and I don't feel like thinking about your guilt on top of it, so just drop it."

Mathias shoved my shoulder with a smile. "You just act tough. I know you're soft inside. And that you're doing me a huge favor."

I opened my mouth to refute him, but Luna hurried to change the subject. "What shoes are you wearing?"

"My black sneakers, I think."

She threw up her arms in dismay. "You are not going to ruin all our work with your worn-out sneakers."

"One sec." I walked into the hall and pulled my biker boots from a box. They were actually winter boots, but the fall was cold this year, so I could easily wear them now. They were black leather, with studs and buckles. I showed them to Luna. She gave me a tortured grimace and looked desperately to Mathias. He furrowed his brows.

"The boots are better than sneakers," he said.

Relieved, I pulled them on.

Luna cursed. "You were otherwise perfect."

Her disappointment sailed over me, and I felt an irrepressible urge to make up for it. They had made a huge effort to get me ready for the party. Luna had even sewn a small black-and-red bag that matched the dress.

"I can wear a piece of jewelry." The words flew out of my mouth, much to my astonishment.

They both looked at me, surprised.

"Do you have jewelry?" Mathias sounded skeptical.

"A piece of jewelry. Singular. And I found it today, out in the barn."

"In the barn," said Luna. "That doesn't bode well."

I showed them the box. Mathias opened it and held up the chain.

"I've never seen anything like this. It's pretty."

Luna took it from him and gasped. "I sense a power in it."

"You do? So do I. Do you think I should leave it alone?"

Luna shook her head.

239

"It's a good power. You *have* to wear it tonight." She wore the same dreamy expression as when she talked about color magic and love. It was pointless to try to argue with her. She held it out to me. "Spit on it."

"What?"

"You need to spit on it. That's how you consecrate an amulet."

"I didn't know it was an amulet."

"Well, it's not, until you spit on it." Luna rolled her eyes as if I were clueless. She doused me with persuasion, and I felt myself form a gob of spit in my mouth, all the while scowling at her.

The necklace's clasp was as hard as a rock. Mathias had to help me get it open. It was an S-shaped metal wire, which he easily twisted to the side, inserted into the final metal ring, and squeezed back together. He took a step back.

"Perfect. The color of the stone is the same as the dress."

"It's weird that it was just sitting out there in the barn," said Luna. "Actually, it's also weird that no one ever came and raided the house. It's been empty all these years."

Agreed.

"I actually also found something you should give to your mom." I grabbed the book, which still sat on the kitchen table. "I think it's hers."

Luna took the book and flipped through it.

"It looks like one of her notebooks. She has a ton of these at home with recipes in them." She smacked the book shut. "I need to get going, too."

She kissed Mathias so intensely that I turned my back and looked out the glass door at the flat landscape to give them a little privacy.

"See you up there, Anna," said Luna. They had finished their make-out session.

I waved with one hand, and she shot out the door and ran across the field like a bolt of golden lightning.

Mathias watched her out the kitchen window. "Will you promise me something?"

"What?"

"Take care of yourself tonight. And Luna."

I nodded, unaware that I would not be able to keep one promise without breaking the other.

 # CHAPTER 15

The sound of whining tires and gravel spraying in all directions reached my ears.

A moment later, there was a knock at the door. Outside stood Elias, and just as he'd said, he was dressed in an attractive, dark suit. I reluctantly admitted to myself that he looked really good. His curls were slightly tamed, for once, and he wore a flatteringly serious expression on his face.

Behind him was a yellow sports car I didn't recognize. But from what I knew of Elias, it was predictably flashy.

Elias studied me without saying anything.

"No sleazy pickup lines?" I asked as I pulled on the black coat I had found in the barn.

His eyes lingered on the coat.

"You're so beautiful, I forgot all my pickup lines." There wasn't so much as a smile on his soft lips.

I made an unladylike *hrmf* sound. "Let's just get this over with."

Elias held the car door open for me, and I lifted the hem of my dress so I wouldn't step on it when I got in.

"Nice boots." He glanced at the heavy, studded leather boots.

"You never know who you'll need to kick," I said with a sweet smile.

Elias leaned toward me. "Glad to hear that the change in appearance hasn't changed your lovely personality."

I put a finger to his chest and pushed him away without saying anything. He laughed and slammed the car door shut.

I accidentally glimpsed myself in the rearview mirror, where my face surrounded by red hair tried to mime something to me. I looked away with a gasp.

Elias slid into the driver's seat. "What do you see in the mirror?"

"Nothing," I mumbled and looked out the windshield at the near-dark landscape as he maneuvered the car down my drive.

"Have you been practicing shielding?" he asked.

"Yes, every day. It's going better. But I still can't be in a room with more than twenty or thirty people without feeling sick."

"It takes years to learn. Just keep practicing."

"How many people are coming tonight?"

Elias turned the car onto Kraghede Road. "About six hundred."

I choked. "I'll have to take some klinte."

"Od has asked that you refrain from doing so."

"Then I hope he'll be there to catch me when I pass out."

"I think you can handle it. If you concentrate."

I moaned and held my head. "This is going to be a living hell."

I suppressed a strong urge to open the door and jump out of the moving car. *Think of Mathias. Think of Mathias,* I chanted internally.

When we arrived at The Boatman, I saw that the parking lot was full of vehicles very different than the last time I was there. There were neither tractors nor scooters, but rather a horde of expensive cars I didn't recognize. An ornamental gold crown and the number one was painted on a large car's license plate.

"Is that what I think it is?"

Elias looked at the car. "Od has always been close to the royal family."

"Define *always*."

He smiled mysteriously and swung around to the back of The Boatman where he parked in front of the back entrance, so close to the precipice that my stomach dropped. The headlights shone out into the air above the steep drop down to the beach far beneath us. Elias turned off the lights, and the depths disappeared from my field of vision.

I stepped out into the dark parking lot, where the wind rustled my dress; it felt like my skin was being sandblasted. I pulled my coat close around me. The air smelled strongly of the sea, and I could hear the seagulls screeching. The crashing waves were constant background music.

"Is it really a good idea to put a bar on the edge of a cliff?" I couldn't help but ask.

Elias shrugged his shoulders. "It's part of the attraction. To drink at The Boatman is to throw the dice of fate. We lose a couple patrons every year."

I shivered and put my arms around my body.

"Are you cold?" he asked, and put an arm around my waist. "Just let me know if you need me to warm you up."

"And you just let *me* know if you want to take a trip over the cliff."

He laughed, opened the back door, and showed me inside with a wave of his hand. We walked down a narrow corridor until we reached a heavy wooden door.

Od's office was hexagonal and had no windows; instead there were doors all the way around. I had never seen such a strange room. Od sat at a large desk in the middle. The desk was made of wood and had various animals carved into it. Wolves, horses, snakes, wild boars. In front of it was a large brown leather sofa, and on the floor lay an enormous red cowhide.

I sensed through my powers that the room had looked like this for a long time. Centuries, maybe. I also sensed that many events had taken place in this space. Dramatic events. I couldn't see anything specific. It was blurry, but the air buzzed with occurrences. One very clear message that my subconscious sent me gave me a violent shock. The message was accompanied by interior alarms and howling sirens. It told me that I had been there before.

244

I tried not to let my face reveal my inner tumult, but focused instead on Od, and like the last time I saw him, I was nearly bowled over by his beauty. I tried to look nonchalantly at him, but I wasn't quite successful.

"Anna. I'm happy to see you." He nodded to Elias, who backed out through the door and closed it behind him with a final smoldering look in my direction.

I almost wanted to ask him to stay. Being alone with Od tore up my already frayed nerves.

I pulled off my coat. He stood, took it out of my hands, and looked me over.

"That's a beautiful dress."

"It was a gift from my friend Luna."

"Sekibo?"

"Yes, do you know her?"

"Not yet." He laid my coat on the sofa and let his hand rest on it for a moment before continuing. "But I know her parents. Always cherish gifts. Especially those from friends. They hold great power."

He stretched out his hand toward me, and I took an instinctive step back. Od stopped mid-motion. He looked me straight in the eyes. Then he smiled. I felt like an ice cube on a hot stove and suddenly couldn't move.

He carefully took the heart necklace in his hand. "Speaking of gifts. This was a gift. But not for you."

I dug deep inside myself and found the small crumb of defiance I had left. "What makes you say that?"

"Because this necklace was a gift for your mother."

"From whom?"

"From me," he replied evenly.

I inhaled sharply. "I hope you and my mom weren't a thing."

Od laughed hoarsely. "Gods no. I would have never dared approach her in that way. Or in most other ways."

245

I had a hard time imagining there was a whole lot that Od didn't dare do, and my curiosity was very much piqued, but I pressed my lips together as I fumbled at the back of my neck to unfasten the necklace.

Od looked kindly at me. "I think you should keep it on. The sympathy I have for your parents, I also have for you."

"And I think you should shut up," I hissed as I tugged desperately at the chain.

Od's eyebrows shot upward.

Oh yeah, Od should be treated with respect, blah, blah, blah.

I got my temper somewhat under control.

"Are you gonna help me or what?"

He appeared to suppress a smile. "No."

My rage bubbled up again. "Oh, well, thanks for nothing."

The sound of Od's hoarse laughter wrapped itself around me like a hot wind.

"Anna, you don't need to be so angry. I have no ill will toward you."

"I honestly don't care what you feel toward me." I tried to avoid eye contact, but he caught my gaze.

Caught as in, I couldn't move from that spot. He laid his hand against my cheek, and I was incapable of stepping back. This was the first time he'd touched me. His hand was warm, and his aura was strong and full of so much goodness that tears sprang to my eyes.

I saw glimmers of his past. Od together with different people. I saw him with Arthur, Elias, Rebecca, Ben, and the dark, curly-haired woman I had also seen in Rebecca's past. She was neither bloody nor holding a baby this time, but she was furious. I had a pretty good guess of who she was, which disturbed me. It also shocked me to see that his past went very far back. Even further than Elias's. Od was a very old man. But these things didn't startle me half as much as the fact that the images I got from Od jumped around erratically and unsystematically. I knew only one other person whose past looked like that, and that was Mathias.

"What are you?" I whispered.

"I'm a person. Just like you." Od's blue-green eyes bored deeper into mine.

I felt like I was spiraling down.

"What are you besides a person?" I refused to blink, out of fear that the tears would overflow and run down my cheeks.

Od took his hand off my cheek and looked down. I nearly collapsed on the floor in front of him.

"It's time to go in," he said.

I couldn't let him think he could get away that easily. "You wanted me to see it."

He cocked his head. "What exactly did I want you to see?"

"You're not stupid, so stop pretending like you are," I snarled. "You told Elias that I couldn't take any klinte, and now I can sense that you're . . ." I didn't know how to phrase it. "That you're something. I want to know what."

I tried to make my voice commanding, but my willpower faltered under Od's mild gaze.

"Your powers are very strong." He didn't answer my question. "I asked you not to take klinte because I want your senses to be sharp tonight."

"They won't be very sharp if I faint."

Od laughed his hoarse laugh again. "I don't think you will."

He held out his arm as a sign for me to take it.

I hesitated for a moment, but then laid my hand on it. I instantly felt his strength and looked down. Small silver threads rose from his arm, swirled around mine, and glided into me. I felt how his strength took up residence in my body. I almost didn't dare to, but I glanced up.

He towered high above me, shining silver. I forced myself to not run away. Where would I run? Over the cliff?

He turned his face toward me, and I saw that his eyes were shining, and that he was, if possible, even more beautiful than before. His aura was gone.

My heart pounded. Suddenly the bar with six hundred people in it was very enticing.

"You're super scary, you know that, right?" I stammered.

He resumed his normal size. The silver glow disappeared, and his aura returned.

"I wasn't trying to be scary. I gave you strength to get through the night."

"I still want to know what you are," I whispered bitterly, as I tried to sense whether anything felt different.

"Patience," Od said lightly. "Are you ready to go in?"

"There's only one way to find out. Lead the way," I said. I didn't care if I broke down in front of all the guests. I didn't want to be alone with Od one second longer.

He turned to one of the many doors and nodded. It opened without him touching it. I had given up on being surprised by these kinds of details, so I just walked through it with a firm grip on Od's arm.

The sounds of a sea of people struck me as we walked into a little hallway covered in mirrors. I kept my gaze trained on the floor. The hall led to the bar. Only now did I realize that it had been quiet in Od's office.

The Boatman was filled to the brim with festively dressed people, and it went completely silent when we walked in. The music stopped, and everyone's eyes turned to us.

I secretly wished that the earth would open up and swallow me. At least I didn't have a headache and nausea, even though I felt a terrible pressure on my mind from the presence of all those people.

Then the lights began to flash, and the applause roared.

Od walked through the space with a smile, while I clung to his arm.

248

"Can't you at least try to look like this isn't causing you pain?" he said out of the corner of his mouth.

"Not part of the agreement," I whispered, but I tried to straighten my back and look with dignity upon the throng. I refused to smile. There had to be limits.

Gradually, the applause stopped, and people went back to talking among themselves.

I had seen several of the guests before. And I don't mean I had seen them at Frank's or in the supermarket. No, I had seen them on TV and in the tabloids. I spotted a well-known businessman and a few actors. There were also people I didn't immediately recognize, but most were extravagant and some even mesmerizing to look at.

Onstage, the band started playing again. When I realized who they were, I stared.

"How in the hell did you get them to play?" I pointed.

Od looked up.

"It was their turn," he said. "They've been waiting years for this."

"How did you lure all these famous people up here to the middle of nowhere?"

"Tonight, the rest of Denmark is nowhere."

Once I managed to tear my eyes away from the various celebrities, I noticed that The Boatman had undergone a transformation since my last visit. Gone were the large pint glasses; round, weathered wooden tables; and fisherman types in casual attire. Instead, nine banquet tables had been set up and loaded with food and drink. Large centerpieces of fruit, nuts, and bread sat on the tables. Whole roasted suckling pigs with apples in their mouths, hams, and platters of vegetables steamed. On the walls hung beautiful woven tapestries and animal hides, along with sheaves of wheat and bunches of onions and garlic. As the pièce de résistance, an ice sculpture stood in the middle of the room. It depicted a nude woman with a baby. The child sucked at one of her breasts. From the other flowed a pale liquid. The guests took turns filling their glasses with it.

Ew!

We stood at the large round bar, which was decorated with branches and fall leaves. Behind it stood the two bartenders: the fair, tall man, who tonight had put his long silver-white hair in an artfully braided updo, and the small, black-haired, tattooed woman, who hadn't even changed her threadbare undershirt. She looked just as dour as last time, and I sensed that the party and the elegant guests didn't mean a single thing to her.

A woman stopped in front of us and held out a tray of glasses. My eyes grew wide when I saw that a large, exposed pregnant belly protruded between the folds of her garment. Then I realized the entire staff consisted of pregnant women, and that their large stomachs poked out between waves of orange, burgundy, and gold fabric.

Od handed me a glass and took one himself. It was already full, so at least I didn't have to fill it at the ice sculpture. The glass was matte, with reddish-brown metal wires around the stem.

"Looks like you brought the nice glassware out for the occasion," I said, and took a sip. The drink was spicy and strongly alcoholic.

"Elias plans these parties with his usual flair for the dramatic," said Od. He put his perfect lips to the glass and drank.

"I'll say."

"The party is a celebration of the harvest and the equinox. The dark, cold time is coming, and we give thanks to the gods that we have provisions for the winter."

I shook my head. *Again with the gods.*

Od continued. "We are grateful that the women are fertile, the harvest has been good, and the animals are fat. The food on the tables is an offering."

"Are you aware that your guests are well on their way to eating all the offerings? Won't the gods be pissed about that?"

Od laughed quietly. "The food and drink symbolize the bounty of fall and the sacrifices we are willing to give. It doesn't matter that we eat it. The gods will get their due."

"So this is a kind of blót?"

Od nodded approvingly. "Do you blót?"

I thought of Rebecca's little ceremony in my yard. "We held a færa-blót when I moved into Odinmont."

"Good," said Od. "I would advise you to stay close friends with the gods."

"Do you sincerely believe in the old gods?"

"Don't you?"

"No, of course not."

"They won't like that."

"I couldn't care less what some gods I don't even believe in like."

"You of all people should have an open mind."

"I'm actually pretty busy trying to shut my mind down. And if I'm going to believe in something . . ." I drained my glass and set it on the bar. The black-haired bartender snatched it with a surly expression. "Then I'd like to see proof that it exists."

Od finished his drink and looked down into the empty glass. "Be careful what you wish for."

I wanted to say something more, but a couple came up to us then. I stiffened.

Od appeared unperturbed. It was probably everyday fare for him to spend time around top-level politicians and their internationally famous actress wives. He smiled and extended his hand to the man, before turning and kissing the woman on each cheek.

"You are more beautiful than ever," he said.

"And you are handsome as *ever*," she replied with a glimmer in her eye.

"Allow me to present Anna." Od waved a hand at me.

The man held out his hand, and I took it.

"Anna what?" he asked.

I was about to tell him, but Od jumped in. "Just Anna for now."

The man looked at Od for a moment before looking back to me. "Okay, Anna-for-now. Are you enjoying the party?"

"No," I answered truthfully. "I hate parties."

He laughed loudly. "Honestly, I do, too. But Od's parties are an exception." He patted Od on the shoulder before turning to his wife. "Will you two be okay without us for a second?"

She nodded and smiled sweetly. "Better than with you."

The two men disappeared through the door to Od's office, and I was left alone with the actress-slash-first lady and had absolutely no clue what to say.

A professional smile was pasted on her lips, and she was constantly aware of which angles she was being photographed from.

"Your dress is exceptional. Is it a Danish designer?" She laid a hand on the lace at my collarbone.

When her fingers brushed my skin, I felt a tingle of intelligence and strength. She had a bit of the same electric energy as Luna, but not as intense.

"Something tells me you're not as into dresses as most people think," I said.

"And something tells me you're more into them than you yourself think," she replied with a subtle smile. "There's no shame in enjoying your own beauty." She looked out over the crowd. "You are in the company of powerful men."

"Yeah, that's typical, they go into the office to talk about important things while we stand here talking about dresses."

The woman smiled again. But she did not reveal whether she agreed with me. Instead, she changed the subject. "Why have I never met you before?"

Because you're the first lady and I'm a juvenile delinquent.

The smooth smile never left her lips. "I haven't always been the first lady, and you don't look like a juvenile delinquent."

I felt my jaw drop. *What the hell?*

"Such language!" She gave me a mock-reprimanding look. "Excuse me."

Then she turned and walked away with a dignified gait.

I stood alone and felt impossibly out of place.

"You've got a clingy spirit haunting you," said a high-pitched voice behind me.

I spun around. Behind me stood a plump woman in a leopard-print dress and an impressive layer of blue eye shadow. She was a head shorter than me, but her bleached hair was teased so high that it almost made up the difference. At her side stood a weather-beaten man with a goatee. The small woman snapped her fingers around me.

I took a step back. "What are you doing?"

"Trying to contact the spirit. I want to know if it's evil or good." She looked at a spot behind me. "Stop hiding!" she shouted.

A couple of the other guests turned around.

"It went away." She focused on me. "I haven't seen you before. What's your name?"

"Anna." I didn't mention my last name. If the prime minister couldn't know it, I was pretty sure I should also keep it secret from this white trash couple.

The woman smoothed her dress. "I'm Ulla, and this is my husband, Jørn."

Jørn flashed me a wide smile.

The woman fluffed her hair up even more. "I'm telling you, you have a clingy spirit. I can help you get rid of it if you want."

I had no idea what to say. In my mind, this woman was competing with Rebecca for the title of Crackpot of the Year. I didn't think I would ever be happy to see Elias, but I actually breathed a sigh of relief when he joined us.

To my surprise, Ulla blushed when she saw him.

"I see you've met Anna. Do you see anything, Ulla?" he asked.

Ulla looked at him warmly. "Not a trace."

I could think of only two reasons for her to lie. Either she didn't know Elias well enough to trust him, or she knew him *too* well.

Ulla continued. "Nothing but a very beautiful girl."

She glanced from me to Elias.

"Anna isn't the only beautiful woman here tonight." He winked.

I got a brief vision of a somewhat younger Ulla and an Elias who looked the same as he does now. *Yikes.*

Jørn put an arm territorially around his wife.

"We should move on." He dragged Ulla away.

She turned, and over her shoulder, she said, "Anna, remember to contact me if you want my help. Ask Elias where to find me."

We watched the couple.

"Friends of yours?" I turned to face Elias.

"Ulla is an old acquaintance. Her husband is none too fond of me."

"Why might that be?"

"She was very pretty when she was younger."

"And one day I'll be old, and you'll be hitting on a new girl who, as of right now, isn't even born yet."

Elias's face was expressionless. "That's how it's been for a very long time."

"Don't you ever get tired of it? There can't be much new happening on that front."

"There are always new women."

"And you were with Ulla. When she was new."

Elias leaned close to me. "Easy now, there's plenty of me to go around."

I pushed him away. "What kind of nutcase is she?"

"She's far from nuts. She's the most powerful medium in Denmark."

I took the bait. "Medium?"

"She can communicate with spirits. The souls of the dead. The ones that are still here."

"Are you telling me ghosts exist?" I asked wearily.

"Spirits, revenants, specters."

"Let me guess. Young Ulla saw ghosts flying around her, you stepped in gallantly to teach her to shield, and romantic music started playing."

Elias looked away. "Something like that."

I looked around in mock terror. "Are the spirits whizzing all around us right now?"

Elias answered sincerely. "There aren't as many as you would think. Most go straight to the realms of the dead. But those with unfinished business stick around."

I was getting tired of all this talk about superstition, gods, ghosts, and sacrificial offerings. "I don't know what kind of mushrooms you've all been eating, but I don't believe in that."

"Isn't it a redeeming thought, that there's something more after you die?"

I shook my head.

"I think that when you die, you die. It's like pulling out a plug. I've seen a dead person." Alice's glassy eyes appeared in my head, but I pushed the image away. "There was nothing. No aura. Her body was just an empty shell."

"Interesting." Elias considered me for a moment before he continued. "But it doesn't surprise me. I've had the same experience."

"What do you know about it? You can't see auras. And you can't talk to dead people, like you claim this Ulla can."

"No." He smiled. "But there are many other things I can see."

I exhaled, annoyed. "I'm actually not interested in what you can do. And I don't believe in ghosts, period."

"Believe me, ghosts are the least of the revelations you have in store." Elias snatched a glass from a passing pregnant woman. He drained it in one gulp before continuing. "It doesn't really matter what you believe when it comes to the spirit world. One day, you will probably find out what happens when you die. You don't need to think about death now. Right now, you should be living."

He ran the back of his hand across my bare back.

"Yes, I'll find out someday. The question is whether *you* will."

He stiffened momentarily, then pulled back his hand and looked at me angrily. "I will also leave this life at some point."

I had hit on something essential. That day, when Elias had willingly allowed me into his innermost core, I had sensed his mixed feelings around death. The only thing Elias feared more than death was the prospect of never dying.

I wanted to apologize for crossing the line, but a sparkling energy I knew well struck me from behind. I turned and saw Luna and her parents.

Elias smiled smoothly at them. "Ben, Rebecca. How nice to see you after all these years."

Two pairs of eyes flashed, one dark brown and one cornflower blue. A cloud of antipathy shot from Ben and Rebecca toward Elias. It hit me in passing and zapped me in the arm. *Ow.* I took a step to the side.

"The feeling is not mutual." Ben's voice was a growl.

Elias faltered slightly but maintained the smile on his lips.

"I don't think I've had the pleasure of meeting your beautiful daughter." He held out his hand to Luna.

Rebecca stepped between them. "And you still won't have it."

I hadn't thought that this otherwise gentle woman could be so terrifying, but in that moment, I was glad not to be in Elias's shoes.

He blanched slightly.

"I can sense that I'm persona non grata." He turned to me. "I'll see you when you need a ride home. Or if there's anything else I can do for you."

He disappeared into the crowd.

"Why is everyone so mad at Elias?" I asked.

"Who else is mad at Elias?" Luna looked at me.

I shook my head. "No one."

Ben's brown eyes had regained their warmth.

"Anna, you look amazing. You look like . . ." He paused as Rebecca gave him a warning look. "You look like a goddess."

"Thanks to Luna. She's the one who made the dress."

Luna smiled. "You looked so good when you came in. Everyone was whispering about you."

Ben took my arm with a firm grip. "There's someone you should meet."

He started walking, and I had no choice but to go along. He stopped in front of a small group of three.

A man of around fifty, flanked by a young woman and a young man, was clearly our target. The man was the diametric opposite of Ben. He was only a hair taller than me, with a wiry build. He wore a neutral gray suit. His steel-gray hair was short, and his glasses were a dark metal. If Ben hadn't planted me directly in front of him, I would never have noticed him.

The two younger people widened their eyes when they saw Ben.

The older man smiled, and his gray eyes sparkled behind his glasses when he saw Ben. They shook hands. "It's been a long time, Benedict. Far too long."

"Niels, you've been missed." Ben turned to me. "Anna, this is Niels Villadsen."

The man aimed his piercing gaze at me. We shook hands, and intelligence and authority shot up my arm.

Niels introduced the two others. "This is Mette and Steen."

The young man looked at me disinterestedly but shook my hand. He took the floor, which I got the feeling he did as often as he could, and spoke to Ben. "I've always wanted to meet you. Or at least, ever since I read about you in my studies."

What is going on?

Ben cleared his throat. "Would you excuse us? We need to speak with Niels alone."

Steen looked unhappy about this, but Mette walked away with him.

Niels watched them go. "They get younger and more ambitious every year."

Ben's deep laughter rumbled. "Are you sure it's not just you getting older and more relaxed over time?"

"Older, sure." Niels's eyes sparkled. "But there's no time to relax. Not as things are now."

I felt like one big question mark.

Ben swung around to me again. "Niels, there aren't a lot of people here tonight who know this, but Anna's full name is Anna Stella Sakarias."

Niels straightened his back and inhaled. He looked intensely at me.

"Ah, now I see it. You have been well hidden. And you are Od's companion tonight. Yes, that does send quite a signal."

"Does anyone care to explain what you're talking about?" I tried to keep my voice restrained, but my tone nevertheless got a couple of heads to turn in our direction.

"Then you'll have to let me tell you about your parents," said Ben.

I pressed my lips tightly together and shook my head.

"She doesn't know?" Niels's voice was incredulous.

"Anna doesn't want to know anything. She is a very headstrong girl."

Niels smiled. "Sound like someone we know?"

The two men shared a knowing look, and I wanted to stamp my foot.

Niels detected my irritation. "I would advise you to reconsider. Before long, you'll probably need all the information you can get. There are several people who can help here. Ben and Rebecca would be my first suggestion. But I will also make myself available."

He handed me a business card. When his fingers touched mine, I saw a glimpse of a younger Niels with jet-black hair smeared with dirt, with scrapes and scratches on his face and arms. Gone were the suit and white dress shirt. Instead, he was dressed in a grimy white undershirt, which revealed that, despite his modest height, he was muscular and agile. He ran through a stone corridor with Ben at his side. Both men had desperate looks on their faces.

I tried to hide the fact that I had just had a vision by looking down at the card. On it was printed the official crown emblem of the Danish government. *Niels Villadsen, DSMA*, it said.

"You're from the government?" I couldn't hide my animosity.

Niels nodded. "We're a small department under the Ministry of the State. Not many people know about us."

"I'm guessing you're just fine with being relatively unknown."

A smile reached his eyes. "And I suppose that's a feeling you're familiar with."

"What does DSMA stand for?"

"It requires a long explanation. I'll be happy to give it to you. When you're ready."

I was about to say something cheeky, but just then the music stopped.

The singer took the mic. "First and foremost, we want to say thank you for the opportunity to play here tonight. It is a great honor for us."

People clapped politely.

"Also, thank you to Od Dinesen for this, as always, extravagant equinox party."

The guests clapped more enthusiastically this time, and a couple shouts of *whooo* rang out.

"With that, I would like to welcome this evening's host."

People clapped like crazy when Od stepped up to the stage. The singer held out the microphone to him, but he shook his head.

"Thank you." Even without the microphone, his voice carried clearly through the large room. "This evening, we are celebrating

259

the knowledge that we will face the winter in warm houses and with full pantries. Times have changed, but we must all still remember what a gift we have received in life and its pleasures."

His gaze panned around The Boatman, and he looked me straight in the eyes. Suddenly, it was as if he were speaking directly to me. I felt like I was being tossed around in his gaze and his voice was close to my ear.

"Cherish your friends. They are the key to your survival." His eyes blazed wildly. "You can't get through this alone."

Then he released me and looked in a different direction. I slumped and looked around, confused.

Everyone in the venue stood nailed to the spot, eyes shining and looking up to the stage, as if they were in a trance.

At the other end of the room stood Elias. His eyes met mine, then he turned his back to me and disappeared through a door.

I realized that I was standing by the bar again. How did I get here? Aside from Od's voice, it was quiet in The Boatman.

A man was standing next to me.

"Drink with me," he said. He ignored Od and the many people standing like pillars around us. The man was taller than most, though he didn't top Little Mads. His left side was hidden in shadow, and what I could see of his face was handsome in a rugged way. Kind of like how a mountain, the sea, or a storm can be beautiful. Thick, dark hair cascaded over his back like a cape. He was strangely alluring, and I couldn't take my eyes off him. It was impossible for me to determine his age.

"Who are you?" I asked, dazed.

The man nudged a full glass—a glass that had not been there before—over to me.

"My name is Svidur." He took a sip from his own glass. "And you are Anna Stella Sakarias."

There was no reason to deny it, so I said nothing.

"You look like your mother."

"Did you know her?"

"I knew her. I know her. I will always know her."

I didn't know what to say.

Svidur nodded toward the bulging tables. "This is an impressive blót we have here tonight. There's plenty of food and drink. But look how they eat. A fool eats without realizing when his stomach has had enough."

I followed his gaze. "They're clearly offerings."

"Offerings. *Pfff.*" He washed down another mouthful. "Offerings are not what they used to be."

"What were they?"

"Hangadrott," he replied firmly. "See, that's something that pleases the gods. I can't imagine any prayer the All-Father wouldn't answer if you gave him that."

"I have no clue what you're talking about."

Svidur changed the subject. "Something you said tonight bothered me."

"It's not uncommon for me to say things that bother people."

He gave a deep, rusty laugh before continuing. "You said you don't believe in the gods. I did not like that."

"That was a private conversation."

"Nothing is private in this place." He looked around. "Why don't you believe in the gods?"

I shrugged. "Why should I believe in a bunch of used-up gods that have nothing to brag about besides some ancient bog bodies and bulldozed burial mounds? I'm sorry, but it's been a few years since they had any adherents."

"They have more adherents than you think," he said.

"Just because a lot of people believe in something, that doesn't make it true."

"What would it take to make you believe?" Svidur straightened, becoming even taller.

"Proof."

Svidur made a *tsk* sound and wagged his index finger. "Proof and belief are opposites. When you have proof, you have knowledge. In order to believe, you have to hold a conviction without actually knowing that it's true."

I chewed on this a bit.

"And where is this conviction supposed to come from?" I threw up my arms. "The gods haven't done a whole lot to help me."

"Maybe they've helped you more than you know."

I set down my glass. "It really bothers you that I don't believe in them. What's it to you?"

Svidur turned to face me, and I let out a gasp when I saw that his left eye socket was a dark hole. His right eye was opened wide.

"Because the people's faith is the only thing separating us from Ragnarök and chaos." He towered over me.

"Who are you?" My voice shook. I was interrupted by roaring applause and squinted my eyes.

Od had evidently finished his speech, and people were clapping their hands ecstatically.

I looked around. Svidur was gone, and instead I stood amid a terrible racket of whooping and whistling people. Whatever Od had said, it had incited excitement on par with a rock concert.

I held my head in my hands. What had just happened? Impressions hammered against my mind. The strength I had gotten from Od had lost its efficacy.

At that moment, Luna came running up to me.

"Wasn't that an amazing speech? I felt like he was speaking directly to me. The things he said about love and peace were so beautiful." She stopped herself. "Are you okay?"

"It's just really getting to me, how many people are in here. I don't feel well." My ears were starting to ring slightly.

Luna put an arm around me. "Let's go outside."

Out in the parking lot, we walked a short distance away from the entrance. I leaned my head against The Boatman's rough wood siding and let the calm wash over me. Aside from a single lamp, it was completely dark, and the sea roared somewhere far beneath us. It was chilly, but the wind had died down a bit. I enjoyed the small shivers that ran through my body.

Luna looked up. Clouds had gathered over the almost-full moon, and there was not a star to be seen.

"It's so peaceful here," she said.

"Mhmm." I lacked the energy to comment further.

"What a party," she said.

"Yeah, I hope it's almost over." I scratched carefully at my scalp with a straightened finger, afraid to ruin my updo.

"I don't know what you mean. This is the best party I've ever been to."

"We must not have been at the same party."

Luna snorted, smiling. "I don't think we experience anything in the same way."

I had to agree with her on that, and I was about to say so aloud, but the feeling of an approaching aura prodded my consciousness. Recognition lashed me like a whip, and fear nearly knocked the air from my lungs.

Luna saw the look on my face. "What's wrong?"

"Go back inside The Boatman. Now," I whispered.

She looked around. We backed cautiously toward the entrance, but it was too late.

The Savage glided out from the darkness. His face had healed a little, but it was covered in scabs and pus-filled blisters. The hair on one side of his head hung in thin clumps, and his scalp glistened in the light of the lamp.

"Should we run?" whispered Luna.

I shook my head faintly. It was imprinted in my memory how quickly and precisely this large man could move.

An angry flame sliced through the Savage's aura when he recognized me. Then he looked at Luna, and his simple impulses shifted from anger to desire. He slowly came closer. His hands and shirt shone dark and wet, and a nauseating, ferrous scent reached my nostrils. The ecstasy of a fresh kill emanated from him, and I saw a short film that was at most an hour old.

I didn't know the girl, but my stomach contracted in sympathy.

Luna's eyes lingered on the dark splotches across the man's shirt. We backed slowly toward the door, but I knew it was useless. I prepared my body to fight and tried to remember everything Varnar had taught me.

The man was now nearly upon us. Just like last time, his stench hit me. It had not improved since Mathias fried him. The smell of blood, shit, and infection surrounded him. He focused on Luna.

I could see that she was fighting to keep the contents of her stomach down. I had time only to think *oh no* before he reached out and grabbed the purple turban. He ripped it off with a jerk, and Luna's bright red curls tumbled over her shoulders. With an unsettling smile that displayed all his brown teeth, he lowered his hand to his belt. His hand rested on his giant knife while his desire fought against the urge to kill her on the spot.

The evening's prior murder had excited him. Killing always turned him on. I sensed that clearly. I prepared myself to jump on him. Maybe Luna could get away before he fought me off.

But he was even quicker than I had expected, and before I was able to react, he grabbed Luna's hair with his enormous hand, squeezed it hard, and disappeared with long strides into the shadows, with Luna dragging behind.

CHAPTER 16

I sprinted into the darkness but could not see anything, and I cursed at the clouds blocking the moonlight. I ran but then stopped abruptly. If I didn't keep a cool head, I had no chance of finding Luna in time. I forced myself to stand still, even though every fiber of my body was screaming to keep running. I listened but could hear nothing other than the waves crashing far below me. Then I attempted something I had never tried before. I extended my extrasensory power into the night. First in one direction, then in another. I visualized casting a large fishing net into the darkness again and again. But I could not detect Luna. Then I realized that her aura was too vague.

The Savage's, on the other hand, was very clear.

I tried again. Finally, I felt his animalistic impulses and zoomed in on them. Right now, they were emanating lust.

I ran toward him in the dark, unable to see where I was stepping. The repugnant aura was my lantern in the night. As I got closer, I saw the very recent past in his mind.

They were in a small beach house nearby. His hands glided over Luna's body as she struggled. He slapped her, and she screamed and turned to get away, but he grabbed her by the hips, pulled her backward, and fumbled to yank her dress up.

I ran as hard as I could, and I finally made it. In a moment of ice-cold recognition, I realized I never would have found them if I had taken klinte.

They were in the living room. The clouds outside dispersed at that moment, and the moonlight tumbled in. The Savage turned toward me, still gripping Luna's lower back.

Rage and fear spread icy tingles across my back. My hands automatically clenched into fists, and I bared my teeth in an animalistic snarl.

Now that I was here, I had absolutely no plan for what to do. An attack was probably the best solution, so I lunged at him and hit him with a series of punches and kicks. Like Varnar had taught me, I hit him all over his body—in the head and the side, and I slammed his knee with a hard kick.

He tossed Luna aside like a rag doll, and she banged her head on the coffee table. Her temple hit the corner of the table, and she looked up at me sluggishly.

The Savage was not particularly impressed by my punches. He took a few steps forward and lurched at me. Although he was a giant brute, he was quick. His one fist struck me hard in the side, and it felt like half of my ribs bent. His other fist flew toward my head, and I only just managed to raise my hands, like Varnar had practiced with me over and over.

The blow stunned my arm, and I had difficulty controlling it, so my next punch landed next to where I aimed, which also exposed my face.

He hit me with the back of his hand. The force of the blow sent me flying sideways into a shelf. If he had hit me with a closed fist, my cheekbone would have been crushed.

Books and knickknacks came crashing down on me when the shelf tipped over. A heavy ceramic bowl hit me in the head, and small golden spots filled my field of vision. I shook my head and remained on my feet.

I heard Varnar in my head: *Do not let your opponent bring you to the ground.*

The man lunged toward me. I grabbed the heavy bowl and held it up in front of me.

He had pulled his giant knife, and it hit the bowl with a harsh *clink*. The knife's edge slid on the bowl's clay surface and cut my hand, and blood ran down my arm.

I swung the bowl as hard as I could, hitting him in the side of the head. A normal person would have fallen to the ground, but he didn't even shake his head.

I held the bowl up in front of me again, this time with both hands. The Savage's free fist whizzed forward and hit the bowl with a clatter, and I was left holding a large shard of ceramic in each hand. The knife flew forward again, this time directly toward my stomach. I would now find out if death really was like pulling a plug.

The man's arm was hit by a kick that changed the direction of his attack, and the knife shot out of his hand.

When I saw who had delivered the kick, profound relief washed over me.

Varnar's timing was, for once, perfect. Had he come one second later, I would have been sliced open from navel to throat. How he had found us, I didn't know, and I didn't have time to think about it. He circled closer to the Savage and resembled a dangerous feline.

The Savage growled, and the two men went after one another.

My relief diminished when the man moved just as quickly as Varnar—and he was significantly larger.

Each time Varnar was hit, I saw small glimmers of pain in his aura. When the Savage was hit, I saw nothing. Just an indestructible, murderous drive.

"Go!" Varnar shouted at me.

"And leave you and Luna?" I yelled back and swung one of the ceramic shards at the Savage.

I missed, and he laughed as he landed a kick to Varnar's solar plexus.

Varnar flew backward but managed to stay on his feet. He returned a torrent of blows to the Savage's face and body.

I tossed the remnants of the bowl aside, ran around them, and tried to join in the fight, but the two men were moving so quickly I was afraid I would do more harm than good.

Varnar did a kind of backflip and, with one hand on the floor, grabbed ahold of the Savage's enormous knife. He continued to attack, and I saw that he was somehow even more elegant with a knife in his hand. Elegant and deadly.

"Get out of here, Anna." He spun around and left a vertical gash across the Savage's forehead, eyebrow, and cheek.

I ignored his ridiculous order to leave.

For each cut Varnar bestowed on the Savage, he himself took several punches, and though the Savage was now bleeding like a stuck pig, he did not react. Varnar made a final lunge at him, but the Savage grabbed the knife with one hand.

The blade sliced into his palm, and blood gushed out between his fingers. He pushed Varnar back with a firm grip on the knife's edge. With his free hand, he grasped Varnar's wrist. Finally, the knife landed on the floor.

Despair and exhaustion emanated from Varnar. I realized that he knew he was going to lose.

On the floor, Luna was struggling to get to her feet.

I looked from her to Varnar. Then I hit the Savage, as many times and as hard as I could.

He swatted me away like an irritating fly, and I crashed sideways into the sofa.

Varnar looked at me in the moonlight. Looked at me as if he were taking in every detail. A strange expression flitted across his face, and for some reason, it reminded me of my knight-in-shining-armor fantasy about him. Then he turned back to the Savage and did exactly what he had taught me never to do. He dropped his arms from their protective position in front of his face.

"Run," he shouted before the Savage hit him in the jaw with full force.

I screamed as blood poured out of Varnar's mouth and he sank to his knees. The man's large boot hit him in the side, and he tumbled to the floor. Varnar was down, and the Savage began kicking him.

Without thinking, I jumped onto the man's back and bit him in the neck, scratched his face, and pulled his hair. Whatever I could do to inflict harm.

From the floor, Varnar gave a strangled shout.

The Savage spun around in a wild dance, with me on his back and my red dress billowing out around us. He swung his fists back, and I clung to him as the blows rained down over me. Finally, he charged backward into the wall.

The impact knocked the air out of me. It was impossible to hold on any longer, and I landed in a heap on the floor next to Varnar.

"You stupid girl," he hissed as he tried to stand.

Before he managed to get up, the Savage kicked him in the temple, and he went out like a light. The Savage had found his knife again, and he raised it over Varnar's lifeless body.

I threw myself between them, and the knife glinted above us in the moonlight.

Varnar had not saved me this time. He had only delayed the inevitable, and I had dragged him down with me. When the Savage was done with us, it would be Luna's turn, and she wouldn't get off so easy.

This thought made me resort to a desperate act.

"Arthur," I whispered. "You once said you would always hear me, no matter what. I have a problem now. A serious problem."

It was laughable and hopeless, and I had just enough time to feel good and stupid when the Savage lowered his knife toward me.

From her position on the floor, Luna let out a sudden shout. "No!"

The Savage stiffened and backed up.

269

I heard a whistle and felt something move across my hips. I looked down. The black brocade snakes were writhing over my dress, and a surprised sound escaped me.

Luna raised her hand, and the snakes rose from my dress and attacked the Savage. One struck him on the cheek, and he grabbed it. The snakes' eyes shone coldly in the moonlight.

Luna's hand turned quickly in the air, and the snakes attacked again. This time, one snake bit the Savage in the thigh, and the other went for his arm.

He swung the knife and chopped the head off one of the snakes. Beads rained down over my legs and the floor. The other snake made to attack again, while Luna shouted something.

The Savage whipped around and looked from her to the snake. Comprehension reached his eyes, and he hit her in the side of the head. She slumped, and the snakes slithered back onto my dress, where they were still once again.

I tried to get up off the floor, but the room spun.

The Savage leaned over Luna and began to unbutton his pants.

Oh no. I crawled forward and grabbed one of his legs, but he kicked back, and his heel hit my cheekbone.

Consciousness drained out of me.

The Savage picked Luna up and threw her onto the sofa. The blood and the fight had made him even more excited. He lifted Luna's dress.

She cried.

I fought dizzily to get up, but my body would not obey me.

Luna screamed when he leaned forward to press himself into her.

CHAPTER 17

Luna was still screaming.

I blinked and looked around. I must have lost consciousness for a second.

The Savage pulled away from Luna and, eyes wild, looked down at his groin, which was in flames. It was a mystery to me why he wasn't bellowing loudly in pain. Luna crawled backward on the sofa.

At that moment, neon-green light streamed in through the open door.

A glowing green and gigantic version of Mathias burst into the little house. He looked around at the chaos with eyes resembling beams of blue light. He grabbed the Savage by the waist with one hand—yes, *one* hand—shook him hard, and hurled him into the wall.

The Savage slid down to the floor and remained lying there, completely still, while his crotch smoldered, and the smell of burnt flesh filled the air.

Mathias knelt in front of Luna and lifted her gently. She looked like a child in his enormous embrace, and she slung her arms around him, crying.

"Are you guys okay?" he asked me with his deep, metallic voice.

"I am." I frantically touched Varnar's face, which was a bloody mess. "Varnar is breathing, but he needs help."

I tried to stand but slipped on the blood and beads.

"What about him?" Luna pointed to the unconscious man with the smoking groin.

"What did you do to him?" asked Mathias.

Tears ran down Luna's cheeks.

"I don't know. I think I'm the one who did it. His . . . caught fire . . . when he tried to . . ." She stopped.

Mathias's blue eyes sparkled ominously, and I thought he would kill the Savage on the spot, but he just clenched his teeth. Then he pulled an electrical cord out of the wall and wrapped it tightly around the Savage's arms and legs.

"Let's wait to decide what to do with him." Mathias's voice indicated that he had a few ideas. Then he picked Varnar up with one arm. Luna was gripped firmly in the other. "Get up on my back," he said to me.

"Can you carry all three of us?"

"Up," he shouted, and his voice sounded like a force of nature.

I commanded my body to obey, crawled up onto his back, and held on to his neck with a convulsive grip.

Mathias ran with incomprehensible speed through the harsh, moonlit landscape.

"How did you find us?" I asked in his ear.

"I was sleeping. Suddenly, someone shouted that you were being killed. So I just jumped out of bed and ran. The voice led me here. Where are we?"

I realized he was wearing a T-shirt and pajama pants.

"We're in Jagd. That's almost twenty miles from Ravensted." I pointed toward the faint light from The Boatman. "We need to go over there."

"It's been ten minutes at most since I was woken up," he said, mostly to himself.

I guided him around to the back entrance. "Who woke you?"

"I know it sounds weird, but it sounded like your friend Arthur."

My entire body felt cold.

Mathias carefully laid Varnar on the ground and held Luna in both arms.

272

"I have to go in and find Od. How do I look?" I asked.

Mathias managed to look at me with a professional expression, though he was standing barefoot in pajamas and glowing a pale green.

"You have a red mark on your cheek, but otherwise you look shockingly good. If you hurry and stay away from harsh light, it's possible no one will notice." He rearranged a few strands of hair. "There."

I exhaled to get my nerves under control.

"Get in and get out."

I ran around The Boatman to the main entrance, where I pulled on the boar-shaped door handle and walked back into the party. It was unbelievable how little time had passed since I had left through that door with Luna.

In the shadows along the wall, I searched for Od. I passed two men deep in conversation. I recognized one from a music program that left the streets deserted every Friday.

"Did you hear Od Dinesen's speech? I loved what he said about art being the most important thing of all," he said.

"I didn't notice that part," said the other, who I knew as a journalist from TV. "However, he did have a fantastic point about always striving to get the truth out."

They continued talking about their very different experiences of Od's speech, and my suspicion that Od dabbled with mass hypnotism in his spare time was strengthened significantly.

Finally, I spotted him in the middle of a circle of devoted listeners. I tried to signal to him, but at that moment, someone caught my arm and pushed me up against the wall.

Elias positioned himself right in front of me and blocked my view of Od. "Where have you been?"

"I need to talk to Od." I took a step forward, but he shoved me back into the wall. My back already hurt after my encounter with the Savage, and I let out an anguished sound.

Elias looked at me, frightened. "Sorry. I didn't mean to hurt you. What happened?"

I briefly debated making up a story but decided I would rather have him as a coconspirator than try to lie to him.

"Luna and I were attacked by the man who killed the red-haired girls. Some friends helped us, but one of them was hurt."

"How did you get away?"

"We beat him and tied him up," I said casually.

Elias looked at me skeptically.

"Do you know who he is?" I asked.

"I know what he's capable of." He evaded my question and ran his fingers tentatively over the mark that was on my cheek. "Did he hurt you?"

"Yes," I said, raising my hand to show him the large, bleeding wound.

Elias rubbed his forehead. Then he spoke with an intensity I had never heard from him before. "Listen to me now, Anna. This is important. You cannot speak of this to Od, Luna's parents, or anyone from the DSMA."

"But . . ."

"Under no circumstances."

"Why not?"

"Just trust me."

I looked at him with contempt. "Trust you?"

Elias leaned forward, and I was wrapped in his aura, which simmered with . . . fear? He spoke quickly into my ear. "If they find out that he touched you, the treaty is broken. It will cost lives. Many lives."

I heard the words but didn't understand them. *What treaty? Whose lives?*

Niels Villadsen passed us then with his entourage in tow.

Elias laid one hand on my bruised cheek and took my bloody hand in the other to hide the large wound. Suddenly, his facial expression was the usual flirty one. He leaned heavily against me and kissed my good cheek.

Niels looked suspiciously at us. Something in Elias's voice had made me believe him, even though I didn't understand what he was talking about. The fear in his aura also made an impression. I tried to appear infatuated with him to shake Niels off, but he was still staring at us with an appraising look.

Okay, then. I would have to sacrifice myself for the greater good, so I pressed my lips against Elias's.

His head gave a jerk, but he recovered astonishingly fast and slipped into the kiss like it was the most natural thing in the world. He moved his hand to the back of my neck.

It was nice, really nice, so I broke off the kiss as quickly as I could.

Over Elias's shoulder, I saw Niels walking away from us.

Elias whispered in my ear: "That was fantastic." He turned and watched Niels. "We need to get you out of here before anyone notices anything."

I cast a long look at Od and then nodded.

At the back entrance, we found Mathias, Luna, and Varnar in bad shape. My stomach flipped in fear when I saw Varnar's bloodied face.

Mathias sat with his back against the wall and Luna in his arms. She appeared to be sleeping, and he glowed a faint neon green. He looked up at us, tired.

"It's good that you came."

Elias observed the glowing Mathias.

"Now I understand," he said. Then he knelt in front of the bloody, unconscious Varnar. "What a mess. Come inside."

Mathias gently shook Luna, who opened her eyes and stood up unsteadily.

I put an arm around her waist to keep her upright.

"Can you get my mom and dad?" she mumbled.

"Shh," I said. "They can't know about this."

"Why not?"

"Trust me." I repeated Elias's words without knowing the reason for the secrecy.

She staggered onward.

"I trust you, Anna," she said drowsily.

Elias opened the back door and ushered us in.

In Od's office, Mathias carefully laid Varnar on the sofa. Elias dug around in his pockets and produced a small ampoule of laekna and a syringe.

"You really are always prepared," I said with a raised eyebrow.

He winked at me, then rolled up Varnar's sleeve and gave him the injection. Right away, the wounds diminished noticeably.

"He's pretty banged up, but he hasn't broken anything. This will take care of the worst of it. He just needs to sleep now," said Elias.

When Luna saw Varnar's wounds close, her eyes grew wide. "What did he give him?"

I looked dully at her. "I'll explain later. Right now, you just need to take a drop so we can get back to the party before your parents start to worry."

She looked down at herself. Her golden dress was torn, bloody, and scorched in the front, and her red ringlets stuck out in all directions. Deep violet bruises adorned both cheeks.

"Don't you think they'll be more worried if they see me like this?" She obediently swallowed a drop of laekna. She flinched when it began to take effect. The bruises first turned transparent, then finally became one with her brown skin.

"Yeah, actually." I looked at her as I took a drop myself. It was becoming a recurring event, Elias dousing me with hard-hitting potions after near-death experiences. I don't know if that said more about him or me. I closed my eyes for a moment as the laekna soothed my injuries. I looked down. The cut on my hand was now just a long scratch.

"You don't seem to need any, do you?" Elias waved the ampoule in front of Mathias.

Mathias looked down at his bare feet. "No."

"Great. Now we just have to make sure no one finds out about this evening's drama." Elias had clearly appointed himself the leader. "Anna, you look relatively normal. You need to stay here until the party is over." He turned to face Luna. "You can't go back in. I think it's best if . . ." He turned to Mathias. "What was your name?"

"Mathias."

"If Mathias here takes you and the young man home."

He did not ask about transportation, or why Mathias was wearing pajamas.

"What should I do with Varnar?" asked Mathias.

"Is this young man Varnar?" Elias studied the unconscious Varnar with renewed interest.

I looked to Mathias. "Do you know where Kraghede Manor is?"

He shook his head.

"Can he stay here?" I asked Elias.

Elias chuckled. "Believe me. That's not a good idea."

"Shit. Then he'll have to go to my house. Put him in the guest room. What about your parents, Luna?"

She drummed her fingers against her lip.

"I can call my mom's cell, but my phone is back home." Elias held out his phone, but she shook her head. "What if she can see that I'm calling from your phone?"

"Don't worry. My number is impossible to trace. The only people who know it are those for whom I am available at all times." He wiggled his eyebrows at me.

Luna took the phone and dialed a number. She quickly explained to Rebecca that she was on her way home with Mathias. I was impressed by her ability to sidestep the truth without technically lying.

Mathias lifted Varnar. "What about the murderer? He's still back at the beach house."

"I'll take care of it." Elias closed his eyes for a second. "I'll see your friends out," he said to me as Luna and Mathias walked toward the door.

I waved at them before they disappeared out one of the many doors. Elias's phone glowed on the desk where Luna had set it down. I bit my lip and snatched it. Then I dug around in the bag Luna had made for me, found my wallet, and took out a business card. I quickly sent a text, deleted it from sent messages, and placed the phone back on the table. Exhaustion washed over me, so I sat on the leather sofa and leaned back, my eyes closed. I had just managed to slip into sleep when I felt a little bump as Elias sat down next to me.

"What now?" I asked without opening my eyes.

"We could pick up where we left off." His fingertips ran across the lace from my shoulder to my wrist.

"Forget it." I pushed his warm hand away.

"I know you're attracted to me. I've never been wrong about that."

"Congratulations on the delusions."

"I will clearly be tormented by unrequited desire tonight."

"Something tells me you have someone else in reserve who can solve that." I looked at him.

He looked down at the floor in an imitation of guilt. "You know me so well already. But just so you know, you were my plan A tonight."

"How romantic! Have you noticed what year it is? It's not ye olde seventeenth century anymore, where girls were nothing but plans for you."

Elias laughed without an ounce of shame. "Come on, let's find Od. You have to make a round and walk out the door together to mark the end of the party. Then I'll drive you home."

"Can I take some klinte?"

Elias shook his head. "Laekna and klinte don't mix. Bad trip."

I straightened my spine. "Then let's get this over with."

Impressions from the crowd of people poured over me as Elias led me inside. Whatever Od had filled me with before the party started had stopped working. The floor buckled ominously beneath me.

Od saw us across the room and reached us in just a few long strides.

"All good?"

"Fine," I said, my ears ringing.

Od took my arm, and a tiny bit of strength seeped from him to me. It was enough to help me hold myself upright. We left Elias and walked through the room together.

People turned and smiled. Many stopped us and thanked Od for the party. A journalist asked my name. I didn't answer her.

"Where have you been? I haven't seen you in several hours," Od whispered to me.

"I was right here." I looked up at him with the sincerest smile I could muster.

"I didn't see you."

"You were probably too busy performing mass hypnosis," I said dryly.

Od laughed hoarsely.

My legs wobbled, and he put his arm around my back without changing his facial expression. We rounded the bar, where Od stopped and shook the hand of a celebrity chef I had seen on TV.

"Thank you so much for the food," Od said. "It was exquisite."

The chef replied, but I wasn't listening. Od's firm grip on my waist was now the only thing holding me up.

We continued on.

"I have a feeling that you've had an eventful evening," said Od.

"And what are you basing that on?" I asked as we passed Ben and Rebecca.

They looked at me suspiciously, and I tried to appear cheerful, which probably did not make them any less suspicious. We reached the mirrored hall that led to Od's office and turned to face the guests, who clapped like crazy, while I tried to hide the fact that I was about to pass out.

"You seem a little out of it," he said between enthusiastic cheers.

A tingling sensation spread across my body, which always happens right before I faint.

"I'm not used to being around so many people."

"You have something that looks like blood on your boots."

"I spilled some wine." I could barely hear my own voice through the howling in my ears.

"The snakes on your dress have moved, and one is missing its head."

I looked down. The black snakes on my dress were coiled in a completely different pattern than at the start of the evening, and the right snake's head had been chopped off.

"Oh."

Od cast a final smile over the guests before we retreated to his office. He practically dragged me the last few steps.

As soon as he closed the door behind us, I collapsed in his arms.

The cord tightened around the girl's neck, and she fell into the snow, her arms and legs fluttering weakly. She made a guttural noise as she tried to breathe one last time.

With a gasp, I woke with my hands placed protectively around my own neck. The necklace had wrapped itself around it, and I loosened it with my fingers.

It was light outside, and I lay in my own bed.

I had a vague recollection of lying in the back of a car, of being carried, and of Elias's scent. I lifted the covers and saw that I was wearing only panties and a bra. Elias could expect a stern talking-to the next time I saw him.

Someone behind me breathed heavily. Maybe Elias wouldn't have to wait so long to receive his scolding. I was about to give him a piece of my mind when a particular fragrance hit my nostrils.

It was the smell of forest and fresh air.

I lay still until the respiration behind me was rhythmic again. Then I turned carefully.

In front of me, just a few inches away, lay Varnar. Was I having another vision? I pinched my thigh. *Ow*. No, he was really lying there. Right there. I could not help but study him now that I finally had the chance.

Sleep softened his features and made him look younger. His hair lay around his face like a dark halo, and for once, his eyebrows weren't furrowed. His thick eyelashes looked like small, delicate fans. His lips, which were slightly parted, curved upward in something that almost resembled a smile. Someone had washed the blood off him, but a bruise covered an entire side of his face. Without the laekna, it would have been swollen beyond recognition, but now it was merely a dark shadow. His shirt sat neatly folded next to the bed, and it was sweetly painful to look at his smooth, muscular torso.

I knew I should look away, but I couldn't. I looked at the burn marks on his arm. Now that I looked at them more closely, I could see they were runes. One of them resembled a strange, twisted M. I resisted a powerful urge to trace my fingers over the scars.

Varnar moved. He was about to wake up.

I quickly turned my head down into the pillow, closed my eyes, and pretended to be asleep. A strand of hair slid down over my cheek. It tickled horribly, but I ignored it. I could sense that Varnar was now awake, but he didn't move. I lay as still as I could and tried to slow my breathing.

Intense relief and something like pure joy flowed from him, and completely unexpectedly, I felt a finger very carefully lifting the hair off my face.

I gathered my courage and opened my eyes.

His hand stopped moving, but he left it on my cheek. Sleep still hung like a fog over his face, and for a moment, I saw the hint of a smile on his lips. Then his eyebrows knitted together into their familiar irritated expression. He pulled back his hand, then rolled over and sat on the edge of the bed with his back to me.

"You jumped on him," he said into the air. "I told you to run, but you threw yourself directly into the fight."

His back was a tense network of small muscles, and my fingers itched to stroke it soothingly.

"He would have killed you," I whispered.

Varnar ignored me. "I was sure you were going to die. He's a lot stronger than you. He's even stronger and faster than me. He would have killed you, but you tried to fight him."

"Isn't that why you're training me? So I can fight if I or someone else gets attacked?"

Varnar turned and looked at me with so much rage I winced.

"I'm training you to keep you alive!" he shouted.

I had never heard him raise his voice that way before, and I was so scared that I sat up and backed down to the foot of the bed.

He was about to say more, but at that moment, Mathias burst in the door wearing nothing but boxer shorts, and though Varnar had an impressive body, I had to admit that the sight of Mathias nearly au naturel made my heart flutter.

"What's going on?" He looked at us. Varnar tense as a spring at the edge of the bed, and me, with tears in my eyes, at the other end. "Are you okay, Anna?"

I nodded but couldn't speak.

Varnar stood and grabbed his shirt aggressively before looking at Mathias. "I don't know how, but somehow, we survived last night.

I'm assuming you had something to do with it. Thank you for that and for helping . . . this stupid girl." This last bit he practically spat out.

Mathias looked down. Varnar said nothing else and stomped toward the door.

"Wait," I cried and jumped out of the bed with the duvet wrapped around me. I could hear the desperation in my own voice.

Varnar stopped in the doorway but did not turn to face me.

"I can't even look at you right now," he said. He exhaled heavily. "I'm coming over tomorrow evening. We can talk then."

He ran down the stairs. I watched him go. At the bottom of the stairs, he stopped to pull on his shirt. Then he flung open the door.

Outside stood Greta, her fist raised in an about-to-knock-on-the-door position. She looked down at Varnar's still-visible abs. Then she looked at his face with its large, dark bruise.

He looked angrily at her before passing her in the doorway and disappearing over the fields toward Kraghede Forest. She shifted her gaze to the top of the stairs, where Mathias and I stood. Me with the duvet around me and Mathias in his underwear.

Oh shit!

"Greta, what are you doing here?" I asked.

Greta slowly lowered her hand.

"I did say I would come for unannounced visits." She stepped into the hall.

"Your caseworker?" whispered Mathias.

"Yep," I whispered back.

At that moment, Luna came bouncing out of the guest bedroom wearing only a bra and Mathias's pajama pants. She didn't notice Greta at the base of the stairs.

"Did you have fun with Varnar last night?" She grinned. "We had to undress you because you threw up all over yourself when Elias brought you here. You were out cold."

Double shit!

I waved my hand rapidly from side to side to signal that she should shut up, but as always, this kind of hint bounced right off her.

"Are you not feeling well? I feel great today. Whatever Elias gave us was really strong."

Mathias went to shove her back into the room.

"Can I borrow some clothes to go home in?" she shouted. "My dress is burnt, and there's blood on it. Both yours and Varnar's. And some of what's-his-face's."

Triple shit!

Greta looked like she was mentally searching through the entire social work curriculum to figure out how to react.

"The two of us need to talk," was all she came up with. She walked stiffly into the living room.

I quickly threw on a pair of pants and a hoodie and rummaged around for my one yellow T-shirt. I handed it to Luna in the guest room, along with a pair of gray joggers. Mathias had clearly informed Luna of Greta's presence.

"I'm sorry. I didn't know your caseworker was here," she said.

"If I'm lucky, she'll be content with throwing me out of the house and back into that little apartment. If I'm unlucky, I'll be going back into a group home or a foster family."

"Why?" Luna pulled on the clothes.

Mathias put his now quite dingy pajama pants back on.

I looked critically at him.

He threw up his arms. "I have nothing else to put on. I was kind of in a hurry to get out the door last night."

I sighed and turned my back to him, pointing to the chain around my neck. "Can you take this off? It's stuck."

Mathias opened the clasp like it was made of butter.

The heart pendant and chain dropped into my hand.

I turned back to Luna. "There are some conditions for me being allowed to live here. I'm not allowed to let people stay here or throw wild parties."

"But you didn't do either of those."

"No, but I can't tell her the truth. And now she thinks we had an orgy last night. What are you guys even doing here?"

"I didn't want to leave Varnar when he was unconscious. I thought this was the best solution," said Mathias.

"You thought wrong," I snapped, and fought to get my temper under control. "Come on, we'd better go downstairs."

In the living room, Greta sat at the very edge of the bench and stared fearfully at the large spear on the wall. Then she moved her gaze to us.

"Where's the dog?" she asked.

"He ran away," said Luna. She smiled knowingly at me and gave me a thumbs-up. She must have figured that Greta wasn't entirely comfortable with Monster.

I struggled not to bury my face in my hands.

"I would like to speak with Anna alone," Greta said haughtily to Luna and Mathias.

Mathias nodded and backed toward the door. He gripped Luna's arm and pulled her with him.

They were lucky they could flee this sinking ship. Of all the times Greta could have shown up, she had chosen the worst. Why hadn't she come yesterday morning, when I was home alone and the house was sparkling clean?

"Anna, I am disappointed in you," said Greta. "I am this close to calling off our agreement, and . . ."

She didn't get to finish her sentence before there was a knock at the door.

What now?

Outside stood Hakim in full police uniform. There were small drops of rain in his dark hair. His intense green eyes gleamed as he marched into my house, leaving wet footprints on my tile floor.

"I need to talk to you." He stopped at the sight of Greta, who stood and looked at him in alarm. "Who are you?"

"Greta Johansen. I'm Anna's caseworker." She looked Hakim up and down with great suspicion. "Who are you?"

"My name is Hakim, and I'm investigating the Pippi Murders." He stood up straight. "I need to speak with Anna alone. It's urgent."

"You can't just come strolling in unannounced and demand to speak with her alone."

She was one to talk. I let out a quiet *ha* and gave me a sharp look. I occupied myself with studying my bare toes.

"I can, and I will," said Hakim. "I have to ask you to leave."

Greta gasped indignantly.

"Okay, okay." I held up my hands and stood between them. "One intrusive public servant at a time."

I turned to Greta. "It's not what it looks like. I can explain everything." I just didn't know how to do so without revealing various paranormal occurrences.

I turned around to face Hakim. "What is it that's so urgent?"

He glanced at Greta. "I would really prefer to speak with you one-on-one."

I looked back at Greta. "Can we talk about it tomorrow? I have to go see you anyway."

She pushed her glasses up her nose. "Do you want me to stay? You are not legally obligated to speak unless he has a warrant or is putting you under arrest."

Despite my irritation, I knew she was only trying to look out for me. Like she had been doing my whole life. I shook my head.

"I should probably talk to him. He's okay."

Greta sniffed. "Fine. I'll see you tomorrow."

When I closed the door behind her, I rested my forehead against the cool wood.

"Hard night?" asked Hakim.

I straightened and rubbed my eyes. "Eventful morning."

"I'm okay, huh?" He looked at me with a slight smile.

"Well, I had to say something to get her out of here. What do you want?"

He looked inquisitively at me. "Have you been crying?"

"That's none of your business."

He was about to say something but changed his mind. "You're right. Sorry. Have you seen the news today?"

I shook my head, and he turned on the TV. It was right at the beginning of a segment.

"A rash of violence in North Jutland apparently came to an end yesterday evening, but not before the murderer claimed the life of yet another teenage girl in the small town of Lønstrup on the west coast."

I recognized the girl; I had seen her in the Savage's past. They showed her school picture. In the photo, she was smiling to the camera. In the vision, she screamed as she ran away from him with her long red hair flowing around her. He caught her with ease and, without further ado, took her life with his large knife. He drew the F symbol on her cheek in blood.

I sensed Hakim looking at me.

"Eighteen-year-old Ida Bendixen was found stabbed to death yesterday evening at nine o'clock behind a movie theater in the small town of Lønstrup in North Jutland. She is thought to be yet another victim of the Pippi Killer. Later last night, following an anonymous tip, the police found the man they believe is responsible for the murders. The man was found in an area populated with vacation homes near the town of Jagd, just six miles from Lønstrup. He himself had been subjected to a brutal assault, and the police believe it may have been a form of vigilante justice."

They cut to a windswept dune. The sea churned in the background, the sky was gray, and there were raindrops on the camera lens.

The journalist I had seen at The Boatman the previous evening was struggling to stay upright against the strong westerly wind. He was still wearing a black suit and bow tie and did not appear to have slept.

"Behind me, you can see the small beach house where last night the police made the unsettling discovery of a man who had been the victim of an almost torture-like assault."

The camera zoomed in on the house where, just hours before, I had located Luna and the Savage.

"At the same time, we can hope that this marks the end of the terror North Jutland has experienced over the past six months. I am here with Chief Investigator Lars Guldager." The journalist turned toward Lars. "What can you say about last night's events?"

Lars looked tired but relieved. "We found another murdered teenage girl. We have reason to believe she is another victim of the so-called Pippi Killer. We subsequently arrested a suspect."

The journalist leaned forward, searching for something sensational. "Is it true that the perpetrator was the victim of a violent assault?"

"For the sake of the ongoing investigation, I have no comment."

"Some are saying his genitals were burned, and that the fingers of one hand were nearly cut off," the reporter pressed.

"No comment," Lars said with a warning look.

"His ribs were crushed, and the skin on his face was scalded, as if someone had poured boiling water on him . . ."

Pffft, I thought. The injury to his face was old. These journalists were total amateurs.

"No comment." Lars's eyes flashed at the reporter, and he added, "You should also keep in mind that he is only a suspect—"

The journalist interrupted.

"Thank you, Lars Guldager." He turned to the camera. "That's all we have for you here in Jagd, where, by all indications, the Pippi Killer got what some would say he deserved after killing five teenage girls over the past six months in North Jutland."

Hakim muted the sound, but the images of Ida Bendixen and the beach house kept rolling. It was hard to tear my eyes from the screen, and even harder to meet Hakim's gaze.

He stood expectantly at my side.

"Did you come all the way out here just to turn on my TV?" I asked into the air in front of me. "I could have turned it on myself."

"I wanted to see how you reacted to the news."

"And how am I reacting?"

"You don't seem particularly surprised."

"Well, you guys were bound to catch him at some point."

"I was the one who arrested him."

"So you'll probably get a medal or something." My eyes were still directed at the TV.

"Someone sent me a text last night about where we could find him. I have been unable to track the phone."

I tried to look like I was listening politely but not understanding a lick of what he was talking about.

"He nearly killed me. He was tied up and practically unconscious, but he still almost strangled me. I had to shoot him. I should have brought someone with me."

"You went out there alone?" I gasped. Only now did I see the purple mark on Hakim's neck. My text had nearly cost him his life.

His eyes sparkled in triumph. "There's the reaction I was look-ing for."

Goddamn it. I had stepped right into his trap.

"Is he dead?" I asked. I suddenly felt very tired.

Hakim shook his head. "No. He's a resilient son of a bitch."

I had to agree.

"He didn't even scream when I shot him. And the way he looked. Whoever tortured him really went for it."

I was silently amused that the police believed the Savage had been lynched.

"I would still really like to know why you're here." It seemed like a good idea to keep playing dumb. "Have I also met this Ida Bendixen before?"

"Not as far as we know. There does not appear to be any link between you two."

"Then I'll ask again: Why are you here?"

Hakim pulled out his phone and tapped it a couple times before holding it out to me.

He'd pulled up a web page on the screen. It was a gossip site with pictures that had been taken at the party the previous evening. The first photo was of Od and a pouting model type. I looked at him, uncomprehending.

"While the attack took place, you were a tenth of a mile away at one of the biggest events of the year. As the host's date."

It was impressive that Hakim could recognize me when I could barely recognize myself. I tried to look nonchalant.

"It's not a crime to attend a party." I looked back at the TV to avoid his green, assessing eyes.

Hakim ignored my defensive tone. "We checked the beach house for evidence."

My pulse rose, and my ability to maintain my mask was seriously put to the test. The fact that Mathias had previously been charged with shooting someone would not be difficult to dig up, and his fingerprints must be registered with the police. Mine were, too, after the saga with Peter and the bat.

"And?" It came out timidly.

"Someone cleaned up out there. We didn't find so much as a strand of hair or a drop of blood."

I exhaled slowly as I racked my brain. *Who?*

"That must complicate the investigation," I said.

"Yes. That, plus the fact that our detainee refuses to say a word."

I wasn't sure if he even *could* speak. I had only heard him growl and grunt.

"Are you even allowed to tell me all this? Isn't it confidential?"

"Let's call it a desperate measure."

I ran my fingers through my hair, which was in serious need of a wash and a brush.

"Hey, shouldn't you be drinking bad champagne from a coffee cup right now? You caught the murderer. Yaaay." I raised my arms in a gesture of victory. Then I caught a fresh memory in his mind. "Ah. Your colleagues actually are celebrating right now. They don't care who tortured him, as long as he's been caught. But you went. Because you do care."

"How did you know that?" Hakim tried to regain his composure by turning and looking out the window toward Kraghede Forest, which was barely visible in the mist. It was one of those days where the fog hung over the landscape like an enormous cloud fallen to earth.

He continued: "Yes. I do care. In a sense, I can understand the people who did it, but they must nevertheless be held accountable. But it's not so much that. I have this hunch."

"Mhmm. Another one of your hunches."

He looked at me, irritated, then stared again at the forest, where the girl would be strangled. "I have a feeling this isn't over."

I more than shared his feeling. "You'll miss out on all the glory of solving the case if you make more out of it."

"Damn the glory," he thundered.

I breathed in sharply before recovering. "I still can't see what this has to do with me. Unless you want to go around and check if all the guests' TVs are working."

Hakim sighed. "I won't get any more out of you. I'll leave now."

He stopped. "There's just one other thing." He stuck his hand in his pocket. "We found no blood, hair, or other biological evidence at the crime scene, but I did find this."

He opened his large hand. In it lay a clear plastic bag with a small pale-blue bead, exactly the same color as my nail polish. "Does this look familiar?"

I did not reply, and he smiled without warmth before turning around. A few long strides brought him to the door.

"If you think of anything, don't hesitate to call." He looked at me over his shoulder with his clear green eyes. "Or text."

I watched him pass my window and slouched heavily over the kitchen table, my head churning. For a while, I just stared out the kitchen window. Then I found my phone and took out the card I had been given by Niels Villadsen. *DSMA*, I searched.

Nothing came up leading me to the anonymous-looking officials from the previous evening. *Niels Villadsen*, I typed instead. Three people showed up, but none of them was the Niels Villadsen I had met. *Clingy spirit*, I wrote, feeling very stupid. I got a fair number of hits, clicked on the first one, and arrived at a gloomy-looking website in black and gray with headings in misty white letters.

Clingy spirits are a type of ghost that "cling" to a specific individual. The spirit is often a deceased person who, in life, had some form of addiction to drugs, alcohol, or specific feelings such as aggression or outright violence. Clingy spirits express their addiction through the person they cling to.

I didn't want to read more. With an irritated motion, I pushed the phone away.

Something piqued my intuition, and an impulse made me get up and go outside.

In the barn, I quickly found the envelope of photos in the chest. Raindrops fell heavily on the tin roof, and I jogged across the yard. My hair was damp when I came back inside.

The first photo I had seen before. It depicted a young Rebecca. The next picture was of the woman with the dark, curly hair. My stomach contracted, and I set the photo aside facing down. With quick movements, I flipped through the next few photos, which all showed Ben, Rebecca, and the woman, either at Odinmont or in front of Ben and Rebecca's house. One photograph showed my first foster parents, Jens and Mia. Sadness hummed through me when I held the picture in my hand.

In another picture, Rebecca and the woman with the black hair stood in front of Kraghede Forest, each with a pregnant belly. There was a fine dusting of snow over the spruce branches. Their stomachs met in the middle, and both women were smiling.

My eyes burned, and I quickly moved on to a picture of three people. I studied it, my brain unwilling to understand who it depicted.

All at once, I understood. For a couple of seconds, I couldn't breathe. Then I stood so quickly that the chair toppled behind me. Without stopping to right it, I ran outside.

In the yard, I spun around in a circle.

"Arthur, come here. Right now," I yelled. "I know you can hear me."

I looked out across the field. It was now so foggy that I couldn't see the end of it.

"Arthur," I shouted again, as insistently as possible.

The outline of a figure formed in the fog. It came closer.

Arthur stepped out of the mist with a nervous expression on his face.

"Go ahead and spit it out."

"Spit what out?" His face was so white, it bordered on gray.

"You heard me last night when I asked you for help in the middle of nowhere. And you got Mathias from almost twenty miles away. You're white as a sheet, and I've never seen you eat or drink anything. And I can neither see your aura nor your past.

"That doesn't necessarily mean—" Arthur began, but I cut him off.

"And try explaining this."

He looked at the picture I stuck in front of him, and he paled further, this time to chalk white.

293

The photo had yellowed. Maybe it had been left out in the sun. It showed the black-haired woman and a young Rebecca. Between them, with an arm slung around each woman's shoulders, stood Arthur. He looked exactly the same, not a day younger than he was now, though the photo must have been at least fifteen years old.

"I'll ask you again," I said slowly. "And if you don't answer, or if you lie to me, I swear, I'll never speak to you again. What are you, and who are you?"

Arthur opened and closed his mouth a couple of times before he spoke.

"Don't be scared by what I'm about to tell you. I'm the same person I've always been. No matter what."

"What the hell are you?" I hissed.

Arthur looked at me with his large green eyes.

"I'm a ghost. I died almost eighteen years ago. And I am your father."

CHAPTER 18

My legs gave out beneath me, and I landed in the damp gravel.

Arthur knelt in front of me and took my hand. "I'm still me."

I swung my head forcefully from side to side. "You're joking."

"If only. I wish I were alive to be a real father to you."

"My parents left me."

"You had to grow up among strangers. But I never left you."

Saying nothing, I simply stared at Arthur. It was like the oxygen refused to remain in my chest, and I was left gasping for air.

I tried to stop hyperventilating. I had not been thrown away as a child, and there was life after death. Talk about existential mental overload. I tried to start from the most logical point.

"Why can I see you?"

Sadness hung like a shroud over Arthur's face. "Because you can see the past, and I am past."

Angrily, I pushed back tears. "I can't see other ghosts."

"Yes, you can. You just don't know that they're ghosts. They don't always know it themselves. Plus, there aren't that many of us." Arthur sniffed. "You have no idea how few people I've been able to talk to all these years."

I pressed my hands hard against my temples to keep my head from exploding.

Arthur saw this and waved his hand. "But you don't need to hear about my problems."

"You were saying something about other ghosts," I whispered.

"The others probably wouldn't come to you because they don't even know they're dead. Only mediums actually attract spirits. They're like magnets for them, and it's their job to help the lost ones cross over."

The thought of ghosts roaming around gave me the creeps. Then I remembered I was in the middle of a conversation with one. I tried to compose myself.

"And I'm not a medium?"

"As far as I know, you're just clairvoyant."

My brain was about to boil over. "I can touch you. Why can I touch you?"

"It's complicated. I'll explain it later. There are a lot of things I need to tell you. Things that will change your understanding of the world and probably shock you."

I exhaled and laughed at the same time—maybe a touch manically.

"I'm pretty sure that process is already well underway." I looked up. "Others can't see you, then? Damn, you're harsh. I've been going around talking to myself. Now I can understand why people think I'm crazy."

I stopped. "Why can Mathias see you? Do you know what he is? The same as Od, right?"

Arthur looked down at the gravel. "I have an idea of what he is. And I know what Od is. But I'm not the person to tell you about them. What someone is is a private matter. You don't talk about it behind their back. Especially when the person themself doesn't know."

"Is that a kind of etiquette for supernatural beings?"

"You could say that."

"What are you called? As a group, I mean."

"We usually say we're part of the hidden world."

"We?"

"There are several of us who are part of the hidden world in some way or another."

"Let me guess: Od, Elias, Ben, and Rebecca?"

"Among others. And you, too."

"What about Luna?"

"Let's just say you and your friends are the next generation, and that you will have to go through the same thing we did when we were your age." Arthur stood. "Come on. You'll catch a cold."

I tried to get up, but it felt like I had an extra hundred pounds pressing down on me. Arthur tried to help me, but there was not much strength in his arm.

"So that's why you're such a weakling?"

"What do you mean?"

"You've never been particularly strong. I've always thought it was a little embarrassing for you."

Arthur placed a hand on my lower back and pushed me inside. "It actually requires a certain strength to keep the realm of the dead at bay and move objects by willpower alone." I walked into the living room, picked up the chair that was still lying on the tile floor, and sat at the dining table, where the pictures were spread out.

Arthur looked wistfully at them. With a pale finger, he pushed them around so he could see the ones at the back. He stared at a photo of the woman with the dark, curly hair.

She was wearing the black coat I had found in the barn. In her hands, she held a bouquet of wildflowers, thistles, and twisted branches. She looked gruffly into the camera, but her eyes shone with something. Joy, I think.

"Is that my mother?" I asked hesitantly.

Arthur's eyes shimmered. Could ghosts cry?

"That was taken on our wedding day. I had never seen a more beautiful woman. I still haven't. Apart from you, of course." He tried to laugh, but it came out hollow. "I see a lot of her in you."

I gathered my courage. "Is she dead?"

There was a pause. "No. She's not dead. But she was cut off from us many years ago. She did not leave you willingly."

"What's her name?"

"Thora."

Saying her name seemed to cause Arthur physical pain, so I changed the subject.

"Where are you when you're not with me?"

"By my body, mostly."

I swallowed once.

Arthur continued. "But I can always sense you. Like last night, when you called."

Something struck me. "Are you my clingy spirit?"

Arthur cleared his throat and looked down. It seemed this type of spirit was not entirely accepted among ghosts.

"I latched on to you when you were four, when you arrived at the orphanage. It's the only way I can always sense you. It was a surprise when you suddenly spoke to me." He smiled at the memory. "You have no idea how happy that made me—and how sad."

"Why were you sad?"

"Because your powers are strong. It's not easy, having a gift like yours. And there was no one to guide you. I knew you would have a hard time, so I chose to cling to you to keep an eye on you."

"I've read about clingy spirits. They're addicted to drugs or feelings, and they feed off the person they cling to. Were you a junkie or something when you were alive?"

"I'm addicted to a feeling that I get from you."

"That's the reason for my temper. The aggression. And all the fights. It makes total sense."

Arthur laughed. "No, no. That part of your personality is all you. And maybe your mom, too. She can be pretty . . . Well, I'll tell you some other time."

"So what's the feeling?"

Arthur answered the question with his warm, green eyes. "Guess."

I looked out the window as I struggled with my feelings. "I met a medium yesterday. She sensed you. She said she could drive out clingy spirits."

Arthur's face grew serious. "Ulla. She's nice enough, but she thinks all spirits should cross over. That's what most mediums think."

"What happens if she drives you out?"

There was real anxiety in Arthur's face. "Then she severs the bond between us. Right now, you are functioning as my anchor, along with Odinmont. I am also bound to this place."

"Oh, right. This is actually your house, huh." I reflected. "Is there anything else I should know about you?"

"Um, yes. That time you were attacked by Peter and those two other boys in the woods, I wasn't able to help you."

"Were you there that day?"

"I saw them follow you and hit you, and there was nothing I could do. A father's nightmare. That put a few gears in motion."

"Which resulted in?"

Arthur cleared his throat again. "I decided to upgrade."

"Upgrade what?"

"Myself." Arthur paused uncomfortably before continuing.

"I chose to become a poltergeist, so I can move and touch things. That way I'm better able to help you."

"How have you helped me?"

"How do you think you got ahold of the bat that time Peter attacked you?"

Okey dokey. "So you're a clingy spirit and a poltergeist? Did you know Peter was in the hospital for a month?"

Arthur flashed a crooked smile. "I may be dead, but I'm no angel."

"How many years have you been waiting to use that line?"

"At least ten." Arthur laughed.

I paused for a moment to think. "Elias said that Ben, Rebecca,

Od, and someone from the DSMA had signed a treaty. What's that about?"

Arthur exclaimed with a highly unfatherly curse. "The *secret* treaty isn't too secret if Elias runs around blabbing about it."

"I think it was only to me, and anyway, I didn't understand a word of what he was talking about," I said cautiously.

"Don't make the mistake of believing that you mean anything to Elias, or that you can trust him. Others have done so before you, and it has cost them dearly."

I would think about that comment later. "What does the treaty say?"

"I can't tell you. It would be against the terms."

"Did you sign it?"

Arthur looked up at the ceiling. "Yes and no."

"Either you signed it or you didn't."

Arthur hesitated. "The treaty was signed by your mother, Ben, Rebecca, Od, Niels Villadsen, and some people you don't know."

"So you didn't sign."

Arthur paused before answering. "They signed it with my blood."

I forged ahead with my line of questioning, mostly to forget what he had just said. "Can you talk to Ben and Rebecca?"

Arthurs twisted his mouth into a regretful grimace. "I've had sporadic contact with them over the years, but they don't have the same powers as you and Mathias."

"But they have powers?"

"Like I said before. I don't talk about that kind of thing."

"So it's true what they say: Dead men tell no tales."

Arthur pointed to himself. "Not this one, anyway."

"Can I tell Mathias and Luna what and who you are? I'll tell them it's a secret."

Arthur bowed his head. "You have my permission."

"How did you die?" The words flew out of my mouth.

Arthur's eyes flickered. Then all of Arthur flickered.

I looked at him, terrified, as he went translucent and appeared to gag.

"What's going on?" I shouted.

Arthur sank to his knees, then rolled onto his back in something that looked like an epileptic seizure.

"Arthur," I screamed and bent over him. I had no idea of how to administer first aid to a ghost.

He shook a final time, then vanished with a *pufff*.

I stood alone in my empty living room.

"Arthur? Come back."

All was quiet around me. What had just happened? Had I killed him?

Nice, Anna. Leave it to me to kill my already-dead father.

I took out my phone with shaking hands and pulled up the number.

Elias answered immediately.

"Good morning. How are you feeling today? It was a highly titillating experience having you all to myself last night, in an unconscious and powerless state. Right up until you puked and ruined my suit." He laughed.

"Elias, I don't have time. How do I get in contact with Ulla?"

"Ulla? What do you want with her?"

"Just give me her number. Now!"

"What do I get in return?"

"How about I don't tell anyone that you breached the secret treaty by blabbing about it to me?"

"I didn't sign the treaty, so I'm not bound by it. Wait, how do you suddenly know that it's secret?"

"What do you think my answer's gonna be?"

"Probably that it's none of my business." Someone said something in the background, and Elias's reply was muffled, so I couldn't hear what he said. He came back to the phone. "Okay, you can have this one for free. Next time it'll cost you."

There was once again noise in the background.

A woman's voice answered. "Hello?"

I balked. "Ulla?"

"Yes, who am I speaking with?"

"This is Anna Sakarias. What are you doing with Elias?" I caught myself. "Never mind. I don't need to know."

Ulla's shrill laughter whined in my ear.

"No, no. I'm happily married. I'm here on business matters. What can I do for you? Shall I drive out your clingy spirit?" She sounded hopeful.

I gasped in horror. "No. Absolutely not. I need to ask you something. I don't really know all the unwritten rules for how you're supposed to talk about these things, and I'm a little busy, so I'm just going to ask you outright, okay?"

"Super. I prefer when people—living or dead—get straight to the point."

"If you're talking to a ghost . . ."

"Yes . . . ?" Ulla's voice was questioning.

"And that ghost suddenly becomes transparent, starts to gag and convulse, and, finally, disappears. What's wrong?"

There was a long silence on the other end.

"Hello, are you there?" I asked.

"Yes, I'm here. Are you a medium?"

"No, I'm clairvoyant. I see the past. It seems I can only talk to this one ghost."

"Hmm. Got it. What were you talking to the ghost about?"

Now it was my turn to be silent while I considered how much I should reveal. "We were talking about his past. And then I asked how he died."

I heard an angry puff of air on the other end. "You didn't."

"Is that not allowed?"

"No, you can never ask a ghost about that. Not directly. They may seem almost like normal people, but even the most well-adjusted among them are horribly traumatized. They can easily talk about the fact that they are dead, but not about how the death occurred. Death comes as a shock to most people."

"I can imagine. Did I kill him?"

"No, honey. He's already dead, after all. But he will need some time to recover."

"What happened to him?"

"This is gonna get a little technical, but when a deceased being is confronted with his own death, he feels the death occur again. It feels wholly physical to them, even though they're in spirit form."

"Yikes." *Sorry, Arthur.* "Can I do anything to help him?"

"Let him rest. He'll take up residence in his earthly remains for two or three weeks."

I didn't want to think about the fact that Arthur's corpse was out there somewhere.

"Thanks."

"Don't mention it, my friend. Next time you talk to him, try to convince him to cross over. They aren't meant to stay here. It always ends in a mess."

Not a chance!

"I'll be sure to."

We hung up, and I sat down heavily on the bench. After a brief pause for thought, I stood and rooted through the stack of photographs. I found one where Rebecca, my mother, Ben, and Arthur were standing together. I recognized my mom's slightly surly expression from having seen it on my own face. Arthur wore a wide grin, and Rebecca smiled serenely.

I stuffed the picture in my pocket and hurried out the door.

As I strode quickly across the field to Luna's house with the hood of my rain jacket pulled up around my face, the fog turned to a fine drizzle that landed on my cheeks and nose like droplets from a spray bottle. I turned and looked at Odinmont, which was nearly swallowed in the mist. The house was hardly visible at the top of the hill.

I pounded on the door while studying the serpent knot which, after the events of the past twenty-four hours, suddenly did not seem quite so crazy.

Ben opened the door. The whites of his eyes shone like polished ivory against their dark backdrop.

"Come in," he said in his deep baritone. "Should I call Luna?"

"I'm here to talk to you. Both of you, actually, if Rebecca is here."

Ben separated his broad lips into an unsettling grimace apparently intended as a smile. He showed me into the living room, where Rebecca sat working at the large loom. She stood when she saw me.

"Dearest Anna Stella. Welcome."

"Drop the *dearest Anna*." I walked into the middle of the room, stopped at their dining table, and slammed the photo down on its surface. With a finger, I pushed it toward her.

Ben joined us and looked down at the picture. His face was difficult to read, but Rebecca's eyes filled with tears.

"Your parents." Her voice faded out.

"Tell me," I said curtly. "I'm ready."

"I don't know how to say this." Rebecca wiped her eyes. "Your mother is in a place that she's unable to leave. And your father . . ."

I looked coolly at them. "My father is dead as a doornail. Deceased. Gone. I know."

Rebecca's eyes widened. "How do you know that?"

"You don't need to worry about how I know anything. You just need to explain to me what the hell is going on."

Ben looked at me calmly. "What would you like us to explain?"

"I'll give you a few key phrases. Treaty, impending bloodbath, oh and not to forget, my father's blood used as ink."

They looked at me in silence. Rebecca's blue eyes displayed shock, but Ben was expressionless. Then he spoke.

"That's something we are bound by blood not to divulge."

"By my father's blood?"

"Among others." His voice revealed no emotion.

Rebecca's voice, however, was thin. "More blood will flow if we talk about it."

"Maybe you don't need to talk." I cast my power toward her.

Ben held up his hand, and a force shot out of it. It hit me in the chest like a heat wave and pushed me backward. The air current blew the photo off the table, and I landed on the floor.

"Stay away from my wife," he roared and towered over me.

"What are you?" I asked, nearly breathless.

Like the last time I asked, they did not have time to answer. Luna interrupted us. She had come into the living room.

"What do you mean, *what are they?*" She held out her hand to help me up. "And what are you doing down there?"

I got to my feet and picked up the photo.

"Your dad . . ." I began.

Rebecca looked pleadingly at me. Apparently, there were a few small details they hadn't shared with their daughter.

"Your dad dropped this." I waved the photo. "I was looking for it."

Luna accepted the explanation and looked at the picture.

"Those are your parents. But I've never seen this picture before. Does this mean you want to know about them now?"

"I found it out in the barn. By the way, did you give your mom the notebook . . ."

Luna put her arm around me and swung me around before I could finish my sentence.

"We're super busy," she said and pulled me into the hall. "Later, Mom and Dad."

Ben and Rebecca watched us and leaned, like the first time I saw them, into one another's force field.

"We're busy?" I asked.

"Well, we do have a shift at Frank's."

Shit. I had forgotten all about work.

Luna pulled on her boots. "Frank called and asked us to come earlier. The whole town is celebrating that the murderer was caught and that girls can have red hair and be safe again. There's an event tonight. I saw it online. Did you see it?"

"I'm not on social media," I said tensely.

"Right, but the rest of the world is. And it looks like the rest of the world is planning to go to Frank's tonight, so we better get going."

"Are you okay to go to work?" I asked cautiously.

"It was terrifying," said Luna. "I keep seeing what happened play out in my head." She pulled on a red raincoat with white polka dots. "But I talked to Mathias about it, and it helped."

Outside, she retrieved her rusty cargo bike from the shed.

"Hop in," she said.

Crouched in the box at the front of the bike, I pulled my legs up under my jacket so my pants wouldn't get wet. Luna maneuvered the large bike down the dirt road.

"Anything new since I last saw you?"

"I've completely lost track," I said. "Let me see. Tomorrow, I have to explain to my caseworker that I neither hosted nor participated in an orgy or drug party, and that I still live alone at Odinmont. The police, aside from Hakim, who is essentially just an intern, believe there will be no more killings of red-haired teenage girls, and I had the vision again this morning, so that murder is still on the agenda. And regarding Hakim, he's figured out that I was in the beach house last night. I found out that my father is dead, and that my mother is imprisoned somewhere. Last night I saw Od's aura, and I'm pretty sure that he and Mathias are the same—whatever that happens to be." During this litany, I had held up a finger for each issue. Now I lowered my hand and clenched my fist. "But worst of all, Varnar is coming over for dinner tomorrow."

"I knew the part about your dad," said Luna. "I would have told you, but you said you didn't want to know anything. I'm sorry. How did you find out that he's dead?"

"He told me."

"Who?"

"My dad." I turned halfway around and looked up at her.

Her forehead creased. "Your dad told you that your dad is dead?"

"Yep." I wiped raindrops off my face. "It turns out my friend Arthur is actually my deceased father. My clairvoyant abilities allow me to see and speak to him."

Luna took this surprisingly well. "Well, I told you ghosts are real."

"You don't think it's creepy that I talk to my dead dad?"

She shrugged. "In Asatru, we believe that when you die, you either go to Valhalla, Fólkvangr, or Hel. Sometimes spirits have a reason to stick around in this world. Death is not an ending, but a portal to the next phase."

"Seriously?" I couldn't help but grimace scornfully. "He also said that they've been in contact. Your parents and him."

Luna straightened on the bike seat. "Have they?"

"Have you ever asked them if they secretly dabble in the super-natural?"

"Nah, I think they're pretty normal."

"Luna. Your parents are not normal by any standards."

"Are they not? How are they different from other parents?"

"Around here, normal parents have a trade or work in an office. The dads don't walk around in red leather pants and batik shirts, and the moms don't hang food from trees. And those are just the external things. They also *feel* different."

"You mean their auras?"

"Yes," I said and looked at the rain-slicked road. The rain had subsided, and the gray clouds covering the sky were beginning to thin out. Behind them, I could see glimpses of blue. "They're definitely different. I just don't know how. Arthur wouldn't say anything. Something about not talking about other people's powers behind their backs."

Luna swung onto Bredgade. "I'll just ask them. And I'll also ask them about the snakes on your dress, and how I set the murderer on fire so he couldn't rape me."

Oh right. Minor details.

"Luna," I said. "You can't tell them about that. There's apparently a treaty, which they signed with my father's blood, that says . . ." I stopped. "I actually don't know what it says. But Elias was very insistent that we could not tell your parents, Od, or Niels Villadsen about the Savage. Something about how it would lead to bloodshed."

"What?" said Luna. "What the Hel have they been up to?"

"I tried to ask them." I imitated Ben's deep voice. "We are bound by blood not to speak about it."

I turned and rolled my eyes exaggeratedly.

Luna made a nasal *ha* noise. "That sounds like him."

"Like I said, I've lost track."

Luna breathed as she pedaled. "By the way, what were you saying about Varnar?"

My stomach clenched. "He's coming for dinner tomorrow. We're going to talk."

"Oooohh," said Luna, teasingly. "What are you going to talk about?"

"No idea. I'm totally panicking about having to cook for him."

Luna slammed on the brakes, and I almost flew out of the cargo box.

"Am I understanding correctly that your biggest concern right now is cooking for the guy you're crazy about?"

I pressed my lips together. "Yes."

Luna's teeth flashed in a warm smile. "You're really in love with Varnar, huh?"

I nodded. "But things always go wrong for us. Right now, he's furious at me."

"Yeah, that's what Mathias said. But he wouldn't be showing up all the time if he didn't also have feelings for you."

"That's true. He tends to be nearby when I need him."

"Okay, I'll do it."

"Do what?"

"Make the food, obviously." She set the bike in motion again.

Frank hugged us when we arrived. The bar was already full, and all the staff had been called in to work.

"Boy, am I glad to see you." Deep wrinkles framed his eyes, and relief floated around him like a cloud. I couldn't figure out if it was the prospect of high profits, or because the Savage had been caught. Maybe both.

"You have no idea how busy we are." He smoothed his pomaded hair. "Can I have your friend Mathias's number? I'm hoping he can help bartend. He's worked in a café before, right? And he's over eighteen?"

Luna nodded before I could stop her. "I'll text you his number."

I didn't know if Mathias had ever worked in a café or if that was just a cover story, but he would have to find his own way out of that one.

"Now get to work," said Frank with a mock-serious voice. He winked at us before we scurried off.

I had never been so busy in my life. I chopped, cleaned, and put things in place at breakneck speed. Luna and the other staff members flew in and out of the swinging doors, delivering full trays and orders. Milas and I worked like robots on an assembly line and, miraculously, managed to keep up. In the middle of it all, Frank came in dragging an empty keg.

"Did you get ahold of Mathias?" I asked.

"Yes. He's coming later. Right now, he's helping his mom with some project."

"What are they doing?"

"I don't know, and I don't care. As long as he comes and helps out tonight." He left.

After a few hours, Luna came into the kitchen. "It's happening now."

"What's happening now?"

"You really should get on social media. Then you would know what's going on around you."

"I think I need more than an online profile for that."

Luna grabbed my hand and pulled me through the bar, which was suddenly almost empty. "There are a ton of people outside. Do you have any of that stuff Elias gave you?"

I always had the ampoule full of klinte in my pocket, and I fished it out and dabbed a drop on my fingertip, which I then placed on my tongue. The relief flowed through my body instantly, and I realized just how much I am constantly sensing the past.

Outside, people had positioned themselves along Algade. It took a moment for me to realize the crowd consisted almost exclusively of men. Luna pulled me through the mob, and I jogged after her.

When we turned the corner, I saw what kind of project Mathias and his mom had been working on.

In smaller Danish communities, shared crises tend to result in torchlit processions, and that was what met us when we rounded the corner of Grønnegade. Unity is not to be underestimated, and while people may well point fingers among themselves and judge one another, they will not tolerate an outsider coming in and disturbing the peace. Especially not a homicidal maniac with a penchant for local red-haired girls.

But it was not the hundreds of lit torches glowing in the early dusk that caused my jaw to drop. It was the sight of woman after woman, young and old, big and small, tall and short. Every single one had red hair.

Luna looked out over the many women.

"It was all planned in one day. The ones who were too scared to do it themselves could have their hair colored for free at Mathias's mom's salon."

I saw a small, pretty woman flitting about with curls dyed orange for the occasion. Her eyes resembled Mathias's, and she smoothed, combed, inserted bobby pins, and spoke to people left and right.

Luna continued. "Some have wigs on, but all have red hair. It's in memory of the murdered girls and a sign that the killer's project was unsuccessful."

I saw that several were holding pictures of the girls.

Mathias joined us.

"Hey, Anna. Isn't it awesome?"

"Yeah, it's impressive." I didn't usually harbor particularly warm feelings for my fellow citizens, but something about this shared gesture touched me.

"I brought something for you." Mathias took my hand and pulled me over to a makeshift hairdressing station. He opened a box.

"No, no. I don't want to." I backed away, but he tugged me back.

"Come on, be part of the group for once." He pulled out a chair and signaled for me to sit down.

"Nope." I wanted to flee but was hit in the back of the neck with a wave of persuasion from Luna. I turned around and looked at her, livid. "Stop doing that."

She grinned cheekily as I sat, powerless, and let Mathias put the red wig in place.

When he was done, Luna looked appraisingly at me.

"Red hair really suits you. It's a lot nicer than the black."

Mathias took her hand. "I have to run over to the men now. This part is just for women."

Someone shoved a torch in my hand, and off we went.

I don't think it had ever been so quiet on Algade as when the hundreds of red-haired women marched with their torches. Even on klinte, I could sense that the air was full of emotions. The women's faces were strong in the glow of the torches, and along the road, I saw several people I knew. Little Mads and Principal Holten watched on reverently; even Suzuki and Niller from my class had appropriately serious expressions on their faces. At the very back stood Hakim. He looked worried when he met my gaze.

We ended at the square in front of Frank's, where a small podium had been set up. The mayor gave a speech, and she, too, had dyed her normally brown hair red.

Someone stood right behind me and wrapped her arms around my waist.

"What are you doing here?" asked a woman's voice in my ear. It was both affectionate and desperate.

I turned around, and the woman's arms remained at my waist. Her face was right up close to mine, and I was staring straight into a pair of brown eyes that looked at me with a wild passion. For a second, I thought she was going to kiss me. I pushed her away.

"Aella, what the hell are you doing? Why are you groping me?"

A torrent of emotions flew across Aella's face, and if I hadn't taken klinte, I would have been able to feel them. As it was, I was blank.

She let go and took a step back.

"I thought you were someone else." She twirled a strand of my wig's red hair between her fingers.

I pushed her hand away. She retreated and disappeared into the crowd.

How weird! I hurried back to the kitchen and Milas.

Milas smiled one of his rare smiles when he spotted me.

"Anna," he said in his thick accent. "You look beautiful with the red hair. It makes me happy to see that girls can be safe again. You are too young to fear for your lives."

I took the wig off. It creeped me out to see the red hair cascading over my shoulders.

We went back to being super busy for a few hours. The bar was packed, and Frank had hired a band that played so loudly the floor shook and the windows rattled. Mathias stood behind the bar together with Frank and Lars. One of the times I came out of the kitchen, I noticed Mathias's end was by far the most popular.

I signaled that I wanted to talk to him. He followed me into the back alley, where I gave him a short briefing.

His blue eyes shone faintly. "I can see ghosts?"

"Apparently."

"Wow." Mathias tousled his thick honey-colored hair. "And Arthur—I mean, your dad—says he thinks I'm the same as that guy Od?"

"No, I think you're the same as Od. But you should ask him directly."

Mathias nodded. "Will you come with me to see him?"

"Of course."

When we closed the kitchen, I went into the bar. The klinte made it bearable for me, and I leaned against the bar and listened to the band.

People were dancing on the little dance floor. Frank was throwing Luna around in a wild dance, and I admired how agile he was—in spite of his age. Mathias appeared at my side, took my hand, and pulled me toward the dance floor.

"No, no." I shook my head frantically. I had never danced in public before.

"Come on, Anna," he coaxed. "It's okay to have fun."

With his superhuman strength, he dragged me after him, and I let myself give in to the music. When Luna saw us, she screamed happily and threw an arm around each of us. Frank beamed at us and did an Elvis dance back to the bar. Luna, Mathias, and I jumped around in front of the stage. I was dancing and singing with friends for the first time in my life. It was a night that inspired joy and optimism.

Too bad it would be the last time we felt like that for a very long time.

CHAPTER 19

Greta clicked the mouse while using her free hand to push up her glasses. I was sitting on the edge of my seat in a cold sweat, awaiting the verdict. She swung around on her desk chair and looked at me with her beady eyes.

"I have given a lot of thought to what I saw at your house yesterday." The memory of Varnar's abs and Mathias wearing next to nothing flickered in Greta's past.

Yes, it seems you've thought a whole lot about it.

"And I have come to the conclusion," she gave a dramatic pause as I held my breath, "that it is hard for me to justify allowing you to live alone in the house any longer."

"It's not what it looked like." This came out like a bark.

Greta smiled cloyingly. "What is it, then? Explain it to me. I want to hear your side of the story."

I tried desperately to come up with an explanation that didn't sound too far-fetched. "My friends spent the night. But that was the only time they ever did that."

"Why did they spend the night?"

"We had been to a party." True.

Greta dug around in her bag and pulled out a newspaper. She flipped through it and found a headline. MURDER SUSPECT FOUND NEAR HIGH-PROFILE EQUINOX BALL. A photograph showed Hakim next to a gurney. The person lying on it was covered up, but it was clearly the Savage. Beneath it was a smaller photo of Od and me. *Equinox ball at The Boatman in North Jutland,* read the caption.

"A party? You were at one of the largest events of the year, and you were there with the host, who, as far as I know, is over thirty years old."

Plus a few hundred.

"It wasn't like that. It wasn't a date."

"Then what was it?"

"A trade," I blurted out. *Oops.* Greta's thin eyebrows flew upward, and I held up my hands in front of me. "Not that kind of trade. He knows my parents. And Ben and Rebecca."

"They apprehended a murderer right near where you were."

"But that has nothing to do with me." *At least not as far as you know.*

"The two other men I met at your house. How do you know them?"

"Mathias is my friend Luna's boyfriend. And the other is my neighbor."

"Why was your neighbor in your bed?"

That's actually none of your business, Greta!

"There was no room anywhere else," I said.

Greta did not ask any more about Varnar. "How well do you know Mathias Jarl Hedskov?"

"He's one of my close friends."

"Do you know that he was charged with shooting someone?"

"He was acquitted," I said defensively.

"Mhmm." Greta typed something before continuing. "Your friend Luna Sekibo mentioned someone called Elias, who had given you something. I don't suppose she was talking about drugs?"

Yes, in fact, mysterious, custom-made drugs.

"No, of course not. He gave us some homemade black-currant schnapps."

"Schnapps." A slight creasing of her forehead revealed that Greta didn't believe a word I said. "Was that why you threw up?"

I nodded silently.

316

"Who is this Elias?"

"He works for Od Dinesen."

"And what is your relationship to him?"

"I have no relationship to him. I think he's highly irritating."
That was true, at least.

"What about the police? In addition to meeting Hakim Murr at
your house, they also informed me that they had questioned you."

"They've questioned tons of people."

"They said that you weren't exactly helpful."

"Am I ever?"

Greta flashed a brief hint of a smile and continued her blitzkrieg
of questions. "Why did Luna have blood on her dress?"

"We fell." I shrugged.

"All of you?"

"Uh . . . yes." Even I knew I wasn't particularly convincing.

"How much does it mean to you to live in that house?"

"Everything. It means everything to me."

"Then you'll need to make more of an effort."

"I am making an effort. I have a job. I go to school. A couple of
weeks ago, I got an A on an assignment. I've made friends. Maybe
not exactly the friends you would prefer, but I do have friends."

I was ready to get on my knees and beg, but it wasn't necessary.
Greta's expression softened.

"You have one more chance."

I exhaled with relief. "Thank you."

"But if you can't make it work, we will put your house up for sale.
We've already been contacted by a potential buyer who is ready to
buy the house on a day's notice."

I stared at her, shocked. "You can't do that. I come of age in
three months. Then I can do whatever I want with the house."

"Until then, we may determine that it's most appropriate to sell.
It's for your own good. Right now, we're trying to reduce the number of socially vulnerable individuals in the municipality."

"But I'm not socially vulnerable."

Greta pushed her glasses up the bridge of her nose. Behind the lenses, her eyes were kind. "I just want you to stay on track. My goal is to get you on the right path before you have to stand on your own two feet. Whatever it takes."

Greta held the cards, so I simply nodded.

"There won't be any problems with me."

I trudged from Ravensted Social Center down to Frank's, where I found Mathias in front of the bar and Luna behind it. Mathias bit into a burger and waved happily to me. Pouting, I clambered up onto a barstool.

"What's up with you?" asked Luna.

I recounted my conversation with Greta.

"But they can't do that. It's your house."

"They've always gone above my head to do all kinds of things. So I'm sure they can also sell my house." I realized something. "Arthur is bound to Odinmont. What if someone buys the house and tears it down?"

"Don't worry." Mathias patted me on the shoulder. "Why would that happen?"

I shook him off. "Greta dug around in your past and came to the worst conclusions."

"Shit. I had hoped no one in town would find out about that."

I stood. "I'm heading back out. I just needed to pick up my bike."

Mathias stood as well. "I'll help you. You can't pull it with that front wheel."

"Anna, I'm coming over around five," said Luna.

"Why is Luna going over to your place?" Mathias asked when we stood out back. He lifted my smashed bike as easily as if it were made of Styrofoam.

I admitted, embarrassed, that she was cooking for me.

Mathias lit up with a smile. "How exciting."

We walked down to Ravensted's only bike shop, Bikes by Timmy. I walked in while Mathias carried the bike to the delivery area at the back of the shop. Timmy himself was standing behind the counter, working on a bike that was suspended from the ceiling on chains. He was covered in tattoos, from his bald head to his wrists, and the town was awash with rumors of his sordid past.

"What can I do for you?"

"There's a red men's racing bike out back. The front wheel is crumpled up, and the back tire is slashed, so it needs a new tire and tube."

Timmy nodded and took notes.

"Do you know who did it?" He was still looking down at the paper, but there were angry furrows across his bald head.

I smiled that this man clearly cared more about bikes than people. "I don't know who it was."

Mathias walked into the shop, and I saw a small flash of recognition in Timmy's aura. It was replaced by something else. Anticipation? *Strange.*

Mathias did not appear to recognize Timmy, so I waved it away. I couldn't keep adding unsolved mysteries to the list.

"You can pick it up on Wednesday," Timmy said and handed me a slip of paper.

Outside, Mathias and I parted ways. He had promised Frank to work a shift that evening.

"Are we coworkers now?" I asked.

"Yeah, Frank hired me. That way I can also work with Luna."

"Wow, you've really got it bad."

Mathias stroked a hand over his attractive face. "I've never felt this way before."

"Have you had other girlfriends?" A small glimpse of his past showed me that he had.

"I wish I hadn't. I would really like it if she were the first. You know what I mean."

"No, I don't know. I don't have a lot of experience in that area."

"Maybe you will soon." He wiggled his eyebrows.

"I don't think that's why Varnar is coming over. I'm pretty sure he's not interested in me in that way."

"I have a really hard time imagining that," said Mathias with a you-are-way-prettier-than-you-think-you-are look.

"It's not low self-esteem. I just don't think he thinks along those lines, period."

"All men think along those lines," Mathias said, and pulled me into a hug that totally caught me off guard.

I let him do it, and I even returned his embrace.

"Good luck tonight," he whispered in my ear. "I wish you the best." He held me at arm's length. "But I really hope he's deserving of you. Or else he'll have to answer to me."

I wanted to say that I was the one who would have to make myself deserving of Varnar. That he would probably tell me I could forget all hope of anything ever happening between us.

"Thanks, Mathias," was all I whispered before I turned around and ran toward Odinmont.

At five o'clock, Luna arrived with a bag that she unpacked on my kitchen table.

I studied the contents. "Are you sure you can put lavender and roses in food?"

"Yes, of course," she said. "They go amazingly well with apple leaves and beet juice." She dug around in my cabinets and pulled out the large cast-iron pot as well as a cutting board and several spoons and knives. From her pocket, she fished out a crumpled paper.

"What's that?"

"The recipe. This dish calls for some really special ingredients, but fortunately my mom has most of them. She's always running around in the woods or on the moors, gathering herbs and roots."

"What are we having?"

Luna looked over her shoulder in an explosion of red curls.

"Loooove soup." She giggled. "The recipe was in my mom's notebook, the one you found in your barn."

I rolled my eyes. "Well, I won't be telling Varnar that that's what it's called."

"Do you want to help chop and slice?"

"Sure. I'm an expert at splitting things apart." I took a sharp knife and began to chop what Luna placed in front of me.

I quickly amassed a pile of finely diced fruits, vegetables, and fresh herbs, half of which I did not recognize.

At the stove, Luna rubbed her hands together and shook them three times in a row.

I felt a little crackling puff of air from her aura. "What are you doing?"

"This is what my mom always does when she cooks." She mumbled something.

"What?"

"Shhh. I'm asking the gods to bless this dish." She continued whispering, and I didn't involve myself further. She began to fry the ingredients in the pot, and when everything had been added, she stirred it. First three times in one direction, then three times in the other. "Take the clams and put them in a bowl."

I did as she said. Then she plopped them into the pot.

"Open their hearts," she said, and once again her aura crackled.

"What are you saying?"

"Clams have heart-shaped shells," she said. "They need to be open. You shouldn't eat the ones that don't open."

"Okay." I glanced at my phone. It was almost six.

Luna declared the food ready and gave me a hug before dashing out.

Soon after, Varnar knocked on the door.

321

I stiffened and, for several seconds, was unable to move. Then I managed to put one foot in front of the other.

Varnar's dark hair lay unruly around his face and framed it in the way that almost always took my breath away. He did not look angry anymore, thank God, but he was very serious. His scent hit me when he walked into the foyer.

I had no words, so I just walked into the living room and let him follow me. A strange nervousness swirled around him, and he, too, was silent. He studied the spear on the wall.

"Where did you get that?" was his opening line.

"It was hanging there when I moved in. It must have belonged to my parents."

He said nothing more as I set the food on the table. We sat down, and I poured two glasses of mead.

Varnar went to take the first bite but set the spoon back down. "There's something I need to tell you now. Before I lose the nerve."

My heart flew up into my throat and felt like it sat on top of my vocal cords, rendering me momentarily mute.

He hesitated.

"I shouldn't have gotten mad at you yesterday." He ran his index finger around the curve of the spoon. "The reason I got so angry was that I can't let anything happen to you." He raised his eyes and looked directly into mine. "You aren't supposed to save me." He lowered his voice to a whisper. "It's me who is supposed to look out for you."

"You did, though. The Savage was about to stab me, but you kicked his arm away. And there was also that time with Peter and his friends." I tried to smile, but it felt like a stiff grimace. "You look out for me, and I look out for you."

"No," Varnar leaned forward and placed his hand on mine. The warmth shot up through my arm, and I sat stock-still with eyes wide. "You can never defend me again. The two of us do not have an equal relationship."

I swallowed back the feeling of scorn. "To be completely honest, I have no idea what you're talking about. And you don't get to decide what I can and cannot do."

Varnar pulled back his hand. "You are very stubborn."

"Thanks. You, too."

A hint of a smile managed to tilt one corner of his mouth slightly upward, until he forced it back down and furrowed his brows again.

"Was there anything else you came here tonight to tell me?" I asked pointedly.

Varnar picked up his spoon and once again stirred it around in the soup, clearly to buy time.

"Yes." He paused for an unbearably long time. "I came to tell you that it's not a coincidence I'm always near you."

My stomach leapt. He lifted the spoon to his lips, as if to gain more time, and tasted the food.

"It's because . . ." He interrupted himself. "What kind of soup is this?"

"Uh. Clam soup." I refused to say the name Luna had used for it.

Varnar tried to speak again.

"I'm always near you because . . ." He trailed off and clenched his fist around the spoon. For a moment I thought he was going to bend it. "Because . . ." The words got stuck in his throat. He breathed heavily, as if he were overheated. "Because . . ."

"Because what?" I asked.

Suddenly, he lifted his face and looked at me, like he had looked at me in my dream.

"I think about you all the time."

This was so unexpected, I just stared at him without responding.

"From the time I wake up until I go to bed. Even when I'm asleep. I dream about you."

I was finding it difficult to speak, so I nodded imperceptibly.

"Me too," I said hoarsely.

Varnar let go of the spoon, and it landed with a clatter on the floor. He grabbed the back of my chair and turned it around roughly.

I suppressed a gasp when the legs of the chair squealed against the tile floor. Whatever I had expected of the evening, never in my wildest dreams—*okay*, so maybe in my very wildest dreams— had I thought this would happen.

"Varnar. Are you okay?" I asked cautiously.

He knelt in front of me, took my hand, and laid it against his cheek.

"Yes. For the first time in years. It feels so right to be with you."

Tentatively, I stroked my free hand across his other cheek. He took this as a signal, and in one gliding motion, he leaned forward and pressed his lips against mine. His strong hands grasped my shoulders, and he lifted us both up as he kissed me with intense desperation.

Hundreds of comets exploded inside me. On top of my own, Varnar's emotions shot into me like a shock wave through his hands and lips. It couldn't be compared to the only thing I had to compare it with: Elias. Kissing Elias had been nice, but it had not felt like I was surrounded by soft electricity.

Varnar pushed me toward the table and leaned us over it. Faintly, I heard bowls and glasses toppling beneath us. The bottle of mead smashed on the floor, but I barely noticed it. I felt only Varnar's mouth against mine and his body over me. I let my fingers glide through his hair, like I had been dreaming of doing for so long. It was even softer than I had imagined.

His hands were on my waist and my back underneath my shirt and ran across my bare skin.

"I have wanted this for so long," he whispered, his mouth against my neck.

I pulled back slightly and looked at him. The words were so much like the ones in the dream, it was almost eerie. I saw that his eyes were closed before he kissed me again. Then I forgot all about the dream and everything else.

We fell into something that felt like both a split second and an eternity.

I sat on the edge of the table with my legs wrapped around his waist and my arms around his neck. He lifted me and walked toward the hall, our lips never parting.

Somehow, with overturned furniture and other smashed items in our wake, we made our way up the stairs and ended up in my bed. Me on my back and him over me. His hair brushed the tops of my cheekbones, creating a little space where our faces were right up against one another.

His shirt was gone—had I taken it off? I let my fingers glide across his back, which felt like iron wrapped in silk.

His finger ran across the long white scar down my breastbone. "Where did that come from?"

"I don't know."

He kissed his way from the top of the scar down to just above my navel. Then he turned his head and laid his cheek against my stomach. His dark hair lay in a soft fan across my torso.

"You are so gorgeous," he said.

"You don't think I'm ugly?" The words were out of my mouth before I could stop them.

Varnar rested his chin in the hollow at my navel and looked up at me in a way that made a heat wave sweep over me.

"Nothing about you is ugly."

"You said I was." It was impossible for me to keep the wounded edge out of my voice.

Varnar furrowed his brows. "I never said you were ugly. I don't say anything I don't mean. I would rather not say anything."

"But you said it that time . . ." I didn't get to finish my sentence before he stroked a hand along my side, and I felt a delightful shiver.

"You are beautiful. I've thought so from the start. And I will always think so." He moved and his face was once again in front of mine. He held himself up on outstretched arms above me. Then he lowered himself slowly and kissed me again.

The feeling of his warm body against mine and his exploring hands was new and exciting. I felt everything twice over, as the same impulses were also flowing from him.

"Have you ever . . . ?" he whispered. He didn't finish the question.

"No. Have you?"

"No," he said and looked at me kindly. "If you don't want to, I understand."

In reply, I pulled him close to me.

Although I had imagined myself and Varnar together many times, I still was not prepared. I heard myself gasp at the same time as Varnar made a noise I will keep in my heart until the day I die.

He was everywhere. He hovered over me, he was inside me, and his scent surrounded me.

Eventually, we lay close together, and his feeling of pure joy descended over me like tiny snowflakes and blended with my own. He rested his cheek against my chest as I stroked his hair with a languid hand. His hot breath tickled my skin, and he held me tight as though he were afraid I would disappear.

"I feel completely different now. This feels so right," he mumbled. He slowly slipped into sleep and his body relaxed.

For a long time, I simply lay there and looked at him in the moonlight that fell in through my sloping window. I caressed his hair and back, and I practically drank in his scent. Again and again, my fingers traced over the burn marks on his arm, and I tried to harvest every detail of the moment. Eventually, I could not fight off my tiredness any longer.

When I awoke, I was alone in the bed. I stretched contentedly and, for once, allowed myself to be happy. I rolled over and laid my hand in the spot where Varnar had slept.

There was a fresh, angry imprint in the mattress.

With a furrowed brow, I pressed both hands to the sheet, but quickly pulled them back. A zap of fiery indignation shot up into me. Varnar had left my bed in a rage.

With bare feet and frightened suspicions, I went downstairs.

Varnar was in the kitchen. I could sense it all the way from the hall. And his emotions were a turmoil of anger and bewilderment.

I hesitated before I entered.

A chaos of shards and broken glass and bowls awaited me. A floor lamp had been toppled over, and I righted it carefully as I slipped in.

Varnar stood at my stove, looking into the iron pot. He cautiously lifted the ladle and sniffed it. When he noticed me behind him, he turned and looked at me with so much hatred that I took a step backward.

"What did you do?" he shouted.

Completely disoriented, I looked at him. "What do you mean?"

He pointed the ladle at me, and I focused on it, uncomprehending.

"Magic," he said. "You performed witchcraft on me."

I laughed incredulously. "What on earth are you talking about?"

Varnar's facial expression quickly wiped the smile off my face.

"It's wrong, not to mention illegal, to use witchcraft on someone without their knowledge."

"Witchcraft? Magic? Those things don't exist."

"Then how do you explain this?" He waved his arms around my mess of a living room.

"Explain what?"

In three large strides, he was in front of me and held my arms in a painful grip.

"You bewitched me yesterday," he hissed. "The food we ate was made with magic."

"I can't even cook," I said in a thin voice. "It wasn't me."

He let go of me and I nearly collapsed on the floor. "Then who was it?"

"Luna," I said. "But I don't think she knows anything about . . ."

I didn't manage to say more before Varnar grabbed my wrist and pulled me out the door. He jogged across the field toward Luna's house with me in tow.

"Varnar, I don't have any shoes on," I protested.

He ignored me and pressed onward. I dug my heels into the black soil.

"Stop," I shouted, as loudly as I could.

Finally, he stopped.

I exhaled. "What is it you think happened?"

"The food we ate was bewitched," he explained with his back to me. "That was why we . . ." He searched for the words. "Did what we did."

From his grip on my wrist, I sensed a strong emotion. Relief? *Shit!* He was relieved that he wasn't personally responsible for what had happened.

"I'm sorry I accused you," he said. "You were the victim of an injustice just as much as I was. Neither of us is to blame for what happened last night."

I neglected to mention that my bowl still sat untouched on the dining table back at Odinmont, but my cheeks burned at the thought.

"I will hold the witch accountable for this."

He dragged me off again.

In front of Ben and Rebecca's house, Varnar bellowed: "Luna Sekibo. Come out here."

It didn't take long before Luna appeared in the doorway. She looked at us, confused. Varnar spitting mad and me shivering in the cold with bare feet, wearing thin leggings and a tiny camisole. Only now did I realize that it was windy and drizzling.

"What's going on?" she asked.

"Own up to your actions, sorceress," Varnar shouted dramatically.

Luna laughed, surprised. "Sorceress?"

He pointed an accusatory finger at Luna. "You bewitched us."

Her smile froze. "It worked?"

I glared at her. "Did you know what you were doing?"

She shook her head. "Not really. I thought it might do something. But definitely not anything crazy. It was mostly for fun. What happened last night?"

I looked away, embarrassed, but Varnar took a step forward. "For fun. For fun! Do you think the misfortune of others is fun? You've done irreparable damage."

Each of his words hit me like a punch. Luna looked from me to him. Her sympathy almost stung more than Varnar's angry words. She had tears in her eyes.

"I just found the recipe in my mom's book. I didn't know what it would do. Maybe I had an idea, but I thought it was what you wanted. That you just needed a little nudge."

"Absolutely not," said Varnar. "It's not at all like that between us."

I looked down at my bare, muddy toes.

Varnar continued. "And it wasn't the recipe that did it. Not on its own, anyway. It was you. What you can do."

"What can I do?"

"Don't you know? You must at least suspect that you would have strong powers, with your parents being what they are."

"Aid workers?" Luna looked completely confused.

Varnar moved his gaze back and forth between us. "You guys really have no idea, do you? Has no one explained anything to you?"

"What?" said Luna and I simultaneously.

Varnar put his head in his hands and spun in a circle. I got the feeling that he didn't get freaked out very often, but when it happened, he was a total mess.

"It's not fair to keep you in the dark, but I'm not the one who should be telling you about these things," he said.

God, I hated this rule.

"Whatever I did, I'm sorry. It wasn't my intention," said Luna.

He nodded solemnly.

"I believe you." He did not look at me. "Anna. We will have to learn to live with what happened last night. We can't undo it, no matter how wrong it was."

I closed my eyes, wishing lightning would strike me and put an end to my suffering. When I opened them again, Varnar was gone.

Luna met my eyes, and I felt my lower lip twist downward. Before I could stop the tears, Luna's arms were around me and I was sobbing into her shoulder.

"Shhh," she said. "Come on. Let's get you inside."

"Where are your parents?" I sniffled.

"My dad drove to Jagd. He needed to talk to Od. My mom is out foraging." She pulled me inside and up to her room. She tossed me a towel and dug around in her closet. "Here. It's brown. It's the darkest item of clothing I have."

I dried my hair and eyes with the towel before changing into the jumpsuit she had pulled out.

"Wow. It looks amazing on you." Luna's voice trailed off when she saw my face. I had so little desire to talk about clothes right now. "What happened last night?"

"I don't know. He came over, and he tasted the soup, just a spoonful, and suddenly he kissed me. And then . . ." I couldn't make myself put it more concretely. "It was crazy," I said instead. I sat on her mattress.

Luna looked at me cautiously. "Were you together? Like, *together together*?"

Despite the hopeless situation, I couldn't help but smile. "Yeah."

"How was it?"

I shook my head slightly.

"Incredible." Then I bit my lip. "Too bad Varnar didn't feel the same way."

"Did he say he didn't think it was incredible?"

"No, he said it was wrong. But that's pretty much the same thing."

"Hey, no it's not. Maybe there's something wrong with him."

"I think we can both agree that there is." I threw myself back onto her gaudy pillows and blankets. "I just have to accept that he doesn't feel the same way about me that I feel about him, and that it took magic to get him into bed with me."

I could feel the tears gathering again.

At that moment, the outer door slammed.

"Mom," yelled Luna. "Can you come up here?"

Rebecca stuck her head in. She had on a long blue cloak, and her silver-white hair was damp. Her feet were, as always, bare.

"What were you foraging for?" asked Luna.

"Hawthorn and willow. It is the first Tuesday after the equinox, you know, and they have to be collected at dawn," she said, as if this made perfect sense.

Luna hesitated slightly. "Mom, yesterday I cooked from a recipe in one of your books."

Rebecca nodded with an absent-minded smile.

"Anna and one of her friends ate it. And something happened."

"What happened? Did you get sick?" Rebecca asked me.

"Not exactly."

"Which recipe was it, Luna?"

Luna dug around in the piles of fabric and drawings on her desk. She found the notebook and held a page up for her mother, who studied it.

"This one."

A very strange look spread across Rebecca's face as she took the book out of Luna's hands.

"Where did you get this?"

"Anna found it in her barn."

Rebecca blushed profoundly. It created a stark contrast to her fair hair. She looked at me with true fear.

"Your mother is going to kill me," she said, nearly breathless. "You . . . ?"

I nodded, pulled my knees up to my face, and buried my head in my arms, more embarrassed than I had ever been before.

"Mom, I think you're gonna have to explain some things to me," said Luna.

"When your father gets home. We'll explain everything then. I need to talk to Anna alone first." Luna protested, but Rebecca held up a hand. "Luna, honey. Go put some water on to boil. Anna needs a cup of tea."

Luna pouted but did as she was told.

Rebecca closed the door behind her. She sat next to me on the mattress. I kept my arms over my head and my forehead against my knees. She laid a warm hand on my back. Her electric energy tickled me.

"Anna, your mom isn't here to talk with you about this." She paused. "When you spent the night with your friend . . ." She took a deep breath before continuing. "Did you use protection?"

I looked up. I hadn't even considered that.

"No," I said. "We didn't think that far."

"I can imagine. It wouldn't be the first time someone forgot it while under the influence of love magic." A memory flickered from her, but it was quickly packed away again, and I wasn't able to make it out.

"Love magic?"

"Yes. I made that recipe many years ago to help a couple get together. Two people who were destined for each other but who

332

needed a little help." She sighed. "This is my responsibility. I have a drink you can take. Then you at least won't have to worry about the fact that you were unprotected."

"Is it, like, a magic morning-after pill?"

"You could say that. If you drink it, you're safe for a year, and it also has a couple days' retroactive effect. I'm assuming you don't want a baby right now."

I shook my head forcefully. Not that I thought protection would be necessary for the foreseeable future, given my luck with love. I thought for a moment.

"The things you can do—is it like what Elias makes?"

Rebecca studied me critically. "What do you know about what Elias makes?"

"Not a lot," I lied, and looked down. "I just know he makes potions."

"No," said Rebecca. "That's not the same as what I can do. My husband and I were both born with our powers."

"What powers?"

She sat for a while without saying anything.

"We're witches," she said finally.

"Witches?" I could feel a smirk spreading across my lips. "As in new-age-Wicca-herbal-tea-making-tree-hugging witches?"

Rebecca raised her hand and wiggled her fingers up and down. A stack of papers lifted several feet up from Luna's desk. She pulled her arm toward herself, and the pile floated slowly toward us. She sat it down in front of us.

"No," she said. "We're spell-casting-white-magic-practicing witches."

A bunch of pieces clicked into place regarding Luna and her mysterious parents.

"Do you fly on broomsticks?" I couldn't help myself.

"If the weather's right for it." Rebecca's facial expression did not change in the slightest.

I didn't know if she was messing with me, and I moved on to the important part.

"Why didn't you tell Luna? She has some pretty crazy abilities herself."

"Luna has a potentially powerful mix of magic in her. We didn't know how the combination of Scandinavian and African magic would manifest itself. Maybe the two would cancel each other out, so there was no reason to put her in danger by telling her about it. If she turned out to have powers, we would cross that bridge when we got to it."

"Well fasten your seat belts and get ready to cross that bridge really damn quick," I said. "Because I've already seen her do some pretty wild things. And why would knowing about it put her in danger?"

"You've probably figured out that some things happened before you were born. Those events complicated everything."

"Was one of those complications the death of my father?" A hardness resounded in my voice.

"He was my best friend, Anna." Sadness flitted across Rebecca's face. "Not a day goes by that I don't miss him. You have no idea how amazing he was."

"I have some idea," I mumbled.

"We've been on the run all these years. We thought it was safest for Luna not to know too much about the past. We moved every time someone tracked us down, and we couldn't come back to Denmark. It was simply too dangerous."

"And it's not dangerous now?"

"It's more dangerous than ever. But we couldn't leave you in the lurch."

"Who is tracking you down? And what do you mean by *leave me in the lurch?*"

Rebecca rubbed her forehead. "I'll have to talk to Ben before I tell you more. This is rooted in political circumstances, which he has a better understanding of."

"Political circumstances?"

Rebecca held up a slim white hand. "I won't say any more now. Would you please wait to talk to Luna about this until we have spoken with her?"

"Of course." I added the question of danger and flight to the long list of mysteries in my life. "What time is it?"

"About eight."

"*Ugh*. Our classes start at nine."

"You can make it. Come downstairs and have some breakfast. Then you and Luna can go to school together."

"I don't have any shoes," I said pitifully.

"How did you get here without shoes on?" She waved a hand. "It doesn't matter. I actually have some old ones of your mom's. Do you wear size seven-and-a-half?"

"Mhmm."

She smiled her angelic smile. "Then everything will be just fine."

I was in total disagreement with this statement.

Downstairs, Luna had boiled water. Rebecca stood in front of the pot. She rubbed her hands and shook them three times, like I had seen Luna do the day before. Then she sprinkled various herbs into the water while she mumbled to herself. I recognized the crackling puff from her aura. She grated a root into the brew and stirred it—first three times in one direction, then three times in the other.

I forced the tea down. It tasted strong, and a bit like hay.

Rebecca found a pair of high-heeled lace-up boots. I put them on, and they fit. A little glimpse of the past shot up into me from them.

My mom and Arthur were running away from Ravensted High School at night. I felt adrenaline and anger. Then I smelled something animal. Sheep or goat.

"They look good with the jumpsuit," Luna said, yanking me back to the present. "It's nice to see you in something other than black."

I was completely indifferent. My appearance was the last thing I was thinking about right now. She pulled a comb through my messy hair, braided a lock of it, and stuck some bobby pins in it. Then she handed me a long pink wool cardigan.

I pulled it on with a groan. I guess I wasn't *completely* indifferent.

In French class, we were met by an eager Mathias.

"How did it go?" he whispered to me behind Luna's back, while our teacher wrote verbs on the whiteboard.

I looked down at the desk without responding. Luna whispered something in his ear. He looked at me over her shoulder.

"No, you're kidding me," I heard him say.

I tried to ignore them. When class was over, I got up and left the room without waiting for them.

Unfortunately for my already dismal mood, Peter whispered to me in passing.

"I saw you got a lift with Looney Tunes this morning. Is your bike broken?" He smiled maliciously.

In the hall I saw Varnar, who had changed into his dark-green work pants and tight black T-shirt. I cast my gaze downward when we passed each other. Varnar turned his head away, but his sense of guilt hit me like a cold crosswind.

Our next class was history. Margit fingered her large amber pendant.

"Today we're talking about the transition to Christianity in Denmark. It was King Harald Bluetooth who, in the year 965, converted the Danes to Christianity, which he did for political reasons, as most of Europe had become Christian by then. After the shift, the old gods were viewed as evil spirits, and people had to get used to praying to Jesus and God instead of the Norse gods. Those who still followed the old faith were considered heathens and prosecuted. At the time, that meant they lost their lives in a variety of horrific ways."

I was only half listening. I couldn't see how events that took place over a thousand years ago could mean anything at all for me.

The secretary, Mrs. Larsen, opened the door and stuck her head in.

"There's someone here who wants to speak with Anna Sakarias," she said.

Everyone looked at me.

"Who?" I asked resignedly.

Mrs. Larsen opened the door a little wider and revealed Hakim in his police uniform behind her. A murmur went through the class. I closed my eyes and breathed in and out a few times before standing up.

Outside the door, Hakim said to Mrs. Larsen: "Thanks. I'll take it from here."

When Mrs. Larsen left us, she looked over her shoulder a couple times.

"Thanks a lot. My reputation needed a little more tarnishing. Being taken away by the police in the middle of class was just the ticket."

Hakim looked at the door to the classroom.

"I hadn't considered that. I didn't think they would let me pull you out of class if I was in street clothes."

I saw a little flash of Hakim, in normal clothes, being looked at with suspicion by a woman. I was well aware of how the world could be mistrustful of someone because of their appearance. The difference was that I could wash off my makeup and change my clothes. I got the sense that Hakim wore his uniform as often as he could, and I understood why.

"And it couldn't wait?" I asked.

"No," he said quickly. I realized then that he had dark circles under his eyes, and that his short black hair was sticking up in all directions. "I need to speak with you. Now."

"Okay." I led the way. "We can sit in The Island."

"You're a bit of a chameleon, aren't you?" he said as we walked down Brown Hall.

"What do you mean?"

"The first couple times I saw you, you were covered in black makeup and had torn clothes on. Then you were at a party with the rich and famous in a designer dress, and the day after you looked like a crackhead. Now you look like something from a fashion magazine."

I looked down at myself. "My friend Luna is just really good at sewing. I borrowed these clothes from her. And I don't usually wear heels."

I didn't say anything more about it. My appearance couldn't possibly be relevant to the police. We reached The Island and sat on the red sofa.

"What is it that's so important?"

Hakim took off his jacket. His pumped-up chest was stuffed into a white T-shirt, and a piece of paper had been tucked into the pocket over his bulging left pectoral muscle. A broad tattoo covered his upper arm, depicting an Arab-style snake biting its own tail. Suddenly, he reminded me more of my old fellow inmates at Nordreslev than a young, ambitious police officer. He stuck his hand into one of his jacket pockets and pulled out some photos. The dead girls. He arranged the photos in a row on the table.

"I haven't slept in two days. I've been thinking nonstop. Will you hear me out for five minutes?"

"Sure." I put my hands in my lap and looked at the pictures.

He pointed. "These are in chronological order of when they were killed. Naja Holm, Tenna Smith Jensen, Alice Gorm, Belinda Jaeger, and Ida Bendixen."

The girls smiled up at us, and I shuddered.

"What do they have in common?" asked Hakim.

This was easy to answer.

"Red hair," I said. "And their age."

"What do they not have in common?"

I studied them again. "I don't know. Is there a point to this?"

"Social background and cause of death," Hakim said, ignoring my question. He planted his index fingers on Alice's and Ida's photos, respectively. "Stabbed to death and normal upbringing." He moved his finger from Alice's picture to that of Naja Holm. "Blow to the head and normal upbringing." He turned the three pictures over. "Alice, Naja, and Ida were all victims of brutal violence, and they all had completely normal middle-class upbringings, but Alice's parents are teachers, Naja's father is a farmer, and Ida's mother is a jeweler, so they're not actually so alike. It seems that their most obvious commonalities are hair color and age." He pulled the photos of Tenna and Belinda closer to him, so they lay side by side. "These two girls were strangled, and we found traces of an unknown type of sedative in their autopsies. Our impression is that they were unconscious when the murders took place. The girls probably did not know what was happening. The other thing they have in common is that they were both socially disadvantaged, with many moves and placements in group homes and foster families in their pasts."

"You don't think it's the same murderer as Naja, Alice, and Ida?"

Then why do all five have the same mark?

Hakim asked himself the same question. I snatched it directly from his head. Images of the girls with the rune in various iterations flickered from him. The one of Belinda lying on a steel table with closed eyes and blue lips made the biggest impression on me.

If Hakim noticed my strange facial expression, he didn't let on. "I can't see how the same man is capable of committing such different murders. Especially not the man we have. He seems almost stupid. Tenna's and Belinda's murders appear well-thought-out. Sophisticated, even. I think the guy we have is only behind three of the five Pippi murders, at most."

"And your colleagues don't believe you."

Hakim scratched at his hair, making it stick out even more. "They think we should close the case. I don't really have much of a say since I'm only a local officer."

"And the Savage hasn't said anything?"

"The Savage?"

Oops. I rubbed my nose. "That's what I call him."

"It fits him," Hakim said and gave me an appraising look. "No, he's not saying anything. He's totally apathetic."

I noticed that Varnar was watching us from the other side of the café. He sat at a table with his hands folded on the tabletop.

My stomach contracted when our eyes met. Whatever he thought, he wasn't happy that I was talking to Hakim. I held my head high and focused on the photos on the table again.

"I totally get that it's frustrating that your colleagues don't believe you, but I don't understand why you keep coming back to me. What does this have to do with me?"

Hakim leaned back on the sofa and bored into me with his green eyes. "You once said it's a coincidence that you are connected with the girls. You've moved around a lot, and in one way or another, you've crossed paths with most of them at some point in your life."

I nodded.

He continued. "I agree when it comes to Naja and Alice. I think it's a coincidence that you have come into contact with them. Ida, you have no connection to. What you were doing in that beach house on Saturday, I have no idea, but I also think that was a coincidence."

I wanted to protest, but Hakim gave me a look that was so weary I kept my mouth shut.

"If we concentrate on Tenna and Belinda, then I suspect that, just like you said, there is a second killer who murdered them. One who is still at large. He's smart, and he's highly selective. He's going after a very specific profile in his victims. Moreover, he's humane. It's almost as if he doesn't want to kill the girls. In any case, he doesn't want them to suffer or be afraid."

"Then why is he doing it?"

"I think he's looking for someone."

"What do you mean?"

"I think he's searching for a specific girl, but he doesn't know who she is and has very little information about her. Her age and social profile, her possible place of residence, and, of course, her natural hair color."

"You may be right. But I still can't see where I come into the picture."

Hakim stuck his hand in his breast pocket. "I visited Joan Flint in Hjørring this morning. Your former foster mother. She gave me something."

The way he leaned forward told me this was the grand finale. He had something up his sleeve, and he was looking forward to seeing my reaction. He was not disappointed, because my face must have displayed shock and horror when he pulled the last photo out of his pocket and placed it in front of me.

It was a school picture of me from fourth grade. I looked glumly into the camera, and it suddenly struck me how much I looked like Arthur.

The picture was from before I started dying my hair black. It was from when I still had my natural red hair color.

"I think he's looking for *you*," said Hakim.

PART III

HER MOTHER'S PATHS

A daughter bright Alfrödul bears
Ere Fenrir snatches her forth;
Her mother's paths
Shall the maiden tread
When the gods
To death have gone

Ballad of Vafthruthnir
10th century

CHAPTER 20

"But that's absurd. Why would he be looking for me?"

"You tell me. And why didn't you mention that you dye your hair?"

"I can't see how it's relevant."

"I'll tell you how it's relevant. Five red-haired girls have been murdered, Anna!" Hakim raised his voice.

"I just assumed he had a fetish," I mumbled. Out of the corner of my eye, I saw Varnar start to get up. I waved my hand for him to stay away.

"Your boyfriend doesn't like that we're talking."

"He's not my boyfriend."

"Then who is he?"

I closed my eyes and rested my forehead against my palm. "I actually have no idea."

Hakim was silent, but his face said it all.

"What does Lars Guldager have to say about all this?"

Hakim's eyes flickered. "Lars thinks the case is closed. I can't convince him of my theory."

"For some reason, I don't think you're telling me everything."

"Why not?"

"Lars Guldager must have a good reason to think you've got the right guy."

My attempt to get Hakim to mention the rune was unsuccessful. He looked at me intensely.

"I think it's more like *you* have a reason to think that Lars thinks we've got the right guy."

Did this man have a built-in lie detector? I was too exhausted and emotionally drained to play mind games.

"You have some more photos you'd like to show me, don't you?" I said tiredly.

A moment passed where Hakim just looked at me.

"You really are a strange girl," he said, before he stuck his hand in his other jacket pocket and pulled out his phone. He tapped it a couple times. "I hope you aren't squeamish," he said before handing me the phone.

The images I slowly flipped through were ones I had seen before. Just not in this format. I forced myself to look at them one by one. I felt like I owed the girls that.

At my side, Hakim sat completely still and watched me. He was certainly looking for a reaction, but I felt how my features froze. From the phone itself, I got countless visions of Hakim going through the photos. He must have spent hours looking at the bloody symbols.

"Do you have any idea what it means?" he asked in a low voice.

"At first glance it looks like an F, but it also resembles the rune for A. Ansuz. I think it means 'god' in Old Norse." I repeated Luna's point.

"How do you know the runes?" He narrowed his eyes.

"We're doing a unit on the Viking Age in history." I was secretly relieved to have gotten this message to the police. "Lars thinks it's the same murderer because the girls all have the same symbol," I concluded. "A lone lunatic."

Hakim confirmed with a nod. "That's what he says, anyway."

"If there are more, this could be big."

"Maybe. It could also just be that there are two lunatics."

Hakim stuck his muscular arm into his jacket sleeve. All the impulses I was getting from him told me he was ready to sprint from the school down to the nearest library and read up on the runic alphabet.

"I would advise you to be very cautious with everyone until I find out whether I'm right." Hakim's warning echoed Frank's from the other night. "If there's one more murderer, it could be anyone."

"You don't seriously think someone is after me, do you?"

"I don't know, but you needed to be the first to know that I suspect it."

"And what should I do with this information?"

"You should be careful. Which I don't think is something that comes naturally to you. For god's sake, don't tell anyone that you naturally have red hair. And if the person has already figured out who you are, he will try to get close to you. You shouldn't be alone with anyone who could potentially be the murderer."

"But it could be anyone, from what you said," I said, defeated.

"So you shouldn't be alone with anyone. It's good that you have your big dog."

"He ran away." My voice cracked.

Hakim sat up a little straighter. "You can always call me if you feel unsafe. I'll come."

"Are you trying to get close to me?" I smiled sweetly. "Maybe I should avoid being alone with you."

"Why would I warn you if I was the one who wanted to kill you?"

"Because maybe you don't actually want to kill me."

Hakim smiled, and I suddenly understood why all the girls looked at him.

"That is exactly how you should be thinking." He turned to leave.

"Hakim," I said and stood up.

He stopped and looked at me expectantly.

"You said that Tenna and Belinda were strangled."

"Yes."

"How did he do it? Did he use his hands?"

"He used a cord. The lab found traces of leather. Why are you asking?"

347

"No reason." I tried to sound casual.

His green eyes rested on me for a moment before he walked away.

My legs gave out under me, and I sat heavily on the sofa.

It rocked slightly when someone sat down next to me. I inhaled Varnar's scent without looking at him.

"What do you want?" I asked.

"To ask if we're training this afternoon."

"I thought you wanted nothing to do with me."

"Our training has nothing to do with . . . the other thing. I think we should continue as if nothing happened."

I can't do that.

"Fine," I said, and felt totally pathetic.

Without another word, he stood and walked away from me with his catlike stride.

"Redhead." Luna stared at me. "Are you really a redhead?"

She, Mathias, and I were huddled at the end of Yellow Hall, where I recounted my conversation with Hakim.

"I've been dyeing my hair black since I was thirteen."

"Damn," she said. "Isn't that crazy, Mathias?"

He looked uncomfortably at her.

"Why do you guys always tell each other secrets and leave me out?" she snapped.

"Did you know, Mathias?" I turned to face him. "When did you figure it out?"

"The first time I saw you. If you know about this stuff, you can tell if a hair color is natural."

"Why didn't you say anything?"

"I assumed you had your reasons for not wanting to talk about it."

"What else did the police guy say?" Luna absentmindedly circled a finger in the air in the direction of a ball of paper on the floor down the hall. It quietly began to roll.

Mathias saw his chance and took her hand, at which point the ball stopped.

At the end of the hall, Mads had stopped to look at us, but he kept walking when I lifted my head toward him. I returned to Hakim's visit.

"We talked about the symbol. I was able to tell him that it was probably a runic A. He also said that both Tenna and Belinda were strangled with a leather cord," I said.

"Your vision," breathed Mathias. "I hope you're planning to keep dyeing your hair."

"Absolutely. I hated being a redhead."

"Then at least the girl in the vision can't be you," said Mathias optimistically.

When Varnar showed up at my house a few hours later, he had Aella in tow as his chaperone. Mechanically, he went through attacks and parries, and I made an effort like never before. Every time he got close enough for me to smell, I pulled away. It seemed he was doing the same with me.

Aella looked back and forth between us, as confusion emanated from her. A couple times, I caught her closely examining my face. But it turned out she was talented at self-defense, and a much better teacher than Varnar. She stood behind me, laid her arms against mine, and grabbed my hands. Then she guided my fists around in the air, slowly at first, then faster and faster.

I finally understood a series of punches that Varnar had tried several times to teach me. Why hadn't he just done like Aella from the start? *Of course!* He had known how I felt about him and therefore didn't want to be close to me.

After they had left and darkness had fallen, Hakim's words began to swirl around in my head. *I think he's looking for you.*

Once you get scared, it's hard to shake it off. Several times I thought I heard steps in the gravel outside and someone at the door. Finally, I took the embarrassing measure of bringing the largest, sharpest knife I could find into bed with me.

As I lay alone with a knife under my pillow, the bed felt far too large and far too empty. Varnar's scent still lingered on the sheets, and I turned my head into my pillow and cried. I cried because I had had him and lost him. Because Monster had run away, my dad was dead, my mom was gone, and because my whole life I had lived with the feeling that no one wanted me. And just when I let my-self believe that that wasn't true, that maybe there was someone who did want to be with me, Varnar had unmistakably shown me the opposite.

The vision was crystal clear, and I inhaled the crisp winter air. I would figure this out once and for all. What was I supposed to do again? Oh right. The moon. I looked out through the trees and raised my hand.

The moon was one hand's width over Odinmont.

The girl walked past me, and I tried to follow her. I was so focused that I wasn't able to move.

The man walked through me just like the first time I had the vision. My body shook uncontrollably as his aura trailed a slimy streak through me, and I felt him all the way in my bones. I stood there, rooted to the ground, as he continued moving forward. And when he placed the cord around the girl's throat and strangled her, as he had done so many times before, my body tingled with recognition.

I was certain. I didn't know where or when, but at some point in my life, I had met the murderer.

CHAPTER 21

"Witch," Luna said, beaming, on Wednesday morning as she slammed her orange bag onto the table and threw herself down on the red sofa between me and Mathias.

"Who's a witch?" asked Mathias.

"I am. Isn't that cool? My parents explained everything last night. It's such a relief to finally know what I am."

Mathias looked at her, crestfallen. "You're so lucky."

She wrapped her arms around him and gave him a big kiss. "Maybe soon you'll know what you are, too. When are you meeting with Od?"

He passed the question on to me with his blue eyes.

"I need to call Elias and set something up." I changed the subject back to Luna. "What else did you find out?"

She rubbed her hands together. "Get this. There's a whole world of magic and supernatural stuff. Those in the know call it," she gave a dramatic pause, "the hidden world."

"Wow," said Mathias.

"Yeah, wow," I said, somewhat half-heartedly.

"Oh, come on. Did you know about the hidden world, too?"

"Arthur told me."

"If there's anything else you already know," said Luna, "can you just spit it out now? Just so the rest of us don't share news thinking you'll actually be surprised."

I considered this. "I don't think there's anything more right now. Except that I'm pretty sure I've already met the murderer."

"What?!"

"But I only found out last night," I added.

"And who is it?" She leaned forward.

"I don't know," I said. "All I know is that I felt his aura in a vision last night, and that it's familiar. But in the vision, it's like it's filtered or distorted, so I can't pinpoint who he is. I also tried to notice the moon this time."

Luna lit up. "Try to draw it."

I laughed. "All things creative are impossible for me because of my retrocognition."

Luna giggled. Then she kicked off one of her shoes. "Pull up your shirt—you know why."

I lifted my shirt.

Luna stuck her ice-cold foot against my stomach, and I made a shuddering *schiiiiii* sound, while Mathias looked on with furrowed brows.

"Get me a sheet of paper and a pen from my bag," Luna said to him.

I tried, to the best of my ability, to describe the placement of the moon over Odinmont.

With impressive speed, Luna was done, and she showed me a detailed drawing of the dark forest and the shining moon.

I shivered upon seeing the scene manifested before me.

"Is this how it looks?" she asked.

I nodded. "You are really good at drawing."

"I know," she said with a wide smile. "I'm super talented."

I would have to teach her to at least feign a Danish sense of modesty.

During the ten o'clock break, I called Elias, who picked up immediately. I was not in the mood for our usual ping-pong match of advances and rejections, so I went straight to the point. "Od owes me a meeting with my friend, Mathias. When is he available?"

Elias laughed. "Well hello to you, too. How's it going?"

"Fine," I replied. "Can you check Od's calendar, or horoscope, or whatever it is you use to plan?"

"One moment please." There was a muffled exchange of words at the other end. I recognized Od's hoarse voice in the background. Elias came back on. "Can you come tonight?"

I thought about it. "We're both at work until ten. Can it be after that?"

"Shall I pick you up?"

"If you drive us home afterward."

"There's nothing I'd rather do."

"See you at Frank's around ten, then."

After school, I picked up my bike.

Bike Shop Timmy was quiet, and a weird vibe scratched the air around him, as if he felt guilty about something.

I examined my bike closely, but I couldn't find anything to suggest that Timmy had cut corners, and once again I had to tell myself that it was not my job to solve all the world's mysteries.

My shift at Frank's was blessedly calm.

When I walked out into the bar after my shift, Frank was talking to Elias. Peter sat in one of the booths along with Johnny-Bum and Niller from our class. My stomach did a somersault when I noticed Varnar sitting alone in a dark corner.

Mathias stood at the other end of the bar, putting glasses away.

Frank waved me over. "Your friend shares my taste in old music. I've never met someone who knows so much about music history." He smoothed his gray, pomaded hair, and the lines around his eyes crinkled.

If only you knew how deep Elias's knowledge of history really goes.

Out loud I said, "Do you go around telling people we're friends, Elias?"

Elias put his hand beneath his chin and gave me his most

353

smoldering look. "If you want to be more than friends, you know I'm ready."

Frank laughed loudly. "I would never dare talk to Anna that way. Aren't you afraid of her like the rest of us are?"

"I'm more afraid that someone else will snatch her right out from under my nose." He looked directly at Varnar.

"There's definitely no risk of that happening," I said sharply.

Comprehension glimmered in Elias's eyes. "If someone had the chance and blew it, then they're dumber than I thought possible. You don't throw away something good."

"Agreed," Frank said, and put an arm around me. "You may be a little rough around the edges, but we love you for it."

Suddenly, Peter was standing next to us.

"Two more beers," he said to Frank, who let go of me. He nodded at Peter, grabbed a couple of pint glasses, and began to pour.

Peter stared at me, unblinking.

Ugh. Just when I was in such a good mood.

"Wouldn't you like to go back to having red hair, psycho, like when you were little?" he said loudly enough for everyone to hear. "Maybe there are more people out there who want to kill red-haired girls."

The music played on, but all conversation died. Varnar raised his head, Frank's hand froze on the tap, and Elias widened his eyes.

I thought Elias or Frank would come to my defense, but they just looked at Peter in shock. Frank handed him the beers and took his payment.

So much for following Hakim's advice to hide my true hair color.

Varnar came over to me and pulled me away. He didn't want to look me in the eyes.

"How are you getting home?"

"I have to do something first. Elias will drive me home afterward."

Varnar's lips turned into a narrow line. He raised his gaze toward Elias, who leaned back on the barstool and wiggled his eyebrows at him. Varnar said nothing, and left, slamming the door behind him.

Frank grabbed Mathias and me.

"Can you lock up?" He put a key ring in my hand. "Should I write down the code?"

Mathias tapped a finger on his temple. "Just tell me. I have a photographic memory."

I exhaled sharply to hide a laugh. Frank didn't notice. He seemed distracted and disappeared quickly out the door.

Mathias and I closed up while Elias waited for us outside. I turned off all the lights, and Mathias put in the code before we slipped out and locked the door behind us.

Elias was leaning against the wall and pushed himself upright with one foot, ready to go.

Out of the dark alley behind Frank's, a man came toward us with one hand behind his back. A scarf was pulled up over his mouth and nose, so all I could see was that he was bald and skinny. He was heading straight for Mathias.

I focused my full attention on him, but a moment too late.

What . . . ?

Triumph and recognition rolled off of him. He brought his arm to the front, and I saw that he had a sawed-off shotgun in his hand.

"Did you think we wouldn't find you?" He raised the gun toward Mathias. "This is a greeting from Big T."

I instinctively stepped between the weapon and Mathias, but Elias grabbed me by the waist and pulled me back at the exact moment the man pulled the trigger.

There was a sharp crack and then a boom, and I was standing so close, I could feel the shock wave.

A cascade of blood sprayed over me when Mathias's rib cage exploded.

The man ran, and his steps echoed in the alley behind us as Mathias collapsed in a bloody heap on the ground in front of me.

I screamed and threw myself forward. My friend was lying on the ground in a pool of blood with a gaping hole where his chest should have been. Kneeling at his side, I held his face in both hands. I knew he would rather have Luna be the last thing he laid eyes on in this world, but he would have to make do with me.

He looked up at me with his beautiful, shining blue eyes and tried to smile. His teeth were covered in blood.

"Anna," he said, but his voice faded.

I sobbed violently when he closed his eyes and lay completely still.

His aura flickered weakly before it was extinguished, like someone blowing out a candle.

 # CHAPTER 22

"We need to go." Elias's voice was gentle, and his hand lay on my arm.

"Why did you pull me away?" I shouted. "I could have saved him."

"Anna," Elias said a little louder.

"Leave me alone." I sniffled as I stroked Mathias's handsome, blood-streaked face.

He lay eerily still.

I took his hand.

It must have been my imagination, but it felt as if it gave a little jolt.

I looked down at our hands.

He squeezed mine weakly.

What?

Neon-green light began to emanate from him, and he blinked a couple of times.

"What happened?" he asked.

I looked down at his shredded jacket. His chest was exposed and, actually, didn't really exist anymore.

"What the . . ." My voice trailed off.

Elias pulled me up by my arm.

"We need to get him to Od. Now!" He helped Mathias to his feet.

"How? It's impossible," I whispered.

"Help me get him over to the car."

Moving mechanically, I did what he said, and Mathias walked with unsteady steps between us.

"Elias, please tell me what the hell is going on?" I hissed. "Is he alive?"

"He's alive. He might go into shock, but for someone like him, this is just a scrape."

"Someone like him?"

"Od will explain everything. Right now, we just need to get him out of here before someone calls the police or an ambulance. The gunshot and your screams must have been audible all the way to Aalborg."

Before we drove off, Elias cut the jacket and shirt off of Mathias. I nearly threw up when I saw the damage the bullet had done. His aura was completely gone, and he glowed a pale green.

It was a strange car ride.

Mathias just sat there in the back seat and looked silently out into the darkness. Next to him, I talked to him, terrified that he would either close his eyes and die or look down at himself and discover the gaping hole he was sporting. I said again and again that he would get through this, but I didn't know if that wasn't a big fat lie.

Elias didn't say anything, either.

When we arrived, I was the first into Od's hexagonal office. His eyes widened in shock when he saw me covered in blood.

"Not me," I said through gritted teeth.

Od regained his usual mild, unfazed expression when he saw who the victim was.

We deposited Mathias on the sofa, where he sat with bloody strands of hair clinging to his face, seeming not to register much around him.

"How did he get in such a state?" Od stood and considered Mathias.

Elias stood behind the sofa, arms crossed. "It seems his past, in the form of a thug with a sawed-off shotgun, caught up to him tonight."

Od examined the injuries without showing any sign of alarm.

He bent down in front of Mathias so their faces were on the same level.

Finally, Mathias focused on him.

"You," he said apathetically.

I looked from one to the other. "Do you know each other?"

"He's the guy who owns my mom's salon," said Mathias with a strange monotone voice that sounded nothing like his own. He looked at Od. "Why did you buy that salon for my mom?"

"To get you here." Od's eyes sparkled. "I've been keeping an eye on you for a long time, Mathias Jarl."

I was surprised that Od knew Mathias's middle name. He never used it.

"Why have you been keeping an eye on me?"

"Because I keep an eye on your kind."

"What am I?" Mathias's voice had regained a hint of life.

Od was about to answer, but I interrupted them with a frustrated moan.

"Isn't there a slightly more pressing question right now?" I pointed a finger at Mathias's chest. "Is that going to be okay?"

I looked diagonally into the hole and saw something in there, beating. Mathias's face revealed nothing, but his exposed heart pumped faster behind his broken ribs as we awaited Od's reply.

Od leaned back against the edge of the desk.

"Mathias will heal very quickly. In a week, there won't be so much as a scar."

Now that I looked, I could see that the wound was gradually beginning to close up at the edges. The bleeding had long since stopped, and a couple of pieces of buckshot were pushed out with a small *plop*.

Good. I exhaled. "Very well. You can return to the other thing."

Od addressed Mathias again.

"I hadn't planned for you to find out this way, but you can never predict these things." His smile was sympathetic.

"Mathias, you've probably known for a while now that you're not like other people. That there's something else, something not human, within you."

Mathias nodded slowly.

"That's because you are a hybrid of two kinds of beings. Half of you *is* human. Your mother's half. But your father is not a human." Od stopped, as if he needed to search for the right words. "Your father is a god," he said finally, and I could feel my mouth drop open. Od held up a hand in my direction to indicate that he wasn't finished. "That means the other half of you is divine. You are what we call a demigod."

I found my voice and could hear that it was bordering on hysteria. "Please stop."

Od looked at me calmly. "You're not making it easier for your friend to understand."

I tried to regain my composure by taking a couple of deep breaths. "Are you also a demigod?"

"Yes."

"How can that be?"

"The gods exist," said Od. There was an unspoken *deal with it* in his statement. "They belong to a different world, but they come here once in a while. And sometimes they see a human they're attracted to. Beings like Mathias and myself are the result."

"When you say, 'the gods,' you mean Odin and Thor and all them?"

Od nodded.

"And they seek out humans, who they sleep with, and demigods come from that?" I asked.

"Correct," Od said and smiled.

"Who is my father?" asked Mathias with his eyes half-closed.

"I don't know which of the gods it is. When the time comes, your father will make himself known to you."

The human half of Od was telling me loud and clear that he wasn't telling the whole truth. For Mathias's sake, I held my tongue.

Mathias wrinkled his brows slightly, as if his brain couldn't fully keep up. Then he closed his eyes, and his breathing grew slow and rhythmic.

"I don't think he can handle any more," I said.

"That happens to most people when they get the news. Some react very violently. He's actually taking it quite well." Od turned toward Elias. "Clean Mathias up and find a bed for him. He can sleep here tonight."

Elias, who had stayed in the background for once, shook Mathias, who drowsily got to his feet. They started walking to the door.

"Elias," said Od.

They stopped, and Elias looked back.

"Burn his bloody clothes and throw the bathwater in the sea. When you're done, you can drive Anna home."

Elias's facial expression didn't change. He nodded, and they disappeared out the door.

"What was that about?"

"Our blood is powerful. In the wrong hands, it can do a lot of harm."

"Are you saying Elias has the wrong hands?"

Od didn't answer. Instead, he pulled out a desk drawer and found a bottle and two glasses. He poured a golden liquid into them and handed me one.

"Straight from Heidrun's udders."

I took the glass and sipped the drink. It tasted strong, sweet, and spicy all at once, and it warmed and calmed every fiber of my body. I sat down.

"So you're half god?"

Od held my gaze in confirmation.

"Who is your father?" I stopped myself. "Oh. Od Dinesen. Odin's son. Am I right?"

Od nodded. "My father is Odin."

I remembered from my history paper that Odin was the main god in Valhalla. "So are you, like, the boss of the demigods?"

"In a way. I have to keep tabs on the demigods and guide the ones who are in the human world. Not everyone handles being superhuman so well."

I sat there, unable to find the words.

"Are there demigods in places other than here?" I asked finally.

Od folded his hands around his glass. "Here, we're called demigods. We're stronger, smarter, and faster than humans, and we're perceived as more attractive."

I raised my eyebrows to indicate that Od was not exactly saddled with low self-esteem.

He continued with a smile. "In Valhalla, there are also some of our kind, but there they're called half gods. The half gods are born to goddesses and have human fathers. They are literally perceived to be half as good as gods and are therefore at the bottom of the hierarchy. Demigods have human mothers and are born here in Midgard. Genetically, we're the same, but we are perceived very differently."

"The half gods must be a little bitter about that, no?"

Od wagged his head at a slight angle. "Some of them."

I leaned back, tired. "How old are you?"

Od didn't answer me.

I threw up my arms. "I mean, I'm past the point of being shocked. You can tell me—unless it's a secret."

"It's not a secret. Not to the initiated, anyway." He looked intently at me. "And you're becoming pretty well initiated now." He smiled again, and I melted as always. "I was born in the year 754," he said breezily, but in a flash, I saw the many centuries resting on his shoulders.

I knew how heavily the past could weigh on a person. I closed my eyes and let his age sink in.

"Is Elias as old as you?"

"Elias has to tell his own story."

Yeah, yeah, I thought. *You don't talk about other people.*

"Is there anything else you want to ask about?" Od spread his hands in an open gesture.

"There is a key question I would really like to have answered," I said. "I saw Mathias get a hole blasted through his chest, but he got back up afterward. Are you even capable of dying?"

"We can die. *He* died, after all." Od tilted his head again. "But there has to be an element of self-sacrifice in it. One could say we're capable of choosing to die. And when we sacrifice ourselves, our deaths have a lot of power."

"*He* . . . ? Do you mean . . . ? But that's a totally different religion. I thought if you followed one religion, that closed off the other ones."

Od emptied his glass and looked down at it. "Some believe that the gods are essentially the same, with different names in different cultures. Odin is the same as Janus, Kali is the same as Hel, Freyja is the same as Aphrodite, and so on. Others think it's a deadly sin to acknowledge other gods than one's own. But one thing's for certain. The gods only exist when people believe in them."

Hmm. "Do you know where the gods come from?"

"Some believe the gods created the universe and humankind, others believe humankind invented the gods, and that they are manifestations of humans' faith."

"A little like the chicken and the egg," I said dryly.

Od laughed his signature laugh. "Exactly."

"And you are both chicken and egg."

"I guess I am."

"So which of your halves created the other?"

Od sat for a while before replying.

"Scientists once conducted an experiment," he said. "They measured the brain activity of religious people while they meditated. It showed that the same center in the brain is active when you hear a god's voice and when you hear something concrete. If you ask the same people to imagine that they hear something, a completely different part of the brain is activated."

I leaned forward slightly. "So that's proof that the gods exist."

"Or it's proof that the human brain is capable of creating something concrete out of pure conviction." Od also leaned forward and caught my eye.

As always, I was unable to move.

"The human brain," he said as he reached out his hand and trailed a finger across my forehead, "is a mystery. Did it create the gods, or did the gods create it? Even after more than twelve hundred years, I don't have the answer."

He pulled back his hand.

I twitched, as if waking from a dream where I was falling.

Od continued, unfazed. "The only thing that's really worth knowing is that the gods are dependent on someone believing in them. Those who are forgotten wither and fade away. Over the years, there have been many different deities. Most of them are gone now."

"Which ones have been forgotten and faded away?"

"There was the Celtic god Lugh. Millions of Celts worshipped him a couple thousand years ago. But when the Romans killed the druids, people gradually stopped believing in him." He shrugged. "And so he disappeared. Like he had never existed."

"Why?"

"Gods need to be worshipped by humans."

"So then it doesn't really matter if it was the chicken or the egg that came first."

Od laughed again. "You've got to stop referring to the gods as chickens."

I ignored him. "If the gods exist—the Norse ones, anyway—what about the mythology? Does Valhalla exist, for example? I mean, is it a real place?"

"Yes. It's a real place. I visit a couple of times a year."

"Where is Valhalla?"

"Valhalla isn't in any geographic location. It's more like a different plane. I picture our universe like a house, where the worlds are separated into the different floors."

"Worlds? Plural?"

"Yes. Did you really think this world was the only one?"

"I've actually never thought about it, so yeah, I guess I did think that."

"If the universe is like a house, then the human world, Midgard, is the ground floor. Jotunheim and several other worlds are on the first floor, and Valhalla is on the second. At the top, on the roof of the house, if you will, the ash tree Yggdrasil spreads its branches over all the worlds."

"What's in the basement?" I asked.

Od's face grew dark. "Let's not talk about that now."

I took a large gulp of the liquid. It burned all the way down, and I exhaled sharply. "Is there anything else I should know?"

"Tons, but let's take it a bit at a time." Od fixed his kind gaze on me. "What about you, Anna? How are things?"

"Well. I've had an eventful few days. For one thing, I found out that Arthur is my father. But I'm sure you already knew that." I gave him a sarcastic stare. "Thanks for sharing that with me, by the way."

"It wasn't my place to tell you. Arthur and I agreed that he should be the one to explain his . . . condition."

"Yeah, yeah . . ." I stopped. "Is it because you're demigods that you and Mathias can talk to him?"

"Yes. It's our divine side that allows us to talk to spirits. The gods do not distinguish between the worlds of the living and the dead like humans do."

"I can see him, too."

"You're far from a normal human." Od refilled our glasses.

"Compared to the rest of you, I'm actually pretty normal." I lifted my glass to him in an ironic toast. "Aside from the fact that a police officer thinks there's a murderer out to get me."

Od once again shook his head, as I had noticed he did when something surprised or frustrated him. "Why does he think that?"

"Because I actually have red hair, and he thinks there's still someone out there who has a penchant for strangling redheaded girls with troubled pasts."

Od didn't have a chance to comment because Elias came in.

"Mathias is sleeping," he said. "Anna, do you want a ride home now?"

Very much so. I nodded to Elias, and he disappeared out the door. I stood and started to follow him, but Od placed himself in front of me. I had to twist my neck to look up at him.

He looked me in the eyes, and I was spellbound.

"Look out for yourself," he said, and he kissed my forehead so gently it felt like a warm breeze. He gave off a faint silvery glow. Then he turned away from me, and it was as if someone had turned off the sun.

I stumbled out to find Elias, who was waiting for me in the car. He was unusually quiet and pensive as we drove, acknowledging my presence only by handing me a bag of candy.

Halfway home, I was ready to crack. "Are you gonna say anything?"

Elias kept his eyes on the road.

"About what?" he said, his voice devoid of emotion. "That you actually have red hair? That tonight you were so stupid you almost got your head shot off?"

He braked slightly where the road split and turned.

He added: "Or that the police think there's someone after you, and yet you still aren't looking after yourself?"

"What do you mean, I'm not looking after myself? And how do you know the police think there's someone after me?"

"I listened to your conversation with Od through the door," Elias replied without shame. "And you aren't looking after yourself in a lot of areas. Not to mention, you knowingly stepped in front of a gun right before it was fired, and then you got in a car way out in the boonies with a person who, just this evening, overheard that you actually have red hair, and who knows your background."

"You and I have been alone several times."

"Not when I knew your real hair color."

"But you aren't going to do anything to me."

Elias slammed on the brakes, swung the car to the side of the road, and turned off the headlights. There were no streetlights this far out in the country. In the distance, I could see the two red lights at the top of a windmill. They looked like a pair of evil eyes.

"How do you know?" he asked into the darkness, and I suddenly heard the age in his voice in the form of a cynical edge that wasn't normally there.

My pulse slowly crept upward. "If you're thinking of trying anything, I should inform you I am capable of kicking ass in a way you can't even comprehend."

I had never considered whether Elias knew how to fight, but I immediately determined that I had a fair chance.

"Two of the girls were drugged before they were killed. I just gave you a piece of candy."

I licked my lips, where the sweet taste of the hard candy still lingered.

Elias continued: "All I have to do is wait for the drugs to kick in, and then I can do what I want with you." He turned on the small light in the car's ceiling and turned to face me. His face looked older in the stark light. He looked at me, unmoving.

I stared back. If Elias was out to get me, he would see it through, regardless of whether I begged for my life.

"If you want to kill me, then why did you pull me back when Mathias was shot?"

"Maybe because I want to have my fun with you before I kill you."

"What are you planning to do?" I whispered, irritated by my faltering voice.

"I'm planning to prove a point."

"What point?"

"That you aren't taking this seriously, and that it could get you killed." His expression shifted to his usual smirk.

I wanted to hit him. "Was that just to teach me a lesson?"

"Yes. Did it work?"

"Maybe a little," I said.

Elias seemed to know a northern Danish understatement when he heard one, and he laughed.

I sighed as he swung the car back onto the road. "For a second there, I thought it was you. It all fit. Including how you heard about my real hair color tonight."

"Nah. I've known you were a natural redhead for a long time."

"How?"

"I saw when . . . It was an honest mistake," he held up a hand defensively. "I surprised you in the shower."

"What? Oh. Ah." I blushed and buried my face in my hands. "I'm surprised you haven't said anything until now," I mumbled through my fingers.

"Despite what most people think, I am actually a gentleman."

I hesitantly lowered my hands. "Is there really someone after me?"

"It's not unthinkable."

We had reached Kraghede Road and turned onto it.

"Your parents ran afoul of a few people before you were born. It's possible that you will feel the fallout." He stopped himself.

"Let me guess," I said resignedly. "You can't tell me more about it."

Elias glanced at me with a mixture of warmth and sadness but didn't reply. We rumbled up the driveway and stopped in front of Odinmont.

"Are you gonna invite me in?"

"What do you think?"

"I saw how you looked at Varnar tonight, and I know when I don't have chance. I've given up on winning your heart—for now."

Laughter bubbled up from my mouth before I could stop it. "Something tells me it's not my heart you're interested in."

"You have, as always, seen through me." He bowed his head. "But I actually just wanted to go over some ground rules for how a possibly hunted young lady can keep herself alive."

It couldn't hurt, and if Elias was planning to kill me, he would have done it out in the middle of nowhere. I waved him in.

At the table, Elias poured yet another glass of mead, while I sipped a cup of tea. I was done consuming alcohol for the day. Elias seemed to feel quite the opposite. He was already on his third glass.

A couple of candles on the table were the only source of light in the house.

I had washed myself off only minimally in the bathroom. It was as if Mathias's blood couldn't dry. Even though hours had passed since he was shot, the blood that soaked my clothes and hair was still warm and wet. The water in the sink had quickly turned bloodred, and with Od's words about demigod blood in my mind, I rinsed it away thoroughly when I was done. In my bedroom, I had put my bloody clothes in a plastic bag and hid it in the back of my closet.

"Rule number one," said Elias. "Never be alone with someone you can't trust."

"How do I find out who I can trust?"

Elias raked his fingers through his wild curls. "You have to use both your logic and your instincts. For example, I know your natural hair color and your background. I have for a while. If I wanted to do something to you, I would have done it ages ago. This is where you should use logic. Then there's Luna and Mathias. Do you believe in your heart that they would do anything to hurt you?"

I shook my head immediately. "No. I trust them both one hundred percent."

"What about if one of them had to choose between you and the other?"

I looked down at the table, unable to make myself answer.

Elias continued without further comment. "Are there other people you trust?"

I reflected on this. "Arthur and Monster."

Elias nodded. "Good. Everyone should choose a few people in life who they never have to question. You just need to know that they're the ones who can hurt you the most if they actually do betray you. Something else," Elias continued quickly. "Just because someone doesn't specifically want to kill you doesn't necessarily mean that you can trust them."

"Does that apply to you, for instance? I have actually been warned not to trust you."

"By Arthur?"

"Yep." I took a sip of tea.

Elias looked down. "It's understandable that Arthur would say that."

I waited for an elaboration that never came. "Luna's parents don't like you, either."

Elias's sad expression transformed into one of bitterness. Then he abruptly changed the subject. "What about young Varnar? Do you think you can trust him?"

Just hearing his name made my stomach contract. "Yes, I think so."

370

"Why?"

I wasn't ready to let my feelings guide me in Varnar's case.

"Logically," I said, "he's known that I'm a natural redhead for a couple days."

"Did you tell him?" Elias emptied his glass and placed his hand under his chin.

"No. He found out the other day. In the same kind of way you found out." I felt heat in my cheeks and looked down.

A scornful feeling shot from Elias, but he didn't show it. "Have you been alone with him since?"

I thought back. "No, actually, I haven't."

Elias didn't say any more, but he let me think that through to its natural conclusion. It sent an ice-cold wave through me.

"Let's move on to rule number two. You should not accept food or drink from anyone if you have even the slightest bit of doubt about their intentions."

"How did you know the girls were drugged?"

"I have my sources."

"Do you know what kind of drug it is?"

"I suspect it's a potion called stjórna. If you drink it, it puts you in a kind of hypnosis, where you do whatever you're commanded."

"Can you make it?"

"Anyone can if they have the recipe. It's very simple to make."

Hmm. In the vision, the murderer seemed to be able to control the girl, and she didn't fight off his attack.

"What if you've been given some strona . . ." I began.

"Stjórna," Elias corrected and poured himself yet another glass.

"Okay, stjórna. If you find out that you've been given it, is there anything you can do?"

"No, you lose consciousness and come under the other person's control. Unless you learn to fight against it." Elias's voice immediately turned doctor-like.

I straightened up in my chair. "How would I fight against it?"

"Practice. I can give you small doses regularly over a period of time, so your body gets used to it." He gave me a crooked smile. "But it requires the aforementioned trust."

"I'll think about it and get back to you," I said. Absentmindedly, I ran my hand along the deep crack in the dining table.

Elias followed my movement with his eyes but didn't comment on it.

"Rule number three," he said. "In a situation where your life is in danger, accept the help you can get and think about the consequences later."

"What do you mean?"

"Often, you will have options that you don't want to use or maybe have even sworn you wouldn't use. But if it can save your life, do whatever it takes."

I had no idea what Elias was babbling about. "It sounds like you have a lot of experience with being in life-threatening situations."

"I have a lot of experience with everything."

For a moment, we just looked at each other. Darkness enveloped Odinmont, and our seats at the dining table must have been the only illuminated spot in a radius of several miles, aside from Ben and Rebecca's house.

"How old are you really?" I stopped myself. "Do you mind me asking? Od didn't want to tell me."

Elias looked down at the table. "No, I don't mind you asking. I was born in 1613."

"Are you also a demigod?"

The corner of Elias's mouth crept up. "I am one hundred percent human."

"Shit" flew out of my mouth. "You aren't a ghost, are you?"

Elias laughed loudly.

I immediately realized that I had seen him both eat and drink, not to mention talk with plenty of people who were neither demigods, clairvoyants, or mediums.

"Then how can you be so old?"

"There are several ways to reach an old age," Elias evaded.

"Would you like to say more about that now?"

Elias slowly shook his head.

Suddenly, exhaustion hit me. "Do you have any more tips, or are we done?"

"I think I've covered most of it." Elias stood up and swayed. "I'll head out now."

"Are you drunk?"

"No, no. I can definitely drive." He took a couple steps away from the table but wobbled.

"I can't let you drive like this. Just imagine if you hit someone. Why did you drink so much when you drove?"

He glanced at the half-empty mead bottle.

"It's been years since I tasted that drink. And I needed to dull the shock of thinking for a split second that you had been shot." He pulled his lips back into a mirthless smile. "I could drink a lot more if I were trying to match it up to my emotions."

I threw up my arms wearily. "Knock yourself out. As long as you promise me you won't get behind the wheel. I'm going to bed. If you so much as come near my bedroom, you should know that I sleep with a knife under my pillow."

Elias placed his hand on his heart. "I give you my word. I'll stay away from your bedroom—until you yourself invite me in."

"Great!" I left Elias in the living room and tromped upstairs, where I fell asleep immediately.

I woke up one time that night from music playing downstairs. Elias must have revived the old record player, and it struck me that the vinyl collection that still sat on the old wooden shelf next to the bench belonged to my mom and Arthur.

The next morning when I came down, sharp sunbeams fell into my living room. There were two empty bottles on the dining room table, where old records were also spread out. The bench was askew, and I pushed it back against the wall as I walked past. The door to the patio was open, and Elias sat outside in the morning sun. His curls were stuck to his forehead, and he sat hunched over a glass that was inverted on the table. He stared intently into it.

A small fly was crawling around inside, along the edge of the glass. It kept trying to climb the translucent wall.

"Did you sleep at all?" I asked. "How much did you drink?"

He didn't answer.

"In vino veritas," I heard him whisper to himself.

I came closer. "What have you got there?"

He looked up at me, his pupils gigantic. He leaned forward slightly in his chair, and for a second I thought he would tip over, but he regained his balance by leaning back again.

"It's a mayfly," he slurred. "Right now it's full of life, but tomorrow it'll be dead. Out of all eternity, it lives only a day."

"Well, at least it got lucky with the weather," I said and looked down at the fly in its sunny glass prison.

Elias focused on me with some difficulty. Then he laughed, but it sounded more like a snort. He ran his fingers through his damp curls and turned back to the glass.

"I'm sitting here wondering how I can keep it alive. Prolong its life. Maybe I can brew a potion. But how do I get the formula right when the creature is so small?" He laughed again with a hysterical undertone.

The fly began to spin around and flap its wings. I reached over and lifted the glass. The fly fluttered off and disappeared.

"What are you doing?" Elias shouted and swung out his arm, hitting the glass, which fell to the stone pavers and shattered. He grabbed my wrist, hard.

"It was suffering," I said in my defense.

"I could have saved it." The drunken rage shone in his eyes.

"Calm down. It's just a fly." I tried to pull my hand back.

"It's your fault that it's going to die today." His face cracked and he closed his eyes. Then he released his grasp and leaned his forehead against me instead, breathing in quick jerks. He wrapped his arms around my waist, and I felt tears soaking through the front of my shirt.

"Why do you all think you'll live forever?" he mumbled into my stomach.

I stood there for a while, looking down at the back of his neck. My hands wavered over him, and I raised and lowered them a couple of times. Finally, I laid them on his head and stroked the curls.

Slowly, he calmed down, and his breathing became regular again. Then he leaned heavily against me. If I didn't get him up now, he would fall out of the chair.

I nudged him. "Come on. Let's get you to bed."

Somehow, I got him to his feet and led him up to my guest room. I got him to lie on the futon and draped a blanket over him. He looked up at me with eyes reduced to narrow slits.

"Thank you," he whispered.

"For what?"

"Thank you for comforting an old man," he said, almost inaudibly. Then he closed his eyes, and his breathing became slow and rhythmic.

I stood for a while and looked down at his youthful face surrounded by soft curls. Then I let my fingertips stroke his smooth cheek, just once, before I left the room to go to school.

At school I tried, as gently as I could, to recount the evening's events to Luna. Unfortunately, gentleness is not my forte, so she was in tears before I even got to the ride home with Elias.

"So Mathias is okay?" she asked.

"Od said he would be within a week."

"Are you sure?"

"No, I'm not sure. The last time I saw him, his rib cage was pulverized, and I could see straight through to his heart."

Luna's eyes rolled back in her head.

"But it was still beating," I was quick to add.

She held a hand up to her mouth, stood up, and ran to the bathroom.

Crap.

No long after, she came skulking back, as close to white in the face as her skin tone could get. She sat heavily on the red sofa.

"I don't want to hear any more. But I'm glad you were there."

"Otherwise, I could have done without it." I picked at the sofa's worn upholstery. "But on the plus side, he found out what he is."

"Yeah, it's pretty crazy that he's half god. That explains some things." She thought for a moment. "Who shot him?"

"No idea. But it was some form of revenge. I just don't know how they found him all the way up here." I stared out into space for a second.

Shit! Bike Shop Timmy. He had recognized Mathias the day we dropped off my bike.

Luna didn't notice my realization.

"We'll probably never find out," she said.

I nodded absently. "What about you? Have your parents told you anything more?"

She lit up in a huge smile. "Tons. I'm going to take witchcraft lessons. We've already started going over a bunch of things. Ground rules and stuff like that."

"No more practicing on me. I have no desire to be turned into a toad."

We both laughed before Luna changed the subject. "Have you talked to Varnar?"

I studied my still-blue nails. "We trained a couple of days ago. But Aella was there, too. And even if she hadn't been, we probably wouldn't have talked about it."

"I could have sworn he returned your feelings."

I made a face. "He's really struggling with what happened."

"Could that be your imagination?"

"No, Luna. I can *feel* it. I'm sure."

Luna bit her lip. "Do you think you can get over him?"

"I guess I'll have to." I changed the subject. "What's going on with you and Mathias?"

Luna pulled her neon-yellow shawl tighter around her shoulders.

"Not much. It just feels right. Like we're meant to be together." She shook her head, so the bright red curls bounced up and down. "Being with him calms me down. I barely need to think about what colors to wear."

"Nice. He said the same thing about you."

"He did?"

"Yeah. It's easier for him to control his divine side when you're together."

Luna looked at her phone and sighed. "Time for gym. Ugh. I'm really not feeling up for physical exertion today."

I didn't mention that I felt just the opposite. I really needed it.

The mom of foster family number six, the ones from the evangelical church, told me again and again that revenge is wrong. *Turn the other cheek, Anna,* she'd said, and when I took her advice literally, I ended up sporting a black eye for a week. That was the year I was in class with Peter for the second time. From then on, I was done with forgiving anyone who messed with me or with any of the few people I care about. Bike Shop Timmy was no exception.

I easily clambered over the fence behind the shop, where there were rows of bikes with small white tags on them. I checked for cameras and alarms but found nothing. Then I reached out with my power and saw a stream of people coming and going. Most of them brought bikes in and out.

After Elias had taught me to shield, I could control my clairvoyance much better. This was an unexpected bonus.

I walked around and touched things at random until I found a useful bit of the past. Finally, I saw a van arriving late at night.

Timmy waved it into the back. Then he opened the side door, stuck his head in, and spoke with someone inside. A pair of arms held a box out to him. Then a face came into view.

Recognition caused me to stiffen. What the hell was he doing here? I would have to think about that later. Right now, I watched Timmy carry the box into a shed. Behind me, the van backed out and disappeared. Timmy locked the shed with a huge padlock. He hid the key under the rafters.

I blinked away the vision and was once again alone behind the shop. Quickly, I fished out the key, which was where Timmy had hidden it. I exhaled a couple of times before I stuck it into the lock.

In the shed, I found the box still sitting inside.

A quick look inside revealed a pile of bags containing red and blue pills, each with a small wolf's head printed on one side.

Shit! It was hundreds of thousands of dollars' worth of drugs. I had seen my fellow residents at various homes swallowing pounds of this crap. In the environment I had involuntarily become a part of, these particular pills were known for being clean and relatively harmless. Above all, they were wildly expensive, which contributed to their exclusive reputation. The red pills, known as Skoll, gave you energy and resulted in a kind of mania, where those who had taken it thought they could walk on water. The blue pills were called Hate and produced a deep, pensive high.

Instinctively, I backed away from the box. Just being in the same room with it could cost me a year at Nordreslev. I hurried out of the shed and clicked the lock into place. I hopped over the fence and ran a short distance down the street, where I stopped and leaned against a wall. Then I pulled out my phone.

Hakim answered on the second ring.

"How seriously do you take anonymous tips? Can you be counted on to allow someone to remain anonymous?"

"I can hear that it's you, Anna."

"Then maybe I don't have anything to tell you."

"Okay. I can't hear that it's you."

I gave a long pause, and Hakim waited patiently on the other end.

"I think you should investigate Bike Shop Timmy. Start with the shed behind his shop."

"Does this have anything to do with the dead girls?"

"I don't think so, but I think you should do it anyway."

"I'll look into it. Where are you? I can come right n—"

I ended the call. Then I walked back to Frank's to get my bike and rode home.

When I got back home, I went directly to bed. I closed my eyes and tried to let the events of the past few days sink in. It was not an easy task, and before I could manage it, I drifted off to sleep.

I landed in the large bed in the strange room with the tapestry-clad walls. It still smelled spicy, and the fire roared in the large fireplace like last time.

Instinctively, I looked around for Varnar.

"He isn't here," said a girl's voice.

I jumped out of the bed and whipped around.

In a lounge chair in one corner sat a figure. She was wrapped in a cape and had the hood pulled up around her head, so I couldn't see her face, but from the contours of her form beneath the fabric, she didn't look very big.

I could definitely take her if this ended in a fight. Mentally, I smacked myself on the head. This was a dream.

"Who are you?" I asked and backed toward the door, fumbling for the knob behind me.

"I wouldn't go out there if I were you," she said. When she spoke, it sounded like a distorted version of a voice I knew well but couldn't place.

"What's out there?" Behind me, my hands continued to search.

"Rivers of dreams," she replied. "You'll get lost in them if you open that door."

I made my voice hard. Dream or not, I was not going to let her scare me. "What do you want from me?"

Something rustled on the other side of the door.

The girl shifted in the chair and spoke quickly. "I will tell you what to do."

"And what do you think I should do?"

Again, something scratched the other side of the door. This time it sounded like claws. Something sniffed or snuffled.

The girl straightened, and a lock of fiery red hair fell from beneath the hood.

"Look in the mirror, Anna."

I woke with a start and looked, heart pounding, at the covered mirror.

"No, oh God, no," I mumbled into the darkness.

 # CHAPTER 23

Two weeks passed. Two long, unbearable weeks.

I missed Varnar, I missed Arthur, I missed Monster, and I missed someone or something I couldn't define.

Mathias was quickly back on his feet again, and just like Od had said, after a week, there wasn't so much as a scar to be found on his chiseled chest. I sensed a new calm from him, but he was also afflicted with melancholy.

We talked about it one day when he proclaimed that my eyebrows and lashes were once again too light for my black hair.

I lay there with my head in his lap while he took a pair of tweezers to my eyebrows. The bleakness seeped into me from his legs and hands.

"Why are you so sad?" I asked. "You just found out that you're practically immortal."

Mathias paused briefly, but quickly resumed his work. "Is it that obvious?"

"For me it is."

He sighed. "I talked to Od. He told me he's over a thousand years old. I might live that long, too."

"That's awesome. Maybe one day you'll go on a space mission to another galaxy," I joked.

Mathias once again paused my facial torture.

"That's just it. You're all going to die before I do. My mom, you," he stopped, and I could tell he was gathering the courage just to utter the name, "and Luna."

381

"But that won't happen for a long time." I tried to comfort him, but the morning with Elias popped up in my memory. Maybe eternal life wasn't as much of a win as one might think.

"If I live over a thousand years, then the next seventy isn't a very long time," said Mathias. He tried to make his voice light, but he wasn't fooling me. "I just have a lot to deal with."

I knew exactly how he felt.

Varnar and I were still training, but he always brought Aella along.

She was a good teacher, and they both threw themselves into my training with a zeal that suggested that they, too, were on the Anna-is-in-danger train. Varnar radiated frustration, guilt, and misery when we were together. He completely avoided touching me and let Aella take the one-on-one exercises.

Elias was evidently busy because Od was away. I didn't hear much from him aside from a couple of phone calls, during which he was his annoying self again. He didn't mention his drunken breakdown and didn't seem to even remember that morning, which was fine by me. I had no reason to remind him that he had soaked my shirt with tears over a fly.

The only good thing that happened during those two weeks was that the police arrested Bike Shop Timmy.

Hakim discovered, as expected, his stash of drugs, and with his usual determination, he unraveled a larger network around Timmy, with sales and distribution of narcotics to all of North Jutland. Hakim never found out, however, who was at the top of the drug supply chain, which did not surprise me.

In the middle of October, the first storm hit, and it tore and gnawed at the flat landscape like a hungry predator. Situated on the only hilltop for miles around, I was astonished that my house stayed standing; it was stronger than it looked.

I looked out my living room window toward Kraghede Forest

and caught myself wondering if Varnar was okay down in the dilapidated manor. And Aella, too, of course.

The power went out right after the news channel had announced that the police were discouraging all travel throughout the country because it was deemed too dangerous.

I lit candles, which flickered on the windowsill, even though the windows were closed tight. I realized that someone was pounding on the door. It was hard to hear over the storm.

Outside stood Ben in a long yellow raincoat, a red top hat, and green rubber boots. He looked like a reggae musician dressed as a biology teacher, or vice versa.

"I wanted to make sure you can make it through the storm," he said in his deep, melodic voice. "May I come in?"

I went through Elias's step-by-step safety guide. If Ben wanted me dead, he would have zapped me, or something, as soon as I opened the door. I waved him in.

"I can't even make you a cup of tea, since the power just went out," I said.

Making himself at home, Ben reached into one of my cabinets, pulled out a couple of mugs, and filled them with water. Then he stuck a finger in each one.

"It's been a while since I spoke to you," he said in his strong accent. "How's it going?"

"Fine." I glanced at the water in the mugs, which was beginning to bubble and steam.

Ben didn't seem to notice that he had his fingers in boiling water. "I understand Od Dinesen has told you what he is."

I nodded.

"So he's told you that the gods exist."

"Yeah, he did say that." I couldn't keep the doubtful look off my face.

"Do you not believe him?" Ben brought out a bag and poured some dried leaves into the mugs.

"I haven't seen any proof that they exist."

"You saw Mathias get shot." Ben moved, elegantly despite his massive size, over to the table. "Mathias survived, and he's only half god. Is that not proof?"

"The fact that Od says Mathias is a demigod is not enough proof for me. There's so much mysterious stuff happening that could have all kinds of explanations that don't involve the existence of gods. So it's gonna take more than that for me to start hanging food from the trees."

Ben laughed his signature predatory laugh. "You have a healthy sense of skepticism."

The storm raged on outside, and I sipped the tea. I realized that if Ben wanted to dope me with stjórna, he had just had the perfect opportunity.

You are so bad at looking out for yourself, Anna.

Ben looked at me, and a strange anticipation and nervousness flickered across his face.

"Go on, say it," I said.

"What do you want me to say?"

"Whatever you came over here to tell me. There's obviously something on your mind."

"You shouldn't be able to read me." His thick, dark brows lowered.

My jaw dropped. "Did Luna tell you I'm clairvoyant? Aren't there all kinds of rules about how you're not allowed to talk about other people?"

"Luna didn't say anything," Ben thundered. "I know it because of my magic. But why can you read me? I put powerful spells on myself to avoid that."

"Calm down, I can barely see your aura," I said. "The spells are working fine. But maybe you should also use something to control your face, because everything I can't see with my clairvoyant abilities, I can see in your facial expressions."

384

"This isn't the first time I've heard that." He smiled to himself. "So what is it you want to tell me?"

"I need to tell you about something I did when you were a kid."

I felt my eyes narrow. "What did you do?"

Ben did not get straight to the point, but instead started telling a longer story.

"I was there the night you came into the world. It was two months early. You were so little, and you came close to dying." His gaze drifted over my scar, which peeked over the neckline of my shirt.

I pulled the top of my shirt up slightly and looked at him expectantly.

"I saw you again four years later, when I had to remove you from Mia and Jens. You were the happiest, most wonderful little girl. You have so much of Arthur in you."

"Was it you who took me away from them? I don't remember you."

"I made sure you wouldn't remember it." He squeezed his hand into a large fist. "I thought you would be safe with Mia and Jens. I thought she was only after us, so we went far away to not put you in danger. She had already managed to kill your father, and she had imprisoned your mother."

"Who are you talking about? Who is *she*?"

Ben shook his head, so his heavy dreadlocks slapped together. "How much has Od told you about the other worlds?"

"He talked about Valhalla and some other make-believe places. I don't remember what he called them, and I didn't believe him, either, if I'm being honest."

"They aren't make-believe. The other worlds are real."

"Do you mean like parallel universes?" I could barely say it without laughing.

Ben nodded seriously. "I didn't believe in it, either, the first time I heard about it. Od was also the one who explained it to me, quite a long time ago now. He described our universe as a house with several stories. On each story there's one or more worlds."

"I thought he was full of shit. He's so weird, I filter out half of what he says."

Ben laughed in surprise.

"Every time I think you're the spitting image of Arthur, your mom shows up in you." Then he continued more gravely. "You should listen to Od and treat him with respect. He's not full of *shit*, as you put it."

"I'll decide for myself who I treat with respect," I snapped. "Tell me about the other worlds."

Ben looked at me for a second before he started to drag his little finger across the boards of my dining table. It left behind glowing blue streaks on the dark wood. A month ago, I would have gasped out loud at the sight, but now I was content just to scold him for ruining my table.

He waved me off with his free hand. "It'll go away."

He continued to draw gleaming blue lines. Before my eyes, a detailed drawing unfolded of what looked like an egg-shaped map.

"As Od probably told you, the Norse universe is divided into worlds. They're located on different levels." He drew two horizontal lines through the middle of the oval, where in a beautiful cursive hand he wrote, *Midgard—Alfheim—Svartalfheim.* "The worlds are separated by a kind of membrane. They're close together, but you can't travel between them except in certain places where there are passageways. On the same level as our world, Midgard, there's Alfheim, where the Light Elves live, and Svartalfheim, where the Black Elves live." Ben drew the worlds with his little finger, and I recognized the outlines of Scandinavia, but the two other worlds were unknown to me.

I wanted to say something, but Ben held up his hand. For the first time, I noticed that his palms were tattooed with small symbols.

"Above us is Jotunheim, home of the giants, and Vanheim, the home of the Vanir," Ben continued. "Muspelheim is here, too, but no one lives there aside from the giant Surt." He drew the areas, wrote the names, then drew yet another horizontal line through the egg.

"Sucks for Surt," I mumbled, which prompted a sharp look from Ben.

Okay then, no jokes.

"Over here is Asgard, where the Æsir live, and where Valhalla and Fólkvangr are."

He denoted this on my table. Then he drew a tree at the top, its branches enveloping the oval map.

"The world tree Yggdrasil spreads its leaves over the entire universe," he said. "That's how it has been since creation, when Odin and his brothers created everything."

I pointed at the bottom part of the egg, which was empty. "What's down there?"

"Niflheim," said Ben. "Among other things."

"Among other things?"

Ben sighed. "In the underworld there is also Helheim. It's a realm of the dead. Those who do not die in battle go there."

Ben looked up from his drawing, which now resembled a glow-in-the-dark techno spiderweb.

"For hundreds of years, the Nordic peoples worshipped the Norse gods, but that changed when Christianity swept across Europe." A bitterness I didn't understand flared in his face. "In time, almost everyone was converted, either with a sword at their throat or alms in their hand. Finally, there were only a few people in Midgard who honored the old faith. The gods knew that if they weren't worshipped, they'd fade away. Therefore, they opened a world for the true believers. A world that had been hidden from time immemorial."

Even though I was getting used to being served mysterious facts, my head was threatening to combust.

387

"What is that world called?"

"Now it's called Freiheim, but its first name was Hrafnheim. It means something along the lines of 'the home of the ravens.' It's named after Odin's two ravens, Huginn and Muninn." Ben wrote the name on the map and drew something that looked like an island.

"Any connection to the name Ravensted?"

Ben's eyes sparkled. "Yes," he said.

I waited for an elaboration that never came.

Ben continued: "The gods' servants here in Midgard gathered the faithful and invited them to settle in Hrafnheim. In 1054, Norse pagans from all over Scandinavia began to migrate there."

I furrowed my brows. "And Hrafnheim still exists?"

"Yes, although these are dark times," Ben said grimly.

"What was it like in the past?"

Ben mumbled something in a language I didn't understand, and got a focused look on his face. "Look into me," he growled.

Suspicious, I reached out with my power and felt a little tear in his otherwise impenetrable mental armor. I cautiously looked inside and saw a landscape so beautiful I brought my hand to my mouth. There were snow-capped mountains, deep green valleys, and steaming geysers.

I saw it all from above, as if I were on the back of a large bird. A majestic forest with orange leaves caught my eye before Ben abruptly tossed me out of his past.

"Hey," I protested. "I want to see more."

"You saw what was necessary," he grumbed.

I rubbed my forehead. "Thanks for the lecture on alternative historiography. Interesting. But what does this parallel world have to do with me?"

Ben exposed his teeth in a truly frightening manner. A couple of his gold teeth reflected the gleam of the candlelight.

"Sorry. I lose myself. It's something that comes with age."

I scanned Ben, who at forty-something didn't look like someone who was approaching a dementia diagnosis.

"Ben, how old are you really?" I asked on a whim.

Ben did not answer my question, but instead, he said, "Bear with me. It's important that you let me explain this."

"You actually came to tell me about something you did to me when I was little," I snapped.

Again, he bared his teeth. "Let me finish."

"Fine. Tell me more about the gods and their strange parallel worlds." I leaned back and interlaced my hands behind my neck in an imitation of patience.

"Hrafnheim was a more or less peaceful place where the Norse gods were worshipped for hundreds of years, but about twenty years ago, a woman by the name of Ragnara raised a rebel army of slaves."

"And she took power?"

"In the end, yes. She rules Hrafnheim now, and she has renamed the world Freiheim."

"Do you know her?"

Ben looked down at the table. "We know her, and she knows us."

"How?"

"To make a very long story short, Ragnara got the idea that your mother was a threat to her."

"Why did she think that?"

"Ragnara has a magician and seer who works for her, Bork. He prophesied that your mother's blood would lead to Ragnara's death, which is otherwise thought to be impossible."

"But everyone dies at some point."

"Not Ragnara. She can't die," Ben said casually, as if he had just said Ragnara had long hair or was of Swedish descent.

"Is she a demigod?"

"Demigods and half gods can die. Even though they're very resilient. Ragnara is a completely normal person. She has no magical abilities like me or clairvoyance like you."

I shook my head. "Then it's impossible."

"Ragnara made a deal with someone—we don't know who. This being ensures that no one and nothing can kill her."

"That sounds like something from a fable. A fairy tale."

Ben's sharp teeth glittered again. "We are in the borderland, where almost everything is possible."

"But this seer guy prophesied that my mom could kill her?"

"No. He prophesied that *her blood* could lead to Ragnara's death. Maybe there's literally something in Thora's blood that can kill Ragnara. Maybe it means that if your mother dies, it will also be fatal for Ragnara."

"So what did she do?"

"She came here."

"She was here, in boring old Ravensted?"

"It definitely wasn't boring. It was bloody. Ragnara and her people performed blót according to the old ways."

I didn't want to ask, but I had to.

"The Windmill Murders?"

Ben nodded slowly. "Ragnara wanted to get ahold of Thora and understand the prophecy. At any cost. Only one god knows the future in detail, but Od's father did not wish to share his knowledge with Ragnara."

"Odin?" I had a hard time suppressing my doubtful tone. Instead, I tried to stay focused. "So Ragnara captured my mom to keep her alive and keep anyone from doing magic with her blood?"

The realization that I had just located my mother hit me like small pinpricks. I leaned toward Ben. His story had suddenly become highly relevant to me.

"Correct," said Ben. "The night you were born, Ragnara took your mother prisoner."

"Did you ever find out what the prophecy meant?"

Ben shook his head. "We still don't know. We do know that Ragnara doesn't dare kill your mother out of fear that it would

390

result in her own death. But the prophecy could mean something else."

He met my eyes with a serious expression.

My whole body went cold. "Me?"

Ben nodded. "You are Thora's blood. I'm afraid that Ragnara believes you might have the ability to take her life."

"How long have you known that?"

"I began to suspect it when you were four. I was sure she wouldn't come after you because we signed a treaty stating that you were not to be touched. We negotiated it under very . . . dramatic circumstances. Ragnara is not known for keeping her promises, but the treaty is written in blood, and a blood pact is a binding agreement."

"Is this the treaty that was signed with Arthur's blood?"

"It was necessary."

I swallowed. "But she didn't keep her word, I'm assuming."

"I don't know if it was Ragnara. If I were certain, I would have the right to start a conflict." Ben did not elaborate on what exactly a conflict entailed, but I got the feeling it wasn't pretty. "There was an attempt to poison you, but Mia and Jens's daughter ate the poisoned apple. She nearly died, and I didn't dare let you live with Mia and Jens anymore. So I hid you by handing you over to Greta."

"How would you have hidden me by handing me over to social services? I have been monitored for as long as I can remember."

Ben cleared his throat. "There are many ways to hide people. Sometimes it's best to put them in plain sight."

He waited a moment before he continued. "Now's when I tell you what I had to do."

"What did you do?" My voice hardened, and I drummed my fingers against the table.

"I cast powerful spells around you. Most people who meet you will be uninterested in you. Some simply don't notice you exist. A small handful will be decidedly repulsed by you."

391

I held my breath, unable to speak.

"I placed another spell on you, which makes it so that everyone who tries to find you will have a very hard time doing so."

My lips pressed together, and my heart began to pound.

Ben spoke faster.

"I exempted Greta from the spells," he said. "But that's probably getting too technical."

Several times, I tried to say something, but I couldn't decide which words should be the first out of my mouth.

"Lift the spells. Right now!" I ended up bellowing.

His eyes were apologetic, but unyielding. "I won't do that until I know you're safe. But I understand your anger."

"Anger . . . anger . . ." I was breathless with rage. "You isolated me. You made me unwanted, unloved, and . . . alone." Again, I had to stop to gasp for air. Realization smacked me with an almost physical pain. "You destroyed my life."

"But at least you have a life. I did what I did to save it. I gave your parents my word that I would keep you alive. I promised Arthur on his deathbed."

I couldn't listen, and it was as if the storm outside had taken up residence within me.

"Have I been walking around with your shitty magic on me for all these years?"

"I added more spells when you were fourteen," Ben said uncomfortably. "Back when there was a fire in your foster family's house. I'm certain Ragnara was behind it."

He squeezed his eyes half-shut and turned his head, as if awaiting an explosion.

I did not let him down. I stood and smashed my mug on the ground, the shards flying in all directions. Then I ran.

Behind me, Ben shouted. "It's dangerous to go out."

I absolutely could not care less. I had to get away from him before I put my hands around his throat and squeezed.

Outside, I was nearly lifted by the wind and blown sideways down the field toward Kraghede Forest. My entire body protested against the biting wind and the ice-cold rainstorm. It was true, what Ben had yelled. Weather like this can be deadly, and anyone who doesn't respect a fall hurricane in northwestern Denmark has to be pretty stupid.

I just had to let the worst of the anger out. But then I saw a figure in the field, almost at the edge of Kraghede Forest.

It was a girl, walking with her back to me.

I screamed as loud as I could. "You can't go in there."

She didn't hear me but continued toward the woods with uncertain steps, wearing only a thin dress with bare feet.

I gasped for air as the wind ripped and tore at me. Was this the girl from my dream? I quickly looked up at the moon. It was only half full, and there was no snow on the ground. It didn't fit at all with the rest of my vision. The girl's hair was also too short, and she was too thin and too small. But a strange feeling swirled in me, and I began to run toward her.

Several times I was knocked down by the wind, and I tumbled into the soft mud. The whole way, I yelled to the girl that she couldn't go into the forest. She would be struck by falling trees or downed branches, but either she couldn't hear me, or she had actually been drugged with stjórna. I stumbled toward her and was alternately held back by the wind and suddenly blown several feet forward by it.

Right at the entrance to the forest, I was caught by a squall and slammed into the trunk of a spruce tree. It hurt like hell, but I couldn't let the girl keep going. Either the murderer would show up and kill her, or she would be killed by the storm. I shouted to her again and again as I was tossed around by the wind.

The girl staggered onward, seemingly unaffected by the wind or my screams.

Walking into the forest was like walking into the mouth of a giant, snarling, wild animal. The trees howled and banged against one another, and everything was moving around me. I went way too far into the woods for my own safety, but I had to try to get the girl out. I breathed in as much air as I could and roared as loudly as my voice would permit.

"Stop!"

Finally, the girl stopped. She turned slowly and looked at me with confusion in her eyes. She grabbed her throat, where a leather cord dangled.

Around me, everything was chaos, but my insides turned to ice when our eyes met.

It was Belinda.

CHAPTER 24

Belinda—or Belinda's ghost, as this must have been—stared hatefully at me. Without even seeing her move, she was suddenly right in front of me. The rune on her forehead shone darkly in the sparse moonlight, and she raised a bone-white finger toward me.

"Ugly-Anna. What did you do to me?" She reached out, but her arm went straight through my chest, and an ice-cold flame cut through my insides. Belinda looked at her arm, eyes wild.

Oh no. She didn't know she was dead.

"I didn't do anything to you, Belinda," I tried to say as I backed away.

She formed her fingers into claws and tried to scratch my face. Again and again, her hands went through me. She looked at them in frustration as ice crystals spread across my cheeks.

"What's going on?" she screamed.

An enormous branch snapped off the tree we were standing under. It only just missed me.

Belinda barely noticed it.

I turned to run out of the woods. Belinda's ghost would have to fend for herself, because right now I was in imminent danger. I felt a pair of cold arms cling to my waist from behind. They went through me like a knife through soft butter, but my hips were numbed by the cold, and I fell forward. I rolled onto my back, and then she was on top of me.

"You can't go," she pleaded. "You're the only person who's talked to me in ages."

I remembered what Ulla had said, about how most ghosts are deeply traumatized. Right now, I was in full agreement that spirits did not belong in our world and should cross over to the beyond as quickly as possible.

Belinda's slightly translucent hands were around my neck. As the chill spread from my windpipe to my lungs, she shouted through the roaring of the wind.

"I remember speaking to you at Frank's. Ever since, everything has been so strange. No one will answer me when I talk to them. And I always feel like I can't breathe." Straddling me, she squeezed my throat, and even though she clearly was not a poltergeist like Arthur, I coughed and had difficulty getting up.

The large spruce tree above us swayed ominously. Another branch snapped and fell close to my face. The ground beneath us moved threateningly as the large tree began to lose its grip. It was about to topple.

"Belinda. Let me go. I can't help you now."

"You. Can. Not. Go," she howled.

Again, the earth shook, and the spruce began to creak.

"The tree. It'll hit us," I choked.

Belinda did not react. Instead, she began hitting me in the face with clenched fists that whizzed right through my head.

The tree was tipping toward us.

With great effort, I managed to roll sideways, away from Belinda and the tree, and I winced when the tree hit the ground with a deafening boom.

Belinda screamed as it crashed down over her, and she was trapped under the three-foot-wide trunk.

I lay there for a moment with my arms around my head. Then I cautiously looked up.

Belinda stuck up through the middle of the felled tree. Her lower body was buried in the knotty trunk. She looked down at herself and screamed again. Then she waded out of the tree as if it were a creek, heading straight toward me with her arms raised in an attack position.

I got to my knees and shouted, "You are dead. You are a ghost. You were strangled with the leather cord you have around your neck."

Belinda's ghost stopped; her lips peeled back. She fingered the cord and looked like she was vaguely remembering something. Then she clutched her neck, as if she couldn't breathe, and fell to the ground.

"I'm sorry. I have to do this," I whispered. Louder, I yelled, "You are dead. You are dead. You are dead." I got to my feet and stood over her.

Belinda writhed on the ground and clutched her throat, coughing. Then she disappeared in a poof, like Arthur had done the day I asked him about his death.

When she was gone, I began to shake uncontrollably. Another tree fell close by, and when the roots wrenched up, the ground moved so much that I lost my footing and landed on the forest floor. I got back up and tried to fight my way out of Kraghede Forest, but I had gotten farther into the forest than I'd realized.

I finally glimpsed the field, but just when I thought I would make it, the ground heaved beneath me again. I was near one of the largest trees at the edge of the forest, which succumbed to years of onslaught from the western wind at the precise moment I passed it. It tipped over as its enormous network of roots released its hold on the earth.

I flew into the air, as if I'd been standing on a catapult. First the tree hit the ground, and then I landed, in a torrent of soil and spruce needles, on my stomach across the trunk. The wind was knocked out of me, and I slid down to the ground, where I lay gasping as small black spots danced across my vision.

I closed my eyes, ready to let myself be enveloped by the void, but then I sensed someone approaching me. At first, I prepared to fight or flee, but then I recognized Varnar's focused aura.

He reached me and knelt at my side.

I flung my arms around him and sobbed, completely indifferent to the fact that he felt disgust at being physically close to me. Right now I just wanted to feel his warm, living body against mine.

First he stiffened, but then he wrapped his arms tightly around me. It was as if his strong lifeblood drove out the chill that Belinda's ghost had left in me.

"We need to get out of here," he mumbled in my ear. He got me to my feet and began running through the forest with me in tow.

"We need to get out of the forest, not farther into it. We'll be killed," I shouted.

"It's most dangerous at the edges, where the trees have more room to fall. We won't make it out to the field without getting hit." He sprinted toward Kraghede Manor, pulling me by the hand.

I couldn't see anything in the dark, but Varnar navigated effortlessly between the plummeting trees and fallen branches. After a short, nerve-wracking run, we arrived. He led me into the living room, where Aella was waiting in a battered armchair.

She stood quickly.

Varnar got me to sit on some blankets on the floor and sat down next to me. I breathed in ragged bursts and paid no attention to anything other than clinging to him desperately.

"Where did you find her?"

"At the edge of the forest."

"What were you doing in the forest in this weather?" Aella's voice was accusatory.

I just stared at her, gasping for air.

"I think Anna needs to rest," said Varnar. "We can talk later."

Aella looked like she wanted to say more but stopped herself. She left us and quickly returned with a pile of dry clothes. Then she disappeared into another room.

Varnar somehow got me out of my wet clothes and into Aella's.

My body gradually warmed up and grew calm. It did, however, continue to give little jolts, and I could not release my grip on Varnar, who waited at my side saying nothing.

"I'm sorry," I said, when I was able to speak again.

"What are you sorry for?"

"I know you don't like me touching you." I didn't care if he was letting me cling to him out of pity, as long as I got to feel his warm body against mine.

A feeling I recognized as acceptance flowed from Varnar. He pushed me down onto the blankets, lay down next to me, and held me.

"It's okay," he said.

I got the feeling he was speaking more to himself than to me.

"When are you going to yell at me?" I looked up at him.

The hint of a smile glimmered in his eyes. "Why would I yell at you?"

"I went into the woods during the storm, and you're always pissed at me when I do something dangerous."

"I know you didn't run in there willingly." He paused briefly. "What were you fighting?"

"You saw me? Were you lurking like that time with Peter and Christian?" My voice developed an acidic edge.

"No. I sensed your fight, but I couldn't sense your opponent."

"What do you mean?"

Varnar's dark brown eyes with their small flecks of green stared into mine, and my body gave another jolt, but this time it wasn't out of fear.

"I can sense everything in the forest," he said. "I knew you were in the forest the moment you ran in. It just took me a little while to get to you. You're always unbelievably difficult to find." He furrowed his brows.

My mind flashed bitterly to Ben's magical Teflon coating. "How can you sense the forest?"

399

"I grew up in the forest. Not this one, but I understand the language of all forests."

"The forests have a language?"

Varnar nodded. Veneration and longing drifted off him as his thoughts reached back. For the first time, I got a super short glimpse of his past.

He was younger. A child. And he laughed and clambered, barefoot, high up into a tree. The clothes he was wearing looked foreign, and he shouted something in a language I didn't understand. Behind him, I saw a settlement that resembled nothing from this world. The leaves on the trees were a golden orange.

This is the same place I just saw in Ben's past.

A thought sprouted in my head. "If I say *Hrafnheim*, what does it mean to you?" I asked him.

He waited a second before speaking. "It means home. Even though it's called Freiheim now. The name 'Hrafnheim' is forbidden."

"You're from Hrafnheim," I whispered. Maybe now would be a good time for me to run back into the deadly hurricane. But my body refused to leave its place next to Varnar, so I would just have to hope that he wasn't the person who was after me. My face must have revealed my thoughts.

"I tried to tell you that night when we . . ." He stopped and fumbled for the words.

I cast my eyes down as he regained his composure.

"What I didn't manage to say is that Aella and I were sent here to Midgard to protect you."

"Sent by whom?"

Varnar hesitated. "By your mother. Your mother sent us."

Mother. The word sounded strange even in my head. I said it several times internally before I realized I hadn't said anything aloud.

"You know my mom," I stammered.

"I report to her," he said.

"What do you mean? Report how?"

"She's my commander."

Commander?!

"Isn't she being held captive by what's-her-name?"

"She is. But she's also leading the resistance against Ragnara. She's done so for years, in secret, from Ragnara's own castle."

I looked at him skeptically. How did I know he wasn't telling me a pack of lies?

"You don't believe me?"

I sighed. "I don't know what to believe anymore. My life was completely different just a few months ago. Everything has been turned on its head."

Varnar looked at me.

"I feel the same way." He did not go into detail, but instead changed the subject. "You were fighting with something tonight. What?"

I chewed my lower lip. If I told Varnar about my powers, he might think I was insane. On the other hand, he had just told me he was a bodyguard sent by my mother, who was the leader of a secret resistance movement in a mythological parallel world ruled by a tyrannical queen—and that he could understand forest language. What was the worst that could happen? I cleared my throat.

"I'm clairvoyant. I can see the past." Varnar's face did not give away his thoughts, so I quickly continued. "And because ghosts belong to the past, I can also see them. Tonight I met the spirit of Belinda Jaeger. She's one of the murdered girls."

"I know who she was," said Varnar. "Was she angry?"

"Well, she wasn't happy. But she didn't like me when she was alive, either. She thinks I have something to do with what happened to her."

"Maybe you do, in a way. Maybe she can sense it."

"Oh, come on. Do you also think there's a murderer after me?"

He did not reply, just gave me a serious look.

"Jesus Christ!" I rolled my eyes.

"Not really the divinity I would refer to, but in principle, yes." Varnar smiled, and I was almost able to forget how repulsed he was by me.

"Do you know why there's someone who wants to kill me?"

Varnar shook his head almost imperceptibly. "I only know what I need to know in order to protect you."

"And what do you need to know?"

"That your would-be killer knows your age and that you grew up in this area with no parents. He didn't know your name or what you look like, apart from your red hair. Before, he was killing girls who matched the description—even though the description turned out to be wrong, but I think he's figured out who you are. I, too, was looking for a red-haired girl. It was lucky that you ran right into me that day."

"Then how did you recognize me?"

"Apparently I know more than the murderer does," Varnar evaded.

"What do you mean?"

He pressed his lips into a tight line, and I knew that I wouldn't get any more out of him about it. But there was something else I wanted to know.

"Now you're talking about the guy who hasn't been caught yet. There's also the other one. The one in police custody."

"That's Naut Kafnar. It's disgusting that Ragnara would form an alliance with someone like him."

Suddenly, I smelled smoke and heard screams. I automatically looked around.

"What's wrong?" Varnar's body tensed, and he started to stand up.

"Did you hear something?"

"Only the wind." He tilted his head to one side and listened.

I realized what had happened, and mentally face-palmed. I must have caught something from Varnar's past. "Sorry," I mumbled.

Varnar looked at me with furrowed brows.

I returned to the other topic. "What do you mean by *someone like him?*"

"He's a berserker."

"I've heard about the berserkers."

"You have? I didn't think you knew Freiheim existed."

"I didn't. But I read about them in my history book. Sounds like they were Viking Age thugs."

"I forget that the histories of our worlds are closely linked." His face grew dark. "In my opinion, it was a mistake to let the berserkers be part of the great migration. They continued the tradition of going on raids. They should have stayed here in Midgard, where they would have been wiped out by the followers of the new faith. But Od Dinesen took pity on them. He's known for being merciful."

"Od?" It was one thing to theoretically know how old Od was. It was something else entirely to be confronted with him being part of Nordic history.

"Od Dinesen organized the great migration. You didn't know that?"

"It's been about an hour since I found out that Hrafnheim exists."

Varnar flinched slightly when I said "Hrafnheim." He didn't mention it, however, instead saying: "I'm surprised that you were kept in the dark for so long. You of all people need to know the truth."

I did not have a chance to ask which truth he was referring to, or why I had a special status in relation to it, because at that moment, Ben's voice boomed outside. Aella protested, but he burst into the living room and caught sight of Varnar and me on the blanket together.

Then Varnar jumped up in one of his typical fluid movements, ready to attack.

Ben snarled at me hotly. "I see you're doing just fine. What are you doing here?"

"How did you get through the forest?" I asked instead of replying. "It's deadly."

Ben chuckled. "A simple storm is no threat to me. You have no idea what I've been up against in my time."

"Speaking of *your time* . . ." I began, but Ben waved me off.

"Not now." He threw up his long arms. "What in the gods' names were you doing? Running straight into the forest during a hurricane. I forbid you from doing anything like that again."

Varnar stepped up close to Ben, who was both larger and older than him, but Varnar looked him straight in the eyes.

"You can't forbid her from doing anything."

Ben focused on Varnar, who, until then, he had not dignified with a glance.

"Who are you, boy?" he growled with his deep voice.

"Varnar of the Forest Folk of the Bronze Forest," Varnar said, straightening up even taller.

"Don't lie to me." Ben's eyes sparkled threateningly.

"I never lie."

"Are you telling me you're the Varnar who led the Varangian Guard, and who *died* while protecting Ragnara?"

Varnar raised an eyebrow. "I'm not quite as dead as the rumors suggest."

Ben shook his head, causing the thick dreadlocks to fly around his ears. "Bork *saw* that Varnar died. He always sees the truth."

"Bork lied," said Varnar.

"And why would he do that?"

"He switched sides."

"Bork has always been on Ragnara's side," Ben spat.

"No. Bork has always been on the winning side. He knows that Ragnara's time may be running out."

Ben mulled this information over. "Bork is a cunning snake.

That sounds like something he would do. What about Eskild Black-Eye?"

Varnar looked down. "Eskild is still on Ragnara's side."

I looked from one to the other and jumped in. "What the hell are you talking about?"

The two men looked at me as though they had completely forgotten I was there.

"These are political affairs, Anna," Ben rumbled. "Knowing too much would put you at risk."

I looked appealingly at Varnar, who nevertheless appeared to be in full agreement with Ben.

Ben continued: "I need to speak with Varnar alone. Stay here and rest tonight."

They both turned to leave.

"Hey!" I shouted.

They turned again. Ben with an irritated grimace, Varnar with an unreadable expression.

"Do I not also have the right to hear what's going on?" I asked.

"You don't have the right to know any more than what's necessary for your protection. If you know too much, it will only bring you more danger," said Varnar. The chill of dismissal lay in his voice, and I felt stupid sitting there in a pile of blankets on the floor.

"I agree," said Ben. "Tomorrow we will resume our conversation, and this time I would appreciate it if you don't storm off like a teenage girl."

The two men left the room.

"I *am* a teenage girl," I yelled after them, and got up. I untangled myself from the blankets and looked for my shoes. Storm or no storm, I wasn't planning on staying one more second in this junk pile of a manor.

Aella stuck her head in. "Where were they going?"

I sneered. "They were going to talk about political affairs." I angrily pulled on my shoes.

Aella spread her arms. "I don't know quite as much as Varnar, but I'd be happy to tell you what I know." This was clearly an attempt to keep me there with bait rather than by force. Though I was certain she wouldn't be shy about resorting to the latter if the bait didn't work.

I took the bait and sat on the armchair. "Okay. Do you also know my mom?"

Aella nodded. "Thora. Yes. But not as well as Varnar does. He practically worships her."

I wrinkled my nose at this information.

"Varnar would go to his death at Thora's command," said Aella.

"And you wouldn't?" I asked.

"It depends on the command," she said with a crooked smile.

"But are you both part of the secret resistance movement?" I felt like laughing as I said it.

But Aella nodded gravely. "I've been part of it longer than Varnar. I've actually been on Thora's side for several years. Varnar had a hard time breaking away from Eskild Black-Eye. But Eskild's most recent actions drove him to it, and when he finally crossed over, he raised quickly through the ranks. Now he's one of Thora's closest advisers."

"So who *is* this Eskild Black-Eye?"

Aella blinked a couple of times. "I forget that you aren't familiar with Hrafnheim. Eskild has commanded Ragnara's army from the very beginning. They say he's also the father of her son, although no one knows that for sure."

"Ragnara has a son?"

"Sverre," hissed Aella. She could have just as well said *maggot*.

"What's he like?"

"He's a little shit, is what he is. And he hates Varnar, because Varnar's skill earned him praise from Ragnara and Eskild." Aella sniffed.

"Why was Varnar praised by Ragnara and Eskild?"

"When we arrived in Sént as kids, we started in the army's training program. This was long before we switched sides to the resistance movement."

"What is Sént?" I was getting tired of feeling so dense.

"Sént is the biggest city in Hrafnheim," said Aella. "The castle is there. Ragnara took it over when she usurped power."

"And you went there?"

"Yes. And from the beginning, Varnar was talented and highly dedicated. At fifteen, he was one of Ragnara's personal bodyguards. At sixteen, he trained all the new bodyguards, and the year after, he was made head of the Varangian Guard."

"Have you known him since you were kids?"

"Yes. We grew up together in the Bronze Forest," Aella said lightly, but a deep sorrow flew across her face as she said it.

"Why did you go to Ragnara's stronghold?"

Aella looked into the flames, taking time to reply. Finally, she spoke. "We no longer had a home. Eskild took all the children from the Bronze Forest twelve years ago."

"Why? What about the adults?"

Again, Aella paused, studying her hands intently. And again I smelled smoke and heard screams. I waited silently until she was ready to speak.

"Varnar is the oldest of our people now," she said quietly.

I considered what I should say, but then Varnar joined us.

"Benedict left. You can sleep here, Anna. I'll sleep in the barn. Aella has her own bed in the kitchen, so she's not far away if you need anything." He gave Aella a get-out-of-here look, and she stood and traipsed off. Varnar stood in the doorway, clenched his fists, and spread his fingers out a couple of times. I looked at him expectantly from my spot on the weathered armchair.

Without saying any more, he turned his back to me and left.

Even though I really wanted to go home, I gave in to the fear of toppling trees and ghosts, and I curled up on the floor in front of the fireplace. The thought that Varnar would rather sleep in a cold, dilapidated barn during a hurricane than in the same room as me was almost unbearable.

I opened my eyes and saw the familiar scene in the forest. I had clearly landed in the precise spot where the girl had just recently taken her last, panting breath. Her back was exposed, and the blood ran from the rune. The man disappeared between the trees. I followed him with my eyes before looking down.

The girl lay there like a rag doll someone had tossed aside in a messy pile. Her hair was partly covering her cheek, so I had to kneel and get very close to her to see her face.

The recognition sent icy shock waves through me, and I stumbled back with a scream.

The facial features were familiar but distorted in a death mask. The hair color, which appeared light gray in the moonlight, was all wrong. But that didn't change the fact that these were my dead eyes staring back at me, and that the girl's face was my own.

 # CHAPTER 25

My screams must have woken Aella, because it was she who hauled me out of the vision. She was kneeling next to my bedding and shaking me forcefully.

At first, I fought against her grasp. Then I recognized her and shook the vision off.

"What did you see?" Aella's voice was tense.

I shook my head, unable to speak.

She looked like she wanted to give me a hug, but my expression must have signaled that she should hold off. She asked me again: "What did you see? Did it change?"

Change!?

"What the hell do you know about what I see?" I sputtered. I wrapped my arms around myself and rubbed. The fire had gone out; only faint embers smoldered in the fireplace.

Aella stood and added a couple pieces of firewood. She kept her back to me. "I have a suspicion that you're a seeress."

"What gave you that idea?"

"I don't know if it's safe for me to say," she said as she poked at the embers.

"Safe for whom?" I was tired of trying to put this puzzle together in the dark.

Aella turned toward me. Her face was closed off.

"Should I sleep in here? I can wake you up if you see it again."

The warmth began to seep into me and drove away the cold that, for the second time that night, numbed my entire body.

"I'm okay. It was just a dream."

Aella pressed her lips together. Then she nodded.

"Call me if you need anything," she said before padding barefoot out of the living room.

I lay down and closed my eyes. Immediately, my inner eye saw my own face with glassy eyes and hair that looked pale in the moonlight. With a gasp, I opened my eyes wide.

I lay there the rest of the night and stared into the fire, not daring to fall asleep again.

The next morning, Varnar walked me home through the razed forest.

The whole way, we had to step over and crawl under large trunks and branches lying across the small path. Neither of us said anything until we reached Odinmont.

"It's good that now you know I'm here on Thora's orders."

You mean, it's good for you that I know you're not spending time with me of your own free will.

I said nothing but turned to go inside.

"Can we train?" he asked behind me. "There's something I really want to show you."

I turned back around toward him. "Now?"

"Do you have something else to do?"

"Not exactly."

He walked around the side of Odinmont and into my garden without saying anything. I trudged after him.

Varnar stood in front of me on the grass. His hand flew forward, and I evaded it with relative ease and retaliated with a karate chop to his throat. He blocked my attack and pushed my arm away. I trapped his arm and punched him in the diaphragm. His free hand struck my arm, but I used the force of the blow to spin around and place one leg behind him while shoving him hard in the chest with both hands, causing him to fall backward. I knew that he let me do it. If we had been fighting for real, he would have won easily, but it was as if we were dancing a rehearsed dance.

A month had passed since we last trained properly, just the two of us, and although Aella was a good teacher, it wasn't the same as fighting with Varnar.

He got up from the grass and wiped his hands together.

"You've gotten better."

I tried to brush off his praise.

"Again." He stood in front of me, and we began another round. I could sense that he was enjoying it, too. He sent a fist directly toward my face, and I instinctively raised my arms, so the punch hit my forearm. I let his force send me a few steps back, so he threw a couple of punches pointlessly into the air. *Ha!* He hadn't been expecting that.

He rewarded me with one of his far-too-rare smiles. Then he ran straight at me, and I prepared for a frontal attack. But suddenly he was gone, and I looked over my shoulder.

Though I had no idea how he had moved, he stood behind me, and before I had time to react, he hit me in the side with a flat hand. If it had been a fist, he would have cracked my ribs.

"How did you do that?" I asked, hunched over.

"Those moves have saved my life on several occasions," he said. "Watch me."

He stood in front of me again. Slowly, he showed me how he ran forward, did a sort of dance move, and then a backflip, and in this way was able to move to a position behind me at the speed of light.

I tried to copy him, but my first attempt was clumsy. I cursed.

"Try again."

I gave it another try. It was a little better, but I was still hopelessly far from Varnar's elegant movements. We kept working for a while, but each time I ended up cursing.

Finally, I lost my patience. "Am I the only one who's horrible at this?" I yelled. "I'm sure the other people you taught were able to figure it out immediately."

Varnar squatted on the grass and looked at me. "I haven't taught this to anyone but you."

I looked at him, uncomprehending. He had trained hundreds of people before me. My thoughts were interrupted by Luna, who stuck her head over the hedge.

"Hey, Anna." She saw Varnar and changed her expression to an anxious grimace. "Hey, Varnar."

He nodded stoically at her.

She looked back at me. "My dad sent me to come get you. Do you have time?"

I looked questioningly at Varnar. He stood and looked from Luna to me. Then he took off running out of my garden and sped across the field toward Kraghede Forest.

Luna tracked him. "He doesn't say goodbye?"

I shrugged. "Pretty much never."

"That's funny."

"What's funny about it?"

"You don't, either. Are you coming?"

We were met by Rebecca. She looked like she wanted to give me a hug but thought better of it. "Come in," she said instead.

I followed her into the living room, which had been completely rearranged for the occasion. The furniture stood along the walls, and on the tile floor, a circle and a bunch of runes had been drawn in chalk. There were candles all around the circle.

Luna sat on the floor with a bongo drum in her lap.

Bongo drum?

Ben stuck his head in.

"Anna." With a nod of his large head, he signaled for me to come with him.

Outside, I stood in front of him with my arms crossed. He looked down at me with lowered brows.

"I don't want to argue with you. You just have to accept that I did what I did to keep you alive."

"Nice life I got out of it."

Ben raised his large, tattooed hands. "I promised Arthur that I would protect you."

"I'm not sure my dad agrees with your way of achieving that task."

"I know more about what Arthur thinks about things than you do. You've never met him, and he was my best friend," Ben said fiercely.

"And what do you think, with your in-depth knowledge of my father, he would say about you having given me a life of isolation with no sense of stability and with pretty much everyone turned against me?"

"He would say the most important thing is that you're alive." Ben's deep voice was far too confident.

I turned the corners of my mouth downward in a grimace of disagreement. "I don't think you're right."

"Why don't we ask him?" Ben's teeth shone behind his broad lips.

For a moment, I was distracted by the sound of drums and Luna's singing voice from the living room. I focused on Ben again.

"What do you mean, ask him?"

"My wife is preparing a seid, during which she can contact the dead."

"What's a seid?"

"It's an Old Norse ritual. The seid-woman can get very close to the world of the dead."

This would certainly be interesting.

In the living room, I saw that Rebecca had changed clothes. Well, "clothes" might be a stretch. Her costume was composed of stitched-together animal skins decorated with feathers, bones, and teeth along the edges. Around her head she wore an iron band with large, twisted horns, and in her hand, she held a long golden staff, which ended in a cast bronze bird's head.

Luna was still sitting on the floor with the drum in her lap. She, too, had a horned band around her head, though a smaller version than Rebecca's. If they didn't both have such serious expressions on their faces, I would have burst out laughing.

Ben turned in the doorway.

I grabbed him by the sleeve. "You aren't participating? Isn't this right up your alley?"

"Seid is not for men," he growled before disappearing, and I was left alone with the freaky costume party.

Rebecca solemnly raised her hand. "I want to try to connect with a departed friend. I must enter the space between the worlds and speak with him."

On the floor, Luna started beating the drum and singing quietly in a language I did not understand.

Did she know it was Arthur they were trying to coax out? Probably not. Otherwise she would have told her mom that I could just talk to him. If he had recovered, that is, after I had sent him back to his corpse.

Rebecca continued: "In the seid, I summon the spirit of the deceased, and both he and I step into the shadowland so we can converse."

She started to walk from side to side to the beat of Luna's drumming. The bones and teeth clinked together on her costume.

I pressed my lips together to hold back my laughter.

Rebecca chanted something, then began to shake her torso in a motion most closely resembling a bizarre samba. I bit my tongue. With eyes closed, Rebecca raised her arms.

"To honor the gods' animal disguises, in which Freyja becomes a falcon, in which Odin becomes a serpent, and in which Njord becomes a fish, I have dressed myself in the skin of an animal. Deceased friend. Best friend," she chanted. "I must speak with you, friend."

On the floor, Luna intensified her drumming. Then I felt a cool hand wrapping around my own. I turned my head and looked into Arthur's green eyes. He smiled at me.

"Arthur, I'm so sorry," I whispered.

"You couldn't have known. It's all right. But I've missed you."

I nodded at him with tears in my eyes as Luna and Rebecca continued, none the wiser.

Arthur looked at them and laughed out loud. A giggle also escaped my lips.

From her place on the floor, Luna looked up at me disapprovingly.

I tried desperately to maintain my mask, but Arthur, who was gasping with laughter at my side, made this quite difficult.

"I don't understand why she puts that outfit on every time she contacts me. And the dance! I can hear her just fine without it." He struggled to get the words out between bursts of laughter.

"But can she hear you?" I asked.

Rebecca gave me an irritated look before closing her eyes and continuing her chanting.

Arthur shook his head. "Barely. It's really hard to get a message across. But it's nice that she can catch even small fragments. It's very rare for those who aren't born with the gift to be able to hear us."

"Can't you just write it down for her? Or use one of those Ouija boards they always have in horror movies? You are a poltergeist, after all," I whispered.

Arthur shook his head. "That would be a bad idea."

I wanted to ask why, but at that moment Rebecca raised her hands and shouted: "My friend. Are you here?"

"Yes!" Arthur bellowed so loudly that I stuck a finger in the ear that was closest to him.

Rebecca shook her head, the large horns nearly hitting the ceiling lamp.

"I can't hear him. Luna, play louder."

Arthur said something to me, but it was impossible to hear over all the noise.

"Arthuuuuuurr," shouted Rebecca.

"I'm here!" Arthur shouted back.

Luna looked questioningly at me, and I nodded and pointed in Arthur's direction.

"Uh, Mom," she said.

"He's close," shouted Rebecca. "I can feel him."

She shook her torso again.

"Mom," said Luna again.

"Luna." Rebecca's voice was sharp. "You cannot interrupt the holy seid."

Luna muffled the drums with a petulant look on her face.

"I spoke with Belinda Jaeger's spirit yesterday," I whispered.

"Belinda Jaeger. She hasn't crossed over?"

At that moment, Rebecca yelled again. "Arthuuur. We need to ask you about something."

"You don't need to shout," shouted Arthur.

Rebecca cocked her head and listened intently.

"I can hear him. He says his hope has not run out."

"No," Arthur roared. "Stop yelling. I can hear you loud and clear."

"That's right, you have nothing to fear. We are taking good care of your girl." She looked triumphantly at me, as if her misinterpretation of Arthur's words excused the isolation magic her husband had cast around me.

Arthur threw up his arms.

"See what I've had to deal with all these years? Communication is difficult. I want to hear more about your encounter with Belinda later." He walked up to Rebecca and placed his mouth right next to her ear. "Is there news about Thora?"

"What?" asked Rebecca with a shout. She shook her body in yet another shimmy.

I couldn't keep up the farce any longer. "He's asking if there's any news about my mom."

On the floor, Luna drummed on.

"Luna, can you stop?" I barked. "I can't hear my own thoughts."

Luna stopped. "You can't interrupt a seid, Anna. It's holy."

"Holy, schmoly . . ." I snapped.

Luna appealed to her mother with a look.

"Quiet, Luna." Rebecca looked at me with both awe and a hint of suspicion. "Can you hear him?"

"He's standing right next to you." I pointed to Arthur, who looked at Rebecca with both love and sorrow.

Rebecca whirled around and let go of the staff. It landed on the tile floor with a clatter. Luna made a frightened sound, but Rebecca didn't notice the noise. She looked around and positioned herself with her face right in front of Arthur's. But she was focused on the wrong spot. Pain swept across Arthur's face. He raised a hand toward her but lowered it again.

"Tell her I miss her. Both of them," he said.

"He misses both you and Ben."

Tears gathered in Rebecca's eyes.

"We miss you, too," she choked out. "We're still trying to find a way."

"A way to what?" I don't know which one of them I was asking.

Arthur's face told me that Rebecca had said too much.

I looked at him demandingly.

"A way to what?" I repeated.

He hesitated.

"They're trying to find a way to bring me back to life," he said.

"What!?" It came out as a shout.

Rebecca's gaze flew around without locating Arthur, even though they stood practically nose-to-nose. "What's he saying?"

I ignored her. "Why didn't you tell me?"

"I didn't want to give you false hope. It's impossible. Or practically impossible."

"Then why are they trying?"

"What's he saying?" Rebecca asked again.

My hands shot up. "That you're trying to bring him back to life. Can that be done?"

"I shouldn't have said anything," she said.

"No, she shouldn't have." Arthur shook his head.

"You should have said something before," I said.

"Is Arthur saying I should have told you before?" Rebecca laid her hand on her heart.

"Ughh," I exclaimed and waved my fists in the air. "This is impossible. I'm saying that you," I pointed at Rebecca, "should have told me. Arthur apparently doesn't think I should know anything about any of it. It wasn't even all that long ago that he told me he was my father. And that he's a ghost."

"How long have you been able to see him?" whispered Rebecca.

"Since I was four."

"I'm so glad he's been with you. And you with him. He was amazing when he was alive, but he's even more impressive in death. The night he died . . ."

Arthur flinched when she said it.

I held up a hand. "Could you maybe not mention when he you-know-what? It seems ghosts are highly allergic to it."

"They are? I didn't know." Rebecca collected herself. "Luna, honey. Could you go get your dad?"

Luna, who had been following the conversation like a spectator at a tennis match, ran off.

Rebecca continued: "Tell him we've done everything in our power to protect you."

"Tell him yourself. Feel free to get specific. He can hear you perfectly well."

"He can?"

I nodded.

A smile flitted across Rebecca's lips. "All these years, I've worn the seid costume and performed the dance of the dead."

Alongside me, Arthur laughed. Rebecca looked out into what for her must have appeared to be empty air.

"We had to cast spells on your daughter to protect her."

I could feel my brows lowering, and I looked expectantly at Arthur, whose expression mirrored my own.

"Which spells?" he asked.

"He's asking which ones."

"Ben placed both a Reka and a Neitt spell on her." She looked nervously into the space where she thought Arthur stood.

Arthur's expression shifted from stunned to understanding.

"Ah, so that's why," he said. "I've never understood why people look straight through you, and why a few get so provoked by you. I thought you had inherited some of your mother's personality, but I only ever saw you as lovable."

"What's wrong with my mom? Is she a monster or something?"

Rebecca's forehead creased. "Your mom? Why is he talking about your mom?"

I moaned in frustration. Though I could see and hear Arthur, communication between the living and the dead was a real pain. I repeated Arthur's words, and again Rebecca laughed.

"No, she's not a monster. She can just be a little . . . scary."

Next to me, Arthur looked pensive. "A Reka and a Neitt. That's intense magic. But you decided it couldn't be any other way. The most important thing is that Anna's alive."

I stared at him, my mouth agape.

"What's he saying?" asked Rebecca.

"Nothing meaningful," I said.

"Tell her what I just said," Arthur said determinedly.

I shook my head.

"Hell no. They destroyed my life." I pointed at Rebecca.

"At least there was a life to destroy. Look how it turned out for me."

At that moment, Ben and Luna joined us. Rebecca had been standing silently next to us and following my half of the conversation.

"Is he here?" Ben asked breathlessly.

"Yes. Anna can see him. And speak to him with ease," said Rebecca.

Ben looked around the room.

I pointed noiselessly to the place where Arthur stood.

Ben walked up to him but, like his wife, did not focus on the right spot.

"There's so much I want to say to you, Arthur," said Ben.

"But there's something I want to ask you first, Ben. Why didn't you tell me you could bring Arthur back to life?"

Ben stiffened. "Because it's nearly impossible to bring the dead back. It requires strong magic or divine intervention. We've looked all over the world for a solution."

"Have you found a way?" I tried not to let my voice reveal my hope.

"We haven't been able to find anything concrete. We've been chasing castles in the sky all these years."

"Are you even aid workers?" Luna looked from one parent to the other.

Rebecca laid a hand on her cheek. "No, sweetie. We are exiled witches fleeing death and searching for a way to fool it. We've even looked into other religions."

"What about your own faith? Asatru?" I asked, mostly to give Luna time to recover. I knew far too well how it feels to have, with the snap of a finger, all of your core beliefs turned upside down.

"Odin can wake the dead," said Rebecca. "But he would never wake Arthur."

"Why not?" I looked at Ben, Rebecca, and Arthur in turn.

Arthur looked down at the floor. Ben and Rebecca looked at each other.

It was Ben who finally answered.

"Because he desires your mother. Maybe even loves her. But she didn't want him. She was the only mortal to ever reject a god. Because she loves your father. Odin has never forgiven Arthur for laying claim to Thora's love."

I had no idea what to make of this. I didn't actually believe in the old gods, even though everyone around me seemed convinced they were quite real.

"So," I said tentatively. "How do you all know that the gods exist? I mean, do you even know what it means to be a god?"

The room was silent for a long moment. Rebecca was about to say something, but next to me Arthur suddenly twisted his head around.

"There's someone coming here. He's heading straight toward us."

At the same time, Ben raised his head with a jerk and looked at his wife. They shared a knowing look. He walked a lap around the room. Finally, he stood before the large front door with eyes closed as he hummed quietly. Rebecca placed herself behind Luna and me.

I looked at Arthur. "Who is on his way here?"

"What do you mean?" asked Luna.

"I was talking to Arthur."

Rebecca's voice was muffled. "Can Arthur see who it is?"

I passed the question off to Arthur with a raised eyebrow.

He shook his head.

Ben positioned himself with his back to the wall, and with an outstretched arm, he laid his hand on the doorknob. I tried to cast my power out and sensed someone slightly familiar.

"Can you feel him?" I asked the room.

"Yes," said Ben, Rebecca, and Arthur in unison.

"Who is it?"

"We can't recognize people from a distance. We can only sense them because we've cast spells on the house. When someone who isn't included in the magic comes near, we notice it immediately," whispered Ben. "And this person is not included. Others tend to keep away because of our magic, but this guy is heading right toward our front door."

He and Rebecca had another silent conversation over our heads, and I felt how the air in the room grew thick with magic and emotion.

"Luna, honey," Rebecca said gently. "Do you remember when I taught you to collect energy in your hands?"

"Yes. You said I should be sure not to drop it, because then it would explode and, worst case, kill someone."

"Well, you should start collecting energy now. And let it just hang out there. If I say 'throw,' you throw it in the same direction as me."

"But . . ." Luna began.

"Shh," said Rebecca.

Arthur placed a cold hand on my arm.

"I'll go out to look." He disappeared through the wall.

Even though I was aware of Arthur's ghost status, it shook me to see him pass through a solid brick wall as though it were made of mist.

A moment later, he was back. "It's a young man. Not anyone I know. But he knows us. And he is very determined," he said.

I repeated this to the rest of the group.

We all stood completely still. Then the gravel outside crunched, and a dark shadow passed the kitchen window.

Rebecca's eyes were wide, and Ben flung open the door and launched himself outside. Soon, he came back in with a man in tow and threw him onto the kitchen floor. He stood over him with his tattooed palms aimed at him.

Rebecca, too, aimed her hands at the man.

Out of sheer terror, Luna dropped her ball of energy, and it whizzed down to the tile floor just a few inches from the man's head. A gigantic boom resounded throughout the house as it blasted a large hole in the floor. The man screamed and curled into a ball with his arms over his head.

"I come in peace," he shouted. "Niels Villadsen sent me."

I recognized the sound of his voice. "I think he's from the DSMA. He was at the ball at The Boatman."

Ben looked down at the man, eyes wild. Then he slowly lowered his hands. The man peered up from behind his arms and looked at Ben.

"Whoa," he said. "I was almost blown to pieces by Benedict Sekibo."

Something told me he thought that would have been a really cool way to die, if it came down to it.

Ben stood up a little taller, and next to me, Arthur rolled his eyes.

"You almost got blown to pieces by my daughter," Ben said, giving Luna a look of approval. He made a brief motion with his head that made Luna and Rebecca lower their hands. Ben extended a large hand to Steen, as I remembered the young man was called.

Steen took it cautiously, and with a powerful jerk, Ben pulled him upright. Steen wobbled before he found his footing and straightened his horn-rimmed glasses.

"What are you doing on my property?" asked Ben.

Steen's gaze faltered under Ben's, and he looked instead at Rebecca, who was still wearing the enormous horns and peculiar costume. He tried to act like this was completely normal, but he only partly succeeded.

"I come with a message from Niels, which I was asked to deliver in person." He finally pried his eyes away from Rebecca, but his gaze landed instead on Luna who, with her smaller horns and chaos of red curls, resembled a crazy, beautiful leprechaun. "Are you in the middle of a seid?" he asked, and looked down at the floor, where the chalk drawings were still visible, if a bit smudged. "I've never been to one."

"It's none of your business," snapped Ben.

Steen nodded rapidly. "Of course not. Allow me to introduce myself. We seem to have gotten off on the wrong foot."

Hats off to his ability to recover quickly.

"I work with Niels Villadsen at the DSMA, and my name is Steen Arneson." He looked at Ben in veneration. "We met at the ball at The Boatman, but I'm sure you don't remember."

"Are you related to Magnus Arneson?" asked Rebecca.

"Yes. He was my father."

"My condolences," she said and held out her hand. "Magnus was a good man."

Steen accepted her hand. Then he turned and held his hand out to Luna.

"I saw you at the equinox ball, but we didn't meet." He looked at her a little longer than necessary.

Luna didn't notice, but Ben emitted a low growl.

Steen stood there for a moment, until Rebecca cleared her throat and pointed at me.

I shook his hand.

"My name is Anna. We've met before," I said quietly.

"Have we?" Steen furrowed his brows. "When?"

"The Boatman. I was at the ball, too."

"Did we speak?" I could see him racking his brain.

"Briefly," I said.

"I don't remember you at all."

I looked angrily at Ben. *Goddamned spells.*

Rebecca cut in. She waved her hand toward the table, which was still pushed against the wall to make room for the seid.

"Come. Sit down. We have been anything but hospitable. You must think we're barbarians."

The gold teeth glinted behind Ben's dark lips when she said this, and Arthur laughed.

Steen glanced at Ben and smoothed his hair before taking a seat. Rebecca removed her horned headband and went into the kitchen to make tea.

Ben sat across from Steen and stared at him without blinking, while the poor man did his best not to squirm in his seat. Luna took her horns off as well and plopped down.

I stood in the middle of the room with no clue as to whether I was invited to take part in the deliberations or not. Rebecca placed a warm hand on my back and pushed me toward the table.

"Just sit. I have a feeling this also concerns you."

I sat, and Arthur stood behind me.

"What message is so important that you would set foot on my land without making yourself known first?" asked Ben.

Steen jumped and accepted the cup of tea Rebecca handed him.

"It was not my intention to not make myself known."

Ben made a rolling motion with a large hand to indicate that Steen should continue.

"I come with news from Freiheim. It's classified, so Niels couldn't risk bringing it himself. We're bending the rules so much, we're on the verge of breaking them."

"What happened?" Rebecca's voice shook slightly.

"Ragnara's seers finally interpreted the prophecy. Without Bork. He was exposed as a traitor and imprisoned. We don't know what Ragnara's other seers figured out, but it caused Thora to flee the castle."

Ben widened his eyes, Arthur exclaimed, and Rebecca gasped. Luna and I looked blankly at each other.

"What does that mean?" I asked.

Ben gathered his thoughts before he spoke.

"It means that the treaty is officially broken." He slammed his fist onto the table, causing the cups to shake. "And if Thora has fled, then her life must be in danger."

Steen interjected. "It's been months—more than half a year—since Thora fled. Intel from Freiheim is extremely delayed now that we no longer have diplomatic relations."

"That fits with the timing of when the first girl was killed," said Ben.

Rebecca looked thoughtful. "And if Ragnara dares to kill Thora, then I'm quite sure what conclusion the seers have reached."

"What?" I asked.

"Thora isn't the key. You are." Ben looked gravely at me. "They think you're going to kill Ragnara if they don't kill you first. The hunt for you has begun."

Steen looked questioningly from me to Ben, who pointed a dark finger at me.

"This is Thora's daughter."

"Ohhhh," exhaled Steen. An intense cone of pure fear shot from him. He stood so quickly his cup toppled over, which he didn't even notice. He backed away from us, and his voice took on an edge of hysteria. "This is all over my head. I was only sent to give you the message. I didn't even know what it meant myself."

He fumbled for the doorknob behind him. Then he yanked the door open and ran out. His rapid steps could be heard in the gravel outside.

"We have to strengthen the spells," Ben said to his wife. "There's no other way."

"Tell them I agree," concurred Arthur.

I shook my head at all three of them. "You can forget that."

"It's not up to you," said Ben.

426

"Ben, maybe we should talk about this," Rebecca tried. "People will have even more of an aversion to her than they do now. Maybe even Luna and Mathias. And ourselves."

"We don't need to talk about anything. It's my duty to protect her, whether she wants it or not."

I could see a force field gathering around him. Rebecca sighed with resignation, and her aura, too, started to crackle.

"No, no . . ." I stood up and, just as Steen had done a moment before, began moving toward the door.

Ben stood, towering between me and freedom. "I will hold you down if I have to."

He reached out to grab me, but Luna threw herself between us. She held her father's dark gaze with her caramel-colored one. Never before had I seen her eyes shine like that. Ben's eyes burned back at her, and I was impressed that she didn't flinch.

"Don't you touch her without her consent," she hissed, and for the first time since I'd met her, she was actually pretty frightening.

Ben took a step back and looked at his daughter with a mix of rage and pride.

"Run, Anna," Luna shouted over her shoulder.

I ducked under Ben's broad arm, stumbled out the door, and ran toward home.

Arthur appeared at my side immediately.

"You can go to hell," I yelled at him. "I'm done letting you guys make bad decisions on my behalf."

"I will do whatever it takes to make sure you're protected," he said.

I came to a stop in the dark soil and turned toward him.

"You all have a very misconceived notion of what it means to protect me. I don't want to be even more isolated. I don't want to lose the few friends I've finally made. I would rather let Ragnara get me." In a flash, I recalled the vision from last night with my own dead face.

Arthur ignored me.

"I'm sorry, Anna," was all he said as he placed a cold hand around my wrist and started pulling me back toward Ben and Rebecca's house.

I tried to resist, but it was as if he had taken over all my muscles and was controlling my body.

"Stop that. What are you doing?"

"Possession. I rarely do it. Only when it's absolutely necessary."

I writhed but nevertheless saw my feet moving in the opposite direction from where I wanted them to go.

"Stop. I will bring up your death. Don't think I won't!"

Arthur exerted himself more, and I now began to run against my will back toward Ben and Rebecca's house.

Damn it.

"You are dead," I shouted in despair. "You died in Benedict's arms."

I sensed Arthur's energy wane.

"No, Anna," he said desperately.

"Yes, Dad," I whispered. Loudly I said: "You. Are. Dead!"

He released his grip on my arm and fell to the ground, where he convulsed until he vanished before my eyes.

I blinked away the tears before once again running toward home. On my way up the steep road toward my house, I cursed. God, I was so tired of other people thinking they knew what was best for me. And I was tired of people who were sent by someone else to boss me around. I muttered breathlessly to myself.

"My dad sent me. Niels Villadsen sent me." I sent a bitter thought to Varnar. "Your mother sent me."

I continued stomping up the dark hill.

When I reached the edge of my yard, I saw the contours of a figure sitting in front of my door. At first, I stopped. Then I took off running, my heart pounding.

Monster sat motionless in front of Odinmont, but his large eyes were simmering with emotion.

I wanted to throw myself to the ground and hold him to me. I wanted to cry with relief at seeing him again. I wanted to tell him I had missed him more than I thought it was possible to miss any living thing. But I did none of those things. Instead, I stood in front of him with my arms crossed.

"And who sent *you*, then?" I imbued my voice with all the hardness I could muster.

Monster tilted his giant head, as if listening intently. Then he opened his large mouth, and sound resonated in his chest. With a voice so deep it sounded more like a purring lion than anything human, he replied.

"Your sister."

PART IV

THE SON OF ODIN, HIS DESTINY SET

I saw for Baldr,
the bleeding god,
The son of Odin
his destiny set:
Famous and fair
in the lofty fields,
Full grown in strength
the mistletoe stood

Völuspá
10th century

 # CHAPTER 26

My mouth hung open. I was unable to say more before I heard crunching gravel behind me.

Aella came speeding straight toward us with tears running down her cheeks. She knelt in front of Monster and desperately grabbed the fur of his shoulders.

"Is she safe?"

I stared at them both and tried to figure out what to say but was again interrupted by the sound of shouts.

It was Luna's voice.

"They're coming!"

I turned and saw her red hair shining in the sun as she ran at full speed across the field toward my house. A bit farther down the hill, Ben and Rebecca moved quickly toward us.

I leaned over Aella and Monster and opened the door as quickly as I could.

"Get inside," I commanded.

We tumbled into the hall, and I whirled around in the doorway as Monster and Aella disappeared into the living room.

The Sekibos were right on our heels, and I reasoned that it didn't matter whether I was inside or outside Odinmont. Ben's and Rebecca's magic was so strong they could likely break down the door with their minds and cast spells on me by force either way. But Luna, who reached the driveway at that moment, leapt up like a gazelle and sailed through the air in a way that should not have been humanly possible.

I jumped aside when I realized she was heading straight for the doorway, feetfirst.

She landed just inside the door but had so much momentum, she kept running and smacked into the wall.

"I still don't have full control over all this," she said. She turned around and was back at the door in one long stride.

Outside, Ben's large figure was quickly approaching. His eyes were shining and wild.

My pulse rose as he barreled straight toward me with hands raised, but in a rapid motion, Luna slammed the door right in her father's face. She flailed her arms, and the magic crackled around her as she yelled: "*Balwark allt.*" Then she expelled a wave of energy so powerful I was knocked backward and landed on the floor.

Around and across my door, something was spreading that at first resembled a spiderweb. It rapidly grew thicker. Eventually it turned into a mass of stretchy, rubbery beige ropes.

When Ben hammered on the door from outside, it caved in, and the ropes made a loud *boing*, but they all held.

Once again, Luna waved her arms, and with lightning speed, thick elastic ropes spread across the walls of my home so all the windows and the door to the garden were also covered. When she was done, Odinmont looked like the inside of a giant cocoon. Light filtered through the web, so the entire house was plunged into a dim twilight.

Luna leaned against the wall, her forehead glistening with sweat.

"I had no idea you could do that," I said as I got to my feet.

"Neither did I," she panted. "I improvised."

I glanced at the door.

"It'll hold," she said. "I'm sure."

I heard Aella's voice from the living room. Monster growled something in response. Oh, right. There was just the matter of a talking dog and the statement about my sister to deal with.

We walked in and stood in front of Aella and Monster.

"Hello, Luna," said Monster with his guttural voice.

"Hi. Glad to see you're back," said Luna. "Uhhh . . . You can talk?"

Monster let out a hoarse laugh.

Unable to blink, I stared at him. "I'm guessing you're also from Hrafnheim," I said.

It took a moment before Monster responded. He sniffed and, by all measures, looked like a completely normal dog. A normal giant dog, anyway. All parameters of normalcy were shattered, however, when he spoke again.

"I am from Hrafnheim," he affirmed.

I shook my head and inhaled a huge gulp of air. "You said something about a sister?"

It was Aella who answered. "You have a sister. A twin sister. You're identical. Except she has red hair. Serén is her name."

"I have a sister," I said, mainly to myself. I stared out into space while my heart raced. "Is she in your world?"

Both Monster and Aella nodded.

Oh. That must be why Varnar had recognized me even with my black hair. Because he knew what my sister looked like.

"Does she know I exist?"

Monster showed his teeth when he spoke: "She sent me. She knows you're in danger."

I sat on the bench with a thump. All my questions were tripping over each other.

"Does she also . . ." I forced myself to finish the sentence. "Does she also have spells on her like I do?"

Aella shook her head. "Everyone likes her. Everyone who doesn't want to kill her, that is."

"Is her life in danger, too?" It came out almost as a scream.

Monster cocked his enormous head. "She is as much of Thora's blood as you are."

I searched for the right words. "Did she grow up with my . . . I mean, *our* mom?" For some reason, my throat hurt when I asked.

"She has always known Thora, but she's only known that she's her mother for a year." I sat for a moment and contemplated. The others gave me some time and kept quiet. The notion of me together with my sister kept mingling with my memories of being alone—on the playground, in a room in yet another foster home or group home.

Outside, I could faintly hear Ben's shouts, but I barely registered them.

"How did she find out that I exist?" I whispered.

Monster's rough voice resounded: "Thora told her about you before she fled."

"Is my sister clairvoyant, too—like me?"

Aella nodded. "She can see the future."

I leaned against the backrest and rubbed my temples.

"Why is she there, and I'm here?"

Aella ran her fingers through her short hair. "It's really complicated, and I'm nowhere close to knowing all of it. Just that you were born here in Midgard, and Serén was born in Hrafnheim."

What? I realized that I hadn't said this aloud, but just stared uncomprehendingly at Aella.

She shrugged, and her gaze rested for a moment on the long scar that extended above the neckline of my shirt. "Like I said. It's very complicated."

I was going to try to formulate another question, but again Ben's voice blared outside, and one of my windows splintered as the rubber ropes surrounding it gave out. Behind him, Rebecca called to her daughter.

"We're going to have to do something about them," I said and exhaled. "They'll smash Odinmont to pieces. And I don't want any more magic on me."

Luna walked over to the busted window, where Ben stood right outside, pounding on the elastic ropes.

"Dad, stop it."

"Luna. I command you to remove this bulwark," he bellowed.

"No," she shouted back. This was followed by a diatribe in rapid French that I didn't catch much of—though I recognized a couple of the more offensive vocabulary words.

Ben responded first in French, then in an African language, and finally in Danish.

". . . and I'll use all my power if I have to."

"Ben," Rebecca pleaded behind him. "Calm down."

"What's going on with the dysfunctional witch family?" I whispered to Aella and Monster.

Luna turned around.

"I can't talk him down. He's out of his mind. Maybe . . ." she wondered.

"What?" I asked.

"There's something about demigods being above witches in the hierarchy. Maybe Mathias can do something." She pulled out her phone and called him.

"Hey, babe," she said. "Are you up for coming out to Odinmont and talking some sense into a couple of agitated witches?"

Mathias said something on the other end.

"They want to put some spells on Anna that she doesn't want. They want . . ." She held the phone away from her ear and looked at it. "Huh. He took off."

About twenty seconds later, I heard Mathias's muffled voice outside.

Ben protested.

Then there was a flash of green light, the sound of Mathias's voice with a metallic timbre, and then silence.

"What's going on?" shouted Luna.

"They left," Mathias shouted back. "Uh, how do I get in?"

Luna's arms made a couple of circles above her head.

"*Balwark burtu*," she said.

The ropes began to droop and slowly slid downward, hitting the floor with a farting noise. They left greasy streaks on all my windows.

"Great," I said. "Three hours of cleaning for me."

Luna crossed her arms, looking pleased with herself. "Hey. I just saved you."

"Thanks for that. Can't you magically clean up while you're at it?"

"I can only do the hard stuff when I'm all amped up. Then it just flows."

The front door opened, and Mathias walked in. He stepped over what now resembled a large blob of beige Jell-O. It stuck to his socks. Evidently, he had once again come so quickly he hadn't had time to put shoes on.

"What did you do to Ben and Rebecca?" I asked.

Mathias looked down at his dirtied socks. "Od said that we demigods can rule over the beings beneath us in the hierarchy. So I just said they should go home and leave you alone. And then they left."

"Ooh, my dad must be pissed now." Luna laughed. "He's not used to having people tell him what to do."

Something tickled my clairvoyance and told me that this was not quite the case. I pushed the thought away.

"Do you think they won't put any more spells on me?"

"They won't touch you unless I say so," said Mathias with a self-assured air that reminded me of Od. He looked around my chaotic home with all the globs of slime and Monster and Aella, who both nodded at him. "What happened here?"

"Long story," I said, then gave him as brief a recap as possible.

Mathias went over to Luna and put an arm around her as if to support himself on something.

"Oh yeah, and Monster can talk," I added.

Mathias stared at the giant dog, who gave him an animalistic grin.

I turned again to Aella and tried to find the words.

"What about my sister . . . Serén. Where is she?"

The fear in Aella's aura was so intense I had to squeeze my eyes shut.

Monster panted briefly with his tongue hanging out of his mouth before he spoke. "She's safe with my people. That was why I had to leave you, Anna. To save her. Ragnara had found out that she was Thora's daughter. I got her out just in time."

It was as if Aella's face crackled, and for a second, I thought she would faint. Instead, she stood up and stared through the glass door, smeared though it was with the remains of Luna's magical barricade.

I looked bitterly at Monster.

"All this time, you didn't say a word, you damn dog. Why?"

He laughed hoarsely. "First of all, I'm not a dog."

"Oh! You aren't really a human, are you? A shape-shifter or something like that?"

"I'm definitely not a human," said Monster, insulted. "I belong to the Wolf Folk."

"Wolf Folk?"

"We descend from the giant wolf Mánagarmr."

Luna furrowed her brows. "Mánagarmr, the son of the wolf Fenrir and the giantess Hyrrokin? He fed off the blood of dying men and caused solar and lunar eclipses by spraying it around."

"And your forefathers burned witches and owned slaves. No one should be held responsible for the crimes of their ancestors," Monster snapped back.

"Good point," she whispered.

"And you know my sister how?" I interjected. I may have spoken louder than necessary.

439

Aella turned halfway from where she stood by the glass door, and she and Monster exchanged a glance. "Serén entered the Iron Forest, where the Wolf Folk live, and sought out Etunaz."

"Who is Etunaz?"

"Me," rumbled Monster.

"Should I stop calling you Monster?"

"I actually quite like it," he said with a wide grin.

"The Wolf Folk don't take too kindly to humans," said Aella. "It took a lot of courage on Serén's part to go in there."

"So why did you listen to her?" I asked Monster/Etunaz.

He looked pensive.

"Your sister," he said, "is something rather special."

Aella bowed her head at his words.

"Serén saw that an alliance could provide the Wolf Folk with the peace they've always sought. The alternative is chaos."

Again, I had to search for the words, and they came out as an accusation.

"Why didn't you ever speak before?"

"You weren't ready," he said and exhaled, causing the loose skin on his jowls to flap. "And, for a long time, I was content just to listen."

"What else did Serén tell you?"

Monster paused before he spoke again. "She has seen that if someone succeeds in killing her or you, it will mean doomsday—Ragnarök. The world will end."

"Which world?"

Monster slowly shook his large head as stillness hung in the room.

"She doesn't know."

 # CHAPTER 27

Later that evening, when the others had all gone home and I had cleaned up after Luna's magic, Monster stretched out on the floor of my bedroom while I lay in bed.

I had forced Luna to magically repair my window. This was a success—kind of. It now had green, nubby glass and an orange frame. But it was airtight and whole.

Monster breathed heavily. It was a little like having a friend over for a sleepover. Except that I'd never had friends to bring home, or a home to bring them to. And that my overnight guest was a giant wolf. Oddly enough, it felt perfectly natural to talk to him. I had been doing that all along, after all. The only difference was that now, he talked back.

"How did my sister know I'm in danger?" I asked.

Monster smacked his lips. "She had a vision of a girl being strangled in the woods. She actually suspected that the victim was her, but when Thora told her about you, she realized that may not be the case at all. Then she started sending you the vision."

I propped myself up on my elbow.

"How does she *send* me the vision?"

"No clue. I just know that the most talented seers can send dreams to one another."

I sank back into my pillow on the floor, and Monster waited patiently for me to collect my thoughts.

"What's it like in Hrafnheim?" I asked, and turned onto my side, facing him.

441

"I grew up in the Iron Forest," he said in his rough voice. "The trees there are gray like iron and have hard, sharp leaves. You walk not on soil but on coals. In some places, they smolder and glow. Other places, they're ice-cold. It's both beautiful and terrifying."

"Sounds festive. Have you been to other places in Hrafnheim?"

"The Wolf Folk have always stayed away from humans. I've only left the Iron Forest a few times in my life."

"How old are you?"

"We don't measure age in the same way as humans."

"Oh, do you count in dog years?" I teased.

Monster growled lightly. "We measure in life stages. First, you're a pup. Then you become a hirdswolf. At some point, you challenge the leader of the pack or decide to remain with the hird. When you get old, you're abandoned by the pack and live alone until you die."

"Harsh," I said.

"Natural," said Monster.

"Which stage are you in?"

"I'm a little atypical," he replied evasively.

"What do you mean?"

"I belong to the Fenris clan. The Wolf Folk's royal family. My father is the leader of the Fenris clan and therefore king of the Wolf Folk."

"You're a prince."

"Prince Etunaz of the Wolf Folk," he said with his rusty voice. "My older brother, Liutpold, would have been king after my father."

"Would have been?"

"He's dead. Varnar killed him." Monster's voice revealed no emotion.

"Varnar killed your brother?" Suddenly, I understood why Monster had reacted so violently the first few times he saw Varnar.

442

"It was Liutpold's own fault. He attacked Ragnara, and at the time, Varnar was the leader of the Varangian Guard. He was just doing his job."

"You're a very forgiving wolf," I said. "Was that where Varnar officially died?"

"After the fight, Varnar disappeared, which isn't anything unusual. If my kinsmen had actually killed him, there wouldn't have been anything left."

I didn't inquire as to why one would disappear after being killed by a giant wolf.

Monster continued: "They say Ragnara laid his skin on the floor next to her bed."

I gulped and hurried to get off the topic of Varnar's staged death and Monster's brother being used as a rug.

"Then you must be some kind of crown prince."

"I've had a hard time conforming," he said instead of answering my question. "I don't agree with the old customs. But I can tell you about that later."

My eyes were starting to get heavy. Monster's return gave me a deep sense of calm, and for the first time in weeks, I truly felt relaxed.

"I haven't had a single friend my whole life," I mumbled. "And when I finally get one, it's Crown Prince Etunaz of the Wolf Folk. Sweet."

I closed my eyes and began to quietly drift toward sleep.

"I actually really like being Anna's dog, Monster," he said and smacked his lips.

"What does Etunaz mean?" I whispered.

Monster laughed hoarsely. "Man eater."

Varnar and I trained together a couple of days after Monster's return. The giant wolf was inside Kraghede Manor with Aella while Varnar and I fought in the old riding hall.

443

I was starting to get the hang of his brilliant trick. We had gone over it lots of times, but right now we were just practicing what had gradually become an arsenal of many different kicks, movements, parries, and punches Varnar had taught me.

His open hand whizzed directly toward my face.

I parried with ease and used the force of his attack to spin in a half circle and place myself at his side. I hit him on the shoulder with a clenched fist and was pretty proud of myself for getting a punch in.

"Monster told me that Serén is sending me visions," I said between blows.

"I know. Aella told me," Varnar said as he performed an elegant backflip and clipped my chin with the tip of his shoe. He only tapped me. Had he moved his foot an inch, he would have broken my jaw.

Damn! I did a roundhouse kick, hit him in the stomach, and brought my leg back in so quickly he grabbed at the air when he tried to catch it. *Yes!*

"She's sending you a vision that ends with what could be either you or Serén dying. Right?" Varnar's voice was indifferent. Cold, even. But his aura blazed with emotion. He lunged at me, but I avoided the hit. "The murderer's face is concealed in the vision."

"I can only see him from behind," I said. I planted a hand on the ground and used my body as a lever, so I could swing one leg up and kick him in the back. "But it doesn't matter who it is. Soon, I'll be so good at fighting that I can take anyone. Even you."

Faster than I could comprehend, Varnar was upon me. His fists moved so quickly I could barely see them. He didn't hit hard, but nevertheless, the multitude of blows all over my body were painful. He hit my head, my shoulders, my stomach, and my chest in rapid succession. Then he pushed me so hard I toppled backward and landed on my back with him on top of me. Straddling me, he put his hands around my throat. He didn't squeeze, but he held me so tightly I couldn't move. He bent his head down very close to mine.

"You can't take me," he hissed. "Never believe that. Overconfidence is a straight path to defeat."

My own hands held on to Varnar's, but I couldn't budge them. I whispered effortfully: "Then it's a good thing you aren't the person who was sent to kill me."

His dark eyes stared into mine.

"Don't you get it? It was me. The order was given. I was on my way here with an entirely different mission than the one I have now. If I hadn't switched to Thora's side, I would have been your murderer."

I looked up into his intense gaze. I refused to believe that.

"You wouldn't have killed me," I said steadily. "You wouldn't kill an innocent person just because you were ordered to."

"I'm a soldier." He said it as if the simple statement explained everything. Then he continued: "And Serén saw it. It was in the future. In yours. In mine." His voice grew soft. "In ours."

I saw another glimpse of what, at the time, I had thought was a dream where I had mixed the vision from the forest together with my many daydreams of Varnar. Had that been Serén, trying to warn me about him?

He slackened his grip around my neck but kept his hands there. "You can't trust anyone. Not even me."

I felt prickles behind my eyes. "I can't help it."

I thought Varnar would say something more, but he let go of me and stood up.

I remained lying on my back for a moment, my heart pounding. Then I sat up.

"Why did you switch sides?" I tried to make my voice neutral.

Varnar had his back to me. "I couldn't be party to Eskild's actions any longer. When Aella confided in me that she was actually fighting for Thora, I made up my mind."

445

"Why did Aella switch?"

"Several reasons. The same as me." He turned. "She also loves the wrong person."

"What do you mean? Oh . . . Is it not allowed in your world?"

Varnar shook his head imperceptibly. "Before Ragnara, it was accepted. Normal, even. But now it's prohibited."

I exhaled slowly. "She's in a relationship with my sister, isn't she?"

It surprised me to see disapproval in Varnar's face.

"Do you think it's wrong to love someone of the same gender?" I asked, astonished.

His face stiffened into a hard mask before he replied.

"I think it's wrong to love, period." Then he turned around and walked with a firm stride out the door of the riding hall.

I remained sitting for a while in the musty sawdust before I could get back up.

On Friday, when I was at work, I voluntarily went behind the bar with a tray of clean glassware and began putting it away.

Frank stood at the other end of the bar and acknowledged me with a surprised grin. He came over to me.

"You're unusually agreeable today," he said, while a hint of concern radiated from him. "I was wondering if you want me to drive you home tonight?"

"No, I rode my bike," I replied. "But thanks for offering."

He nodded with a serious face and ran a hand over his hair.

The next time I came out into the café, I saw Elias was sitting at the bar and talking to Frank. He waved when he saw me.

"You're radiant," said Elias.

I scowled at him. "What do you want?"

"Ah, now there's the Anna I know. Looks like a flower but she stings like a bee."

I shot him daggers with my eyes.

"Why are you mad at me now? Last time I saw you, you put me to bed and stroked my cheek. A sure sign of warm feelings. If not romantic, then at least caring."

I crossed my arms. "Drop it, Elias."

He ran his fingers through his curls. "What did I do?"

"I saw you in a vision," I snapped. "At the bike shop. You delivered a box."

Comprehension spread over Elias's face and aura. With irritation, I noted he felt neither anger nor shame.

"Do you prefer Skoll or Hate?" he asked. "I'll give you a friends and family discount."

"I don't touch that shit. Why the hell are you selling drugs? I've known people who were addicted to those pills."

Elias shrugged. "If I don't do it, others will. I can make them cleaner than anyone else, they're safe and have no side effects, plus they're a fantastic trip."

"Is that how you rationalize it to yourself?"

"Yes," he answered honestly. "I have to make a living somehow."

"You have a job. With Od. Aren't you his stand-in while he's away?"

"Let's just say I want to have my independence."

"How paradoxical that your independence is tied to other people's dependence."

"Paradoxical is my middle name." He grinned and winked.

I held up my hands in frustration. "*Egotistical* should be your middle name."

"Not in all situations," he said with a smoldering look.

"Tell me why you're here. You have ten seconds."

"It's related," he said. "I'm here to offer to help you build up a tolerance to stjórna."

"You're here to offer me a drug, where I'll be one hundred percent in your control, and you can do with me as you please?"

"Yep. And I'll do it for free."

447

"And why would I agree to that?"

"One day it might save your life," Elias said gravely. "Believe it or not, I actually want to help keep you alive."

"Only until there's something to be gained by helping someone with the opposite," I said.

Elias's lips pressed together, and he stood up.

"We don't have to be alone. Your saintly Mathias can be there. Or innocent Luna. Or the flawless Varnar, although I personally wouldn't trust him for a second. He's trained to follow orders without thinking. I at least decide for myself what I do." Then he disappeared out the door and slammed it behind him.

Frank appeared at my side again. "Your men are hard on my door," he commented as he scratched his gray sideburns. "It wasn't too long ago that that thuggish-looking guy almost smashed it after talking to you."

"Who?"

"The guy who's always around you, looking longingly at you when you aren't paying attention."

When I still looked confused, he continued: "With curly dark hair?"

Varnar.

"They aren't my men. None of them." I stomped back to the kitchen, where I loaded the dishwasher so angrily that poor Milas nearly dropped the food in fear.

When I got home, I had to sit at the table with a cup of tea and stare into space for a long time to calm down. I turned off all the lights apart from a candle that was burning on the table. Finally, I was able to relax a little, and I started getting ready for bed.

There was a light knock at the door. Monster jumped up and let out a single bark that made the windows rattle.

I looked at my phone; it was after eleven. Then I trudged over to the door and opened it, knowing that Monster would live up

448

to his name and eat the murderer raw if he was dumb enough to announce his arrival.

Outside stood Od, whom I hadn't seen in weeks. He looked enormous in the moonlight, and he had a slight metallic sheen.

"May I come in?"

I stepped aside, and suddenly he filled my entire doorway. Then he ducked inside and into the living room. He sat at the table and let his huge hands glide over the wooden surface. His index finger found the deep crack and rested in it.

"It's been many years since I was here, but the place is familiar to me. Before the house was built, people worshipped the gods here." He appeared to be lingering in the distant past.

I stood in the kitchen and didn't know quite what to do.

"Can I get you anything?"

Od looked at me as if he had forgotten I was there. His eyes shone with a hint of phosphorescence.

"Mead," he said with a deeper voice than usual.

I pulled a bottle out of the cabinet and wiped off the dust. My parents' mead stash was getting noticeably smaller. I placed two glasses on the table and poured. The glass almost disappeared in Od's giant hand.

We drank in silence, and Od closed his eyes and sat still as a marble statue. It was hard for me not to stare at his perfect face.

From his place on the floor, Monster looked at him with concern and raised a bushy brow.

I also thought Od was behaving strangely. He was far from his usual mild and controlled self.

"Where have you been the past few weeks?" I asked.

Od partially opened one eye. I was pretty sure a silver beam shone through the crack. He set the glass down.

"I've been in Asgard." He opened his eyes fully and held a sparkling hand up in front of himself.

"You're glowing," I noted.

449

Od's hand froze in the air, and he directed his gleaming eyes toward me.

"And you seem taller." I tried to make my voice steady.

He smiled and, as always, I was completely under his power.

"It's because I've been with the gods," he said. "Just as humans affect the human in me, the gods affect the god in me. Right now I'm stronger, more attractive, and wiser than usual."

"Congratulations," I mumbled and rolled my eyes.

Od's eyes shifted from shining to blazing. A slight unease spread through me.

"It's a good thing that you're strong," I said carefully.

"I don't want this strength," he bellowed and slammed a huge fist on the table, causing it to shake. He exhaled with a hiss.

I was struck by a wave of heat that also extinguished the candle. With Mathias's steam breath in mind, I scooted my chair back, stood up, and took a couple of stumbling steps backward.

Od seethed coldly in the darkness, and his dazzling eyes were directed at me.

At that moment, Monster stood between us with his front paws on the table and, growling, stuck his mastodon head right in Od's face. They stared at one another, and I admired Monster's courage. Despite his impressive size and strength, if they came to blows, he wouldn't stand a chance against a demigod.

But it was Od, however, who first cast his eyes down. He collapsed in his chair.

"I'm sorry." He buried his face in his hands. "When the god in me is strengthened, the human part is diminished, and I lose my mercifulness."

Monster's hackles lowered slowly, and I felt the danger pass. He put his paws back on the floor but remained standing between Od and me.

"It's okay, Monster. Isn't it?" The last part was addressed to Od.

He once again focused his eyes on me. "Can I spend the night in your bed?"

I sat in my chair, completely taken aback, and another growl rumbled from Monster's chest.

Od waved his hand. "Not like that. I need your humanity, so I can feel like myself again."

I wanted to say no as firmly as I possibly could, but when I saw the desperation in Od's face, I nodded curtly.

Monster rolled his eyes as if to say, *oh, come on.*

I curled up under the blanket while Od was in the shower, not knowing what to expect.

Monster and I had had a wordless conversation in the living room in which he, with what I took to be an older-brother-like look and a gesture with his snout toward the bathroom, urged me to throw the insolent demigod out. In reply, I had pressed my lips together and raised an eyebrow stubbornly. Offended, Monster went to sleep in the guest bedroom.

A dim light appeared in the doorway. It was Od's glow-in-the-dark body.

I closed my eyes as he lifted the cover and crawled in with me. When he was in place, I opened them again.

We lay face-to-face without touching one another. Then he took my hand, and I shuddered when I felt a current of something flowing from him to me.

"What is that?" I looked at Od's radiant face.

His eyes were closed, and I could see his long dark eyelashes against his shimmering skin. He smiled, and I saw that his inner turmoil had dissolved into relief.

"What you see and feel is divinity."

I touched my feet to his legs and once again felt the cool current. I had the thought that I was like a rechargeable battery in a plug.

"Isn't it unpleasant, losing your strength?"

451

"I'm both losing and gaining strength right now," he said. "And it's nice lying here with you. It's also pleasant for you."

It wasn't entirely clear whether he was asking me or telling me.

I engaged my senses and let the strength be absorbed by my body.

"Yes, it is pleasant."

Od took my shoulder and gently turned me over, so my back met his chest.

His silvery arms were wrapped around me, and, swimming in a sea of divinity, I fell asleep.

In the morning, I gathered my courage and looked at myself in the mirror over my vanity. I turned my head from side to side and found that I looked like myself. No red hair or sweet smile. But I was a prettier version of myself. My skin looked healthier than normal; I had fresh, pink cheeks, and my black hair had a glossy sheen. The whites of my eyes were very bright, and when I bared my teeth, I saw that they, too, were white as chalk.

I met Od's eyes in the mirror as he stood behind me, stooped down, and rested his chin on the top of my head. His strong hands, which had returned to their normal size, ran through my hair and landed on my shoulders. His silver glow had disappeared.

"Side effect?" I said dryly, twirling one of my gleaming locks between my fingers.

He let go of my shoulders and cleared his throat.

"You won't get sick for the next several months. Your bones and muscles are stronger for a while, and you're faster than usual. And if you die a natural death, I've added about ten years to your life." He turned quickly and sat on the edge of my bed.

I swung around and glared at him.

"And you didn't think to tell me that before you filled me with godliness?" I got up and stood in front of him. "What if I don't want to live ten extra years? What if I didn't want free teeth whitening?"

Od looked down at the floor.

I completed the thought. "Why didn't you give it to an old person, so they could live longer? Or a sick person. A child? You call yourself merciful."

Od looked up at me with pain in his eyes. "When the god in us is dominant, we become selfish. We do what we want rather than help others."

I raised my eyebrows when he said *we*. "I think you're shunting your responsibility here."

Od continued. "Yesterday I wanted your company, so I took it."

"Took my company? As I recall, I gave you permission to sleep here."

Od bit his lip and stared at his hands.

"You wouldn't have forced me!" I was certain of that. Almost.

"No, I would not have forced my way into your bed." He looked up and smiled slightly, but even that almost put my willpower out of commission.

I realized that demigods had several options when it came to force.

Od continued: "I don't allow myself to stay with the gods for very long."

"If you had spent more time in Asgard, then maybe you would have . . ."

Od did not respond, and that was response enough.

Something rattled in the back of my mind.

"That's why Elias is so old, isn't it? You tap his humanity when your divinity is all pumped up."

Again, Od's silence answered my question.

"You should tell Mathias that. He's freaking out at the thought that Luna will get old and die someday. This way she could keep living."

Od met my gaze. His eyes were still full of sorrow, and I didn't understand why. "Elias should have died many years ago. I broke a rule and saved his life. On that occasion, he got a couple of hundred years added to his life. But he also sometimes does for me what you did last night. That's why he doesn't age."

I tried to stop myself from picturing Od and Elias spooning, but the image kept popping into my head.

"Are you and Elias like . . . together?"

"Do you want to know what Elias is to me?"

I nodded silently, but I actually wasn't sure I did.

"Elias is the child of a woman I knew many years ago. In every way but blood, he is my son."

Od's eyes looked far into the past. I knelt in front of him and took his hands. In that instant, I saw the past of Od the human. Like with Mathias, the images bounced around and there were black holes. But I saw men and women in old-fashioned clothes. I saw water, wooden ships, and towns that stank of decay. A sea of faces and scenes swam past. The stream of images stopped at a pair of blue-gray eyes in a woman's freckled face. When she smiled, I felt a wave of warmth. She reached out her hand to me and caressed my cheek. It suddenly felt wet. I took her hand and saw that it was bloody.

"If you have to choose, save Elias," she said. I looked down, where a boy lay on the ground in a pool of blood.

The woman collapsed with her free hand on her stomach. My stomach turned when I saw what she was trying to hide. The room we were in resembled a slaughterhouse. There were weapons. There were instruments. *Oh no.* In my vision, Od opened his mouth and bellowed with a powerful, metallic voice: "Help me, Father. Help me, Odin."

The vision stopped abruptly.

The god side of Od must have taken over, which shut me off from the rest of the action. I landed in my body on the floor of my bedroom, with Od's hands still in mine.

He studied me intensely.

"That's why you haven't told Mathias," I whispered. "You don't want to give him false hope that Luna will live forever with him. She can be killed in other ways. Even if his powers are keeping her alive."

Od bowed his head and looked down at our interlaced hands. Then he looked up, now with his usual calm, controlled expression. The conversation was over. He let go of my hands and stood up.

"Can I stay for breakfast?"

I got to my feet. "Yes, of course."

Monster refused to even glance at us when we made our entrance in the kitchen, but when Od made him a plate of scrambled eggs and bacon, his desire for food trumped his irritation over Od's behavior the previous evening. As we ate, they exchanged anecdotes from Hrafnheim.

For the second time in twelve hours, there was a knock at my door.

I opened it, and for once I was not happy to see Varnar. I glanced into the kitchen, where Od was clearing plates and coffee cups from the table. It would be a little tough to explain the barefoot demigod's presence in my kitchen at nine o'clock on a Saturday morning. I decided that I didn't owe Varnar an explanation and waved him in.

A strangely despondent, angry mood emanated from him when he saw Od, but he nodded respectfully.

"It's an honor to meet you," he said.

"Likewise," smiled Od. "I've heard epic stories about you, Varnar of the Bronze Forest."

Monster, whose hackles had risen, got up and stood before Varnar. Wolf and man looked at each other, and the air grew thick with emotion. Varnar looked Monster straight in the eyes, looking neither triumphant nor apologetic.

"You are my brother's slayer," growled Monster.

I held my breath.

Varnar nodded.

"If you were able to kill Liutpold, then you're also the right body-guard for Anna. Thank you for protecting her in my absence."

"Your brother was a worthy opponent. He fought bravely," replied Varnar.

Monster snorted. "Liutpold was a fool."

I raised an eyebrow.

"He was my brother, but we disagreed on a lot of things," continued Monster. "I told him not to attack Ragnara, but he wouldn't listen. It cost him his life." He laid a large paw on Varnar's shoulder. It looked like it weighed a ton, but Varnar didn't budge under the weight. "Friends?" asked Monster.

Varnar placed his hand on Monster's back. "Friends," he replied.

I exhaled slowly. Next to me, Od appeared to do the same.

"Come sit," I said. "What do you want?"

Varnar sat at the table, anything but relaxed. "There was someone in the forest last night. Someone who doesn't belong there. I think he was heading for your house, but someone or something up here scared him away. By the time I got here, there was no trace of him. I patrolled the area all night."

"When did he disappear?" I asked.

"Just before midnight."

Od met my gaze.

"Who was it?" I moved my eyes back to Varnar.

"I don't know. But my suspicion is someone from Freiheim."

"Why don't you say Hrafnheim?" I snapped.

"Habit." He looked at me coolly.

"Ragnara has forbidden everyone from using the old name. It can cost a person their life to say Hrafnheim," said Monster.

"Does that rule also apply to giant wolves?"

"It costs us our lives just to be what we are."

456

"How do you know it's someone from your world?" asked Od, wisely neutral in the Hrafnheim-versus-Freiheim discussion.

"The forest told me it was someone who doesn't belong in Midgard."

No one questioned Varnar's ability to understand forest language.

"He probably ran off when he saw me. I spent the night here," said Od. "I arrived just after eleven o'clock."

Thanks a lot, Od! He really hadn't needed to say that.

Varnar's face flared with anger.

Od continued: "Thank you for the intel. You are a talented soldier."

Again, a flash of fury in Varnar's eyes.

The testosterone level had gotten too high, so I jumped in.

"I have to go to work soon, and I'm nowhere close to ready. Feel free to head out if there's nothing more."

Od looked at me with his head slightly tilted.

I pursed my lips. "I'm not one of those people who think you should be treated with subservience."

"Subservience is not the same as respect," replied Od.

"I haven't seen any behavior from you lately that really commanded respect," I said, drumming my fingers on the tabletop.

From the floor, Monster laughed hoarsely.

Od smiled his most breathtaking smile, and to my great irritation, I melted. He leaned across the table and laid a hand on my cheek. Trapped as I was, I leaned forward toward him. A corner of my consciousness was screaming that I was doing this right in front of Varnar, but I couldn't do anything about it.

"If you wish, I will leave. But thank you for the gift you gave me last night." A statement that could easily be misunderstood. Od's god side was apparently still dominant enough that he needed to display his power.

I blushed, but still couldn't move.

Od got up and nodded to Varnar and Monster before leaving Odinmont.

I blinked and shook my head as if I'd just woken from a deep sleep. Varnar had also stood and was staring at me with his lips pressed into a thin line.

"He just slept here," I began. "Nothing else happened . . ."

"It's none of my business," he interrupted. "You should treat a demigod with deference. Fear them, even."

He strode toward the door.

I stayed seated and stared after him with tears in my eyes. Monster watched me with concern. He whined.

"Stop looking at me like that," I pleaded.

He sniffed deeply.

"The policeman is on his way," he said with his rough voice.

I walked over to the door, which Varnar had not closed behind him, and saw Hakim coming toward me across the driveway. He looked over his shoulder at Varnar, who sprinted across the field toward Kraghede Forest. Then he turned his head and watched Od's tall figure disappearing at a quick trot down the road.

"You sure have a lot of guests," he said when he saw me in the doorway.

"The point of moving out here was to be isolated from other people," I said. "I don't really think isolation lives up to its reputation."

Hakim was, for once, not in his police uniform, but rather in jeans and a black hoodie. He looked more like the cross-the-street-to-avoid-them segment of the population than an upright policeman.

"What are you doing here?" I asked more harshly than I meant to.

Hakim tousled his short black hair. "I'll make it quick."

"Go on." I didn't invite him in.

"The man I arrested in the beach house in Jagd, the one you call the Savage, is dead."

"Dead?"

"He was found this morning."

I didn't mourn the Savage's passing, but nevertheless, goose bumps spread up my arms.

"How did he die?" My mouth was suddenly bone-dry.

"Someone broke in and poisoned him. The door to his cell was open."

The Savage had not slipped gently toward death. I plucked the images directly from Hakim's head. Whatever he'd been given, it had killed him violently. I saw him lying stiff with blood running from his eyes, nose, and ears. The foam around his mouth was pink. In the vision, Hakim was bent over the Savage's corpse with rubber gloves on. Hakim's eyes were a little puffy, and his hair stuck up in every direction. He was wearing the same clothes as now.

I found my voice. "Do you know who did it?"

Hakim shook his head. "The strange thing is, there's no sign of a struggle. It's almost as if he willingly allowed someone to poison him. I found a mark from an injection on his arm."

"You don't have anything from the CCTV cameras?"

"The entire security network had a system failure for an hour after midnight."

"Anything else?" I asked. I might as well hear it all now.

Hakim pulled out his phone and tapped around on the screen before holding it out to me. It was a picture of the cell's worn linoleum floor. Carved into it was a symbol I already knew alarmingly well. The rune Ansuz. The camera had zoomed in on the symbol in the soft, gray-painted material, but in the corner of the photo I noticed a sturdy, bluish finger caked with dried blood. Under the nail, a gray line was clearly visible.

"He scratched it into the floor before he died," I observed.

"That, or someone guided his hand," replied Hakim.

I felt nauseous, but I tried to make my voice calm. "As much as I appreciate being served with a picture of a blue, bloody finger first thing in the morning, I don't understand why you came all the way out here to show it to me."

"Do we have to go over this again? I think someone—"

"—is after me and wants to kill me in the most terrible way. Got it. But you could have just called. It's not like I'm in more danger now that the murderer is dead. Quite the opposite."

Hakim looked down at his sneakers. "I tried to call. You didn't pick up."

"Oh. My phone is in my bag." I still wasn't used to carrying a phone.

Hakim cleared his throat.

"You thought something had happened to me."

"The murders have stopped, even though there's now a surplus of local red-haired teenage girls. That tells me that the murderer has homed in on the specific person he wants to kill. Your identity is well-known, and everyone knows by now that you're a natural redhead. Our primary suspect is dead, and either he or his killer carved the murderer's signature into the floor, most likely as a message that this isn't over. And then you don't pick up the phone when I call you. Yes, I thought something had happened to you."

"Well, nothing did."

"I thought I would come out here and find your mutilated corpse, so from now on, can you please have your phone on you so you'll hear it if I call?"

"I'll try."

"*Try?*" yelled Hakim. "You don't need to try. You need to get yourself together and realize what grave danger you're in."

At his outburst, Monster came running. He snarled, and for a split second, even I was a little scared of him. He leapt in front of me and barked right in Hakim's face.

Hakim jumped back.

"It's okay, Monster," I said and laid a hand on his enormous head,

460

which was trembling with agitation. To Hakim, I said, "As you can see, I'm protected. Monster is always with me."

Hakim breathed raggedly, and his hand had reached behind his back. No matter how big and strong Monster was, he probably couldn't survive a bullet to the forehead.

I inserted myself between them.

"Thank you for checking up on me. I'll be sure to pay more attention to my phone in the future."

Hakim nodded and appeared to be at a loss for words. His dark green eyes were wide beneath his thick brows. Then he composed himself.

"Can I ask you one last thing?" His voice shook slightly. Mine would, too, if Monster had jumped up in my face like that.

"Ask away," I said.

"I didn't tell anyone that you tipped me off about Bike Shop Timmy, and I'm not going to. And I won't ask how you knew what he was up to. But it frustrates me that I can't go higher up than him. There's someone above him, and this person hasn't stopped producing the drugs. They're already on the market again. Between you and me, do you know anything that could help me?"

I moved my head slowly from side to side. "No."

I didn't know whether I was lying to protect Elias or to protect Hakim.

In my bedroom, I got ready for that evening's shift. The weather had gotten colder now that it was almost November, so I rummaged in my closet to find a sweater. My hands found a plastic bag all the way up against the back wall. It was the one I had put my bloody clothes in the night Mathias was shot.

I pulled the bag out and opened it. To my amazement, the clothes were still wet and warm. I took out the black undershirt, and my hand was immediately colored bright red. Mathias's blood hadn't dried even though it had been—I counted on my fingers—

461

almost a month. I put the undershirt back, tied the bag in a knot, and stuck it back in the closet.

At Frank's, everyone was talking about the Savage's death.

The patrons raised their glasses and rejoiced that he would never hurt any red-haired teenage girls—or anyone else—ever again. A number of details had gotten out, and they were discussed and repeated across the tables.

I didn't harbor any warm feelings for the Savage, but nevertheless, my stomach simmered with unease at the collective enthusiasm over the macabre death of another human being.

A welcome side effect from my night with Od was that I found it tolerable to be in the café, even though it was full. I therefore willingly made a round with the tray. I made eye contact with Frank across the room, and he looked soberly at me as, on the small stage, Johnny-Bum and Niller performed a graphic reenactment of the Savage's death with the help of ketchup and beer foam. I quickly returned to the kitchen.

As I emptied the dishwasher, I heard shouts from the bar. I stuck my head out the swinging door and saw Christian Mikkelsen, AKA the psychopath who had both beat me up and jacked up my bike within the past two months. When he spotted me, he completely went off.

"You bitch," he shouted, pointing his index finger in my direction. "The police picked me up again today. What did you tell them?"

"Go back to the kitchen, Anna," said the other bartender nervously, though he himself was a sturdy northerner.

I remained standing there. "I didn't say shit about you. They probably brought you in because you're a total psychopath," I shouted back.

Christian took a few threatening steps toward me, but the bartender pushed back against his chest.

"Hey, hey . . . We don't want any trouble," he drawled.

"Then you shouldn't have her around," spat Christian.

At that moment, Frank came in. He immediately took stock of the situation and was in front of Christian with two long strides. An aggressive vibe shot off of him, and I could barely recognize the aura as Frank's.

"If you don't leave my bar now, you'll make it worse for yourself." Despite Frank's age, I didn't doubt for a second that he was fully capable of following through on that statement.

Just like the time Christian attacked me, he lashed out at Frank without warning. He was fast, but Frank was faster.

I barely saw what was happening before Christian was lying on his stomach with Frank on his back. His arms were twisted painfully backward, and though he was writhing around, he couldn't move much at all. He seethed with rage, yelling and screaming. The other bartender and Frank got him upright and dragged him off.

Before they tossed him out, Christian shouted: "You're going to regret ever hiring her."

Then the two men sent him flying out the door. The patrons at Frank's applauded.

I went up to Frank. "I'm sorry."

"It's not your fault he's an idiot." Frank smoothed his hair, which had gotten mussed during the scuffle. "Better in here than out there, when you're on your way home. I'm driving you home tonight, whether you rode your bike or not. In case he's waiting for you."

This seemed like a distinct possibility, so I nodded. "Okay. Fine. If you want."

He patted my shoulder with a chuckle and pushed me back toward the kitchen. "Now get a move on. I'm not paying you to stand here and chat."

463

The bar was empty, and Frank wiped off the counter while I swept the floor.

The final guest had tottered off, and my ears rang in the silence after the many hours of noise. A pile of beer labels, dirt, and a couple of coins gathered on the floor in front of me.

Frank came toward me with a dustpan. His usual friendly features had been replaced by a mask of exhaustion. He crouched down and held the dustpan while I pushed the dirt into it. Distractedly, he picked the coins out and jingled them in his hand.

"What is it about you that makes some people so angry at you?"

"I don't know," I lied. "I think that Christian guy is just angry, period. He's decided he hates me, but it could just as well have been someone else."

Frank looked up at me. "But others, too. Most people don't even notice you. I just don't get it. I think you're such a lovely girl."

I tapped the broom on the floor before hurrying toward the narrow cabinet behind the bar where we kept the cleaning supplies. Behind me, Frank stood up and followed. He stuck the dustpan into the cabinet and closed it with a click.

"Want an after-work beer?" he asked.

"If people knew you served alcohol to minors, it would tarnish your good name."

"What people don't know can't hurt them." He smiled.

He was absolutely right about that, so I climbed onto a barstool while he pulled a couple glasses down from the holder on the ceiling.

Something scratched at the door, and Frank jerked his head up. I could make out the silhouette of Monster's gigantic body behind the frosted glass.

"That's my dog," I said. "Can I let him in?"

A swell of relief flowed from Frank as he nodded. Had he thought it was Christian out there?

"That solves the mystery of your good mood," he said, and the friendly glimmer was back in his eyes. "I told you he would come back."

I held the door open so Monster could lumber in. He sat and looked longingly at the two draft beers.

"Do you like beer?" I asked him, and he nodded imperceptibly. I looked at Frank. "Can Monster have one, too?"

Frank clucked, then poured a beer for Monster in the only glass that was big enough for him to fit his snout into.

I convinced Frank to let me ride my bike home now that Monster was back. He said that no one was stupid enough to go after both of us at once. But he made me promise to let him drive me home if one day Monster wasn't there to escort me.

Monster wisely held his tongue but nodded in agreement. He was immensely satisfied to have drunk a beer. When we got home, he raved about the culinary experiences he had had in this world— not that I had contributed to them.

I tumbled into bed, and he threw himself on the floor with a thump that sent shock waves up through my mattress.

"There's something I want to ask you," I said, my eyes already closed.

"What?" If he'd been a human, I would have said he had whiskey voice.

"That was my sister I saw in the mirror, wasn't it? The times I saw myself with red hair?"

Monster nodded.

"Did she say anything about the messages she sends me?"

"Like I said, I don't know a whole lot. Just that it's risky when she contacts you in dreams or through mirrors."

"Risky how?"

"They can be monitored. And people can be traced through them."

465

I remembered the snarling sound when I spoke with Serén in the dream. We must have almost gotten traced.

Monster continued: "Now that Serén is known to be Thora Baneblood's daughter, you can be certain they're looking for her. The smallest trace will send Ragnara's entire army after her."

"So I shouldn't count on hearing from her anymore?"

"Not unless it's an emergency situation." Monster smacked his lips.

"But she's in the Iron Forest? Is she safe there?"

"Safer than at the castle in Sént," he said evasively.

Hmmm. "Do you know where my mom is?"

"No. And she doesn't send messages that way. She's not a seer."

That explained why Ben and Rebecca hadn't had contact with her in all these years.

"Do you think Ragnara will send others after me, now that the Savage is dead?"

Monster let out a yawn that ended with a very doglike whining noise.

"I'm certain they're already on their way."

 # CHAPTER 28

On Monday morning, Luna's hair was purple.

"Why?" I asked, my forehead creased.

She twirled around with a huge smile in front of the plush red sofa in The Island. The violet curls danced around her face.

"Because purple is the color of magic and spirituality. I need all the help I can get to learn about witchcraft. And I don't need the red anymore. I figured out the date. The day when either you or your sister will die."

I don't think she even considered how inappropriate it was to smile as she said that. Pride emanated from her, so I chose to attribute the smile to that.

"When?"

"Well, if it's this year, then it's just after midnight on December 21," she said. "It's the winter solstice."

"That's funny," I said from my spot on the sofa.

Mathias focused on me. "Funny isn't quite the word I would use, considering the seriousness of the matter."

"No, not that it's the winter solstice. December 21 is my birthday."

They both looked at me, and Luna stopped her pirouettes. "Why didn't you tell us when your birthday is?"

"Why would I?"

Mathias adopted the facial expression he used when he saw me as socially illiterate.

"You know. Presents. Cake. And happy-birthday-to-you." This last bit was delivered in song.

"I'm not really into birthdays. Mostly it's fallen right in the middle of a move, or when I had just arrived in a new place."

"Have you never celebrated your birthday?" Luna bit her lower lip.

"No. And I haven't missed it."

"This year I'm throwing you a birthday party with everyone you know," she said decidedly.

"If I don't kick the bucket first," I said.

"Don't say that!" Her eyes flashed, and I took a step back. It felt like tiny needles were boring into my skin.

Mathias stepped between us.

"There are many of us making sure that doesn't happen." He looked at me with one of his most charming smiles, and my legs wobbled. Then he turned toward Luna. "It's great that you figured out the date. That will help us a hell of a lot. Now we know we have to be extra vigilant on December 21."

"What if it's Serén who dies that day, and I'm predestined to die before then?"

"God, stop being so pessimistic," said Luna.

"In Asatru, which you yourself profess to believe in, fate isn't something you can just get out of. I think we can keep clearing potential killers out of the way all we want, and the result will be the same. At one point, Varnar was supposed to kill me. When he switched sides, the murderer was just replaced by someone else."

Mathias's jaw dropped. "What?! Varnar?"

"It doesn't matter. My point is, there may not be very much we can do."

"Rewind a second," said Luna. "Did you say Varnar was going to kill you? How do you know that?"

"He told me." *While he sat on top of me with his hands around my neck.* "And Serén sent me a vision of it."

Mathias squeezed the bridge of his nose and closed his beautiful blue eyes. I caught just a glimpse of them shining first.

"You can't be alone with him."

"That's not up to you to decide," I snarled.

"What if he switches sides again!" He opened his eyes, which now resembled gas flames.

"He won't."

"You can't see the future. I don't think you should train with him anymore."

"Well, it's too bad for you that you don't think so."

Mathias grew and developed a green glow. "I can command you. You're beneath me in the hierarchy."

"I'll tell you where you can stick the hierarchy. And if you ever start to think you can make decisions on my behalf, you might as well join Ben, Rebecca, and Arthur's camp."

He pursed his well-shaped lips. Then he relaxed again and ended with a warm smile.

"I'll never command you do to anything. I respect your choices, even though I think your judgement is crap."

"And I think you should be careful not to let your divine side go to your head." I thought back to Od's behavior the day before. "If we're done discussing my maybe-maybe-not-imminent death, there's one detail I think you should hear."

I told them about Elias's relationship to Od and the effect that long-term companionship with demigods has on humans. "It's not a guarantee, but if you stay together, chances are good that Luna can live into the space age with you," I concluded.

Mathias's face was unreadable. He looked from me to Luna.

I expected him to whoop or run a victory lap, but that didn't happen.

"This is good news. Hello?" I waved a hand in front of him.

Luna, too, stood completely still, with large, round eyes.

"What's up with you?"

"Eternal life together is a big deal, Anna," said Mathias. "I don't know if Luna wants to be with me long-term. Let alone forever."

Luna broke into a smile.

"Oh, that was what you were nervous about?" She flung her arms around him, and they toppled onto the sofa. "Of course I want that. I've wanted that since the first day I met you."

"You have? You hid it well."

"I was a little busy suppressing my magical powers, meeting my future best friend, and stopping myself from telling Anna everything I knew about her parents."

I looked down at my studded boots.

Mathias stroked a hand over her purple curls. "Now we just need a way to let Anna live forever, too."

I exhaled loudly to hide a derisive laugh. I would actually be perfectly happy if I just made it through the rest of the year.

At the ten o'clock break, Luna and Mathias left the history classroom arm in arm while I packed up. When I came out, a figure was standing down the hall, arms swinging anxiously at her sides.

I jogged over to her.

"Aella, did something happen?"

"There's something I need to tell you. I should have told you before, but there's always so many people around you. And I think only you should hear it."

I inhaled a big gulp of air. "So no one's hurt?"

Aella started walking and signaled that I should go with her.

"No. Not recently, anyway. Do you have a minute?"

"Of course."

We found a deserted corner between the Blue and Brown halls.

"What is it? You're making me nervous," I demanded.

Aella hesitated.

"When Thora told your sister that she was her mother, she also told her about the night your father died. Serén repeated it to me. I don't know if this is useful to you, but I think you should know what I heard. Varnar doesn't even know."

My brows furrowed. "Just tell me what you know."

Aella sighed and went ahead: "Your mother was pregnant with you, but only Thora and Arthur—and probably also Od Dinesen—knew that she was expecting twins." Aella stood up straighter before she continued. "Ragnara and Eskild captured your mother, and they cut her stomach open and pulled you out."

Yikes!

"Ragnara didn't dare kill Thora. Apparently, there's a prophecy that that says Ragnara herself might also die from that. I'm not quite sure how it all fits together. But in any case, she wanted to kill the child Thora was pregnant with."

"Why did Ragnara dare to kill me? Can't she die from that, too?"

"The prophecy says something like *the blood that flows in Thora's veins* . . . blah, blah, blah." Aella made a rolling motion with her hand. "The interpretation is that it doesn't apply to the blood of Thora's offspring."

"So, it's okay for Ragnara to kill me, but not my mom?"

Aella nodded.

I tried to stay focused. "My mom was lying there with her stomach cut open." I shivered. "And I was ripped out. Then what happened?"

Aella continued unwillingly. "Thora healed immediately after they took you out."

I leaned my head back. "Why did she heal?"

Aella threw up her arms. "No one knows. Serén remained inside. Ragnara didn't know there was another baby. And then . . ." Again, Aella stopped as if to collect herself. "Ragnara stabbed you in the chest. In order to . . . you know."

Involuntarily, my hand reached for the knobby scar along my sternum.

"But you healed, too. She stabbed you again and again, but the wounds closed immediately."

I exhaled hard with both hands on my chest. "Then what?"

Aella rubbed her nose. "It was utter chaos. You were lying there all . . . gooey. Eskild and Ragnara tried to grab Thora, and then Arthur stepped in." She looked down and kicked at the artificial acrylic carpet. "Eskild stabbed him."

My eyes burned. "But he didn't heal, I'm guessing."

Silently, Aella shook her head.

I rubbed my forehead.

"So how did they proceed from there?"

"Bear in mind that I heard this from Serén, who heard it from Thora, who lived through it almost eighteen years ago."

"Just spit it out! Tell me what you know!" My voice resounded loudly, and a few students looked in our direction.

Aella bit her lip.

"Od Dinesen and Niels Villadsen arrived—and they had a solution."

"Which was?" I almost didn't dare ask.

"To sign a blood treaty, so all parties would be forced to uphold it. That way Ragnara, Thora, and you would survive."

"What's a blood treaty?"

I could see that Aella did not want to explain, but she forced the words out. "You use someone's blood—all their blood—so you harvest their life force. That makes the treaty nearly unbreakable."

I closed my eyes. "I assume Arthur signed up willingly."

"Yes. He was already seriously injured," said Aella. "It was Eskild who finished him off." She quickly moved along. "The terms of the treaty were that Thora would go to Hrafnheim as a prisoner. Ben and Rebecca would take care of you. And Ragnara wasn't allowed to touch you for as long as the treaty held, which, in principle, was forever. Or until someone broke it." She shrugged her shoulders. "And it's broken now, because Ragnara tried to kill you, and Thora fled."

"What else?"

"There's nothing else."

"There has to be!" Again, I spoke so loudly that people looked at us.

"I swear, I don't know any more. Now you know as much as I do." Her teeth ground against one another. "And believe me, I didn't want to tell you. But it would have been wrong not to."

She turned around and ran off with the same catlike stride as Varnar.

I stood and watched her go with my hands placed protectively on my scar.

After school, it was time for my monthly visit to Greta. I was beyond confused after Aella's story, and my thoughts kept returning to my sister.

While I waited on the cobalt-blue sofa outside Greta's office, I thought about how my remaining consultations could be counted on one hand. When I turned eighteen, I'd be a legal adult; there would be no more getting checked up on by social services. Even though for the past several years I had been counting down the days, the thought nevertheless imparted a strange sadness on me.

Greta opened the door, and an older man left her office.

When I walked in, she opened the window to let the worst of the alcohol fumes out. I sat in the chair at the corner of the desk while Greta pushed her glasses up her nose and began typing something.

"How's it going?" Her voice was a little distracted, but she wasn't fooling me.

I therefore thought carefully before answering.

"Good. I'm doing well in school, and my dog came back. I go to work two or three times a week, and it seems like my boss is happy with me."

Greta nodded and kept her gaze on her screen. "Have you heard more from the police?"

I chewed on my lower lip. There was no reason to lie—not too much, anyway.

"That young police officer, Hakim, has gotten in touch a couple times."

"Why?"

I shrugged. "I'm sure they're talking to a lot of people. But he's dead now, the guy who did it, so maybe he'll find another case to investigate."

I hoped Greta would accept my fabricated theory. I knew full well that Hakim wasn't planning to stop investigating anything.

Greta fixed her beady eyes on me. Then she pushed her glasses, which had once again slid, up the bridge of her nose. "Hakim Murr contacted me for information about all your previous foster families. I hope he hasn't been bothering you."

I turned my head from side to side and pushed my lower lip out. "Nope." I left it at that.

Greta swung her chair back to face the computer. "If you feel harassed by him, I can only help you for the next couple of months. When you're eighteen, that's the end of my authority over you. Unless . . ." She stopped mid-sentence.

"Unless I mess up and end up back in the system."

"Yes."

"I'm not planning on messing up."

"Good." Greta scratched her forehead. "Have you considered selling your house?"

"Absolutely not. Why?"

"The potential buyer has increased their offer."

"Who is it?" I held my breath.

"I don't know. He—or she—communicates via lawyers. But a very favorable offer has been made. You could buy something more suitable for a young girl."

"The house has sentimental value for me. It belonged to my parents, you know."

Greta's thin eyebrows shot up. "I've known you for thirteen years, Anna, and until a few months ago, you didn't want to know about your parents. I wasn't even allowed to mention them. And now their home suddenly has sentimental value. Has something happened that I don't know about?" She leaned toward me slightly.

Parallel worlds, ghosts, blood treaties, demigods, and witches.

"No. I just like living there."

Greta straightened with a disappointed expression and looked at her watch, the thin gold band hanging loosely on her wrist. "I hope you reconsider. It could really pay off for you financially."

"I'll think about it. And I still want to know who the buyer is."

"I'll see if I can find out." She stood and made a sweeping motion toward the door. "Remember that you can still be subject to unannounced visits."

She pushed her glasses into place again before she opened the door for me.

"I won't forget."

How could I?

In rural towns, even small events are a big deal. And the semi-annual Ravensted Open by Night event, which took place a few days later, was no exception.

By night was a stretch, as the event lasted from six o'clock to ten o'clock on a weeknight. *Open*, however, lived up to its promise, as all the businesses and shops flung open their doors and everyone for miles around who could walk or crawl showed up in the center of Ravensted. There were popcorn machines, bargains on athletic socks, and sausages, and the little stage was set up in the square in front of Frank's, so local bands could play. Farmers from the area set up booths and handed out samples of cheese, jam, and bread.

The community theater's members ran around in costume, performing skits and pulling pranks. Halloween was just around the corner, so Ravensted was decorated with pumpkins and people dressed as witches and ghosts.

On the way to Frank's, Luna and I laughed as we passed a witch-ghost couple. The witch had a fake wart-covered nose and a pointy hat, and the ghost was covered by a sheet with holes for the eyes.

Because I was chopping vegetables and washing dishes, I missed Niller and Suzuki's band, the Ravensted Dog Trainers' Association show, and the clown run. But we closed the kitchen at eight o'clock, and I was free to walk around town. Luna and Mathias were still at work, but we agreed to meet up later.

Oddly enough, for the first time in my life, I enjoyed the revelry around me. I passed a face-painting booth, where children were being painted to look like fairies, skeletons, trolls, and butterflies. From a distance, I saw Hakim tasting a piece of bread at a booth. He was accompanied by a dark-haired woman I took to be his mother.

Our eyes met, and he nodded at me. The woman looked at me curiously.

I noticed Varnar a bit farther down the street, clearly in his role as my discreet bodyguard. I rolled my eyes. *No, he couldn't just walk around with me normally.* Irritated, I turned and stomped off. I wove in and out of a few side streets to shake him off. I was counting on Ben's Teflon magic to help me.

Finally, he disappeared, and I hit the walking street again, where I was passed by a girl on a unicycle and a boy on stilts.

A guy from the community theater wrapped in a dark cape walked by with a basket full of cookies. They were decorated with skulls drawn in white icing. He smiled at me under the hood of his cape. What little I could see of his face was handsome. He looked a little like Varnar.

I automatically smiled back and took one of the cookies he handed me.

He bowed with a provocative smile and took a couple steps backward with a courteous, twirling hand motion.

My teeth sank into the cookie. It tasted sweet, spicy, and a touch bitter. I chewed once and only just managed to think *uh oh*, before a tingling feeling spread from my throat, down to my stomach, and throughout the rest of my body.

Then darkness.

Then nothing.

* * *

My legs moved beneath me. I walked forward with no control over my movements.

The cape-wearing young man had a firm grip on my arm.

"Smile," he whispered.

I smiled against my own will.

Then it was once again just darkness.

* * *

Someone shouted. There were several voices. One of them was familiar.

I heard snarling and a roar.

A terrified scream.

Then the sound of fighting.

Another scream—this one from pain. The scream turned into a rattle.

Silence followed by a crunch, then the sound of something being dragged.

"Anna?" The voice sounded feverish. My brain tried to place it, but my concentration kept slipping.

I didn't know if I was standing or lying down.

A hand closed around my neck. At first, I thought it would squeeze. But then I felt that it was either wrapping something around it or taking something off.

Then I slid back into nothingness.

 # CHAPTER 29

My hands found something soft and prickly. Grass? This time I was sure I was lying down. I cautiously opened my eyes and looked up into a blue-black, starry sky with a half-moon that was blocked when Varnar stuck his face in front of it.

His hair was matted, and he had four dark streaks on one cheek.

"You're alive," he said, his relief transferring to me. From one of his hands dangled a leather cord.

"What happened?" I managed to say. My voice sounded strangely hoarse.

"Why did you run off?" he yelled. "You know you're almost impossible for me to find."

"I got mad that you didn't want to walk with me," I croaked.

Varnar furrowed his brow. "I will never understand you."

"The guy with the cookies. Who . . ." My voice broke, and I coughed. Only now did I notice how sore my throat was.

"One of Ragnara's men. Geiri."

"Do you know him?" I wheezed.

"Yes. I knew him."

"Knew?"

Varnar's face closed up and disappeared from my field of vision.

I got myself to a sitting position, although the ground was spinning, and my stomach protested.

I saw that we were in a deserted industrial area on the outskirts of town.

How the hell did I get all the way out here?

Varnar had leaned back on his heels, and I saw that Monster was sitting just behind him, unmoving. I turned my attention back to Varnar.

"Where do you know him from?"

"The Bronze Forest. We arrived at the fortress at the same time."

I didn't know what to say. "Where is he now?"

"Gone," said Monster with his deep voice. He licked his lips.

"Oh." I could no longer hold the contents of my stomach down, so I stood up, stumbled behind a bush, and threw up.

Man and giant wolf wisely stayed back.

I wiped my mouth with the back of my hand and slunk back over to them. "What now?"

"We go home and act like nothing happened," said Monster.

"I'm not sure I can do that."

Varnar stood. "Geiri won't be the last person to come after you."

I nodded silently. Then I finally found the words. "I'm sorry he's dead. Even though he did try to kill me."

Varnar bowed his head. His dark, shiny hair caught the moonlight. Then he raised his face, and I could barely recognize him with the hard look he gave me.

"He was a soldier, and I'm a soldier. There's a war, and we each fought on our side. That is the only truth I can live by. I would kill him over and over and over again." He took off running and disappeared.

Monster's fur shone dark and wet. "Come on, Anna. Let's go home."

I ordered Monster into the shower, despite his protests. I didn't want him in my bedroom with blood in his fur.

When I had soaped him up under the shower head, I let him rinse off on his own and looked at myself in the mirror. A thin, red stripe adorned my neck. I leaned forward and studied the mark. When I swallowed, it felt like having strep throat.

"What actually happened?" I shouted to make myself heard over the splashing water.

Monster stuck his large head—which, when wet, was quite a bit sleeker than usual—out from behind the shower curtain. "I mostly stay where I can either hear or smell you. Varnar shouted for me when you disappeared. Together, we found you in the square. Geiri already had the rope around your neck. It's amazing that you held out so long."

I wondered if it was because of the divinity Od had poured into me. My index finger traced the red line. "Which one of you . . . finished him off?"

Monster snorted, the water droplets forming a cloud around his head.

"We divided the task," he said and pulled his head back into the shower. "One of us killed him, the other got rid of the body."

All right, then.

Some things are better not to think too much about. I looked into the mirror and tapped lightly on it. Was my sister in there? Now that I really wanted to see my red-haired reflection, she no longer appeared to me.

"I guess I'm clean," Monster said. "Can you turn off the water so I can shake off? It's probably best I do it in here."

"Yes, please," I said. I stuck an arm in and turned the knob.

Monster shook forcefully, and the cascade of water hit the plastic curtain loudly. He came out, disheveled and with the expression of indignity that only a wet dog can have.

"Oh, stop it," I said. "You needed it."

I pulled out my largest bath towel and rubbed him until his fur regained some of its fullness.

We clambered upstairs, where Monster laid down on the floor and was snoring before I had even gotten under the covers.

As I lay in the dark, struggling to settle down, it struck me that it could have been Varnar on Geiri's mission. And that Geiri at some point could have decided to switch sides, and that my mom could have sent *him* here to protect me.

Instead, he was now lying disassembled in Monster's stomach, while Varnar lived his life at Kraghede Manor.

The cool phone lay heavily in my hand on Thursday morning.

Do it—don't do it.

I called. As always, Elias picked up immediately. There was no trace of anger in his voice.

"What a lovely surprise. Why are you calling?"

"I changed my mind."

"About what, I dare only hope."

"About you getting me used to taking stjórna."

"Oh, that," said Elias. "May I ask why you changed your mind?"

"You can ask me whatever you want. Just don't expect an answer."

Elias laughed on the other end. "Are you as aggressive in bed as you are in conversation?"

"I take it back. You can't ask me whatever you want."

Elias laughed again. "When?"

"Whenever. Just not Saturday. I have work then."

"Tomorrow afternoon?"

"Fine. Monster is here. Just so you know."

Pause.

"Elias?"

"I didn't know he was back."

"Od didn't tell you?" I asked.

"Od?" Elias's voice revealed that he knew nothing about Od's visit with me.

"Forget it. Yes, Monster is back. And I know what he is, and how it all fits together."

"Even after a very long life, I still don't know how it all fits together. So I highly doubt that you do."

"Well, it doesn't matter," I snapped. "I don't need to discuss it with you. I just need you to give me the drugs."

"In that case, I'm your man," Elias said and ended the call.

Monster galloped alongside my bike on the way to school, and today he followed me all the way up to the door. People gave him a wide berth, and with the events of the previous day in my mind, I suddenly thought that was quite sensible.

I found Luna and Mathias entangled outside the dance room in Blue Hall.

Even though I had wrapped a yellow scarf around my neck, which Luna had optimistically given me, Mathias immediately spotted the mark. He released his grip on Luna and pulled on the yellow knit.

"What happened?" His eyes began to glow slightly.

I dragged them down to the end of the hall and gave them a quick summary. Luna's face had turned an odd color by the time I was done.

Mathias put an arm around her again. "Pretty crazy that he could get you with all those people around. All this time I thought you were most vulnerable when you were alone."

"Apparently not."

"What can we do?"

"First of all, I asked Elias to build up my tolerance to stjórna. He's coming over tomorrow."

Luna gasped, and Mathias exclaimed angrily.

"What?" I threw up my arms. "I can train with Varnar from now until the end of the world. If the murderer poisons me anyway, then it doesn't really help much if I can kick ass."

Mathias snorted. "I don't like it."

"You don't have to like it," I said, but when I saw the look on his face, I continued with a softer voice. "I don't like it, either. But I can't think of any other options."

Luna drummed a pink fingernail against her plump lips. "Maybe my parents know a spell."

I raised my hands.

"I don't want more of their magic in my system." I stopped. "Did you guys make up? I thought your dad was mad at you."

"He was. But he was also proud that I conjured that sticky web. We've reached a kind of truce, so they can keep teaching me." She lit up. "Should we try to form one between them and you, too?" She brushed a purple ringlet away from one eye with the back of her hand. "It is a plus for you to be on speaking terms with them. They know a lot of things that could help."

Before I managed to respond, she cast a cloud of persuasion over me.

I coughed and waved my hand. "Haven't we talked about this? I don't want any more magic on me."

"Sorry. I can't always control it." She brushed my arms, but it was no use. Her spell was already in my system.

"Ugh, okay, fine. Ask them."

In Danish class, Mr. Nielsen was pumped.

"Today we'll be looking at some Old Norse texts." Excitedly, he waved around a stack of stapled photocopies. "We will read excerpts from a collection of Icelandic texts dating all the way back to the eighth century."

"Wow," Niller said, his voice dripping in sarcasm.

Luna took a copy and lit up. "This is 'Hávamál.' Words of the High One. I know it."

She recited a series of words in a language I couldn't understand.

Mr. Nielsen stared at her. "You know the *Poetic Edda* in the original language. You know Old Norse?"

"Well, yeah," she said. "I learned it at home."

He gave her a skeptical look as he distributed the rest of the papers and returned to the front of the room. "The *Codex Regius*, or *Poetic Edda*, was written down around the turn of the millennium. The poems are about the old gods and heroes. We're starting with one of the oldest and most important poems. 'Hávamál' or the Words of the High One, as Luna rightly said."

Lunas beamed and pointed to herself with both index fingers.

"The High One is the god Odin," said Mr. Nielsen. "The poem is his story about how to behave in society. Mads, would you please read the first stanza."

Little Mads sat up straight in his chair and looked down at the paper. He began to read in his deep and actually quite nice voice.

Within the gates ere a man shall go,
(Full warily let him watch),
Full long let him look about him;
For little he knows where a foe may lurk,
And sit in the seats within.

"Thank you, Mads. Just stop there. Does anyone know what this means?"

Luna put her hand up so high she almost lifted off her chair.

"Luna," said Mr. Nielsen.

"It means you should be careful when you're in a new place because you don't know if the strangers will be your enemies."

Mr. Nielsen nodded. "Correct. Odin advises us to be cautious around strangers. Mads, would you read stanza seventy-six?"

Cattle die, and kinsmen die,
And so dies one's self;
But a noble name will never die,
If good renown one gets.

"Who knows what this is saying?"

Again, Luna stretched in her seat with a hand in the air.

"Does anyone aside from Luna know what this is saying?" Mr. Nielsen asked, exasperated.

No one answered. No one wanted to be marked as the loser who was actually interested in these old texts.

I looked down at the paper and read to myself. "Cattle die. Kinsmen die. And so dies one's self. But a noble name will never die, if good renown one gets."

I cautiously raised an arm in the air.

Mr. Nielsen looked at me, surprised. "Yes, Anna."

"We all lose everything in the end. Our stuff, our friends, and even our own lives. But if we've made a good name for ourselves, that never goes away."

Mr. Nielsen clutched his pen and pointed it at me. "And what does that mean?"

I was starting to regret having signed up for this. "That life is about gaining a good reputation."

Peter laughed maliciously. He was clearly thinking that I had not managed to secure myself a good reputation. For once, he was actually right.

"How does one do that?" Mr. Nielsen stepped closer to me.

"Uh, I don't know," I said.

"You shouldn't think too much about death or loss," Mathias helped me, "because it's inevitable anyway. It's about living with honor, so posterity thinks highly of you."

"Yes!" Mr. Nielsen shouted excitedly. "One had to live with honor. It was very important at that time to leave behind a proper reputation. Because that was the only thing that would live forever. That's quite nice, isn't it? They really weren't all bad, the old guys. But what if we read on? Mathias, would you please continue with stanzas one thirty-eight and one thirty-nine?"

Mathias read.

I know that I hung on the windy tree,
Hung there for nights full nine;
With the spear I was wounded, and offered I was
To Odin, myself to myself,
On the tree that none may ever know,
What root beneath it runs.
None made me happy with loaf or horn,
And there below I looked;
I took up the runes, shrieking I took them,
And forthwith back I fell.

Mr. Nielsen waved a hand toward Luna, who was squirming in her chair with her arm raised. "I can see that you really want to share what you know about this passage, Luna."

"Odin sacrificed himself and hung for nine days from the World Tree with a spear through his body. When the nine days were up, he could read runes. That's why they're associated with the gods."

"Good, Luna," said Mr. Nielsen. "That's also a very nice message, that he made a sacrifice to gain knowledge. But something else came out of this myth in particular. Something that's maybe not so nice about the old Vikings. Does anyone know what it is?"

Luna looked gloomily down at the table.

"What's wrong?" I asked her.

She just shook her head.

"Hey. Your aura is pitch-black," I whispered.

"Anna and Luna. I assume that whatever you're whispering about has to do with the poem. Please enlighten us."

"*Hangatyr*," whispered Luna.

"What?" Mr. Nielsen placed a hand behind his ear.

"Hangatyr," she said louder.

"What is Hangatyr?" asked Mr. Nielsen.

"It's one of Odin's names. It means 'the hanged god.' And it resulted in human sacrifices."

A chill spread through the room, and the hairs on my arms stood up.

Mr. Nielsen nodded. "Here we see a more brutal side of the Vikings. They sacrificed people. It was completely accepted and part of their societal norms."

Something jogged my memory as Mr. Nielsen talked on. Hangatyr. No, that wasn't it. Something with *hanga* . . . Where had I heard that before?

After class, I asked Luna. "Is there anything else in Norse mythology that's called *hanga*-something?"

She shrugged. "It just means 'hanged' or 'hang' in Old Norse. *hangatyr* can refer both to the individual, meaning Odin, and to the sacrifice victims. But we can ask my parents. They know a lot more about it than I do."

"Okay," I said as I continued pondering.

On Friday afternoon, Elias was standing in front of my blue front door when Monster and I came home from school. He was leaning up against the door and looked like he felt very comfortable there.

Monster looked at him. "Brewmaster."

Elias bowed his head in response to Monster's greeting. "Prince Etunaz."

"Brewmaster?" I said.

Elias shrugged his shoulders. "A beloved child has many names, as they say."

"'Beloved' is a bit of an overstatement. Not to mention 'child.'"

Elias smiled. "I'm young at heart."

"I could agree with 'childish.'" I leaned my bike against the whitewashed wall. "If you want to come in, you'll need to move. You're standing in front of the keyhole."

Elias's eyes didn't move from my face as he reached his arm back and grabbed the doorknob.

The door opened behind him.

"Are you also a locksmith now?" I walked toward him.

He took a few steps backward into the foyer before stopping and holding out a flat hand. In it lay a key identical to the one hanging from my own key ring.

"Where did you get that?"

"Arthur gave it to me many years ago."

"But he can't stand you. Why would he give it to you?"

The key disappeared into Elias's pocket. "The not-being-able-to-stand-me thing is a more recent development."

"Give me that key. I don't like you having it."

"I won't come here unless you want me to. I promise."

"I still don't like it."

Elias walked into the kitchen.

"That's not my problem," he said over his shoulder. "You can't take back someone else's gift."

"Hey!" I walked after him. "You can't do that. It's my house."

"Technically, right now it belongs to the county."

"If you don't give me the key, I'll have the locks changed."

"Go ahead, but this key will always open Odinmont. No matter how many new locks you put in the door." He filled my kettle and set it on the stove.

I growled. "You are the most irritating person I've ever met, and believe me, that's saying something."

"Good to know I stand out." He started rummaging in the cabinets and dug out a couple of mugs. "Coffee?"

"Uh . . ." As always, I was on the verge of throwing him out. I looked to Monster for help as he ambled after us.

He smacked his lips. "Brewmaster, I'd love to try your coffee."

I gave the giant wolf an annoyed look.

"I've always liked the Brewmaster." Monster laughed hoarsely.

"What? Do you know each other?"

"Have you not noticed by now that we all know each other?" Monster slumped on the floor.

489

Elias handed me a cup of scalding hot coffee and set a steaming bowl on the table for Monster.

"Let's sit," he said.

I sighed, recognizing I'd lost the battle over the key.

"Okay, how are we doing this?"

"I'll give you a very small dose of stjórna. After a minute or two, you will lose consciousness. Your loss of consciousness will only be short-lived, but during that time, your body will develop a slight tolerance for the drug. The more times we do this, the more immune you'll become."

I raised the cup to take a sip of coffee. Elias was about to say something, but my phone rang.

"Just a sec, Elias." I fished the phone out of my bag and looked at the screen.

It was Hakim.

"What do you want?" I asked with no introduction.

"Uh, hey," he said. "I'm glad you picked up."

"I don't dare not to after the shit you gave me last time. Why are you calling?"

"We've received the autopsy report for the man you call the Savage."

"And you thought you'd entertain me with his stomach contents?" I blew on my coffee and took a sip.

Across the table, Elias looked nervously at me.

I could tell Hakim was trying to keep his cool.

"I was right; he was poisoned," he said. "He was injected with a common, fast-acting poison."

"So you're calling to brag?"

"Anna, stop it. I may have found out why he was almost supernaturally strong."

"Okay. I'm listening."

"Our medical examiner is freaking out. She found something else in his blood. Something that had been there longer."

490

"What?"

"It sounds really weird, but she found traces of blood in his blood. Someone else's blood."

"What kind of blood?"

"Apparently some kind of human blood, but she can't figure out the blood type. And even weirder, it doesn't coagulate, even though the Savage is dead."

"What does 'coagulate' mean?"

In front of me, Elias's ears perked up.

"It doesn't dry," said Hakim. "It's like it's still alive, even though it's in a dead body. And the blood is very potent. The medical examiner thinks he may have gotten his strength from that. She's going to run more tests on it."

"Uh-huh." I looked at Elias, who returned my gaze. "Why do I need to know this?"

There was a pause.

"I have a feeling you know something," Hakim said finally.

"Why would I know something about the Savage's blood?"

Another pause. "Maybe I shouldn't have told you."

"Oh, stop. I love it when you show me photos of murdered girls and blue fingers and share the contents of autopsy reports with me. That's just the kind of thing girls like me are into."

"Bye, Anna," said Hakim. "Call me if you think of anything."

"Bye," I said distantly and hung up while looking at Elias. "Does it mean anything to you that the Savage had blood in him that doesn't dry, even though he's dead as a doornail?"

Elias looked solemnly at me. "Unfortunately, yes."

"Do you have something to do with that?"

"Again, unfortunately, yes."

"Did you give him demigod blood so he could get stronger?"

Elias opened his mouth but closed it again without answering.

"Did you break into his cell and poison him?"

Elias bowed his head and looked down at the table.

I was starting to feel light-headed.

"That's why he willingly let you inject him," I mumbled. "That's why there wasn't a struggle. Because he knew you and trusted you. He thought you had come to give him more demiblood."

Next to the table, Monster had stood up and was growling quietly.

My head took another spin, and a familiar tingling feeling spread through my esophagus.

"Why am I dizzy?"

Elias raised his face and looked me straight in the eyes. "There's stjórna in your coffees."

Monster snarled. "Your medicine doesn't work on giant wolves, Brewmaster."

"I'll keep that in mind," said Elias.

Before everything went black, I managed to tell Monster: "Don't eat him. I want to hear his explanation first."

Then I spiraled downward.

 # CHAPTER 30

The first thing I saw was blood. There was a pool of it on the tile floor at the edge of my field of vision. Then I heard someone moan.

I managed to sit up, although the world was spinning around me.

Elias sat across from me, holding one arm. Monster stood between us with bared, bloody teeth.

"I told you not to eat him," I gasped.

"You didn't say I couldn't take a taste," Monster replied with a hiss.

"So how does he taste?" I asked, and fought to remain conscious.

"Awful. Too many chemicals," Monster said, and coughed.

"You know full well how I taste, Anna," said Elias with a weak smile.

I made an irritated sound. "How long was I out?"

"Five minutes, tops. You took a very small dose. And I would have told you. I just wanted to prove how easy it is to sneak drugs into everyday foods and beverages." He grunted with pain. When he raised his hand slightly, blood poured from his arm. "I need some laekna. Otherwise I'll bleed out."

I stood up, but the floor swayed beneath me. I fell forward and landed painfully on my knees.

"Right now I'm inclined to let it happen," I hissed. "Do you realize it's your fault that five girls are dead?"

Elias's eyes wandered. "I think I only had something to do with three of them. Help me. Then I'll explain everything."

"As always, your focus is exclusively on your own survival."

"Come on, Anna. I have a bag on a cord around my neck. There's laekna inside. And a lot of other stuff, which I'll let you have unlimited access to if you help me," he bargained.

"Kiss my ass!"

"I'll also tell you a secret that could have significant implications for you."

I looked at him coldly, but inside I was faltering.

"A secret that could have significant implications for Arthur," he corrected.

I thought for a second. *Damn it!* Then I crawled over to Elias, as my legs still couldn't support me.

He moved a little so I could unbutton his shirt. When I got up close to him, I felt his warm breath against my neck. He breathed raggedly. My hand glided across his chest to grab the little pouch hanging from a leather cord around his neck.

"You're so close to my heart," he whispered with some effort.

"Shut up, Elias," I said as I fumbled with the opening of the pouch. Finally I succeeded in getting it open, and a couple dozen ampoules in every color of the rainbow fell into my hand. One of them I recognized as the pale green laekna. "Nice home pharmacy you've got here."

"You never know what you might encounter."

I put the other colorful ampoules back in the pouch. "Do you drink this?"

"No. The wound is too big. You'll have to drip the laekna into it."

I helped him take off his bloodied shirt, and it did not help my nausea any to see Monster's deep bite marks in Elias's arm.

"Hot," I said sarcastically.

"You should see me fully naked," he replied weakly.

"Watch your mouth, Brewmaster," growled Monster.

I dripped a couple of drops into the bloody holes.

Elias closed his eyes as it took effect. The wounds began to close, and eventually there was nothing to be seen.

"There won't be any scars?" I asked.

"No, not with laekna. It doesn't work in the same way as healing. There's a tiny bit of Od's blood in the laekna. That ensures the full reconstruction of the tissue. And a combination of different chemical elements compensates for blood loss. Finally, a good portion of opium soothes the pain."

"You sound like a scientist. That is, a conceited, crazy one."

Elias smiled darkly. He stood up and walked over to my kitchen sink, where he rinsed the blood off his arm. His curls hid his face, but I could see that the muscles in his back were tense.

"Tell me," I said. "Was it Od's blood you gave the Savage?"

Elias turned to face me as he dried himself off with a dish towel. "No, the blood came from someone else."

"Who?"

Elias shook his head slightly. "Secret. I have to protect my suppliers."

"But why did you give the blood to the Savage? How do you even know him?"

"The berserkers have a tradition of taking euphoria-inducing substances. I've sold them potions for centuries."

"But this guy got injections."

Elias tossed the towel onto my kitchen table. "That was a special agreement."

I found the courage to ask. "Did you know what he would do with the extra strength?"

"No," Elias said quickly. "I had no idea that he was coming to Midgard, or that he was after you. I thought he was going to fight the giants or the dark elves. But I never ask what my products will be used for."

"Maybe you should."

"I've had bad experiences with that."

495

"You amoral little shit," I spat.

Elias took a step forward. "As soon as I knew he had been sent here to kill you, I tried to stop him. I had the chance the night of the equinox ball, but your policeman made it out to the house before I could finish him off. You're welcome, by the way, for removing all the evidence. The whole lot of you would have been sitting in jail right now if I hadn't."

"It was you who cleaned up out there?"

"Yes. Of course. I am on your side, after all. Haven't you figured that out?"

"No. I haven't figured that out. And I'm very unsure of how much I can trust you."

"I'm almost always neutral," Elias whistled. "Nothing else is worth it in these political affairs. Conflicts come and go and cost a lot of people their lives. Meaningless deaths. Century after century, and people never learn. Do you know how many years it's been since I chose a side in any controversy whatsoever?"

"Something tells me it's been about eighteen years. I'm just not sure exactly which side you ended up on, and whose life it cost."

It was quiet for a moment.

Elias's lips were pressed together. Monster stood with his hackles raised and teeth bared.

I sat in a heap on the floor in the pool of Elias's blood.

"I tried . . ." Elias began, but his voice gave out. "Your father's death is one of the worst things that ever happened to me."

My anger faded slightly. "Were you friends?"

"I don't know if we were friends. But he gave me the chance to be his friend. He was one of the very few who at least gave me the chance."

"And you burned that chance?"

"I don't know yet," he whispered.

I furrowed my brows. "What is it you can tell me that will make a difference for Arthur?"

Elias looked out my kitchen window. "Are you able to hold yourself up?"

"Why?"

"I need for you to not fall down a very long, steep flight of stairs. If you're still unsteady on your feet, then it's better we wait."

Stairs? The stairs that led to the upper floor were neither long nor steep. I saw no reason to reveal my confusion to Elias.

"I suggest that you show me right now what's so damn relevant for me and Arthur," I said as, with difficulty, I pulled myself to standing. "And on a related note, let me just remind you that I forgot to feed Monster this morning."

Behind me, Monster laughed hoarsely.

Elias gulped. "Okay. Then let's do it now."

He put his bloody shirt back on, walked over to my bench, and began to pull on it.

"What in the hell are you doing?"

Noisily, Elias dragged the massive piece of furniture across the floor. "This hill is very old, and it's man-made. When I was kid, I found a chamber inside. It's still there."

"Is there something hidden under there?" I looked at the bench.

"There's almost always something hidden under everything. You'd be smart to remember that," said Elias with a bleak smile.

"And you found that out hundreds of years ago?"

"Yes. I lived nearby."

My jaw dropped and I tried to make sense of the information I had just received about my home and about Elias.

"Are you from here? I mean, were you born here in Ravensted?"

Elias paused his effort to move the heavy bench. "I was born at Kraghede Manor."

"In the 1600s?"

"Yeah," he said and resumed pulling on the bench. "Back then, the old ways were banned, and the hill was just sitting here. But I loved to spend time here. Even then, I must have been drawn to

497

this place. Like I am now. But now it probably has more to do with my fascination with the place's inhabitant." He winked and, for a second, looked like his usual flirtatious self. "It was also here that I met Od for the first time," he continued offhandedly.

Aha. I grabbed on, too, and with our combined efforts, we managed to turn the sturdy bench. On the floor beneath it was a narrow wooden door with a large iron ring attached.

I stared at it. "Has that always been there?"

Elias looked at it. "No. When the house was built, it cut off access to the chamber below. For many years, you couldn't get down there. When Arthur moved in, we worked together to break up the floor."

I gathered myself and brushed my hands together.

"Are we going down there?"

"Yep."

"What's down there?"

"It's better you see for yourself," said Elias, grabbing the thick iron ring and pulling.

The door creaked open, and the smell of dirt and damp hit us.

I looked down. Just below the hole was the start of stone steps, but they were quickly swallowed by darkness.

"Let me just find my flashlight," I said.

"Good to see you aren't scared of having to go underground." Elias chuckled.

Who said anything about not being scared?

I walked into the hall and found the flashlight. Out of Elias's sight, I clenched my shaking hands a few times. Then I straightened my back and returned to the living room.

"Lead the way," I said, and we began our descent. I went after Elias and fumbled at the side, where I found a wooden handrail.

The flashlight's beam did not illuminate much beyond the stone walls and stairs. Cold, clammy air enveloped me, and behind me I heard Monster's claws on the stone steps.

After what felt like an eternity, we reached the bottom. Elias handed me the flashlight, and after a quick inspection, I saw that we were in a short hall that ended in a low opening. If we were planning to go through it, we would have to crawl.

Elias fumbled with something on one wall, and a warm glimmer blazed. He crouched down and rolled a lit torch through the opening, so the chamber inside was illuminated. Then he turned and looked up at me. In a flash, I saw the old age in his face, which was bathed in the cold light of my flashlight.

"Shall I go first?"

I nodded, and he started crawling into the hole. Once he was inside, I exhaled forcefully before following suit.

Behind me, Monster struggled with a groan to get through the opening.

Inside, I stood up again. Elias had picked up the torch and clenched it in his hand. Monster stood so close to me that I could lay my hand on his back.

In front of us in the dark room, two figures were waiting for us.

CHAPTER 31

Arthur walked toward us. He stood between me and a stone table with an unmoving, covered figure on it. A sheet was laid over it, but it was clear that the contours of a person were concealed beneath.

"Oh, so this is where you spend your time," I said, trying to keep my voice steady.

"I did tell you that I'm bound to Odinmont," he said with a sad smile.

"I want to see you." I nodded toward the covered figure.

"You're looking at me right now." Arthur laid his hands on my shoulders. His green eyes stared straight into mine. In the warm torchlight, he looked more like a living person than ever.

I shook his hands off. "That's not what I mean."

"I don't want you to see me like that."

"Why not? That's how it is." I felt my chin jutting out stubbornly.

Next to me, Elias moved. "Is Arthur here?"

"You know he's here. He's lying right there." I pointed at the stone platform.

"You know what I mean," replied Elias.

I ignored him.

Arthur stood very close to Elias, who shivered as if struck by a cold wind.

"I can't believe you dare to keep coming here," said Arthur.

Elias did not react, for obvious reasons.

I sighed. "Okay, Elias. You've revealed that my father's body is buried in a crypt beneath my own house. Very symbolic—if you're into psychoanalysis, anyway. What about it, exactly, is important for me and him?"

Elias took a few steps toward the sheet-covered silhouette. Arthur stepped between them and pushed him in the chest with both hands. Elias waved his arms in the air and continued forward with some effort.

"Stop it, Arthur. I'm doing this to help."

"I know your way of helping," Arthur hissed.

Again, Elias did not register his voice. But Arthur's poltergeist abilities were enough to make it difficult for him to move forward.

"What is going on?" I asked.

"Elias has regularly come to visit my corpse these past eighteen years," said Arthur. He gave Elias a proper shove, so he staggered backward a few steps.

"Anna needs to see you," Elias said into the air, toward the place where he thought Arthur stood. "Otherwise she won't understand."

"Understand what?" I asked.

"I will explain to you what it is I'm trying to do."

I shifted my gaze to Arthur. "What's he trying to do?"

Arthur's face was suddenly despondent and very tired.

"An insane project. An impossibility. I thought we were over your bullshit." He was speaking to Elias again. "I don't want to be your new obsession."

I sensed a very old argument.

"I know what you're saying, Arthur," snapped Elias. "Even though I can't hear you. But it's different this time."

"How is it different? Are you not saving up money for your experiments right now? If I know you, you're selling drugs, and worse."

"Demigod blood," I said.

Elias looked sharply at me. "What's he saying?"

"That you're working on a crazy project that you're saving up money for." Some things suddenly made sense.

At once, Arthur looked like he was about to explode. "It was you. You sold demigod blood to Naut Kafnar? That nearly cost my daughter her life. It cost other people's daughters their lives. I'll kill you."

He put his hands around Elias's neck, and they toppled backward. Elias threw punches into the air as Arthur squeezed.

Monster and I exchanged a look. He rolled his large eyes.

"Sometimes I'm reminded why we giant wolves stay away from you humans."

"Stop it, Arthur. Let him go." I went to grab his shoulder, but my hand went straight through him. I shivered when I realized I could touch my father only when he wanted me to.

Elias made a gurgling sound.

"Get him off me," he squeaked.

With two long strides, I walked up to the stone table and grabbed the sheet. I pulled, suppressing a shriek when the cloth slid away from the body underneath.

Arthur's clear, dead eyes looked back at me. He lay on his side and stared blankly into space. His coloring was almost completely white; his lips were blue, and his skin resembled wax.

On the floor, Arthur stopped and looked up at me. He let go of Elias, who rolled, coughing, onto his side.

Monster sniffed Arthur's corpse. "He smells fresh."

"Don't get any ideas," I said weakly.

"I don't even like human flesh," said Monster, insulted. "I only eat you in extreme circumstances."

I felt Arthur stand at my side. Behind me, Elias had gotten onto all fours, while still coughing.

I walked around the stone platform, where I saw that Arthur's back was decorated with a large, bloody splotch.

Arthur had followed me. "Ben put a stasis spell on my body. That's why it doesn't . . . spoil."

"Magical preserves," I said dully. "Why?"

"Ben and Rebecca are hoping to reverse my death with magic or divine intervention."

"Then what is Elias trying to do?"

"Elias has always been obsessed with the idea of reversing the process by scientific means. He's been trying for hundreds of years."

"I know I can do it, Arthur." Elias coughed from the floor.

"What can you do, Elias?" My interest was piqued.

"I've been a scientist since the mid-1600s, and I started working on something in the late 1700s. There were some men in England . . ." He was interrupted by another cough.

"Who were they?" I asked.

"Does the name Frankenstein mean anything to you?" said Arthur.

"The monster?"

"No, Frankenstein was the scientist who created the monster."

I furrowed my brows. "But that's a horror story. Fiction."

"Let's just say it's based on real events."

Elias had gotten to his feet.

"If he starts going on about Frankenstein, stop him," he said and brushed the dirt off his hands.

"He's already going on about Frankenstein."

"Oh, Arthur. You know full well I've moved past that. That's not what I'm working on. Galvanization is only a small part of my work."

Arthur raised his hands in frustration.

I felt completely out of the loop. "So, what are you talking about, then?"

Elias grabbed my hand and pulled me over to a dark corner. On the way, he snatched the torch from the ground where he had dropped it when Arthur tackled him.

"You need to see this." He held up the light, and I saw that there was a table I hadn't noticed at first. It, too, was covered with a dark sheet. Elias pulled it off.

Under it stood flasks, instruments, and microscopes—most of it looked antique.

"What is all that?" I asked.

"Years of research," Elias mumbled as he rummaged around the table. He lifted a stack of paper that appeared to contain miles of notes. He leafed through them.

"What's this?" I asked and picked up something that resembled a pair of metal spoons connected to a generator.

"That's the predecessor of the defibrillator."

"The *what?*"

"The thing that restarts a person's heart." He took the spoons out of my hands and placed them on his chest. "You send electricity to the heart to make it start beating again if it's stopped. For many years, we worked with electricity as the central focus of reanimation."

"So that's what all this is about? Reanimation?" I asked.

Elias set the spoons on the table and looked at me. "That's what everything is about."

Then he resumed digging in the piles.

"How do the gods, or whatever they are, fit into all this?"

Elias replied to me over his shoulder: "The gods move between the worlds of the living and the dead. Odin can even revive the dead. I want to have the same power as him."

I glanced at Arthur, who shook his head. "Elias is manic and insane. Before you moved in, he came here regularly. I regret giving him the key, but I thought he should have access to this place."

"Why?"

"His mother's earthly remains are buried in this hill."

"Oh, come on. How many dead parents have you got hidden down here?"

"Quite a few," said Monster.

I shined the flashlight in front of me. Along the wall lay a skeleton, neatly arranged in a little pile. The skull lay on its side, so the empty eye sockets faced out into the room.

Monster continued around the space. "There's more over here," he said.

Along the walls and in slat-like alcoves lay skulls and bones. "For God's sake. I might as well be living on top of a graveyard. How am I supposed to be able to sleep from now on?"

"Eh," said Elias without looking up from his stack of notes. "There aren't too many people who *don't* live on top of a pile of bodies. Humans have always buried their dead. Over the past several thousand years, they've accumulated beneath us. And the human body is made of the same stuff as the earth. There's really no difference. They don't affect you."

"That's actually true," Arthur conceded. "You shouldn't be afraid of them."

"Why are they down here?"

"Odinmont is a burial mound. They've been burying the greatest and most important people here for over a thousand years. It's thought that they're closer to the gods in this sacred place."

"And are you? I mean, you of all people should know," I said to Arthur.

"It's a good place to rest," he said simply.

Okay. I tried to compose myself and returned to Elias. "I've now been informed that I live on top of a pile of skeletons, Arthur's magically fresh corpse, and your mother's grave."

He looked up from the papers.

"I'm sorry for your loss, by the way," I added quickly. I didn't really know how to give condolences for someone who had died almost four hundred years ago. "But you still haven't said what's so important about it."

"I wanted to show you that his body is still intact. And you should hear this next part, too, Arthur, if you can resist attacking me for a second."

505

"Okay," Arthur said curtly and folded his arms across his chest.

"He says okay," I said.

Elias scratched at his curls.

"I became an alchemist in the mid-1600s." I was about to say something sardonic, but he stopped me. "It's just an old word for chemist. It's a total misunderstanding that it's only about making gold—although that wouldn't be a bad skill to have." This last bit was added in a low voice. "After my mother died, I rejected God and all other gods. It wasn't because I didn't believe in them. I just refused to have anything to do with them."

"What about Od? You must have had contact with him. Otherwise you wouldn't be so old."

Elias cleared his throat. "Od is like a father to me. And he prolongs my life. He was the only divinity I had contact with."

Typical Elias, I thought. *If something can benefit him, he holds on to it.* I gestured for him to continue.

"Over time, I became a natural philosopher and practiced natural philosophy with a nearly religious fervor."

I tried to follow along. "When was this now?"

"The 1700s. I observed chemical reactions to find ways for humans to become stronger, get well, heal their wounds, and also safely and temporarily forget their sorrows and worries."

"Narcotics?" I could hear the critical note in my own voice.

"I call it a balm for the soul," said Elias with a grin. "And a good source of income." He continued: "Then I met a few men, right at the turn of the century. The promising nineteenth century. Whereas I previously thought it was the task of science to find a way to control nature, I then discovered a world in which it was possible to contribute to nature. Create. Build. The field in which, until then, the gods had had a monopoly."

"Wasn't that tampering with some dangerous forces?" I asked.

"Yes." Elias's eyes sparkled, and for a moment, I saw the insanity Arthur thought he possessed. He fished a piece of paper out of

506

the stack and handed it to me. It was a drawing of a dismembered human body connected to wires and devices.

"Jesus Christ."

"No, it's beautiful. If only for a fraction of a second, we brought dead tissues back to life. With electricity. That was in 1803."

Arthur exhaled in irritation. "That was just what the public saw." He pointed to the drawing. "You don't even want to know what went on behind closed doors. By the way, I've heard this spiel countless times before."

"Okay, but I haven't," I snapped back.

Elias looked uncomprehendingly at me, and I waved a hand for him to keep going.

"For years, I experimented with electricity, physics, and chemistry. On their own and together in every different combination imaginable. But I couldn't make it work."

"When you say *it*, you mean reviving the dead?" The thought was both morbid and enticing.

"Exactly," said Elias. "When I met Arthur, I had almost gone mad with frustration."

"And your condition hasn't exactly improved over time." Arthur sniffed.

Elias bowed his head. "You helped me, Arthur," he said. "You helped me find life again. To live with the living rather than the dead."

I knew Arthur well enough to see that he was somewhat appeased by this.

"Which made it all the more ironic that you died an unnatural death." He furrowed his brows. "My obsession returned with full force. And then I made a discovery that made me suspect that maybe the gods weren't completely useless after all."

Arthur narrowed his eyes. "I've never heard you say that before."

"Arthur has never heard me say this before," echoed Elias. "I discovered by coincidence that Od's blood has healing and strengthening properties. I started experimenting with it. That was how I created laekna."

"Why is demigod blood different?" I asked.

"I've analyzed it forward and backward without figuring it out. There's nothing chemical about it that differentiates it from the known elements. And then it hit me. There must be something else in it."

"Something else?"

Elias scratched his chin. "When I worked with alchemy in the 1600s, there were tales of something called the philosopher's stone. A component that can change the unchangeable. For example, it was said to be able to change a different metal into gold. The philosopher's stone was also called the elixir of life. The idea is found in many cultures. Including Scandinavia. I had always seen it as a myth, but with the discovery of the properties of demigod blood, my conviction wavered."

"Something that can change the unchangeable," I repeated.

"Yes. And what's more unchangeable than death?" asked Elias. "I kept working with the demigod blood. I acquired more. It's wildly expensive, by the way. But I still could not bring life back into the dead."

I had no desire to think about how Elias had tested this.

"When are we now?"

"This is within the past few years. Fifteen years, thereabouts."

"Only a four-hundred-year-old refers to fifteen years as 'a few,'" I said.

"Four-hundred-and-two-year-old," Elias corrected with a little smile.

"Belated congratulations on the milestone birthday."

"Thanks." Elias laid his hand on his chest and did a little old-fashioned bow. He returned to the matter at hand. "I was circling around the problem, but I couldn't figure out what made demiblood different. To clear my head, I tried to concentrate on something else for a while. Just a couple of years. So I read up on the art of poetry. I was something of a romantic poet in my day." He winked at me.

Arthur straightened with an air of warning. "I really hope nothing happened between the two of you. If he so much as tried something, I . . ."

"Of course not," I lied. To Elias, I said: "I don't really think you're getting to the point."

"I think I found out what the unknown element is."

"So what is it?"

"It's the divine essence. And you can find it in the blood of the gods. Diluted in human blood it doesn't have the same effect, but undiluted in gods' blood it's the same as the philosopher's stone, the elixir of life, the holy grail . . . all those mythical things."

"No, no," said Arthur. "The gods don't bleed. Everyone knows that."

"They say the gods can't bleed," said Elias, almost as if he had heard Arthur. "I didn't believe they could, either, but when I started reading the old Icelandic texts, I came across something. Do you know the Edda poems?"

"We just started reading them in Danish. But we haven't gotten very far. What did you find?" I was quickly running out of patience.

"It's from the tenth century poem 'Völuspá.'"

Elias recited:

I saw for Baldr,
the bleeding god,
The son of Odin
his destiny set:
Famous and fair
in the lofty fields,
Full grown in strength
the mistletoe stood

Arthur's eyes landed absently on the stone platform with its unsettling load.

"I've never thought about that. It's true that Baldr bled, and Ægir brews the mead of life with his blood," he mused. "Could it be . . . ?"

Unable to hear what Arthur said, Elias nodded. "I know what you're thinking, Arthur. Maybe that's how it works."

I understood nothing. "How what works?"

Arthur began excitedly. "Did Ben tell you that Ragnara is immortal?"

"Uh, yeah."

"We've never been able to figure out why or how, but we thought Odin might be behind it. She was a dedicated follower of his before they parted ways."

I shook my head. "One topic at a time, please."

"It's the same topic. If someone gave her some of, for example, Baldr's blood, then that explains why she's immortal," said Arthur.

"However, I do think the divine essence is ephemeral," said Elias. "Like a chemical gas. In humans, it disappears over time. That's what my experiments with demiblood have shown."

"So she has more of the blood. Somewhere. Or else someone is supplying her with it. So she can stay immortal."

I repeated Arthur's words to Elias.

Elias spread his arms. "Yes," he said. "I am almost certain that's how it works."

Arthur clutched his forehead. "So there's a way to kill her."

"Arthur says this is how we can kill her," I translated.

"Again: yes." Elias looked like a great weight had been lifted off his heart. "What's more, I think that if we can get ahold of that blood, that's how we can bring you back to life without you becoming a zombie, Frankenstein's monster, or a corpse. I think if we combine it with magic and science, then we'll have the solution I've been trying to find for most of my very long life. All these years, we've been going around, each trying in our own way. Me with science, Ben with magic, and Rebecca with religion. In reality, we need all three to work together."

Arthur snorted. "My reanimation doesn't really matter. The most important thing is getting Ragnara out of the way. So she can't kill my kids."

I didn't translate this for Elias.

We all stood in silence for a while.

"Now we just have to figure out how to steal the blood from Ragnara," I said finally.

Elias looked around as if to locate Arthur. "We need to put our heads together."

Arthur nodded. "Okay. We'll work together on this. But I still haven't forgiven you for what you did that time."

"He agrees," I said, without repeating the last part. At some point I would have to find out what role Elias had played in my father's death, but right now, I couldn't handle any more revelations. I was suddenly incredibly tired.

"I think I'll have to go back up soon," I said. "I really need to rest."

"Of course," said Arthur.

"Can you come up with me?" I asked.

"Not yet, Anna," Arthur said. "I need to rest, too."

"Oh. About that. I'm sorry I sent you down here, but I didn't have any choice."

"I'm sorry I tried to possess you. That was wrong of me." He put his arms around me, and I pulled him close. He felt alive and real.

"Can we agree to never do that again. Either of us?" I wiped my eyes with the back of my hand.

"Yes. Agreed. I don't want to lose you."

"Are you okay down here?"

"I actually really like it here. One way or another, it's home."

"Come back when you can. Maybe I'll come down here."

"That would be nice." He smiled warmly.

I turned with a final look at the stone table, which Elias was covering up. Monster and I squeezed out through the low opening to the hall and began climbing the stairs. Behind us, I could hear Elias's feet on the steps.

As we walked up toward the light, it struck me that death wasn't the only thing commonly known to be unchangeable. The same, in fact, was true of the past.

But maybe there was a way to change both.

 # CHAPTER 32

When I saw Luna and Mathias on Monday, Luna announced that I would be going to her house on Thursday evening. Ben and Rebecca wanted to form a truce. I flat-out refused, but she fished a book out of her bag and dangled it between two fingers.

"What if I give you this?"

"What is it?"

"Something I stole from my mom. It's her notebook about Hrafnheim. There's all kinds of stuff in here about the different lands, the history, and the traditions."

I reached out for the book, but Luna pulled her arm back.

"Are you coming on Thursday?"

Ughh . . .

"Only if Mathias and Monster come, too," I said finally.

She slapped the book into the palm of my hand.

"Yes!" She laughed. "What did you do yesterday?"

All in all, they took it well.

"Am I correct in understanding," asked Mathias, "that Elias thinks we can revive Arthur through a combination of gods' blood, magic, and science?"

"Yep. Although I didn't understand a whole lot of Arthur and Elias's pseudo-conversation. Elias couldn't hear Arthur, and Arthur was mad about something or other from their past." I waved a hand. "It was pretty confusing."

"So that means," Mathias interjected, "my blood also has something in it?"

"Yes, but it doesn't provide immortality. You just get very resilient and strong from it. Oh right, I forgot to tell you, Hakim called right before I blacked out. The autopsy report on the Savage shows that he had an unknown type of blood in him."

"Was it demiblood?" asked Luna.

"Yes. And he had bought it from Elias."

She gasped. "I'm starting to understand why no one trusts him."

"He said he didn't know what the extra strength would be used for."

Why am I defending Elias?

"Why did you black out?" Luna's forehead crinkled slightly.

"Elias snuck stjórna into my coffee without me realizing." I shrugged. "But Monster took a big bite out of his arm as revenge."

"Elias's moral compass seems to be a bit skewed," Mathias mused.

"You don't need to tell me. I don't think he even has a moral compass. If he does, it follows its own logic."

The following days were abnormally undramatic. I went to school and work and hung out with my friends, and I could almost convince myself that I was a normal Danish teenage girl.

On Wednesday evening, I studied the book about Hrafnheim that Luna had stolen from her mom. It was full of drawings and notes, and on the center pages, there was a map depicting something resembling a large island, which was divided into nine smaller realms.

My fingers stroked the area in western Hrafnheim where the name Bronze Forest had been added in fine cursive. Below the Bronze Forest, in the southwestern part of the island, was a dark gray blotch with the name Iron Forest.

I flipped back to the map and saw that Ván was the realm in which the capital of Sént was located. That was where Varnar and Aella had grown up after they left the Bronze Forest, and where Ragnara's castle was.

I spent most of the night reading the notebook, and when I finally got too tired to keep my eyes open, I placed it in my closet along with my mother's coat.

On Thursday, I trained with Varnar.

I now had a good grasp of the different parries, kicks, and punches. Varnar's trick of moving quickly with a backflip was also coming along. This put him in an unusually good mood, and he almost smiled a couple of times.

"You're ready for a weapon," he said.

"A weapon?"

"Yes. If someone goes after you with a spear or a sword, you can't kick and punch your way to victory. I started with the basics, but I think you've got them down now."

"Thanks," I said quietly as I picked at a loose thread on my sleeve. "I don't know how much you know about this world, but the age of swords and spears is actually over. People here rarely go after one another with antique blades. They mostly use firearms."

With a shudder, I recalled Mathias's exploded chest.

Varnar looked seriously at me. "The people who are after you probably don't use firearms."

I shrugged my shoulders. "Well, it can't hurt to learn."

"Let me go get something." Varnar disappeared from the old riding hall.

I remained there alone and looked out through the hole in the roof at the opposite end of the hall. The sky was dim, and a pair of dark birds sat and watched me from the exposed beams. They made a hissing sound before flapping away. Varnar had lit some oil lamps and hung them from the hooks along the walls of the hall. I shivered in my thin workout top. Now, on the cusp of November, the bitter cold had crept in.

Varnar came back and handed me a branch that had been stripped of twigs. He held one in his hand as well.

"I was expecting a saber or something like that," I said as I turned the knotty stick in my hand.

"Anything can be a weapon," said Varnar with a grim grin. "And I don't want to risk chopping your arm off by accident."

"I appreciate that." I smiled back.

After a split second of eye contact, he turned away quickly.

"The parries are the same ones you already know," he said over his shoulder. "Your weapon is just an extension of your arm."

He turned again and swung at me with his branch.

At lightning speed, I parried with my own. Varnar nodded in acknowledgment before lunging at me again.

Unaccustomed to fighting with a weapon, I worked hard to keep up. I even tried to hit back, but Varnar blocked me and, in the same motion, swung his stick in a semicircle, striking me on the arm. It didn't hurt, but it stung my pride.

The next time he made an attack on me, I copied his motion from before and extended my parry with a swing of the branch. To my surprise, I hit him on the shoulder. Pretty hard, in fact.

"Sorry," I said quickly. "I didn't think I would hit you. I didn't mean to hit so hard."

Varnar ignored my apology. "Nice. No one's ever hit me on the first try before."

He continued, and yet again, I had to fight to avoid being hit. I defended myself and tried to hit back. At the same time, I observed Varnar's movements. Then I tried something I'd never done before.

At the same time as I was fighting, I reached out for the very recent past. When Varnar attacked me, I rewound to find a similar situation and copied his movements. Soon, I could perform his attacks almost as well as him. I hit him more and more frequently.

His aura sputtered with surprise as we fought. Eventually, I could sense he wasn't holding back like he normally did. He was putting his full force into trying to defeat me. He did in the end, when he swept his stick along the ground to knock my legs out from under me, and I landed on my back in the soft sawdust.

Breathless, he sank to his knees at my side.

"How did you do that?"

I turned my head to look at him.

"I think I used my clairvoyant abilities to remember how you moved. And then I copied it." I, too, was breathing hard.

He gave me a look I couldn't interpret. Then he leaned toward me and looked at me, almost as if he were studying a rare animal.

Nervousness simmered in my stomach. "Did I do something wrong? Should I change something?"

He slowly shook his head.

"Don't ever change anything about yourself," he whispered.

My pulse quickened.

"Anna," came a voice, and we both jerked. Monster stood in the doorway. "Aren't we going to visit Luna and her parents? We need to hurry if we want to get there by dinnertime."

You annoying, food-obsessed giant wolf!

Varnar stood up quickly and brushed his hands on his pants. I ordered my body to get up.

Monster's bushy eyebrows rose as his eyes moved from me to Varnar. Then he turned and lumbered back out to the yard outside Kraghede Manor.

Varnar said nothing. He just vanished through the door and into the twilight.

Monster and I showed up at Ben and Rebecca's after wading across the field through a strong headwind and drizzle.

In the foyer, I removed my muddy boots as Monster shook himself off.

The living room looked like itself again after the seid. The lines of chalk had been washed off the floor, and the furniture was back in place.

517

"Dearest Anna Stella," said Rebecca. "I am so happy to see you."

I wanted to respond flippantly, but a look from Monster forced me to content myself with nodding and pressing my lips tightly together. I stood, at a loss, in the middle of the room.

Luna came bounding down the stairs with Mathias behind her. He had a happy, goofy grin on his face.

I studied him intently.

"What's up with you?" I whispered as Luna helped her mom in the kitchen.

He looked at me with a distracted smile. "What?"

"You look like you're stoned."

"I'm not, but . . ."

"But what? What were you and Luna just doing?" Out of sheer habit, I reached into his past. "Christ! No way," I said with a surprised smile as I rapidly backed out of his memories. I took a couple steps back as I almost burned myself on his aura.

The front door slammed, and Ben poked around in the hall before coming into the living room. "Anna," he said with a nod in my direction.

I stood behind Monster, and Mathias also stepped directly between us.

"I'm not an oath breaker," Ben grumbled. "I promised not to put any more magic on you against your will. I will keep that promise."

He looked bitterly Mathias. Was someone offended that a whelp had pushed him around?

Rebecca quickly called us to the table, and we sat down. She pressed her palms together and said a prayer over the food.

"On this night of Samhain—All Hallows' Eve, the end of summer, the transition from light to dark, and the feast of the dead— we give thanks for this life-giving food, and we remember all who have gone before us to the realms of the dead and the shadowland."

Oh, right, tonight was Halloween. I had seen a few kids running around Ravensted in costumes on my way home from school.

We began eating, while an awkward silence hung in the air.

Luna tried to kick-start the conversation. "Anna has a question about 'Hávamál.'"

Rebecca smiled, relieved that someone had spoken. "The Words of the High One. What did you want to ask?"

I cleared my throat, uncomfortable with suddenly being the focus. "It's because we read the poem in Danish class. And Luna mentioned the word *hangatyr*."

Both Ben and Rebecca stopped moving.

"That is a dark part of our religion, which we do not participate in," Ben growled.

"I know," I said quickly. "It's just that I've heard another word that sounds like hangatyr. Hangabot or -dot."

Luna's parents looked intently at me. Rebecca set down her fork. "Hangadrott?" she said.

"Yes, exactly. That was it!" There is no greater relief than hearing a word that's been on the tip of your tongue for days. My relief was dampened, however, when I saw Ben's and Rebecca's facial expressions. "What is it?" I asked weakly.

"*Drott* is the Old Norse word for 'king.' *Hangadrott* is when you sacrifice a royal to the gods. It's the greatest sacrifice that can be made."

"Where did you hear that?" asked Ben. There was a threatening edge to his voice.

"A man at the equinox ball mentioned it," I said cautiously.

Ben stood. The pointy fork he still held in his hand suddenly looked like a weapon. "What else did he say?"

"Uh," I sat up a little straighter in my chair. "I was talking to him when Od gave his speech. He said a bunch of strange things, including that the All-Father would give me anything if I gave him a hangadrott."

Ben's eyes flew to Rebecca.

"Did he tell you his name?" Rebecca's voice was low and controlled.

"He said his name was Svidur," I said. "He also said he knew my mom."

Rebecca brought a hand to her mouth, and Ben made a noise that was halfway between a snarl and a cough. He put his hands on the edge of the table, and his fork hit the floor with a clatter.

"He's back," said Rebecca.

Luna, Monster, Mathias, and I looked at one another, disoriented.

"What is it?" asked Luna.

Ben sat down heavily. "Svidur is one of Odin's names."

"Odin?" I couldn't keep the skepticism out of my voice.

"This could be our salvation," said Rebecca.

"Or our downfall," added Ben.

"I really don't think I was talking to Odin. I don't even believe in Odin or the other old gods. I said as much to that Svidur guy."

Rebecca closed her eyes.

Ben's eyes flashed with anger. "What exactly did you say to him?"

"That I don't believe in the gods. That the last people who believed in them are bog bodies in museums now. And when he tried to convince me, I said it's none of his business what I believe in."

"Anna Stella Sakarias," Rebecca said authoritatively, and for once I was actually a little scared of her. "You have to treat your superiors with respect."

On the other side of the table, Mathias looked down at his plate.

"Some mentally unstable dude who thinks he's a god does not get to decide who or what I believe in."

"Young people these days," thundered Ben. "You think the world revolves around you. You're used to having everything served to you on a silver platter."

"I should think that I, in particular, am an exception, and that you bear a good deal of the blame for that being the case," I hissed back.

So much for a pleasant reconciliation dinner.

Silence hung over the table.

Monster looked longingly at the curry-cheese tart, though he had enough of an understanding of human drama to stop eating.

I scooted my chair back and stood up. "Thanks for the one bite of food I was able to have before you started lecturing me. I'm leaving now. We can't be in the same room until you understand that only I get to decide who I respect."

Then I left the dinner.

Monster trudged after me into the hall with a sulky expression.

"Wipe that look off your face," I grumbled as I quickly pulled on my boots and coat. "We'll go down to Frank's and get some food."

When we left, I slammed the door hard.

On the way across the field, Monster looked expectantly at me.

"What is it?"

"Hangadrott is a big deal. If it really was the All-Father you spoke with, he promised to grant your wish if you sacrifice a royal to him."

"First of all," I said as I tromped with difficulty through the soft dirt, "I'm not gonna have my own private genie in a bottle. Second of all, I really don't think it was Odin. And third, I have no intention of sacrificing a member of the Danish royal family."

"You know other royals. One, at least."

"Who?"

"I'm a prince."

I stopped and looked at him. "I don't even want to hear you say that kind of thing as a joke."

"It's not a joke. You can ask Odin to vanquish Ragnara. Our entire world is in danger for as long as she reigns."

A lump scratched my throat. I knelt in front of him and put both hands on his shoulders. They sank into the thick fur. My knees got all muddy in the damp dirt, but I didn't care.

"If you die," I said, "then I'll die, too. Of sadness. You're my best friend, and I can't lose you." My voice cracked, but in front of Monster it didn't matter. "You have to stay alive."

Monster laid his heavy head on my shoulder and breathed into my hair. "You're my best friend, too, and I'll do anything to make sure you survive."

I flung my arms around his neck and hugged him.

We sat that way in the middle of the field in the dark for a while as the biting northern wind tried to pull us apart.

Then I stood, and we walked the rest of the way home to Odinmont, where I immediately jumped on my bike and steered it toward Frank's.

We passed quite a few people walking along the side of the normally deserted road into town. When we passed, they turned and looked severely at me. Some of them had on old-fashioned clothes. What the community theater was up to and why they were running around in costume in the countryside at night was a mystery to me, but that was their prerogative.

In Ravensted, the streets were also teeming. I parked in the back alley behind Frank's since there wasn't any space out front.

Was there some event for Halloween?

Nah. The bar looked like its usual self when I walked in. There were some locals I knew, and also a number of costumed people I hadn't seen before, but all in all, it resembled a completely normal evening.

Frank looked at me with surprise when I came in. "Did you feel the need to be social?"

"I just need some food." I smiled. "My dinner plans were canceled."

"What would you like?"

"A sandwich. And would you ask Milas to pack a bag for my dog?"

"Of course." He disappeared into the kitchen to get the food.

A clammy aura hit me from the side. I turned my head and saw that Peter had climbed onto the barstool next to mine.

"Your friend the Paki pig is sitting over there." He nodded toward a corner, where Hakim sat alone eating a burger, engrossed in something on his phone. "Huh, I never knew the police hired illegals. But I guess plenty of places do. Luna works here, after all."

I clenched my fists on the bar and counted silently to ten. There was no point in getting into a fight at my workplace, especially not in front of a police officer. To stop myself from smacking Peter's head into the bar, I jumped down from the stool and walked over to Hakim.

Behind me, I saw Peter pull his phone out and call someone.

"Hey, Hakim," I said, standing in front of his table.

He looked up at me and hastily turned off his phone, but not before I saw what he was looking at. It was a photo of the Savage's face, stiffened in a surprised death grimace.

"Would you like to sit?"

"If you promise not to show me pictures of dead bodies or tell me about the contents of autopsy reports while I'm eating."

"Okay." He smiled. "I promise."

I sat at the little café table and sighed deeply.

"Is something wrong?" he asked.

I scratched my neck without answering him. "Can I ask you something?" I asked instead. "I hope you won't get mad."

"You don't usually seem to care if I get mad."

I couldn't help but laugh. "Am I that bad?"

"Well . . ." He had a warm vibe I hadn't felt from him before.

"Are you religious?"

He furrowed his brow, taken aback. "You meet a man of Arab descent, and you naturally assume he's religious?"

"I'm not assuming anything," I snapped. "I passed that point a long time ago."

Hakim relaxed a little. "Okay, fine. I am religious."

"Good. If you're religious, then you must believe in something. I want to hear from a person of faith about what it's like. So what do you believe in?"

He reflected. "That there is only one true god. You can't worship others and . . ."

I held a hand up. "Stop right there. I had a Christian foster family who followed the Bible down to the last comma, so I know religious parrot talk when I hear it."

Hakim's eyebrows shot up, and he laughed in astonishment.

"Try again. What do *you* believe in?" I pressed.

He stroked his large hand over his chin thoughtfully.

"Okay. I believe in truth and justice," he said. "I believe that everyone is responsible for their actions—both good and bad. I believe that throughout our lives, every human builds up a kind of ledger, which in the end is settled by a higher power."

"So you think there's a power that's higher than us?"

Hakim nodded. "We're responsible for our own actions, but yes, there is a higher power."

"What do you mean when you say it's 'higher'?"

"It's . . . you know. Almighty."

"Why is it almighty?"

"I don't know. It just is."

"I would have expected a more clever answer from you."

Frank arrived at our table with my sandwich. "Who's your friend, Anna?"

"This is Hakim." I made a sweeping gesture with my hand and rolled my eyes dramatically. "He's from the police, and he's here to make sure I don't violate my probation."

"I'm your boss, so I think I would know if you were on probation. I've seen your papers," Frank said with a crooked smile.

His eyebrows lowered, and a clear image of the little boy I occasionally saw in his past sailed toward me. The boy screamed desperately.

Hakim spoke. "I investigated the Pippi Murders. That was how I met Anna. Now I can't seem to get rid of her."

Frank crossed his tattooed arms over his chest.

"I'll admit that Anna is hard to ignore. I can't escape her, either." His eyes sparkled at me. "Let me know if you want a ride home." Frank tossed his head in the direction of the other bartender. "He can surely handle the bar himself on such a slow night."

I looked around the half-full bar, confused. I would have said it was fairly busy.

I quickly changed the subject when Frank left. "I have two follow-up questions about the religion thing. One. You mention justice. Is the justice you're talking about objective? I mean, is there someone up there," I pointed toward the ceiling, "who decides what is fair?"

"Yes," said Hakim without hesitation. "What's your second follow-up question?"

"Do you believe in ghosts and witches and stuff like that?"

Hakim laughed. "No. Definitely not. For the most part, I only believe in what I can see. I'll admit that sometimes mysterious things happen, especially when you're around, but that's just because I don't know the whole truth."

I considered him. "And the truth is important to you?"

"Yes." He leaned forward in anticipation. He was counting on me bringing out the big reveal. I had to disappoint him, and for some reason, the memory of Od telling me I wasn't ready for the truth popped into my head. I slowly folded a napkin around my sandwich.

"I left my dog outside. I don't like for him to wait too long." I stood.

"You're leaving? Just like that? I want to know what's going on."

I snorted. "Good luck with that."

"I will figure it out. Even if you don't want to share your secrets with me. It'll just take a little longer."

"For your own sake, you should stay out of it," I said before heading out.

Monster sat stoically by the dog-leash hitch when I came out with a bag of leftovers in one hand and my napkin-wrapped sandwich in the other.

"You look pissed," he mumbled.

I didn't reply, just stomped toward the back entrance of Frank's to get my bike. When I turned the corner to the back alley, I stopped abruptly.

Not again!

Both tires were slashed, and the seat was mangled.

At my side, Monster growled threateningly.

"Is that your bike?" came a voice from behind us. Hakim had followed me.

I didn't even bother turning to face him. "Yep."

A shout rang out from the street.

What now?

The shout rang out again, and I recognized the shout as Frank's. I ran in the direction of the shout, my heart pounding.

Fortunately, it was only Frank's truck that had suffered damage. However, it had suffered a lot of damage. Spray paint decorated the sides. The windows were smashed, and the tires were flat.

A stream of curses and expletives flowed from Frank's mouth as he walked around the truck.

I walked up to it and placed a hand on the hood. As expected, I saw Christian Mikkelsen in full swing. He hadn't been bluffing when he said Frank would pay for employing me. The feeling of guilt made my stomach clench.

Frank paced frantically back and forth, and people were starting to gather and stare at the smashed truck. Hakim made a surprised noise when he saw Christian's work.

"It's a good thing you're here," Frank said to him in a hoarse voice. "I think I know who did this. There are countless witnesses who heard him threaten me. I don't know his name, but I know what he looks like."

"Christian Mikkelsen," I said.

Hakim's head jerked. "Belinda Jaeger's boyfriend?"

"I don't know what they were. But it's the guy you showed me a picture of."

"Anna's bike didn't fare much better," Hakim said to Frank.

"You're kidding me," said Frank. "Was it also him the last time your bike got smashed?"

"Last time?" Hakim asked pointedly.

Crap! I touched my forehead. "He was mad at me because you brought him in for Belinda's murder. He thought I had ratted him out."

"Why didn't you report that he was harassing you?"

I made a derisive *heh* sound. Good thing Hakim didn't know what Christian, Markus, and Peter did to me that night Varnar came to my rescue. "I didn't think it would help his opinion of me. Also, I thought he had stopped."

"Did you really think he would stop? What about the night we were celebrating the death of the Pippi Killer? He almost knocked me down to get ahold of you," said Frank.

Okay. Here it comes.

With eyes closed, I awaited the explosion.

"I could have done something," yelled Hakim.

I turned toward him. "What could you have done? It would only have made matters worse if I got the police involved."

"I'm not just *the police*."

"In this context, you are."

Hakim bared his teeth in a frustrated grimace. "We'll file a report. Let me just call a colleague."

"I don't want to report it," I said.

527

"I do," said Frank.

"Anna, it needs to be recorded. Otherwise I can't build a case against him."

"He's not important," I said. "I have bigger problems than him."

"I would very much like to hear about those problems later, but right now I want you to report Christian Mikkelsen."

"I really don't care what you want," I snapped back.

Even more people gathered around us.

"Jesus, they're really staring," I said. "Don't they have any manners?"

"Who are you talking about?" asked Frank.

Hakim also looked around, confused. I studied the people who had gathered around the truck. They said nothing, just watched us silently.

Oh, of course.

"Nothing," I said to Frank and Hakim.

The gathered people—ghosts—did not appear angry or frustrated. Just curious. They didn't have the desperation I had seen in Belinda, or the sadness that surrounded Arthur. On closer inspection, I saw that they were wearing clothes from different time periods.

Hakim made a phone call, and Frank studied his smashed truck, on the verge of tears.

A young man stepped forth from the crowd. "You can see us."

I nodded and walked up close to him so I could whisper without Hakim and Frank noticing. "Why are there so many of you?"

He smiled. "Tonight is the Feast of the Dead. We're just visiting." His hair was so pale it was almost white, and he looked about twenty years old.

Monster had ambled closer. "Who are you talking to?"

The young man widened his eyes. "Whoa. A talking dog." He gasped.

I put a hand on my hip. "Whoa. A talking dead guy!"

528

"True." He laughed.

To Monster, I said quietly: "There are others here besides us."

Monster looked around. "Spirits?"

I nodded. Addressing the young man, I said: "You guys are different from other . . ." I didn't quite know how direct I should be. ". . . others of your kind," I concluded diplomatically.

"We *have* crossed over. So we have a different kind of peace."

I glanced at the others, who silently came closer and looked at me with curious, probing eyes.

"Peace or no, you're giving me the creeps."

The young man nodded understandingly. He turned to them.

"There's nothing to see here. Move along. Remember, you're only here for tonight. I'm sure you have people you want to see or places you want to revisit." He made a motion as if leading a flock of chickens.

The crowd dispersed, and the spirits vanished into the dark.

"How long are you guys here?"

"Until midnight."

"Just tonight?"

"Yes. And only if we have business here."

I looked at him in the light of the streetlamps. He looked more transparent than Arthur ever had.

"Do you have business here?"

He looked solemnly at me. "Yes. I need to give a message to someone I think you know."

"Someone I know? Who?"

"A dead person who is bound to Odinmont." His voice was probing.

"There are quite a few dead people at Odinmont, but I'm guessing you mean my dad, Arthur."

"Exactly," he said. "We knew each other when we were alive. I need to talk to him, but I have to be let in. The place is enveloped in strong magic that keeps most uninvited guests out."

Good to know.

"I'm on my way home, but my means of transportation have been destroyed." I stopped. "Hey, what's your name?"

"Thorsten."

"Okay, Thorsten. Can you just meet me out there? I'll try to find a way to get home quickly."

Thorsten agreed with a nod and backed into the shadows.

I walked back over to Hakim and Frank, who seemed to be wrapping things up.

"Does one of you have a bike I can borrow? Just until I can get mine fixed."

Frank looked at me. "Sorry. And where will you get your bike fixed? The town's only bike repair guy is in jail."

Hakim and I exchanged a look.

"I'll drive you home," he said.

"I can do it," said Frank. "We'll just take my van."

Hakim laid a large hand on Frank's shoulder. "I'll drive her. You just stay here." It sounded friendly, but it was really an order.

Hakim disappeared into the back alley and came back with my bike under his arm. He started walking. "Come on, Anna."

"My dog has to come, too," I said as I jogged after him.

"Fine."

We arrived at Frederiksgade, where Ravensted's largest housing complex is located. The parking lot was illuminated by streetlamps that shone coldly over the rows of cars.

Hakim approached a station wagon and unlocked it. He laid my bike in the large cargo space, while Monster jumped in and filled the entire back seat. Hakim closed the tailgate and joined me in the front.

"Your dog is giving me a weird look. I don't think he's quite normal," he said as he started the car.

In the back seat, Monster sniffed.

"You don't need to tell me." I concealed a smile by turning my head and looking out at the streets of Ravensted. They were still full of people, but now I knew that only a few of us could see them.

"You know you can tell me things," said Hakim. "Like how Christian is on your back. I can keep it to myself if you don't want to report it. It'll only help my investigation of the Pippi Murders. The more I know, the better."

"What do your colleagues have to say about the fact that you haven't closed the case?"

"Oh, it's closed. It's very closed."

"What does Lars Guldager say about it?"

"Also that it's closed. He doesn't know I'm still working on it."

"How can you keep working on it? Don't you have other stuff to do?"

"I use my free time." Hakim's voice did not invite further questions.

We continued out of the town in silence, and no one said anything before Hakim pulled into the driveway in front of Odinmont.

He pulled out my bike and leaned it against the whitewashed wall. Then he illuminated it with his phone.

"Come here," he called.

I walked over to him. In the sparse light from the phone screen, I looked down at the seat of my bike.

There was a cold rush in my stomach when I realized the seat hadn't been cut up randomly. On closer inspection, the slashes formed the rune Ansuz.

Hakim cursed as he put on rubber gloves. "We've both touched it. There could have been evidence on it."

"Maybe it's just an expression of Christian's sick personality that he carved that. Maybe he knows that symbol was on the girls. It was on Belinda, after all."

"Or maybe it was Christian Mikkelsen who killed Tenna and Belinda."

The cold crept into me. I cautiously placed a hand on the bike seat.

"Don't," shouted Hakim. "You'll ruin the few remaining traces."

I pulled my hand back pensively and was surprised not to see Christian slashing it. There was an aggressive energy on my bike, but it was foggy. I knew the aura but couldn't place it. I pulled out my phone and took a picture of the seat.

"I'm not sure it was Christian who did this," I said.

"Why not?" Hakim stepped in front of me and bent over the bike.

"It's kind of hard to explain. I just don't think it was him," I hedged.

Someone made a grunting noise behind me. That voice, by contrast, I did know, and the sound sent ice-cold tentacles of fear up and down my entire body. I turned around slowly and came face-to-face with the Savage.

The giant knife was in his hand, and he laughed cruelly as he lunged so quickly I didn't have time to move.

The knife buried itself in my stomach.

The Savage's eyes held mine in triumph as he moved his arm up in a long, smooth motion. The knife moved up through my stomach, diaphragm, and lungs, finally landing in the middle of my heart.

CHAPTER 33

I made a gurgling sound, and Hakim turned toward me.

All the hairs on Monster's back were standing up, and he spun around, confused.

I looked down at my chest, in which the Savage's entire arm was now buried. He stared at my torso with eyes wide as he stabbed again, his knife doing no damage. Just like Belinda, he didn't realize he was dead.

"What's going on?" Hakim asked and grabbed my shoulder. He pulled me aside and out of the Savage's reach.

My entire body was shaking. The chill of death had embedded itself deep inside me.

The Savage followed and pounded his translucent knife into Hakim's back.

"Watch out!" I screamed.

Anna, you idiot!

Hakim jumped in the air and flinched as if someone had thrown a snowball at the back of his head. He looked over his shoulder into what, to him, must have looked like nothing. Then he turned back to face me.

"What is wrong with you?"

The Savage walked up to me and stabbed again. This time he hit me in the throat. I coughed and clutched my neck.

Just then, Thorsten was standing at the Savage's side. He touched him gently on the shoulder.

The Savage turned and looked at him with a snarl.

"You're not alive anymore," said Thorsten quietly. His voice was soft and persuasive. "You need to cross over now. You don't belong here."

I thought uneasily of the ghosts I had driven away by mentioning their deaths. I guess my method had been pretty brutal to them, but I hadn't known it at the time.

The Savage looked uncomprehendingly at Thorsten.

"Anna," I heard Hakim call again, but I didn't have the energy to answer him.

"No," growled the Savage. This was the first time I had heard him utter a word. He took another step toward me, and I cowered in Hakim's grasp.

"Yes." Now Thorsten's voice grew firm. "You must cross over."

The Savage extended a blue finger toward me. "But she . . ."

"Shhh. It doesn't matter now. Nothing matters. You need to move on."

"Nooo," the Savage sniveled.

"You're dead now, Naut Kafnar," Thorsten said decidedly.

The Savage's chest rose and fell several times. Then he fell to the gravel and convulsed in death throes for a few moments before he dissolved and vanished.

"Are you okay?" Thorsten asked me.

I was hyperventilating, but I found my voice. "I'm okay."

"Good," said Hakim. "What just happened?"

I shifted my gaze from Thorsten to him. "Uh . . ."

Behind him, Thorsten began gesticulating to indicate that he didn't have much time.

"Nothing's happening," I said, which wasn't too far from the truth. "If you're done with my bike, you're free to leave now."

The chill had spread to my voice.

"I don't want to leave you alone in this state."

"Alone." I laughed and looked at Thorsten and Monster. With Arthur in the basement, we had enough for a party. Then I composed myself. "I thought I heard something, but it must have just been a bird. You can go."

I looked at my phone. It was twenty to twelve. If Arthur and Thorsten were going to talk, we would have to hurry.

Hakim furrowed his dark brows. "You are the absolute strangest person I've ever met."

"Believe me. I'm nothing compared to some."

"What do you mean?"

"Nothing, Hakim. Now get out of here."

"A minute ago you were clinging to my arm. Now you're desperate to get rid of me."

"Yes." I looked him straight in the eyes.

"Are you sure you're okay?"

"Yes." I took out my keys and walked up to the door. "Do you want me to call you in an hour so you can hear that everything's fine?"

"Okay," he said. "But I'm taking your bike so I can examine it."

"Go right ahead. I can't use it in this condition anyway."

I kept my back to him and fumbled with the lock. To my relief, I heard the car door slam behind me and the roar of the motor as Hakim barreled down my driveway.

"Go in. Hurry," I told Thorsten and opened the door.

"Who's here?" asked Monster.

"A ghost named Thorsten. He says he knew my dad."

"How do you know you can trust him?"

I looked at Thorsten. "I don't. But he says he's Arthur's friend."

Monster rolled his large eyes. "I've never met someone so bad at looking out for themselves as you."

"Ahem," said Thorsten behind us. "If I don't want to wait another year to deliver my message, we'd better find Arthur."

I hurried over to the heavy bench and started tugging on it, but it moved only slightly. Monster took one of its wooden legs in his teeth and pulled it quickly across the floor. I didn't dare think of what else that set of teeth could do. The hatch in the floor appeared, and I opened it.

"We're going down here." I grabbed the flashlight that still sat on the windowsill.

"Has that been there all along?" Thorsten asked and pointed down. "I came out here for years when I was alive. I had no idea there was something under the house."

"Not some*thing*. Some*one*," I replied and began the descent.

The others followed suit.

At the end of the hall, Monster and I had to crawl to get through the low opening. Thorsten simply walked through the wall.

Inside the chamber, I tried not to look at the sheet-covered figure on the stone table. Arthur rose from a seated position on the floor. He stared at Thorsten before the two of them embraced.

While the two dead men were hugging, I realized that I found myself in a burial chamber on Halloween along with two ghosts, a fresh corpse, a ton of skeletons, and a man-eating wolf. What did it say about me that I didn't find this particularly creepy?

"What are you doing here, Thorsten?" asked Arthur.

"I come with a message for you. I'm sure you can guess who it's from."

Arthur bowed his head. "Yes," he whispered.

"She doesn't want to wait for you much longer."

"Who doesn't want to wait?" My voice was sharp.

"The goddess Freyja."

"Not more gods and goddesses." I threw my hands in the air.

The two ghosts exchanged a look before Thorsten spoke again. "She has the claim to Arthur's soul."

Panic spread through me. "Claim? How?"

"How long do I have?" asked Arthur, ignoring my question.

"To the end of the year, at most."

"What are you two talking about?"

Thorsten turned toward me. "Arthur shouldn't even be in this world. He has to go back to Fólkvangr, Freyja's home in Asgard. She has the claim to the people who fall while protecting their families. Arthur was given permission to stay here because of you. But now that you're about to come of age, his time is running out."

I was more scared now than I was when the Savage planted a knife in my stomach. More scared than when Belinda held me down under the falling tree in the hurricane.

"He's not going anywhere."

Thorsten shook his head at me. "We don't belong here."

"Arthur does," I said.

"Not anymore." He addressed Arthur again. "You have to come with me. It's so peaceful in Fólkvangr. It's beautiful there." I recognized the persuasive tone he had also used on the Savage.

Arthur's outline was suddenly a little blurred, and he had a wavering expression on his face.

Oh no! Thorsten wasn't just sent with a message for Arthur. He was sent to try to bring him back.

"Drop it," I said threateningly.

"There's no sadness. No longing," he continued and took a step toward Arthur. He reached out his hand.

I stood between them. "You are no longer welcome here. Leave my home."

He ignored me. To Arthur he said: "Come with me."

Arthur took a drowsy step in Thorsten's direction.

"Anna, I don't want to leave you, but it's so hard to hold on. Especially tonight. The veil between the worlds is so thin right now."

"Wake up, Arthur," I yelled. "You can't go with him."

I tried to bang my fist on his chest, but my hand went straight through him.

"I'm so tired," Arthur mumbled.

Time to bring out the big guns.

"Thorsten, how did you die?" I asked feverishly.

Finally, Thorsten focused on me. He looked down at himself and pulled his jacket to the side. A thick rope hung around his neck. On his T-shirt, the rune Ansuz was drawn in blood.

"Windmills," he whispered, seemingly reliving the moment of his death. "It's such a long way down."

"*Oh.* You were one of them."

His nearly transparent body stretched, as if hanging from something. "Would you do something for me?" he asked with a—literally—strangled voice.

"What?"

"Tell my dad I'm fine. That I'm at peace."

"Okay. Who's your dad?"

"Preben," Thorsten coughed.

"Your dad is Janitor Preben?"

Thorsten didn't manage to answer before he dissolved into nothing.

Immediately, Arthur shook his head hard as if to clear his mind.

"You were about to go with him. What the hell were you doing?"

"Freyja tries calling me to her once in a while. Her power is very strong."

"Why does she call to dead people? Isn't she the goddess of love?"

A strange expression flew across Arthur's face, but he gathered himself quickly. Since I couldn't see ghosts' auras, I had no idea what that was about.

"It's true, she is who you go to with matters of fertility and growth. But she's also a goddess of war and death. She and Odin split the dead among themselves. Those who die in battle, anyway. She takes her share to Fólkvangr."

"Why didn't you go there when you . . . you-know-what?"

"I did."

"You were there?"

"Yes. But I was brought back here to Midgard."

538

"By whom?"

"Od."

"What? Od brought you? Why?"

Arthur's face was gentle. "Because of you."

Just then, the sound of shouting rang out in the hall.

"Anna?" Varnar's voice was desperate.

"In here," I called. To Arthur, I said: "Is your resting place secret?"

"Is this someone you trust?"

I thought for a second.

"Yes," I replied. "He was sent by my mom to watch over me."

"If Thora sent him, then you can tell him."

Varnar appeared beneath the opening. His pants were covered in clay dust, and his eyes were opened wide.

"I thought something had happened to you. I was in the woods when you got home, and then I heard you shout. When I got here, the door to the house was open, and you were gone." He looked around at the chamber, which was lit only by my flashlight. "What is this place?"

"It's a grave," I said. *A mass grave, to be precise.*

"I can see that." His eyes swept across the skeletons. "What are you doing down here?"

Monster looked like he was asking himself the same question.

"It's my dad's resting place," I said, and pointed at the cloth. "Because of my powers, I can talk to him."

Varnar spun around. "Is he here now?"

"He's standing right next to you."

Arthur gave Varnar a good look over. "This is the protector Thora sent you?"

I nodded.

"What's he saying?" asked Varnar.

"He's asking if you're my protector."

Varnar stood up straight. "I would give my life to save your daughter's."

"Thora hasn't changed a bit," Arthur mumbled with a laugh. "And in some areas, she still doesn't get it."

I made an uncomprehending grimace at him.

"Tell your protector I appreciate him being here," Arthur said formally. "And that I'm grateful for him taking care of you."

"He's glad you're watching out for me," I abbreviated.

Varnar's face was serious, but Arthur smiled deviously.

"Thanks for checking on me," I told Varnar, who was walking along the walls of the round chamber and studying the skeletons.

"These people were buried according to the old customs, with grave goods for the gods and diversions for the journey to the realms of the dead." He bent over something that resembled an advanced chess set. It was next to a long skeleton that clutched a sword in its bony hand.

"This is old in our world, too. This mound must be over a thousand years old."

"We have a handful of these kinds of mounds in Freiheim, but most of them have been plowed under. The bones have been crushed and spread to the wind."

Arthur clenched his fists. "Would you ask him if all the original customs are now banned in Hrafnheim?"

I conveyed the question.

"Worshipping the gods is punishable by death. All rituals associated with them are forbidden. Monuments and memorials have been removed, and the old names have been changed."

"What about Njordvík and New Odense?"

Again I had to pass on the question.

"Njordvík," I could hear how it made Varnar uncomfortable to say the name, "is now Norvík. And what used to be called New Odense is now called Hedeby."

"Why did everything change names?" I asked.

"I think Ragnara is punishing Odin for something," said Arthur.

"What's she punishing him for?" I asked.

"Who's punishing whom?" asked Varnar.

Ugh. "I really need to get you reanimated, Arthur. If for no other reason than to facilitate communication between you and everyone else." I looked at Varnar. "My dad says Ragnara is punishing Odin by removing all the place names that have anything to do with the gods."

"She's angry at the gods, in any case. She says they only serve to keep the people in invisible chains, and that the powerful use them to maintain their dominance."

"It's terrible to take people's faith from them," said Arthur.

I looked at my phone.

"Do you two have anything else you want to discuss through me?" I asked. "Because if not, I do actually have to get up for school in the morning."

"Would you ask him if Thora's okay?" Arthur said quietly.

I cleared my throat. "He's asking how my mom's doing."

The muscles in Varnar's jaw tensed.

"It's been many months since I saw her. But I can tell you that Thora Baneblood is fighting. She wants to save the worlds and her children and kill Eskild Black-Eye and Ragnara."

"She's taken the name Thora Baneblood?" Arthur shook his head as he smiled slightly to himself. "She's always had a flair for the dramatic." He grew serious. "I wish I were with her. I'm afraid that she'll fight so hard she'll forget all the good things in life."

Up in the living room, we worked together to return the bench to its place.

Monster immediately announced that he was going to bed and hurried up the stairs. Maybe he actually did have a little bit of situational awareness.

"Can I stay for a little while?" Varnar asked when we were alone.

"Yes, of course," I said. This was the first time Varnar had expressed a desire for social interaction that didn't involve violence, training, and/or lecturing me.

I leaned against the kitchen table. "There's something I've never gotten to ask you."

"What?" He came and stood right next to me.

The short distance between us made me want to reach my hand out, but I quickly rejected that impulse.

"What do you know about Preben?"

"He doesn't tell me much about himself, and I don't ask."

"Can you help me get him to talk?"

Varnar nodded. "Yes. But don't count on much of a response. He's very reserved."

Coming from you!

"Can I ask you something?" Varnar's hand gripped the tabletop.

"Sure. Ask away."

"Why did the policeman take you home tonight?"

Caught off guard, I had to fumble for the words. "My bike got smashed again, so he drove me home."

He let go of my kitchen table and leaned toward me. "Who smashed it?"

"Hakim—the policeman—thinks it's that guy Christian, the one who attacked me."

Varnar swore. "I should have finished him off when I had the chance. But Thora's orders are that I can only kill if you, Aella, or myself is in grave danger."

"I would like it if you continued to follow that rule. There's been plenty of deaths around here, and I'm not even convinced it was him."

"Then who was it?"

I shrugged. "I think it's someone I know, but for some reason I'm having a hard time recognizing his aura."

"What happened to your bike?"

"The tires are slashed. And that rune was carved into the seat."

"Which rune?"

"This one." I got out my phone and showed him the picture I had taken of it.

Varnar cautiously took the phone and looked at the screen. "This is a very old symbol."

"It was on all the girls. You didn't know that?"

Varnar was still staring at the phone. "No. Well, now that you mention it, it was on the girl Naut Kafnar killed in town."

"But when . . ." I had a hard time completing the sentence. "When Ragnara sent you here, you weren't instructed to put the symbol on me when you . . . when you killed me?" I blurted.

"I didn't get any details about my mission. I only knew I was supposed to neutralize a threat to Freiheim."

Leave it to me to be seen as a threat to national security.

"But the girls all had the symbol on them. The ones Naut Kafnar killed as well as the others. I always thought it was a message from Ragnara. Evidently, she also used that symbol last time she was here, before I was born." I thought of Thorsten's bloodied T-shirt.

Varnar shook his head. "She banned the old writing system after she broke with the gods. It's a capital offense to use most of the oldest runes."

"But you have runes on your arm." This flew out of my mouth before I had time to consider that it revealed how much I had studied his body.

He rubbed his upper arm. "These are different runes," he said without elaborating. "But I think you're right in thinking it's a message."

"Why would Ragnara use the forbidden runes to send me a message?"

"I don't think it's for you. I think it's a message for the gods."

Varnar left shortly thereafter. As always, he took off running toward the door when I was in the middle of a sentence.

Flabbergasted, I followed him, and he turned around in the doorway. He looked solemnly at me. Then he put his hand on my shoulder and gave it a slight squeeze before running off.

I stood there, flustered. He had never made such a friendly gesture before. At least, not outside the influence of love magic.

Exhausted, I put on my pajamas and crawled into bed.

Monster was already snoring in the guest bedroom. Embarrassed, I realized he had been trying to give Varnar and me some privacy. He sure was optimistic on my behalf.

I didn't have to cringe for too long, however, because I fell asleep within five minutes.

A loud ringing woke me up soon after. Dazed, I sat up in bed and spotted my glowing phone on the floor. The display told me it was Hakim.

Crap.

I had completely forgotten that I'd promised to call him. I quickly snatched up the phone. I didn't even bother with a hello.

"I know," I said, stumbling over the words. "I forgot to call you. I'm really bad at holding up my end of agreements—especially when it comes to my own safety. You must be pissed. Next time, I promise I'll remember. Everything's okay. I'm fine."

It was quiet for a moment on the other end. "Were you sleeping?"

"Yes. I had just fallen asleep."

"Should I take the unusually long flow of speech to mean you've actually started to respect me a little bit?" His voice was teasing.

"Oh, I wouldn't go that far."

Hakim grew serious again. "I've examined your bike very thoroughly. There are no prints on it aside from yours and mine. But Frank's truck is covered in Christian's fingerprints."

"Aren't you making a big deal out of a simple vandalism case?" I yawned discreetly. "I didn't think you had these kinds of resources. Doesn't the police department's evening and night staff consist purely of an answering machine these days?"

"I did say I'm using my free time."

"And they let you mess around with evidence like this?"

"The answering machine didn't object." Although Hakim's voice was neutral, I knew he was smiling.

I hesitated. "Hakim, can I ask you something?"

"As long as it's not another theological question. It's simply too late at night for that."

"No, this one's totally down-to-earth." I searched around for the words. "What did you think of me the first time you met me?"

"I didn't like you," Hakim said after a short pause.

"Was it just a matter of antipathy?"

Hakim sighed on the other end before he replied. "I wanted to get very far away from you. Or hit you."

Good to know how Ben's magic worked in practice.

When I didn't say anything, Hakim followed up. "Well, you asked."

"I have that effect on most people. It's not your fault."

"I don't think it's your fault, either."

"What do you mean?"

"I have no reason not to like you. You're a decent and intelligent girl. After I recognized that, I started to like you."

"So you *decided* to like me?"

"Well, yeah. Can't you tell?"

"If lectures and gross details of horrific murders are a sign of affection, then yeah."

He laughed.

"Do you like me?" he asked.

Even through the phone, I could sense that he was holding his breath. I tried to make my voice breezy. "I meant it, that time I told Greta you're okay."

"Am I just okay?"

"Yes, Hakim. You're just okay." I hurried to change the subject. "So what have you concluded after the events of this evening?"

545

He waited a second to answer. "I am now even more certain that you are at the center of a bunch of strange, sinister occurrences, and that you're lying every time I ask you about it."

I chose to neither confirm nor deny this. "That's not what I meant. What do you make of the fact that there were prints on the truck but not on my bike?"

"I don't know. Maybe Christian is craftier than I thought. Maybe he did both but got rid of the prints on your bike."

"Why did he carve the symbol into my bike seat?" My tired brain was having a hard time following along.

"To send you the message that the murderer, whether it's Christian or someone else, has now definitively tracked you down, and that he's coming after you."

 # CHAPTER 34

"Sorry," was the first thing Luna said when I met her and Mathias at the end of the driveway up to Ben and Rebecca's house the following morning.

I had sent her a text to ask for a ride to school.

Her hair was blue today, and for that reason, I had a hard time concentrating on what she was saying.

"Sorry for what?" I climbed into the bike's cargo basket, and she pedaled as Monster galloped alongside us and Mathias followed on his own bike.

"For my parents' behavior yesterday."

"They're just concerned," I said. "But I don't think I want to be around them unless they stop forcing things on me."

"I'll talk to them. We're having a session tonight where I'm gonna learn about the different kinds of magic."

I turned around in the basket and looked up at her. "What's up with your hair?"

"Mathias did it last night. I can concentrate better with this hair color. I have so much to keep track of with all the magic on top of school. Plus it's cute, right?"

"Well, it sure is blue," I said diplomatically. "How can your hair survive being colored so many times?"

"I have a trick," said Mathias, a little uneasily.

"What trick?"

"I discovered it by chance a few years ago when I was helping my mom in the salon. I was washing the hair of a client who wanted to change her hair color. When I ran my fingers through her hair in a certain way, I was able to pull the old color out. Plus her hair was healthier than before. This method is much gentler than traditional chemical lighteners," he added. Sometimes Mathias sounded like a fifty-year-old hairstylist.

"That must be a demigod specialty. My hair was also noticeably softer after that night with Od."

Neither Luna nor Mathias commented. They just exchanged a knowing look.

"It wasn't like that. Not at all."

Monster snorted on my other side.

"Then why did he sleep there?" asked Luna.

"I told you. His god side, or whatever you call it, was supercharged, so he needed my humanity."

"But you say you don't believe in the gods," said Mathias.

"I believe in what I can sense, and I sensed a person who needed help."

"So what do you believe? You have to admit that Mathias and Od are different from normal people," Luna said as she stood up on the pedals, panting.

"I've actually been thinking about it," I said. "I'll gladly admit that there are some beings that are different from us. Genetically, I mean. So you can call them gods or extraterrestrials or something else. But I don't buy that they rule over humans. I definitely don't think we should sort the races into a pecking order. That's totally old-fashioned, isn't it?"

"Agreed," said Mathias. "I also don't like the idea of people being under me."

"You seemed pretty happy about it yesterday." Luna laughed.

"Oh my God," I said and covered my ears.

"Luna!" Mathias's face was appalled, but his eyes shone adoringly.

In Blue Hall, Luna's hair almost blended in with the walls as we headed to Danish class, where Mr. Nielsen was still pumped about the Icelandic texts. We would be going over "Völuspá"— The Prophecy of the Seeress—and I was reminded of Elias's theory.

"This text," said Mr. Nielsen, "is over eleven hundred years old. However, it talks about something that hasn't happened yet. The future. Maja, what is your interpretation of the poem?"

Maja from my class blushed, while Tine chuckled.

"Uh." She looked blankly at her papers.

Although the enthusiastic smile stayed plastered on Mr. Nielsen's lips, his eyes were despondent. "Try reading it aloud, Maja. Maybe that will refresh your memory."

The wide-seeing völva
Wolves she tamed
Seid she performed
Seid she loved
Always was she sought
By evil women

Maja looked like a giant question mark as Mr. Nielsen looked expectantly at her.

"It's a description of the völva," said Mr. Nielsen. "Völva is an old word for seeress."

Luna nudged me in the side with her elbow. She leaned toward me. "Notice any similarities? Wolf taming, and that evil women are after her? And talking to the dead is also a form of seid. You do love to talk to your dad."

Mr. Nielsen continued. "Read a little more, Maja."

Maja began again with a look of suffering on her face.

The sun, the sibling
of the moon, from the south
Its right hand cast

Over heaven's rim;
No knowledge it had
where its home should be,
The moon knew not
What might it had,
The stars knew not
Where their stations were

Luna whispered: "Moon." She pointed at herself. "Luna." She pointed at me. "Stars. Anna *Stella*. And Serén is an old Celtic word for star. Mathias is also quite golden. Like the sun. That's so strange." She laughed. "And at first none of us knew what powers we had."

Hmm. Very strange indeed. My head began to spin.

"Maja, skip down to stanza forty," said Mr. Nielsen. "Here the völva tells of the events leading up to doomsday."

She saw there wading
Through rivers wild
Treacherous men
And murderous wolves,
And workers of ill with the wives of men.
There Nithhogg sucked the blood of the slain
And the wolf tore men;
Would you know yet more?

The final line was delivered into my head in a different voice than Maja's. As if it were speaking directly to me. I gripped the edge of the table as the room began to spin.

The giantess old
In the Iron Forest sat
In the east, and bore

The brood of Fenrir;
Among these one
In monster's guise
Was soon to swallow
The moon from the sky.

Wasn't Monster's home in Hrafnheim called the Iron Forest? And hadn't he said he descended from Fenrir? No, that couldn't be right. The poem had been written over a thousand years ago. It couldn't be a real prophecy. It couldn't have something to do with us.

There feeds he full
On the flesh of the dead,
And the home of the gods
He reddens with gore;
Dark grows the sun,
And in summer soon
Come mighty storms:
Would you know yet more?

Again, the last line was shouted by an unfamiliar female voice inside my head. It was almost as if the poem were screaming: *Do you get it?*

Images of war, fighting, and blood splatters pounded in my head.

"Is there something wrong, Anna?" I heard Mathias whisper as Maja continued mercilessly.

The sun turns black,
Earth sinks in the sea,
The hot stars down
From heaven are whirled;
Fierce grows the steam
And the life-feeding flame,

Till fire leaps high
About heaven itself.

A collective scream from a terrified crowd of people resounded in my head. An intense heat burned my face as an ice-cold wave pummeled me. My stomach dropped like I was in an elevator as it whizzed downward. I stood and put a hand over my mouth to keep from both screaming and throwing up. I ran to the door.

Fortunately, the bathroom at the end of Blue Hall was empty—and thank God I made it there in time. I vomited more violently than I ever had before, and my entire body writhed with cramps. Then I sat, dazed, on the floor in front of the toilet. A loud ringing in my ears hinted that I had exactly one second to lean against the wall before I passed out.

Then the darkness enveloped me.

An intense pressure told me a crowd of people were gathered around me. I heard Mr. Nielsen's voice and sensed his revulsion. But he managed to keep his voice professional: "Give her some air. I think she's coming to."

I kept my eyes squeezed shut as the pressure abated slightly, until only Mr. Nielsen was close by. Then I looked out.

"What's wrong?" He sounded authoritative and grown-up, but his vibe was panicked. I think he was considering everything from overdose to Ebola.

"I think I have the flu," I said timidly.

Behind him, Mathias piped up. "I threw up last night. It must be a virus."

"Me too," lied Luna. "All weekend. There's definitely something going around."

"I've been sick, too," came Little Mads's deep voice.

I turned my head and looked at him in surprise. He wasn't difficult to spot, despite being at the very back of the crowd.

552

He winked at me.

Thanks, I mouthed.

Mr. Nielsen relaxed noticeably. "So there is a good explanation."

"It's nothing serious," I said. *Aside from the fact that I've just seen the coming of doomsday, marking the end of everything.* "I think I just need to go home and rest."

"Yes, that's probably best," said Mr. Nielsen. He wanted to get me out of his care and away from his scope of responsibility. "Is there anyone who can help Anna get home?"

I protested, but a voice said: "I'll take her."

It was Varnar.

How embarrassing, for him to see me this way.

"Do you know each other?" Mr. Nielsen's voice was both relieved and suspicious.

I nodded. "Yeah, we're friends."

"Okay. The rest of you go back to class," said Mr. Nielsen over his shoulder. "That includes you two," he said to Luna and Mathias, who were trying to stick around.

Mathias was about to puff himself up, but Luna took him by the arm and pulled him back to the classroom.

"Call me," she said.

"Anna, I'll just make a note that you went home sick," said Mr. Nielsen before he, too, started walking away.

I got unsteadily to my feet as the crowd of people dispersed. Thankfully, I noticed that someone had flushed the toilet. I slumped over the sink and filled my mouth with water.

"What happened?" asked Varnar.

"I don't know. I actually have no idea." I turned toward him but wobbled.

He gripped my arm.

Normally, visions did not affect me to this extent, nor for this long. And I hadn't even had a vision. I couldn't see the future, after all. I inhaled deeply to clear my head.

"We were reading an old poem in Danish class. Suddenly I felt sick, like when I have a vision. But I don't think I was seeing the past."

"But you saw something?" His scent wrapped around me, we were standing so close.

"Yes. I saw war. A bloodbath. And I saw everything disappear."

"Everything?"

"Everything. The sun. The moon. The stars and the earth. Everything."

"Which poem were you reading?"

I wriggled out of his grasp and took a step back. "'Völuspá.' Do you know it?"

"I heard it when I was a kid. Before it was banned to believe in the gods. It's about Ragnarök. The apocalypse."

"I thought it was just a story," I said.

"You don't sound so sure?"

I sighed. "Serén has seen that doomsday will come if Ragnara succeeds in killing her or me. Maybe someone a thousand years ago saw the same thing. Maybe I was seeing the past. I mean, a vision of the future seen by someone in the past."

Varnar looked like he was struggling to follow. "You saw the future in the past?"

I put my hand over my eyes. "I don't know. I'm a little confused right now."

"But you're feeling better?"

"I feel fine. But I have to go home. Mr. Nielsen thinks I have the flu."

"So let's go."

"You don't have to come," I said.

"Yes, I do. Protector. Remember?" He pointed at himself with a smile that nearly made me faint again.

We walked back to Odinmont, and the crisp fall breeze did wonders for my head. Neither of us said anything, so nothing new there.

At home, Varnar parked me in front of the dining table while he rummaged around in the kitchen.

"You must be hungry," he said. "You threw everything up."

I closed my eyes. "You saw?"

"No, I heard it."

I laid my forehead on the table. "Ugh."

Varnar was by my side immediately. "Do you feel sick again?"

I looked up. "No. I'm embarrassed."

"Why?"

"Throwing up is gross."

"So?" He looked at me blankly.

"Hello? Girls don't want to be gross."

"I don't know very many girls, and the few I do know are like Aella. She has no problem with that kind of thing." He went back into the kitchen and started pulling out bread and cheese. He returned to the table with a plate of food and two cups of tea.

"Thanks."

We ate in silence.

After a while, he spoke. "You said something today."

"Oh no. What did I say now?"

He smiled slightly. "You said something that made me happy."

"What was it?"

"You told your teacher that I was your friend."

"Why did that make you happy?"

He looked down at his mug.

"I've been plagued by the thought that I could have killed you." He stopped and looked up. "What do you think of me?"

"I think you're very dedicated to whatever task you take on."

"But do you think I'm unquestioning? That I'll do whatever I'm ordered to do?"

I looked down. "No. You did break from Ragnara. And that Eskild guy. You did that because you don't like the things they do."

"Yes. And I agree with the things your mother does. I've also begun to see that you're important. I mean, that you have the ability to change all our fates. It's no longer just because of my promise to Thora that I would give my life for yours."

"Let's hope it doesn't come to that." I smiled, deflecting.

My attempt to lighten the mood did not work on Varnar. His face was still serious. "I want you to trust that I'm not disloyal. For you to know that I won't switch sides again. That's why I was happy to hear that you consider me your friend."

"Is that the only reason?" came a hoarse voice from the door.

I scooted my chair away from Varnar. Without realizing it, I had leaned in toward him.

Monster's voice grated. "Next time you should let me know when you're leaving somewhere."

"I'm sorry. I don't usually think about telling others where I am."

Monster's face was expressionless.

Varnar stood and swept out the door without another word.

I again laid my forehead against the table with my arms over my head.

Monster came over to me and breathed into my hair. "What's going on?"

"I had a horrible vision of a war and what looked like a natural disaster. I saw and felt a ton of people die. Then I threw up and fainted in front of a huge crowd of people, including Varnar," I mumbled into the table.

"That's not what I mean. What's going on between you and Varnar of the Bronze Forest?"

"Ugh," I whined. "Is it that obvious?"

"Wolves have mates, too."

I turned my face, so my cheek was now pressed to the cool wood. Monster rested his giant head on the table and looked at me.

"Do you have a mate?" I asked.

"Yes. I have pups, too. Except they aren't pups anymore. They're hirdswolves now. But of course, in my head they'll always be little puppies." His large eyes were warm.

I smiled weakly. "You're a dad."

"To two strong boys and a fearless girl. My mate's name is Boda. She's beautiful and strong and brave."

"What does she say about you being here?"

"She understands."

"But you miss her? And you must be scared that you'll never see her again."

Monster turned and walked over to the glass door. His sharp claws clicked against the tile floor. He looked out across the land.

"Boda takes care of the pack in her way. I do it in mine."

I sat up in my chair. Then I stood and joined him at the door, where I also looked down at the flat North Jutland landscape. Red and gold fall colors adorned the trees and bushes, the sky was gray with rain-heavy clouds, and the brown fields and charcoal-gray roads divided everything into a neat system. The large windmills turned in the wind, and here and there small whitewashed houses gleamed. Suddenly, I saw the landscape with different eyes. A transparent film, in which everything collapsed and flames licked across the fields, was overlaid atop the calm scene.

I laid a hand on Monster's back and, for a long while, we stared out through the glass door.

That afternoon, I decided it was time to speak with Od. Monster and I had to take the bus to Jagd, since my bike was still in Hakim's care.

I walked into The Boatman, which had now been reclaimed by the locals after the glamorous equinox ball a month earlier. Songs in the local dialect streamed into the bar over the speakers, and people engaged in lively conversations over beers, sodas, and endless cups of coffee. As always, it surprised me to see the place so full of life. I realized that even though the area seemed deserted at first glance, people were still around, and they were just as lively and tough as always.

There was no trace of Od, but the small, black-haired, tattooed woman was standing behind the bar. I walked up to her.

"I need to talk to Od."

She focused on me with eyes that were so dark, iris and pupil nearly blended into one. With some effort, I held her gaze.

Then she ducked behind the bar, where she stayed for quite a while. It sounded like she was digging around for something down there. I tried to look over the bar.

"Hello," I called.

Like a feather, she was upright again, and I jumped back.

"The beach," she said and pressed a large towel into my hands. Her septum ring swayed slightly when she spoke, and her voice was so deep that if I had heard it in isolation, I would have thought it belonged to a man. Then she grabbed a tray and walked out past me, banging her shoulder into mine along the way.

What the hell?!

Monster looked at me curiously when I came out with the towel in my arms.

"Why are you coming out here with a blanket?"

"I honestly don't know. But apparently, we have to go down to the beach." I approached the cliff and looked down the approximately 120-foot drop. "Who knows how we get down there."

Monster went to investigate and quickly came back. "There's a footpath, but it's steep."

We walked over to it, and my stomach dropped when I saw the narrow path leading down at an almost vertical angle. But there was no way around it, so we began our descent. The closer we got to the bottom, the more the sandpaper-like wind whipped at me. My long hair was blown around, and a strong smell of seaweed, salt, and fish enveloped me.

When we made it down, I saw the full breadth and length of the flat beach. It was white and smooth like a polished bone, and a mixture of wind and sand snaked its way along the ground like a smoke screen.

Monster stopped in the middle of the beach and let me continue alone up to the waterline.

I walked toward the sea, which today was bluish green and crashing and foaming wildly. Bewildered, I gazed upon it as it lay there, rough and beautiful. For some reason, I thought of Svidur. The wind yanked at the towel, and I fought to hold on to it.

After some time, a figure emerged from the water. A tall, muscular, solid person, who waded through the waves toward the shore.

Od stepped onto the beach, looking more than ever like a mythological figure. A very naked, very handsome, very frightening mythological figure. When he reached me, I handed him the towel, which he accepted almost ceremonially.

"Thanks." Then he bent over and kissed my forehead. His lips were ice-cold, and his wet hair dripped salt water onto me.

"You're welcome. I got it from your bartender."

Od let out a hoarse laugh. "Veronika. She's not mine."

"All righty." I looked out over the sea. "What were you doing out there?"

"I was visiting Hlen and Ran on Jan Mayen island."

"I have no clue who or what you're talking about."

Od looked down at his bare feet. "It would take a long time to explain. Time we don't have."

Okay, Mr. Mysterious.

"How did you hold your breath so long?"

He smiled mysteriously and started taking long strides toward the tall bluff on which The Boatman was perched. I jogged after him and followed the tracks he left in the moist sand.

"To what do I owe the pleasure?" he asked as we walked.

"Is this when I'm supposed to say the pleasure is all mine?"

"You can say what you want."

We had reached Monster, who nodded at Od.

"Prince Etunaz," Od said and did a half bow.

Monster was about to say something, but I jumped in.

"I'm sorry to interrupt your formalities, but I need to talk to you about your blood."

Od looked pointedly at me. "My blood?"

"What does it do?"

"You're talking about dangerous forces." He paused. "Humans gain strength from demigod blood, but few can tolerate it. Most go insane. You can only share our strength in very small doses. For example, in combination with the laekna Elias makes. Or through skin contact." He did not elaborate, which was fine by me. "And even then, our energy is intense."

I thought of the Savage, who had seemed simpleminded. Maybe that was the effect of the demiblood.

"Relax, I'm not planning on drinking your blood. I'm just trying to figure something out."

Od resumed his progress toward the cliff. "What are you trying to figure out?"

"What it is about your blood that's different."

"Even I don't know that."

"If your father is really a god, then you must have gotten it from him?"

"I'm sure I did. But I don't like that you're questioning whether he's a god."

"I couldn't care less what you like." I stopped.

The others also came to a halt. Monster looked at me despairingly, and Od tilted his head.

I backpedaled. "Sorry. I'm not questioning that he must be something special. You do glow, and you're strong, smart, and handsome and all that. I just don't know why that's the case."

Od's handsome face broke into a smile. "I must say, your outbursts are very refreshing. It's been decades since I met such opposition."

One-two-three-four-five, I counted mentally to keep from exploding again.

"Glad I could entertain you," I said with restraint.

"You know I don't mean it that way." Od's eyes were kind.

I tried again. "I get that your blood is potent, and that it can be dangerous. But in your body, it's mixed with human blood. What if you get the pure stuff? From your father, for example?"

"My father doesn't bleed."

"But Baldr did."

"How do you know that?"

"From the Prophecy of the Seeress. We read it in Danish class." I left out the fact that it was Elias who'd pointed out to me that Baldr was the bleeding god.

"Ah. 'Völuspá.' The ballad of the greatest seeress of all."

"Was she real, or is it just a story?"

"The völva Hejd? She was very real."

"Did you know her?"

Od squeezed his eyes shut, as if looking into the past. "Yes, many centuries ago."

"Did she really see all those horrible things in the poem?"

"Yes." A pained expression flew across Od's face. I suspected it did not have to do with the brutal prediction. More likely, he had known and cared about her. Time to change the subject. "So if a human consumes pure god's blood, what happens?"

Od shook his head as if to drag himself back to the present. "I would think the human would die. God's blood is as unstable as a radioactive atom."

561

"What if they don't die?"

"If the human doesn't die from the blood, they would probably acquire some of the god's powers."

"Do you know how Ragnara became immortal?" I asked quickly in an attempt to copy Hakim's trick of shocking the truth out of people.

Od, however, kept his expression neutral. "I don't know. But I've always thought a god plucked out her life force and hid it somewhere."

"Which god?"

Od's saltwater-soaked hair had dried a little in the strong wind and fell around his face in thick locks.

"I don't even dare guess at that," he said and resumed walking.

I ran after him. "But could it be the other way around? Could she have *consumed* something?"

We had reached the narrow path by the cliff. It twisted upward for what looked like forever. We began the ascent, and it was only thanks to all my workouts that I was able to talk and climb at the same time.

"It's not impossible," said Od over his shoulder. "But what god would give her divine abilities? In my experience, the gods are stingy with their powers. And they're jealous of those who acquire godlike strength."

"What if it's not a god? Could others have access to god's blood?" I panted.

Od didn't respond. He simply walked up in silence.

When we finally reached the top, both Monster and I were gasping for breath. Od appeared unfazed by both skinny-dipping in November and the steep climb. He finally answered my question.

"Yes. People other than the gods could get access to god's blood, but it would take considerable cunning and a lot of courage to get hold of it. And for what? I would advise you to forget about all this god's-blood stuff. Humans shouldn't mess with it." He turned to leave.

"What about the dead?" I shouted. "What happens if the dead mess with it?" I was still out of breath.

Suddenly, Od was right in front of me. His torso, which appeared to have been chiseled by a master sculptor, was at eye level. I leaned my neck back and looked straight into his blue-green eyes, which at that moment were the exact same color as the sea. As always, I had the sensation of being pushed down by a strong current. He smelled like salt water, air, and earth, and his unruly locks made him look less human than ever. A thin layer of sand coated his eyebrows and lashes, and there was a piece of seaweed stuck to his neck.

"This is not a warning, Anna. It's an order. Do not get involved with these forces."

Although the world was beginning to spin around me, I held his gaze.

"If I'm not mistaken, I have to believe in my heart that you are half-god, in order for these hierarchical orders to work. And I am not convinced. Not in the sense of becoming religious about it, anyway. So you can't order me to do or not to do anything."

Od activated his full strength, and the weight of his persuasive power pressed against me.

"There is only one god who wakes the dead, and he does not take kindly to others—especially humans—imitating him. I've said the same thing to Elias."

"Doctors revive people every single day. What's the difference?" I would have liked for my voice to sound more assertive, but right now I was just glad to be able to squeeze a word out at all.

"Arthur has been claimed," said Od, as if he had read my thoughts. "He was claimed by a goddess. That's the difference."

"I don't believe in those rules. Who made them?"

"The gods make the rules!" Od's voice had taken on its metallic timbre.

"If the human brain created the gods in the first place, then what?" I snapped back.

Od shrank back a little. The softness returned to his face, and he laid his hand against my cheek.

"Someone before you had the same thoughts. It will likely cost her her life, and she'll take one or more worlds with her when she falls." He pulled back his hand. "I care about you, Anna Stella. Be careful," were his last words before he turned his back to me and disappeared through the back entrance of The Boatman.

"We're not done talking," I yelled, but my voice was swallowed up by the wind. Cursing, I ran up and grabbed the doorknob, but it was locked. I pounded on it.

After a while, someone fumbled with the lock on the other side, and Elias stuck his head out.

"Anna," he said, surprised. "What are you doing here?"

"Where did Od go?"

Elias furrowed his brows. "Od? He's not here. He's in Norway."

"I just spoke to him. He came out of the sea, stark naked, and talked nonsense before disappearing in here."

Elias accepted this unquestioningly. "Did he say anything useful?"

I reflected. "If Od warns you that something is very dangerous and orders you to forget all about it, does that mean you're onto something?"

Elias's eyes sparkled. "That is exactly what it means."

Elias drove us home. In the car, I revealed what I saw fit.

"Od said that god's blood is just as unstable as a radioactive atom, and that it would probably kill a human to drink it straight."

Elias made a sharp turn, and there was a bump as Monster rolled off the back seat.

"Are you okay?" I asked over my shoulder.

Monster growled. "I think that was the Brewmaster's way of

thanking me for taking a taste of his arm," he said as he clambered back onto the seat.

Elias looked in the rearview mirror, and I think the two of them made eye contact for a second.

"Can't we try to work together?" I asked, tired. "I have enough to deal with keeping immortal queens, berserker ghosts, witches with repulsion spells, and the police at bay. I don't need to have you two fighting on top of that."

Elias clucked. "Does that mean you've finally understood that I'm on your side?"

I ignored him.

"But he said that there's god's blood someplace, and that someone other than the gods has access to it?"

"Od said someone could have access to it. I don't think he knows for sure."

"Did he say anything else?" asked Elias.

"A long series of warnings, but I get that kind of stuff all the time."

"I can imagine. What else?"

"That he's spoken to you about the possible consequences of meddling with these forces." I turned my head to look at him.

Elias kept his eyes aimed at the road. "Not too long ago—just over a hundred years—he warned me. That was when I was experimenting. A lot."

"What were you experimenting with?"

He looked at me with a crooked smile.

"Everything," he replied. "But especially the medical sciences. Let me know if you ever want to play doctor."

Behind me, Monster barked so loudly the whole car shook. "Have some respect, Brewmaster!"

Elias jerked the wheel in alarm, and the car swung into the other lane, which, thanks to the area's depopulation, was free of cars.

"Monster, you were sent to protect me. Not to get me killed in a car accident!" I shouted. "Elias doesn't mean anything by these comments. He can't help it. To be honest, I think it's an acute verbal tic he has."

"I have full control over myself." Elias sniffed.

"Like hell you do, you neurotic, sex-addicted, traumatized junkie." I struggled to control my pounding heart. "Are you guys done with this crap?"

"Sorry," groaned Monster.

Elias pressed his lips together, which I took as a yes.

I tried to concentrate and laid my hand on my forehead while exhaling. "I think someone—a god or some other being—is supplying Ragnara with god's blood, which makes her invincible. If we cut her off from the blood, she can be killed." I could not keep the emotions out of my voice as I sat there and plotted the murder of another person—fundamentalist dictator or not. "What's more," I added quickly, "we have a chance to revive Arthur if we get ahold of the blood. I just don't know exactly how."

"That's where I come in," said Elias, who seemed to have recovered.

"I hope your centuries of amoral experiments have paid off."

"They have. But we'll need magic, too," he said.

"For what?"

"Do you remember the defibrillator I showed you? The heart starter."

"Yeah."

"We'll have to jump-start Arthur, but electricity isn't strong enough. His body has been dead for too long." He glanced quickly at me to see if I could handle what he was saying.

I kept my face devoid of expression. "Do you think Luna can supply the necessary magic?"

"I don't know her, but based on what you've said, she is already very powerful."

566

"What exactly does she need to produce?"

"Magical energy."

"I've seen her make balls of energy with her hands."

Elias nodded thoughtfully. "Good. She needs to learn to channel the magic into a conductor, but it sounds like a good start if she can already make balls of energy."

"So we need god's blood, your heart starter, and for Luna to learn to channel her magic into a wire," I summarized. "That sounds doable."

Monster stuck his large head between us from the back seat. "What about how Odin doesn't want anyone but him to bring people back from the dead?"

"I couldn't care less what he wants," I said.

Elias inhaled. "I have an unresolved issue with the All-Father anyway. I would like to defy him on this very matter."

Monster smacked his lips. "What about the whole Freyja-has-claimed-Arthur thing?"

"I mean," I said with a shrug. "I have the same attitude toward her as toward Odin."

Elias braked hard and pulled the car over. I jerked forward against my seat belt, and the front half of Monster's body came between us.

"What?" yelled Elias. "Freyja claimed him?"

"Yes. He's supposed to go to that place. Fólkvangr. Od struck a deal with Freyja, so Arthur can be a ghost here in Midgard until I come of age."

"Od did that?" Elias spoke rapidly. "Where did you hear that?"

"Arthur told me."

"He'll say whatever it takes to get you to give up."

"That other ghost said it, too."

"What other ghost?"

"His name was Thorsten."

I thought Elias's jaw might hit his chest. "You talked to Thorsten?"

"Yes. Last night. He was here because it was All Hallows' Eve. Apparently, he gets a pass to come here that day every year. Did you know him, too?"

As I'd seen happen once in a while, Elias's age suddenly shone through. He looked impossibly tired and sad.

"I knew them all," he whispered. Then he sat up straight. "What did Thorsten want?"

"To tell Arthur he has until the end of the year. Then he has to go to Fólkvangr."

A stream of curses shot from Elias's mouth. Some of them sounded like they were from the olden days. Others were quite up-to-date. He smacked both palms against the wheel. "The end of the year. We don't have enough time. And we don't stand a chance against Freyja."

"Why not? She doesn't get to decide where Arthur's spirit goes."

"She certainly does not share that opinion."

"Doesn't she stand for peace, love, and harmony? Can't she be convinced to change her mind?"

"Not when it comes to Arthur."

"Why not?"

Elias shook his head. "I shouldn't tell you."

"You normally don't hesitate to blab to me about all kinds of crap."

"It's between your dad and the goddess. And maybe also your mom."

Oh . . .

"I don't want to know that kind of thing about him." I shuddered.

"Even when I try to do the right thing, I do the wrong thing," Elias muttered to himself. Then he sighed. "Freyja's always had a thing for your dad. And she can be a little territorial. When your mom came into the picture, she wasn't happy about it. Can we just leave it at that?"

"And Odin was in love with my mom, who didn't want him. How many gods and rulers did my parents manage to piss off before I was born?"

Elias raised an eyebrow. "A few."

"Wait a second. Ben said my mom was the only human to ever turn a god down."

Elias looked down. "Yes."

"So Arthur was what . . . Freyja's boyfriend?"

"Yeah, you could call it that," Elias said evasively.

I get the point.

I looked out at the road ahead of us, which had been enveloped in darkness. We were all deep in thought the rest of the way home.

When we pulled up in front of Odinmont, Monster jumped out first. I was also getting out but stopped.

"Elias, do you think I could talk to another clairvoyant? I need . . . uh . . . feedback about a vision."

I was certain Elias was thinking: *What can I get out of this?*

I had to disappoint him. "I can't offer anything in return."

"How about you owe me one?" He winked at me.

"You nasty . . ." I wanted to jump out of the car, but Elias stopped me. "Even though you act tough with me, I know *deep down* you really like me."

I ignored his inappropriate emphasis on *deep down*. "How much I like you varies. Oddly enough, it's based on how you behave."

"And when have I behaved the best?"

I reflected and tried to give him an honest answer. "The night Mathias got shot."

"You like 'em vulnerable. I'll remember that."

I raised my hands in an irritated gesture. "Why do you keep this up?"

"I told you. It's been decades since I felt this way about another person."

"You're only interested in me because I'm abnormal. A freak."

I expected a flippant reply, but Elias grew serious.

"Is that what you think? No." He searched for the words. "I'm prepared to stop . . . I would change my lifestyle for your sake."

"You mean set your lifestyle on pause for a while," I said. "I age. You don't."

"That actually wasn't what I had in mind." He reached out and took my hand.

First Hakim. Now Elias.

"Why are you all so sentimental?" I pulled my hand back.

"All? Do you have other suitors besides Varnar?"

"Varnar isn't my suitor. And no. There aren't any others."

Elias wasn't listening to what I said.

"I knew it wouldn't take long for others to notice your charms." He took a breath. "I'll ask you for a favor now. In return, I'll find a clairvoyant you can talk to."

"All right, then. What's the favor?"

"When you start a relationship with someone, tell me right away."

"I'm not going to be with anyone."

"It will happen. And when it does, I hope to be so close to you that I'm the first to know." He wiggled his eyebrows, clearly back in the role of Don Juan. Then he got serious again. "Do you promise to tell me?"

I shook my head. "Okay, okay. If it means that much to you."

At school on Friday, Varnar pulled me aside. "You wanted to talk to Preben."

"Yeah."

"He's in the office now." Varnar followed me to the end of Brown Hall, where a staircase led to the basement.

When we reached the foot of the stairs, I saw what a large network of corridors and rooms there was under the school. The system appeared to be twice the size of the building aboveground.

The ceiling was so low that if I stood on my tiptoes, I could touch the exposed pipes. The floor was made of concrete, and fluorescent tubes cast everything in an unreal light. If I hadn't been used to hanging around in burial chambers and dilapidated manors, I would have thought it was creepy. A strange vibe hung over the halls, as if dramatic events had once taken place here, but they were either removed or diminished with time.

It took several minutes to get to Preben's office.

Varnar cleared his throat in the doorway. "Anna here would like to talk to you."

Preben looked up from his place at the worn but tidy desk and nodded.

Varnar nodded back, and I got a clear sense that the two men normally communicated as nonverbally as possible, which suited them both just fine. Varnar disappeared through the door, and I was alone with Preben.

"Come on in," he said. I could hear that he was fighting not to speak in dialect.

I pulled a beat-up office chair to the desk, and he folded his large, calloused hands in front of him. His hair was thick and nearly white, his glasses an older model, but his eyes were alert and quick. A badass, humorous vibe mixed with melancholy flowed from him.

I picked at the visible foam rubber on the seat of my chair.

He leaned back as if to indicate that he had plenty of time.

"Your son, Thorsten, knew my parents," I began.

The pain that emanated from Preben was so deep I had to make an effort not to scoot my chair back.

"Who are your parents?"

"Thora and Arthur Sakarias."

Preben widened his eyes but said nothing.

I continued without knowing how to convey my message. "Do you know what they were up to back then? Your son and my parents."

Preben gave me an appraising look. "I have a feeling."

"If I say I have a message for you, can you figure out who it's from?"

He gave me a nearly imperceptible nod.

"He's doing well," I said. "It's very beautiful and peaceful where he is."

Preben opened his mouth a little, but no sound came out.

"He asked me to tell you."

"Thank you," Preben said with slightly furrowed brows.

I stood, exhaled, and left the office.

Varnar was waiting for me down the hall. I walked past him, and he fell in at my side without saying anything.

Back in Brown Hall, I took a few gulps of air, which was significantly fresher than down in the corridors under the school. Varnar looked like he wanted to say something but didn't manage it before someone shouted from the other end of the hall.

Luna came storming up to us. Her blue hair and neon-yellow jumpsuit clashed violently with the brown walls and carpeting.

"What's wrong?" Alarm boiled in my stomach.

"You've been super unfair," Luna said Varnar.

He took a step back in surprise.

"What are you talking about?" I asked. "What did he do?"

"The shit he gave me about the love soup."

"Oh no," I moaned. "I thought we had repressed that whole thing."

"He owes you an apology, too," Luna huffed.

"Me?" I refused to look at him. "Luna, tell me what's going on."

"Yesterday I had a session with my parents, where they taught me about the different kinds of magic, including love magic."

I could feel my cheeks flush. "What about it?"

"Love magic only works under very specific circumstances."

"Which are?"

Luna's jaw jutted out angrily, and she pointed a finger at Varnar.

"Magic is totally normal in Hrafnheim, so you knew full well that my magic only worked because you were already in love with Anna."

What? I crossed my arms and turned slowly toward Varnar.

He stared down at the floor. His dark hair flopped forward and hid his face, so I couldn't read it. He didn't meet my gaze. He turned around and took off running down Brown Hall.

It was raining when I ran home from school with Monster at my side.

In front of my house, a figure stood leaning against the white-washed wall with its head bowed.

My heart was pounding hard as I shifted from running to walking and covered the remaining distance with cautious steps.

Monster remained standing in the middle of the drive.

Varnar's clothes and hair were wet with rainwater. When I came closer, he looked up. The eyes that met mine burned with a pain I didn't understand.

I couldn't say a word when I stood in front of him. He furrowed his brows and appeared to be undergoing an inner battle.

"I'm responsible," he said. "You are without blame."

"Why do you say that?"

He continued as if he hadn't heard me. "I have inappropriate feelings for you."

I reached out for him, but he stepped away.

"I have failed my mission and brought dishonor on you and myself." He took a few more steps back. "You will never see me again."

Then he turned and ran toward the woods.

His back grew smaller and smaller.

I cursed loudly and kicked at the gravel.

And—for the first time ever—I ran after him.

PART V

THE SKY OF DREAMS

The sky of dreams with driving clouds
red were they as dripping blood
Wounded was I and forth I sought
our haven and your care
Ravaged was I by wounds more numerous
than you had chance to heal
The dread dream vision
of coming death its silent speech foretells

The Saga of Gunnlaug Serpent-Tongue
13th century

CHAPTER 35

It may well be true that Varnar is a better fighter than me. He is much stronger and moves like a dancer. Add to that his almost acrobatic abilities, not to mention his precision, which would make any dart player or surgeon jealous. It is highly plausible that he excels in all these areas.

But I can run faster than he can.

I closed in quickly and caught up to him halfway across the field. It was now pouring rain, and with every stride, I sank farther into the muddy ground. Without thinking, I stuck out my foot and tripped him.

He fell with an ungraceful stumble very uncharacteristic of him.

Because I hadn't planned on tripping him and was also by no means thinking clearly, my foot slid in between his legs, and I, too, tumbled onto the wet ground.

He rolled around, and we ended up lying tangled together.

"How dare you run away?" I shouted.

He looked at me, uncomprehending. "I promised to stay away from you. I'll ask Thora to replace me with a different, more suitable bodyguard as soon as I can."

"What if I don't want you to be replaced?"

Varnar's eyes darted away. "If I remained your protector, I obviously wouldn't be able to stay away from you."

"I don't want you to stay away." I pounded a fist against his chest.

He made a sound, and I wasn't sure whether it was my strike or my words he was reacting to. Then he furrowed his brows in the expression I had come to know so well.

"Why not?" His voice was controlled.

"You idiot. Why do you think?"

"It's not possible. Not for me. No one can . . ." His voice cracked.

"No one can what?"

He closed his eyes as the rain streamed down his face.

"Love me," he whispered.

I had no idea what to say. I already found myself dumbstruck whenever I was with Varnar, but this was so unexpected I just lay there in the rain and mud and stared at him.

"I can," I said finally. "I already do."

With eyes closed, he lifted his hand and took mine, which was still resting on his chest. He laced our muddied fingers together.

"I've done things . . . If you knew what I've done, it would be impossible for you."

"I don't care what you've done."

"*I* care. My penance is a promise to never be with a woman."

I laughed, but it sounded more like a desperate sob. "Well, that particular ship has sailed."

He opened his eyes and looked directly into mine. "Don't you get it? I broke my oath."

"I don't believe in unbreakable oaths. And I certainly don't believe in promises of self-torment."

"Then what do you believe in?"

I reflected intently. I had asked others about this, but never myself. I squeezed Varnar's hand so hard it must have hurt, but he didn't move it.

"I believe in the now," I said. "Not the past or the future or fate or condemnation. I believe in right now."

"Why?"

"Because maybe this moment with you is the only one I'll get."

The words flew out so quickly I couldn't stop them. I could hear their despairing tone.

Varnar looked at me for a long time without saying anything. Then he moved his muddy hand to the back of my neck, and a combination of dirt and water scratched my skin when, with an abrupt motion, he pulled me to him. He pressed my body against his, and I clutched his wet shirt as his scent blended with the smell of rain, spruce, and soil. A force pulsed up through the ground and into us. I felt that everything was dissolving, and that we were part of a greater whole in which our small, individual lives meant little.

Varnar's warm breath tickled my neck. "You're shaking. Are you cold?"

"I don't know." I was honestly having trouble remembering my own name.

He got to his feet and helped me up. Then he ran into the woods with my hand in his. We flew through the tree trunks and across the moss-covered forest floor.

Then we reached the old, dilapidated manor, where Aella was fortunately nowhere to be seen.

In the living room, he turned to face me and suddenly looked uncertain. When I saw his muddy, soaking-wet appearance, I laughed.

I must have looked about the same because he flashed me one of his rare smiles, and I flung my arms around him.

At first, he stiffened, but then he slowly ran his fingers through my hair. Then he tentatively brought his mouth to mine and waited, taking ragged breaths. Just when I couldn't stand it any longer, he kissed me. There was a desperation in his kiss, which I returned after many months of longing.

We ended up on the floor on a bed of blankets, where he carefully pulled off my wet shirt before kissing me again.

He was more restrained than he had been the night he was under the influence of love magic.

Several times, he stopped and asked if we should keep going, and to make sure I was okay. This was an attentive side of him I hadn't seen before.

Afterward, we lay close together. The back of his hand slowly traced down my side before ending on my hip.

My eyes were closed, and I absentmindedly ran my fingers through his thick hair.

"Ahen Drualus," he whispered.

"What?" I opened my eyes.

"The first time I heard your name, I thought you were called Ahen. It reminds me of a song I haven't heard since I was a kid. Ahen Drualus."

"What does it mean?"

"The druids' herb. In this world, you call it mistletoe." He quietly sang a couple bars in the language I had also heard Aella speak. He translated it for me.

She who wanders alone
But is lovely as two
The druids' herb she bears in her heart
And to her
Your heart must you lose

He hesitated. "When I've allowed myself to think of you in the past few months, I've called you Ahen Drualus."

"Where does the song come from?"

"I don't know where the ballad comes from originally, but the men sang it to the women at midsummer. It's a very old tradition among my people. Or it *was*."

I moved my fingers to the scars on his shoulder. Some of them were rough and clumsily done, others were fine and even. One of them resembled a strange M, and one at the bottom still had a little scab, as if it had been made recently.

He watched me. "I didn't think I could fall in love. Or that anyone could fall in love with me. And even if it happened, I was sure I would be able to resist."

"You must have a really distorted self-image." I smiled.

His lips pulled upward, too. "I was starved, tormented, and exhausted for days to test my willpower. I withstood everything. But it only took you a moment to overpower me."

"The way I remember it, it took me months."

"I didn't know you reciprocated my feelings."

"That makes one of you in the entirety of the greater Ravensted area. Even my dog noticed it."

Again, his hand followed the curve along my side from my hip to my chest. Then he carefully ran his finger down the long scar on my sternum.

"I found out how I got that," I said. "Ragnara did it the night I was born."

Varnar's finger stopped. "She did that to a newborn?" His eyebrows drew together. "It was all lies. Everything she said about protecting the weak and the innocent." He studied the scar. "This is a fatal wound. How did you survive?"

"It's a mystery. I healed in her hands."

"She's not a healer." Varnar's forehead crinkled. "Someone else must have stepped in."

"Who would have done that? My mom was badly injured—although she was also healed by Ragnara's touch. Eskild was apparently there, too, but he probably wouldn't have helped me, even if he could."

When I mentioned Eskild, Varnar abruptly turned his head and looked up at the ceiling.

"What is it about this Eskild guy? I can sense that he's significant to you."

Varnar was silent for a moment. "My people have lived in the Bronze Forest for generations. We are peaceful," he said.

I raised an eyebrow. "Aren't you living evidence to the contrary?"

"I chose the warrior life. I wasn't born into it."

"Why did you choose it?"

He lay on his back.

"Necessity." He kept his hand on my chest. "And to atone."

"For what?"

"A mistake." He retracted his hand. "I should have been home when the berserkers came. My parents needed me, but I wasn't there."

"The berserkers?"

"They plundered our settlement. Killed all the adults. Captured the children so they could be sold as slaves."

Small, cold tingles spread across my body as Varnar's memories flowed into me. I pretty much never saw concrete images from him, but I heard screams and could smell the smoke. Worst of all, I felt his panic. A child's panic.

"Where were you?"

"In the trees. That's how it always was. I forgot everything else when I was in the woods."

"What happened?" I asked even though I had a pretty clear idea.

"The forest told me that there was unrest at our settlement. When I got there, everything was in chaos. I climbed up a tall tree and saw it. The berserkers were plundering and rampaging. The children had been gathered together in a group between the piles of their dead parents."

I let the few images I got from him seep into my head, even though I would have much preferred to shut them out. I caught a glimpse of Aella as a little girl. She cried and clung to a slightly older boy. On closer inspection, I saw that it was Geiri. The one who had tried to kill me with the poisoned cookies. The one Monster had eaten.

Oh, shit!

Varnar said nothing.

I didn't want to ask, but I did anyway. "Your parents?"

"I saw my father right away. He was lying with an axe in his hand. He wasn't a warrior, and it was made for chopping wood. But he must have tried to fight." Varnar paused. "My mother was alive. But not for long."

I wanted so badly to put my arms around him. To hold him close to me. But I got the sense that he wouldn't be able to continue his story if I did.

He turned his head and looked at me, and his face had the hardness that sometimes came over it. "I should have been there. I failed."

"How old were you?"

"Eleven."

"What in the world could an eleven-year-old do against a group of berserkers?"

"Distract them so my parents could have fled."

"But then you would have been killed."

His face showed that he would have gladly given his life to save theirs.

"I think," I said cautiously, "that your mom and dad died knowing you were in the forest. Parents can withstand a lot if they know their children are safe."

Again, Varnar looked at me as if what I said was completely irrelevant.

I changed the subject. "How did the children get away?"

Varnar rolled over onto his side, and I tentatively laid my hand on his. Distractedly, he interlaced his fingers with mine.

"Eskild Black-Eye came with the Varangian Guard. They didn't spare any of the berserkers. Afterward, he took us to the castle in Sént, where we were all given a home. Ragnara told us how she had freed the slaves and forbidden the deities that served to control the people. Now her goal was to protect the defenseless."

Aha.

"So you devoted yourself to the Varangian Guard and became the best protector in Hrafnheim."

"The Varangian Guard's purpose is to protect the defenseless."

"Which is why it was hard for you to break with Eskild."

"Eskild is the most talented warrior, strategist, and commander in the worlds. I still think that." His gaze turned gloomy. "But he has lost his honor. I was convinced that Ragnara's reign was about fighting for the weak. But I found out," Varnar's finger once again found my scar and traced it, "that I was mistaken."

"But that's not your fault."

"I got so close to both of them. I could have killed them."

"Not Ragnara." I raised myself up on my elbow. "Unless you know where she keeps the god's blood."

Varnar widened his eyes. "What are you talking about?"

Who knows how much Varnar knows. And how much I should tell him.

"You do know she's immortal, right?"

He nodded slowly. "But we still didn't take any chances. She thinks there is a flaw in her immortality. Someone or something can kill her. I have seen men die to protect her."

I sniffed. "What a waste of life."

Varnar didn't comment. "What did you say about god's blood?"

I decided that I could use an ally. "There's a theory that Ragnara's immortality is due to her regularly consuming god's blood. It makes her invulnerable."

"Ragnara hates the gods."

"Maybe so. But even if you hate someone, they can still be useful to you. It's not *my* theory, anyway."

Varnar narrowed his eyes. "Then whose theory is it?"

I looked into the fireplace. "I don't want to say."

"Don't you trust me?"

I looked back at him. "No. Not fully. You yourself warned me against that."

He smiled contentedly. "I taught you well."

"You taught me to be a suspicious, murderous machine." I laughed.

He put his arms around me.

"To be a survivor," he corrected. "Even though you've been one all along. I'm just teaching you to survive in a slightly more organized fashion."

"Maybe," I whispered into his shoulder, "right now we should just focus on living."

I spent that night at Kraghede Manor. I slept in Varnar's arms. That night, I was the one who fell asleep first, and he was staring expectantly at me when I opened my eyes, as if he had been looking forward to me waking up. I quickly found out why.

A little later in the morning, I met Aella in the kitchen. She fought to keep her face in a nonchalant expression but ended up giving me a giant hug.

"He's like a brother to me," she whispered. "He hasn't been happy since we were kids. If you can get him to allow himself just a bit of happiness, I will be eternally grateful."

I stood completely stiff as she hugged me, and didn't know how to respond.

Varnar walked me home, where Monster was waiting. He nodded at Varnar, and I thought I saw acceptance in his eyes.

Varnar bowed his head toward him in greeting. Then he gave me a look that made my stomach somersault before he ran back toward the forest.

I watched him and sighed.

"Finally," said Monster. "It took you guys long enough."

"Are you okay with it? I was scared you would be overprotective and big-brother-like."

"I want you to be happy. And I much prefer Varnar of the Bronze Forest to both the Brewmaster and the policeman."

"What did Hakim ever do to you?"

"He said I was weird," Monster said sharply.

"You *are* weird. You're a gigantic talking wolf that eats people."

"But he doesn't know that."

"Varnar killed your brother. Isn't that worse?"

"He was just doing his job."

I unlocked the door and we walked in.

"Have you talked about the future?"

"Yes. I told him about my vision of the end of the world."

Monster rolled his eyes. "*Your* future."

"Oh. No. I don't know how much future there is left."

"You never know," said Monster.

Later, as I stood in the kitchen with my wet hair in a towel turban, I heard a car door slam. Someone walked across the gravel, after which the car door slammed again, and a motor rumbled down the drive. I stood on my tiptoes and looked out the window at my driveway, which was now devoid of both people and cars. Tentatively, I walked outside.

My bike was leaning against the wall in pristine condition. The seat had been replaced, and the wheels were good as new. My fingers stroked the frame, and I got a glimpse of Hakim repairing it. He was smiling to himself as he tightened a nut.

Hmm.

Monster stood next to me and sniffed the bike.

"Do you think he expects me to tell him all my secrets just because he fixed my bike?"

Monster snorted. "I think he expects more than that."

I shook my head. "He doesn't think that way."

"In some areas you really aren't very bright," said Monster before lumbering back inside.

I followed him and started gathering my things so we could go.

As I stood with my jacket on and my keys in my hand, my phone rang. I fished it out of my bag as I wrapped Luna's yellow knit scarf around my neck with one hand and tried to button my denim jacket with the other.

"Hello," I said. My voice was strained from clamping the phone between my ear and shoulder.

Elias laughed on the other end. "What are you up to?"

I dropped my keys and cursed. "Too many things at once."

"Isn't that your style?" he asked. "I don't know anyone else who plots to oust rulers, steal the gods' blood, and avoid certain death while also working and getting an education."

"That's not what I meant. I'm just trying to talk on the phone and get dressed at the same time."

"Am I lucky enough to catch you while you're undressed?"

"Elias. What do you want?"

"I have a seeress for you."

"When can I talk to her?"

"Tomorrow."

"That's fine." I knelt and picked up my keys. "Where does she live?"

"Do you know Sømosen?"

"Yes. But no one lives there. It's a bog."

"Haven't you grasped that the world is so much more colorful than most people know?"

"Okay. A clairvoyant lives in a creepy bog." I led Monster out and closed the door. "And, obviously, I have to go meet her. How exactly do I get there by bike?"

"I'll escort you, of course. I can be there at nine."

"See you then." I had unlocked my bike while we talked and wanted to wrap things up, but then I thought of something. "Uh, Elias."

"Yes."

"You made me promise to tell you if something happened between me and . . . someone."

Elias's voice was suddenly ice-cold. "Who?"

"Varnar."

Some time passed before Elias replied. "Then I guess congratulations are in order."

"Don't be like that. You were the one who asked me to tell you."

"And I predicted that it would happen. I knew someone would claim you soon."

"He didn't claim me. I actually chased after him."

"And to the best of my knowledge, he has no clue how lucky he is."

The call was disconnected.

I stood for a moment and looked at my phone. Then I pushed away the strange knot in my stomach and biked toward Ravensted.

In the kitchen at Frank's, my head was in the clouds. At one point, Milas had apparently called my name several times.

"Sorry. What did you say?" I looked at him distractedly.

He laughed.

"Why are you laughing?"

"Envy," he said. "What I wouldn't give to be seventeen and in love for the first time again."

My cheeks grew hot.

Luna joined us in the kitchen with a full tray in her arms.

"Wow." She stared at me.

"Wow, what?"

"I can't see auras, but there's a gold frame around you. What happened?"

Milas looked at her in wonder.

I grabbed her arm and pulled her into the back alley. "Shhhh. Milas doesn't know that I can see auras."

She held a slim hand in front of her mouth. "Oh right. But seriously, what happened?"

As soberly as I could, I recounted the events. Though I couldn't stop breaking into a goofy grin.

Luna jumped up and down. "I knew he was in love with you. Why did it take him so long to admit it?"

"He swore an oath not to be with anyone."

"Will you see each other again?"

"I guess so. We're still training."

"But see each other as boyfriend and girlfriend?"

"I don't think he even knows those words."

"But you have to talk about what's going to happen. He comes from a totally different world. How will you make it work?"

"Honestly, I'll just be happy if I don't kick the bucket in the next few months. We can handle the rest once I know if I'm even going to make it."

Luna's eyes reflected the stark light overhead. "Stop saying that. I can't stand it."

"But it's true."

"Yeah, but you don't have to talk about it all the time."

I was going to brush her off but remembered how I had reacted when Monster made the insane suggestion of sacrificing himself. Maybe that was just part of having friends: They would be sad if you disappeared.

"We'd better go in. A ton of people have come in in the past half hour." Luna wiped her eyes and placed her hand on the door handle. Then she stopped, turned toward me, and flung her arms around me. "I'm so happy for you."

I let her hug me and even returned her embrace a tiny bit.

I resumed my work but was interrupted an hour later when Luna came into the kitchen again. She had flushed red blotches on her cheeks. "Can I convince you to come out and help a little? I just can't keep up."

"You know what happens to me when there's so many people."

"Can't you take a little klinte?" she whispered. A cloud of persuasion sailed forth from her, and I didn't manage to duck. "Oh, sorry."

She fanned the air as if to disperse a bad smell, but it was too late. I tried to give her a dour look, but my sunny mood made it totally impossible.

"Okay, then." I smiled.

Luna flashed her pearly whites in thanks as I discreetly dug the small ampoule out of my pocket and dabbed a drop onto my lip.

The bar was packed with people in a festive mood. There had apparently been a handball match at Ravensted Arena, which had ended in a home team victory, so people were ecstatic.

Suddenly, someone in the crowd placed a warm hand on my upper arm.

I jumped, unable to identify the hand's owner due to the klinte.

It was Hakim who stepped out in front of me. He had on jeans and a royal-blue sweater, which suited him quite a bit better than the uniform.

"Oh, it's you," I said.

"I just wanted to say hi."

"Oh, hi." I was about to keep walking but stopped. "Thank you for fixing my bike. Why did you just drop it off? You would have been welcome to come in."

Hakim flashed me a smile that caught the attention of several female bar patrons.

"You often emphasize your desire to be left in peace, so I didn't want to disturb you. It's better if you come to me when you want my company."

"Uh, okay," I said. "Are you here to investigate something? Do you have a hunch again?"

"I'm having a night out with some friends." He pointed at a group of guys standing a short distance away, stealing glances in our direction.

"A night out?"

"You don't have to sound so surprised." He smiled again and was about to say something else, but then we heard shouting from the bar. He turned his head in the direction of the shouts. The voices rang out again, and I recognized one of them as Frank's.

We ran toward the noise and saw Christian Mikkelsen standing in an aggressive stance in front of Frank, who was equally riled up.

"You're going to pay for every cent of the repairs," yelled Frank.

"You brought it on yourself. I told you to fire her," Christian yelled back.

Hakim stood with all his muscles tensed, ready to jump in, but as of yet, no one had raised a hand against another.

Frank took a step forward, and immediately Christian lunged at him without warning. He hit Frank in the jaw. Frank wobbled but threw a punch back at Christian. It hit him in the solar plexus, making him double over.

Hakim threw himself between them.

Frank raised his hands. "It was self-defense."

Christian was already on his way out but managed to send me an evil look.

"I'll come after you later," he hissed before dashing between the bar patrons.

Hakim squeezed through the crowd after him.

I went up to Frank. "Are you okay?"

He wiggled his jaw back and forth. "I've been through worse."

Then he clapped me on the shoulder and returned to his place behind the bar.

I followed him. "Why was he here?"

Frank said nothing.

"Frank?"

"He was looking for you," he said with an uneasy expression. "I wanted to get him out before you found out."

Hakim came back.

"He ran away," he growled. "Do you want to report the attack?" he asked Frank.

This was my cue. I backed, as discreetly as I could, toward the kitchen.

Milas hadn't been aware of the drama, and I felt no need to enlighten him.

"The whole bar is talking about it," said Luna. "You should watch out. People say he's ruthless."

"Monster will come when it's time for me to go home. Maybe Varnar, too." My stomach flopped a little at the mere thought. "Christian can't get anywhere near me."

"No, it sounds like you're pretty well covered." She wiggled her eyebrows.

I laughed and turned to the cutting board while she headed back to the bar. At some point, I dumped a pile of half-eaten fries into the trash can and noticed that it was nearly full. Milas was in the middle of making an advanced dessert, so I pulled the bag out of the holder and slipped out the back door. In the alley, I quickly threw the bag into the dumpster and ran back to the door.

The whole operation took less than twenty seconds.

When I placed my hand on the handle, someone stood close behind me. In a flash, this *someone* reached over my head and put a cord around my neck.

And then he pulled.

 CHAPTER 36

You would expect me to make a strangled noise, but I didn't. I didn't have enough air for so much as a single little wheeze. My airways were completely blocked, and I knew I had thirty seconds tops before I passed out from lack of oxygen. After that, I would be dead in about two and a half minutes. I had no voice with which to call for Arthur or Mathias, and even if Monster sensed I was in danger, it would surely take him too long to get to me.

So I worked quickly.

Varnar and I had practiced standing with him behind me, and even though I was well on my way to dying of strangulation, my arms were still free. A strange context in which to think that things could be worse.

I folded my hands in a kind of double fist, slammed them backward at an angle, and hit my attacker on the shoulder. He made a muffled sound and loosened his grip just slightly on one side before pulling again. In that split second, I managed to slide a pinkie finger in between the cord and my neck. I also managed to gulp a bit of air, which bought me another few seconds. At the same time, I kicked backward.

Just then, he raised one leg, and I missed.

Varnar had taught me that an opponent attacking from behind in close combat will expect me to kick backward, and that he would react by raising his leg. I timed it so when he raised his leg, I set my kicking foot on the ground in a straddling position, and using my body as leverage, I leaned forward and pulled on the cord with my pinkie finger. It made a little *pop* as it snapped under our weight. A sharp pain shot up my arm, but because the attacker was a bit off-balance on that one leg, I had room to fling my head backward. I think I hit his jaw.

He cursed, and something about his voice was familiar. If I hadn't taken klinte a few hours earlier, I might have recognized his aura, but as it was, I had no idea who he was. But he let go. *He let go!*

I sucked in air with a gurgling sound and spun around. Then I attacked, instinctively firing off all the punches and kicks Varnar had taught me.

"Help," I wheezed. "Help me."

The man did not strike me again, but expertly parried my blows, and I didn't manage to hit anything but his arms and legs. His head was shrouded in a hood resembling the one the murderer wore in my recurring vision.

Hakim came around the corner and caught a glimpse of me in action.

"Stop. Police," he bellowed and reached for him.

The man avoided him deftly. He took a couple of steps backward, and it was almost as if he'd dissolved into the shadows. Hakim stormed after him into the darkness.

"This is the police," he yelled again and ran along the alley. "Where the hell did he go?"

I didn't have the breath to reply.

Monster came galloping, his hackles raised. Varnar was right on his heels.

"Glad you could make it," I choked out. I may have sounded just a little sarcastic.

"Who was it?" asked Varnar.

I shook my head, still laboring to breathe, and leaned against the wall. But I let out a gasp of pain when my fingers touched the wall.

"Ow, damn it," I howled.

Varnar came to my side immediately. "Did he have a weapon? Are you hurt?"

In response to his question, I raised my hand to him. My pinkie finger stuck out at a strange angle.

"I'll survive," I said dryly.

He smiled, and even though I couldn't sense his aura because of the klinte, I could almost feel his relief wash over me.

Just then, Frank stuck his head out the back door.

"What's all the commotion?" When he saw us standing in the alley, his forehead creased. "What are you doing out here?"

"Anna was attacked," said Hakim.

"Was it Christian?" asked Frank.

"No idea. He had his hood pulled up, and I couldn't feel . . ." I stopped myself.

"You couldn't feel what?" Hakim asked sharply.

"Nothing." I carefully supported the wrist of my bad hand with my good one. "Frank, I can't work anymore tonight. My hand is kind of busted."

"I'll drive you to the emergency room," said Hakim. "And afterward, we'll report the attack."

"Who would we report? I couldn't see him, and I don't want to go to the hospital."

"The attack *needs* to be reported. And you need to go to the hospital. That hand won't heal right without a doctor," said Hakim.

Varnar examined my finger with a professional look on his face. "The bone is broken and displaced," he said. "It just needs to be set in place and put in a splint. I can do that."

"Are you completely out of your mind?" asked Hakim. "You can't play amateur surgeon on Anna's hand."

Varnar looked at him uncomprehendingly.

"I'll drive her to the emergency room," said Frank. "And then I can drop her off at the station afterward."

"I would prefer it if Varnar takes care of my finger," I said. "We just need to find some kind of stick or something else he can use as a splint."

Both Frank and Hakim stared at me, shaken.

"That is absolutely out of the question," said Hakim. "It's fine with me if your boss drives you to the hospital. That way I can get started on the paperwork."

We stood for a moment—our strange little flock—before we pulled ourselves together.

Frank and I walked toward his van, which was parked on Algade. Hakim headed toward the station, and Varnar and Monster remained standing there.

When we got there, Frank fumbled with the keys, his forehead deeply furrowed. He got in and leaned over the passenger seat to open my door for me. Before he was able to, someone next to me grabbed the handle. It was Varnar, who had approached in complete silence.

"I'm coming with you," he said.

"Thanks," I whispered.

We climbed into the front seat.

Frank glanced at Varnar but didn't say anything. Then he started the car and drove us to Hjørring Hospital.

I was quickly given X-rays, which revealed that the bone in my finger—exactly as Varnar had diagnosed—was broken and displaced. Then I was sent back to the waiting room, where Varnar and I sat in the blue chairs while Frank got coffee.

I studied a mysterious three-dimensional artwork on the wall as I gratefully felt the effect of the pain pills a harried nurse had given me. The effect of the klinte was also starting to fade, and I felt a deep peace emanating from Varnar.

"You aren't mad at me?" I asked. "I did go into the back alley alone."

596

Varnar didn't turn his head, but kept his eyes on Frank, who was bent over a table of thermoses and plastic cups.

"No," he said. "I'm not mad at you."

"And you aren't feeling guilt-stricken that you weren't there to help me?" He clearly had issues with not being there when people needed him.

Now he looked at me. "I didn't need to be there. You handled it yourself. I taught you to defeat a trained fighter in hand-to-hand combat."

A cold jab prickled in my stomach. "So your work here is done?"

"No. Now I need to teach you to defeat two of them."

Frank joined us and handed me a cup of steaming coffee. He had a purplish-blue bruise where Christian had hit him.

"Don't you want to get that checked out?"

Frank wiggled his jaw. "Nah. I deserve to be reminded of my carelessness."

I had no idea what to say, so we waited in silence until a doctor called me in.

Frank stayed outside, but Varnar came with me. Even though the young, freckled doctor didn't appear to pose a threat, he had no intention of letting me be alone with him.

While the doctor worked on my hand, Varnar followed along. A couple of times he even asked intelligent questions. I got the sense he was asking out of professional interest. A warrior evidently needed to know a little of everything. He didn't so much as flinch when the doctor and nurse set the bone, even though I cried out in pain.

When we came out of the small hospital room, Frank looked uneasily at my bandaged hand.

"Was that you screaming?"

I nodded resignedly. "They set the bone."

Frank's gaze shifted to Varnar. "Do you still think you should have done it?"

His sarcasm flew right over Varnar's head. "The doctor was skilled. I couldn't have done it better myself. I learned a lot from watching him lift the bone back into place without damaging the skin. A broken bone can be very sharp."

Frank shuddered.

"I've heard enough." He took the medical chart from my good hand and quickly flipped through it. "The fracture occurred when the patient had a beer keg fall on her hand at work."

He looked at me angrily.

I shrugged.

"You can't say that."

"Hakim will be mad at me, but he's always mad at me."

"I'll get a workplace safety violation."

"I hadn't thought about that."

Frank stomped over to the desk, where he spoke loudly and gestured wildly with his arms.

The nurse stretched her neck and stared at me, so I turned my back to her.

"Anna, come over here," came Frank's voice through the waiting room.

I grudgingly walked over to him and the curious woman dressed in white.

"Tell them what happened," he said firmly.

I sighed. "It wasn't a keg. A man attacked me."

The nurse widened her eyes. "Why didn't you say so?"

I gave her an ambivalent look.

Frank sighed. "I don't want any problems. Just tell them the truth so it can go in your chart, and we can go home."

"I was attacked in the back alley at my work. I went out there alone with a bag of trash, without my boss's knowledge and completely against his wishes. He always takes extremely good care of his employees, and he would never put me in a situation that was in any way dangerous to me." I gave Frank a cheeky smile. "Happy?"

He raised his hands in frustration and turned his back to me.

The nurse wrote it down with pursed lips. "Anything else? Did you see the attacker?"

Frank turned to face me again. "Did you lie about that, too? Or did you really not see him?"

"No. I didn't see him."

"That's too bad." He took my revised chart and guided me back to Varnar, while he nodded apologetically at the nurse over his shoulder.

We drove back to Ravensted in silence. Varnar looked out the windshield, and at some point, his hand found mine in the dark. What I felt when his fingers carefully stroked the back of my hand was unlike anything I had ever felt.

When we reached the police station, Monster was standing outside.

Varnar jumped out and ran over to him.

In the van, I fumbled with the seat belt.

"Uh. Help," I said to Frank and waved my bandaged hand.

He unbuckled his own seat belt and twisted his torso toward me.

"You end up in life-threatening situations, which you keep surviving against all odds. If you can't handle it yourself, someone comes and helps you. Why do so many people want you dead?"

I pressed my lips together. The more Frank knew, the more danger he would be in himself.

Frank's face softened. "Anna. I care about you. Do you understand that I don't want anything to happen to you?"

I inhaled. "Can you just help me with the seat belt?"

For a moment, I feared he would close the door, which Varnar had left open. Then, Monster stuck his large head into the van.

Frank twitched at first out of fear. Then he laughed and unclicked my seat belt. "What did I say? There's always someone who comes to your rescue."

I scowled at him before hopping out of the van.

"Anna," he said from behind me.

"What?" I turned around.

"I'm sorry that you had to go through that."

"It's okay, Frank. I survived."

"Yes, you survived." The smile lines crinkled around his eyes.

"Thanks for the lift to the hospital."

"It was the least I could do."

I slammed the door and walked over to Varnar with Monster at my heels.

Varnar started to say something to us, but then Hakim showed up. "Why are you standing out here?"

Varnar looked at Monster. "Don't let her out of your sight."

Then he ran off into the darkness.

"Your dog can't come into the station," said Hakim.

"Then I'm not coming, either."

Hakim looked at the sky.

"What did I ever do to deserve meeting such a difficult girl?" He waved us in. "You're lucky it's so empty here tonight."

He led us into a small office that became unbelievably cramped with him, Monster, and me inside. He squeezed in behind a desk.

One wall was a macabre collage. Most of the pictures were ones I had seen before.

Hakim followed my gaze. "I didn't think about that. Should we move to another room?"

I shook my head and sat down on a chair facing away from the pictures. I gestured behind me with my thumb. "Aren't you scared your colleagues will think you get off on that stuff? The case is closed, you know."

Hakim looked at the computer screen. "Lots of officers have old cases they can't let go of. Cases that become obsessions. You should see what's hanging around in these offices."

"I'm good, thanks."

A little smile curled up one corner of his mouth.

"Is that what this is for you?"

"What?" He looked up.

"An obsession?"

Hakim placed a large hand on the desk. "No."

"Then what is it?"

"Unresolved. Everything has a beginning and an end. This case is somewhere in between." He hesitated. "You are somewhere in between."

"So you think I'm heading toward the end?"

"Maybe a happy ending."

I turned and looked into Alice's crystal-clear eyes in the photo right behind me. "For whom?"

Hakim ignored the question. "Did you recognize nothing at all about the person who attacked you?"

"Something about his voice was familiar. But I can't place it."

Hakim looked at me intently. "So you think it's someone you know?"

I shrugged my shoulders. "Maybe."

I remembered the vision I had had, where the murderer walked through me. I had recognized the aura then. But because I had gotten the vision from Serén, I hadn't been able to pinpoint it.

"We should make a list of people you know."

"You mean men."

"Could it have been a woman?"

"In principle. But I have the feeling it's a man. And the voice was deep, too."

"But the voice could have been distorted because of the hood."

"Maybe."

"So the women you know should also be included on the list."

"That'll take a while," I said. "I know pretty much everyone around here."

"I have all night."

On the other side of the desk, there was a quiet rumbling from Monster's chest.

I looked down but a thought distracted me. The first time I had the vision, the murderer had also walked through me. And that time, I hadn't recognized him—or her. So it had to be someone I had met within the past couple of months.

"I think it's someone I've met recently," I said. "The voice is, like, fresh in my memory."

"Is this where I'm supposed to just accept your explanation and trust that at least some part of what you're saying is true?"

With my lips pressed together, I nodded.

To my surprise, he didn't push further. "What does it mean that you *recently* met the person? Was it in the past few weeks?"

I rewarded his trust. "Since August 20 at 7:30 a.m."

Hakim leaned back with eyebrows raised. "That's specific."

"I remember because it was my first day of school."

Hakim opened his mouth to say something but closed it again. "So let's make that list."

It took over an hour to piece together my acquaintances from the past few months—and I left some out without quite knowing why. Svidur and Veronika were two of them. Niels Villadsen and Ulla were two more. But most of my new connections were typed into Hakim's computer and printed out. It struck me how much my life had changed when I looked at the names. Ben, Luna, Frank, Elias, Od, Rebecca, and Varnar. The other students in my class. The staff at Frank's, Christian, and many more.

"Is that all of them?" asked Hakim.

"No, we're missing one."

"Who?"

"You."

"I surprised the attacker tonight. You saw. That rules me out."

"What if you're working together?"

Hakim stood up. "That's a good point, but it's getting late. You've had a long night. I think you should leave the police work to us."

"Then what should I do?"

Hakim let his muscular arms glide into his jacket before making his way toward the door. "You should do what you already do so well."

I stood, too. "And what is that?"

He stopped with his hand on the doorknob. "Survive."

It was cold, early November, and I shivered in my thin denim jacket as we walked toward Frederiksgade, where Hakim's car was parked. Using my good hand, I tried to wrap the yellow scarf tighter around my neck, but I fumbled with the end that was behind my back.

Hakim stood in front of me and grabbed the scarf. He wrapped it carefully around me and made sure it fully covered my neck. His large hands landed on my shoulders.

"Better?" he asked.

I flinched involuntarily but made my face stony. I shrugged his hands off my shoulders, turned my back to him, and started walking. "That's the second time tonight someone's wrapped something tightly around my neck." With some effort, I stopped myself from hyperventilating.

He fell into step next to me. "I just don't want you to freeze."

We walked the rest of the way to his car. I sank into the soft seat. Monster took the back seat, and Hakim started the car.

In no time, we passed the city limit, and darkness surrounded us.

"Where did you learn to fight like that?" asked Hakim.

I didn't answer.

"I know that you've tried to become a member of all the martial arts clubs in the region. At some point, it was added to your case file that you weren't allowed to practice any form of martial

603

arts. All of your foster parents were told you would be taken away if they let you train."

"I didn't even know that," I said. "I was just always told no when I asked."

Hakim kept his eyes on the road. "You haven't been treated fairly."

"I don't believe in fairness."

"I do."

"Good for you." I turned my head away from him and looked out at the darkened landscape. There wasn't much to see apart from small lit-up windows here and there and the headlights of the few other cars in the distance.

"What I saw you do in that alley can't be learned without instruction. Where did you learn it?"

"The Internet," I lied. "There's a ton of videos."

We reached the driveway leading to my house, and Hakim turned onto it. "I've trained in martial arts since I was ten. You can't learn that from watching a video. Someone trained you. Who?"

"Are you asking in a professional capacity? Am I required to answer?"

Hakim stopped the car in front of my house. "It's hard for me to be professional with you. I'm asking as a . . . a friend, I think."

"Then I choose not to answer you. Neither as a friend nor as anything else." I changed the subject. "What kind of martial arts have you trained in?"

Hakim unfastened my seat belt. "All kinds."

"Because you like to fight?"

"To avoid it. I hate violence."

"Hmm."

"Do you like it?"

I thought about it. "I don't know if I like it, per se. It just feels natural to me."

"I can believe that." Hakim laughed.

"Why do you hate fighting?"

Hakim's large hand stroked his chin. "I grew up with conflict. Violence is one of the earliest memories I have."

"Did your dad hit you or something?"

"No. My father was killed in the war when I was little."

"You weren't born here in Denmark?"

"We fled when I was eight." He looked directly at me.

I searched for comforting words, but nothing came out. Instead, I clumsily pushed the car door open and hurried out, opening the back door for Monster.

Hakim rolled the window down. He had recovered quickly from my awkward exit.

"Remember to go over the list of names again, and add any you may have forgotten," he said before he started the car and disappeared down my driveway.

# CHAPTER 37

The next morning, when Elias came over, he didn't mention that Varnar and I had gotten together, but I got some clear glimpses of his very recent past, which included a lot of alcohol, medications, and several women.

I raised an eyebrow. "Are you even okay to drive?"

"I'm okay to do anything."

"I don't want to ride with you if you're intoxicated."

"You can ride with me, no worries. I have a potion that makes me sober no matter what, and how much, I've consumed."

"So typical of you to make a solution to a problem you yourself created. Maybe it would be better if you put your energy toward fighting your substance abuse."

"I should do that," he said as he examined me, squinting. "But not today."

I had succeeded in hiding my bandaged finger behind my back, but when I turned to grab my jacket, he spotted it.

"What happened *now?*"

As briefly and undramatically as I could, I recounted the evening's events, but Elias was nevertheless distraught by the time I finished telling him.

"First of all, let me see your finger." He grabbed me by the arm and led me over to the dining table.

I laid my bandaged hand on the tabletop. "It's fixed. It just needs to heal now. The doctor was really good. Varnar said so himself."

"And Varnar, of course, is right about *everything*," he said quietly and began taking the bandages off.

"Hey. It took them forever to do that yesterday."

He ignored me and completely unwrapped my hand to study it.

The finger was swollen. It had a strange yellowish hue, and the nail was blue.

Elias, who was engrossed in his examination, said to himself: "The doctor did well. But he doesn't have over three hundred years of medical experience or the remedies I have."

"No, I don't think anyone can top you in that area."

He looked up and suddenly had his usual brazen expression.

"That's not the only area," he said, and winked. He carefully laid my hand on the table and stood up. "Don't move."

He disappeared through the front door.

I looked at my mangled hand.

Elias returned with an old doctor's bag. From it, he fished out a cloth and a syringe.

"This is going to hurt a bit," he said. He gently grabbed the end of my finger and pulled.

I let out a pained howl, but it was as if the bone fell right into place.

Monster, who had been watching us from the floor, stood up with an agitated expression. I waved him away.

Elias took the syringe and inserted the needle into my finger until it hit the bone with a little click. I squirmed in my chair as a cold sweat broke out on my forehead.

"I'm injecting concentrated laekna straight into the fracture. That way your bone will regenerate." He squeezed a bit of the liquid into my finger, and an intense heat shot into it and continued up my arm. My cheeks turned red, my pulse rose, and my breathing grew heavy.

"If only I had the same effect on you," he mumbled.

I let this comment go. Elias had had a hard night.

He took my hand in a tight grip and squeezed the finger as if to brace it while it healed. It made a crackling noise, like when you pour boiling water over ice.

Then he let go of my hand. My finger resembled itself again. I flexed it tentatively, amazed to feel neither pain nor discomfort.

"Thanks." I made a fist.

"Are you okay?" he asked.

"The hand is a start," I said.

Elias's blue-gray eyes came to rest on me. "What's wrong?"

"What makes you think there's something wrong?"

"Physical ailments aren't the only kind of pain I have hundreds of years' experience in spotting."

I rubbed my forehead.

"I'm scared that I'll never get to meet my sister because one of us might die soon, which will bring about the end of the world. It's becoming clearer and clearer to me that Ragnara needs to be gotten out of the way."

Elias stared at me. "Sister?"

Shit! I had to get better at keeping track of my stories. "Twin sister." I sighed.

He laughed in surprise. "There're two of you?"

"Don't get any ideas. And anyway, she's into girls."

Elias leaned back in his chair with a wide grin. "You're killing me."

I threw my arms up. "Forget it."

"I never forget anything."

"Of course you don't. Should we get going?"

Neither of us said anything on the drive.

Monster lay in the back seat and looked out at the North Jutland scenery. The area around Sømosen is hillier and greener than the flat landscape surrounding Ravensted. We drove up and up and up, until we finally stopped in the parking lot in front of Dronninglund Forest, where Sømosen is located.

I got out of the car.

The forest towered before me. I leaned my head back. Most of the trees were much taller than the ones in Kraghede Forest. Centuries of activity seeped into me from my surroundings. Although there were only a couple of cars besides Elias's in the parking lot, I felt clearly how much this place had thrummed with life.

Elias began walking with long strides into the forest, and we followed suit. The smell of damp, moss, and forest surrounded us, and a force that nearly threatened to pull me down into the swampy ground pulsed beneath my feet.

We rounded a bend in the path, and a placid pond surrounded by golden autumn leaves lay before us. Small tussocks formed paths across the water, and in several places, birch trees shot up directly from the murky depths. The pond sat in an indentation, and around it rose hills covered in trees and bushes.

"It's beautiful here," I exclaimed.

"Don't let it fool you," said Elias. "The bog is deadly. It's bottomless, and if you step on what look like mounds of earth out there, you'll go straight through." He picked up a stone and handed it to me. "According to superstition, you have to throw a stone before walking into the bog."

"Why?"

"To avoid accidents along the way."

I accepted the stone. "Are accidents likely here?"

"The place is enshrouded in myths," he replied cryptically.

I weighed the stone in my hand and flung it as far as I could out into the pond. It hit the surface with a splash that sliced through the silence. "Tell me about the myths."

Elias resumed walking. "They say beautiful elven boys and girls will lure you out into the bog and drown you. They look like humans in front, but they're hollow in back."

"Is that true?"

"It was. But most vætter were resettled in Hrafnheim during the migration."

"Vætter?"

"It's an umbrella term for mythical beings."

"Is Hrafnheim like a dumping ground for nonhuman entities?"

"You could say that. It's rumored that Fenrir and the Midgard Serpent also ended up there, but I've never gotten that confirmed."

We had reached one end of the pond, where there was a natural indentation in the hill. Elias walked right up to the earthen wall and began lifting up the trailing plants. He knocked on a hollow tree trunk that lay at the foot of the hill.

Monster and I followed him. "What are we looking for?"

"The opening."

"To what?"

Elias didn't answer.

"Justine," he called.

Someone tugged on my arm, and I looked down.

A little boy stood at my side. He looked up at me with large brown eyes. His clothes were torn, and his head was surrounded by soft, dark curls.

"Where's your mommy?" I asked him and crouched down.

The boy pointed at a large stone that was embedded in the hill.

Elias looked at me. "What did you say?"

"This boy seems to have gotten separated from his parents."

"You see a boy?" Elias looked around.

I looked again at the child, who smiled back at me.

"It's probably a myling. There are still some left out here," he said.

"What's a myling?"

"It doesn't matter," Elias said quickly.

The myling started to walk, and his small hand waved for me to follow him.

"Is it here?" I asked and laid my hand on the large rock that was embedded in the hill.

"There it is," Elias said, leaning his shoulder against it and pushing. "The entrance to Justine's place is always hard to find."

The stone rolled aside to reveal a dark passageway leading into the hill.

"Are we going in there?" I asked, slightly uneasy.

In response, Elias stepped into the darkness. The little myling boy followed with silent footsteps.

I went in, and behind me, Monster's claws scratched against the hard-packed floor. Unsettlingly, I heard the stone glide back into place behind me, and for a second, we were all cloaked in utter darkness. Only the little myling's eyes burned phosphorescently. Then torches sputtered to life along the walls and illuminated the earthen corridor.

"What kind of place is this? We aren't in an elf mound, are we?" This last part was meant as a joke to lighten the grim mood.

"I would never take you into an elf mound," Elias replied seriously. "It's far too dangerous."

As is always the case when a paranormal fact is shared with me in passing, I was a little freaked out. "Wait, so elf mounds exist? Have you been in one?"

"One night. The wildest party I've ever been to," he said. "But that's forty years I'll never get back," he added quietly.

We continued into the belly of the hill, and echoes of voices from the past whizzed around me. Foreign languages and laughter rang out. Footsteps ran up and down the passage. Once in a while, I was struck by an intense smell of unwashed bodies and animals.

We stepped into a warm, illuminated cavern. Inside stood a woman with matted gray hair. She had sparkling black eyes, and I looked straight into them. My clairvoyance flared.

It was like standing between two mirrors and seeing an infinity of reflections both in front of and behind you. Our two-way view of one another's visions of the past and future flowed into one large mass, and for the first time, I saw time as an enormous surface onto which I had been plopped down in a random location. What came before the present had already happened, just as what came after was also determined, while simultaneously both the past and future seemed to be in constant flux.

Justine stared at me with an expression that must have resembled my own.

The little myling ducked behind her.

"What's going on?" I asked.

Justine, who was significantly shorter than me, looked up at me.

"Have you never been around another seer before?" Her vision of Monster, Elias, and me tromping through Sømosen on our way here appeared in my mind.

"Never. This is really strange."

"It's completely normal that our powers are testing their strength with one another." She sat cross-legged on the floor and waved a wrinkled hand toward a small bench to indicate that we should sit down. "Take a few deep breaths and relax. Then it'll quiet down."

I obeyed. I immediately started to choke on the smoke-filled air. I looked around and noticed that we were in a cave whose only light source was a hole high above us that let in a sliver of greenish light. A fireplace smoldered in the corner, and a narrow band of smoke snaked its way along the sloped walls toward the hole in the top of the cavern.

Justine pulled her worn red shawl tighter around her shoulders. "Welcome to Pondbottom."

"That sounds like a place where you drown," I said and coughed discreetly again.

"Not as long as you stay on my good side."

All righty, then.

"The Brewmaster says you wish to speak with me. Do you want a reading?"

"No. Definitely not." The last thing I needed was more grim predictions. And I was already far too familiar with my past. "Can you see the past or the future?"

"Both."

"I can only see the past."

"Lucky girl."

"What do you mean? I would much prefer to see the future."

"Yes, we always want what we don't have. And especially what we can't have." This last bit was aimed at Elias.

He looked down at his hands.

"I have some questions," I said. "I just experienced how I can see your visions of the future in your past. And you must be able to see my visions of the past as well."

She confirmed this with a nod.

"But we're in the same room now," I continued. "Have you ever been able to see another seer's vision without them being physically present?"

"If I touch one of the seer's belongings. And if they had the vision recently."

"Have you ever tried to see someone else's vision simply by hearing that person's words?"

"You mean on the phone?"

"Read aloud. And translated from another language. And before that, possibly passed on orally before they were written down."

Justine narrowed her black eyes. "How old were the words?"

"About eleven hundred years. Maybe a little more," I said tentatively.

Justine's gaze shifted to Elias. "Who have you brought me?"

Elias, who had now turned his head in my direction, answered quietly: "I'm not sure. Never before have I met someone like Anna. Not with such strong powers, anyway."

Justine crawled over to me and gripped my hands. Slightly stunned, I leaned back but was unable to evade her grasp. She

613

closed her eyes and squeezed my hands as she rocked from side to side and hummed to herself.

"The seeress on the hill," she mumbled. "So lovely. The bloody god's fate. She and her mirror will hear the whisper of the ravens." She furrowed her brows as if she was struggling to understand something. "She will bear a name given in love. A name of fate." She let go of me and rocked back on her heels. "The half man will know her."

"I didn't ask for a reading."

Justine's eyes were clouded. "And I didn't give you one. That was someone else I was reading through you. But this other person saw you. A very long time ago."

I swallowed. "Who?"

"The mother of all seers."

"The völva Hejd?"

Justine nodded slowly. "She knew you."

Elias looked from Justine to me. "Not *that* Hejd. She died over a thousand years ago. Od laid her in her grave himself. There's nothing that connects her with Anna."

Justine shrugged. "That's what I saw. In your very distant past, when you were just a glimmer of a speck of dust, Hejd saw you." She closed her eyes and listened intently. "She sent you a message. A warning."

"That's not possible."

"What do you know about what's possible? But you'll grow wiser. I'm telling you this. You'll grow wiser even than you would like to."

"Don't you get it? I didn't want a reading."

Justine held her head high, and anger shot out of her.

"That was a presumption. I see death holding you in its arms. And I see a silver thread between the two of you. Your fates are linked. In love or death. Or both." Her delicate hand waved back and forth between me and Elias, as if she were splashing us with invisible water. "There's your reading."

I stood. "You're a quack."

She leaned toward me and hissed: "Just because my powers don't function like yours, that doesn't mean I'm a fraud."

I turned to Elias. "What did you tell her, you manipulative little shit? She's very convincing, but I'm not that stupid." I stomped out of the little cave with Monster running after me.

"We'll meet again, beautiful seer," Justine shouted after me.

Outside, I squinted against the light of the autumnal no-man's-land until Elias came running. He was angry.

"I haven't met a single past-clairvoyant in my life who can control themselves. And then I put two of you together. What was I thinking? Oh right. I was thinking of helping you!" He kicked at the dirt. "I risk meeting elves, mylings, and trolls in this damned bog, only to once again end up getting an earful from you."

I crossed my arms. "You told her to say that stuff."

"Why would I do that?"

"To make me believe something's going to happen between us."

"I don't need a clairvoyant to tell you that."

"That's a very romantic statement, in light of what you did last night."

For a moment, Elias looked a little shaken, but he recovered quickly. "I'm free to do what I want, with whomever I want, until you want me."

"Until . . . Are you clairvoyant now, too?"

"As I've said, I'm never wrong about that."

"And what exactly are you basing this on? Our warm, friendly relationship?"

"Why do you think we fight all the time?"

I threw my arms out. "First, because you're extremely annoying. And second, because I fight with everyone."

"Not in the same way as you fight with me. Do you ever feel like it's almost like arguing with yourself?"

I refused to answer him.

"The two of us, we're a lot alike."

"I'm not a four-hundred-year-old lying, pompous egomaniac who only does things for my own gain."

"But if you were to live another four centuries, what do you think you'd be like?"

I looked up at the bright blue sky.

"I can tell you," Elias said. "Either you'd be exactly like me . . . or you'd be much worse."

I racked my brain for a response. But no matter how hard I tried, I was unable to contradict him.

When we pulled up in front of Odinmont, two figures stood at my front door.

One was significantly taller than the other. It was Mathias and Little Mads.

Elias stared at the steering wheel and refused to acknowledge my presence. Without saying goodbye, I got out of the car and opened the door for Monster. I slammed it hard after him for good measure.

Elias swung the car around in a spray of gravel and sped off. I didn't need to see the future to know how he would spend the rest of the day. I pushed away a twinge of guilt and walked up to Mads and Mathias.

"What are you doing here?" I may have sounded a little exasperated.

Mathias's voice was serious. "Mads needs to talk to you."

I dug out my keys and opened the blue front door. "Can it wait? I have a lot to think about."

"It's important."

Monster and the two boys followed me into the house. Monster looked inquisitively at Mads with an expression I couldn't fully interpret.

"He wants to ask you something," Mathias continued.

Mads ducked his head slightly as he walked through the doorway from the hall to the kitchen. When he straightened back up, there were only a couple of inches separating his head from the ceiling beams.

I tossed the keys onto the kitchen table and turned toward Mads. "So ask me."

He looked helplessly at Mathias, who gave him a reassuring nod. "Let's sit."

I pulled out a chair, sat down without taking my jacket off, and exhaled. "I'm ready."

Mathias tilted his head. "Mads has been observing us lately. You, me, and Luna."

"What's so special about that?"

Mathias continued, putting on a patient grimace. "Mads is struggling with some things himself. He's always had a hard time fitting in."

I nodded for him to continue. So far, Mathias hadn't said anything that was news to me.

Mads finally spoke. "It's not just my height that sets me apart," he muttered with his deep voice.

I looked him up and down, trying to figure out what he might mean, to no avail. "What else is different?"

Mads spread out his large hands. He held them a quarter inch above the table, and something started to crackle.

I looked down at the table and discovered small blossoms of frost spreading across it.

Mads clenched his fists, and a wind blew through my living room. A few papers fluttered to the floor.

What?

"What are you?" I whispered.

Mads shrugged his large shoulders. "I was hoping you could tell me."

"How am I supposed to know?"

Mads looked at me with desperation. "I want to know if I can join."

"Join what?"

"Your group."

I stared at him, uncomprehending. "We don't have a group."

"Yes, we do," said Mathias. "And I've already shown him some of what I can do."

"That's on you," I said.

"You have to help Mads. Maybe he can talk to Od or Elias. Or Luna's parents."

"So introduce him."

"I thought I should get your okay first," mumbled Mathias.

"Who made me the leader?" With a small shock, I realized that was how Mathias saw me.

Mads's face said the same thing when he looked at me pleadingly.

I leaned back in my chair. "I don't know what impression Mathias has given you, but this whole undertaking is highly disorganized. Most of the time, we have no idea what we're doing. I'm sorry, Mads, but I can't help you. I have enough problems of my own."

"Have you considered," said Mathias, "that Mads might be able to help you?"

"Uh."

Monster, who had been following the conversation intently, came closer to the table.

"I need to know what I am. I don't even know my father," Mads begged.

Mathias looked down at the table. "At first, I thought he was the same as me. But he's not. He's not the same as Luna, either. But he's *something*."

Monster spoke up. "I think I know what you are."

Mads's mouth hung open, and he appeared to be shocked beyond all comprehension.

"I think," Monster said in his deep, hoarse voice, "you're related to me."

 # CHAPTER 38

"It can talk," Mads said breathlessly. "The dog. It just said something."

"He's not a dog," I said and stood up. "Who wants coffee?"

Mads didn't answer my question. "If he's not a dog, then what is he?"

"Ask him yourself," I said, peeling my jacket off and tossing it onto the bench.

Mads turned his large body to face Monster.

"I descend from the giants," Monster rumbled.

Mads looked like he was considering pinching his arm.

"I think you're a giant, too," he continued. "Or part giant."

"A giant?" Mads's breathing was still labored. "They don't exist. That's just mythology."

"Did you guys want coffee or what?" I asked from the kitchen.

"How can you talk about coffee right now?" This was the first time I had heard so much as a hint of annoyance in Mads's otherwise calm voice.

I set the kettle on the table with a bang. "If I stopped eating and drinking every time I engaged with supernatural phenomena, I would die of thirst and hunger. If you want to join our *group*," I said more gently, "then you'll have to deal with these things."

Mads seemed to pull himself together. "Okay," he said.

"Okay, what?"

"I would like some coffee."

"Me, too," added Monster.

Again, Mads stared at him. I looked at Mathias, who nodded subtly. Then I got out three cups and a bowl.

Mads let out a deep breath. "Why do you think I'm a giant?"

"I can see," said Monster, "that you have giantlike qualities. Giants have a close connection with nature, and some of us have dominion over the elements."

"I wouldn't call that 'having dominion,'" I interjected. "He just produced a gust of wind and a little frost."

"Well, he is only part giant. Like how I'm both giant and wolf."

Mads pried his eyes away from Monster and looked at me. "What are you?"

I leaned my head back. My greatest flaw was becoming common knowledge. "I'm clairvoyant."

"Clairvoyant?" Mads wavered slightly in his chair.

"I can see the past and auras."

"And ghosts," Mathias added.

"Oh, yeah, and ghosts." I nodded and set the coffee in front of him and Mads.

Mads was very pale.

"It's okay, Mads," Mathias said and laid a hand on his shoulder. "We've all been there. It's a lot to take in, to find out what you are and what the hidden world contains."

"What's the hidden world?" whispered Mads.

"A world that's full of witches, giants, ghosts, and more," I said.

Mathias shook his head. "Give Mads a minute."

"And alternate history," I said, wiggling my eyebrows.

"Anna!" said Mathias.

"And super annoying people who think they're demigods but are most likely mutants or aliens," I concluded. When I saw Mads's face, I wished I could eat my words. "Sorry, Mads. Mathias is right," I said more gently.

"We've all experienced the reveal. It's overwhelming."

Mads leaned back in my poor, creaking chair. "It's also a relief."

Mathias smiled. "When I found out what I am, I was relieved, too. But that may also have been because I had just survived getting shot in the chest. But I know what you mean."

Just then, I think Mads was wishing he had never confided in us.

Mathias waved a hand. "I'm sure that won't happen to you."

"What's special about half giants?" I asked Monster.

Monster lapped up a couple mouthfuls of coffee. "They're closely linked to nature and the elements."

"Can you control the weather, too?"

Monster looked a little regretful. "I didn't receive that gift."

"What else?"

"We're hardy. Our bones are strong as stone and very difficult to break."

Mathias cut in. "I thought giants were evil."

Monster sniffed. "The gods conquered us, and afterward they fed the humans a bunch of lies. Yes, there are bad giants who do bad things. But the gods aren't always all that nice, either."

"How can I be a giant?" asked Mads. "Giants aren't part of the real world."

I scratched my forehead. *Here we go.*

"Uh, Mads. There's something I have to tell you about the world. Or worlds. Because there's several of them."

And so I began to talk.

Mathias had his arm around Mads's shoulder when they left my house. Fortunately, Mathias had gone into "god mode," so he was tall enough. I watched as the two enormous young men—one greenish and one pale as a corpse—lurched down the driveway.

At this time of year, darkness dominated with long nights and overcast days, but today the sun shone miraculously from a cloudless sky. It was heartrendingly beautiful to see the feeble beams bathing the black and winter-green fields.

I stood for a while and looked out over the landscape. I thought about the murderers Ragnara kept sending after me. About Arthur, who was already dead; my mother, who was among Hrafnheim's most wanted; and my sister . . . I gasped for air. My sister, who I might never get to see.

With a jump, I took off across the field and stormed toward Kraghede Forest in the weak winter sun.

I heard Monster running after me, panting. I ignored him and ran into the woods, quickly reaching the entrance of Kraghede Manor.

Just then, Varnar strode out of the riding hall. He shot me a wild look and jogged over to me.

Monster stayed in the woods, where he paced back and forth in a very wolflike manner.

Varnar's strong hands gripped my shoulders. "What is it?"

"Let's train now. Right now. I'm done with just protecting myself. I want to learn to attack."

Four hours later, I was drenched with sweat, and I had scratches on my arms and across my cheek where Varnar's branch had struck me. We fought in the old riding hall.

"Let's stop," he said. "You're exhausted."

I ignored the suggestion and went after him again. He protected himself elegantly without hurting me.

"Stop it." He swung and hit the stick out of my hand. Then he reached out to grab me.

I spun around, kicked, and hit his thigh. If it hurt, he didn't show it.

"You haven't eaten, you have no weapon, and you've barely slept. And last night, you were almost killed."

"I'm sure Ragnara and Eskild will be very understanding when we meet someday and I postpone our confrontation because I'm feeling hungry and need a nap."

Varnar took another step forward and reached out to me, but I drove a fist into his stomach. This time, he grunted in pain.

"Enough!" he shouted and moved so quickly with his dance-like footwork that my eyes almost couldn't follow him. All of a sudden, he was behind me and held me tight.

I tried to break free, but he squeezed me against himself.

"I know you're scared."

"Scared!" I hissed. "I'm not scared. I'm furious at Ragnara and Eskild. I swear, they're going to pay for everything they've done to my family."

"Anger and thirst for revenge are good fuel in a fight, but they also cloud your vision. It'll spell death for you if you attack them with those as your only thoughts."

"Better to die in battle than to just sit here and wait," I spat, and swung my heel back.

It hit Varnar's shin, and he let go so abruptly that I toppled forward. He cursed, and I suddenly noticed the dark circles under his eyes. As if all the worries of the world lay on his shoulders.

The anger subsided, my legs gave out beneath me, and I landed in the sawdust. Varnar sank down at my side.

"You don't think I'll make it," I said.

"What makes you say that?"

"I can sense your feelings."

He looked down. "What else can you sense?"

I leaned into him, drained. "That you care about me."

"I more than care about you." His arms intertwined around me. "I would do anything to keep you safe."

"*Anything* can be pretty wide-ranging."

"I'm afraid that even with protection from witches, Varangian guards, a demigod, and two half giants, we're fighting against a superior power." I noticed that he counted neither Od nor Elias among my defenders. "It's going to take wide-ranging tactics if we're going to defeat Ragnara."

I closed my eyes and let myself be in the moment. It was just the two of us in this large, empty, echoing space. My hand searched for his and found it.

We sat that way for a while without saying anything.

Then my phone rang from the bottom of my bag, and I spluttered with fright before I got up and dug around for it. The display said it was a hidden number.

"Hello," I said hesitantly.

"Anna Sakarias?" The voice was authoritative, and it took me a second to place it.

"Yes."

"This is Niels Villadsen from the DSMA. We met at The Boatman, at the equinox ball."

"I remember you."

"I'm calling because of new information from Freiheim, which I'm hoping you can help shed some light on."

"How would I be able to help? I don't want to know anything."

"My sense is that you're at the epicenter of the events we've been hearing about lately."

"What events?"

"Mysterious killings of red-haired girls, earthquakes, a detainee who was poisoned in his cell. An enthusiastic police officer named Hakim Murr is collecting evidence and connecting the dots."

I ignored his enumeration. "What's the new information?"

"I've been contacted by Eskild Black-Eye from Freiheim."

"Eskild?" I exclaimed.

I could see Varnar's ears perk up.

"He thinks someone has interfered in Freiheim's affairs."

I didn't reply.

"Have you heard of Serén, daughter of Thora Baneblood?"

"Serén. Nope. I've never heard that name before." My eyes met Varnar's.

625

"So you don't know why Eskild is saying that someone helped Serén flee?"

"Didn't she leave a long time ago?"

It was quiet at the other end for a while before Niels spoke again. His otherwise neutral voice quivered slightly. "So Eskild's telling the truth? She got away?"

I didn't respond, and Niels continued.

"Do you associate with Varnar of the Bronze Forest?"

"Varnar is dead."

Varnar stood up and looked intensely at me.

Niels continued: "Eskild claims we are harboring Varnar here in Midgard. He demands that we hand him over so he can be prosecuted in Freiheim."

"It's a little difficult to hand over a dead person who was devoured by giant wolves."

Niels laughed on the other end. "You're well-informed for someone who doesn't know anything."

"What do you want me to say?"

"I want you to confirm that we in Midgard continue to be neutral in the conflict between Ragnara and the insurgents in Freiheim. That you haven't been subjected to attempted attacks or threats. That you don't know Varnar, and that your dog is a dumb mutt born in this world."

"Confirmed," I lied.

"Good," said Niels. "I'll tell that to Ragnara's people next time we talk."

"Was that all?"

Niels lowered his voice: "I feel obligated to tell you that I know the berserkers are now fighting for Ragnara." There was a brief pause before Niels quickly continued in a whisper. "You should tell that to Varnar, even though he's dead and you have no idea who he is."

"Wait, do you know something about my . . . ?"

626

But the call was already disconnected. I stared at the phone. Varnar looked at me, tense.

"Ragnara is planning something," I said. "Niels said she now has berserkers on her side."

Varnar's body stiffened, and I smelled smoke and heard screams from his past.

"An attack is imminent." The words came out almost like an exhalation. "And there are still a lot of things about you that I don't understand."

I went right up to him. "But you know everything about me."

He took my hand. First, he caressed it. Then he held my pinkie finger. "This was broken yesterday."

This was a statement, so I didn't reply. I just looked down at my hand.

"Who healed you?"

I raised my head, looked him right in the eyes, and pressed my lips together.

"You healed. I healed the night I fought Naut Kafnar. Who do you know who can do that?"

I concentrated on not blinking.

He looked at me with an expression I had never seen before. Awe mixed with dismay.

"You have power. You don't realize it, but you do. Demigods protect you. Witches care about you. Half giants form bonds with you. And humans, we carry out your wishes and defend you. I didn't get it when Aella said the same thing about Serén. When Etunaz said it about both of you. But now I understand."

"I have no power," I said weakly. "I always feel like I'm powerless."

He let go of my hand. "Whether you like it or not, everyone's fate depends on you and your sister."

CHAPTER 39

On several occasions, I held my phone in my hand with Elias's number typed in, but each time, I failed to call him. Finally, I sent him a text asking for his address. I expected a call or a smarmy reply, but he just sent a message containing some numbers, which upon review I determined to be GPS coordinates.

On Thursday, I pulled myself together and hopped on my bike.

The temperature had fallen even further now that it was mid-November, and after rummaging through my closet, I realized that my mother's coat was the warmest piece of outerwear I owned.

I typed Elias's coordinates into my phone and headed across the flat landscape in the direction of Jagd.

In the middle of the bogland, halfway between The Boatman and Ravensted, the cold voice in my headphones told me to turn. I stopped and looked around. There appeared to be nothing but windswept fields, but on closer inspection, I discovered a fresh tire track running along a ditch to the right of the road. I followed it, mostly because I didn't know what else to do.

After a little off-roading, my bike's narrow tires skidding several times in the rich soil, the track led into a small cluster of trees. The ditch alongside me appeared bottomless, and pale branches stuck out of the dark water like white fingers grasping at the sky.

"I don't like this," grumbled Monster. "We're vulnerable in there."

"If I held myself back every time something was dangerous, I wouldn't be able to leave my house."

"Actually, that's not a bad idea," he muttered.

We entered the grove and ended up at a small red house I would have never noticed from the main road. Its age was indeterminable. It may have been rebuilt many times over the years. Next to it stood a wooden tower whose top was adorned with a spangled star of gleaming metal.

I parked my bike and looked up.

"Welcome to my laboratory," Elias said from behind me.

Because my ghost dad always made his entrance in the same way, I was able to act like I wasn't frightened.

"And what is that?" I pointed at the tower.

"My observatory." Elias's face was unusually serious.

"Your interests spread over many areas."

"What can I say, I'm a Renaissance man." He bowed with his hand on his heart.

I rubbed my cold hands together.

"Come inside." Elias walked toward the house.

"Do I dare enter your bachelor pad?" I asked, slightly concerned that I would be met with sultry music and a king-size bed with silk sheets.

"I only let a very select few visit this place." He gave me a typical Elias look. "My short-term acquaintances never come here."

"Yeah, yeah . . . I'm something special. Blah, blah, blah . . ."

"Mocking people's feelings is never a good look," he said quietly.

Inside, I looked around the house, which in some ways surprised me and in other ways screamed Elias. The walls were covered in shelves stuffed with books. The kitchen looked like an old apothecary full of large jars with labels and formulas. The spicy scent I associated with him permeated the house, and the furnishings were simple and practical. There was a total absence of Elias's cheeky, calculated side.

I took the coat off and draped it over the back of a chair. Elias's eyes lingered on it for a moment, but he said nothing.

He turned his back to me, rummaged in a cabinet, and pulled out a couple of glasses. "Can I offer you anything?"

"Whatever you've got with a high ABV." I sat down in a worn leather armchair.

"You've come to the right place." He held a dusty bottle in his hand.

"How do you actually get to Hrafnheim?"

Elias's back stiffened slightly. "Why do you ask?"

"Just curious."

He relaxed and turned around. "One of the doors in Od's office leads to the kingdom of Njordrvík in northern Hrafnheim, but since Od is neutral, he allows neither members of the resistance nor Ragnara's people to pass."

"What about you?"

He smiled. "I have free passage because of my business dealings."

"But there must be other ways."

"The Earl has a passage somewhere near Ostergaard. I would guess he was the one who let Varnar and his swarthy friend and Prince Etunaz pass."

I thought about my neighbor, who was evidently involved in all this.

"How involved is Paul Ostergaard?"

Elias looked at me without answering.

"What about Mina—his daughter. Does she know anything?"

"I'm trying to follow the rules. And you're not supposed to talk about other people."

I changed the subject with an irritable snort. "How did Naut Kafnar get here?"

Elias filled the two glasses. "I don't know. Ragnara must have allies here in Midgard that even I don't know about."

He held out one of the glasses to me.

I looked at it without moving. "Put a splash of stjórna in it."

Monster growled. "Don't take any chances. The Brewmaster can't be trusted."

Elias's eyes met mine, and I stared back. "That's why I'm doing it. I take no chances with Elias."

"Fight it!" Elias's voice reached me. "Resist the tranquilizer."

I fumbled around in the dark.

"Anna," growled Monster. "Wake up."

I strained toward the two voices.

A third voice spoke. It was deep, hoarse, and familiar.

"You can change everyone's fate, little seeress."

Svidur?

I woke with a start and looked straight into Monster's worried eyes. Elias stood behind him with his empty glass in hand. The bottle's contents had been significantly diminished, and his eyes were glazed.

I got to my feet, swayed a little, and leaned on Monster's shoulder for support.

Elias took a step toward me, but Monster snarled, so he backed up. "You shouldn't ride your bike in this state. I'll drive you home."

"And you shouldn't drive a car in your state." I exhaled heavily and pushed the nausea down.

Elias conjured an ampoule filled with an orange liquid. He placed a drop on his tongue and closed his eyes. When he opened them, they were clear again. He held out the ampoule.

I opened my mouth.

"No," said Monster.

"He just took some himself," I snapped. "He wouldn't poison himself, would he?"

"That's all he does." Monster stepped aside and let me take some of Elias's potion.

It tasted of citrus and mint and immediately refreshed my brain. The nausea vanished.

"Practical medicine," I said.

"You would think edrú would be worth some money." Elias smiled. "But it doesn't sell well. I think people want to be martyrs of their debauchery."

I twitched my head and took my coat. "Am I immune to stjórna now?"

"As immune as you can get. But you'll still need to fight your way out of the darkness."

I left Elias's home without saying more, but I looked back over my shoulder once.

He stood in the doorframe, encircled in light, with his face in shadows.

Then I looked ahead again and rode into the darkness.

On Friday evening, Frank's was quiet.

Mathias came into the kitchen with a tray around nine, when Milas and I were closing the kitchen. "How's it going?"

I pulled the trash bag out of its holder and went into the back alley. Mathias understood and followed me.

I gave him a brief summary as I threw the bag in the dumpster.

"Do you think Elias is playing both sides?" Mathias asked.

"I don't know, but he always has hidden motives."

"Maybe he isn't that bad."

"And maybe you're too trusting."

Mathias smiled in the cold light of the exposed bulb over the back door to Frank's. "Trust could be the answer here."

I scoffed and changed the subject. "How about you?"

"Od showed up at my house yesterday. I have to go down to Copenhagen with him. All demis have to register with the DSMA."

"Don't tell him anything. Niels Villadsen already knows that Hakim has been digging around. And if he finds out that both sides broke their agreements, we risk a conflict between Hrafnheim and Midgard. Oh . . . and remember, Varnar is officially dead."

"What's going on with you two?"

I shrugged and tried to look nonchalant, but my stomach turned to ice. "No clue. I haven't talked to him in days." I brushed my hands together and hurried to find something else to talk about. "When do you leave?"

"In two weeks. It was supposed to be on the solstice, but I moved it."

"Why?"

"The solstice is the day before you-know-what," he said. "I want to be here to look out for you." He smiled his most captivating smile, and, annoyingly enough, it paralyzed me a little. "And of course, we also have to celebrate your birthday."

"You really don't need to make a big deal about it."

"Good luck talking Luna out of throwing you a party." He laughed. Then he grew serious. "I'm really not happy to be leaving now, either. If anything happens, call on Arthur. He can reach me. I've figured out that I can get here in about fifteen minutes."

I tried not to look too impressed.

"Monster, Aella, Luna, her parents, Arthur, and Varnar are here to look after me. I'm sure you're totally unnecessary."

Back home, I sat on the bench and stared into space as Monster snored on the floor. I had turned off all the lights in the house and could neither force myself to do anything nor go to bed.

When there was a knock at the door, Monster opened one eye a crack.

"It's your bodyguard," he muttered before going back to sleep.

I tiptoed through my dark house. Heart pounding, I opened the door.

Varnar stood outside.

"Can I come in?" he asked quietly.

I stepped aside, unable to speak.

He walked into the foyer and closed the door behind him,

633

enveloping us in darkness. Because I couldn't see anything, all my other senses were heightened. His scent wrapped itself around me, the chill of his clothes radiated toward me, and I heard his heavy breathing.

"What do you want?" I stammered.

"We aren't finished," he whispered.

"With training?" I asked, a little downhearted.

"No." He stepped right up to me and leaned his forehead against mine. His hands wrapped around my waist. "I don't need to train you anymore. You're as skilled as my best soldier. But the two of us aren't finished with each other."

My fingers ran through his hair. "I was scared you'd had second thoughts."

"I was worried," he mumbled, "that my love would make me a worse protector. But I've found that my feelings for you are your best defense." He leaned down and kissed me.

I lay on my stomach as Varnar's fingers traced a line down my spine. He laid his cheek in the hollow between my shoulder blades.

My own breathing was slow and relaxed.

"Do you know where my mom is?"

"No. But Eskild is looking for her, so my men are following them. If he finds her, I'll make sure she is protected."

"Does Eskild know that the resistance fighters are close to them?"

He rolled onto his side and kept his hand on my lower back. "Yes."

"Will you tell me why you switched sides?"

Varnar's brows furrowed, as they always did when something was hard for him to talk about.

"What did Eskild do to you?" I asked quietly.

"You should really be asking what he made me do." Varnar closed his eyes.

My neck grew cold, and I waited until Varnar was ready to talk again.

His hand left my back, and a chill crackled from him.

"What's wrong?"

"There's something I need to tell you."

"Okay." I took his hand.

He let me do it, but I could sense that he wanted to pull it away.

"Normally, I was alone in the field with my troops, but one day Eskild came with us on patrol."

"What happened?"

"We found a circle of Odin worshippers in the middle of a ceremony."

"Isn't that forbidden in Hrafnheim?"

"Yes. It's illegal to worship the gods."

"Did you often find believers?"

"Once in a while. Normally, we arrested them and brought them to Sént."

"But this time?" I asked, fearing his response.

"Eskild ordered us to attack, even though they were unarmed."

"What did you do?" I whispered.

Varnar was silent for so long I wasn't sure if he would answer at all.

"First, I told them to surrender, but they threw themselves at us. And so . . ."

I saw the images. The worshippers had been barefoot and dressed in white. Out of respect for the dead, I watched the vision to the end.

I looked at Varnar's hand in mine. The same hand that had killed unarmed men and women.

I dried my cheeks, but stopped when I saw a tall, muscular man with one blue eye and one black, holding a young woman by the hair. She screamed in a foreign language, and her feet were dangling above the ground.

"Who's the girl?" I asked.

635

"Can you see . . . ?" Varnar's voice carried a streak of fear. Then he composed himself. "She was your age."

The man, who must be Eskild, held a knife to her throat.

"I asked him to spare her. But . . ." Varnar gathered his courage before continuing. "He ordered me to kill her."

I trembled. "Why?"

"A soldier must do as he's ordered. So I didn't ask any questions."

"So you did it?"

The images flowed, but this time I shut them out.

He looked intently at me, as if he suspected I saw what he had done. "I had killed before. And I've killed since. As a soldier. But that day, I became a murderer."

Without realizing it, I had placed my hand over my mouth. I slowly lowered it.

"Then what?"

"We left the dead behind. When I got back to the capital, I spoke with Aella and Serén. I admitted my disapproval. They told me about the resistance against Ragnara. And about your mother's plans. So I swore two things."

"That you would switch sides, and what else?"

"That I would never take a woman. I don't deserve love. I should have told you before. I understand if you can't accept what I've done."

Again, I looked at his hands. Mostly to avoid meeting his gaze. I whispered so my voice wouldn't break. "You believed in Ragnara's project. You thought you were doing the right thing. It's not your fault."

"Even if I save everyone's life, if I give my own in battle—on judgement day, I will still be guilty."

On Monday, it was time for my monthly visit to Greta. The second-to-last one ever. Unless I screwed up, which I had no intention of doing. I was therefore as honest as possible.

"I kind of got a boyfriend," I said.

Greta's small eyes focused on me. "It isn't Od Dinesen, is it? He's far too old for you."

She's right about that.

"It's my neighbor. He's twenty-four."

Greta pushed her glasses up the bridge of her nose. "Does he have a job?"

"He's a janitor at the high school." *And a military commander, bodyguard, and resistance fighter.*

"Good."

I cleared my throat.

"Is it okay if he sleeps over? Just a few times," I added quickly. I needed to officially get permission in case Greta came over un-announced again and found Varnar there. I wasn't taking any chances when my birthday was so close.

"Well, it is only natural." Her thin eyebrows lowered, and she pulled her lips back slightly. "You don't have your mom to talk to, so I'll have to do it. Woman to woman."

I held up a hand. "Rebecca Sekibo has already had the talk with me."

"All right," Greta said, relieved. She stood. "I'm happy to see that things are going well for you. The school tells me you're get-ting along fine. Your boss says you're one of his most reliable em-ployees, and the police say you've been helpful in the investiga-tion. All in all, I think you're on the right track." She opened the door and fidgeted a little with the thin watchband on her wrist. "I haven't followed anyone else for this many years. I . . . I'm very proud of you. You have demonstrated that you are responsible enough to live alone. I can't imagine anything happening that would make it necessary for us to sell your house."

Greta was half right. What actually happened was something she never could have imagined.

I floated around in a happy daze. The nights blended into the days, and Varnar and I were as one. Aella said he smiled more in those days than he had in the past thirteen years.

I was free from attempted attacks, so I almost managed to forget how close we were to the winter solstice—and my or my sister's death. In my overriding joy, the threat of my imminent and violent death seemed unreal.

At the end of November, the Christmas decorations made their appearance. Varnar poked at some of them, mystified, as we sat on the red sofa in The Island one day.

"Tell me, what kind of creature is this?"

"It's an elf."

He tossed it away. "Ugh."

"What makes you say that? They're cute."

"Cute? In Freiheim, we fear them. They can do a lot of damage."

"Elves don't really exist."

He smiled his now-familiar smile and caught a lock of my black hair. "What do you know about what really exists?"

"Do you also have Santa Claus hidden away in your world?" I laughed.

"Who?"

"No one. Do you even celebrate Christmas?"

"We observe jól or jólablót. The completion of the Wheel of the Year. The days when the light returns."

"I thought everything religious was forbidden?"

His warm hand slid under my hair and rested on the back of my neck.

"Ragnara has let the people retain a few customs. Midsummer celebrations are also allowed. And the two equinoxes."

I leaned into him. "Will I ever get to see your home?"

"I don't have a home. The closest I get is being with you."

Mathias came to my house the day before he was supposed to go to Copenhagen for his initiation.

"I'm staying home," he said. "What if something happens?"

I was lying on my back on the bench with green goo on my face while he sat next to me and filed my nails.

"I couldn't be any safer. Odinmont is enchanted. If I just stay here, no one can come in. Monster is capable of eating an adult man, and Varnar and Aella are pure killing machines. I'll stay inside until you get back." A cold breeze and a hand on my leg made me smile. "And it seems I also have protection from the spirit world."

Mathias looked up from my nails. "Hey, Arthur."

Arthur sat on the bench by my feet.

"We were just talking about the strategy for while Mathias is gone. I promised to stay home."

"We agreed that if anything happens, Anna will call on you, and you can get me. You can teleport to Copenhagen, right?"

"Teleport?" Arthur laughed. "Sure, you could call it that. And yes, I can."

"So there's no danger ahead," I said.

"Can I talk to you?" Frank asked that evening, and gestured to the back door.

"Just a second," I said and cut the last slice of the tomato before following him.

"Maybe just leave that there." He pointed at the sharp knife in my hand.

"Oh, right."

Varnar was planning to come to Odinmont after my shift, and I was having trouble concentrating on anything else. I set down the sharp blade and dried my hands on my apron. Standing in front of the dumpster, I shivered in the cold.

"What's up?"

Frank looked soberly at me and let out a deep breath. The smile lines that usually surrounded his eyes had vanished. As always happened when his feelings were in disarray, I saw images of the little crying boy.

I focused on him. "Is there something wrong?"

"It's about the future." The toes of Frank's pointy boots carefully poked holes in the thin layer of ice on a puddle of water.

The crackling sound made me tremble again. "The future?"

What does Frank know about that?

"I need to . . ." He took a step toward me.

There was a rumbling from the shadows. Frank flinched as an enormous figure stepped out into the sharp light. He slumped a little when he saw that it was only Monster.

"That dog scares the crap out of me."

"I'm freezing my ass off. What is it?" I stomped on the puddle and smashed the last of the ice.

Frank exhaled, and the warm breath hung like a cloud around him. "You're coming of age next month. Until now, the municipal government has been giving me a subsidy in exchange for employing you, but that ends when you turn eighteen."

"Are you firing me?" I gaped.

The smile lines were back and formed deep furrows around his eyes. "I was actually afraid you would quit, now that you aren't required to have a job."

"That didn't even cross my mind. I like working here."

"I want to keep you here, too. And give you a little more responsibility. You can tend bar."

I actually hadn't thought about anything past my birthday. And the thought of working in the crowded bar wasn't particularly attractive. But with klinte and a little more practice with shielding, it might be possible.

"It pays better," Frank tried to entice me.

"I'll think about it."

Frank opened the door for me. "Of course."

I walked into the warm kitchen, glancing over my shoulder at Monster, who would remain at his post in the back alley for the rest of my shift.

When we got home, Varnar was waiting for me by the front door, and my mouth involuntarily pulled into a smile.

I unlocked the door, and Monster and Varnar walked in. Monster quickly disappeared into the guest bedroom, and Varnar and I occupied ourselves with other activities. Despite the looming threat to my life, I was unconcerned.

That night, I slept in Varnar's arms for the last time.

CHAPTER 40

On Saturday afternoon, Varnar, Aella, Mads, Monster, and I sat in my living room.

Monster was in the middle of telling Mads stories about giants when several auras flickered at the edge of my consciousness. They were aggressive and reminded me of the Savage.

"And then my ancestor Fenris bit off Tyr's arm when Tyr tied him up. They say Fenris is still bound, but that he'll be freed during Ragnarök." Monster stopped and sniffed the air as the fur on the back of his neck stood up.

The gravel crunched, and dark shadows moved past the kitchen window.

Varnar and Aella jumped to their feet in an elegant, fluid motion.

I looked out into the twilight and saw four people positioning themselves in my yard. A woman and three men, all dressed in the same kind of skins and clothing as Naut Kafnar. Something else about them reminded me of him, but I couldn't pinpoint it. The four figures stood motionless.

"What are they doing? They know we won't go out there," I said.

Varnar rummaged in my kitchen drawers and found a couple of sharp knives. "There're more."

"What?" I managed to say before I heard the gravel crunch again. A chill spread over my body when a fifth man walked up. He was even bigger than Naut Kafnar and had long, fair, tangled hair. But he did not have the same moronic facial expression. He was dragging something. A bound figure with a hood over its head.

The person kicked and protested weakly.

I reached out with my power and almost screamed out loud when I recognized the aura as Luna's. I ran toward the door and went to fling it open, but Varnar grabbed my arm and held it.

"I don't care. I have to go out there and help her," I yelled.

"That's what he wants."

I shook my head forcefully. "Nothing can happen to Luna!"

"You stay here. We'll go out there." He signaled to Aella and Monster, and the three of them walked to the door leading to my garden.

"What can I do?" Mads's voice was even deeper than usual.

"You look after Anna." Varnar handed Aella a knife.

"What about me?" I asked.

"The house is enchanted. You're protected by two half giants and two Varangian guards. Don't worry."

I rolled my eyes. "That's not what I meant. What can I do?"

"Call your father."

Varnar looked at me one last time before he disappeared into the oppressive darkness.

"Arthur," I said.

He manifested himself immediately. "What is it?"

"We have company." I pointed outside.

"What are you saying?" asked Mads.

"I'm not talking to you."

"Then who?"

"My dad."

He looked around. "There's no one here."

"My dad is dead."

Mads paled and took a step back.

I continued speaking to Arthur. "They have Luna. Get ahold of Mathias, and then see if you can also get the message through to Ben and Rebecca."

Arthur looked out the window and grew even whiter than usual.

"Berserkers." He turned toward me. "Whatever happens, do not go out there. Promise me."

"Just hurry up," I begged.

"Promise me."

I looked my father directly in the eyes.

"I can't," I whispered.

Arthur cursed but became transparent and disappeared.

Out in the yard, the berserker who was clearly the leader yelled: "Do you want your friend back?"

I opened a window a crack.

"If you do anything to her, I'll kill you." I put as much force into my voice as I could, but it sounded more like a squeak.

The berserker laughed. He spoke, like Aella and Varnar, with a slight accent, but it was different from theirs.

"What do you mean by *do anything to her*? I do not understand your language very well." His face twisted into a mocking grimace. Something flared, and he now held a torch in his hand. He yanked the hood off Luna's head.

She was gagged but her eyes flashed, and she writhed around. In vain, unfortunately, as her hands were bound tightly behind her back.

The man held the torch closer to her, and her eyes grew wide. "They say witches burn like paper."

The air was nearly knocked out of me, and it was only because Varnar and Aella attacked at that moment that I was able to resist throwing myself directly at his throat.

They resembled dangerous wild cats, and I was proud of them, until the berserkers started in on them.

They moved with inhuman speed. Although they received several gashes, they were unfazed. I realized why the four of them reminded me of the Savage. Their auras had the same degenerated edge as his. They must have taken demiblood.

Elias!

644

Monster attacked with a roar worthy of a lion. His large teeth closed around a berserker's arms, and I heard a loud snap when the bone broke. Another attacker grabbed him around the chest and squeezed until his ribs cracked.

Mads flung open the door and threw himself into the fight. He tore Monster away from the berserker but took a punch to the face that brought him to his knees.

Arthur appeared just then. "Mathias is on his way. So are Ben and Rebecca."

"Help them," I pleaded.

He passed through the wall and grabbed the female berserker by the throat. She gurgled and flailed, but all her punches went through him. Arthur's poltergeist abilities were not strong enough, however, to hold on to her for long, and she fought her way toward Varnar.

A giant ball of energy hit her in the back. Flames burst on her rags and in her hair, but she kept fighting.

Ben's large figure approached across the field with arms raised, Rebecca behind him. Her wild eyes cut through the darkness all the way up to me.

"Let my daughter go, you coward," thundered Ben.

The leader of the berserkers seemed more clearheaded than the others, and he avoided direct combat with my friends. He must not have taken demiblood.

"Let her go? Gladly." He waved the torch over Luna's dress and pushed her toward Ben and Rebecca.

Blue flames surrounded her immediately, and it actually did appear that witches were highly flammable. She rolled around on the ground in a sea of flames.

Rebecca threw herself forward.

Varnar and Aella were fighting as hard as they could, but it was not enough.

A knife glimmered and struck Aella in the arm. She screamed

and simultaneously took a fist to her side. She collapsed and received a kick in the stomach. The blade flashed again, and it would have landed in her neck if Varnar hadn't gotten between them.

The knife dug into his shoulder, and it remained there as he defended himself with the other arm.

Arthur whizzed around and tried to help, but he couldn't do much against the demiblood-enhanced berserkers.

Ben sent cascades of fireballs and flames toward them. The smell of burnt skin and hair spread through the air, but they fought on, unbothered.

Mathias was still several minutes away. I was struck with the chilling realization that he would not get here in time.

One of the berserkers was holding on to Varnar, who tried to twist himself free, the knife still sticking out of his shoulder.

Aella lay lifeless on the ground. Monster snarled and gnashed his teeth. Some of his ribs bulged strangely under his bloody fur. Ben and Mads tried to get past the last three berserkers to reach Varnar, but they held their ground. And Rebecca knelt at her daughter's side, mumbling spells.

I realized that my friends were losing. They would all die.

The head berserker grabbed Varnar's hair.

"I can see that the story of how you were ripped to shreds by the Wolf Folk is grossly exaggerated, Varnar of the Bronze Forest." He turned his face toward the house. "Shall we see if he'll come back from the dead again?" he called. "Or will you come out here and get him?"

"Stay inside," Varnar yelled with great effort as the berserker gripped the knife that was still buried in his shoulder.

What the hell am I supposed to do?

With hands that grew clumsy from working quickly, I tore the business card from my wallet, which had Niels Villadsen's number on it. My fingers trembled as I typed the number.

"Anna," Niels said on the other end. "Od and Mathias were just here. Do you know why they suddenly . . ."

I cut him off. "There's a group of berserkers here. They're about to kill Varnar."

"Varnar?" Niels balked.

My breath caught as I heard Varnar cry out in pain. I looked out the window and saw the berserker twisting the knife. Then he pulled it out slowly and laid it against Varnar's neck.

"I'm giving you one hundred heartbeats," he shouted, "before I slit his throat."

I spoke rapidly into the phone.

"Send a strike team—or do something diplomatically."

The voice at the other end was tensely neutral.

"If Varnar of the Bronze Forest is alive, he's a wanted man. It's Ragnara's right to apprehend him."

"But he'll be killed," I yelled.

"I'm sorry. There's nothing I can do in this case. My hands are ti—"

I threw the phone aside as I heard another howl of pain from the yard.

Desperate times call for desperate measures, so I ran upstairs. As I heard shouts and struggle outside, I fumbled around in the dark of my bedroom. Finally—after having rummaged in the closet for what felt like a lifetime—I found the bag. The knot was tight, and I couldn't get it loose. Eventually, I tore the plastic to pieces and pulled out my bloodstained shirt.

I ran downstairs and pulled the rusty spear down from the wall. In my hand, it shook with energy and began to glow.

I yanked open the front door.

Outside, I was met with a horrific sight. Monster lay panting on his side. Mads was on his knees, and over him stood a berserker with a raised axe. Rebecca was trying to protect her daughter, who lay smoking and sooty on the ground, while the female berserker attacked unabated, and no matter how many energy bombs Ben sent toward the frenzied fighters, they fought on like half-charred robots. The leader was still holding the bloody blade to Varnar's throat.

When he saw me leaving Odinmont, Varnar shouted desperately: "No, Anna!"

The berserker grinned. "Thank you for joining us." His smile stiffened when he caught sight of the glowing spear.

Something that felt like a snake unfurled in me and twisted around in my body. It hissed its venom into me. I could taste Mathias's blood.

I swung the spear and hit the berserker who was holding Varnar. Like white-hot metal through butter, it pierced his chest with a whistling sound. He let go of Varnar, and to my surprise, he cried out in pain.

Inside me, the snake hissed and grew.

I stabbed the man who stood over Mads. The spear slid, smoking and sputtering, into his stomach, and he, too, screamed loudly.

The snake inside me became a dragon that threatened to combust inside of me.

I stabbed the woman and the last berserker. They both howled when the spear pierced them.

Its power buzzed in me, and it spoke inside my head.

I was forged by the Sons of Ivaldi using rune magic. Kill. Create fear.

I now turned to the leader. My eyes were flamethrowers against his, and the breath from my mouth was scalding hot.

He walked backward with wide eyes.

"Do you understand my language now?" I asked with a voice that sounded nothing like my own.

Fear radiated from him, and I laughed. My laughter was caustic, and I reveled in the reaction it produced. Pure, unadulterated fear. I saw his entire past unfurling behind him. All those he had killed stood there, silent and angry.

I grew taller. Fire flowed from my mouth, and the spear spoke to me again.

I am Gungnir. Kill with me, it whispered. *Destroy. Dominate.*

I raised Gungnir to chop the berserker into pieces.

The ghosts behind him urged me on.

Gungnir, in my hand, pulled me forward.

The dragon inside me roared.

A cool hand stroked my cheek. "Stand down."

I spun around and looked into Od's gentle eyes. His whole long life stretched out like a tunnel behind him, and shining silver threads oozed from him.

Behind him, Mathias knelt at Luna's side. He was gigantic and beautiful, shining green. Ben and Rebecca stared at me. Their pasts wrapped around them, too. Ben was in tattered clothes and chains, and white wings sprang from Rebecca's back. I blinked a couple times.

"Drop the spear," said Od.

I held tight.

"He must be killed." Once again, I pointed the glowing spear at the berserker, who fell backward and squirmed on the ground.

"He'll get his punishment. Drop it." Od's voice was commanding, and he placed all his divine powers of persuasion on me.

It bounced right off me. The demiblood surged through me, and Gungnir laughed.

"You'll succumb to the blood if it remains in your body. And the spear will consume you."

"I'm strong right now." My voice had a metallic whine to it.

"The blood and Gungnir are strong. You yourself are weak in relation to that power."

I wavered, and the dragon inside me snarled.

On the ground lay Aella. I saw her as a little girl with long dark hair.

Varnar looked at me, and behind him stood him as a boy. The

boy was dirty and had a dead, murderous look in his eyes. He held a bloody axe in his little hand.

I shook my head.

"She's hallucinating." Od's voice was muffled behind the dragon's buzzing and Gungnir's laughter.

"She's falling," Ben's voice shifted into an incomprehensible language. An overwhelming scent of sunshine and spices hit me when I landed in his arms. His face was painted with a white, gritty substance, and above us, Rebecca hovered on her angel wings.

My body shook with spasms.

Mathias's voice had a hysterical edge. "She's not breathing. What do we do?"

"We must pray that she survives, and that her mind isn't damaged." Od's words reached me through the many visions that were racing toward me from all sides.

On the ground, the berserkers' leader gave a gloating laugh.

The ghosts of his victims looked expectantly at me from behind him.

Before I slipped completely into the nightmare, I urged: "Take him!"

The dead smiled and threw themselves upon him.

I don't know how many days I was tossed around in the troubled sea of dream visions.

Hooded figures hunted me through endless darkened forests. No matter how fast I ran, I never reached the snow-covered fields. Ghosts held me back with their icy hands, and knives pierced my heart again and again.

I saw distorted versions of everyone I knew. Frank with the crying boy, Mathias as a golden, shining god, Luna ice-cold and nearly transparent on a bonfire of blue flames, and Little Mads as a tree with a rough trunk. Monster looked at me with red eyes, and above him rose a gigantic wolf, its teeth dripping with blood. Hakim was there at one point. He and Ben fought each other with spears and swords, and they were both dressed in strange leather armor. Hakim wanted to reach me, but Ben forced him back.

Through the nightmares, Od talked to me the whole time. His hoarse voice was the rope I clung to through the hurricane.

"Let Elias heal you," he said several times.

"No," I rasped through chapped lips.

Svidur lay on the ground, impaled by Gungnir. He looked at me with his single eye.

"I lack your faith," he moaned. "I need for people to believe in me."

Finally, Elias appeared in my dream. He had longer hair and wore old-fashioned clothes. He smiled teasingly and gave a gallant bow. Then he did some odd dance steps.

"You betrayed me," I moaned as a serpent knot wrapped itself around me and threatened to squeeze the life out of me. One of the snakes tightened around my neck, so I had difficulty breathing.

He nodded and held out a beautiful, long-stemmed glass. It was filled with orange liquid.

"That is what I do," he said. "I betray those I love."

I swung my arm and knocked the glass out of his hand.

The shards slashed him, and he looked down. When he raised his head again, he had snake eyes, and green scales spread across his body.

"Hold her arm," he hissed to the serpent knot, and the snakes obeyed. Then he bit down with his razor-sharp teeth. They punctured my forearm, and I screamed as he interlaced himself with the other snakes. "This should help," he spat as the potion spread through me.

Slowly, the visions were banished, and I heard trickling water and smelled live greenery. Under my bare feet there was soft moss, and sunshine hit me through a screen of leaves.

A woman came toward me. Her dark hair was shiny and smooth, and she had a ruddy, bare face.

"Hejd?" I asked.

She spoke, and although the language was foreign, I was able to understand it.

> She knows of the horn of Heimdall, hidden
> Under the high-reaching holy tree;
> On it there pours from Valfather's pledge
> A mighty stream: would you know yet more?

"What is the horn of Heimdall?" I asked.

She took a step forward but her feet sank into the ground, up to her ankles. I saw that the moss was only a thin film over water and mud.

> One did she see in the wet woods bound,
> A lover of ill, and to Loki like;
> By his side does Sigyn sit, nor is glad
> To see her mate: would you know yet more?

Hejd tried to pull her feet out of the mud with a frustrated expression, and she gesticulated wildly as if to explain something to me.

I reached out to her to help. "Loki? Why are you talking about Loki?"

Hejd tilted her head, as if she was making a great effort to understand me. She continued.

> A hall she saw, far from the sun
> On Nastrond it stands, and the doors face north;
> Venom drops through the smoke-vent down,
> For around the walls do serpents wind.
> There feeds he full on the flesh of the dead,

And the home of the gods he reddens with gore;
Dark grows the sun, and in summer soon
Come the mighty storms: would you know yet more?

She had sunk down to her thighs.

"What serpents are you talking about? I don't understand."

I took her hands and tried to pull her up, but the force that was pulling her down was too strong.

Surt fares from the south with the scourge of branches,
The sun of the battle-gods shone from his sword;
The dead throng Hel-way, and heaven is cloven.

She sank quickly to her waist, then to her neck, and finally the water began to close over her head. Then she leaned her head back, so only her mouth protruded.

Now she must sink.

Her hands slipped out of mine, and she was gone.

CHAPTER 41

I awoke to a quite different reality than the one I had left.

The first thing I saw was a pile of colorful pillows. Then I saw Mathias's burning blue eyes, followed by Luna's concerned gaze. I lay in the small room in Ben and Rebecca's house that Luna had set up for me before we had even met.

"You aren't burned at all," I said to Luna. My voice was raspy and dry.

She looked at me and laughed shakily. Tears ran down her cheeks. Mathias cautiously took my hand.

"It's good to see you," he said. "And good to see you alive and well. You've been out for almost two weeks."

Luna ran out of the room.

"Mom, Dad," she shouted. "Anna's awake."

Two weeks . . .

Alone with Mathias, I figured I might as well get it over with.

"Did anyone die?" I whispered, my voice raw.

"The berserkers were in bad shape, but you didn't kill anyone," said Mathias. "And everyone else survived, too."

I exhaled slowly. "How are they?"

"Fine. Elias is a miracle worker. Luna's burns are gone, although some of her hair got fried. The others have also healed. His potions don't work on giants, so Monster and Mads will have to heal on their own, but they're healing quickly, thanks to their giant blood."

"Speaking of blood . . ."

Mathias squeezed my hand. "I can't figure out if I'm mad or impressed that you drank my blood. I, of all people, know what you had to fight against."

I remembered the creature that had threatened to blow me up from the inside.

Mathias continued: "But you saved everyone. You saved Luna, and for that I am eternally thankful."

"She wouldn't have been in danger in the first place if it weren't for me," I pointed out.

Mathias didn't respond.

"Why did I have such a violent reaction? The berserkers were only a little dazed from the demiblood."

"Because you drank it. That's apparently a big no-no. And combined with your clairvoyant powers, your brain just boiled over."

I didn't want to think about it anymore. "Where's Varnar?"

Mathias didn't manage to reply before the entire Sekibo family came bursting in.

"Anna," cried Rebecca. "I'm so glad you're okay."

Luna jumped up and down, and I noticed that her blue curls were somewhat shorter.

I tried to get up but couldn't even support myself on my elbows. "I want to go home."

An uneasy feeling spread through the room. Mathias avoided my gaze, Luna's eyes filled once more with tears, and Ben and Rebecca looked at each other.

With difficulty, I pulled myself halfway to sitting up. "What's going on?"

"It was all very chaotic," said Mathias. "Elias treated people at Odinmont. After he had given them laekna, they lay sleeping all over the place. And we had to lock the berserkers' leader in the barn, because he was yelling and screaming. Something about the dead being after him. Do you know anything about that?"

"No," I said curtly. "Then what happened?"

"Your caseworker came by."

I stared at him, aghast.

"Or, actually, first Hakim Murr came, but he left again after he and Ben had a huge fight over whether you should be hospitalized. Maybe he was the one who got in touch with Greta."

"And what did Greta see when she came?"

"She saw unconscious people lying around, while that guy shouted psychotically in the barn. And she found you hallucinating. You were lying in bed with Od."

"With Od?!" I sat up fully and nearly collapsed from the effort.

Luna rushed to prop a few pillows behind me.

"Od gave you strength to prevent you from becoming permanently insane," she said. "I believe he saved you."

Right now it was almost tempting to flee back into my visions.

"We couldn't tell the truth, of course," Ben rumbled.

"Couldn't you hypnotize her?" I moaned.

"There are some images that even I can't remove from the retina. We said we had found the house and you in that state, which is not far from the truth."

"Oh no," I groaned and hid my face in my hands. "What did she do?"

Silence.

"Say it," I shouted.

Mathias exhaled forcefully as if to prepare himself. "She called a doctor. He concluded that you had ingested a powerful, unidentified narcotic, and that only time, care, and luck would bring you back. So she asked us to pack your things and move you here. We did, and Od and Elias took the berserkers with them."

"What else?" I knew Greta. There had to be something else.

"Then . . ." He hesitated but then forced the words out. "Then she sold Odinmont."

Odinmont was sold? To whom? And what about Arthur's body?

656

I realized that I hadn't asked any of the questions aloud but was just staring mutely at Mathias.

He read them anyway. "We don't know who bought the house."

"But . . . but . . ." I attempted. "But it's my house."

"Not anymore," said Luna, but when she saw my face, she added: "We'll get it back."

I tried to compose myself. "How?"

"I don't know, but we'll figure it out."

I closed my eyes and sank back into the pillows.

Someone cleared their throat at the door, and I looked up.

I couldn't place the muscular, gray-haired, bearded man who filled the entire doorframe.

"I'm your new bodyguard," he said with a deep voice. "I'm from Freiheim. My name is Une."

I looked around the room in confusion. "Did I get more? Where's Varnar?"

"The commander . . ." Une managed to say, but he was pushed aside by Aella, who showed up just then. She only came up to his shoulder.

"I need to speak with Anna alone."

Reluctantly, people slunk away.

"What's going on?" I wasn't sure I could handle more bad news.

Aella sat on the mattress and took my hand. I pulled it back.

"Tell me. What the hell is going on?"

She smiled weakly. "I'm glad to see you're doing well."

"*Well* is an overstatement."

"But you're yourself again." She picked at a tassel on a yellow pillow and, several times, prepared herself to speak.

"Aella . . . where is Varnar?" I dreaded the answer.

She looked up, and her face held both fear and empathy. "He left."

"Left?"

"He went back to Hrafnheim."

657

I bit my lip, hard. "Why?"

"He thinks your relationship prevents him from protecting you properly."

I sat up again, and this time my fury held me upright. "Can he make up his mind? Last time we talked about it, he said his feelings make him a *better* protector."

Aella's eyes were sympathetic. "Your feelings for him are the problem."

"My feelings?"

"You risked your life and your sanity to save him. And that was the second time you did so. That night with Naut Kafnar you did the same thing."

"But . . ."

"He wants you to forget him," she said quickly. "He said you're free to be with someone else, if that would make you happy."

I wanted to protest, but she continued. "He took Etunaz with him. He needs care, and they agreed that he would only be a hindrance here."

Monster is gone, too?

"Hindrance? I would be more than happy to take care of him."

Aella smiled weakly. "I'm actually inclined to agree with them."

"About what?"

"That your feelings for others are a threat to your own safety."

At school on Monday, I sat there like a bike with a flat tire.

I had lost Varnar, Monster, Odinmont, and two weeks of my life. It's incredible how quickly everything can be turned upside down.

And suddenly my feelings for people were a danger to me, which was a bit of a twist after having not known or liked very many people before. I tried to ignore my deep longing for Varnar and Monster.

I had tried, on several occasions, to approach Odinmont, but someone had cast a spell on the entire hill, and I hit an invisible wall no matter how hard I tried to get in. Even the witches' magic was no match for it.

Luna chattered next to me. It was now the middle of December, and there was just over a week until my birthday. She had big plans for the evening, and she talked about them as we sat side by side on the red sofa, while I stared apathetically through the rain-streaked windows.

The official story was that I had thrown a wild party at Odinmont. We had consumed dangerous homemade drugs, and it had all gone wrong. Some of the guests had nearly died, and I and an unknown man had had bad trips. Luna and Mathias, the Goody-Two-shoes, had come to my rescue and called in responsible adults in the form of Ben and Rebecca. Od and Elias managed to keep themselves anonymous, but the story of me in bed with a strange man over thirty had spread far and wide. I had, as unlikely as it seemed, managed to obtain an even worse reputation.

The official story in the hidden world was that some berserkers had acted of their own accord. Od had stepped in on the strength of his neutral position and held them back. The peace between Midgard and Freiheim was intact, although it balanced on a knife's edge. One of the berserkers had gone a little psychotic upon being attacked by his deceased victims and mixed Varnar up with them. He insisted that it was Varnar's ghost he had met in Midgard. If he suspected that he had seen Varnar alive, he kept it to himself, and Varnar was therefore still officially dead.

"We can have it at Frank's." Luna was still talking. "Are you even listening?"

"What? No. I mean yes. Will Frank let me have my birthday there? Hasn't he heard all the rumors?" I assumed I had lost my job thanks to the "orgy."

Mathias patted me on the shoulder. "Frank's first reaction was that it must have been some kind of misunderstanding."

"You didn't say anything, did you?"

"No, of course not. He can draw his own conclusions. But he wanted us to tell you to just call when you're ready to work again."

One point for Frank. I looked out the window again as Luna prattled on. Once in a while, I contributed a *mhmm* to her stream of words.

After school, I walked down to Frank's. I could sense Une behind me the whole way, but I couldn't be bothered to either shake him off or walk with him.

Frank jumped out from behind the counter when he saw me. He pulled me to him.

"Anna. It's so good to see you. I've been so worried." He held me out with straightened arms. "You must have lost at least ten pounds. Come on, I'll have Milas make some food for you."

Une slid onto a high stool slightly apart from us.

I took off my mom's coat and crawled up onto a barstool as well. Frank came out with a large plate of fries and two burgers shortly thereafter.

"I can't eat all that."

"You can bring the rest to your dog."

My facial expression betrayed me.

"Not again," said Frank. "Did he run away?"

"He got hurt. The night . . ." I stopped myself.

Frank's brows wrinkled slightly. "What really happened there? Everyone's asking me. Including your policeman."

"He's not mine." I sighed. "And I don't really know. I don't remember much."

Frank accepted my vague answer and changed the subject. "When can you work again?"

"There are so many problems with me. I can't believe you're keeping me on."

Frank laughed, and the smile lines formed a fan around his eyes.

"Of course I'm keeping you, now that I finally have you." He winked and let me eat in peace while he went down to Une and took his order.

Une fumbled a little with the coins, and I resisted the urge to help him.

If he wanted to be a secret bodyguard in a foreign world, it was his responsibility to master the currency.

"Anna," came a familiar voice behind me.

I didn't turn toward Hakim, but instead stuffed a couple fries in my mouth. He sat next to me.

"Am I about to get a lecture?" I asked between two mouthfuls. "Or did you come to arrest me?"

"I actually wanted to know if you're okay."

"That's a bit hard to answer."

"Try."

I sighed. "I'm okay."

"Why is that man following you?" He nodded toward Une.

"Is he?"

"Yes. And where's the other guy who usually follows you?"

I placed the fries I had just picked up back on the plate. "What do you want, really?"

"You weren't on drugs. I've seen people on bad trips. That's not what was going on with you."

"What was going on with me, then?"

"I was hoping you could tell me."

For a moment, we just looked at each other. Then I picked up my burger and bit into it so I had an excuse not to talk.

"I've received an invitation."

I shrugged to indicate that I had no idea what he was talking about.

"To your birthday on Saturday."

I coughed and swallowed my food with difficulty. "Did Luna invite you?"

"I figured it wasn't your idea."

"It wasn't my idea to throw a party at all. She took advantage of the fact that I was unconscious."

Hakim suppressed a grin, but then grew serious. "Is it okay with you if I come?"

"Why would you want to go to my party?"

"Because . . ." He collected himself. "There was something you said when you were delirious."

"Oh no. What did I say?"

"That you were going to die on your birthday. That he would come after you on that day. So I would like to be here, even though I have a hunch that you're pretty well protected." He glanced again at Une, who was looking down at his beer.

I closed my eyes. "You and your hunches. I was hallucinating. I probably also said the moon is made of green cheese."

"No, but you said that Luna is the moon. And that Mathias is the sun, and you and your sister are the stars. I didn't know you had a sister."

I opened my eyes and looked at him with the sincerest expression I could muster. "I don't."

"Liar." He stood.

Frank came back over at once.

"What did you call her?"

Out of the corner of my eye, I saw Une stand halfway with a Varnar-like movement that pierced my heart.

Frank continued: "I don't care that you're a policeman. You have no right . . ."

I stood, too.

"Stop it. Both of you. You, too." This last bit was directed at Une, who was walking toward us. "I have enough problems already."

The three men looked at one another. Then they nodded.

"Thanks!" I pulled my coat back on. "Should I come to work tomorrow?"

Frank looked indignantly at me. "No. You're on sick leave until after your birthday."

"Fine," I mumbled.

Frank disappeared into the kitchen and came back with two wrapped sandwiches. He handed them to me.

"For both of you," he mumbled and nodded at Une.

How much has Frank figured out?

I took them and hurried to leave.

Une slunk silently after me.

"Do you want to fight?"

Une, surprised, coughed on his soup. The drops hung in his long beard, and he wiped them away with his sleeve.

A couple of days had passed. Aella had forced me to eat at Kraghede Manor, and just being there caused all the memories of Varnar to assault me. I could in no way sit still, let alone eat anything.

"Who would we be fighting against?" Aella asked, picking her bread into little crumbs.

"Me."

She smiled. "Whose team do you want to be on? The girls against the boy, or you two against me?"

"I'm alone. It's you two against me."

Une shook his head. "I'm here to protect you, not to fight you."

"Oh, is it too hard for you to defeat a teensy little girl?" I said these last words in a baby voice.

"Anna," said Aella. "There's really no reason for it."

Une gnashed his teeth. "You're bold. Bold and stupid. I've been a Varangian guard for fifteen years. And with Thora for three. You wouldn't last two seconds against me."

"Against both of you," I corrected. "Come on. I need to train."

"You don't need to train when I'm around."

"What about when you aren't around?"

663

He stood. "Do you doubt my loyalty?"

"Good, you stood up. I was starting to worry you were more interested in Aella's food than in keeping me alive. Then I would really be in trouble. She's almost as hopeless in the kitchen as I am."

"Hey!" Aella stood, too.

I ran out of the kitchen and into the yard. They cursed in unison and followed after me.

"You can't run out alone," Une bellowed after me. "Tell me, how have you kept her alive for so long?" This was directed at Aella.

"Believe me, it hasn't been easy," she grumbled. "Come back, Anna."

I snuck through the shadows and led them on a wild-goose chase for a while.

Finally, they found me in the old riding hall. I sat cross-legged on the ground.

"Glad you could make it," I said calmly.

Une was breathing angrily, and Aella's eyes were wild. They were in precisely the state of mind I was hoping for. Provoked and ready to hit me. I did a backflip and struck Une's arm with my foot.

"I don't want to fight you, Thora's daughter."

I knocked Aella's legs out from under her, and she landed on her back in the sawdust.

"I promised your sister that nothing would happen to you in my presence," she said and stood up as she brushed off her hands.

Once she was up, I repeated the move, and she landed on her back again. She shouted a few most unladylike curses.

I laughed and did the same to Une.

He got up with a gliding, feline movement, and I could all too easily guess who had taught it to him. This made me kick him in the shin a little harder than I'd actually meant to. I bit back an apology.

"You . . ." He hopped on one leg and reached out to me.

I whipped around, and he grasped at the air.

Aella also tried to catch me, but I ducked and planted a fist in her bicep.

"We'll take off the kid gloves if you don't stop," she hissed, clutching her arm.

"By all means, take them off." I bowed to them, and they threw themselves at me.

After a short time, I had seen and memorized both of their fighting styles, so I could calculate their next moves. It cost me a couple of kicks and punches to figure it out, but afterward, I was ahead of them almost every step of the way.

The two of them were talented, but not like Varnar. Not even close. I realized just how good Varnar was. Agitated, I wiped my arm across my eyes, but it was that split second that made the difference.

Aella hit my cheek with her open hand, and Une grabbed me from behind, so my arms were locked.

I kicked, but he was prepared and stood in such a way that I couldn't hit him.

"Are you done?" Aella asked quietly.

I scoffed and writhed.

"I know you miss him. Both of them."

"You know nothing." I sniffed to hold back the blood in my nose.

"Surely you don't mean that? I left Serén to save your ungrateful ass."

The anger seeped out of me. I relaxed in Une's arms.

"Just let me go."

He let go, and I landed on the ground, gasping for air. Une went to the door, where he assumed a guard position.

Aella knelt over me. "We'll take you home, and we'll stay in the living room tonight. We won't go near your door unless you call for us."

It would take a person who knew me well to know that was precisely what I needed.

"*Now* what's happened?" asked Mathias the next day in front of the classroom on Yellow Hall. He took my jaw and turned my face from side to side.

I pushed his hand away. "Nothing."

"Who hit you?"

How the hell can he see the tiny mark on my cheek?

"Aella."

"Why on earth did she hit you?"

"I attacked her and Une."

He threw up his hands. "Don't you have enough enemies?"

"No. I need a few more." I made a face.

Just then, Luna arrived.

"I'm almost done with your dress," she announced. "Oh. Are you two mad at each other again?"

"Anna attacked two Varangian guards. The ones who, it's worth noting, are supposed to protect her."

"I needed to blow off some steam," I mumbled. "Wait, what did you say? What dress?"

"The one for your birthday. It's so pretty. It's blue and white and has beading here." Her hand stopped over her chest when she saw my expression. "You said yes."

Mathias scratched his forehead. "I'm not sure I understand why we're throwing a party. On that specific day. Isn't it better to keep Anna home with you?"

"She can't get any better protection than at Frank's, surrounded by all of us," said Luna. "If Ragnara comes after her, it's more likely that she'll attack our house. My parents also agree that it's better for her to be away then."

I interrupted her.

"When did I willingly agree to wear blue and white? Not to mention a dress!"

"The other day, when we were sitting in The Island."

I put my head in my hands. "You can't do that to me."

"You can*not* back out when you give your word to a witch."

"Who came up with that rule?"

She grinned. "The witches."

The dress really was pretty, but I put it on only because I was under the influence of powerful persuasion magic. It was deep blue and snow white and made of a slightly transparent material, and something about it tickled my memory, but I couldn't put my finger on it.

It was Saturday afternoon. We were at Ben and Rebecca's house, where I had been living since the news of the sale of Odinmont reached me. Mathias had refreshed my hair dye, so it was now a sparkling black. Luna was ecstatic.

"Happy birthday," she said several times.

"It isn't yet. I wasn't born until just before midnight."

"Okay, then happy solstice," she chirped and did a couple dance steps. She had also sewn herself a new dress of orange silk, and it hugged her body tightly. To top it all off—literally—Mathias had dyed her hair the exact same shade of orange. "Aren't you excited for tonight?" she asked.

"I wish I could skip it. I'm not in the mood to be around a bunch of people."

"But you never are." Luna produced the box with the green velour cover. "Look what I saved from Odinmont."

She opened it and displayed the red necklace.

"I don't want to wear it. Od gave it to my mom, but she didn't want to wear it for some reason."

Mathias frowned with disappointment. "But it goes so well with the dress."

"And there's a power to it," agreed Luna. "I think it can protect you."

Rebecca came in at that moment. She clapped her hands. "Don't you all look nice."

"Mom, have you seen this before?"

Rebecca took the box from her hands and looked down. She traced a long, slim finger over the red crystal. "Where did you get this?"

"It's Anna's. Od gave it to her mom."

"But my mom didn't want to wear it," I added.

A smile flitted across Rebecca's lips. "So typical of her, to refuse a gift like this."

"A gift like this?"

"This necklace is priceless. But she's very strong-willed." She smiled at me. "The stone is a goddess's tears." She pointed at the two curves of the heart, joined vertically by a small gold band. "It's two drops put together."

I squinted and looked at the heart again. "Ohhh . . ."

"Gods don't cry like we humans do. Their tears are hard like metal or gemstones. And the gold is sacred gold. Obtained in a less than legitimate way, but sacred nonetheless." A faint amusement curled the corners of her mouth, but she suppressed it. "The night you wore it, Mathias must have had to help you with the clasp."

"You noticed? How did you know I couldn't do it myself?"

"Of course I saw that you were wearing it at the equinox ball. And I know you couldn't open it yourself, because only gods and demigods can bend the gold. And dark elves, of course."

"Dark . . . what?" I shook my head. "It doesn't matter. Why did my mom end up with it?"

"Because the goddess shed the tears over your father."

My lips tightened. "Freyja?"

"Normally she cries over her husband, who left her, so she was happy when Arthur died and went to Fólkvangr. But she had to let him go when her husband came back."

"It was Od who took Arthur from Fólkvangr," I said.

"Od *is* her husband."

We all stared at her.

668

"He's what?" I finally stammered.

Rebecca once again smiled her ethereal smile. "You need to read the mythology. Then you'll have a better overview."

"But . . ." Luna interjected. "I know the story of Freyja's husband, Od. It just never occurred to me that there was a connection to Od Dinesen."

"Don't you know by now that connections are everywhere?" Rebecca smoothed her nearly white hair with her hand. "Od left Freyja because he wished to be more human. He felt he took on too many of the gods' qualities when he was with them."

I thought of the night he showed up at my house, silvery and unstable.

"But he's there once in a while," I said.

"Od made an agreement with Freyja. She would release Arthur's spirit until you're of age, and he would spend a month with her after every equinox."

"He's doing that for my sake?"

She nodded. "To protect you."

I bit down hard on my lip. "I didn't ask him to do that."

Rebecca stroked my cheek. "But your father did. And the goddess cried when she let him go."

I pushed her hand away.

"I don't want to wear the necklace." Out the window, I could make out Odinmont and, behind it, Kraghede Forest. My hands instinctively went to my throat to protect it. "Shouldn't we get going?" I asked sharply and turned around.

Luna's large eyes looked at me, pleading, but I shook my head stubbornly, so she swallowed her protests.

"Yes," she said simply. "We should go. Come on, Mathias."

We all walked out to the orange Volkswagen bus, where Ben met us wearing a fur hat and an ankle-length overcoat.

"Even after all these years, I'll never get used to the temperature in this country," he grumbled.

I realized that the chill had shifted from humid and clammy to bone-dry. A fine sprinkling of snow had settled over the fields.

Trembling, I realized that this was how they looked in the vision.

Frank's was festooned with balloons and flags, and I marveled at the decoration before I realized it was for me.

Luna bounced around. "Frank, it looks great."

There weren't many people at the bar yet, and none of them were there for me. I considered how many people Luna could have persuaded to come. Not many, I guessed.

"Nothing but the best for Anna," Frank said with a crooked grin.

My *thanks* remained on my lips, and I walked, flustered, into the kitchen to set down my coat. Alone in the kitchen, I exhaled a couple of times. Then I got out the ampoule of klinte and dabbed a little on my tongue. Demiblood, longing for Varnar and Monster, and my otherwise nervous state made it impossible for me to shield. If I was going to make it through the evening with all these people without ending up on the floor, I needed to take klinte.

"Why are you standing in here alone?"

I jumped when Frank spoke to me. I hadn't heard him come in, and I once again was reminded how much I used my clairvoyance to gauge other people. I laughed nervously.

"I just needed a minute alone before it gets going."

"Should I . . ." Frank pointed toward the bar.

"No, stay."

"Then can you help me with this? It needs to go out back." He kicked one of the refrigerators. "It went kaput yesterday. Don't tell Milas I told you this, but his back isn't so good, so I don't want him dragging it."

"Of course." I laid down my coat, glad to be able to do something practical.

Together we dragged the large block outside and stood for a moment in the twilight.

"Did I already say happy birthday?" Frank put a hand on my arm.

"No. And you don't need to, either. I don't like all the attention."

"I only asked for your help with the fridge as an excuse. Milas's back is fine."

I stopped and backed toward the door with my heart pounding. "Why?"

"I have something for you." He came closer and dug around in his pocket. He pulled out his hand and laid something in my palm.

I looked down. It was a key.

"It's to the apartment over the bar. It's no house, but it has a kitchenette and its own shower and toilet. You can live there as long as you want."

"What do you know about my housing situation?"

He looked down. "Mathias told me. Do you know who bought Odinmont?"

I shook my head. "I went up there, but it was locked up and empty." I left out the fact that the whole hill had a spell placed on it. I squeezed the key. "This is seriously the best present I could have asked for."

I don't know what made me put my arms around him. He squeezed me close to him, almost desperately.

"Uh, Frank. That's hard enough," I coughed with a grin.

"You need to take better care of yourself," he said into my ear.

"Hold on. We've talked about this. I've gotten much better about that."

"Have you?" asked a voice from the shadows.

 # CHAPTER 42

Christian Mikkelsen stepped out of the shadows. Markus slipped behind us and stood in front of the back door. Peter stepped closer, and a fourth man—I recognized the aura as the thin man who had shot Mathias—placed himself in front of the exit to the alley.

"You," I hissed.

The thin man looked at me. "I have never seen you before."

Ben's magical Teflon must have worked on him.

Frank stood between us with his arms spread out. He was good at fighting, but even he couldn't take on four jacked men, so I flexed my hands and rolled my shoulders. God, I really wished I hadn't taken klinte. I tried to buy a little time.

"Did you bring your little friends to beat me up because I hurt your feelings?" I bent my knees to ready for the first punch.

Christian ran a large hand over his tattooed scalp. "Not at all. I'm just supposed to hand you over to my anonymous employer. Though I must admit, I'm mixing work and pleasure."

Ragnara?

"The pleasure is all mine," I said and clenched my fists.

"Are you sure?" asked Christian, and I stiffened when he showed me what he had in his hand. A leather cord. "My employer wants you dead or alive."

Shit! This cord is identical to the one in the vision.

The reactions of his three companions did not surprise me. The thin one smiled expectantly. Peter glanced at Christian, and Markus didn't seem to have a clue what was going on.

"I'm sorry you got dragged into this, Frank," I whispered.

"You don't need to be sorry about anything," he whispered back.

Christian advanced.

Frank moved between us before Christian hit me, and took the punch to his chest. He grunted in pain but hit back and struck Christian's nose, which crunched and turned bluish white. Christian roared angrily.

The thin man had pulled a knife that was laughably small compared to those of the berserkers, but which could still cause fatal damage if it hit you the wrong way. I approached him.

"A little girl in a fancy dress." He laughed and swung the knife.

After having trained with Varnar, I could see how inexpertly he handled the weapon. I did a roundhouse kick and struck him in the wrist.

He shouted in surprise but held fast to the knife and thrust it again toward me.

Out of the corner of my eye, I saw Christian launch himself at me from the side.

Meanwhile, Markus and Peter were defending themselves against Frank, who was a far superior fighter. I recognized the fluid movements of the Varangian Guard.

What is going on?

When I did a backflip to avoid the knife and simultaneously kicked the thin man in the shoulder, knocking it out of its socket, I caught Frank's surprised expression. Our eyes met for a split second before fighting on.

Christian barreled toward me. He hadn't counted on me being able to fight so well. I had also been far less skilled the last time he attacked me, but now I danced around and struck him with punches and kicks.

"Arthur and Mathias," I yelled.

Arthur manifested himself immediately. He flickered like a defective neon sign, and a moment passed before I realized that it

673

was because of the klinte. With a shiver, it dawned on me that the drug could potentially cut me off from my father.

"Not again," he sighed when he saw that I was in trouble. Then he recognized Markus and Peter. "I've wanted to do this since you were kids," he hissed and approached Markus. He grabbed Markus's wrists and twisted them so they pointed toward his own face.

Markus screamed in surprise when he hit himself in the head.

"This is what you get for attacking my daughter," Arthur breathed into Peter's ear, which turned bluish and was covered in frost. Then he stepped into Markus and took over his body. He hurled it at Peter, who looked at his friend in shock.

Markus, possessed by Arthur, attacked Peter, and they all tumbled into a big heap. If I hadn't been so busy avoiding getting chopped to pieces, I would have laughed out loud at the sight of Markus alternating between hitting Peter and himself.

Frank took a couple seconds to breathe before running over to help me.

Both Christian and the thin man clearly regretted the attack, now that half of their group members were fighting among themselves, and Frank and I had proven ourselves to be dangerous opponents. And when Mathias arrived just then, enormous and glowing green, they were ready to split.

The thin man paled when he recognized him. "You . . . you're dead."

"I am?" asked Mathias with a creaking metallic voice. He grabbed him by the throat with a large hand.

The man's feet lifted from the ground, and he swung the knife and cut Mathias on the cheek. The gash closed quickly, and the man threw the knife away as it made a sizzling sound in his hand.

Christian held his hands in the air and stood still to signal surrender.

"Mathias," I said. "Don't kill him."

Mathias turned his head and gave me a wild look.

I had to take a step back, but I held his gaze. Then he relaxed, lowered the man, and tossed him on the ground.

Arthur rose from Markus's body. He was more transparent than ever, and I wasn't sure if it was because of the klinte or because he had used up all his strength.

I soon got my answer.

"It's hard on me, possessing someone. I'm going to have to rest for a few days."

"It's okay, Arthur. We did it. The danger is averted," I said as he faded and vanished into the ice-cold air. "See you later."

"Police," came a voice from the alley. There were several voices, but I recognized this one.

"I can't let Hakim see me," I said and ran to the back entrance. The others slipped in, but I managed to catch a glimpse of Hakim as he rounded the corner.

"Anna," he shouted.

I dashed through the back door right after Frank and Mathias. We holed up in the kitchen, and Frank locked the door.

His eyes scanned back and forth between us. They landed on Mathias.

"I hired a demi," he observed. Because of the klinte, I couldn't tell if he was proud or afraid. He bowed.

"Stop bowing at Mathias," I snapped. "And why do you fight like a Varangian guard?"

"Why do *you*?" he shot back.

Just then, Hakim pounded on the door. "Anna. Open up. I saw you."

"Shit," I cursed.

Mathias spoke quickly: "I have an idea." He grabbed a lock of my black hair.

"What are you doing?"

He pulled and suddenly held dark flakes in his hand.

675

"I'm changing your hair color." He pulled again and extracted another handful of dye from my hair.

"I hate my red hair," I whined.

"Anna!" bellowed Hakim. "Open the door. This is an order."

"Okay, then hurry up," I grumbled to Mathias, who quickly ran his fingers through my hair, while Frank looked on, dumbfounded.

"There."

Red tresses draped across my shoulders.

Hakim was now about to kick the door down.

I opened the door and stuck my head out. "What's going on?"

Hakim looked at me with his mouth agape. He tried to speak a couple times, to no avail. On the ground lay my four attackers with their hands tied behind their backs and two police officers standing over them.

"Oh my God," I said as innocently as I could. "What's going on here?"

"You know better than I do," he managed to stammer out.

I shook my head and uneasily brushed a red strand out of my line of sight. "I've been in here for the past half hour."

"I saw you run in just now."

"Did you guys see that, too?" I asked his colleagues.

"All I saw was a black-haired woman," said one.

I lifted a lock of red hair. "So then it couldn't have been me."

Hakim's eyes sparkled. "Why are you always lying to me?"

I leaned in close to him. "Mainly to protect you."

Frank squeezed past me. "Can I be of any assistance?"

"I suspect this man," Hakim pointed at the thin man, "is responsible for some of the Pippi Murders. And Christian Mikkelsen has previously been linked to one of the victims."

"Didn't you already catch the killer?" asked Frank. "Several months ago?"

"I suspected that the case was not solved. We heard shouts coming from here, so I feared that the murderer had struck again."

His eyes lingered on my red hair. "It would appear that I was right."

"I wish I could help," Frank apologized.

Mathias and I headed back to the bar while Hakim and Frank continued talking.

Luna ran up to us. "Mathias, why did you run out so abruptly? And Anna—your hair." She fingered a red tendril.

I shivered, and an uneasy feeling I couldn't fully interpret spread through me.

Mathias gave her a brief summary.

"Does that mean your vision was averted?" Luna smoothed my red tresses pensively.

"It sure looks that way. Christian mentioned his *employer*. That could only be Ragnara. And he had a leather cord like the one in the vision." I carefully removed her hand and tossed my hair behind my shoulders, so I didn't have to look at it.

"What about Frank?" asked Mathias.

"He fights in the same way as Varnar. And he could tell you're a demi."

"Why didn't he say anything?" asked Luna.

"He must not have known that we were also involved. Why does this all have to be so complicated?" I put my head in my hands.

Someone cleared their throat behind me. I twitched and wished, for approximately the twentieth time that night, that I hadn't taken klinte.

I turned and came face-to-face with Elias. He was struggling to keep his face neutral.

"You . . . You look incredibly like your father right now." He fingered a red tendril. "I'd like to speak with you alone."

"So you can stab me in the back again?"

"You have my word that I did what I did for a good reason. To protect our common interests." He raised an eyebrow pointedly.

"You gave the berserkers demiblood," I hissed.

677

Elias did not deny this. "I had a good reason."

I sighed. "You always try to weasel your way out of things. You have five minutes. Luna will stand right over there and keep an eye on you. She'll bomb you with energy balls if you try anything."

Mathias and Luna left reluctantly. Luna stood at the bar and stared at us, unblinking. She extended the index and middle fingers of one hand and pointed them first at her eyes, then at Elias.

I crossed my arms. "Did you tell the berserkers where they could find me?"

Elias looked down without answering, which was answer enough.

"Why the hell did you do that? And why did you sell them demiblood?"

Elias bit his soft lower lip. "Justine saw that you would lose Odinmont."

"Justine?" I put a hand on my hip. "I don't even believe she's clairvoyant."

Elias's gray-blue eyes rested coolly on me. "You shouldn't let your distrust of me carry over to her. She's for real, and you know it."

I refused to answer and stared at him stubbornly.

"She knew the house would fall into Ragnara's hands."

"Ragnara." I couldn't hold the name in and had to fight not to shout it.

"Ragnara isn't coming to Odinmont. She just wanted to chase you out because you were better protected there. The house was purchased by an intermediary."

"But does she have Arthur?" I whispered.

"I have his body. In return for the demiblood, I was allowed to take what I wanted from the crypt. Ragnara didn't know Arthur was there. She thought I was taking my mother."

"Let me get this straight. You helped to create a situation that caused me to lose Odinmont, because you knew that it would happen, so you could be sure to get Arthur's body? But that's all backward. If you hadn't done it, I would still be living there."

"No. Then it would have happened in a different way. It was sure to happen."

"Well, we'll never know, will we?" I snapped. "And make up your mind. Can the future be changed or not?"

He sighed. "I believe that fate can be changed. But also that time can sometimes point strongly in the direction of certain events, which are very difficult to change. I didn't dare take any chances. I did it to help you."

I threw my hands in the air. "I'm not sure how I feel about your way of helping. Where is Arthur?"

"At my home."

"Do you know that people were seriously hurt? I almost went insane. A war almost broke out between Midgard and Hrafnheim."

Elias looked calmly at me. "Justine was almost certain that none of those things would happen. And I did heal the wounded. Even the berserkers."

"Your logic is completely backward."

"But it is logical, nonetheless. If it hadn't been for me, Arthur would now be in enemy hands."

"In a way, he is."

"I'm not your enemy."

"I don't know what you are."

"I'm your most valuable ally." His warm hands landed on my shoulders.

I shrugged them off.

I saw a glimmer of resignation before he once again smiled gallantly. "I didn't even get to say happy birthday. I have a present for you."

"Unless it's my father's body, I'm not sure I want it." This sounded totally wrong, but I maintained the stubborn expression on my face.

Elias produced an orange ampoule.

"And this is?"

"Edrú. According to Justine, you'll need this in the coming days."

"I may not have any coming days." I twisted my lips into a sarcastic smile.

"What do you mean?"

"My sister had a vision that the murderer will attack either me or her tonight."

Elias furrowed his brows. "That can't be right."

"Why not?"

"Justine says you both will live, at least until sometime next year."

"Yay . . ." I made an ironic thumbs-up. "So I can relax tonight?" I shook my head. "It doesn't matter. I don't think it's going to happen now."

Uncertainty simmered in my stomach when I looked down at myself and caught sight of the red hair.

"Don't tell me any more," Elias said with a teasing smile. "I'm just abusing your trust."

Before I could reply, he planted a kiss on my forehead and sauntered off.

Luna rushed over to me. "What do you have there?"

"A birthday present." I stuffed the ampoule into my cleavage.

"Oh, right. That reminds me, I have something for you."

"The dress and this party aren't my gift from you?"

Luna handed me a small package. "It's from Mathias, too."

I opened it, and inside lay a ring with green stones.

"We made it together. The night you were in the worst throes of hallucinations, we didn't know if you were going to make it. Mathias cried, and as with the gods, stones came out instead of tears. I forged the iron into a ring using magic energy."

I examined the simple ring. The green drops were arranged like

680

a flower. I let it slide onto my finger. Although it looked massive, it weighed nearly nothing.

"Thank you."

Luna flashed a huge smile.

Mads came over to us. He held something out to me with his good arm. The other was bandaged up, and he still had bruises and scratches on his face. He gave me a transparent crystal the size of a tennis ball.

"Wow. What is it?"

"I made it," he said. "I just took a flintstone and squeezed it."

"That's wild!"

"It's nothing special." He shrugged. "It can't really be used for anything."

"I can throw it at my enemies." I laughed.

"Well, yeah. You could do that." He smiled crookedly.

"It's a giant-crystal," said a hoarse voice from behind me. "It's highly valuable."

I turned around and looked into Od's gentle face.

"Excuse us," he said to Luna and Mads.

They left immediately, and even smiled as they went.

"There's no reason to hypnotize people. You could have just asked nicely."

He laughed and stroked my hair. "It's so nice to see you as you should be."

"There's no particular way I *should* be." I weighed the giant-crystal in my hand.

"Oh, Anna. Always on edge with everyone." He grasped my hand and studied the ring. "A giant's gift in one hand and a piece of jewelry created through magic, divinity, and humanity on the other. Gifts from beings that are otherwise mortal enemies are in your hands. This can save you or destroy you."

"I don't like it when you speak in Old Norse."

He cocked his head slightly.

"I mean, when you talk like a poem from the olden days."

"I *am* from the olden days." He placed a finger under my chin and tilted my head up.

I was lost in his eyes. "What did you do with Gungnir?" I asked drowsily.

He released me and looked up at the ceiling.

It grew cold when he looked away, and I realized that all of Elias's drugs combined could never measure up to the dependency humans develop in the vicinity of demigods.

"The spear is back on the wall in Odinmont. My father left it there years ago, so that's where it must stay." Od looked at me again, and my legs wobbled beneath me.

"Aren't you worried the new owner," I tried to keep my voice steady, "will take it?"

"He would go up in flames. Humans can't touch it."

"*I touched it.*"

"You had god's blood in your body."

"So does Ragnara, as far as I understand."

"Ragnara won't go to Odinmont. Only the new owner will."

"Do you know who bought the house?" I was about to grab ahold of him.

"Let's not talk any more about that. Do you want to know what your present is?"

I pouted in response.

Od ignored my teenage behavior. "I've spoken with my wife regarding your father."

The pout was immediately wiped off my face. "What did she say?"

"He gets one more year in Midgard."

"Thank you," I exhaled. "What did you have to do in exchange?"

Od's face stiffened for a second before he once again smiled his unaffected smile.

"I gave an offering," he said curtly. He did not leave room for further questions, and frankly, I didn't really care.

682

"I'm glad," continued Od, "that you made it to your eighteenth birthday."

"I haven't made it until midnight."

"Then we'd better take good care of you tonight." His fingers interlaced with mine, and divine power spun from him into me.

I blinked. Od was gone, and I stood amid a crowd of people. The large clock over the bar showed that more than two hours had passed.

Goddamned demigod hypnosis.

I looked around and saw the bar was half full. Most of the people from my class were there. Niels Villadsen was talking to Ben and Rebecca, and Mathias was chatting with Frank. Luna and Mads sat with Une and Aella, who smiled at me from the bar.

I sent Niels and icy glare, and he looked back apologetically.

"I'm sorry I couldn't get here earlier," said Hakim, who had apparently just come up to me.

I shook my head to clear my mind. "It's okay. Time has flown by."

"There was a ton of work to do with the arrests."

"Do you think you have the right people?" I tried to focus.

He took me by the elbow and pulled me aside. "Everything points to yes. This isn't official, but we found sedatives in both Christian Mikkelsen's and Jon Hviid's apartments."

"So that's his name?"

"Have you met him before?"

"Briefly," I said evasively, remembering the bloody hole in Mathias's chest.

"They also both had leather cords in their possession," said Hakim. "We're in the process of analyzing whether they're the same ones that strangled the girls, but it seems we have a match."

"So it's over?"

Hakim squinted and looked questioningly at me. "It appears so. What do you think?"

"I don't think anything else will happen tonight," I said with Elias's words in mind. "What does your gut say?"

He smiled, and several women looked in his direction. "I don't know what my gut says. I can't figure out if I'm noticing you because I still think you're in danger, or because . . ."

"Because what?"

He didn't answer, but instead searched his pocket. He handed me a silver chain with a pendant in the shape of a finely decorated hand. "Here's your present."

I took the necklace. "What is it?"

"It's a khamsa. The Hand of Fatima. It protects against evil."

"And I need protection against evil?"

"Well, it can't hurt. May I put it on you?" He didn't wait for an answer. Instead, he walked behind me and waited. I lifted my hair so he could put the chain around my neck. His rough hands brushed the back of my neck, and I shivered in a not entirely unpleasant way.

"It's not particularly reassuring that you're so keen to wrap things around my neck," I said brusquely and moved away slightly. My hand rested on the cool pendant.

He ignored my comment.

"I need to get back to the station." He took a few steps but reconsidered and came back.

"Anna . . ."

"Yes."

"The red hair . . ."

"What about it?"

"It suits you," he whispered in my ear before leaving.

I was left standing there, dumbfounded, but was quickly flanked by Mathias and Luna. When I caught sight of Frank, I stomped toward him.

"Come to the back alley," I said and walked past him, through the kitchen and out the door.

Frank followed and looked from Luna to Mathias, who stood on either side of him with arms crossed.

"You can start talking now," I demanded. "You're connected to Hrafnheim."

Frank didn't bother denying it.

"Are you from there?"

"I was born in this world."

"Are you something supernatural?"

"Full-blooded human," he replied.

"Thora is my mother."

"I know." Frank smoothed his gray pompadour.

I closed my eyes. "What is your role?"

"I was sent here to look for you. You were unbelievably difficult to find. I searched for more than three years."

"Why should I believe you? Varnar, Aella, and Une didn't recognize you."

"Thora's army has many factions. Not everyone knows each other. It's one of the precautionary measures."

"But Varnar is high up. He should know you."

"He didn't join up with Thora until after I left. And I couldn't reveal my identity to anyone, even my allies."

Because of the klinte, I wasn't able to determine if he was telling the truth. "Why didn't you say anything?"

"I feared you would tell Varnar. I wasn't sure of his role. He did work for Ragnara, after all."

I leaned my head back and looked up at the clear sky. The moon had the exact same shape as in my recurring vision, but it hung lower in the sky. I tried to follow Elias's advice and use my logic.

"We've been alone together several times. You fought alongside me tonight. And you've always helped me and looked out for me."

I couldn't feel his relief, but I could see it in his face.

"I absolutely do not wish you harm," he said. "I have my mission, but I've also come to care for you very much."

685

"Yeah, yeah . . . Welcome to my personal guard," I said and waved my hand.

Luna threw her arms around Frank. "I'm so glad you're on our side."

Mathias extended a hand, and Frank took it with a smile, nearly toppling under Luna's embrace.

We returned to the party, where yet another surprise was waiting. Frank had hired a band, and they were playing loud enough to make the walls shake. Luna and Mathias dragged me onto the dance floor, and we danced until I was about to collapse from exhaustion—which, for me, is saying something.

Frank's was closed, and we were hanging out at the bar over a final beer.

Une and Aella sat on one side of me, while Mathias and Luna sat on the other. Frank stood behind the bar putting glasses away.

A faint ringing in my ears was the only reminder of the evening's noise and festivities. The klinte still kept me from sensing the many people I had been around, but it was starting to wear off. The ringing grew louder. At that moment, Frank's phone buzzed. He grabbed it lazily.

"Hello." He immediately stood up straight. "She's right here. I'm standing here looking at her."

He paused while the other person spoke.

"When?"

He looked at me as the other person replied.

"We'll wait here." He hung up.

We were all looking at him, and Mathias glowed faintly green.

"That was Hakim," said Frank. "Someone helped Anna's four attackers escape. He thinks they'll try to find you."

He pounded the counter angrily, then disappeared into the kitchen.

Une and Aella stood, and electricity crackled in Luna's palms. Mathias had grown noticeably larger.

I started to feel somewhat light-headed as the ringing sound increased.

Everyone looked at me, and I would have said something if it weren't for the intense howling in my ears. The room started to spin, and my friends' faces mixed together in a blur. Then I slid off the barstool, unconscious before I hit the floor.

I woke in the familiar dark forest with its view of Odinmont. In front of me, the scene I had witnessed so many times before was playing out.

A hand closed around mine, and when I turned my head, I was looking into my own face. "Serén?" I said.

She spoke quickly and desperately. "I've been trying to contact you all night."

"I took klinte."

She pulled her lips back. "But why? Klinte takes away our gift."

"I don't see my clairvoyance as a gift at all."

She looked at me in bewilderment before continuing. "One of us is still in danger."

In front of us, the man strangled the girl.

I finally recognized her dress. I hadn't noticed it because the moonlight removed all color, and in the vision, I saw it from behind.

"It's me," I said resignedly. "She has my dress on."

"Or it could be me in your clothes."

"I don't get it. I'm surrounded by protectors. And you're in another world."

"The future is seldom easy to understand."

We looked on as the girl lost her struggle in front of us and had the rune cut into her back.

When the man ran toward the field, Serén pointed at the dead girl on the ground.

"That," she said, "is either you or me. And it's happening soon."

I awoke on the floor at Frank's. A swarm of concerned eyes stared down at me.

Luna was tugging on my arm. "Did you see something?"

She pulled me up onto a chair.

I twisted my head. "My sister contacted me. The murder still happens."

"You need to get out of here," said Une. "Ideally to somewhere protected by magic."

"Our house is," said Luna.

"This bar is, too," said Frank. "But probably not as well as Ben and Rebecca's home."

"She'll be in danger as soon as she leaves this place," said Aella. "We need to get ahold of the witches so they can escort her to their home. I'll get them right away."

"I'm faster," said Mathias. His voice now sounded metallic, and he was gigantic. "I'll take Luna with me and get her to safety."

No one dared contradict him, and they were out the door in a flash.

"You should keep watch at the front and back doors," Frank said to Une and Aella with a voice that almost sounded like Varnar's. "I'll show you the best positions."

They disappeared, and I sat alone for several nerve-racking minutes until Frank came back. "The Varangian guards are outside. The witches and the demigod will be back soon, and the police should be here any minute. You couldn't ask for better protection."

I had started to sense his aura faintly. It was aggressive and focused. It reminded me of Varnar's.

He focused on me. "You're white as a sheet. Is it because of the vision?"

"I always feel nauseous afterward. How long have you known I'm clairvoyant?"

He gave me a crooked smile. "Since I figured out who you are." He handed me a glass of water. "Here. This will help."

I took the glass and drank. Then I set it down. "Frank, there's something I want to say to you now. If anything happens . . ."

He leaned over the bar.

I hesitated. "Tonight. The party. And you gave me a job when no one else would have me. And now the apartment."

He took my hand. "I care about you so much."

"What I'm trying to say is, I don't have a whole lot of friends. But you are my friend."

Frank's eyes were sad as he squeezed my hand.

"Frank, what is it?"

"Anna . . ." he said. "I'm not your friend."

I cocked my head. "Then what are you?"

"I'm your killer."

⟨HAPTER 43⟩

I pulled my hand back. Frank didn't hold on to it.

With a leap, I was on my feet.

"Aella—Une!" I yelled as loud as I could.

He slowly straightened up. "They're not coming."

My insides turned to ice. "Did you kill them?"

"I tried to avoid it."

"Traitor."

"I'm sorry, Anna." He stepped out from behind the bar.

"That wasn't even Hakim who called."

He walked toward me. "It's been difficult to get you alone. I've been trying for months. Ever since I found out who you are."

I took a defensive position.

He came closer. "Don't fight it. I don't want you to suffer."

Something dawned on me. "You killed Tenna and Belinda."

A muscle tensed in his jaw. "They fit the profile."

"They were innocent."

"So are you."

"Was it you who hired Christian Mikkelsen and the others tonight?"

"I wanted to win your trust. And that of your friends."

"*You* carved the rune into my bike seat while Christian smashed your car," I reflected. "And that night when I broke my finger. That was you, too. And you planted the sedatives and leather cords on Christian and Jon Hviid." Hakim would be livid when he found out that he had been played. If he ever found out.

"I really don't want to do this."

"Mathias will be back soon."

"Six berserkers on demiblood are waiting for him near Ben and Rebecca's house. He and the witches will be busy for a while."

It was all a setup. Frank had planned everything.

"Why are you doing this?"

He stood in front of me with tears in his eyes. "I'm doing this for love."

I mentally ran through Elias's survival guide.

Rule number one: *Never be alone with someone you can't trust.*

Too late.

Rule number two: *Never accept food or drink from someone if you're even the slightest bit doubtful of their intentions.*

I looked at my half-empty water glass as a tingling sensation spread through my throat. *Shit!* The floor swayed beneath me.

Rule number three: *In a situation where your life is in danger, accept any help you can get and consider the consequences later.*

I took a deep breath and used the precious remaining seconds to call out a name.

Frank's forehead creased when he heard it.

Then the earth opened up, and I disappeared down into it.

* * *

My own voice shouted inside my head. *Wake up!*

I stood in the back alley before the lifeless shapes of Une and Aella. I took a couple of unsteady steps forward to check if they were alive.

I heard a snarl, and when I turned drowsily, I saw Frank's rottweiler with hackles raised and teeth bared.

Frank came out. He slammed the back door and took my hand.

"Walk," he said, and I couldn't object, so we walked toward his car hand-in-hand.

Just then, Mads turned the corner of Grønnegade. "Mathias said we should meet here and make sure you got home safely. Where are the others?"

Relief spread through me, but Frank leaned in close to me.

"Say good night," he whispered.

I obeyed, while my inner voice screamed in protest. Mads looked back and forth between us.

"The others left. Luna had too much to drink." Frank laughed. In my ear, he said quietly: "Act like you got drunk and I'm helping you home."

I swayed and gave Mads a knowing grin. *Help me, Mads*, I tried to shout, but the words remained trapped in my throat.

Mads's brows were furrowed. "Are you okay?"

Frank squeezed my hand.

"I'm fine." I was surprised by how normal my voice sounded. "Go home."

Frank took my hand and pulled me away, while Mads watched. Pitch blackness.

* * *

I sat in Frank's car.

A giant hammered against my window. No, it was Mads, his large head twisted in desperation. On the ground behind him, Frank's dog lay dead or dying in a pool of blood.

The car shook every time Mads threw his body against it.

Frank cursed and practically stood on the accelerator.

Mads continued leaping toward the moving car, but Frank jerked hard on the wheel—there was a bump and a roar of pain and despair. Then Mads was gone.

I was once again sucked down into nothingness.

* * *

Something cold hit my cheeks. "Ugly-Anna!"

I blinked.

Before me lay Kraghede Road like a black snake in the headlight beams.

We passed Ben and Rebecca's house, and I saw flames from the roof and the silhouettes of people with raised swords and spears. Something green glinted up there.

Cold hands wrapped around my neck. Belinda's spirit sat straddling my legs. "You called. I was fast asleep." She squeezed, and I coughed as the chill spread.

This sharpened my senses a bit. I lifted a hand that felt like it weighed a ton and pointed at Frank.

"Look," I whispered.

Belinda's wide eyes fixed themselves on him. She let go of me and fiddled with the leather cord around her neck. Her other hand found the rune on her forehead. "I remember him. I let him in myself. He had brought beer for us."

"It was him," I managed to say. "He . . . did that to you."

She bared her teeth and formed her hands into claws.

Frank looked at me. "How can you be conscious? I gave you a huge dose."

At that moment, Belinda's ghost scratched at his face. "I'll kill him."

Frank twitched but didn't appear to sense anything.

"You . . . not strong enough," I breathed to Belinda. "Find Christian."

"What are you saying?" asked Frank.

I didn't intend to waste a single precious breath on him.

Belinda hissed. "Chris? He treated me badly."

I fought against sleep. "Get him to . . ." I passed out for a moment. ". . . To say your killer's name."

She placed her face right in front of mine, staring intently at me. Her blue lips were next to mine, and she smiled. The sticky symbol on her forehead gleamed. Then she flickered and disappeared.

And so did my consciousness.

* * *

I was back in the old vision, and almost relieved by the familiar sight. Maybe it was all a dream, the party and Frank as murderer.

I looked down at my toes and felt the chill creep up my bare legs and arms. The moon shone on the snow-covered fields, and I could just make out Odinmont between the trees. I prepared myself for what I would once again be forced to see.

But there was no one in front of me. No girl and no killer. I heard spruce needles and dry branches cracking as someone tramped behind me.

"Stop," said Frank.

I could do nothing but obey.

Watch out, shouted my own voice.

Frank stood behind me and breathed rapidly in and out. He laid his cheek against my hair.

"I wish it weren't you." He leaned heavily against me and placed the leather cord gently around my neck. It brushed against the silver pendant Hakim had given me earlier that evening.

I wanted to flee, but I was nailed to the ground. My arms hung uselessly at my sides. I tried to lift them, but it was impossible.

He inhaled shakily. "Goodbye, Anna."

Then he pulled.

* * *

Fight, shouted my voice, as oblivion called out to me. *Kick him. Hit him. Do something.* It was so tempting to just let go and let myself fall.

The cold bit into me from the earth, and small needles prickled

694

my cheek. Out of the corner of my eye, I saw the bottom of the spindly birch tree. It was still intact, and this gave me hope. My airways were blocked, and a knee bore down painfully on my back. Above me, Frank sobbed violently.

"Why isn't she dying?"

Good question. The divinity Od had topped me up with earlier that evening probably had something to do with it. Plus, the silver hand was wedged between the leather cord and my neck. It delayed my death, but it couldn't prevent the inevitable.

The more Frank pressed me down into the forest floor, the more a small, hard object dug into my chest. The pain made my head slightly clearer.

It was the ampoule of edrú Elias had given me a few hours before, and which I had tucked into my cleavage. I flapped my arms weakly in an attempt to grab it, but I managed only to brush a bit of snow away.

"Why are you fighting?" Frank's voice was strained as he struggled with the cord.

So far, the vision matched exactly with what I had seen again and again, and there was nothing to suggest that it would not end precisely as my sister had predicted.

There was a roar above me as a large body crashed into Frank. He loosened his grip on the cord, and I painfully gasped all the oxygen I could before he pulled it tight again.

Someone tried to beat him away, and he turned around, letting go of me entirely. They tumbled to the ground behind me.

I tried to roll over, but my powerless body wouldn't obey. Finally, I was able to tip myself onto my side.

The newcomer was Hakim, and he hadn't been lying when he said he'd been practicing martial arts since childhood. But he was no match for Frank's lethal Varangian Guard moves.

Just like in my recurring vision, Frank wore a light-colored jacket with the hood pulled up.

I fumbled for the ampoule, but my fingers felt leaden and were stiff from the cold.

Frank pulled out a knife, and for an instant he looked like Varnar as he swung it expertly at Hakim, who just barely avoided taking it to the neck.

My frozen fingers searched for the ampoule, and it took all the willpower I had not to sink back into the warm, pleasant daze.

Frank struck Hakim in the thigh. He groaned in pain as a dark spot spread across his leg. This hampered his speed, and he got another slash under his arm.

Finally, the little ampoule lay in my palm. Getting it open was the next challenge, and it turned out to be quite a bit more difficult than I had expected.

Meanwhile, Frank hit Hakim with a punch to the head.

"I've mortally wounded you," he yelled. "If you leave now, you can get help before you bleed out."

"I'm not leaving Anna."

"Do you understand who she's up against?" Frank's eyes were red. "I'm at least killing her mercifully."

Hakim reached behind his back and pulled out his pistol, and I instinctively feared for Frank's life, but with a roundhouse kick he knocked the pistol away. "You've lost, Hakim. I'm giving you the opportunity to save your own life. Turn around. No one will ever know."

"I would know," Hakim snarled.

My trembling fingers scratched at the lid.

Hakim threw himself forward, and Frank hit him in the throat with the side of his hand. I knew from my training with Varnar that he would have died on the spot if Frank's hand had been clenched in a fist.

"Don't make me kill you, too," he yelled as Hakim hit the ground, coughing.

I gave up on unscrewing the ampoule and bit into it. Shards

of glass cut my lips, and blood mingled with the fresh flavor of citrus.

I swallowed the mixture, and an icy wave billowed through my body. The klinte was expelled, and my brain was clear within a split second. The adrenaline also helped me to my feet.

Hakim was down and grasping at Frank's legs, but Frank kicked him in the stomach. I threw myself between them as Frank's boot sailed toward Hakim's neck.

Frank shouted in surprise but recovered shockingly quickly and circled around me.

"You're unbelievably difficult to kill." He slashed the blade at me.

I did Varnar's trick and was behind him before he could hit me.

He whipped around with a yell. "How do you keep surviving?"

Warm blood flowed over my lips. "I have good people on my side."

Belinda's ghost manifested itself. She snarled and pounded a cascade of blue fists into Frank's chest. He shook with each blow.

"And some not-so-good," I added. "Thanks, Belinda."

Frank gasped for air and clutched his chest. "Belinda Jaeger is dead."

"Yes, she is. But that doesn't mean she isn't still mad at you."

Behind me, Hakim got up. He dragged one leg and gasped in pain, but he held his pistol steadily in both hands, the barrel aimed at Frank's chest.

Frank slowly raised his hands as relief emanated from him.

"You don't actually want to kill me," I said in wonder.

The smile lines appeared around his eyes. "You're such a nice girl."

"I should have known it was you."

"Why?"

"Of course Ragnara's assassin is immune to my repulsion spells."

697

He shook his head sadly from side to side. "I had quit. I was out of Ragnara's grasp. But . . ." He shook his head again. "Believe me. I don't want this."

Suddenly, he jumped toward me with a fluid movement, knife raised. Its point was aimed directly at my throat.

There was a sharp crack as Hakim fired the pistol.

I screamed as Frank collapsed. Without thinking, I knelt and held his face.

"No," I cried.

Hakim kicked the knife out of his hand and aimed the pistol at him again. Blood ran down his arm with frightening speed from where Frank had slashed him.

Frank looked up at me with glassy eyes. "I really wish . . ."

"What?" I sniffed.

"That I had killed you." His eyes rolled back, and his life force flickered.

Hakim's legs gave out beneath him, and he landed on his knees on the forest floor. His aura, too, was thin and transparent.

I sat between the two dying men with Frank's head resting in my lap.

"Belinda," I cried. "Get Od Dinesen and Elias Eriksen."

She bared her teeth grudgingly.

"He doesn't deserve to live." She pointed at Frank, whose white jacket was quickly turning to shining black in the moonlight.

"Do it for Hakim. He never gave up on finding your killer. Even when no one believed him."

She cocked her head. "People don't care about me."

"He cares."

She became a bit less translucent. Then she backed into the shadows. Her glowing eyes were the last thing to disappear in the darkness.

Hakim leaned heavily against me. "Was that Belinda Jaeger you were just talking to?"

"What are you talking about?"

"Don't lie to me." His voice was weak. "Not now."

"Yes, I was talking to Belinda." I sat up straighter to support more of his weight. "How did you figure it out?"

"That you're clairvoyant? I've had a hunch for a while."

"You and your hunches . . ."

He laughed quietly, but it ended in a cough. "And there's something about a magical underworld. Maybe even a parallel universe. I haven't quite figured that part out."

"It sounds like you're getting close."

His breathing was labored.

I had keep him talking so he wouldn't lose consciousness.

"How did you find me?" I asked.

"There was noise from the cell where Christian Mikkelsen and Jon Hviid were being held," he whispered. "When I got down there, Christian was beating himself up. He was punching himself in the face and shouting that Frank was the killer and that he had you. It was like he was possessed."

"*Well done*, Belinda," I mumbled.

"What?"

"He *was* possessed. Belinda must have upgraded herself to poltergeist. Which is pretty impressive. She's barely coherent. That's truly an achievement."

"P-pol . . .?" Hakim breathed heavily.

"It's overwhelming to hear about all this stuff. We've all been where you are now." I waved a hand. "Don't sweat it. It'll pass."

"Thanks for the confidence."

"What do you mean?"

"You could have sent Belinda's ghost anywhere, but you sent her to me."

I cleared my throat. "How did you know we were here?"

"When you were hallucinating, you said you could see your house from the place where you were going to die. I've been out here several times since and found the places where Odinmont is visible. I've always thought that this was the most obvious place— for a murderer, anyway."

"Good guess. Did you also have a hunch that it was Frank?"

No reply.

"Hakim?"

His head fell forward.

"Shit!" I shook him. "Od," I yelled. "This would be a good time to show up."

A silver gleam answered my prayers.

Od, with Elias and Niels Villadsen behind him, came walking up to us. He was enormous and shining silver threads sparkled around him.

"Elias, find some laekna, now!" I called.

Elias passed Od and pulled out ampoules and syringes as he ran. When he reached us, I had already rolled Hakim's sleeve up.

Elias injected him with a smooth, practiced motion.

Hakim spluttered and blinked his eyes. He tried to get up but toppled forward.

"Take it easy," said Elias. "You almost bled out just now."

Hakim scoffed and stood like a wounded bear.

"Tough guy," commented Elias.

Before me, Frank's aura flickered threateningly.

"Give Frank some, too," I said.

Elias's youthful face was stony, and his soft curls appeared gray in the moonlight. "He tried to kill you. Repeatedly."

"He's still my friend."

"What's in it for me?"

It didn't surprise me that Elias was negotiating. "What do you want?"

"Can I pick anything?" He looked me up and down.

"You . . ." I clenched my hands into fists.

He interrupted me. "I want for you to someday do the same for me. No matter how angry you are with me. I will betray you again. And you'll hate me for it. But nevertheless, I want you to save my life, if it's in your power."

I didn't even stop to consider. "Deal. Hurry up."

Elias tore the unconscious Frank's shirt apart.

I looked at the hole in the right side of Frank's chest. Had it been on the opposite side, his heart would have been pulverized. The damage was nowhere near what Mathias had suffered, but Frank wasn't a demigod.

Elias had a professional demeanor. "The bullet went through."

I looked away as he plunged the syringe between Frank's ribs.

Something within Frank made a squishy, pumping sound. His aura resembled an ember someone was blowing on, and it grew stronger and stronger until it was burning solidly. He remained unconscious.

Elias looked at me with scrutiny.

"Your lips," he said.

I felt them and held back a sob.

He held my jaw, and like the first time we met, he let his thumb slide across my lower lip, leaving behind a fluid. The deep cuts closed up.

I stood up and didn't thank him.

Od stood in front of Hakim, who already looked a bit livelier. Od laid a large, shining hand on his shoulder. "My sincerest thanks. You saved someone I care for immensely. We'll take over from here."

Hakim swayed but stared Od right in the eyes, a feat requiring both courage and strength. "This is a police matter. You aren't taking over anything."

Niels stepped forward and displayed an official-looking badge.

Hakim's eyes widened.

"You've carried out an impressive bit of police work," Niels said, pulling him away.

I shouted after them. "You aren't going to do anything to Hakim, are you?"

Niels looked at me through steel-rimmed glasses. "Of course not."

"Then what do you want with him? He knows a lot."

Niels smoothed his gray suit. "I was actually thinking of hiring him."

"Oh."

"And, young lady . . ." Niels looked sternly at me.

"Yes."

"This never happened."

EPILOGUE

It was Christmas Eve. I sat with a blanket wrapped around me in Ben and Rebecca's living room, while Luna decorated an astonishingly mainstream Christmas tree.

The last three days had been surreal. After Od and Niels left with the unconscious Frank, Hakim and Elias accompanied me to see whether Mads, Une, and Aella were still alive. We found them in bad shape, but thankfully not so bad that they couldn't be patched up with laekna. Elias didn't try to exchange anything for healing them, and I didn't thank him for it.

Then we checked on Mathias and the Sekibo family, who were unharmed but frothing with rage over having been prevented from helping me.

A soot-blackened Ben unleashed curses and oaths over the fact that enemies had managed to get through his magical bulwarks and set fire to the house. Apparently, the relationship between witches and fire is very fraught.

The berserkers left after a while, and the fight did not cost any lives. It seemed the purpose of the attack was to keep Mathias occupied while Frank killed me.

It did not take long for the witches to repair their roof using magic, so no traces of the attack remained, apart from a couple of black spots on the white plaster walls.

Odinmont was still impossible to get near, and Frank's Bar & Diner was closed, a sign in the window claiming the owner left for personal reasons.

No news had come from Varnar, and the mere thought of him made my eyes burn.

"Rudolf, the red-nosed reindeer . . ." Luna sang as she planted a silver star on top of the tree.

I blew on the cup of tea she had put in my hand. "I'm surprised you guys have a Christmas tree. It seems so . . . normal."

She dangled a paper pig on a string.

"Christmas trees originate from Norse blót rituals." She found a branch for the pig. "It's the same as when we hang food from the trees outside." She took a handful of pebernød cookies and distributed them among the paper cones hanging from the tree.

"Is that really what Christmas decorations are?"

"Yep." She continued humming the song.

"What about hangatyr? Human sacrifices?" I asked.

"Gingerbread men and women," came a deep voice from the doorway, where Ben stood in stocking feet, snow in his dreadlocks.

I swallowed. "That's what they symbolize?"

He nodded solemnly but lit up when he reached Luna.

"It looks great, chérie." Then he turned and looked at me. "I just met with Od Dinesen. He invited us to a New Year's Eve party at The Boatman."

"Isn't that kind of . . ." I searched for the word. "Gregorian?"

Ben clucked. "Od is pretty well assimilated to modern times."

"The new year has been celebrated on that date for hundreds of years in this country."

"Like I said," he smiled menacingly, "modern times."

I raised an eyebrow. "What do you know about that?"

Luna hummed on, unaware that I was hinting at her father's true age.

"Let's go. I'm ready to celebrate the fact that I made it all the way to Christmas. Thanks, by the way, for letting me have it here. I didn't think you celebrated Christian holidays."

"There's nothing wrong with the carpenter's teachings. We're happy to honor his birth. But our jól will probably be a bit different from the yule you're used to."

"I've spent Christmas in fourteen different places. Some people eat goose, others eat roast pork. Not to mention what you win for finding the almond in the rice pudding."

Ben once again flashed his large teeth. "That's not what I meant. For one thing, we don't celebrate jól. We drink jól."

The Sekibo Christmas was indeed very different from anything I had ever experienced. It lasted three days, during which we placed sheaves of wheat in the fields, danced to the beat of a drum, made offerings of food, and drank incredible quantities of mead. Ben ran around in fuzzy pants and a he-goat mask, and Rebecca wore her ritual animal skin costume and the horned headband. By day two, I had to say no to alcohol, and on day three, I boycotted heavy food.

Ben pushed the goat mask up on his forehead. "But eating barley porridge with duck fat and blood sausage keeps oskereia away."

I suppressed the urge to vomit. "Who?"

"The restless dead," said Rebecca before she leapt barefoot onto a spruce bough and tramped on it.

"Belinda can come on over," I said. "If you mean people like her."

I couldn't bring myself to ask why she was jumping on spiky spruce needles.

Ben and Rebecca exchanged a look.

"Belinda can go both ways," Ben said and replaced his mask.

I was relieved when the jólablót was finally over.

Od's New Year's Eve party was, as expected, spectacular. The Boatman was decorated with strange, enormous bubbles, so it felt like we were underwater. The bar was packed with humans and other beings. It seemed this evening was reserved for those who were part of the hidden world. The rest of the country was not invited.

Elias met me at the door wearing a suit and his usual cheeky smile. He pulled me onto the dance floor, where the music immediately switched from an upbeat song to a slow dance. The scoundrel.

"You're more beautiful than ever. Survival suits you." He twirled one of my red locks between his fingers.

I pushed his hand away, ready to give him a verbal smackdown, but he chuckled and laid his cheek against mine. It was warm and smooth, as it had been for the past four hundred years.

"Don't say anything. We shouldn't fight at the end of the year. It colors the year to come."

"Then what should we do?"

"Right now?" he whispered in my ear. "Dance, of course. Just dance."

And so we danced. For a brief moment, my thoughts ceased, and I was fully in the present in Elias's arms. I let the music envelop me and closed my eyes. But the moment passed, and again my thoughts circled around what I had to do. I opened my eyes, and over Elias's shoulder, I met Od's gaze.

He crossed the room, and the crowd parted imperceptibly for him. They didn't even notice themselves doing it.

He laid his hand on Elias's shoulder. "I'll take it from here."

Elias separated himself from me but managed to plant a kiss on my collarbone before slipping back into the throng.

Od put his arms around me. "I know what you're planning to do. I don't know when you're going to do it, but when it happens, I hope you'll take someone with you."

"So you're a mind reader now?"

"No, but I've gotten to know you pretty well." His brow lowered slightly. "I'm warning you. What you're asking of yourself is nearly impossible. And so dangerous. I'm of half a mind to forbid it."

"You can't forbid me from doing anything."

He smiled, and it was like the sun shining on my face. As always, my willpower was subtly weakened.

"Actually, I can." He narrowed his eyes slightly. "But tell me. Are you doing this to find Varnar?"

I looked down. When I spoke, it was so softly I could barely hear myself, but I knew Od could hear me perfectly well.

"Varnar chose to leave me. He can do as he likes." I chewed on my lower lip. I hadn't even discussed Varnar with myself. It was far too painful to think I meant so little to him that he could leave me so easily.

"I am certain Varnar of the Bronze Forest loves you."

I shook my head subtly.

Od stroked my cheek with the back of his hand. "I know you don't believe me, but you actually are quite lovable. Many people care about you." His finger rounded the silver hand that hung around my neck. "I love you, too."

"You don't count. You notoriously have a crush on all things human." I looked up.

Od gave a hoarse laugh and said nothing more.

We stood close together until the final notes of the song, and I felt his strength seep into my body. I suspected that he was intentionally boosting me with divinity. He didn't say goodbye before letting go of me and disappearing into the crowd, which once again parted for him.

I retreated to the edge of the dance floor and stared out at the partygoers. Luna and Mathias jumped around in a wild dance together with Une and Aella. Luna waved at me, and I waved back. Mathias gave me one of his dazzling smiles. Elias was deeply engrossed in a conversation with a pretty girl who casually played with her long blond hair. I didn't need to see the future to know that Elias would start the new year with a bang.

Ben and Rebecca sat at a table with their hands interlaced, and Mads was talking with the tall, fair bartender.

Even Hakim was here. We hadn't seen each other much because he had spent most of last week in Copenhagen. He was talking to Niels Villadsen, but once in a while, his gaze strayed to me.

I made a discreet waving motion, and he nodded back with a little smile.

I looked around again. Some were missing. Arthur, who, before I met my new friends, had been the only one to make me feel somewhat likable. Monster. My heart twinged. I didn't know how he was, or if he was even alive. Varnar . . . I refused to think about him. I even missed Frank, despite his new status as my killer. I had no idea what Od and Niels had done with him.

My eyes landed on the large clock displaying a quarter to twelve. I turned and left the crowd of humans, demigods, witches, and half giants. Just over six months ago, I hadn't known any of these people, and now several of them had risked their lives for mine.

That was why I had to go alone.

In front of the door to Od's office, I stopped and looked into one of the large mirrors.

The forest-green dress, which Luna had sewn me for the occasion, was the exact same color as the stones in the ring that adorned my finger. Red waves flowed over my bare shoulders. After I had decided what I had to do, I'd determined that it was most practical to keep my hair red.

I looked at myself one last time before slinging my bag over my shoulder. It would be a long time before I could put on party clothes again, if at all. I was figuring on a fifty-fifty chance of coming back. The odds were even lower for coming back successful.

The door opened with a little creak. I had been worried that I wouldn't be able to get in, but I entered Od's office without a hitch.

The strange room with its many doors looked the same, except there was now a cage inside. Bars and all. My first impulse was the joy of reunion, a split second before my brain took over.

Behind the bars sat Frank, his hands folded, but he raised his head when I came in. He looked okay—physically, anyway. But his face was gray, and the wrinkles around his mouth and eyes were deep-set.

"Have you come to take revenge?" His voice was placid.

"I had no idea you were here." That was the truth. "There's another reason why I'm here, and I would appreciate it if you don't tell anyone you saw me."

"I owe you that much." He smiled warmly. "I meant it when I said I wished it weren't you I had to kill."

"I'd just like to know why."

Frank stared at his hands again.

"I can't tell you that," he whispered.

"Who are you doing this for?" I asked. "It's someone you love."

Frank looked at me, shocked. Then he shook his head with his lips pressed tightly together.

I did it without thinking. It was dangerous, and it was stupid. But I reached between the bars and took Frank's hands. Then I pushed my power into him and pulled the past out. Frank's mind gave it up with ease.

I felt the empathy in my eyes, which overflowed with tears.

"The boy," I said and turned my head slightly. "Is he your son?"

Frank stared at me.

"Ah. Your grandson?" I concluded. "Ragnara has him. My life for his."

Frank's eyes widened in fear.

"She'll kill him if you say anything?"

Frank was immobile but looked up and down. Yes.

"Do you know where he is?"

Frank looked from side to side. No.

I pulled back my hands.

Frank didn't try to hold on.

"What will happen to you?"

"I expect I'll be executed."

"Neither Od nor Niels is executing anyone." I tried to keep my voice calm.

"No, but they'll deliver me to Ragnara."

I gathered my courage, and then I asked: "Will you kill me if I let you out?"

"Yes," Frank said firmly.

Evidently, the deal still stood. His grandson's life for mine.

"As far as I can tell, there's no magic keeping this door locked." I pointed to the door of the cage. "And if I were to give you, let's say, a letter opener, you could get the lock open. After a little while. I get a head start."

"One hour, max."

"Until early tomorrow morning."

He considered. "Deal."

"Turn around. I need to change."

Frank turned obediently.

I pulled a pair of jeans, my biker boots, a black hoodie, and my mom's coat out of the bag. My high heels were kicked off and tossed in a corner, but after giving it some thought, I laid the green dress in the bag with the rest of the items I'd packed, including the last bit of klinte, Mads's giant-crystal, Rebecca's notebook about Hrafnheim, Freyja's tears—which, if nothing else, I could sell—and various other things I imagined I might have use for. I was dressed in a matter of seconds.

Outside the door, I heard people counting down. Ten—nine—eight.

"Turn back around." I pulled on the coat.

Seven—six—five.

I took a letter opener from Od's desk. "Which door leads to Hrafnheim?"

"It's too dangerous. They'll kill you."

I raised an eyebrow. Ironic.

Four—three—two.

"Do you want the opener?"

Frank exhaled a hiss through bared teeth. Then he raised a finger and pointed to a blue door.

One—Haaappy New Year!

I tossed the letter opener to Frank and just managed to see him grab it before I flung the door open and threw myself into the dark.

CHARACTERS

AELLA [EYE-ELLA]	a girl who came from the Hidden World with Varnar
ALICE	classmate of Anna's
ARTHUR	Anna's lifelong friend
BENEDICT SEKIBO [SE-KEE-BO]	Luna's father
CHRISTIAN MIKKELSEN	Peter's friend, who Anna calls "the psychopath"
ELIAS [EH-LEE-AHS] ERIKSEN	potion maker and Od's assistant
ESKILD BLACK-EYE	Ragnara's adviser and commander of her army
FRANK	owner of Frank's Bar & Diner
FREYJA [FREY-A]	the goddess of love
GEIRI	one of Ragnara's men
GRETA	Anna's social worker
HAKIM [HA-KEEM] MURR	a young police officer
JANITOR PREBEN	in charge of taking care of the school Anna attends
JUSTINE	a clairvoyant friend of Elias's
LARS GULDAGER [GOOL-DAY-ER]	a police officer
LITTLE MADS	a tall boy in Anna's class
LUNA SEKIBO	Anna's new friend
MATHIAS HEDSKOV [MA-TEE-AHS HEDH-SKOH]	Anna's new friend
MIA AND JENS	Anna's first foster parents
MONSTER	Anna's dog
MR. NIELSEN	Anna's Danish teacher
NAUT KAFNAR	Anna calls him "the Savage"

NIELS VILLADSEN [NEELS VIL-ADH-SEN]	a government agent
OD DINESEN [DEE-NE-SEN]	owner of The Boatman
ODIN	the All-Father, the primary god of the Norse pantheon
PETER NYBO [NEE-BO]	Anna's nemesis at school
RAGNARA	the ruler of Freiheim
REBECCA SEKIBO [SE-KEE-BO]	Luna's mother
SERÉN [SE-REN]	a red-headed girl from the Hidden World
TENNA SMITH JENSEN	a girl who used to live in the same group home as Anna
THORA BANEBLOOD	Ragnara's enemy
TIMMY	bike shop owner
ULLA	a medium
VARNAR	assistant janitor at Anna's school and watches over Anna
VÖLVA HEJD [VOHL-VA HAIT]	the mother of all seers

PLACES

1. THE BOATMAN	a bar in Jagd
2. THE BRONZE FOREST	home of the Forest Folk
3. FÓLKVANGR	Freyja's domain, where she takes her share of those who die in battle
4. FREIHEIM	another name for Hrafnheim
5. HRAFNHEIM	a world created for believers in the old faith
6. THE IRON FOREST	home of the Wolf Folk
7. THE ISLAND	the school's café
8. JAGD [YAGD]	a coastal town

9. KRAGHEDE [KRAG-HEY-THE] FOREST — a forest bordering Ravensted

10. KRAGHEDE [KRAG-HEY-THE] MANOR — an abandoned manor in Kraghede Forest

11. MIDGARD — the human world

12. NORDRESLEV YOUTH CENTER [NORT-RES-LEF] — a juvenile detention center

13. ODINMONT — a hill with a house sitting on it

14. RAVENSTED — a town in northern Denmark

15. THE HIDDEN WORLD — the world of the gods and other supernatural beings

16. VALHALLA — Odin's domain, where he takes his share of those who die in battle

CONCEPTS

1. ASATRU [AH-SA-TRU] — Norse paganism

2. BERSERKERS — a group of warriors

3. BLÓT [BLOHT] — a ceremony

4. CLAIRVOYANT — someone who can see the past and/or future

5. CLINGY SPIRIT — a type of ghost

6. DEMIBLOOD — the blood of a demigod

7. DEMIGOD — someone who is half human, half god

8. EDRÚ [ED-RU] — a potion that erases the effects of other intoxicants

9. KLINTE [KLINT-A] — a potion that dulls the senses

10. LAEKNA [LEK-NA] — a healing potion

11. MEDIUM — someone who can communicate with the dead

12. RAGNARÖK — doomsday

13. RETROCOGNITION — the ability to see the past

14. **SEERESS** a female clairvoyant, also known as a völva

15. **SEID [SAIT]** a ritual for contacting the dead

16. **STJÓRNA [STYUR-NA]** a sedative potion

17. **THE VARANGIAN GUARD** Ragnara's army

18. **VÖLUSPÁ [VO-LU-SPA]** a 10th century poem

AUTHOR
MALENE SØLVSTEN made her debut in Denmark in 2016 with the first volume of the fantasy trilogy Whisper of the Ravens and was nominated for the Readers' Book Prize in the same year. The series quickly became a bestseller in Denmark, for which the author received the 2018 Edvard Prisen, awarded annually by the Danish Library Association. An economist by training, she lives with her family in Copenhagen, where she now works as a full-time author.

TRANSLATOR
ADRIENNE ALAIR is a literary translator working from Danish, Norwegian, and Swedish into English. She studied Scandinavian Studies at the University of Edinburgh and has lived in Sweden and Denmark. She is now based in Charlotte, North Carolina.

The thrilling fantasy adventure continues ...

Malene Sølvsten
Fehu
(Whisper of the Ravens Book 2)
On sale Fall 2024
ISBN 978-1-64690-027-5

In an unknown parallel world full of gods, demigods, and creatures, Anna is picked up by soldiers of the ruler Ragnara. When she is freed by a renegade officer, they set out to free her twin sister, Serén, who has been captured by Ragnara. The road to the capital is fraught with deadly dangers, and the vision of her own murder still plagues Anna endlessly. But she begins to understand more and more that Ragnarök, the downfall of the world, is directly linked to her own fate.

Discover the exciting Rosenholm fantasy trilogy!

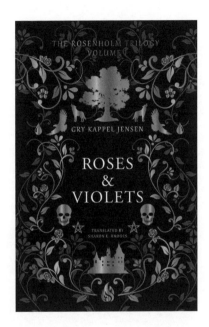

Gry Kappel Jensen
Roses & Violets
(The Rosenholm Trilogy Volume 1)
On sale now!
ISBN 978-1-64690-012-1

Four girls from four different parts of Denmark have been invited to apply to Rosenholm Academy for an unknown reason. During the unorthodox application tests, it becomes apparent this is no ordinary school. In fact, it's a magical boarding school and all the students have powers.

Once the school year begins, they learn that Rosenholm carries a dark secret—a young girl was murdered under mysterious circumstances in the 1980s and the killer was never found. Her spirit is still haunting the school, and she is now urging the four girls to bring justice and find the killer. But helping the spirit puts all of the girls in grave danger . . .